TIRANT LO BLANC

by Joanot Martorell &

Martí Joan de Galba

TRANSLATED AND WITH

A FOREWORD BY

DAVID H. ROSENTHAL

Schocken Books

NEW YORK

First published by Schocken Books 1984
10 9 8 7 6 5 4 3 2 1   84 85 86 87

Library of Congress Cataloging in Publication Data

Martorell, Joanot, d. 1468. Tirant lo Blanc.
Bibliography: p.
1. Galba, Martí Joan de, d. 1490. II. Rosenthal, David H., 1945–   . III. Title.
PC3937.M4A27 1984   849.9'33   83–40465

Designed by Jane Byers Bierhorst
Manufactured in the United States of America
ISBN 0–8052–3852–2

Parts of the Foreword and an earlier draft of the "Tirant in
Sicily and Rhodes" episodes originally appeared in *Allegorica* magazine.

The preparation of this volume was made possible by
grants from the Joint U.S.-Spanish
Committee for Educational and Cultural Affairs and
the Translations Program of the National Endowment for
the Humanities (an independent federal agency).

· for Stephanie Smolinsky ·

· Contents ·

"God help me!" shouted the priest. "Here's *Tirant lo Blanc!* Give it here, friend, for I promise you I've found a wealth of pleasure and a gold mine of enjoyment in it. Here's that brave cavalier Sir Kyrieleison of Muntalbà, his brother Thomas of Muntalbà, the knight Dryfount, Tirant's fight with the mastiff, Pleasure-of-my-life's witty comments, the Easygoing Widow's loves and schemes, and the lady empress in love with her page Hippolytus. I swear to you, my friend, that it's the best book of its kind in the world. The knights in it eat, sleep, die in their beds, dictate wills before they go and many other things you cannot find in other works of this sort. For all that and because he avoided deliberate nonsense, the author deserved to have it kept in print all his life. Take it home and read it, and you'll see everything I've said is true."[1]

With these words, and especially the phrase "the best book of its kind in the world," Cervantes established *Tirant lo Blanc* as an underground classic, a category in which—outside the Catalan Lands—it still belongs today. Yet for its wit and vivid realism, *Tirant* deserves to be placed in an entirely different group of works: those medieval and Renaissance masterpieces like *The Decameron, The Canterbury Tales, Gargantua and Pantagruel,* and *Don Quixote* itself that remain both "great books" in the academic sense and very enjoyable reading for anyone who happens to pick them up. The novel has also had its admirers in our own century, particularly the Peruvian writer Mario Vargas Llosa, who described its author Joanot Martorell as "the first of that lineage of God-supplanters—Fielding, Balzac, Dickens, Flaubert, Tolstoy, Joyce, Faulkner—who try to create in their novels an 'all-encompassing reality.' "[2]

Why, then, has *Tirant lo Blanc* failed to win the acclaim it deserves? A number of reasons could be advanced, but the basic one is simple enough: it was written in Catalan.[3] When *Tirant* was published in 1490, the Catalan language and its literature were about to enter a three hundred and fifty year decline during which the outside world would take very little notice of them. *Tirant* shared in this general oblivion, from which it has only partially recovered in the Castilian-speaking world. Had the outcome of the Spanish Civil War been different, this process might have accelerated, and perhaps translations into other modern languages would have been published or reprinted by now. Instead, Catalan culture was brutally suppressed for twenty years and benignly neglected for fifteen more, thus making the literature almost inaccessible to interested foreigners. This translation, then, is the first modern version of *Tirant lo Blanc* to appear in any non-Hispanic language.[4]

Though exact estimates differ, there is a general consensus that something like three-quarters of *Tirant lo Blanc* was written by Joanot Martorell.[5] Much remains to be learned about his life, but what we do know illuminates many aspects of his masterpiece. Our author's father, Francesc Martorell, was one of King Martin the Humane's chamberlains and a magistrate in the city of Valencia.[6] His wife, Damiata de Montpalau, bore him seven children: Galceran, Joan or Joanot, Jofre, Jaume or Jaumot, Isabel (first wife of Ausiàs March, the outstanding fifteenth-century Catalan poet), Aldonça (who married Galceran de Montpalau), and Damiata, to whom we shall return shortly. While not great lords, Joanot and his relatives were respected members of the fighting Valencian nobility. They usually lived in the town of Gandia, where Joanot may have been born in 1413 or 1414. His name first appears (as Sir Johanot Martorell, meaning he had been knighted) in 1433, together with his father and his brother Galceran.

Like most of the Valencian aristocracy, Joanot's family was frequently involved both in military expeditions (Francesc, Galceran and Jofre participated in King Alphonse the Magnanimous's 1420 campaign in Sardinia and Corsica) and in private duels. In his introduction to *Tirant*, Martorell tells us he had been to England, and his quarrel with Joan de Montpalau—the first extensive information we have about him—explains the reason for his voyage. The quarrel can be followed through their cartels of defiance, beginning with Joanot's letter of May 12, 1437. Montpalau was his second cousin (Joanot's mother was Damiata de Montpalau and his sister Aldonça was Galceran de Montpalau's wife), and Martorell begins by reminding him that: "whenever you came to my father's house, which is now mine, we trusted you as a friend and relative and all doors were open to you, nor did anyone watch you, for no one thought you would do anything wicked or shameful to us or our family" (1193). But "coming and going to your heart's content, you promised and swore a sacred oath to wed my sister Damiata and quickly celebrate your engagement, something you have not yet done. Instead, in the meantime you have used your oath and promise and my sister's trust in your friendship and kinship . . . to steal her honor and mine, and you have dishonestly and incessantly sullied and shamed her" (1193).

Since "such wickedness and treachery" (1193) cannot go unpunished, Martorell declares that if Montpalau denies all or part of the accusation, he will fight him on foot or horseback with arms of his choosing before any impartial judge he can find until one is killed or surrenders. If Montpalau refuses to seek a judge, Martorell offers to do so himself under the same conditions. Secret marriages like the one between Damiata and Joan de Montpalau, in fact, were standard themes in much chivalric literature, including *Tirant lo Blanc* itself.[7] Church weddings did not become obligatory in Catholic countries until the Council of Trent in 1564, and under Scottish church law any marriage before witnesses remains binding today. We should also remember that cartels of defiance were not only sent by messenger, but were also posted on doors, street corners, and churches for all to see. In challenging Montpalau, Martorell was jeopardizing his sister's good name and future happiness.

Three days later, Montpalau accepted the challenge, specifying that the duel be on horseback with two swords and one lance apiece and authorizing Martorell to seek a judge. In replying to the charges, Montpalau denied that he had offered to marry Damiata; he did not attempt to refute the charge that he had deflowered her. On May eighteenth, Martorell promised to find a referee within six months. Another thirteen letters were exchanged, all signed in Valencia and mostly concerned with technical details of the bout. It is worth noting that for both Martorell and Montpalau, "man of letters" is an insult used with the same scorn Martorell later heaped upon lawyers and notaries in *Tirant*. In chapter 41, for example, the author cheerfully has three lawyers hanged and proposes the liquidation of almost all the rest. In his correspondence with Montpalau, Martorell, who was certainly one of the more eloquent knights of his age, declares that he will write no more "because it is unworthy of knights and gentlemen and suitable only to women and jurists, whose sole defenses are their tongues and pens" (1203). What the passage reveals is how much Martorell accepted the standard attitudes of his class and continued to define himself as a knight despite his literary accomplishments.

Since the King of Aragon could not judge duels between his vassals except in cases of treason, Martorell was forced to look elsewhere. His final letter to Montpalau, dated April 1438, comes from London. In it, he declares that the King of England will oversee their duel and encloses an invitation and safe-conduct from Henry VI of Lancaster. These documents were brought to Valencia by Francesc Oliver, presumably one of Martorell's servants who had accompanied him on his voyage. Oliver was arrested on arrival, however, and the documents were confiscated.

Months went by, and in February 1439 Montpalau's friend, relative, and business agent Perot Mercader arrived at the English court. There he accused Martorell of leaving Valencia without the permission of Prince Henry of Aragon or his mother Queen Mary of Castile. Martorell replied by challenging Mercader himself to a duel.

From all these chivalric shenanigans, one can conclude that our author was in England for at least eleven months (March 1438 to February 1439). Though we do not know what happened to Mercader, we can assume that Montpalau never reached London. The quarrel was finally resolved by Queen Mary who, with Alphonse the Magnanimous's written permission from Naples, ordered Montpalau to pay four thousand florins directly to Damiata Martorell "and not to the aforesaid Sir Joanot or anyone else."[8] The next time we meet Lady Damiata is in 1462. Naturally, she is still a spinster. By dragging her name so persistently through the mud, her brother had made it impossible for her to marry.

Various other documents (an arrest warrant dated October 19, 1440, battle challenges exchanged with the Valencian knights Jaume Ripoll and Felip Boyl, who appears on the jacket, and with Gonçalbo de Híjar) complete our picture of Martorell: quarrelsome, boastful, and tough-talking. Though we have no proof that he actually went to war, many details of *Tirant lo Blanc* lead one to suspect that he did. He was definitely in Portugal (though we do not know exactly when), and he was probably in Naples in 1442 and was certainly there in 1454–1455 for at least a year. He died a bachelor in 1468 and left no known illegitimate children.

What we do not know about Martorell far exceeds what we do know, but a number of traits emerge from the documents discovered so far. First of all, our author and his family were knights accustomed both to private duels and full-scale battles. As such, they accepted knighthood as a profession and the chivalric code as an ideal. If there were no knights, who would lead armies to war? And war, in fifteenth-century Valencia, retained the crusader connotations it had lost in most parts of Western Europe. The Moorish kingdom of Granada still existed when Martorell began work on *Tirant* in 1460. We have also seen him offer to risk his life to defend his sister's honor. One of the great differences between Martorell and his admirer Cervantes, then, is that although Martorell was capable of laughing at almost anything, knighthood itself was a sacred institution for him. His reason for existence was war and killing, and his attitude toward what twentieth-century mercenaries would call "pen-pushers" is clear from his correspondence with Joan de Montpalau. Martorell was a knight who also wrote (and wrote partly in order to justify his class), not a writer who happened to be a knight.

Virtually all the secondary literature on *Tirant lo Blanc* has been concerned with factual matters such as the novel's sources and date or Martorell's life. Scholars like Constantin Marinesco, Lluís Nicolau d'Olwer, and Martí de Riquer have also discovered a number of imitations and plagiarisms in the book, and undoubtedly there are more still to be unearthed. The reader, however, should bear in mind that Martorell's work is primarily based on what he saw, felt, and heard about and not on his readings.

The only part of *Tirant* where literary sources play a determining role in the action is the William of Warwick sequence (chapters 1–28). This group of chapters is partially a revision of Martorell's only other known work, the until-recently unpublished *William of Warwick,*[9] which covers the same ground as chapters 1–39 of *Tirant.* In both versions, the main doctrinal source is Ramon Llull's *Book of the Knightly Order,*[10] a religiously oriented treatise on a knight's duties and the meaning of his station, arms, and armor. The plot comes from a thirteenth-century Anglo-Norman romance entitled *Guy of Warwick,* which was later translated into English, Irish, and French.[11] The French prose version is the one Martorell probably read. It seems to have originally belonged to John Talbot, son-in-law of Richard de Beauchamp, Earl of Warwick, who died in 1439.[12]

Beauchamp revered the memory of his legendary ancestor and contributed generously to Guy's Cliff, the hermitage where, according to tradition, Guy had retired to do penance after a life of wars and tournaments. Beauchamp himself was devoted to the chivalric code and once jousted for three consecutive days: first as *Le Vert Chevalier* (The Green Knight), then as *Le Chevalier Attendant* (The Waiting Knight), and finally as himself. He helped defeat the French at Rouen and was one of Henry VI's tutors. Beauchamp was close friends with the Venetian humanist Pietro da Monte, who in turn was friendly with the Valencian clergyman Vicent Climent, who had lived in England since 1433. It is not at all improbable that Martorell knew Climent, and therefore da Monte and perhaps Beauchamp as well.

We find the French prose version of *Guy of Warwick* in a handsome book of hours presented by John Talbot (Beauchamp's son-in-law) to Henry VI of England and Margaret of Anjou, either at their engagaement (May 1444) or at their wedding (March 1445). This book, which can now be found at the British Museum (Old Royal, 15 E VI), also includes two other items relevant to *Tirant:* a French translation of the statutes of the Order of the Garter, and Honoré Bouvet's *Tree of Battles,* mentioned in chapters 28 and 32. When Martorell declares, in his first version of *William of Warwick,* that "This is a treatise on the knightly order taken from a book belonging to the King of England and France," he may well be telling the truth.[13] Our only problem is that the book was not given to the king until 1444 or 1445, and our author had left England in 1439. These facts, in turn, have led William Entwistle[14] and Riquer to postulate a second voyage in 1450 or 1451. What seems certain is that—whether through Talbot or Henry VI—Martorell was impressed by the same manuscript we now admire in the British Museum.

A word should also be said about Martorell's treatment of the Order of the Garter. According to English specialists, the first written account of its founding appears in the Italian Polydore Vergili's *Anglicae Historiae* (Basil, 1534). The story, however, is actually first told in *Tirant,* which was written some seventy-five years earlier and published in 1490. It is possible that Martorell heard it from the king himself, for when Diaphebus relates the tale, he declares that he is telling it "as I and all these knights heard it from the king's own lips" (282).

All this information may also shed some light on Martorell's initial statement, in his dedication, that *Tirant* is translated from English into Portuguese and then into "Valencian vernacular" (that is, Catalan). Since the book is dedicated to Don Ferdinand of Portugal, and since we know Martorell was at least once and perhaps twice in England, the statement cannot simply be dismissed as a fiction. Such fictional translations are commonplace in chivalric literature, but almost always involve languages more exotic than English or Portuguese—Arabic or Hungarian, for example. Clearly the first part of *Tirant* is an adaptation of an English legend. Though it is unlikely that Martorell knew Portuguese well enough to translate into it, there was nothing to stop him from dictating *Guy of Warwick* to a Portuguese scribe who could then complete the translation and polish the style. In 1439, the date of Martorell's first trip to England, Don Ferdinand was only five or six years old, but on our author's second voyage—the hypothetical one of 1450 or 1451—his "prince of the royal line" might have asked him to collaborate on a Portuguese translation.

The next section of *Tirant* for which important sources have been found takes place in Sicily and Rhodes. In this case, however, the basis is not literary but historical: the Egyptian siege from August 10 to September 18, 1444. The Catalan and Valencian colony on Rhodes—both knights of the order and bankers, merchants, sailors, and the like—was considerable, and until 1437 the grand master (Antoni de Fluvià) had been a Catalan. So great, in fact, was the Catalan influence that the Genoese accused the order of serving Alphonse the Magnanimous and allied themselves with the Egyptians.

We know Martorell was in Valencia during the siege, but he certainly had plenty of opportunities to obtain all the information he wanted. To begin with, Francesc Ferrer composed a long and accurate poem about the siege and defense of the island.[15] The Valencian privateer Jaume de Vilargut, however, was probably Martorell's primary source of information. We know they were friends, because in one of his letters to Joan de Montpalau, Martorell proposed Vilargut as an arbiter. At the beginning of 1444, Vilargut helped to intercept and capture the *Doria,* a Genoese vessel taking provisions to the Muslim fleet anchored outside Rhodes. He fought during the siege and was later captured by the Grand Karaman and imprisoned in Alexandria. Two and a half days later, he escaped with a group of merchants and returned to the island. All this occurred in 1446. In 1447, Vilargut was back in Valencia, where he could have given Martorell a long, firsthand acount of the siege.

In addition, there are numerous parallels between Tirant's exploits in Rhodes and those of the Burgundian knight Geoffroy de Thoisy.[16] Martorell could have learned about Thoisy's role in relieving the siege through two contemporary accounts: one anonymous and the other in *Ancient Chronicles of England* by Jehan de Wavrin, nephew of Thoisy's commander, Admiral Walerand de Wavrin. The connection—which Romanesco establishes through a series of coincidences—is further solidified by Thoisy's oath in 1454 at the famous Vows of the Pheasant in Lille:

> I vow to do my utmost to be among the first ready to set out on this holy voyage with my lord and the last to abandon him if he does not order me elsewhere. I shall always obey his commands.[17]

In Martorell's book, Tirant makes a similar vow before the King of France:

> I swear before God, His saints, and my lord the Duke of Brittany, admiral of this fleet and the most excellent and Christian King of France's representative, that today I shall be the first ashore and the last to retreat. (358)

The one aspect of the Sicily and Rhodes sequence with literary precedents is the story of the Calabrian philosopher whom Princess Ricomana summons to learn whether Prince Philip is as loutish and miserly as she suspects. A number of models are used, the first of which is Joseph's interpretation of the Pharaoh's butler's and baker's dreams in Genesis 40. The discovery of the king's illegitimacy initially appears in *The Arabian Nights* (night 469). The tale is then retold in Clemente Sánchez de Pascual de Gayango's *Libro de los enxemplos* (*Book of Fables,* early thirteenth century), but Martorell's model was probably the Italian *Cento novelle antiche* (*A Hundred Old Tales*) or *Novellino* (*Tales*) of the late thirteenth century.

More than half of *Tirant lo Blanc* takes place in the Byzantine Empire, which our hero saves from the Turks while also wooing and finally winning Princess Carmesina. Apart from certain brief inserts (Abdullah Solomon's speech in chapter 148, for example, is a translation of Petrarch's Latin epistle, *Familiarum rerum,* 12, 2), most of the action is either Martorell's own invention or based on historical events and personages. The plot—in an extremely general way—parallels *Guy of Warwick,* in which Guy saves Constantinople from the Sultan of Babylon. As a reward for his labors, he is offered the emperor's daughter Laurette, but he rejects her out of loyalty to his beloved Felice.

Martorell's real motives for writing about Byzantium, however, probably had more to do with its recent fall (in 1453) than with any literary models. At a moment when all Europe spoke of a crusade against the Turks (Trebizond was not conquered until 1461, and Rhodes held out until 1522), Martorell would have had ample reason to make this the subject of his novel. In addition, there are two historical models with whom a number of parallels can be established: the adventurer Roger de Flor (1280–1305) and the Hungarian general János Hunyadi (1407?–56).[18]

The real Roger de Flor was one of the shadier characters in Catalan history. He began his career as a Knight Templar in the Holy Land, and after the fall of Acre amassed a fortune by blackmailing refugees. When the grand master learned of these activities, he denounced Roger, who fled to Genoa and became captain of a company of Catalan mercenaries (the *almogàvers*). He and his band then sailed to Sicily, where they fought for the Catalan King Frederic III against the pretender from the house of Anjou. Shortly after the peace of Caltabellota (1302), Roger was summoned by the Byzantine Emperor Andronicus II. The Catalans won a number of victories in Asia Minor, but Roger's primary goal was to found his own principality. The *almogàvers'* savage looting aroused the emperor's distrust, and Roger was recalled to Adrianople, where he was assassinated in 1305. The immediate result was the famous "Catalan Revenge," in which his mercenaries ravaged Macedonia and Thrace. Before his death, Roger had wrested a number of concessions from the imperial court: he was appointed first megaduke and then Caesar and was promised the Bulgarian tsar's daughter (also Andronicus's niece) in marriage.

Objectively considered, Roger de Flor could perhaps best be described as having played a minor supporting role in the fall of Byzantium. Catalan sources, however—from Ramon Muntaner's *Chronicle,* still widely read in Martorell's day, to the current *Great Catalan Encyclopedia*—are more discreet about his vices and more flattering about his undeniable military talents. In any case, one can easily see several parallels between Roger and Tirant. Roger was welcomed enthusiastically when he arrived in Constantinople with a fleet of twelve ships (Tirant has eleven). Both Roger and Tirant are distrusted by some of the groups in the empire (Tirant by the Duke of Macedonia, Roger by the Alans and the Genoese). Roger was made first megaduke (Tirant becomes captain general) and then Caesar. Roger was promised the emperor's niece; Tirant is given his daughter. Roger and Tirant fight the Grand Karaman in Anatolia. And finally, Roger and Tirant both die in Adrianople.

Hunyadi, Tirant's other historical model, was the most successful fifteenth-century general against the Turks. He became governor of the
kingdom of Hungary and led an army of thirty thousand men in the "long
campaign" of 1443–44, during which he broke the sultan's power in
Bosnia, Herzegovina, Serbia, Bulgaria, and Albania. A series of setbacks
followed, notably at Varna (1444) and Kossovo (1448). In 1456, Sultan
Mehmed II besieged Belgrade. Hunyadi, at the head of a small trained
army and a mass of ragged and unequipped peasants, succeeded in relieving the siege and even made sorties into the enemy camp. He was unable
to take advantage of his successes, however, because a few days later he fell
ill and died of a plague that had broken out in his camp. Nonetheless, the
relief of Belgrade was celebrated throughout the Christian world with
processions and thanksgivings ordered by the Valencian Pope Calixtus III.
Hunyadi had also corresponded with Alphonse the Magnanimous and had
offered to be his vassal in exchange for aid against the Turks.

The most obvious link between Hunyadi and Tirant is their names.
Though of Hungarian ancestry, Hunyadi had been born in Transylvania
(among his other feats, he replaced Vlad Drac or Dracula as lord of
Wallachia). Because of his origins, the Hungarian general was often referred to as Valachus or Balachus—a name frequently corrupted to Blach
and, by extension, to Blanc or Blanch in Catalan, Bianco in Italian,
Bianchus in Latin, and so forth. He appears in French chronicles as "*le
chevalier Blanc* / the white knight" and in Catalan as "*lo comte Blanch* / the
white count," "*lo rey Blach* / the white king" or simply "*lo Blach.*"
Furthermore, Hunyadi's symbol was a raven, and in chapter 125 of *Tirant
lo Blanc,* Martorell tells us Tirant has a raven depicted on his banner.
Finally, Hunyadi and Tirant both die attended by Franciscan friars (in
Hunyadi's case by his great friend and comrade Giovanni di Capistrano).

Most of the episodes in North Africa and the final relief of Byzantium
were probably written by Martí Joan de Galba, following Martorell's
previous plan and including certain chapters written before his death
(315, for example). Though Galba is more precise in his place names (he
seems to have frequently consulted Sir John Mandeville's *Travels*), both
authors display a solid knowledge of the Mediterranean and, in Martorell's case, of southern England as well. Their primary source of information was certainly fourteenth-century Valencia itself, where Christians,
Muslims, and Jews traded freely with the entire area. Epirus and parts of
Greece (including Athens) had been Catalan possessions, and medieval
Jewish Catalan cartographers were among the finest in Europe. The
kingdom of Tlemcen, which plays such a large role in the North African
episodes, contained a substantial contingent of Christian renegades,
among them the famous vizier Hilal the Catalan. The kingdom was not
annexed by Morocco until 1389. Bougie, likewise, was independent of

Tunis during parts of the thirteenth and fourteenth centuries. Information of this sort would have been common knowledge in Galba's and Martorell's city. A far more striking detail is the inclusion of Bornu, a sub-Saharan kingdom generally believed to have been "discovered" by Europeans in the eighteenth century.[19] In *Tirant,* it is accurately situated on the border between Barbary and Black Africa. Like medieval Catalan maps, this description indicates an exact and extensive knowledge of caravan terminals far beyond the Christian world and the geographic imagination of most Europeans.

King Escariano, Tirant's black friend and ally, combines imaginary traits with those attributed to Prester John. The historical background— apart from Mandeville's fanciful commentaries—is as follows. In 1427, several Ethiopian ambassadors arrived in Valencia. In 1450, a certain Pietro Rombolo disembarked in Naples, accompanied by an Ethiopian with a message from Prester John, as well as by an Arab who probably acted as interpreter. Three years later, Alphonse the Magnanimous dispatched several ambassadors to Ethiopia.[20] Only in 1530 did Europeans realize how little use the Ethiopians could be to them militarily and how much they differed religiously. *Tirant* was written at a time when many Christians still hoped to find a powerful ally on the other side of Muslim North Africa.

All these sources—both literary and historical—help us to understand the background against which *Tirant* was written: a European (and above all Mediterranean) world for which central Spain was a remote and primitive outpost. The novel, however, is far more than the sum of these factors, which do not tell us why—or whether—it is a major literary work. What, then, are *Tirant*'s distinguishing features as a novel? Perhaps the one that has most impressed critics is its realism. Compared to the stylized dreaminess of chivalric romances and the realism-by-type of authors like Chaucer or Boccaccio, *Tirant* is full of characters with sharply defined individual personalities. The hero himself is a case in point. Brave in war, he is so shy in love that even when Pleasure-of-my-life slips him into the princess's bed, he declines to take advantage of the opportunity. Yet he is generally at ease with ladies, and skillfully maneuvers Princess Ricomana of Sicily into the arms of his loutish friend Philip. The princess, for her part, is a kind of adolescent *demi-vierge,* seductive and priggish by turns. Pleasure-of-my-life, Tirant's helpmate, is likewise a complex character. The freest in speech, she is also the only one without a lover (though we do see her play sexual games with the princess). The empress is alternately cynically pompous and openly lascivious. Her seduction of the young knight Hippolytus, whom she often addresses as "my son," provides some of the book's most entertaining moments.

The sexual episodes in *Tirant* take place in an environment that, while ostensibly Byzantine, probably bears a far closer resemblance to Marto-rell's Valencia. The characters alternate high rhetoric with colloquial speech. Sometimes the transition can be hilariously abrupt, as in this passage where the princess tries to persuade Tirant not to consummate his affair with her:

> Tirant, do not change our glorious reunion into bitter woe but calm your-self, my lord, and abjure bellicose violence, for a delicate damsel cannot resist a knight. Do not treat me thus, as love's battles should be won through clever flattery and sweet deception, nor should you employ treachery except against infidels. Do not cruelly defeat one already vanquished by love! Will you brutally prove your mettle against a helpless damsel? Give me part of your manhood that I may resist you! Oh my lord, how can you delight in forcing me? Oh, how can you hurt the one you love? By your virtue and nobility, please stop before you hurt me! Love's weapons should not cut; love's lance should not wound! Alas, cruel false knight, be careful or I shall scream! Lord Tirant, show your compassion and pity a helpless damsel! You cannot be Tirant! Woe is me! Is this what I longed for? Oh, my life's hope, you have slain your princess! (1089, 1090)

This speech begins in one of *Tirant lo Blanc*'s typical modes: the repeti-tive, baroque "Valencian prose" in which its characters so often address each other. Thus, in addition to the standard medieval war-sex meta-phors, we find a mode of speech where redundancy and ornamentation are cultivated for their own sakes, as in the phrases *treballosa pena* ("bitter woe") and *bel·licosa força* ("bellicose violence"). The ornamental quality of the Catalan is underlined by placing the adjectives before the nouns. As Tirant's "assault" draws to its conclusion, however, these devices fall away and the princess's voice becomes that of a real adolescent girl losing her virginity.

This crystallization of a real human voice out of a generalized (and often indistinguishable) rhetoric is one of the peculiarities of *Tirant* and a major difficulty in translating the book. Another example, much earlier on, is when William of Warwick takes leave of his wife. After a long exchange of courteous speeches and set-piece lamentations, he suddenly bursts out:

> "Lady countess," the count replied, "let us put an end to these words. I have to set out, and you can stay or leave as you like." (122)

There are two likely explanations of these abrupt shifts in tone of voice, both of them probably correct. One is that aristocrats in Martorell's Valencia really did affect a ponderously verbose style in much of their conversation, only breaking into what we would consider "normal" speech in certain circumstances: under pressure, for example, or when especially relaxed. Martorell's letters have sometimes been cited as proof of this penchant for verbosity, but since they were intended for public consumption it is difficult to draw any conclusions from them. The other explanation is Martorell's own sense of irony, as well as the limits of his patience. In the princess's speech, this irony is carried by the phrases "clever flattery" and "sweet deception," as well as by the deflating sentence that follows her words: "Do not think the princess's pleas persuaded Tirant to leave the job unfinished" (1090). Often, one feels that there were limits to Martorell's endurance of his own rhetoric, since such abrupt deflations are not infrequent in *Tirant*.

This mixture—or more exactly, sudden succession—of styles leads us to the confusing question of Martorell's own intentions. We know he died before completing the work, and we are also fairly certain that Galba interpolated passages of his own in the manuscript Martorell left behind. It is therefore logical to assume that Martorell never had a chance to revise what he had written. *Tirant* does often feel like a first draft written by someone groping his way toward a new style. The William of Warwick episodes, though partially marked by Martorell's personality, are much closer to standard medieval literature than the rest of the work. They are followed by Tirant's exploits in England, which, despite their chivalric trappings, are essentially a realistic account of a warrior's training. For this reason—and also because of the tough-guy attitudes struck in many of the speeches—they sound at times more like a prizefighter's memoirs than what we would usually consider knightly adventures:

> "Knight," replied Tirant, "I am not unaware of your station, rank, courage, and powers, but this is no time or place to discuss lineages. I am Tirant lo Blanc. When I take my sword in hand, no king, duke, count, or marquis can refuse me. Everyone knows that. In you, however, one can quickly find all the seven deadly sins, and to think that with shameful words you seek to frighten and degrade me! I cannot be insulted by a loose-tongued knight like you, nor would I feel praised if you spoke well of me, since it is commonly said that being praised by vile men is as bad as being praised for vile deeds. Let us waste no more words, for if one hair fell from my head, I would not want you to have it or let you take it." (227)

In this section, Martorell seems to be reorienting himself and moving away from his original intentions. Instead of the usual monotony of literary jousts, we are offered exact descriptions of a wide variety of possible situations, including a fight with a mastiff. Sex also enters the book in this section, first in the guise of the prostitutes in the king's wedding procession and then with the brooch Tirant takes from between Fair Agnes's breasts. Nonetheless, one has to wait until the Sicily and Rhodes expedition for a radical shift in tone. As has often been noted, with the change to the Mediterranean Tirant ceases to be a knight-errant and becomes a general. He no longer jousts; he leads armies and plots strategy. Likewise, sex and humor enter the book in a far more decisive manner. From this point until Tirant's shipwreck in North Africa (when Galba's intervention becomes obvious), the action in *Tirant* revolves around war, love, and politics. It is also with the shift to the Mediterranean that the characters become fully three-dimensional, with peculiarities, ambivalences, and sometimes—as with the empress's and Hippolytus's overtly Oedipal relationship—noticeable subconscious lives. Thus, toward the end of the book, when the emperor finally dies, we are told that Hippolytus

> was certain that the enamored empress would lay aside her shame and take him
> as her husband and son, for old ladies usually wish to marry their sons to repair
> and atone for the sins of their youth. (1171)

Under the politics and war heading, we see Tirant's constant emphasis on battlefield discipline and cunning strategy, which are credited for his frequent victories over larger forces. In the course of his North African campaign, for example, he and King Escariano are besieged by a mighty coalition of real and imaginary Muslim potentates with more than five thousand oxen, cattle, and camels—so many that the Christians can barely get in or out of the main city gate. Tirant routs this horde by two stratagems, one relatively traditional and the other a clever ruse suggested by the Genoese Almedixer.

First, Tirant divides his army so as to trap the Saracens between two attacking forces. He sends one half under King Escariano to hide in a wood on the other side of the Saracen camp, ordering them to attack only when he gives the signal. Then Almedixer sets fire to a mixture of goat's hair and mutton fat, and fans the smoke toward the enemy camp. The Saracen livestock catch the scent and stampede, ripping up tents and goring men and horses in their flight. When the enemy camp is in a thorough uproar, Tirant hoists a flag and he and King Escariano attack simultaneously from the front and rear. The battle is still fierce (after all, what good is a victory over cowards?), but the enemy's advantage has been lessened by Tirant's clever generalship.

Off the battlefield, too, we notice the realistic precision of Martorell's descriptions, as in this passage in which Tirant puts Constantinople on a war footing:

> Furthermore, Tirant had heavy chains stretched across the streets and left
> there until he rang a bell in the palace that could be heard throughout the city.
> Since there were many thieves in the town, he ordered half the houses on each
> street to hang lanterns in their windows until midnight and the rest from

midnight until dawn. Once the emperor had retired, he rode through the streets till midnight, when Diaphebus, Richard, or another would take his staff and make the rounds till morning, and in this manner the city was preserved from all evil. Moreover, Tirant told the aldermen to search every house, bringing all the wheat, millet, and barley they found to the market square. After letting each family keep as much food as it needed, they distributed the rest at two ducats a cartload. Within a few days the city was well provisioned, whereas before Tirant's arrival the people had been unable to buy bread, wine, or any other food. (394, 395)

This attention to such unchivalric details as crime prevention and rationing was part of what led Vargas Llosa to describe Martorell as the first novelist seeking to present an "all-encompassing reality." Such passages also reflect a gift for "circumstantial realism" (the piling up of believable details to create the illusion of a factual account). This technique, so frequently used in nineteenth-century novels, is here being placed at the service of an impossibility: the defense of a city that had fallen at least seven years earlier. In any case, for Martorell it was probably not a consciously employed technique but a natural result of his fascination with everything he saw or heard about.

Reading *Tirant,* one often feels that Martorell wanted to include *everything* in his book. Elaborate courtly speeches and brisk exchanges, knightly protocol and descriptions of how to set fire to a ship at anchor displace each other and accumulate a staggering abundance of detail. What sometimes seems to be missing is the capacity to prune all this *copia.* In the end, unfortunately, that task fell to Galba, who was a competent rhetorician but a bad novelist and who shared nothing of Martorell's insatiable appetite for the sensory world. The result is a book with an unusually improvised feeling. At times we seem to be in a literary universe close to our own; at other moments we are almost drowned in boring and repetitive speeches. Yet the thrust of much of *Tirant*—more than in otherwise more consistent and polished medieval authors like Chaucer and Boccaccio—is toward the modern novel. Perhaps the very audacity of Martorell's conception kept him from realizing it as consistently as he might have otherwise (and perhaps would have in a final draft).

Nonetheless, what he did leave behind is fascinating. In addition to the grimly realistic descriptions of warfare and military training (the besieged citizens of Rhodes eating rats, or the Enedasian knights completing their training with a year in slaughterhouses), we also find a group of sexual relationships free from both puritanical remorse and medieval typology. Sex, in *Tirant,* is never the occasion for guilt. If the princess withholds her favors from the hero, it is out of fear of pregnancy and scandal. In general, the only morality with any psychological impact is the chivalric code: fair play, a clean fight, etc. In the area of sex, *figura* (how things appear, not how they are) is what counts.

In sexual and psychological terms, perhaps the most developed relationship in the novel is between the empress and Hippolytus. The attitudes that will dominate it appear clearly in Hippolytus's reply to the princess (he has just declared himself to the empress), when she asks him to give several of her hairs to Tirant as a sentimental keepsake:

> "May God punish me," replied Hippolytus, "if I take them unless you tell me the significance of their being three instead of four, ten, or twenty. Really, my lady! Does Your Highness think these are the old days, when people followed the laws of grace and a damsel who loved some suitor in extreme degree would give him a well-perfumed bouquet of flowers or a hair or two from her head, whereupon he considered himself exceedingly fortunate? No, my lady, no. That time is past. I know quite well what my lord Tirant desires: to see you in bed, either naked or in your nightdress, and if the bed is not perfumed, he will be just as pleased. Offer me no hairs, as I am unaccustomed to bearing such gifts, or else tell me why you have pulled them from your head." (738)

Compared to Tirant's and the princess's never-ending pleas and rejections, Hippolytus's and the empress's courtship is straightforward. The fears she expresses—that Tirant is using Hippolytus to gain political power, that she will look foolish, that she will not be able to keep pace with Hippolytus's appetites—are what one would expect from an older, more experienced woman about to begin an affair with a young knight:

> Your kind words deserve an answer, but not the one you desire, for you have troubled my spirit. What leads you to court a woman so much older than yourself? If this becomes known, people will say that I am enamored of one who could be my grandson! I also know that foreigners are neither true nor steadfast lovers, and blessed is that woman who has no husband to impede her! I am so unused to love that I would have trouble satisfying your appetites, wherefore your hopes are tardy and vain, as another possesses what you desire, though if I wished to cuckold him I could do so. Your youth and sweet disposition make me forgive your audacity, and any damsel would rejoice in your devotion, but I would rather see another win this prize than perish myself for love of a foreigner. (747)

She and Hippolytus then arrange to meet ouside her bedchamber. The empress has the room perfumed and redecorated, and she retires early complaining of a headache. When she reaches her rooms, Eliseu, one of her maids, sends for the doctors, who prescribe a glass of malmsey with candied marijuana seeds. There is a hilarious exchange with the doctors:

The doctors said: "If Your Highness will eat a few candied marijuana seeds and drink a glass of malmsey, they will rid you of your headache and help you sleep."

The empress replied: "My illness is such that I do not think I shall get much sleep or even rest, since the way I feel now, I shall be tossing and turning all night."

"Your Highness," said the doctors, "if this proves to be the case, send for us at once, or if you prefer, we shall spend the night here or outside your door and observe you every hour."

"That will not be necessary," replied the empress, "as I want my bed all to myself and prefer not to be observed when I am making merry, nor is my ailment one that can bear too much scrutiny. This woman will show you out, for I wish to go to bed." (752, 753)

We then see the empress eat a big box of the seeds and wash them down with wine. After dismissing Eliseu, she goes out onto the roof and finds Hippolytus lying there. She is pleased by his discretion and thinks how well he will "protect her honor." They lie down on the roof and consummate their love then and there. We next see them in bed, where we are told that:

> Anyone who saw her then would have recognized her peerless beauty, for while Carmesina resembled her in many respects, you could see that in her time the mother had excelled the daughter. (755)

The lovers do not fall asleep until daybreak, and shortly thereafter Eliseu returns to see how her mistress is faring. She finds Hippolytus beside her with her nipple in his mouth. The maid's first instinct is to call for help, but then she remembers her lady's preparations the night before. Meanwhile, the emperor and the doctors have come and are waiting outside. Eliseu thinks the empress has been discovered, but when Her Majesty goes to the door she realizes nothing is wrong:

> She hurried back to Hippolytus, pulled his ears, and gave him a big kiss, saying: "My son, please go into that alcove and stay there till I can dispose of the emperor and his doctors." (758)

Once Hippolytus is safely hidden, the emperor and the doctors are shown in, and the empress tells them her dream: that her dead son had returned, climbed into bed with her, kissed her breasts, and told her he was in Heaven with other knights martyred by the infidel. He asks her to take Hippolytus as his replacement, for he loves him as much as his sister Carmesina. In the course of the empress's description, the dream—which might have been a kind of grotesque joke—becomes quite moving. The reader is drawn into the empress's own psychological state, where the double-entendres reflect her real incapacity to distinguish between Hippolytus and her dead son, as well as her emotional condition after their night together:

> "Alas, my lord," cried the empress, "what a rude awakening! I held him in these very arms and felt his sweet mouth on my breasts. Many early morning dreams come true, and he will surely return if I go back to sleep." (760)

Martorell's ability to give form to these feelings lifts the scene out of the sphere of vaudeville (though it certainly has its humorous elements) and gives it an individualized emotional charge rarely found in medieval literature. It was scenes like this one, of course, that evoked Marcelino Menéndez y Pelayo's outrage, as when he declared that *Tirant* "slithers about amid the lowest kind of sensualism."[21] The Catalan scholar Martí de Riquer, in his far more sympathetic treatment of *Tirant,* implicitly accepts these moralistic terms by claiming that Martorell's sense of humor saves the novel from being pornography. To my mind, however, both points of view are equally alien to the author's perspectives. Exactly what these perspectives were is a bit difficult to pinpoint. Martorell certainly accepted Christianity and did not perceive himself as a rebel against the Church. On the other hand, he refused to make the connection between religion and sexual morality. Sex, in *Tirant lo Blanc,* is something intrinsically pleasurable and good but which may involve practical dangers. There is a good deal of humor in his description of the circumstances surrounding sex (as there is in his descriptions of many other things), but the humor is not designed to deflate or paliate the sexuality. On the other hand, all the characters remain themselves in sexual situations, with the same seriousness they have outside them and—in many cases, since the dialogue is more intense and intimate—more three-dimensionality than they usually display on public occasions. In fact, Martorell is at his best in bedroom scenes and military campaigns.

In translating *Tirant,* I have tried to stay as close as possible to standard modern English and to avoid the false archaisms that used to mar many renderings of medieval texts. In addition, I have eliminated as many redundancies as possible, both to make the book more readable and in the belief that Martorell might have done the same, had he lived to complete his project. I am indebted to Martí de Riquer for his advice, encouragement, and most of the information contained in the footnotes, as well as to the Joint U.S.-Spanish Committee for Educational and Cultural Affairs and the National Endowment for the Humanities for their generous financial support.

Though I realize the category "great medieval and Renaissance classics" is usually considered a closed one, my hope is that *Tirant* will eventually find a home there. Certainly the novel deserves it, for in its literary innovativeness, its realistic dialogue and description, and its vivid presentation of major characters, it equals and often surpasses other masterpieces of fifteenth-century literature. As always, however, the proof is in the reading, and therefore perhaps my best advice would be to again quote Cervantes's words: "Take it home and read it, and you'll see everything I've said is true."

David H. Rosenthal

TIRANT LO BLANC

To the honor, praise and glory of Our Lord Jesus Christ and His glorious and holy mother, Our Lady the Virgin Mary, the words of the present book entitled TIRANT LO BLANC *begin, dedicated by Sir Joanot Martorell, knight, to His Most Serene Highness Prince Don Ferdinand of Portugal.*

Most excellent, brave and glorious prince of the royal line:

Though I knew of your virtues by repute, I am far more mindful of them since Your Highness revealed his will concerning the deeds of those glorious knights of old, whom poets and historians have praised in their works, perpetuating their memories and noble exploits, and especially the distinguished and chivalrous feats of that famous knight Tirant lo Blanc who, as the sun outshines the planets, in his knightly deeds outshone all others. He bravely subdued many kingdoms and provinces, offering them to others and desiring only the simple honor of his victories, and later he conquered the entire Greek Empire, winning it back from the Turks who had brought the Christians under their yoke.

Since the aforesaid tale was written in English, and Your Illustrious Highness has been pleased to beseech me to translate it into Portuguese, believing that as I spent some time in England, I must know the language of that isle better than others do—which request I consider a most acceptable order, for my chivalric vows oblige me to make known the valor of former knights, and even more so because the book's main theme is the code and order of chivalry—and considering my insufficiency and the administrative and family affairs that weigh upon me, as well as the adversities of Fortune that give my thought no rest, I could have justly excused myself from the task but, confiding in The Sovereign Good that aids all noble enterprises, compensating for men's weaknesses and bringing all virtuous tasks to conclusion, and trusting that Your Highness will excuse any failings in style or presentation that may have entered this book through carelessness or ignorance, I shall dare to translate it not only from English into Portuguese but also from Portuguese into Valencian vernacular,[2] that my native land may receive joy and instruction from the many worthy deeds recounted. Therefore, I pray Your Highness to accept the present work of his affectionate servant, for should it contain any faults, the blame lies with the English language, some words of which are impossible to translate. Be mindful of my affection and constant desire to serve you, and excuse my clumsy rendering of the various thoughts. Impart them to your servants and others, that they may extract the kernels of wisdom hidden therein, urging on their valor never to shrink from harsh deeds of arms but to champion noble causes, upholding the common good for which the knightly order was founded.

Likewise, this book will be a light unto knights of the spirit, as it attacks vice and unnatural acts, and lest others be blamed if any fault be found, I, Joanot Martorell, assume all the responsibility and wish to share it with no one, since I have translated this book in the service of that most illustrious prince of the royal line, Don Ferdinand of Portugal. Begun January second, fourteen hundred and sixty.

PROLOGUE

As manifest experience shows, the weakness of memory, consigning to oblivion not only those deeds made old by time but also the fresh events of our own era, has made it appropriate, useful, and expedient to record in writing the feats of strong and courageous men of old. Such men are the brightest of mirrors, examples and sources of righteous instruction, as we are told by that noble orator Tully.[1]

In the Holy Scriptures we read the stories and saintly exploits of the holy fathers, of noble Joshua and the Kings, of Job, Tobias, and mighty Judas Maccabaeus, and likewise that exquisite poet Homer recounts the exploits of Greeks, Trojans, and Amazons, as does Titus Livius with Romans like Scipio, Hannibal, Pompey, Octavian, Mark Anthony, and many others. We also study the battles of Alexander and Darius, the adventures of Lancelot and other knights, the versified histories of Virgil, Ovid, Dante, and other poets, the holy miracles and wondrous acts of the apostles, martyrs, and other saints, the penitence of Saint John the Baptist, Mary Magdalene, Saint Paul the Hermit, Saint Anthony, Saint Onophrius and Saint Mary of Egypt. Innumerable stories have been compiled lest they fade from memory.

Worthy of honor, fame, and eternal glory are all brave men, and especially those who risk death for their fatherlands, for we read that honor cannot be won without valiant deeds, nor happiness without courage. Brave knights have always preferred death to shameful flight. That saintly woman, Judith, with manly courage dared to slay Holofernes, thus freeing her city from oppression. So many books have been written and compiled from old stories that the human mind can scarcely encompass them all.

In ancient times, the knightly order was held in such esteem that only the brave, prudent, strong, and dexterous in arms were received into it. Physical strength and courage should be employed with wisdom, for through prudence and strategy, the few at times have vanquished the many, laying low their enemies through astuteness and cunning. For this reason, the ancients ordered jousts and tournaments, teaching their young bravery and dauntlessness before their enemies. Knights should be accorded respect and reverence, without which kingdoms and cities could not live in peace, as we are told by Saint Luke.[2] A courageous warrior deserves honor and glory, and since among other knights of glorious memory we find brave Tirant lo Blanc, this book celebrates his deeds, as the following stories tell us.

WILLIAM OF WARWICK

· I ·

*H*ERE THE FIRST PART OF TIRANT'S BOOK
BEGINS, RECOUNTING CERTAIN NOBLE
EXPLOITS OF COUNT WILLIAM OF WARWICK
IN HIS SAINTLY LATTER DAYS

The knightly estate excels in such degree that it would be highly revered,
if knights pursued the ends for which it was created. Divine Providence
has caused the seven planets to influence our natures, giving us varied
predispositions to sin and vice, but Our Universal Creator has allowed us
free will, which, if we use it well and live virtuously, will mitigate our
weaknesses. For this reason, the present book will be divided into seven
main parts, showing the honor and sovereignty knights deserve among
their fellow men.

The first part will discuss the origins of chivalry; the second, the
knightly order and calling; the third, the tests to which any lord or
gentleman aspiring to knighthood should be subjected; the fourth, the
manner in which he should be knighted; the fifth, the significance of his
weapons; the sixth, the life and customs appropriate to a knight; and the
seventh, the honor due him. These seven parts of knighthood will be
treated in due order in a later chapter. Now, to begin, we shall recount
certain valiant deeds of that noble and spirited knight and father of
chivalry, Count William of Warwick, in his saintly latter years.

· II ·

*H*OW COUNT WILLIAM OF WARWICK, HAVING DECIDED TO VISIT THE HOLY SEPULCHER, INFORMED HIS WIFE AND SERVANTS OF HIS IMPENDING DEPARTURE

In the rich, fertile, and pleasant isle of England lived Count William of Warwick, a brave knight of noble birth and even greater virtue who, through his wisdom and ingenuity, had served the cause of chivalry with great honor and whose fame had spread throughout the world. In his virile youth, this knight had often risked his life in battle, making war on land and sea and winning many jousts. He had bested seven kings and princes, leading armies of ten thousand, and had tilted in five great tournaments, always winning glorious victory.

When this valiant count had reached the age of fifty-five, he was moved by divine inspiration to make a pilgrimage to the Holy Sepulcher in Jerusalem, which every Christian should visit to atone for his sins. This virtuous count wished to do penance for the many deaths he had caused in wars and tournaments.

Having made his decision, one night he told his wife. Despite her virtue and wisdom, she was greatly distressed, and her womanly heart quickly revealed its anguish.

The next morning, the count summoned his servants, both men and women, and spoke the following words: "My children and faithful servants, God is pleased to part me from you. My return is uncertain, as my journey is one of great peril, and therefore I wish to reward you now for your services."

Having sent for a great chest of gold, he paid them so generously that they were all well pleased. Then he entrusted his lands to the countess, though they had an infant son, and he ordered a gold ring made with two coats of arms: his own and hers. This ring was so cunningly fashioned that it could be split into two halves, but only when they were joined could one see both sets of arms.

Once all this had been done, he turned to the virtuous countess and, with gentle demeanor, uttered the following words:

· III ·

HOW THE COUNT TOLD HIS WIFE OF HIS DEPARTURE, AND WHAT SHE REPLIED

"The evidence I have of your love and sweet disposition, lady wife, redoubles my grief, for your virtue has won my heart and my soul is saddened by our parting, yet hope also consoles me, as I know of your good works. I trust you will accept my departure with forbearance, and, God willing, through your prayers my journey will soon be over. I commend my son, servants, vassals, and manor to you. Keep half of this ring and cherish it as you would my person."

"Alas!" cried the afflicted countess. "Can it be true that you wish to forsake me? At least allow me to accompany and serve you, for I would sooner die than live without Your Lordship. Should you spurn my pleas, on my deathbed I shall feel no greater woe. I only wish you knew the sorrow that burdens my weary heart. Tell me: is this the joy and solace I longed for? Is this the comfort of love and conjugal faith I expected? Where are my hopes that Your Lordship would stay with me until I died? Have I not spent enough time as a widow in mourning? Woe is me, for I see my prayers are denied! Let death come; nothing can help me—neither thunder nor lightning nor mighty tempests—in persuading my lord to stay and not abandon me!"

"Oh lady countess! Well I know that love has conquered your great wisdom," the count replied, "but consider that when Our Lord shows His grace to a sinner, making him repent of his misdeeds and wish to do penance, the wife who so loves his body should love his soul still more, and instead of lamenting should thank God for His mercy. Thus should you behave in my case, for I have sinned greatly, wounding and killing many people in time of war. Is it not better, now that I have retired from battle, for me to serve God and seek absolution than to live for worldly gain?"

"That all sounds very sweet," the countess said, "but it is I who must drink this cup of grief, and bitter it is for one orphaned so long and a widow with neither husband nor lord. Just when I thought my misfortunes were over, I see my woes increase and can truly say that I have only this poor son to remind me of his father."

Then she grabbed the little boy's hair, pulled it, and slapped his face, saying: "My son, weep for your father's departure and keep your grieving mother company."

The infant, who was only three months old, began to cry. Seeing the mother and child in tears, the count was much distressed, but although he sought to comfort her, he could not restrain his own sobs of love and pity.

For a long time he was speechless, while the three of them wept together and the countess's maidens also made great moan, since they loved their mistress dearly.

Having learned of the count's departure, the gentlewomen of the city went to bid him farewell, and as they entered his chambers they saw him consoling the countess.

Upon beholding these honorable ladies, the countess waited till they were seated and then uttered the following words: "The cruel assaults of harsh decisions and grave abuses torment my womanly spirit, oh ladies, and reveal my unjust afflictions, just as bitter tears and deep sighs, the results of my defeated suit, proclaim my sorrow. To you, oh married ladies, I address my tears and show my affliction. Consider my woes your own, as you may find yourself in my situation, and by bemoaning your future ills you can also pity mine. Let my hearers lament the evils that await me, for there is no steadfastness to be found in men. Oh cruel death! Why do you pursue those who fear you and flee those who invoke you?"

The noblewomen rose, urging the countess to vent her grief, and together with the count they comforted her as best they could, while she said: "Abundant tears are nothing new to me, having always been my lot. Often and for many years, when my husband was at war in France, I wept every day, and I shall now die of a broken heart. Would that I had slept my life away and escaped such cruel sorrows. Tortured by your departure and deprived of all hope and comfort, I declare that just as the glorious saints endured martyrdom for Jesus Christ, so I wish to be martyred for my lord and master. Henceforth act as you like. Fortune allows me nothing better, since you are my husband, but I swear that without you I am in Hell, whereas by your side I am in Heaven."

When the countess had finished her dolorous lamentations, the count replied in the following manner:

· I V ·

THE COUNT'S WORDS OF COMFORT AND FAREWELL TO THE COUNTESS, HER REPLY, AND HOW THE COUNT WENT TO JERUSALEM

"My spirit is soothed, oh countess, by the last words you spoke, and, God willing, I shall quickly return with my soul fortified, but wherever I may be, my spirit will remain with you."

"What good is the spirit without the body?" the countess retorted. "I trust that for love of your son, you will think of me from time to time, but love of those far away is like pollen on flax. Do you want to know something, my lord? My grief is greater than your love, for if you loved me as you pretend to, you would stay by my side, but what good is holy oil to an unrepentant Saracen? What good is my husband's love if he does not show it?"

"Lady countess," the count replied, "let us put an end to these words. I have to set out, and you can stay or leave as you like."

"Since I can do no more," said the countess, "I shall retire to my chambers and bewail my cruel misfortune."

The count sorrowfully said goodbye to her, kissing her many times and weeping bitter tears. Then he sadly took his leave of the other ladies and set out with one squire.

Having left the city of Warwick, he took passage on a ship, which sailed with a favorable wind and arrived safely in Alexandria. There the count went ashore and made his way to Jerusalem, where he confessed all his sins thoroughly and diligently, receiving Christ's precious body with the greatest devotion. He visited His sepulcher, offering fervent prayers with so many tears and such great contrition that he truly deserved Our Lord's pardon.

After visiting the other holy places in Jerusalem, he returned to Alexandria, where he boarded another ship bound for Venice. Once there, he gave all his money to the squire who had served him well, arranging a good marriage for him to ensure that he would remain in Italy. Then he had the squire spread the word that he had died, so that some merchants wrote to England saying Count William of Warwick had perished during his voyage from Jerusalem.

When the countess heard these tidings, she was overcome by grief and ordered a funeral service worthy of so brave a knight. A while later, the count returned to his own country. He was all alone, with hair down to his shoulders and a long white beard that reached his waist. Dressed as a Franciscan friar, he begged for alms in the streets of Warwick and dwelt in a nearby hermitage dedicated to Our Lady.

This hermitage was on a high mountain blessed with thick woods and a clear spring. The count retired to this isolated place, where he led a solitary life, shunning worldly affairs and doing penance for his sins. No one recognized him because of his long hair and beard, though in the course of his weekly rounds he visited the virtuous countess. Seeing him beg with such humility, she gave far more to him than to other paupers, and for a while he persevered in this miserable existence.

· V ·

HOW THE KING OF CANARY INVADED ENGLAND WITH A MIGHTY FLEET[1]

Some years later the King of Canary, a hardy youth whose virile and restless soul was stirred by dreams of conquest, had a great fleet of ships and galleys built. He planned to descend on the isle of England with a mighty host, for English pirates had assaulted some of his towns. Great was his rage and indignation at this affront, and, setting sail with a favorable wind, he soon reached England's green and peaceful shores, where under cover of darkness his fleet entered the harbor of Southampton. He and his Saracens landed without being heard by the inhabitants, and once ashore they began to ravage the island.

The peace-loving English king, when he heard of their arrival, mustered his forces and attacked his foes. A great battle ensued, in which many men were killed, but the Christians got the worst of it, for the Saracens outnumbered them and carried the day. The English king's power was broken, and he had to retreat with his remaining troops to the city of Canterbury, where Thomas à Becket's holy bones lie buried.

As the English king was regrouping his forces, he learned that Saracens were pillaging the island, killing or enslaving Christians and dishonoring their wives and daughters. Knowing his foes would pass by the shore, the king hid his men in a pass under cover of darkness. At dawn there was a cruel battle, in which many Christians perished. Those who survived fled with their hapless sovereign, while the Saracens again carried the day.

Great was the misfortune of this Christian king, for he lost nine battles in succession and finally had to take refuge in the city of London. When the Saracens learned of his whereabouts, they besieged the city and tried to storm it. They broke through the Christian ranks and advanced halfway across London Bridge. Each day there were many noble feats of arms, but in the end the afflicted king fled to avoid starvation. He made his way toward the Welsh hills and stopped in the city of Warwick.

When the virtuous countess heard of the unlucky king's approach, she had food and lodgings prepared. Being a woman of great prudence, the countess considered how she might fortify and defend her city, and once the king had arrived she addressed him in this manner:

"Sire, I see you and all your subjects in great peril, but should you wish to abide in this city of yours and mine, you will find it abundantly provided with everything necessary for war, since my husband, Count William of Warwick, who was lord of this land, equipped his castle with bombards, crossbows, muskets, cannon, and many other types of artillery. God in His mercy has granted us four years of good harvests, so that Your Highness may safely remain here."

The king replied: "Countess, I feel your advice is good, as this city is strong and well provisioned, and whenever I wish to leave I may easily do so."

"By Saint Mary it is so, my lord," said the countess. "Though there were many more Saracens, they would still have to attack from the plain, because on the other side there is a river that flows down from the Welsh hills."

"I shall be happy," the king replied, "to stay here, and I pray you, countess, to make ready everything my army needs, for which you shall be duly paid."

The countess immediately left the king. Then she, two damsels, and her city aldermen went through the houses requisitioning grain, oats, and everything else they needed. When the king and his men saw such plenty, they praised the virtuous lady's solicitude.

Knowing the king had left London, the Saracens pursued him until they heard he was in Warwick. On their way, they took a castle called Kenilworth[2] about two leagues from the city. The desperate English king climbed to the top of a tower and looked down upon the Saracen hordes, who were burning towns and castles and slaying as many Christians as they could, both men and women. Those who managed to escape ran toward the city, crying for help. From a good half a league away, you could hear them weeping and lamenting, for they were doomed to die or be enslaved by infidels.

As he beheld his enemies and the destruction they wrought, the king felt he would die of grief. Unable to gaze further upon this desolation, he descended the tower stairs and entered a little room. There he began to sigh, while bitter tears rolled down his cheeks. His stewards standing outside the room heard their master's laments, for when he had wept and moaned a long time he began to speak thus:

· VI ·

*T*HE KING'S LAMENT

"If God wishes me to be both wretched and shamed, then let death, the final deliverance, overtake me, as my infinite sighs are such that if our religion did not restrain me, I would end my own life. Woe is me, hapless king! My sufferings move the world to pity, and yet I find few defenders of my just cause. Oh God of sovereign glory, if sorrow and distress hamper my tongue, compensate for my shortcomings, since Your just gaze always finds the straight and true path. Lord, by Your pity, redeem this Christian nation however greatly it may have sinned. Preserve and defend us, that we may glorify Your name. Alas, I am like a sailor lost at sea who begs the Virgin for help. Oh Holy Mary, free us from enslavement, that your Son's holy name may be glorified in my kingdom."

As he was lamenting, the king laid his head on the bed, and he thought he saw a fair damsel dressed in white damask enter the room with a little child in her arms. Many other damsels followed her, all singing the *Magnificat*. He fell silent as the lady approached him, placed her hand on his head, and spoke these words: "Have no fear, oh king, for the Son and the Mother will aid you. When you see a man with a long beard begging for alms in God's name, kiss his lips in sign of peace and humbly beg him to lay aside his habit and lead your army."

The grieving king awoke and saw nothing. He was amazed by the dream and puzzled over it for a long time. When he left the room, he found his finest knights awaiting him. They said: "Sire, our enemies have surrounded the city." The king did what he could and had the walls well guarded.

The next morning, the count climbed the mountain to gather the wild herbs that sustained his life. Upon beholding the Saracen hordes that had ravaged the lands below, he left his hermitage and went down to the city, which he found filled with woe.

The poor old man, who had spent many days eating nothing but grass, saw the city's affliction and went to beg for alms at the castle. As he was entering, the king came out of Mass, whereupon the count knelt before him and begged for charity. Remembering his dream, the king lifted him up and kissed his lips. Then he took the old man's hand, led him into a chamber, and began to speak thus:

· VII ·

H OW THE KING OF ENGLAND PLEADED WITH THE HERMIT

"The glorious expectations I have of your great virtue, oh reverend father, give me courage to beg your help and counsel in our dire need, for I see you are a man of saintly life and a friend to Jesus Christ. I hope you will be moved by the great terror these infidels have wrought. They have destroyed most of the island, defeating us time and again and slaying our finest knights. Should you feel no compassion for me, take pity on those Christians who will be enslaved and dishonored. Though this city is well supplied with food and arms, we cannot resist much longer, as the Saracens are many and have conquered most of our kingdom. They will not stop until they triumph, and our sole hope is Your Reverence. For the love of God I beg you, if any pity dwells in your heart, to put aside your penitent's robes and don those of charity, which are knightly armor."

When the king had finished these sad words, the hermit replied:

· VIII ·

*T*HE HERMIT'S REPLY

"I am astounded that Your Highness should request help from one so poor and weak as I. Your Majesty is not unaware of the decrepitude of my feeble person, caused both by age and the harsh life I have endured. I lack both the strength and the prowess to do battle, and yet you ask my advice when there are so many brave knights around you, men dexterous in arms who can counsel you better than I. Truly I say to you, my lord, that were I a hardy knight and skilled in warfare, I would gladly serve you and risk my frail person for Your Majesty, as it would be a great pity if in your youth you were dethroned. Therefore I must beg Your Highness to excuse me."

The sorrowful king, grieved by this reply, began to speak thus:

· IX ·

*T*HE KING'S REPLY

"Such a just request brooks no excuse if any compassion dwells within you, for you know that, to defend the Catholic Faith, holy saints and martyrs have battled the infidel and won glorious crowns of martyrdom, their noble spirits comforted by God. Therefore, reverend father, I kneel at your feet and with bitter tears again beg you, by Our Lord's holy passion, to act as a true Christian and pity me, the most afflicted of kings, and all the Christian folk, whose only hope lies in God's mercy and your virtue. I am certain that your goodness will not deny my request."

The sorrowful monarch's bitter tears moved the hermit to pity. His pious heart was softened, and tears of compassion rolled down his cheeks. He had always intended to help the king, but first he wished to test his constancy.

After a short while, the hermit raised the king to his feet, and, drying his tears, addressed him thus:

· X ·

THE HERMIT'S FINAL REPLY TO THE KING

"On you, wise young king of blessed life, all eyes are justly fixed as you plan your defense. Only at great risk can one my age win fame through deeds of chivalry, and in his senectitude, a bold knight need only avoid base acts to sustain his honor. Your sad words and bitter tears have touched my heart, but had you not begged so piteously, reason would have obliged me to refuse. Oh grieving king, how little spirit you show! Save your doleful laments for some greater occasion! I see your pleas are humble and sincere, and for love of God, whom you invoked, and of yourself, my natural lord, I submit to your commands and shall use all my skills to free you. I am willing, if necessary, to do battle, old though I am, and to defend Christianity against the haughty Islamic sect. With God's help, I shall give you honor, glory, and victory."

The king replied: "Reverend father, since you show such kindness, I give you my word as king that I shall not alter a hair of your commands."

"Now, my lord," said the hermit, "when you go into the hall, turn a smiling face to your knights and subjects. Show your cheer, speak in a jovial manner, and eat a hearty lunch, that those who have lost hope may swiftly regain it. A lord or captain, in whatever adversity he may face, must never display a gloomy countenance lest he dismay his followers. Send for some Saracen clothes and you will see what I plan to do, for on my way to the Holy Sepulcher I stopped in Alexandria and Beirut. There I studied the Arab tongue and learned to make a kind of explosive that takes hours to ignite, but once lit, can destroy the whole world. The more water you pour on it, the brighter it burns, and it can only be doused with a mixture of oil and pine resin."

"What an amazing thing!" the king exclaimed. "I thought water could put out any fire on earth."

"No, my lord," the hermit replied, "and if you will allow me to go to the castle gate, I shall bring back something that mixed with plain water or wine will light a torch."

The hermit went straight to the castle gate, for upon his arrival he had seen some quicklime there. He picked up a handful and returned to the king. Then he took a little water, threw it on the quicklime, and lit a candle from it with a straw.

The king said: "I would never have believed this had I not seen it with my own eyes! Now I am convinced that men can do anything, and those who can do the most are people who have traveled. I beg you, reverend father, to tell me what ingredients you need for these explosives."

"Sire," replied the hermit, "I shall fetch them myself, for since I have often made such explosives, I can tell if the ingredients are good or bad. Once they are ready, my lord, I shall go alone to the Saracen camp and place them near the king's tent, where they will ignite around midnight. The Saracens will hurry to douse the fire, while Your Majesty waits to attack. When you see a great blaze, sound the trumpets, and you may be sure that ten thousand Christians will suffice to defeat a hundred thousand of them. I can tell Your Highness that when I was in Beirut, I saw a similar case of one king against another, and with God's help and my advice the city was saved from its besiegers. Therefore Your Majesty, or any knight, should learn all he can about weapons to dismay his enemies and succor his friends."

· XI ·

*H*OW THE KING OF ENGLAND THANKED THE HERMIT

The hermit's wise words cheered the sad king, who thanked him profusely for his gracious offer and swore to obey all his orders.

When they had finished talking, His Majesty went into the great hall, where he showed himself to his subjects with cheerful mien and spirited gesture. His knights were astonished to see their lord looking so merry, for it had been many days since he had laughed or jested.

The hermit soon returned with the ingredients for the explosives. Then he told the king: "Sire, we lack only one item, but I know the countess has it. Her husband, William of Warwick, stored it in great quantity, as it has many uses."

The king replied: "Then let us visit the countess and request it."

The king sent word to the countess that he wished to speak with her. Upon leaving her chamber, she saw him standing with the hermit.

"Countess," the king said, "by your kindness and virtue, grant me a little of that sulfur that never stops burning, the sort your husband used to make torches the strongest wind could not extinguish."

The countess replied: "Who told Your Highness that my husband knew how to make such torches?"

"Countess," the king said, "this hermit informed me."

The countess quickly entered her stores and brought out so much sulfur that the king was well satisfied.

When the king had returned to the great hall and lunch was ready, he took the hermit's hand and seated him by his side. The royal servants were amazed at the honors their master bestowed upon the old man. The countess was even more surprised, since she was used to giving him charity and had always derived great pleasure from his soothing words. When she saw how the king revered him, she wished she had given him more and told her maidens: "Oh, how I rue my ignorance, for I showed little honor to this poor worthy hermit, and yet I believe he must be a saintly man. Though he lived long in my county, I was blind to his worth, and now the king, who is so generous and pious, has seated him by his side. All the days of my life I shall grieve for the little honor I did him. Oh virtuous king, father of charity, you now atone for my failings!"

· XII ·

*H*OW THE ENGLISH KING TOLD THE HERMIT TO PREPARE THE EXPLOSIVES

Rising from the table, the comforted king asked his friend to prepare the explosives. A few days later, when they were ready, the hermit told His Majesty: "Sire, with your leave I shall now execute our plan while Your Highness awaits the signal to attack."

The king quickly consented, and under cover of darkness, the hermit donned some Saracen clothes and slipped out through a secret door. No one recognized him as he made his way to the Saracen camp.

When he thought it was time, he hid the explosives near the tent of a mighty captain who was a close relative to the king. Shortly before midnight, a huge and terrifying blaze burst forth. The king and his unarmed men rushed to douse the flames, but the more water they poured on the fire, the brighter it burned.

The brave King of England, who had gathered his remaining knights, sallied forth from the city and fiercely attacked his foes. The Christians wrought such destruction that it was pitiful to see, for they spared no infidel who crossed their path.

When the Saracen king saw the roaring blaze and his countless dead comrades, he leapt on his steed and fled to Kenilworth Castle, where he fortified himself with those who had escaped the massacre.

He and the other Saracens were dumbfounded at their defeat. They could not understand it, for they were fifty times more numerous than their foes. Once they had fled, the Christians pillaged their camp, and the next morning, the English entered the city in great triumph.

Four days later, the Saracen king sent ambassadors to challenge his opponent to battle. The letter they brought was of the following tenor:

· XIII ·

*T*HE KING OF CANARY'S CARTEL OF DEFIANCE

To you, Christian king and former ruler of England, I, Abraham, Lord of Canary, make the following offer: that all bloodshed may cease between us, though I command more towns, castles, infantry, and cavalry, I shall meet you in single combat, for though Allah has given you one victory, I have bested you many times in your own country. Therefore, if you wish the killing to end, let us enter the lists under the following conditions: if I defeat you, you will rule England as my vassal, paying me two hundred thousand gold nobles every year on Saint John's Day. On that day, you will don certain robes that I shall send you and show yourself in one of four cities: London, Canterbury, Salisbury, or Warwick. Since it was here that you discomfited me, here I shall first celebrate my coming victory, but if Fortune favors you, I shall quit your land, and furthermore I shall restore all the towns and castles I have conquered.

These words are not spoken vaingloriously or in scorn of your royal crown, but because Allah is great and will give each his just deserts.

· XIV ·

*H*OW THE KING OF CANARY'S AMBASSADORS BROUGHT HIS CHALLENGE TO THE KING OF ENGLAND

Two of the noblest Saracen knights prepared to depart with their lord's cartel, but first they sent a messenger to ask the English king for safe-conduct.

When the messenger reached the city gates, the guards told him to wait while one of them hastened to the king and informed him of what had happened. After taking counsel, His Majesty ordered the gates thrown open and the Count of Salisbury cried: "Messenger, our king declares that your ambassadors may come in safety."

The count gave him a silk robe and a hundred nobles, and the messenger went away contented. As they awaited the ambassadors, our hermit advised the king: "Sire, let us give those Saracens a sight they will long remember. Send two mighty lords to welcome them with a multitude of bareheaded knights, while three hundred soldiers guard the main gate. Station women in windows and on rooftops along the streets, with big cloths covering their bodies and helmets on their heads, for thus our guests will mistake them for soldiers. Once they have entered Warwick, send the three hundred men back into the city, that the ambassadors may see them on corners and in squares. Dismayed by the sight of so many soldiers after that battle they lost without knowing how or why, they will believe we have received reinforcements from Spain, France, or Germany."

Thinking the hermit's words very wise, the king and his council chose the Duke of Lancaster and the Count of Salisbury to welcome the ambassadors. Four thousand men escorted them, each with a garland of flowers on his head, to meet their foes a good mile outside the walls. Then the Duke of Bedford said: "Tell me, father hermit, since these ambassadors have to go through so many ceremonies, how should the king receive them: naked or clothed, armed or unarmed?"

"If there is no malice in your words," the hermit replied, "you have asked a good question, but I see that your intentions are more evil than good. Since I am only an old hermit, you think you can insult me before my lord. Mind your tongue, for otherwise I shall place a bit in your mouth that will chafe at every step."

Upon hearing these words, the duke rose, drew his sword, and cried: "Were you not so old and dressed in Saint Francis's robes, I would take this sword, the avenger of insults, and trim your skirts up to the waist."

The king rose angrily and ordered the duke seized, disarmed, and locked in the keep. All the other lords soothed the hermit, saying a man of his age and monkish habit should forgive such affronts. The hermit offered to do so, but the king would not hear of it, and though everyone pleaded with him, he wanted to fling the duke out of the city with a trebuchet to welcome the ambassadors.

While they were discussing these matters, word came that the Saracens were on their way, whereupon the men who had been chosen left to carry out their tasks.

When the ambassadors were before the king, they gave him a letter of credence and the cartel. Once it had been read aloud, the hermit approached his lord and whispered: "Your Majesty, accept the challenge."

The king declared: "I accept your king's challenge and his conditions."

Then he invited the ambassadors to stay the night, saying he would give them a more complete answer on the morrow. He ordered comfortable lodgings prepared, and all their needs were attended to.

The king convened a general council, and while his knights were gathering, the hermit approached him with some other lords. He knelt before His Majesty, kissed his hand and foot, and humbly begged for the keys to the keep. The hermit and the other lords pleaded so much that the king was forced to give in, and upon reaching the tower where the duke was imprisoned, they found him with a friar who was hearing his last confession. When he heard the door open, his face turned white as chalk, for he thought they were coming to take him to trial.

Instead the hermit said: "Lord duke, you and I have exchanged harsh words. I beg you to forgive me, and I shall gladly forgive you too."

Then they returned to council, where the king and all his dukes, counts, and marquises awaited them. They read the Saracen king's challenge again, and since the king and everyone else loved the hermit, recognizing his holiness and wisdom in the arts of war, they asked him to speak first, and these were his words:

· X V ·

*H*OW THE KING'S ENTIRE COUNCIL ASKED THE HERMIT TO SPEAK FIRST

"Since natural duty and reason oblige me to obey Your Majesty's commands, and since despite my small knowledge you order me to speak first, I shall tell you what I think without prejudice to these magnanimous lords, though, feeling myself unworthy to discuss military matters, I must protest and beg your indulgence if I speak foolishly. I hope you will be pleased to correct or discount my suggestions, for I have lived long in a hermitage and know more about wild beasts than arms. I say, my lord, that Your Highness should accept the Saracen king's challenge, and once you have accepted, as a good and valiant king should—knowing that to die in battle is better than to live in shame—and considering that your foe is a brave and mighty warrior, I think Your Majesty, having pledged his faith before Our Lord God, should practice no deceit if he wishes to best his enemies. Nonetheless, our king is young and frail, though his spirit is bold and chivalrous, and it would be neither suitable nor just for him to enter the lists with one so strong. Therefore, his uncle, the Duke of Lancaster, should do battle in his stead, and the king should abdicate in his favor lest the Saracen king be deceived."

When the hermit finished these last syllables, three dukes rose in great fury: the Duke of Gloucester, the Duke of Bedford, and the Duke of Exeter. They began shouting that they would never permit the Duke of Lancaster to fight the battle and become king, since by right they were all closer to the throne.

The king refused to hear them and instead spoke these words:

· X V I ·

*H*OW THE KING OF ENGLAND ARGUED THAT HE SHOULD DO BATTLE WITH THE KING OF CANARY, AND WHAT HIS COUNCIL REPLIED

"Truly, such an unnatural request should not be heard. Better you had tried my courage with doubting words, for I shall allow no man to do battle in my stead. I accepted the challenge and I shall meet it."

A mighty baron then rose to speak: "My lord, forgive me for what I am about to say, but this cannot be. God may have given you the will but He has not given you the strength, and we all know Your Highness is unequal to such cruel battles. Submit to our counsel, since if we deemed you fit for such a task, we would willingly obey your orders and permit you to fight."

All the other knights praised this baron's words.

Then the king replied: "Since you, my loyal vassals and subjects, think me incapable of fighting the Saracen king, I thank you for your devotion and submit to your will, but let no man, under pain of death, dare to say he will replace me. I shall choose my successor and give him my crown, kingdom, and royal scepter."

They all said they were satisfied, whereupon the king spoke these words:

· XVII ·

*H*OW THE KING OF ENGLAND, WITH THE CONSENT OF ALL HIS KNIGHTS AND BARONS, YIELDED HIS CROWN, SCEPTER, AND KINGDOM TO THE HERMIT

"Thus does iniquitous Fortune flatter those she wishes to undo, concealing part of their adversity lest they be forewarned. Oh evil destiny that awaits the lucky, who consider small afflictions great and cannot withstand great ones! Therefore, oh dukes, counts, and marquises, since Divine Providence has been pleased to deprive me of force and bodily health, and since you all declare me unfit to do battle, I acknowledge your good will, stripping myself of all my powers and giving my title, scepter, and royal crown freely and without constraint or obligation to my beloved father hermit, who is present today."

Then he removed his robe, saying: "Just as I remove these royal vestments and place them on this hermit, likewise I divest myself of all sovereignty and lordship and place them in his hands. I ask him to accept them and do battle with the Saracen king."

When the hermit heard the king's words, he leapt up and tried to speak, but all the great lords rose as one man and surrounded him, stripping him of his monkish habit and dressing him in the king's clothes. Before a notary, the king yielded all his powers to the hermit in the presence of his whole council. When the Hermit King saw the barons pleading with him, he accepted the kingdom and called for some armor, but nothing they brought satisfied him.

"On my faith," the Hermit King said, "at this rate there will be no battle even if I go in my shirtsleeves. I pray you, my lords, to go to the countess. Beg her by her great virtue to lend me the armor her husband wore."

When the countess saw so many noblemen and heard their pleas, she gave them some old armor of little value. Having seen it, the Hermit King said: "This is not the suit I want, for she has others that are far better."

The barons went back again and asked for the good suit of armor, but the countess told them there was no other. When he received her reply, the Hermit King said: "Lords and brothers, let us try our luck together."

Once they were before the countess, she said: "May God take my little son, who is all I have in the world, if I have not already given it to you."

"Quite so," the king said, "but that suit is not the one I wanted. Lend me the suit in that little alcove in your chamber: the one covered with green and white damask."

The countess knelt and said: "Sire, please tell me your name and how you met my lord, Count William of Warwick."

· XVIII ·

THE HERMIT KING'S REPLY, AND HOW HE RECOUNTED HIS FEATS OF ARMS AT THE CITY OF ROUEN

"Countess," the Hermit King replied, "this is no time or place to disclose my name, as I must attend to other matters far more pressing to everyone, and hence I beseech you to lend me the armor, for which I shall be eternally grateful."

"Sire," said the countess, "I shall happily lend it to you, but please—and may God grant you victory over the Saracen king—tell me what you know about my husband."

The king replied: "My lady, since you urge and beseech me so, I shall gladly tell you because of your great merit. You surely recall that great battle in which your husband defeated the King of France at Rouen.[3] Defending the city against sixty thousand soldiers on foot and horseback, the count rode forth with only a handful of men. There at the bridgehead, his knights slew more than five thousand Frenchmen. Then he retreated toward the city, while the battalion from Picardy pursued him. They tried to storm the gates, but William of Warwick stood his ground. Finally the king charged with all his men, a mighty clash ensued, and, seeing himself outnumbered, your husband withdrew into the city. Those guarding the portcullis let a throng of Frenchmen ride through, but they lowered it just before the king could enter. When William of Warwick had killed or disarmed them all, he saw the king still assaulting the city. He sallied forth from another gate and charged with all his might, wounding his foe twice and killing his mount beneath him. One French knight, seeing his lord unhorsed and badly wounded, gave him his steed, but by retreating the king lost the battle. Countess, you will recall that a few days later your husband was summoned home by the King of England, who welcomed him with great honor and made a breach in the walls. All alone atop a chariot hung with brocade and drawn by horses with silk trappings, he entered London in shining armor, his naked sword held aloft. Later they came to Warwick and spent several days here, and I was always in his company, for we were comrades-in-arms."

· XIX ·

THE COUNTESS'S REPLY WHEN THE KING ASKED TO BORROW HER HUSBAND'S ARMOR, AND HOW HE PREPARED TO BATTLE THE SARACEN KING, OVER WHOM HE WON GLORIOUS VICTORY

"With unspeakable joy, sire, I recall everything you have recounted. It comforts my soul to hear of my husband's noble feats of arms, as I loved him dearly and held him in the highest esteem. His peerless valor was worthy of a royal crown, but the Fates have not befriended me, for they oblige me to live in mourning. Since I lost him, I have not spent one good day or night, and all my hours have been filled with sorrow. I shall speak no more lest I offend Your Highness, and I only apologize for having given you so little. Had I known of your comradeship with my lord, William of Warwick, I would have offered far more honor and charity."

The king was pleased by the virtuous countess's words: "Without error there is no need for apologies. Your virtues are great beyond telling, and I can never thank you enough. I only beg you, by your gentility, to lend me the armor I requested."

The countess quickly sent for another suit covered with blue brocade. When the king saw it, he exclaimed: "Lady countess, how well hidden you keep your husband's harness! After all our pleading, you still refuse to part with it! This is the armor William of Warwick wore in tournaments. The suit I want is hanging in an alcove, covered with white and green damask that shows a lion wearing a gold crown. Well I know this was the armor he wore in cruel battle, and, lady countess, with your leave, I am certain I could find it there."

"Woe is me!" cried the countess. "You act as though you had been raised here! Go and take whatever you want."

Seeing the countess's good will, the king thanked her and entered her chamber, where he found the armor and had it brought forth.

The king, who knew he would do battle on the morrow, went to the cathedral and spent the night there, kneeling before Our Lady's altar. The next morning, after hearing Mass with great devotion, he donned his armor in church and ate a partridge to fortify his body. Then he rode to the field of battle, while the women formed a barefoot procession. The maidens also went bareheaded, praying God and the Virgin Mary to grant them victory.

When the hermit had arrived, the Saracen king appeared with a great entourage, riding onto the field with bold knightly spirit. The infidels climbed a hill to watch the battle, while the Christians assembled near the city walls. The Hermit King bore a well-sharpened lance, a shield, a sword, and a dagger. King Abraham, who carried a bow, a quiver of arrows, and a sword, wore a round helmet wrapped in a turban.

As soon as the two knights had taken the field, they charged each other with great valor. The Saracen let fly an arrow that transfixed our king's shield and then quickly shot another that struck his opponent's thigh. Though it failed to pierce the Christian's armor, the arrow hampered his movements. The Hermit King had been struck twice before he could even approach his foe, but he hurled his lance as soon as he came within range. The infidel monarch, who was skilled in arms, knocked it aside with his bow, yet the Hermit King was now so close that the Saracen could no longer use his arrows. As the hermit came within striking distance, he shouted: "Oh Lord, help me vanquish these pagan hordes!" while the Saracen's heart sank at the sight of his foe.

The Hermit King drew his sword and charged, landing a mighty blow on the Saracen's head, but it did little damage because the turban was so thick. The infidel used his bow as a shield, parrying thrust after thrust until at last the Christian severed his arm and buried his sword in the pagan's side. Seeing his foe on the ground, the Hermit King swiftly beheaded him, and with the dead king's head on his lance, he returned triumphantly to the city.

Imagine how joyous the Christians felt, thinking themselves freed from slavery! When the king had entered the city, they brought doctors to treat his wounds.

The next morning, our king summoned his council to the room where he was resting, and they decided to send two knights as ambassadors to the Saracens, urging them to keep faith and saying they could depart with all their possessions.

Having chosen the ambassadors, they sent a messenger to request safe-conduct, and once it had been granted, the ambassadors set out for the Saracen camp. There they were well lodged while the invaders considered their reply, but this was only a ruse, for grief over the slain king had increased their malice.

They had a great argument over whom to elect king, as some preferred Salah ben Salah,[4] while others favored the king's first cousin Aduque-perec. In the end they chose Salah ben Salah, who was a good and valiant knight. He immediately ordered the ambassadors and their entire party seized and decapitated, whereupon their heads were stuffed in a saddlebag on an ass. Two Saracen knights then led the beast toward Warwick, whose watchmen spied them as they approached the walls. As soon as they were nearby, they released the ass and galloped away. The chief watchman, who had seen everything, dispatched ten men on horseback, but when they beheld the bloody heads, they wished they had never been born and hastened to inform the king and his council of such perfidy. Stunned by this news, His Majesty then uttered the following words:

· XX ·

*H*OW THE HERMIT KING SWORE A SOLEMN VOW WHILE STILL RECOVERING FROM HIS WOUNDS

"I risked my life for eternal fame, considering stillborn those who dwell in obscurity, dragged from this world by the implacable Fates before men learn of their existence, being less than stones and trees, which for their usefulness and fruits are cherished. I deem noble a life lived with ardent spirit, dying in the certainty that one's glory will endure forever. Oh cruel infidels of little faith, you cannot pledge what you lack! I swear a solemn vow, wounded though I am, to enter no house but God's until I drive these Saracens from my kingdom!"

He quickly called for his clothes, rose from his bed, and had the trumpets blown. The first one to ride forth was the king himself, and he ordered all those between the ages of eleven and seventy to take up arms under pain of death and follow him. That day, they gathered where the king had defeated the Saracen, while he sent for his artillery and everything else necessary in war.

When the virtuous countess learned that the king had ordered everyone over eleven to arms, she was dismayed, for she knew her son would be among them. She hurried to the monarch, knelt on the hard ground, and began to speak in a piteous voice: "To Your Majesty, wise king grown old in saintly ways, the afflicted justly look for compassion. Therefore I, a grieving countess, have come to beseech you, who are so kind and endowed with every virtue, to pity me, for my sole comfort is this son who is too young to be of use to you. Remember your love and comradeship with my husband, to whom Your Highness was such a friend in time of war and battle, and I also remind you of all my alms and charity. May it please you to yield to my supplications—that is, to spare my son who has no father, nor have I more solace than this wretched child. Therefore, sire, since you are the father of compassion, grant me this favor, for which we shall be eternally grateful."

The king, who recognized the countess's error, quickly replied:

· XXI ·

*H*OW THE HERMIT KING EXPLAINED WHY HE COULD NOT EXCUSE THE COUNTESS'S SON

"Gladly would I obey you, lady countess, if your request were just, for I prize your son's honor as my own, but it is well known that young men must gain practice in arms and the gentle ways of chivalry. It is both needful and customary for men of honor to do battle in their tender youth, since at that age they learn better, both in jousts and in warfare. As your son is of an age to see the great honor knights may win through bravery, I wish to have him with me and promise to treat him as my son, according him every honor for love of his father and respect for you. Oh, what glory for a mother to have a son who longs for fame! Tomorrow I shall knight him that he may imitate his father's glorious deeds, and if he accompanies me now all ardent warriors will approve. I, who so loved your husband—for I never felt so much love or good will toward any man—now wish to love and honor his son in his stead, wherefore I beg and counsel you, virtuous countess, to return to the city and leave your son here with me."

"On my faith, sire," the countess replied, "your advice is neither sound nor pleasing. Do you wish me to understand that this art of chivalry is blessed? I say it is cursed, sorrowful, and useless. Would Your Majesty like an example? Yesterday you were healthy and cheerful, and now I see you sad, lame, and sickly, and woe unto those who lose their lives in combat! If I were certain of my son's safety, I would gladly let him go, but who can guarantee the outcome of a battle? My soul shudders with grief, for his spirit is so bold that he will seek to imitate his father. Sire, the dangers of battle allow my mind no rest. The best advice Your Highness can give me is to exempt my son from battle."

The king replied very gently: "Everything sounds good in a woman's mouth. Lady countess, waste no more words. Go in God's peace and return to your city, for you will gain nothing here."

The countess's relatives urged her to depart without her son and promised that the king would look after him. When she saw she could do no more, she wept and spoke these words:

· X X I I ·

*T*HE COUNTESS'S LAMENT UPON LEAVING HER SON

"Oh unjust fate, that my grief should exceed all others'! Oh bitter tears that reveal my undoing! Win over these witnesses to my irrevocable loss! Let my cries be heard with moans, sighs, and sobs! They are the cries of a mother whose only son has been torn from her and offered up to bitter death with feigned love and friendship. Oh mothers, you are like sheep, for your sons are slaughtered in cruel battle, but what use are tears when all hope is lost?"

The Hermit King was moved to compassion by these doleful lamentations. Great tears rolled down his cheeks as he drew the countess's relatives aside. Two knights then carried her to the city gates, calming her as best they could.

"Perhaps you believe you are consoling me in my woe," the countess cried, "but the more you say, the more you torment my troubled soul! If my only child dies in battle, what will then become of me? Sad and ill-fated, I shall lose son, husband, and everything I had in this wretched world! Would that I might die before bearing such grief! What use are worldly riches, when I am despoiled of all my joy? May merciful God carry me to the other sweet green shore of that great river where, forgetting my past ills, I may abide in eternal peace."

When the countess had finished, her son replied: "My lady, I beg you not to trouble yourself for my sake, and I kiss your hands in thanks for the great love I know you bear me, but you must realize that I am old enough to leave my mother's wing. I am ready to bear arms, to do battle, and to show whose son I am and who was my father. If God wishes, He will shield me from harm, letting me perform feats that will please Him, comfort my father's soul, and fill your heart with joy."

Having heard these words, the countess turned to the relatives who were carrying her and said: "Let no one die for a son! I thought my child's will accorded with mine and that he would shun the perils of battle, but now I see that he will do the very opposite. Certainly there is truth in that old saying: 'Hunting comes naturally to a hound.' "

Once they had reached the city gates, the knights said goodbye and returned to their camp. The countess's son knelt before her, kissing her hands, feet, and lips and asking her blessing. She made the sign of the cross and said: "My son, may God protect and preserve you from all evils."

Then she kissed him many times, crying: "How sad is this parting! It is all I needed to complete my misery!"

When her son had gone, the countess entered the city, lamenting bitterly. Many honorable ladies accompanied her, consoling her as best they could.

· X X I I I ·

*H*OW THE KNIGHTS WHO HAD ACCOMPANIED THE COUNTESS RETURNED TO CAMP WITH HER SON AND TOLD THE HERMIT KING OF HER LAMENTS

Having returned to camp with the countess's son, the two knights told the king everything that had been said. Feeling very pleased by his son's wise words, he ordered the camp well guarded and had his men sleep in their armor. When the sun rose the next morning, he dispatched scouts to see if anyone was nearby. Then he had the trumpets blown and moved his troops closer to the Saracens. The Christians pitched camp on a great plain, and only after the tents were all up did the king allow his men to eat and drink. By this time it was past midday.

The Saracens were astonished at their enemies' approach, since only a short while before the English had not dared to leave the city. Some captains said it was because their king, Salah ben Salah, had broken his word, and in the meantime perhaps reinforcements had arrived from Spain or France: "Wherefore they now have come to look for us, and you may be certain that anyone they catch will be hacked to bits."

One of the ambassadors who had brought the challenge to the Christians spoke up and said: "They treated us with great honor in their city, and we saw crowds of soldiers everywhere, for I swear by Mohammed that there were at least two hundred thousand of them, but now this cursed king of ours has unjustly killed their ambassadors."

Once the Saracens had heard this ambassador's words, they also summoned the others. After listening to their reports, they killed Salah ben Salah and elected another king, but nonetheless they armed for battle and rode forth to meet the Christians.

By now the sun had almost set, so they decided to pitch camp on a nearby hill. When the Hermit King saw them, he said: "On my faith, they must be frightened if they have chosen such high ground. Now tell me, lords and brothers: shall we defeat these invaders by force of arms or strategy, for with God's help and the Virgin's I shall give you victory."

They all replied: "Sire, our victory will be difficult if God and Your Highness do not help us. Now that their king is dead, they have marshaled all their troops. Their numbers are far greater than ours, and therefore we fear we shall get the worst of it."

"My lords," said the king, "I beg you not to be dismayed. Really! Have you never seen a battle where the few have vanquished the many or the weak the strong? Pay heed to what I say: in war, strategy is worth more than strength. Though we are few and they are many, our triumph will be all the greater, and those who come after us will cite our deeds as an example of undying glory. I, as a hermit, hereby absolve you of all sin and penance. Show your dauntless knightly spirits, as it is better to die a Christian than to be enslaved by Saracens. Therefore, each of you should prepare to perform noble feats of arms. Let us give battle, for our cause is just and we shall conquer. No prince on earth can rebuke us if we do our utmost against these traitors, who seek to steal our lands and enslave our wives and daughters."

When the Hermit King had finished his brave words, the former king spoke with manly spirit: "Your royal and lordly acts, kind father, show clearly who you are. Raise your trenchant sword, which is our hope and salvation. Urge us to perform glorious deeds, and we shall readily obey you. Let us take no further counsel but attack with cruel and avenging arms, as it is better to die bravely than to live in cowardice and shame."

The former king's brave words pleased the Hermit King, who began to speak thus:

· XXIV ·

HOW THE HERMIT KING HAD A TRENCH DUG AROUND HIS CAMP AND ASKED THE COUNTESS TO SEND HIM TWO BARRELS OF CALTROPS

"Indescribable is my joy, sire, at your bold knightly spirit, and therefore I shall speak no more. Since God and Your Majesty have crowned me, let everyone follow my lead, for with His help I shall give you victory over your enemies."

And seizing a straw basket in one hand and a shovel in the other, he set out from the camp. When the great lords saw what their king was doing, they all imitated him.

After leaving Warwick, the Hermit King had gathered everything necessary for war. Now he had a stockade built with a trench four yards deep outside it. The trench went as far as the river on one side, but with a gap through which a hundred and fifty men could ride abreast. On the opposite side, they dug another trench from the river to a high cliff near the camp.

The king said: "Well, that is done and we still have two hours until daybreak. Now, Duke of Gloucester and Count of Salisbury, hurry to the countess and ask her, for love of myself and you, to send me two barrels of copper caltrops."

They left immediately and, asking and ordering her on the king's behalf, they obtained the barrels, though the countess was still angry. She knew their need was urgent and gladly obeyed, but she could not help exclaiming: "May God preserve me! How is it this king is so familiar with my house? He knows where to find everything connected with arms and war. Is he a diviner or sorcerer?"

The barons had the two barrels of caltrops loaded on wagons and brought to the camp. When they were before the king, they told him everything the countess had said, whereupon the good king laughed and made merry with them for a while.

Then he had the caltrops brought to the gap and stuck in the ground so the Saracens would tread on them. He also had many pitfalls dug to ensure that once they got past one obstacle, they would find another. The Christians worked all through the night.

As soon as dawn began to break, the Saracens made a great din with drums, trumpets, clarions, and fierce battle cries. They came charging down their hill to do battle with the Christians, while the Hermit King ordered all his men to lie down and pretend to sleep. When the Saracens were almost within shooting range, the Christians suddenly leapt up as though they had been taken by surprise. As the Saracens came through the gap, the king cried: "My lords, be not dismayed! Turn your backs and pretend to flee!"

Beholding their foes in flight, the Saracens hurried forward even faster. As they poured through that gap—which was the only place they could enter—the caltrops pierced their feet. Meanwhile, the king had halted his troops. Seeing some Saracens pulling out the caltrops while others fell in the pitfalls, he shouted:

· X X V ·

*H*OW THE HERMIT KING VANQUISHED THE SARACENS

"Knights worthy of honor, gaze no more upon the city, but rather turn to face our enemies and those of the Christian faith. Attack with great ardor, for the day is ours! Give them cruel battle and show mercy to none!"

The king charged first, followed by all his men. When the Saracens saw the Christians' bravery and how many of their own men were wounded, they lost heart and gave up the fight. Those behind them, beholding the great destruction wrought by their adversaries, fled toward Kenilworth Castle, where they fortified themselves.

The Christians gave chase, beheading as many infidels as they could catch, while, exhausted by his wounds, the king halted for a moment. His men had captured a Saracen so huge he might have been a giant. Having knighted the countess's son, His Majesty decided the boy should slay that

Saracen. The lad drew his sword and stabbed him again and again till he was dead. Then the king seized the boy's hair and flung him on the infidel. He kept him there until the boy's face was covered with gore and made him stick his hands inside the wounds, thus baptizing his son in infidel blood. The child grew up to be a valiant knight and most fearless in battle. So great was he in his day that in much of the world one could not find his equal.

Seeing that the battle was won, the good king pursued the Saracens, killing all those he caught. It was the greatest slaughter seen in that era, for in two days ninety-seven thousand Saracens perished. Finally the king, weakened by his wounds, could walk no further, and they brought him a horse.

"On my word," said the king, "I shall do no such thing. Everyone else is on foot. If I rode it would be unfair."

They advanced slowly toward the castle where the Saracens had taken refuge, and when night fell they pitched camp and celebrated their victory. At dawn the trumpets sounded while the king's men seized their weapons, and he donned a tunic emblazoned with his coat of arms.

Then he led the assault on the castle, from which they were pelted with arrows, lances, and stones. The Christian monarch attacked so fiercely that he alone reached the walls, and the countess's little son cried: "Hurry, worthy knights! We must hasten to save our king, who is in grave peril!"

Seizing a shield that a page had brought him, he dived into the moat and swam to his lord's aid. The others, when they saw the lad break through, all rushed the castle. Many were killed and wounded, but with God's help no harm befell the boy.

Once they had reached the walls, they built a great fire and burned down the gate. The flames spread through the ground floor, and the boy began to shout: "Oh English ladies, regain your freedom, for your deliverance is at hand!"

Three hundred and nine women were inside the castle. When they heard that voice they all rushed to a hidden door, for the main gate was in flames, and the Christians helped them escape. Among them there were many noblewomen.

Seeing the castle in flames, the Saracens tried to surrender, but the king refused and they all burnt to death. Those who fled were quickly killed or forced back at lancepoint, and twenty-two thousand infidels perished on that day.

Then the Hermit King and his men set out to reconquer the kingdom. Showing mercy to none, they made their way to Southampton, where they flung the Saracen crews into the sea and burnt their entire fleet. The king decreed that any infidel who entered England on any pretext whatsoever would be slain instantly.

When he had recovered the kingdom and fulfilled his vow, the king returned to the city of Warwick with all his men. Having learned of his approach, the countess hastened to welcome him with all her ladies, for there were no men left except the sick and wounded. As soon as they saw the king, the ladies knelt and cried aloud: "Welcome to His Majesty, our conquering monarch!"

The noble lord smiled, embraced them one by one, and took the countess by the hand. They walked along talking until they reached the city, where the countess thanked him profusely for the honor he had done her son, and afterward she thanked the other great lords.

· XXVI ·

*H*OW THE HERMIT KING REVEALED HIMSELF TO HIS WIFE THE COUNTESS

After vanquishing his foes and restoring peace to England, the Hermit King rested for a while. One day when he was in his chambers, he decided to reveal himself to one and all, as he was eager to restore the former king's sovereignty and return to his life of penance.

He summoned one of his stewards and gave him half the ring he had divided with his wife, saying: "My friend, take this to the countess and repeat what I have told you."

The steward hurried to the lady's chambers, where he knelt before her and said: "My lady, this ring has been sent by one who has borne and still bears you infinite love."

The countess took the ring, examined it, and fell into a study. Then she hastened to her bedchamber, but before opening the jewel case, she knelt before a little oratory with an image of the Holy Virgin and prayed: "Oh humble Mother of God, compassionate lady, *ab initio et ante saecula* created *in mente divina,* only you were worthy to bear the King of Glory in your virgin womb for nine months. My lady, grant me this favor—you who were yourself so favored—and by the solace your blessed soul received from the Angel of the Annunciation, comfort my spirit. If it please you and your precious Son, oh glorious lady, grant that this ring be from my brave husband, for I promise to serve you for a year in your convent at Puy-en-Velay, to which I shall donate a hundred silver marks."

Then our countess opened the jewel case where she kept the other half of the ring, and upon placing them together she saw that the arms fitted.

Knowing her husband was nearby, she said in a troubled voice: "Tell me, good sir: where is my lord, the Count of Warwick?"—and the steward thought she meant her son—"Tell me, by your goodness, if he was captured by Saracens in those fierce battles. Had it been within his power, he certainly would have joined the fight. Ah, woe is me! Tell me where he is, that I may join him."

She tried to leave her chamber but was so befuddled that she could not find the door, and this was due to the unspeakable joy she felt at her husband's return. So great was her distress that she fell in a swoon.

Seeing their lady in such a state, her maidens cried out and wept, while the steward returned to his master, feeling very sad and looking much altered. The king asked: "My friend, what is wrong? What tidings do you bring?"

The steward knelt and said: "Sire, I would not have performed that errand even for a great city. I know not what evil power that ring possesses or if you obtained it from our foes, but as soon as the countess slipped it on her finger, she fell down dead. Truly, I am amazed by its devilish powers."

"Saint Mary preserve us!" cried the king. "Can it be that I have caused the virtuous countess's death?"

The king hastened to her chamber, where he found her more dead than alive, surrounded by doctors who were trying to revive her. Astonished at such a sight, he asked them to do everything they could, nor did he leave her side until she had regained her senses.

When the countess awoke and saw her husband, she quickly rose, knelt before him, and tried to kiss his hands and feet, but he refused and raised her up, kissing and embracing her many times. Shortly thereafter, he revealed his identity to the lords and townsfolk.

As word spread through the castle and city that the Hermit King was Count William of Warwick, all the knights and ladies, both great and small, hastened to the countess's chambers, where they joyously paid homage to the king and their new queen.

The Hermit King's son also hurried to kneel at his father's feet, kissing them many times with folded hands. Then the barons escorted their monarchs to the cathedral and thanked God for sending such a valiant champion.

Having finished their prayers, they returned to the castle in great triumph, accompanied by many trumpets and tambourins. Once they had reached the great hall, the countess invited her husband and those with him to dine with her that evening and for the rest of their stay.

The countess then left the king and gathered her ladies and damsels, who quickly changed clothes, rolled up their sleeves, and set to work decorating the dining hall, which they adorned with fine hangings richly embroidered in gold and silver. Other ladies worked in the pantry and kitchen, and a noble supper was soon prepared.

Once everything was ready, the countess sent word to the king that whenever he liked he and the others could come to table. When they entered the dining hall and saw how festively it was adorned, with all the food laid before them and the sideboard piled with gold and silver, he said: "If God has preserved my person, it is surely due to the countess, for she is the most diligent woman ever born."

He ordered the former king seated first, followed by the countess. Only then did he take his seat, together with the dukes in order of rank, while the marquises, counts, nobles, and knights were seated at other tables. They were abundantly served in accord with their merits, and for the rest of their stay, they feasted and made merry at the Hermit King's expense.

Nine days later, four hundred wagons arrived bearing gold, silver, jewels, and other spoils taken from the Saracens. The king entrusted the riches to four lords: the Dukes of Gloucester and Bedford, and the Counts of Salisbury and Stratford.

On the morrow, our king convened a general council, at which he appeared in a brocade robe that trailed behind him and an ermine-lined crimson cloak. Bearing a crown on his head and a royal scepter in his hand, His Majesty seated himself and began to speak:

· XXVII ·

*H*OW THE HERMIT KING RESTORED THE FORMER KING'S ROBES, CROWN, SCEPTER, AND KINGDOM AND RETURNED TO GOD'S SERVICE

"We should rejoice and offer thanks to God for our victory, as all blessings flow from His goodness and mercy. By His grace, we have vanquished our enemies and those of the Christian faith. With our naked swords we have avenged their affronts and abuses, wherefore I command that these spoils be divided among you. Those wounded recapturing any castle, town, or city shall have two parts. Those deprived of any limb and incapable of bearing arms shall have three parts. Those who have come to no harm shall have one part and honor, which is the most valuable part of all, and you, my king and lord, should be grateful for God's favors, since with your vassals' help you have reconquered this entire isle. Therefore I now, in the presence of these magnanimous lords, restore your kingdom, sovereignty, crown, scepter, and royal robes, asking Your Majesty to accept them from his loyal servant and vassal."

He immediately removed his royal robes and donned his monkish habit again, while the king and his barons thanked him profusely. Then the sovereign put on his crown and robes, took his scepter, and earnestly begged the hermit to grant him the honor of remaining in his court. He offered to make him Prince of Wales and to share his authority with him, and all those in the council urged him to consent, but the hermit excused himself, saying he could not abandon God's service for such worldly vanities. Here one can see this knight's great virtue and nobility. He refused to reign, though his wife and relatives pleaded with him.

When the king beheld our hermit's determination, he decided to grant some favor to his son. He gave him most of the kingdom of Cornwall and the right to wear a steel crown, which he would display at the Feast of Epiphany and again at Whitsuntide. All his descendants have preserved this custom and wear steel crowns to this day.

Knowing what great favors the king had granted his son, the hermit knelt at his feet and kissed his hand, though His Majesty tried to stop him. The count, after thanking him many times for his generosity, said farewell to the king and those in his court, who grieved over his departure, since they preferred him to his successor. The common folk were also sorry to hear that he had abdicated.

Having said goodbye to the king, the hermit left the city and dwelt for some days in a town one league distant. The king and his council sent him thirty wagons loaded with Saracen jewels, but as soon as Count William saw the wagons, he told those driving them: "Take them back to the king and tell him I want nothing beyond the honor. Let the worldly gain be for him and the others."

When the king and the other lords learned that he wished nothing for himself, they all said he was the most generous and virtuous knight the world had ever known, for he had gained nothing but glory, danger, and wounds from his victories.

The virtuous countess went to join her husband without saying a word to anyone, and a few days later, the king also visited the count, with whom he wished to take counsel about the state of the kingdom and other matters.

One morning, when they were talking together, the countess entered the room and the king told her: "My lady, take no offense at my words, but through your fault I have lost your husband, to whom I would happily have given a third of England."

"Woe is me!" cried the countess. "How, my lord, was I to blame?"

"Because he cherishes you above all else, and had you pleaded with him, he would have stayed."

"On my faith, sire," replied the countess, "I am worried about something far more serious, for he may soon return to his hermitage."

After talking a long while, His Majesty returned to the city, and within three days he and his retinue were ready to depart. The Hermit Count told his son to serve the king with all his heart, and if disputes arose, never to side against His Highness:

"No matter how much evil he may do you, always obey your natural lord. Though he may seize your lands, never oppose His Majesty, as whatever he takes he can also restore. Learn this lesson well: even if he strikes you with his hand, staff, or sword, your natural lord can never shame you, though he may harm your person. Once I was in the emperor's court and saw a duke under imperial authority. Shortly after Christmas, as the emperor was leaving church with a crowd of noblemen, he spoke some harsh words to the bishop who had celebrated Mass. That duke, who was the bishop's friend and relative, replied to the emperor's words, and His Majesty, who had little patience that day, raised his hand and gave him a resounding slap. The duke said: "Sire, you may slap me and do much more, yet I shall bear it patiently, for I am your subject, but if any other king or emperor touches the least hair on my head against my will, I shall make him regret it." Therefore, my child, I beseech you never to oppose your king."

The son promised to obey his father.

The Hermit Count provided his son's retinue with fine clothes, jewels, mounts, and pack horses, whereupon the lad took leave of his parents and awaited the king's order to depart. His Majesty then rode to the main city gate and called for the boy, whom he appointed Grand Constable of England.

When the countess learned of their departure, she asked the count to return to Warwick with her. He consented, but after dwelling with his wife for five months, he asked her not to be offended, for he was obliged to fulfill his vow to serve God. The countess replied: "My sorrowful spirit has been pining for some days, as my suffering heart knew the relapse would be worse than the illness. If you will let me accompany and serve you, we shall build a hermitage with two apartments and a church between them, and I promise to bring only two old women and a priest to say Mass."

The countess pleaded so much that her husband was forced to consent, but, disliking the hermitage where he had dwelt before, she chose another spot that was far more pleasant. It was in a thick wood, near a clear brook that murmured sweetly as it flowed through a fair green field, in the midst of which stood a pine tree of unequaled beauty. Wild beasts came to drink there, and it was a great pleasure to behold them. Once a hermitage had been built and furnished with everything necessary, the count and countess left orders for the governance of their domains. Then they found places for all their maidens and prepared to set out, but at that moment the Count of Northumberland brought a letter from the king. His Majesty invited the hermit and his countess to London, where he had arranged to wed the King of France's daughter.[5] If the hermit was unwilling, he begged the countess to attend, since he had great need of her to welcome the queen and teach her English ways, and as she was a lady of high degree and great understanding, the king wished to show her the honor she so richly deserved.

The Hermit Count replied in the following manner: "My lord, tell His Majesty that I would gladly obey him, but I cannot abandon my vow to God. I shall, however, allow the countess to satisfy him on her behalf and mine."

The virtuous countess preferred to forgo such festivities, but when she saw the count's will and that she could not justly refuse the king, she consented and prepared to set out. After bidding her farewell with innumerable tears, the count retired to his hermitage, where he dwelt in peace for many months. Every day after his prayers, he sat beneath that splendid tree, watching the beasts who came to drink at the clear brook.

TIRANT AND THE HERMIT

· XXVIII ·

*H*OW THE KING OF ENGLAND MARRIED THE FRENCH PRINCESS, AND THE GREAT FESTIVITIES AT THEIR WEDDING

The English knights' martial spirit slackened day by day, for they had enjoyed many months of peace, idleness, and calm repose. Lest they be overcome by sloth, the King of England decided that, since he was going to marry, he would summon all his knights to a great tournament. Word of the glorious festivities quickly spread throughout Christendom.

It happened that a gentleman of ancient Breton lineage set out with a noble company to attend the celebration. He fell behind his companions and dozed off on his mount, for he was weary after his arduous journey. His horse wandered from the high road, following a path that led to the delightful brook by our hermit's dwelling. At that moment, the hermit was amusing himself by reading a book called *The Tree of Battles*. As he read, he continually thanked God for the grace he had won serving knighthood.

Seeing a man approach on horseback and noticing that he was asleep, the hermit put down his book and wondered whether to wake him. When the horse beheld the brook, it tried to bend over and drink, but since the reins were tied to the saddle horn, it could not reach the water. It strained so much that the young gentleman awoke, and, opening his eyes, he saw a ragged hermit with a long white beard, pale and emaciated. This was caused by his ceaseless penance, and his eyes were red from weeping. His aspect was that of a wondrous holy man.

The gentleman was astonished at such a vision, but his good sense told him it must be some saintly man who had retired there to do penance and save his soul. Unabashed, he quickly dismounted and bowed before him. The hermit welcomed him with a smile, and they sat down on the grass. The hermit spoke first: "Young gentleman, I beg you to tell me your name and what business brings you to this fair spot."

The gentleman promptly replied:

· XXIX ·

*H*OW TIRANT DISCLOSED HIS NAME AND LINEAGE

"Reverend father, since you wish to learn my name, I shall gladly tell you. I am called 'Tirant' because my father was from the Tiranian March that borders England¹ and 'lo Blanc' because my mother Blanca was the Duke of Brittany's daughter. Word has spread that the Most Serene King of England will soon wed the French princess, whom men say is the fairest maiden on earth and endowed with many peerless beauties. I myself witnessed one last Saint Michael's Day in Paris, for on that day the marriage contract was signed and the King of France held a great feast. The king, queen, and princess ate at one table, and I can tell you in all truth that when the princess drank red wine, her whiteness was so extreme that one could watch it go down her throat. People also say the English king will be knighted, and that he will knight any other nobleman who wishes to enter the order. I have asked heralds and kings-of-arms why His Majesty did not do so during the war, and they said it was because he never won a battle until Count William of Warwick came, routing the infidels and restoring peace to his kingdom.

"Furthermore, they say the queen will arrive in London on Midsummer Day, and the festivities will last a year. Thirty Breton noblemen skilled in arms have set out for the wedding. They are all eager to be knighted, and I decided to join them. As we were riding, I fell behind because my horse and I were weary, having departed after the others and traveled for many days. As I was daydreaming, I fell asleep, whereupon my mount left the high road and brought me here."

When the hermit heard that the young gentleman was on his way to be knighted, he thought of what the order meant and how a knight should conduct himself. He heaved a deep sigh and fell into a study, recalling the great esteem in which chivalry had once been held. Seeing the hermit so pensive, Tirant began to speak thus:

· X X X ·

*H*OW TIRANT ASKED THE HERMIT WHAT HE WAS THINKING ABOUT

"Father, may it please Your Reverence to tell me his thoughts."

The hermit replied: "Dear child, I am pondering a knight's duty to uphold the noble code of chivalry."

"Father," Tirant said, "I beg Your Reverence to tell me if he is a knight."

"My child," replied the hermit, "it is fifty years since I was knighted in Africa before a great battle with the Moors."

"Lord and knightly father," Tirant said, "I hope you will tell me, since you have served the knightly order so long, how one can best uphold that order, which Our Lord has placed in such high degree and dignity."

"But really!" cried the hermit. "Do you not know the code of chivalry? How can you seek knighthood if you are ignorant of its duties? No knight can uphold a code of which he is unaware, for a bad knight is he who knights another but cannot explain his obligations."

Having heard the hermit justly reprimand him, Tirant felt very happy and replied with deep humility:

· X X X I ·

*H*OW TIRANT ASKED THE HERMIT TO TELL HIM ABOUT THE KNIGHTLY CODE

"Oh, how God has blessed me in bringing me to this place! Here I may be instructed in what my soul most longs to know, and by such a saintly knight who, after serving his order, has retired to this fair spot, fleeing worldly affairs to serve his Creator! In all my time at the German imperial court and those of France, Castile, and Aragon, I never heard the knightly order spoken of in so lofty a fashion. Should Your Reverence not object, I would consider it a great honor if you would tell me the meaning of knighthood, for I am ready and eager to serve chivalry."

"My son," the hermit replied, "the entire chivalric code is written in this book, which I read sometimes to remind myself of the grace Our Lord has shown me. I upheld the knightly code with all my strength, for just as knighthood gives a knight many blessings, so a knight should honor knighthood with all his powers."

Then the hermit opened the book and read Tirant a chapter, which explained how and why the knightly order was founded:

·XXXII·

*H*OW THE HERMIT READ TIRANT A CHAPTER OF *THE TREE OF BATTLES*[2]

"When charity, loyalty, and truth were lacking, ill will, treachery, and lies took root, sowing great error and confusion among God's peoples, and that God might be loved, known, honored, served, and feared on earth—though in the beginning justice was little cherished because charity was absent—it was necessary and proper that justice be restored to honor and prosperity. For this reason, the people were divided into thousands, and each thousand chose the man who was most loyal, strong, kind, wise, brave, and noble. Then among the beasts they sought the fairest, swiftest, most rugged and serviceable, and this was the horse. They gave one horse to each man chosen, and thus these men were dubbed cavaliers. Following this practice, when Rome was founded by King Romulus, 5031 years after Adam and 752 years before Jesus Christ, the king chose the thousand youths most dexterous in arms, that his kingdom might be renowned for valor and nobility. He armed and knighted them, gave them titles and honors, and charged them with the defense of Rome. They were called *miles* because there were a thousand of them, and they were all knighted together."

Upon learning how one knight was chosen from each thousand to serve the noblest calling, Tirant grew thoughtful and said: "Glory be unto You, oh God, who are the Sovereign Good, that You brought me here to learn the truth of knighthood. Long had I revered this order in ignorance of its great nobility and the honor and magnificence of those who loyally uphold it. My wish to be a knight is now greatly increased."

"In my opinion, you should be much loved for your many virtues," replied the hermit, "and thus I know you deserve to be knighted. Do not think that in those days anyone could be a knight, for only the strongest and most righteous were chosen, compassionate men and true who would fearlessly defend the commoners from wrongdoing. Therefore a knight should be valiant, gracious, kind, and accessible to everyone, whatever his station, as the burdens of knighthood are onerous indeed."

"So, my lord," said Tirant, "a knight should have more force and might than others?"

"By no means," replied the hermit, "for there are men as strong as knights, but a knight should have virtues other men do not possess."

"On my faith," said Tirant, "much do I desire to learn what knights possess that others lack."

"My son," replied the hermit, "I wish you to know that, living in solitude as I do, every day I ponder those excellent deeds, worthy of glorious memory, that have been done by the blessed knightly order. Knights were created to uphold faith and righteousness above all else, and do not imagine that knights are of higher lineage than others, since we all come from a mother and a father."

· XXXIII ·

HOW THE HERMIT READ THE SECOND CHAPTER TO TIRANT

"First of all, knights were created to uphold and defend Christianity," said the hermit. "They should not return evil for evil, but rather humbly forgive their enemies. A knight's first duty is to protect the Church, which would be lost without him. We read in the Scriptures that no man dared to ride a horse until knights were created and armed to chastise the wicked. Once knights were armed, they felt secure in their might, and now, my son, I shall tell you the meaning of offensive and defensive arms. Knights were armed for a reason, and their weapons have great significance, for thus they may protect the Church, preserving it from evil as good sons should. Take a lesson from that famous captain Quinto the Elder, who won such glory in this world and the next. The Pope sent him on a mission to the Emperor of Constantinople, but after disembarking, Quinto learned that some Turks had turned the cathedral into a stable.[3] He went with a few of his men to pay homage to the emperor, whom he asked: 'My lord, how can Your Majesty permit these wretched Turks to defile so magnificent and peerless a temple? I am astonished that you allow it, since your heart must be weeping blood.'

" 'My dear knight,' the emperor replied, 'I am not obliged to do the impossible, for they are such a multitude that the whole city is in their hands. They break into houses and do what they like with the women and girls, while anyone who objects is quickly killed or imprisoned, wherefore we must keep quiet, even if we dislike what we see.'

" 'Oh emperor of scant courage!' exclaimed the knight. 'Are you too craven to halt these abuses? Call your men to arms, and I shall show you what must be done!'

" 'Knight,' the emperor replied, 'please do not increase my woes. If you disobey me, I shall expel you, for I would sooner submit than be destroyed.'

"Quinto cried: 'Oh man of little faith! Bad Christians are those who forsake their Lord. I swear here and now that the first man who objects will taste my trenchant sword, and his cries will be heard all the way to the cathedral.'

"Hearing him speak with such fury, the emperor kept his mouth shut, while our knight summoned the few men aboard his two galleys. Then he boldly entered the church, knelt before Our Lady's altar, and prayed. As he was praying, he saw a gang of Turks come in and start dismantling the main altar. He quickly rose and asked for their captain, who was going through the church having stables, barracks, and other vile things built. 'Tell me, recreant captain:' Quinto said, 'why do you dishonor God's house? Order your men to cease and restore everything to its former state, for otherwise, I shall grind your blood and theirs in a mortar.'

" 'Who are you to speak so boldly?' asked the captain. 'Where do you hail from, and whom do you represent?' The knight replied:"

· XXXIV ·

HOW THE POPE'S AMBASSADOR THREATENED THE TURKISH CAPTAIN IN CONSTANTINOPLE

" 'I come from the Holy Roman Empire and I represent the Pope. My mission is to punish you, defiler of Christianity. With this cruel and naked sword, I shall slay those who soil God's house.'

"The captain replied in the following manner: 'Knight, your threats are nothing but wind. You must be mad to insult me when we so outnumber you, but knowing the Pope's great virtues, I shall oblige His Holiness.'

Then the captain told his men to restore the church to its former state. It was quickly done, and in the end the cathedral was more splendid than before. The Turkish captain set out from Constantinople with all his troops, promising never to trouble the emperor again. His Majesty then thanked our knight, who set sail in his galleys, and a favorable wind quickly bore him to Rome. Having heard how nobly he had performed his mission, the Pope sent forth his cardinals, bishops, and a multitude of commoners to welcome him. They brought Quinto in triumph before His Holiness, who greeted him with much love and rewarded him so generously that he and all his descendants after him were rich. When he died, he received great honors and his body was laid to rest at the foot of the altar in Saint John Lateran.

"Having shown how much honor this knight won through his courage, I shall now tell you the significance of a Christian warrior's armor. It symbolizes the Church, which should be guarded and armored by the knights who protect it. Just as the helmet shields the loftiest part of the body, so should a knight's spirit be lofty, that he may shield the people from wrongdoing by kings or anyone else. The vambraces and gauntlets symbolize his duty to champion those in distress, sending no one in his stead to defend the Church and its flock but punishing the wicked with his own arms and hands. The rerebraces mean that no knight should permit murderers or sorcerers to befoul a house of worship. The cuisses and greaves mean that if a knight learns that infidels or anyone else seeks to destroy Christianity, he should quickly defend his religion on horseback or foot if necessary."

"Oh father of chivalry," cried Tirant, "how my soul is comforted to learn the mighty secrets of this lofty order! Now that Your Lordship has told me the meaning of a knight's armor, I hope you will also enlighten me about his weapons."

Delighted by Tirant's eagerness to learn, the hermit replied:

· XXXV ·

*H*OW THE HERMIT EXPLAINED THE MEANING OF A KNIGHT'S WEAPONS

"The good will I bear you, Tirant, obliges me to reveal what I know of chivalry. First the lance, which is long, signifies a knight's duty to defend the Church, which is also long in years and generosity. A knight should perform deeds that will make him feared as a lance is in battle, striking terror into the wicked and championing the good. The sword's significance lies in the fact that it cuts two ways and may be used in three fashions. It slays and wounds with both edges, and its point also stabs. The sword is a knight's noblest weapon, and he too should serve in three ways. First, he should defend the Church, killing and wounding those who oppose it. Just as a sword pierces whatever it touches, likewise a knight should pierce all heretics, attacking them mercilessly wherever he may find them.

"The sword belt means that, just as a knight wears his sword girded to his body, so he himself should be girded with chastity. The pommel symbolizes the world, for a knight is obliged to defend his king. The crosspiece symbolizes the true cross, on which Our Redeemer died to preserve mankind, and every true knight should do likewise, braving death to preserve his brethren. Should he perish in the attempt, his soul will go to Heaven. His horse symbolizes the common folk, whom a knight should shelter in peace and justice. Just as a knight should protect his horse in battle and see that no harm befalls it, so should he see that the common folk are not abused. A knight should harden his heart against those who are false and impious, but he should be gentle toward those who are peaceful and good. A knight who spares one who deserves death will surely damn his soul. A knight's golden spurs symbolize many things, for by placing the precious metal near his feet, he shows his duty to commit no evil that might disgrace his order. His spurs are sharpened to goad his steed just as a knight should goad the people to virtue, but a virtuous knight should also make himself feared by the wicked.

"A knight who betrays his honor for gain befouls the good name of chivalry, and when this happens, all the kings-of-arms, heralds, and pursuivants must approach the king. If they have the knight with them, he should be armed from head to foot, as though he were about to enter a battle or joust. They should place him on a scaffold for all to see, while thirteen priests recite prayers for the dead. As they pray, first his helmet should be removed, since a knight's head is the most important part of his body, and it was with his eyes that he first erred and shamed his worthy order. Next they should strip the gauntlet from his right hand, as that is his striking hand, and if he betrayed his vows for gold, that is the hand he took it with. Then they should strip off his left gauntlet, for he defends himself with his left hand and it is the right hand's accomplice. Finally, they should strip off the rest of his armor and weapons, throwing each of them on the ground while the kings-of-arms, heralds, and then the pursuivants call out their names."

·XXXVI·

*H*OW A KNIGHT IS EXPELLED FROM HIS ORDER

" 'This helmet belonged to a treacherous defrauder of the blessed knightly order.' As these words are spoken, a gold or silver basin of hot water must be brought forth. Next the heralds will shout: 'What is this knight's name?' to which the pursuivants should answer: 'So and so,' saying his title. The kings-of-arms should reply: 'Not so, for this recreant knight has disgraced his order!' Then the priests will cry: 'Let us give him a name!' while the messengers should ask: 'What name shall he have?' The king must answer: 'Let this wicked knight, who disgraced his order, be banished from all my lands and dominions.' Once the king has uttered these words, the heralds and kings-of-arms should throw hot water in the knight's face, saying: 'From now on, traitor, you shall be known by your family name.' The king will be dressed in mourning, making a great show of grief with twelve other knights all dressed in blue tunics and cowls, and each time they strip off part of the traitor's armor, they will pour hot water over his head. When he is completely disarmed, they must remove him from the scaffold, not leading him down the stairs but flinging him to the ground. Then they should take him to Saint George's Church, abusing him as they go, and throw him down in front of the altar. As he lies there, priests will recite the psalm of malediction[4] before the king and the twelve knights, who represent Christ and the twelve apostles. Finally, they must sentence him to death or life imprisonment, cursing him all the while.

"So my son, you can see it is a serious matter to be a knight, for you must succor children, widows, orphans, and married women whenever you see them insulted, hurt, or robbed. A knight must risk death for any woman who seeks his aid, since when he is knighted, he swears to do his utmost to protect the helpless. Therefore I tell you, my son, that knighthood is a great burden. Its duties are many, and any knight who neglects them will go to Hell, so it is better to live simply than make promises one cannot keep. I have not yet told you what the ideal knight requires, as men are not agreed on the conditions for his perfection."

Eager to learn how a good knight must behave, Tirant began to speak thus:

· XXXVII ·

*H*OW TIRANT ASKED THE HERMIT TO TELL HIM IN WHAT ERA THE BEST KNIGHTS HAD LIVED

"If my words will not offend, I would be most grateful if Your Reverence could tell me whether the first knights were as courageous as those who followed them."

"My son," replied the hermit, "according to the Scriptures, there have been many brave warriors in the world, for in the stories of the holy fathers we read of noble Joshua, Judas Maccabaeus, and the Kings of Israel, as well as the dauntless Greek and Trojan knights, those invincible captains Scipio, Hannibal, Pompey, Octavian, and Mark Anthony, and so many others that it would be impossible to name them all."

"And have there been knights of equal valor since the birth of Jesus Christ?"

"Yes," said the hermit, "for the first was Joseph of Arimathea, who bore Christ away from the cross and buried Him in the Holy Sepulcher, and many others of his lineage: bold warriors like Lancelot of the Lake, Galahan, Boors and Percival, and above all, Galahad, who through his ardor and chastity deserved to win the Holy Grail."

"And in our own time," said Tirant, "whom should we honor?"

The hermit answered: "Certainly George Castriota Scanderbeg⁵ is worthy of praise; and the Duke of Exeter, a strong and stalwart youth who preferred imprisonment by infidels to shameful flight; and Sir John Stuart of Darnley, very brave in his order; and many others whose names I shall not mention."

Still feeling unsatisfied, Tirant spoke these words:

· XXXVIII ·

*T*IRANT'S REPLY

"Respected father, why does Your Lordship omit William of Warwick, whose glorious deeds I have often heard recited? Through his courage, many battles were won in France, Italy, and other lands, and he rescued the Countess of Bell Estar from her husband and three sons. They had accused her of adultery and were about to burn her at the stake, but William approached the king, who was administering the cruel punishment, and cried: 'Your Highness, have the fire doused, for I shall defend this lady from her slanderers.' Her husband came forward with his sons, saying: 'Oh knight, this is no time to champion an evil woman, but after she receives her just deserts, I shall satisfy you in combat or however you like.' The king praised these words, whereupon William raised his sword and beheaded the husband with one mighty blow. Then he hurried to the king, served him in like fashion, and slew two of the sons, though the other escaped.

"A great crowd, angered by the king's death, assailed the knight, but he entered the circle of flames and cut the ropes that bound the countess. When the countess's relatives saw how ardently he strove to free her, many joined him, and together they brought the lady to a convent. Before he left, William of Warwick escorted her back to the city, restoring her county to her with everyone's blessing.

"As he was setting out from the city, they say he met a huge lion with a little boy in its jaws, pursued by such a multitude that it dared not stop and devour him. Upon beholding the beast, William dismounted and drew his sword. The lion saw him, dropped the babe, and prepared to defend itself, and many people still recount the splendid battle that ensued as they wrestled, sometimes one on top and sometimes the other. In the end, the count overpowered the lion and killed it. Then he picked up the infant, whose mother had not yet weaned him, and, leading his horse toward the city, for he was too badly wounded to ride, he met the mother and restored her child to her.

"Only a short while ago, when Saracens had conquered most of England, William of Warwick was crowned king and slew their chief in single combat. Then, with his victorious hand, he killed innumerable infidels, delivering the English Christians and restoring the former king's crown and sovereignty. This count has performed more noble deeds than could be told in an entire day."

To conceal his identity, the hermit replied:

· XXXIX ·

*H*OW TIRANT LEFT THE HERMIT, HAPPY WITH THE KNOWLEDGE HE HAD GAINED

"It is true, my son, that I have heard tales about William of Warwick, but having never seen or met him, I omitted his name, though many knights in this kingdom have been killed or wounded defending Christianity."

"Now," said Tirant, "father and lord, since there have been so many outstanding knights and they have done such noble deeds, I beg you not to be offended by what I am about to say. How base and loathsome I would hold myself if I shunned knighthood's duties! Each man should know his worth, and I declare that though chivalry were infinitely more hazardous, nothing could deter me from joining that noble order."

"My son," replied the hermit, "since you wish to take knightly vows, do so with fame and renown—that is, the day you are knighted show your skill in arms, for thus your friends and relatives will know you worthy of your order. Now, since the hour is late and your friends are far ahead of you, I think you should depart lest you lose your way in the forest. I beg you: show this book to the king and all worthy knights, that they may learn the true meaning of chivalry, and when you return, please stop and tell me about the celebrations."

Tirant bowed deeply, mounted his horse, and went on his way. It took him so long to overtake his companions that they began to worry. Wondering if he were lost, some turned back to search for him. They found him on the road, reading about knightly deeds and the order of chivalry.

When Tirant reached the town where his companions were staying, he told them about his fortunate encounter and showed them the book, from which they read aloud till it was time to ride forth again.

After several long days they reached the city of London, where many English and foreign knights had already gathered, since by now it was only thirteen days until the wedding.

As soon as Tirant and his company arrived, they donned their finest clothes and went to pay homage to the English king. The princess was only two days away, in the city of Canterbury, where Thomas à Becket lies buried.

On Midsummer Day the celebrations began, and on that same day the king and his betrothed showed themselves to the people. After a year and a day of festivities, everyone returned to his native land.

While leaving London with his companions, Tirant remembered his promise to Count William. As they drew near where he lived, Tirant said: "Lords and brothers, I must pay my respects to the hermit."

All his friends asked to accompany him, and Tirant gladly consented. When they arrived, the hermit was saying his prayers beneath the tree.

Seeing such a crowd, he wondered who they might be. Tirant led the way, and when they were near enough they dismounted. They approached the hermit, humbly knelt before him, and tried to kiss his hand, though the noble lord refused to permit it.

The hermit, who was versed in courtly ways, welcomed them with great honor, embracing his guests and asking them to sit with him on the grass. They tried to dissuade him, saying they preferred to remain standing, but he would not hear of it and made them all sit around him. Once they were seated, they waited for him to speak, whereupon the hermit, seeing the honor they showed him, expressed his pleasure in this manner:

THE FESTIVITIES
IN ENGLAND

· X L ·

*H*OW TIRANT AND HIS COMPANIONS, RETURNING FROM THE KING OF ENGLAND'S GREAT MARRIAGE FEAST, STOPPED AT THE HERMITAGE WHERE COUNT WILLIAM DWELT

"I cannot tell you, magnificent lords, how your worthiness delights my eyes, and I would be much obliged if you could say whether you come from the king, for I am eager to learn who the new knights are and what the festivities were like, but first I ask you, Tirant lo Blanc, to reveal these lords' names."

Tirant turned to his companions, since some excelled him in rank and lineage, and said: "Oh valiant knights! I beseech you to answer this reverend father, whose wisdom and holiness I have often mentioned."

They all replied: "Speak on our behalf, Tirant, since you met him before we did."

"Then I beg you," said Tirant, "as you insist and the reverend father commands, to correct me if I err."

They all said they would and Tirant, removing his hat, began to speak:

· XLI ·

*H*OW TIRANT SPOKE OF THE GREAT
FESTIVITIES, SOLEMNITIES,
MAGNIFICENCES, AND NOBLE FEATS OF
ARMS AT THE KING OF ENGLAND'S
WEDDING, THE LIKES OF WHICH CANNOT
BE FOUND ELSEWHERE IN WRITING, AND
OF AN ARGUMENT THAT AROSE BETWEEN
TWO GUILDS

"Most reverend and holy lord, you should know that a year ago on Midsummer Night, the king summoned his ladies, damsels, guilds, and those foreigners who had come from every Christian land to take part in his wedding feast, for he had sent many kings-of-arms, heralds, and pursuivants to spread the word. First, however, I shall describe the king's generosity, the like of which has never been read or heard of, as he fed all those who came to any port, domain, or highway on their way to the festivities, and from the day they arrived until the day they left, they ate at the king's expense.

"On Midsummer Day, the king donned his finest robes: a sable-lined cape, stockings embroidered with big pearls, and a shirt of spun silver, though, having not yet been knighted, he wore no gold except his crown. Astride a splendid steed, he set out from his palace and rode toward the central square, accompanied by all the gentlemen of four quarters in the city.

"When the king reached the square, fifteen thousand horsemen rode forth, captained by the Duke of Lancaster, to whom the king bowed and whom he ordered to lead the way. The duke swiftly obeyed, riding past the king with his men in formation, all well armed, on mounts with beaten gold or brocade trappings, and holding canopies and long plumes above their Lombard-style helmets.

"After the duke came the knightly orders, and each man bore a candle in his hand. Then came the guilds, dressed in robes of their own devising, and such a fierce argument arose between two of them that I thought there would be bloodshed."

"What was the cause of the argument?" the hermit asked.

"My lord," replied Tirant, "I shall tell you. The disagreement was between the blacksmiths and the weavers, for each guild claimed it should take precedence over the other. There were ten thousand of each, and their lawyers were the cause of it all, since those on the weavers' side argued that Mass could not be heard nor Communion taken without linen, while those on the blacksmiths' side argued that their trade came first, as all looms contain iron, and therefore the blacksmiths' profession is older.

"So many allegations were made that I cannot remember them all, and had the duke not been armed and mounted, the dispute might never have ended. Seeing His Majesty unable to resolve the case, the duke rode into the crowd, chose three lawyers from each side, and led them away. They thought the duke wanted them to help decide the issue, but once they had begun to cross the river, he posted a thousand soldiers at the bridgehead with orders to bar everyone but the king. The duke dismounted in the middle of the bridge and had two gallows erected, on which he showed those lawyers the utmost honor, hanging them by their feet, nor did he leave before sending their wretched souls to Hell.

"When the king heard what had happened, he rode after the duke and said: 'Uncle, you could not have done me a greater service or given me more pleasure, for those lawyers only seek to enrich themselves at England's expense. Therefore, I order that they be left here until tomorrow, when they shall be quartered and displayed on the public highways.' The duke replied: 'Sire, if you take my advice, you will allow only two lawyers in your entire realm, and those two should decide all cases within twelve to fifteen days. Pay them well, and if they accept bribes give them the same punishment I have meted out.' The king quickly ordered it done.

"When the people learned of the duke's virtuous acts, they praised him heartily, whereupon the festivities continued."

· XLII ·

*H*OW THE KING LEFT THE CITY, LEADING A GREAT PROCESSION OF ALL THE ESTATES AND THE CLERGY

"After the tradesmen came all manner of entertainers, followed by the clergy: archbishops, bishops, abbots, canons, and priests bearing relics. Then came a splendid canopy, covering the king and those betrothed gentlemen who wished to be knighted. They wore silver brocade or white satin to symbolize their virginity, and even if their beloveds were not in the kingdom, they could still walk beneath the canopy.

"After the king came his great lords clad in silk brocade, red velvet, or damask; their wives attired in similar fashion; the widowers and widows, all clothed in fine black velvet, as were their horses; and finally the maidens and bachelors, dressed in green or white silk brocade and cloth of gold. Everyone wore gold chains and brooches set with pearls, diamonds, and precious stones.

"Then came the nuns, many of whom wore silk habits, at times in violation of their vows, for the king had obtained a papal dispensation saying they could leave their convents and dress as they liked, so long as they respected the colors of their orders. The king gave money to the poorer convents that they might celebrate his marriage, and the young and gallant nuns—and even many older ones—were attired in silk habits and carried burning candles. Then came the tertiaries, dressed in silk, bearing candelabra with three branches, and singing the *Magnificat*. They were followed by officers and foot soldiers in the king's red and white uniform, on which his coat of arms had been embroidered in ermine.

"Then came the prostitutes, kept women, and pimps, dancing to tambourins. These ladies wore garlands of flowers or myrtle on their heads, and those who had left their husbands held little flags in their hands.[1]

"In this manner, my lord, the estates made their way to a place three miles from London, while the princess set out from the palace at Greenwich. She rode in a little wooden castle atop a two-wheeled carriage, drawn by the thirty-six biggest and strongest horses in France and accompanied by one hundred and forty betrothed maidens.

"Surrounded by a host of dukes, counts, marquises, noblewomen, and damsels, she awaited His Majesty in the midst of a great meadow. The first to arrive was the Duke of Lancaster, armed and leading all his cavalry. They promptly dismounted and bowed before the princess, who stood at the castle door receiving each group's homage."

· XLIII ·

HOW THE KING OF ENGLAND AND THE FRENCH PRINCESS WERE BLESSED

"Once the king and his retinue had dismounted before the castle, the princess rose to her feet and a silver staircase was brought forth. The Duke of Berry's daughter took her arm and the Duke of Flanders's daughter carried her train, while the betrothed knights descended before their lady and her maidens followed behind.

"The princess curtsied before the king, who bowed his head in salutation. Then everyone in her party, both men and women, kissed His Majesty's hand, and the English cardinal came forth to say Mass at a portable altar.

"As soon as he got to the reading from Scripture, he pronounced the king and princess man and wife. After the service was over, the king and his bride talked for a long while, laughing and flirting as young lovers will.

"When they had finished, the king's uncle, the Duke of Lancaster, came forth and knighted him. Many other gentlemen wished to follow suit, but the kings-of-arms, heralds, and pursuivants forbade it on that day."

· XLIV ·

OF THE GREAT FESTIVITIES ON THE KING OF ENGLAND'S WEDDING DAY

"Once he had been knighted, the king entered a little pavilion and removed his clothes, giving them and two large towns to the Duke of Orleans's son, who was the princess's cousin. His Majesty emerged in a crimson robe of double brocade lined with ermine, and in place of his crown he had donned a black velvet cap with a brooch worth fifty thousand *escuts*. We then set out for the city, led by the king and his retinue.

"Now I shall tell Your Reverence how the princess was dressed. She wore a scarlet silk brocade gown with gold embroidery, and wherever the silk showed, one could see silver thistles with gold and enamel tips. Her mantle was covered with precious metals and studded with rubies and emeralds, while her hair shimmered like gold and hung down to her ankles. Never before had anyone seen such beautiful tresses, nor were her face and hands less exquisitely fair. In truth, her every gesture was graceful and feminine, and her hidden parts must have been still more comely.

"The ladies who accompanied her were the flower of French nobility, and her entire retinue was richly attired. The procession halted in a great meadow, about a mile outside the city, where we found many tents and musicians playing.

"After dismounting, the king and his companions climbed the stairs to the princess's castle. He took her hand and led her down, attended by the other betrothed couples, who began to sport and make merry in the midst of that fair meadow. Once the king and his princess had danced, the others did likewise, followed by the estates in order of rank and dignity. Each time one estate had finished and another was waiting to begin, the king danced with his bride, and then with the fairest lady in that group.

"When the estates had all danced, refreshments were served: malmsey with ginger, which the English drink because of the cold weather. Then we continued on our way until we reached the Thames, where we found a splendid park full of trees with tables beneath them. Each estate had a wooden house or a big tent with fine beds, so that even if it rained they could remain in that park.

"I can assure you, my lord, that each estate was served the finest foods, both on meat and fish days, and the generous king maintained this practice for a whole year. The first day was nothing but galas and celebrations, and as the second day was Friday, we heard Mass in the morning. Then we went fishing in more than two hundred boats, all of which were covered in silk and satin brocade.

"After lunch the king summoned his noblest guests, while his chief huntsman came forth with bloodhounds, whippets, and weapons, whereupon we went hunting and killed many wild beasts.

"On Saturday morning, a council was called of all the companies, both men and women, and the kings-of-arms, heralds, and pursuivants announced the activities for each day of the week."

· XLV ·

*T*HE FEATS OF ARMS THAT TOOK PLACE AT THE CELEBRATIONS

"First of all, on the holy day of Sunday, all the knightly orders and guilds performed. Those that danced best and offered the wittiest masques were awarded ten pounds of silver as well as their expenses, and the whole day was devoted to dances, mummery, games, and other merrymaking."

· XLVI ·

*M*ORE ON THE SAME MATTER

"On Monday, those who wished to joust with blunted arms might do so, using lances with four waxed points mounted on a flat piece of iron. Anyone who preferred real weapons also had to have a flat piece of iron on the end, with five sharp diamond-shaped steel points joined together within it.[2]

"The man who fought best and broke the most lances won three pounds of gold. They jousted with real arms and blunted ones on alternate Mondays."

· XLVII ·

*M*ORE ON THE SAME MATTER

"On Tuesday, any knight or gentleman who wished to do battle on foot might do so, either one against one, two against two, ten against ten, or twenty-five against twenty-five, which was the limit, since there were only twenty-six champions. The victors received gold swords weighing five pounds or more, and the vanquished had to serve them till they were ransomed or set free."

· XLVIII ·

*M*ORE ON THE SAME MATTER

"On Wednesday, there were combats on horseback between those who wished to fight to the utterance. The victors were given little gold crowns weighing more than twelve pounds."

· XLIX ·

*M*ORE ON THE SAME MATTER

"On Thursday, any knight or gentleman who wished to fight to the utterance as described above, one against one or two against two, might do so. The victors received gold statuettes of the princess, and since this is the most perilous exploit a knight can undertake, the statues weighed more than sixteen pounds. The vanquished had to swear before a judge never again to challenge any knight or gentleman to mortal combat, nor could they wear swords for a year or do battle against Christians. Then they had to pledge to serve the princess and obey all her commands."

· L ·

*M*ORE ON THE SAME MATTER

"On Friday, since it is the day of Christ's Passion, no fighting was allowed. Instead, we all went hunting after Mass and Vespers."

· LI ·

*M*ORE ON THE SAME MATTER

"Saturday was reserved for those who wished to take knightly vows. After questioning them, the king knighted those he thought fit to join the order.

"In this manner, father and lord, we divided the days of the week, and twenty-six irreproachable knights were chosen as champions."

· LII ·

*M*ORE ON THE SAME MATTER

"Once council had been held and the week's activities determined, they were publicly announced by kings-of-arms and heralds, whereupon His Majesty's guests all went to lunch. After Vespers, the king, his knights, and many servants made their way to the champions' camp, which was within a crossbow shot of the royal lodgings. There was a wooden palisade around the camp, so high one could only see the champions through the door. Thirteen of them were seated on each side, wearing shining armor and solid gold crowns. As the king and his bride entered, they remained still, merely nodding, for none of them dared to address His Highness. The king and his retinue stayed there a little while, and when they seemed about to leave, four richly dressed damsels of indescribable beauty offered them some refreshment. The monarch gladly consented, and an abundant repast was brought forth: marzipan, cakes, and sweets of all kinds. Everyone was well served, and each knight or gentleman ate sitting on a damsel's lap.

"Having eaten, they went into a meadow and began to dance. The champions quickly removed their armor, donning identical coats of mail, gold jackets, and red caps adorned with splendid brooches. Once the dancing ended, the king and his retinue went to inspect the lists and stands, which they found very well constructed and hung with fine satin.

"When the king had seen all this, a message came from the champions, who invited him and his knights to sup with them that evening. After supper, the kings-of-arms announced that any knight, group of knights, or gentlemen who wished to joust should present themselves on the eves of the days they had chosen, with lists of the arms they wished to bear on red pieces of paper. They had to bring their entire companies and two ladies, one on each side, with musicians preceding them. When they drew near the palisades, they were to call out their names, nationalities, choice of arms, and whether they fought in the name of a married lady, damsel, widow, or nun. If they wished to champion a damsel, the two ladies would depart and two damsels would join and honor them, while all the other maidens cried: 'May Our Lord grant victory to this knight, who deserves glory and a damsel's love!' If it was a widow, nun, or married lady, two of them would call out the same exhortation.

"Then they would enter the castle where the twenty-six knights dwelt, never knowing which ones they would be obliged to combat. The challenger would hand his piece of paper to a lady, damsel, widow, or nun, who would mount a platform where the twenty-six knights stood and place it on a golden box. All the knights would rise to their feet in honor of the lady who had brought the paper. Then she would descend, and everyone would return the next day for the combat."

· LIII ·

HOW TIRANT TOLD THE HERMIT ABOUT THE WONDROUS ROCK

"Then we walked along the river toward London until we reached a shady meadow, in the middle of which we saw something that had never been seen before."

"I pray you:" said the hermit, "please tell me what it was."

"My lord, I shall do so," replied Tirant. "In the middle of that meadow, we found a big rock made of wood so cunningly crafted that it made one continuous surface, and on the rock stood a high castle with mighty walls, guarded by five hundred men in shining armor.

"First the duke rode up with all his men, demanding that the doors to the rock be opened. Those inside refused, claiming their lord had forbidden it. 'Have at them!' cried the duke. 'Everyone follow me!' He dismounted and his soldiers followed him, drawing their swords and assailing the rock. Those guarding the walls fired catapults, muskets, and cannon. They hurled bars that looked like iron but were made of black leather, just as the stones were white leather, some big and some small. They were filled with sand, and if they hit a soldier they could fell him. Certainly it was a most genteel battle, but at first we thought it real. Many of us dismounted, drew our swords, and hastened to aid the duke, but then we realized that it was only a masque.

"Then the estates came forth one by one, asking those inside to surrender, but they refused to admit anyone, including the king.

"Seeing their obstinacy, the queen approached the castle with her maidens and asked who its master was. They told her it was the God of Love, and he stuck his head out the window. As soon as Her Majesty saw him, she curtsied and began to speak:

· LIV ·

*H*OW THE QUEEN PLEADED WITH THE GOD OF LOVE

" 'My opinion of your excellence, oh God of Love, is much diminished, for you seek to conceal your beatitude and glory. You, who rule the souls of all true lovers, should not deny your worshippers. Experience shows that Your Majesty torments his most faithful servants, forbidding them the sweetness of your much-desired bliss. Therefore, I beg you, as I am among your slaves: open your glorious abode to one ignorant of such delights. Allow me to dwell with you in blessed repose and desired glory.'

"When the queen had finished her humble pleas, the door in the rock suddenly opened with a crash of thunder. The king, his queen, and the estates entered a courtyard adorned with silk tapestries of gold and silver, cunningly worked to depict various stories. The sky was hidden by blue brocade, and above the hangings there was a gallery. Angels in white robes and gold tiaras played music upon it, while others sang songs so sweet that their listeners were transported.

"Then the God of Love appeared at a window, smiling and resplendent, and replied:"

· LV ·

*T*HE GOD OF LOVE'S REPLY

" 'Your great merits, noble queen, oblige me to do your bidding. You shall be my obedient daughter, dispensing the graces of this paradise. I grant you power to reward and punish all men and women who sail love's seas, giving some dire storms and others favorable winds. Be merciless only with those who employ fraud and deceit.'

"Having spoken these words, the God of Love vanished. Neither he nor his angels appeared again, and the tapestries started shaking as in an earthquake. I went up to the queen's apartment, and when we looked down on the courtyard, all the tapestries were gone and we saw only a fair meadow.

"Now I shall tell Your Lordship the strangest thing about that rock: as soon as the tapestries disappeared, it split into four parts. The king and his retinue were lodged in one, the queen and her compatriots in another, and in a third were all the foreigners from Germany, Italy, Lombardy, Aragon, Castile, Portugal, and Navarre.

"Each part housed many beautiful chambers whose beds were hung with splendid canopies, and had there been twice as many guests, they would all have been well lodged. Foreigners who had traveled the world over said they had never seen or heard of such lavish festivities.

"In the king's apartment, there was a silver statue of a lady with a few wrinkles on her belly and breasts that sagged a little. As she squeezed them, water spurted from her nipples into a crystal basin, having been brought from the river in silver pipes. In the queen's apartment, there was a gold and enamel statue of a lady with her hands on her pubis, from which an exquisite white wine flowed into a glass basin. In the third apartment, there was a silver statue of a bishop wearing a miter. His hands were clasped as he gazed Heavenward, while oil poured from his miter into a quartz basin. In still another apartment, there was a gold lion with a wondrous bejeweled crown. Clear white honey gushed from his mouth into a chalcedony basin. Where the four parts met, one saw a courtyard with a dwarf in the middle, holding one hand on his belly and the other on his head, while fine red wine jetted from his navel into a porphyry basin. Half-steel and half-gold, he wore a cape over his shoulders. No one could enter without seeing him, and all were free to drink their fill. Nearby, there was a silver statue of an old man with a white beard. He was hunchbacked and held a staff, and his hump was full of white bread for one and all.[3]

"My lord, none of this was done by witchcraft or sorcery, but rather by subtle artifice. Everything was as bountiful the last day as the first, and I can tell you the breadbasket always had at least thirty thousand loaves in it. His Majesty's tables were only cleared to change the linen, and there was always food in great abundance. Each dining hall had a long sideboard piled high with silver, and we all drank from pure silver vessels.

"I could go on forever praising the king's largesse, for each company had its own dining hall and was served with so many kinds of fowl, delicious soups, wines, and sweets that all the foreigners were astounded.

"Behind the rock was a shady grove where the king often took his ease, and in the wall around that grove, there was a door opening onto a park full of wild beasts: panthers, deer, chamois, wild boars, and other animals His Highness had brought. There were so many tents that it looked like a royal encampment.

"That whole day, my lord, was devoted to mirth and pleasure. The next day was Friday, and after Mass we went out in many boats covered with fine silk, satin, and brocade. We rowed up and down the river, fishing and making merry with trumpets, clarions, and tambourins. After lunch, the master huntsman brought the dogs and we went hunting."

Having heard Tirant's report, the hermit smilingly replied:

· LVI ·

*H*OW THE HERMIT ASKED TIRANT WHICH KNIGHT HAD FOUGHT BEST

"Great is the glory of worthy knights who bravely vanquish their foes, and therefore, my lords, I beg you to tell me who the best knight was and who won first prize at the solemn festivities."

"My lord," replied Tirant, "many knights of great authority and lineage came to the celebrations. There were kings, dukes, counts, marquises, and infinite gentlemen of ancient families. Almost everyone who was not a knight beforehand was knighted, and always after proving himself in a joust or mortal combat. The Duke of Acquaviva fought with surpassing courage. Many young gentlemen accompanied him, of whom more than sixty were knighted, all of noble lineage and dexterous in arms. This duke did battle on foot and horseback and almost always emerged victorious. The Duke of Burgundy's brother also displayed his mettle, and in addition, the Duke of Cleve was much praised and honored. Many other lords battled like noble knights, and I can tell you that more than fifty of them died.

"Now I shall tell Your Reverence a remarkable story: a boy who looked no more than fourteen or fifteen years old, though everyone called him the grand constable, came one day to our lodgings and asked for me. Being ignorant of my name, he had to describe my appearance. We are almost exactly the same size, and when he saw me he asked to borrow my horse and armor, as the king and his mother refused to let him fight. They were afraid he might be wounded, but he pleaded so much and with such grace that I could not deny him.

"The champions gave armor and horses to all who requested them, but he insisted on borrowing mine. I said: 'Constable and lord, do as you like with my goods and person,' yet my heart ached to see so young and handsome a knight in peril. All the same, he had his way and entered the lists, though neither the king nor his mother knew until it was over.

"I tell you that of all the jousts, none was so splendid as his, for on the first pass he struck his adversary's visor and ran his lance through the knight's head. When the king heard that his constable had done such a noble deed, he summoned him. The boy was afraid and tried to excuse himself, but in the end, more by force than willingly, he was brought before the king. His Majesty reprimanded him severely, showing his concern and scolding him for fighting a knight like Lord Scales without permission, as everyone said Lord Scales was the strongest and bravest champion. The king enjoined the constable never to enter the lists again without his leave.

"Having heard his lord's rebukes, the constable angrily replied: 'Your Highness, in that case I shall be deemed the most craven knight alive, since you refuse to let me fight lest I be slain in battle. To be a knight I must act like one, the same as everyone else. If Your Majesty does not wish me to brave the perils of combat, order me to dress as a woman and serve the queen, as Achilles did among King Priam's daughters.[4] Do you not recall how my father, when he was king and with his trenchant sword conquered the Saracens, seized my hair and made me kill one, despite my tender age? He taught me to win bloody victory like a courageous knight, and may God strike me dead this instant if I cannot be like him. There-fore, if I wish to imitate my father's knightly valor, you should not impede me but rather let me fight to the death tomorrow.'

"The king replied:"

· LVII ·

*T*HE KING'S REPLY TO HIS CONSTABLE

" 'May God preserve my station, honor, and royal crown! This boy will be the best or worst knight on earth, for his life will not last long. By the faith I owe to chivalry, I shall not permit it. Since you were lucky enough to win one battle, you should be satisfied with your prize.' And he refused to hear another word. 'Great is my tribulation,' cried the constable, 'if my lady the queen will not help me!'

"He hastened to the queen's chamber, knelt before her, and kissed her hands many times. Then he asked her to urge the king to let him bear arms, and beholding his distress, she promised to do what she could. Shortly thereafter, the king summoned his queen, who begged him most earnestly to let the constable fight as often as he liked. 'What, my lady!' cried the sovereign. 'Do you want to let a boy who barely knows how to buckle on his sword fight to the utterance? He asks you to intercede and you, for love of his worthy mother, should try to dissuade him, but instead you plead against his best interests. I shall never allow it, as his father has done so much for me and England that I could never repay him and would sooner die than endanger his son. Bearing arms is perilous! The lad could easily be hurt or dishonored.'

"Seeing her lord's great love for his constable, the queen decided to hold her peace. When she returned to her chamber, the constable was waiting outside. She repeated her husband's words, saying that for the moment there was no hope of his request being granted.

"Filled with despair, the constable came to my lodgings and asked how I thought he could joust with another knight. I told him my opinion: that since he had killed the mightiest champion and won such honor, he should do nothing further to vex the king."

"May God bless you and grant all your wishes!" cried the hermit. "This constable you speak of: did he have parents or close relatives there?"

"Certainly," replied Tirant. "His noble mother was present. As soon as the queen arrived, the king and his council asked the countess to care for her. I neglected to ask about his father, being more interested in arms than lineages, nor would I ever have found out had his mother not summoned me. When I was before her, she asked if I had a wife or children. I inquired why she wished to know, and she replied: 'I shall tell you. If you have a son you should love him, and if you have a wife you should protect her, as it is hard for a lady of honor to see her only son in danger.'

"Then she sweetly asked why I had lent my horse and armor to a young boy who might as well have been an orphan, for though she was alive, she was so distraught that if by chance the other knight had killed him, her only wish would have been for the earth to open up and swallow her. She begged me, as Divine Providence had spared her son's life, not to be the cause of his death and her undoing, since he was all she had left. I swore by my knightly vows to do nothing that might harm her son and everything possible for his good. Then I asked whether her husband had died of illness or in battle. The virtuous lady replied, without lifting her eyes: 'Brave knight, my sins and misfortunes have widowed me in my husband's lifetime. In my youth, I married Count William of Warwick. His courage was famed throughout the world, and he could have been king had he so desired.' I regretted having asked and questioned her no more."

"Tell me," asked the hermit, "since you have spoken so much about this constable: who won the prize of honor?"

"My lord," replied Tirant, "it is certainly difficult to judge, for many great lords were present and most bore arms very nobly. It is well known that when great lords joust, the good are often honored above the best."

"That may be so," replied the hermit, "but in this kingdom it is customary in royal tournaments for the kings-of-arms, heralds, and pursuivants to go forth with criers and musicians, announcing the best knight's name. This was a solemn tourney, publicized and trumpeted throughout the world, where valiant knights truly fought to the utterance. Therefore, I would like to know who won the honor and glory."

Tirant fell silent, hung his head, and stared at the ground.

"Tirant, my son," asked the hermit, "why do you not reply?"

A knight named Diaphebus rose and said: "My lord, some questions cannot be answered, but I swear by the holy order of chivalry, into which I was unworthily admitted on the Day of the Assumption, that I shall truly relate everything that happened. Your Reverence should know that the best knight of all, the one awarded the prize by the king and all the kings-of-arms, heralds, pursuivants, and great lords in Christendom, who wrote out their decision and stamped it with their seals before twenty-five notaries with royal authority and license to witness such acts and seal such letters, which I can show Your Lordship . . ."

"Oh, I should love to see it!" cried the hermit.

Tirant could remain seated no longer, and, rising to his feet, he ordered the pack mules unloaded, the tents pitched, tables set up near the stream, and supper prepared.

Having called for a little pouch where he kept the letter, Diaphebus began to read it:

TIRANT'S EXPLOITS IN ENGLAND

· LVIII ·

*H*OW DIAPHEBUS READ THE KING OF
ENGLAND'S LETTER, IN WHICH TIRANT
WAS DECLARED THE WORTHIEST KNIGHT

We, Henry, King of England by God's grace and Lord of Great Britain, Wales, Cornwall, and Ireland, standard-bearer of the Church and Our Holy Father in Rome, hereby declare that after the tournament held by us in praise and honor of Our Lord, His Holy Mother, and all those knights who have braved death, it behooves us to honor those who have fought best, triumphing without a single defeat or reproach. Therefore, we order and command that all worldly glory, honor, and fame be accorded that noble knight Tirant lo Blanc. Kings-of-arms, heralds, pursuivants, criers, and musicians shall announce our decision at the four corners of the lists. Furthermore, he shall mount a white horse while everyone else walks behind him, both men and women, and he shall ride beneath a canopy to the church of that glorious knight Saint George. There a solemn Mass shall be sung, with a sermon reciting Tirant lo Blanc's deeds of chivalry. We also order and command that, after leaving Saint George's Church, he shall walk through the lists, taking possession of their keys in token of his victory. We order, moreover, that two weeks of festivities shall be held in honor and praise of the aforesaid knight, and that all may know the veracity of these words, we have signed this letter in red and stamped it with our royal seal, published in our city of London this July fourteenth, in the year of Our Lord etc. Rex Enricus. Sig+ned by all the judges. Sig+ned by all the kings-of-arms, heralds, and pursuivants. Sig+ned by all the magnates and great lords in attendance.

"Great is my desire to hear his feats of chivalry," said the hermit, "for he sounds like a most remarkable man. He nobly left to avoid uttering or listening to his own praises, and therefore I beg you to recite his deeds."

"My lord," replied Diaphebus, "I would not want you to think ill of me, since Tirant and I are from the same land and of the same will, wherefore I shall tell you the plain truth. Tirant was the first man the king knighted and the first to bear arms. On that day, my lord, he gathered all his companions, both gentlemen and maidens, and led them to the king's lodgings. Finding the doors closed, we began pounding upon them, and after some time had passed, a king-of-arms appeared at a window and asked: 'What do you want?' The maidens replied: 'We have a gentleman who asks and wishes to be knighted, for he is worthy of the chivalric order.' The doors were quickly opened, and those who wished to enter did so. When we were in the middle of a great hall, a king-of-arms asked Tirant to sit in a silver chair covered with green canvas. Then they questioned him to see if he deserved to be knighted, inquiring about his habits and whether he was lame or lacked a limb. Having found him of sound body, they summoned the English archbishop, who entered dressed as a deacon with an open missal in his hands, and there, in the king's presence, administered the following oath:"

· LIX ·

THE OATH THE KING MADE ALL GENTLEMEN SWEAR BEFORE BEING KNIGHTED

" 'Oh gentleman received into the knightly order, do you swear before God and on the four Gospels never to contravene the most lofty and excellent King of England except in the service of your natural lord, and then only after returning the chain with his arms that he now places upon your neck? Only thus may you oppose him without incurring worthy knights' reproaches, for otherwise you will commit treason and deserve ill repute, and should you be taken prisoner, you will risk death at his hands. Therefore, do you now swear to champion ladies, widows, orphans, damsels in distress, and also married ones, should they request your aid, cheerfully braving death if one or more of these should call upon you?'

"The oath having been sworn, two noble lords, the greatest in attendance, brought Tirant before the king, who placed his sword upon his head and cried: 'May God and Saint George make you a worthy knight!' and kissed him on the lips.

"Then seven maidens approached, all dressed in white to represent the seven joys of the Virgin Mary. When they had buckled on his sword, the four noblest English knights fastened his spurs. These knights symbolized the four evangelists. The queen and duchess seated him on a royal throne upon a dais, with the monarchs on either side and all their maidens and knights standing below them. A sumptuous meal was then brought forth, and this ceremony was observed each time someone was knighted."

"Tell me, if you please," said the hermit, "of Tirant's exploits in arms."

"My lord, on the eve of his first joust, Tirant rode forth with all his companions in the aforesaid manner. They made their way to the champions' camp, where he presented a cartel saying anyone who wished to tilt with him had to stay in the field till they had drawn blood twenty times or one knight surrendered. His request was quickly granted, and we returned to our lodgings. On the morrow, a crowd of damsels escorted him, fully armed, to the lists. There they entrusted him to the judges, who welcomed him with great honor. The king and queen watched from the stands as Tirant entered bareheaded, holding a fan with Jesus painted on one side and the Holy Virgin on the other.

"When Tirant was in the middle of the field, he bowed before the king and queen and went to the four corners of the lists, blessing each of them with his fan. Having done this, he dismounted, while the champions led him to a little pavilion. There they brought him food and sweets, that he might refresh himself if he wished to. Then he again took his arms and mounted his steed. Finding the champion in position, he rode to the opposite end of the field, and, since everyone was seated, the queen ordered the joust to begin. Each one quickly spurred his mount and steadied his lance in its rest. They encountered so fiercely that their weapons splintered, whereupon they requested new lances and returned to the field of battle.

"On the twentieth pass, the champion struck Tirant's visor and drove it against the top of his breastplate, wounding him slightly in the neck. Had the lance held firm, our knight would have perished, and as it was, he and his horse both fell to earth. Tirant quickly rose and asked the judges for a better mount and lance, to which they replied that each knight could take as many as he liked. Tirant and his foe both chose heavy lances and clashed with great fury, but this time Tirant struck his adversary a little below the lance-rest. The Breton's lance held firm, and the shock was so great that the champion flew off his horse and fell to the ground dead. Tirant's maidens hurried to the entrance and asked the judges for their knight. Then they took Tirant's horse by the reins and escorted him to his lodgings, where they removed his armor, examined his wound, and called for surgeons to treat him. Tirant was well served by the maidens, who rejoiced in their first champion's victory.

"After entering the tent where the dead knight lay, the king and his great lords brought him to Saint George's Church, where there was a chapel for knights who had died in battle.

"My lord, as soon as Tirant had recovered, he gathered his company and we went to see the champions. He gave them a cartel requesting mortal combat on foot, and his wish was quickly granted. The next day, he entered the lists most courageously, armed with sword, battle-ax, and dagger. When each man was in his pavilion, the judges prepared for battle. They stationed them so that the sunlight was evenly divided, and neither had more in his face than the other. The king and all the companies entered the field and mounted the stands, while both knights waited with their axes at the ready. Beholding the king, they knelt and bowed before him, and the maidens all prayed for Tirant's victory.

"Once the spectators were seated and the pavilions had been removed, the trumpets blew and the heralds forbade anyone to speak, make any sign, or cough under pain of death.

"Then four knights approached Tirant and four approached his foe. They led them to the middle of the field, where there were three lines. The two knights clashed so bravely that no one could predict the outcome, but though the battle lasted a long time, at last the champion began to falter. Toward the end he could barely hold up his ax, and his behavior showed that he desired peace more than war. Beholding his adversary's condition, Tirant grasped his ax in both hands and dealt him a blow to the head that crushed his helmet and nearly felled him. Then the Breton shoved him to the ground, cut his helmet strap with a dagger, and, after removing the helmet, spoke these magnanimous words:"

· LX ·

TIRANT'S WORDS TO HIS OPPONENT

" 'Valiant knight, your life and death are in my hands. Command me as you wish, for I am ready to obey you: to kill you or set you free, as I would sooner do good than evil. Order my right hand to pity you and spare your life.'

" 'It grieves me more,' replied the knight, 'to hear your vainglorious boasts than to perish, since I prefer death to begging your arrogant hand for mercy.'

" 'My hand is accustomed to sparing the defeated,' said Tirant. 'If you like, I shall gladly free you.'

" 'Ah, how men love to make speeches when they have triumphed by good luck or bad! I am the irreproachable knight Highmount, loved and feared by many. I have always been merciful and treated my foes with compassion.'

" 'Thus would I serve you,' said Tirant, 'for your great bravery and virtue. If you kneel and cry mercy before the king, I shall generously spare you.'

"The knight replied with mortal fury: 'God forbid that I should perform an act so shameful to me and mine, and to noble William of Warwick who received me into this bitter order. Do as you like; I would sooner die bravely than live in shame.'

"When Tirant saw his ill will, he said: 'Any knight who seeks renown must expect a place in Hell.'

"He plunged his dagger into the champion's eye, slamming his other hand down on it so hard that it transfixed his skull. What an ardent knight was he, preferring death to disgrace!

"There were twelve judges of the field. Six kept a list of the victors, while the others recorded the names of the defeated. Those who died worthily were honored as martyrs, but cowards were covered with shame and infamy, and this practice was followed throughout the festivities.

"A few days later, my lord, it happened that the king and queen were dancing and making merry in a meadow near the river. One of the queen's relatives was there, a maiden named Fair Agnes. She was the Duke of Berry's daughter and the most gracious damsel I ever saw. The queen's beauty is unsurpassed, as she is courteous, friendly, chaste, and more generous than any lady alive, for generally women incline to avarice, but Fair Agnes would also part with jewels, clothes worth a whole city, and other riches, so gentle was her condition. On that day, Fair Agnes wore a lovely brooch between her breasts. When the dancing ended, Tirant approached the noble lady, knelt before her, and said:

" 'My knowledge, sweet lady, of the beauty, grace, wisdom, and other virtues that dwell within a body more angelic than human, obliges me to serve you, and therefore I beg you to grant me that brooch between your breasts, which I shall proudly wear in your service and honor, fighting to the utterance with any knight, on foot or horseback, armed or unarmed, in the manner of his choice.'

" 'Holy Virgin!' exclaimed Fair Agnes. 'Are you ready to die in battle for something so small and worthless, heedless of death and the dangers that may await you? Nonetheless, for the sake of all ladies, damsels, and worthy knights, I consent in the presence of the king and queen, and lest you forfeit the prize of your noble deeds, I permit you to take the brooch with your own hands.'

"Tirant rejoiced in Fair Agnes's reply, and since the brooch was tied to her bodice by a ribbon, he was forced to touch her breasts as he removed it. After kissing the brooch, he knelt on the ground and said:

" 'I thank you for this brooch, which I prefer to all of France, and I swear that whoever takes it from me shall lose his life.' Then he pinned it to his cap.

"The next day, while the king was at Mass, a valiant French knight named Lord Barrentowns visited Tirant. 'Oh knight,' he said, 'wherever you may hail from, you have exceeded your rights in touching Agnes's pure body, for never did anyone make so loathsome a request. Therefore, you must relinquish that brooch willingly or by force. It is mine by right, as ever since I was a lad I have loved, served, and worshipped this lady who is worthy of all good things. After my travails and sufferings, I deserve this glorious prize, and if you do not surrender it, your life will soon end. Give it to me peacefully, lest some greater harm befall you.' "

· LXI ·

HOW TIRANT RESPONDED TO LORD BARRENTOWNS

" 'Great would be my shame,' replied Tirant, 'if I lost the brooch she so generously gave me. Truly, I would be held the vilest and most recreant knight alive, and should I ever do such a thing, may I be crowned with a flaming helmet. By your bold speech, my good knight, you reveal the pride I shall soon humble.'

"The knight tried to seize the brooch, but Tirant was ready. He unsheathed his knife and his men followed suit, whereupon a great brawl started, in which twelve knights and gentlemen were slain. When the queen, who was nearby, heard the cries and commotion, she plunged into the crowd and separated the two rivals. I can tell the tale because I myself received four wounds, and I had a great deal of company. By the time the king found out, everything was over, and less than three days later the French knight sent a page with this letter:"

· LXII ·

L ORD BARRENTOWNS'S CARTEL OF DEFIANCE

To Tirant lo Blanc, instigator of bloodshed:

If your soul can brave the sight of those arms used by knights, tell me if you wish to fight armed or unarmed, on foot or horseback, clothed or naked, or in any manner you like, that your sword and mine may duel to the death.

—Written in my hand and stamped with my seal: Lord Barrentowns

· LXIII ·

H OW TIRANT ASKED A KING-OF-ARMS'S ADVICE

"When Tirant had read the letter, he took the page into a little room, gave him a thousand gold *escuts,* and swore him to silence.

"Then Tirant went out to search for a king-of-arms, and, having found one, took him three miles from their camp and addressed him thus: 'King-of-arms, by the trust placed in you and the oath you swore to His Majesty, keep my words secret and counsel me well, as is your chivalric duty.'

"The king-of-arms, whose name was Jerusalem, replied in the following manner: 'Lord Tirant, I promise by my oath to keep secret whatever you tell me.'

"Then Tirant showed him the letter. When Jerusalem had read it, Tirant said: 'Friend Jerusalem, great would be my glory if I could satisfy Lord Barrentowns, but being only twenty years old, I am ignorant of many things. Therefore, I trust in your wisdom and good advice, for you know the customs of knighthood far better than I do. Do not think I speak out of fear or cowardice, but lest I offend His Majesty who has shown me such honor and who has proclaimed bans of chivalry, which I fear to contravene.' "[1]

· LXIV ·

*T*HE KING-OF-ARMS'S ADVICE

" 'O blessed and brave young knight beloved by all, I shall gladly defend you before the king and his judges! You, Tirant lo Blanc, may satisfy this knight with honor, as he is the challenger and you are the challenged. By initiating the quarrel, he absolved you of all wrongdoing. I take the responsibility upon myself, and if any knight condemns you, I shall uphold your honor. Do you know in what circumstances you would be guilty? If you had been the challenger, thus offending the king who knighted you and defying his bans. Then you would surely be cursed by worthy knights, but you have broken no law and have shown your valor. If you want my opinion in writing, I shall gladly give it to you. Accept this challenge, for you have nothing to fear.'

" 'I am much comforted,' said Tirant, 'by your advice, since you tell me I cannot be reproached by the king or worthy knights. Now I ask you, Jerusalem, by the office you hold, to judge our duel and recount it to whoever may ask you.'

"Jerusalem said: 'I shall gladly arrange the terms, though I cannot be the judge, for no knight, king-of-arms, herald, or pursuivant who gives advice can also judge. Not even the King of England, if he wishes to judge a duel, may aid or counsel one of the combatants. If he does so, the fighting should be halted lest His Majesty the emperor annul the outcome; and lest you or Lord Barrentowns lose the prize of battle, I shall find a competent judge on whom you both can rely. He is of our profession, a sworn king-of-arms, and his name is Clarós of Clarence.'

" 'I know him well,' replied Tirant, 'and shall gladly have him if Lord Barrentowns agrees, for he is a worthy king-of-arms and will award the honor to whoever deserves it, but I fear we shall be discovered, as a page brought me this letter and, if I send an answer with another page, it could easily be read. Let us return to my lodgings, where I shall give you a signed answer. Though Lord Barrentowns is the challenger and has given me the choice of arms, I shall let him devise the weapons, however deadly they may be, as my glory will thereby be all the greater.'

"Having returned to his lodgings with the king-of-arms, Tirant immediately wrote his reply, which he signed, sealed with his arms, and handed to Jerusalem. Then he offered the king-of-arms a fine sable-lined brocade robe, asking him to wear it for love of his young friend.

"After vainly seeking Lord Barrentowns among the king's and queen's retinues, Jerusalem decided to enter the city. There he found him making his confession in a monastery. When he had finished, the king-of-arms led him outside, for no one may speak of killing in such a place, and said:

" 'Lord Barrentowns, as a king-of-arms, I wish to restore peace and good will between you and Tirant lo Blanc, but if you refuse, here is your letter and his reply, signed and sealed with his arms, requiring and authorizing me to arrange the terms of this duel. Without prejudice to his rights as the challenged party, he allows you the choice of arms, provided they are equal and with no concealed advantages. Let the duel take place this evening if possible.'

" 'Great is my satisfaction,' replied Lord Barrentowns, 'at brave Tirant's gentility. I accept the power he has given me, and these are the arms I devise:' "

· L X V ·

*T*HE ARMS LORD BARRENTOWNS CHOSE

" 'I propose that the duel be fought on foot with French linen shirts, paper bucklers, garlands of flowers, and nothing else. The weapons shall be double-edged Genoese knives, a foot and a half long and with well-sharpened points.[2] In this manner, we shall fight to the utterance, and I am surprised, king-of-arms, that you make discord out of concord. We had arranged to fight a duel, yet now you speak of peace.'

" 'My office obliges me,' replied Jerusalem, 'to seek reconciliation.'

" 'Then you have done your duty, and I acknowledge Tirant's acceptance. It seems we are in agreement and not disagreement after all.'

" 'I am glad,' replied the king-of-arms, 'that you both are satisfied. Now let us obtain the arms and whatever else we need before night falls.'

"After purchasing the knives, they bought some French linen and had two long shirts made, with short sleeves lest the knights' movements be impeded. Next, they found a sheet of paper and divided it to make two shields. Imagine how much protection a half-sheet of paper would afford! When they had everything, the knight told Jerusalem: 'You have arranged the duel and are on Tirant's side, but I desire no aid except God and these hands. Choose one set of arms, and I shall take the other.'

" 'Lord Barrentowns, I am not here to take sides between worthy knights. My office obliges me to advise them without showing favor, for though you offered me your entire fortune, I would never betray my office. Therefore either let us act as we should, or else dismiss me and find someone you trust.'

" 'By my God and Creator, king-of-arms, you misunderstand me. Let us go and fight our duel, for I see the day is waning. Since you are our judge, see that the end comes quickly.'

" 'My lord, this is how it must be,' replied Jerusalem. 'I cannot be your judge after counseling both combatants, but I shall bring another knight who is above suspicion: the king-of-arms Clarós of Clarence, a man wise in war. He would sooner die than dishonor his office.'

" 'Just as you like' said the knight, 'as long as the duel is fair and secret.'

" 'And I promise,' replied the king-of-arms, 'to say nothing except to Clarós of Clarence.'

" 'Now,' said the knight, 'take these arms to Tirant and let him choose the set he likes, while I await you in the hermitage of Saint Mary Magdalene. If anyone from my company sees me there, I shall say I went to pray.'

"Jerusalem went in search of Clarós of Clarence, who said he would gladly preside. By now the sun had completed its rounds, and, as Clarós had no wish to endanger two worthy knights in the dark, he said he would judge their duel the next morning while the king was at Mass.

"Jerusalem then returned to Tirant, told him how and when the duel would take place, and asked him to choose one set of arms.

" 'As our duel will not be tonight,' replied Tirant, 'I refuse to keep the arms, since if I triumph, some might say I had altered them and won by treachery. Thus did men accuse that knight who slew his adversary in the harbor, for, people said the fatal lance had been enchanted. I refuse to see or touch them until we are about to fight. Give them to Lord Barrentowns, and tomorrow he will test my mettle.'

"Hearing Tirant speak thus, Jerusalem looked into his eyes and said: 'Oh brave and dexterous knight! With Fortune's help, you will wear a royal crown.'

"The king-of-arms then went to the hermitage, where he told Lord Barrentowns that it was too late to judge a duel. They would fight in the morning, while the king was at Mass and some knights would be with His Majesty, others with the queen, and still others would be watching the gallant ladies. Lord Barrentowns said he was content.

"Early the next morning, lest anyone see them, Clarós and Jerusalem led the knights to the middle of a deep wood.

"When he saw they were ready, Jerusalem began to speak thus: 'Brave knights, behold your doom. These are the arms devised by Lord Barrentowns and accepted by Tirant. Let each man take his pick,' and he placed them on the green grass.

" 'Now,' said Clarós of Clarence, 'lords of great nobility, you are in this deserted spot where no relatives or friends can aid you. You are only one step from death, so trust in God and in your strength. Tell me: whom you wish to judge this duel?'

" 'What do you mean?' asked Lord Barrentowns. 'Have we not agreed on you?'

" 'And you, Tirant: whom do you wish to judge?'

" 'I accept whomever Lord Barrentowns chooses.'

" 'Since you both accept me as your judge, you must abide by my commands.'

"Once they had sworn to do so, Lord Barrentowns told Tirant: 'Take the arms you want, and I shall take those you leave.'

" 'No,' replied Tirant. 'You devised and had them made. Choose first, since you are the challenger, and then I shall take mine.'

"As the knights could not resolve this point of honor, the judge finally picked up the arms. Having placed one set on the right and one on the left, he plucked two blades of grass, one long and one short. Then he said: 'The long blade wields those on the right; the short blade wields those on the left.'

"When each had his arms, they disrobed and donned those fateful garments that could only be called cruel hair shirts. The judge drew two lines on the ground, placing one knight on each and ordering them not to move until he gave the word. They cut some branches from a tree, that he might have a little platform. When everything was ready, the judge told Lord Barrentowns:"

· LXVI ·

*T*HE KING-OF-ARMS'S SPEECH

" 'I am judge by the powers you two have granted me, but by the rules of my profession, I am obliged to warn and ask you—and you first, as the challenger—to stop while you still can. Keep God before your eyes and do not die in sin, since you know He cannot justly pardon a suicide.'

" 'Let us leave such words for the moment,' replied the knight, 'for each of us knows his strength, both temporal and spiritual. Bring Tirant before me, and perhaps we may be reconciled.'

" 'That would not be right,' said the judge, 'as you two are equal in the field. Why should he come to you? Jerusalem, ask Tirant if he is willing to come and speak with this knight.'

"Jerusalem went to Tirant and asked if he would come. Tirant replied: 'If the judge commands me, I shall do it with a good will, but to me that knight is not worth one step forward or backward.'

"Jerusalem told him that by his oath, the judge was obliged to seek reconciliation. Then Tirant said: 'Jerusalem, tell the knight I see no reason why I should go to him. If he wants something, let him come to me.'

"Jerusalem returned with Tirant's answer. The judge said: 'It seems to me that Tirant has acted correctly, though you can both meet in the center of the field.'

"So it was done, and when they were together, Lord Barrentowns began to speak thus:"

· LXVII ·

*H*OW TIRANT AND LORD BARRENTOWNS DUELED

" 'If you, Tirant, wish peace, love, and good will to reign between us and want me to pardon your youth, I shall do so on the condition that you restore noble Agnes of Berry's brooch, together with your knife and paper shield, which I shall display before all ladies of honor. You know you deserve nothing from so lofty a damsel, as your estate, lineage, and condition make you unworthy even to remove her left clog, nor are you my equal, though I have generously stooped to fight you.'

" 'Knight,' replied Tirant, 'I am not unaware of your station, rank, courage, and powers, but this is no time or place to discuss lineages. I am Tirant lo Blanc. When I take my sword in hand, no king, duke, count, or marquis can refuse me. Everyone knows that. In you, however, one can quickly find all the seven deadly sins, and to think that with shameful words you seek to frighten and degrade me! I cannot be insulted by a loose-tongued knight like you, nor would I feel praised if you spoke well of me, since it is commonly said that being praised by vile men is as bad as being praised for vile deeds. Let us waste no more words, for if one hair fell from my head, I would not want you to have it or let you take it.'

" 'Since you refuse to be reconciled,' the judge asked, 'do you want life or death?'

" 'The death of this haughty young man pains me,' Lord Barrentowns replied. 'Let us return to our places and prepare to die.'

"The judge climbed onto his platform of branches and cried: 'Go to it, valiant knights! Let each man show his mettle!'

"They leapt at each other furiously, the French knight holding his knife aloft, while Tirant held his a little above his breast. When they were close to one another, the lord lunged at our knight's head, but Tirant parried the blow and struck him on the ear. He cut off as much as he could and almost reached the brain, whereupon the other knight sank his knife a hand's depth into Tirant's thigh and then quickly stabbed him in the left arm as deep as the bone. They both fought so fiercely that it was gruesome to behold, for they were at such close quarters that every thrust drew blood. It was pitiful to see their cruel wounds and their shirts red with blood. Woe unto the wretched mothers who had borne them! Jerusalem kept asking the judge to stop the duel, but his friend replied: 'Let them reach the desired end of their cruel days.'

"After a while, both knights had reached the point where they would have preferred peace to war, but being doughty and spirited youths, they kept fighting and gave no quarter. Finally Tirant, seeing himself near death from loss of blood, got as close as he could and plunged his knife into his foe's heart. The other drove his knife into Tirant's head, and both duelists fell to earth. Had Lord Barrentowns been able to keep his feet, he might have killed Tirant, but the French knight's strength was gone and he quickly breathed his last.

"Seeing the two enemies looking so peaceful, the judge leapt off his platform and said: 'On my faith, you have both behaved like worthy knights!'

"Then he made the sign of the cross over each one and found four sticks to fashion crosses, which he placed on their bodies, saying: 'I see Tirant's eyes are still a little open, but though he may not be dead, he is certainly close to it. Now, Jerusalem, I order you to stand guard over these bodies, while I go and tell the king and his judges.'

"He found the king coming out of Mass, and spoke these words before everyone: 'My lord, there is no doubt that two brave knights who were in your court yesterday are now at the point of death.'

" 'Who are they?' asked the king.

" 'Sire,' replied Clarós of Clarence, 'one is Lord Barrentowns and the other is Tirant lo Blanc.'

" 'I am very sorry,' said the king, 'to hear such tidings. Let us go to them before lunch and see if we can save them.'

" 'On my faith,' replied Clarós, 'one has already left this world and I believe the other will shortly join him.'

"When the duelists' friends and relatives heard this news, they seized their weapons and hastened to where the knights lay. We arrived first and found Tirant soaked in blood. He was unrecognizable, and his eyes were nearly shut.

"As soon as the others saw their lord dead, they rushed over to slay our knight, but we divided into two groups on each side of his body, standing back to back because there were more of them than us. Wherever they attacked, they found men facing them, but they also shot a storm of arrows, one of which struck poor Tirant.

"A short while later, the grand constable rode up with many soldiers and stopped the fight. When the king and his judges arrived and saw the two knights—one dead and the other apparently close to it—they ordered their bodies left there until they had taken counsel.

"While the king was in council hearing Clarós of Clarence's and Jerusalem's testimonies, the queen appeared with her retinue of ladies and damsels. Seeing the two knights' condition, they wept bitter tears of pity, and Fair Agnes approached the queen and cried: 'My lady, here you see great honor and great woe!'

"Then she turned to Tirant's relatives and said: 'Knights who love Tirant, how can you let your comrade perish? Here he lies on the cold ground, bleeding to death. If he stays here half an hour longer, not a drop of blood will remain in him.'

" 'My lady, what can we do?' a knight asked. 'The king ordered us on pain of death not to touch them or remove their bodies.'

" 'Woe is me!' cried Fair Agnes. 'God never seeks to kill a sinner, yet the king does! Bring a bed and place him on it until the council ends, for the cold wind is blowing on his wounds and causing him great pain.'

"We immediately sent for a bed and a tent, but while we were waiting Tirant suffered terribly, for his wounds had chilled and he was still losing blood. When Fair Agnes saw his anguish, she said: 'On my conscience, I do not wish to be blamed by parents, brothers and sisters, or by my lord and lady the king and queen, for my intentions are pure.'

"Removing her velvet robe, she spread it on the ground and had Tirant placed upon it. Then she asked her maidens to do likewise and cover him with their cloaks. When Tirant felt the warmth, he opened his eyes a little wider, while Fair Agnes took his head in her lap, saying: 'Alas, Tirant! Cursed be the brooch I gave you! Cursed the month and day I had it made, and still more when I relinquished it. Had I known how this would end, I never would have let you take it, but everyone deserves his fate and I, alas, now must mourn your misfortune, for I may be called the cause of all this evil. I beg you, chivalrous knights, to bring me Lord Barrentowns's body. Though I never loved him in life, I wish to honor him now in death.'

"Having brought him, they placed his head in her lap beside Tirant's, whereupon the damsel cried: 'Here is love and grief! This Lord Barrentowns had inherited thirty-seven castles in cities girded by towers and strong walls. One such was called Barrentowns, and hence his name, Lord Barrentowns: a man both rich and of unequaled courage. Trusting in his valiant spirit, he came to this sad end. He wasted seven years wooing me, and death has been his reward. Many were his noble feats as he tried to win me for his wife, but I never would have consented, for I am of greater wealth and lineage. I gave him no comfort, and now this hapless knight has been killed by jealousy.'

"Having received a full report from Clarós and Jerusalem, the king dismissed his council. He summoned three archbishops, his bishops, and all the clergy, who formed a procession in the dead knight's honor. Tirant's relatives sent for doctors, a bed, a tent, and everything else they needed to care for him. They found he had eleven wounds, four of which could have been mortal, and five mortal wounds were discovered on the other knight.

"When Tirant had been treated and all the clergy was present, the king had Lord Barrentowns placed in a coffin covered with a splendid gold shroud reserved for knights who had died in battle. Tirant followed him on a big shield, and, though he could barely lift his hand, he made them tie it to a staff while he gripped his naked dagger.

"The clergy went first, bearing crosses, followed by the dead lord and the other knights. Then came the king, his great lords, Tirant on his shield, the queen with her noblest ladies, and finally the grand constable with three thousand soldiers. Thus they entered Saint George's Church, where a solemn Requiem Mass was celebrated. When they laid Lord Barrentowns in his tomb, they passed so close to Tirant that he seemed to be showing them where to place the body with his dagger, for such were the judges' orders.

"Once everyone had left the church, they escorted Tirant to his lodgings, where the king visited him every day until he was out of danger. They accorded this same treatment to all the wounded, and thirty damsels were assigned to serve Tirant continuously.

"It was midday by the time they put Tirant to bed, and the king had not yet eaten. His lords asked if he wished to lunch before returning to Saint George's Church, where he planned to announce his judges' decision on the duel. The judges gave their consent, since it was past midday, and so it was done.

"When it was time for Vespers, the king, his queen, and all the companies assembled in Saint George's Church. They summoned Tirant as well, and once Vespers had been said, the judges read their decision, which was of the following tenor:"

· L X V I I I ·

*H*OW THE JUDGES ANNOUNCED THAT TIRANT HAD WON THE DUEL

"Since our serene lord the king has granted us, his judges, license to decide all battles fought during these noble festivities, in lists or palisade, plains or mountains, on foot or horseback, in armor or without, in public or private, by the powers given us we announce and declare: that Lord Barrentowns has died a worthy knight and thus may not be given a church burial without our consent. We therefore declare that he should be interred within the precincts and with the intercession of our Holy Mother Church, while the glory of said battle belongs to Tirant lo Blanc. Once the prayers for the deceased have been said, Lord Barrentowns shall be entombed with those knights who have died bearing arms without reproach. This is our decision, sealed with our arms.

"When the sentence had been read, all the clergy sang a beautiful litany over the knight's coffin. The honors lasted till almost midnight, for he had never disgraced himself and had died in combat.

"Then the monarchs and their companies returned to Tirant's lodgings, where they honored him as they did all victorious knights."

"May your beloved give you joy and solace," cried the hermit, "for you have told me how Tirant vanquished three noble knights! Great is my comfort, as I knew him before, and now I see he has distinguished himself in battle, yet I am surprised that they gave him first prize after only three victories. It must have been more through the others' defects than through his own virtues."

"No, my lord," Diaphebus replied, "for he performed many other feats that I have not yet recounted."

"Great would be my pleasure," said the hermit, "if you would kindly relate them."

"Your Reverence should know that two months after Tirant left his bed and could bear arms again, something very strange occurred, but to avoid prolixity, I shall omit many other worthy knights, men who also triumphed in battle. I merely wish to describe Tirant's deeds and prove he was truly the finest knight.

"The Prince of Wales had come to London with a great retinue of noblemen. Being fond of hunting, he kept many fierce mastiffs in his lodgings near the city walls, and by chance, one morning the king and three or four knights went to visit him, for the prince and His Majesty were boyhood friends. Since the prince wished to joust, he asked the king to summon his judges, with whom he took council until four o'clock, the hour when people are wont to rest. Tirant was returning from the city, where he had left a robe that he wished to have embroidered with precious stones. As he passed the prince's lodgings, he saw a mastiff that had broken loose and run out into the street. A great crowd was trying to catch it, but the dog was so ferocious that no one dared to approach.

"When Tirant reached the square, the mastiff started to chase him, whereupon our knight dismounted and unsheathed his sword. Beholding the weapon, the mastiff halted, and Tirant said: 'I have no wish to lose this life or its honors for an animal.'

"Then he remounted, while the king and his judges looked on. The Prince of Wales said: 'On my faith, sire, I know that mastiff's nature, and if that knight has any courage in him, we shall see a noble battle.'

" 'That knight,' replied the king, 'looks like Tirant lo Blanc, and he has already frightened your mastiff once. I doubt that the beast will come back a second time.'

"When Tirant had ridden some twenty paces further, the mastiff bounded after him with great ferocity. Tirant had to dismount again and said: 'Is this dog under a spell or the Devil himself?'

"He drew his sword and hurried toward the mastiff, which circled around him but kept its distance because of the weapon.

" 'Now,' said Tirant, 'I know you fear my sword, and I wish no one to say I bested you in unequal combat.'

"He threw his sword behind him, whereupon the mastiff took two or three mighty leaps, ran as fast as it could, and seized the weapon in its teeth. Having carried it to the other side of the square, the dog dashed toward Tirant.

" 'Now that we are equal,' said Tirant, 'I shall vanquish you with the same arms you plan to use against me.'

"They locked together with great fury, biting each other with all their strength. The mastiff, which was huge and vicious, knocked Tirant down three times and pinned him to the ground. The fight lasted half an hour, but the Prince of Wales told his men not to interfere until one or the other had emerged victorious.

"Poor Tirant's arms and legs were covered with bites, but finally he seized the dog's neck, squeezed with all his might, and bit its jowl so hard that it fell down dead.[3]

"The king and his judges immediately ran out and brought Tirant to the prince's lodgings, where they sent for doctors to treat his wounds.

" 'On my faith,' said the Prince of Wales, 'I would not have let you slay my mastiff for the finest city in England.'

" 'My lord,' replied Tirant, 'may God quickly heal my wounds, for I would not care to be in this state for half your principality.'

"When the queen and her maidens heard what Tirant had done, they hastened to his side. Seeing his dreadful condition, Her Majesty exclaimed: 'Tirant, honor can only be won through travails and suffering. As soon as you escape from one predicament, you encounter another.'

" 'Most serene lady endowed with all human and angelic virtues, let Your Majesty judge if I have erred,' replied Tirant. 'I was minding my own business when the Devil appeared disguised as a dog. Naturally I wished to fight him, and his master did nothing to stop it.'

" 'You should not feel downcast, no matter what harm befalls you,' said the queen, 'for thus you will prove your courage.'

" 'No one, most serene lady,' replied Tirant, 'has ever seen me saddened by reverses or cheered by triumphs. It is true that a man's thought wavers, and at times his heart appears joyous or distressed, but one accustomed to toil, anguish, wounds, and mishaps is dismayed by nothing. I am more troubled when I see harm done than by all the harm that may befall me.'

"At this point, the king and his judges appeared. They told Tirant they had watched the battle and seen him throw away his sword. Therefore, they declared him victorious as though he had defeated another knight, and after ordering their kings-of-arms, heralds, and pursuivants to announce his triumph throughout the camp and city, they escorted him to his lodgings with the same honor they had shown him previously.

"We know, my lord, through the reports of many knights and gentlemen, that shortly thereafter two brothers, the Kings of Friesland and Poland, decided to go to Rome. They loved each other dearly and longed to be reunited, and since it was a jubilee year, they hoped to receive the Pope's indulgence. The two kings met in Avignon and set out for Rome, along with many other great lords who also desired absolution.

"Having reached the Holy City, the brothers went to Saint Peter's Church on the day the Veronica and other holy relics were displayed there. Though they had come disguised and with very few retainers, one of the Duke of Burgundy's pages spied the King of Poland. He approached him, bowing deeply as befitted a sovereign, and the king asked if his master was nearby.

" 'Yes, sire,' replied the page, 'he is praying in that chapel.'

"The king said: 'I am delighted, but I shall be even happier when I see him!'

"The kings waited outside the chapel, while the page hurried to tell his lord, who was overjoyed and quickly left his devotions. Great was their pleasure when they beheld each other, for Burgundy is near Poland and they were close friends. They spoke for a long time about their journeys to Rome.

" 'Now,' said the king, 'since I have been lucky enough to meet you, I beg you to dine with me today and as long as we remain here.'

"The duke thanked him and replied: 'Sire, today you must excuse me, for I have invited Duke Philip of Bavaria and the Duke of Austria.'

"The king asked: 'Is Duke Philip the one who bore witness against his mother and forced her to die in prison?'

" 'Yes, my lord, and he is the German emperor's son. All emperors must be of Bavarian or Austrian lineage, and his father was the one elected.'

" 'My friend,' replied the king, 'either all of you must be our guests or my brother and I will lunch with you, but I hope you will consent to share our table.'

"They mounted their steeds, and as they were riding through the city they met the Dukes of Bavaria and Austria. The Duke of Burgundy introduced them to the kings, whose acquaintance they were pleased to make. They all dined together very merrily and were abundantly served.

"Throughout their stay in Rome they ate together, and afterward for the rest of their lives until they were dead and buried.

"One day when they were talking after lunch, the conversation turned to the King of England and his queen, whom men said was among the fairest women living. They spoke of the honor shown those who went to London, both Englishmen and foreigners, and likewise they discussed the noble feats of arms. Then they talked about the many knights who had gone, some to joust and others to see the wondrous rock. The King of Friesland said: 'I should love to go too, now that I have received this holy indulgence.'

"He was twenty-seven years old, and the King of Poland was thirty-one.

"The Duke of Austria replied: 'On my conscience, were it not for the wars and rebellions in my lands, I would happily join you and test my strength against those twenty-six champions.'

"Then the Duke of Burgundy said: 'My lords, let us take advantage of these festivities, the likes of which are seldom seen. If you want to go to England, I shall forget my business with the Holy Father, and I swear not to return home till I have fought to the utterance with some knight.'

" 'My lords,' declared the King of Poland, 'since my brother wishes to go, I shall gladly accompany you.'

" 'As we are all in agreement,' replied the King of Friesland, 'let us swear an oath of love and loyalty, and let none of us command but rather all be equals, brothers, and comrades-in-arms.'

"Having praised and approved the King of Friesland's words, they went to the Church of Saint John Lateran and swore a solemn oath before the altar. Then they gathered everything they needed—armor, horses, and many other items I shall shortly describe—and after a six-day journey by land and sea, they reached England's pleasant shores without revealing their identities. Having informed themselves of the king's protocol, they arrived one night and erected four big tents about two crossbow shots from the rock.

"At daybreak, the knobs atop their tents gleamed in the sunlight, shining all the brighter because they were on a hill. The first people who saw them went to tell the judges, who advised the king to send his king-of-arms, Jerusalem.

"Wearing a tunic embroidered with His Majesty's arms, Jerusalem set out for the tents and when he was at the door to one of them, an elderly knight emerged, with a long white beard and a heavy staff in his hand. He wore a long black velvet robe lined with sable, a thick gold chain hung from his neck, and in his other hand he held a rosary with chalcedony beads. Puzzled to see the knight by himself, Jerusalem doffed his hat and bowed, while the elderly knight did likewise. Then the king-of-arms said: 'My lord, whoever you may be, the king and his judges have sent me to learn your name and whether you command this company. I beg you to tell me, and if by my office I can serve you, I shall gladly do so.'

"The knight, having heard Jerusalem's words, silently doffed his hat again and bowed his head in thanks. Taking his guest's hand, he led him to a tent containing four mighty Sicilian chargers with polished saddles and golden bridles. Then he brought him to another tent, where there were four sumptuous and singular beds."

"In what way were they singular?" asked the hermit.

"My lord, I shall tell you. They all had fine mattresses and green brocade canopies, lined with scarlet satin and adorned with jewels and gold tassels. All the beds were the same color and style, and none was better than the others. At the foot of each bed was a gallantly attired damsel of indescribable beauty, and that, my lord, is why I say the beds were singular. Two beds stood at one end of the tent and two at the other, while above the doorway four handsomely painted shields had been hung.

"Then the knight brought his guest to another tent where four crowned lions lay just within the doorway. Seeing Jerusalem, they rose, and he felt very frightened. A page quickly hit each of them with a switch, and they all lay down again. When Jerusalem had regained his composure, he saw four suits of shining armor and four cunningly decorated gold swords. At the far end, a little to one side, there was a green velvet curtain. A page opened it, and the king-of-arms saw four knights sitting on a bench. A long strip of white silk hid their eyes, that they might see without being recognized. They wore spurs and their swords were drawn, with the points resting on the ground. When their guest had gazed at them awhile, the old knight led him to another tent.

"All the tents were lined with scarlet satin, just like the canopies on the beds. As they entered the last tent, they saw a big sideboard heaped with gold and silver and many tables set for a meal. Those who entered had to eat and drink whether they wished to or not, and if they did not consume everything, a lion would block the door. The servants honored the king-of-arms greatly, and when he had dined and was ready to leave, the old knight gave him a heavy silver platter inlaid with gold.

"Having returned to his lord, the king-of-arms described what he had seen and said he had never felt so frightened in his life.

"The king replied, 'No one should be surprised by what he sees, for men have strange fancies, but if they are worthy knights they will come and salute me.'

"The king went to Mass, and that same day after lunch, he learned that his noble guests were on their way. His Majesty then sat down at the door to the rock with his queen beside him, while their retinues crowded around, making a pathway for the knights.

"Now, my lord, I shall tell you what magnificence they displayed. They were preceded by four pages clad in silver doublets, sleeveless tunics with openwork to the waist, and splendid hose embroidered with large oriental pearls. Each page led a lion by a little silk leash attached to a golden collar. Then came the four knights, riding white jennets with purple velvet trappings, all embroidered in the same style and color. They wore dark grey damask robes, scarlet brocade doublets, black velvet hoods with eyeholes, and straw hats covered with gold plates. Their boots were black satin, with long curled toes, golden spurs, and scarlet linings. Though hoods covered the visitors' faces, their every gesture breathed nobility, and of all the mighty lords who came, none had so genteel and pleasing a manner.

"Having reached the king, they dismounted, nodded, and bowed slightly to the queen, for she was a lady. The monarchs returned their greeting and sat down, while the knights stayed where they were for more than half an hour, just looking at the people and their royal hosts. No one could recognize them, but they recognized many knights and vassals.

"When they had looked to their satisfaction, a page led his lion to them. One of the lords placed a sheet of paper in the beast's jaws and then whispered something in its ear. The lion approached the king, bowing just as a person would. When the queen saw it coming, she leapt up from her husband's side. The king put his hand on her shoulder and bade her be seated, as it was unthinkable that such knights would trouble anyone with their animals. More by force than willingly, Her Highness obeyed him, nor is it surprising that she was anxious, since it was a frightening sight.

"The lion, which was far too tame to hurt anyone, went straight to the king with the letter in its jaws. Once the brave monarch had taken it, the lion lay down at his feet, whereupon His Majesty had the letter read aloud:

Know all men by these presents that four brothers-in-arms have appeared before the Roman Senate, the Cardinal of Pisa, the Cardinal of Terranova, the Count of Saint Peter's of Luxembourg, the Patriarch of Jerusalem, Sir Alberto di Campobasso, and Sir Ludivico della Colonda, asking me, a notary by imperial license, to declare publicly that they are knights of four quarters, for their fathers, mothers, grandfathers, and grandmothers were nobility, and therefore let no lord reproach their lineage. To verify the aforesaid, I stamp this letter with my customary notarial seal. +Ambrosino di Mantova. Signed in Rome March the second, the year one thousand . . . "

· LXIX ·

*H*OW THE FOUR KINGS AND DUKES GAVE KING HENRY A NOTE STATING THEIR DESIRES

"When His Majesty saw they preferred to remain silent, he dictated an answer, welcoming them to his court and promising to do his utmost for their pleasure, honor, and comfort.

"The king placed this note in the lion's jaws, and the beast quickly rose and returned to its master. The knight took the note and showed it to the others, who doffed their hats and bowed humbly, thanking the king for his courteous offer. Then another page led a second lion to another knight, who placed a note in its mouth as the first knight had done. The king took the note and had it read aloud:"

· LXX ·

*H*OW THE SECOND KNIGHT SENT THE KING ANOTHER NOTE

We four comrades-in-arms learned in the great city of Rome that the lofty King of England had offered hospitality and honor to all knights who came to London, and since we wish to engage in mortal combat, we beg Your Highness's leave to fight in the manner we propose.

"The king dictated a reply, saying he would gladly assign them whatever place, day, and hour they liked once they had rested from their journey. He invited them to his lodgings, promising they would be treated as they deserved. Then the king placed this note in the lion's jaws, and it returned to its master.

"Seeing the king's generous offer, the knights doffed their hats again and bowed their heads, while His Highness graciously returned their greeting. Then the third knight did as the others had done, sending a note of the following tenor:"

· LXXI[a] ·

*H*OW THE THIRD KNIGHT ANNOUNCED THE ARMS THEY WISHED TO USE

Let all knights who seek mortal combat come to our lodgings, where they will find a platform nailed across a tree called dryloves, that bears neither fruit nor leaves nor flowers. On the sides of this platform, they will behold four shields painted with oriflammes, and each shield has a name: Courage, Love, Honor, and Lesserworth.

The knight who smites the shield of Love must battle on horseback, clad in one layer of armor and with a cloth screen between him and his opponent, until one of the combatants is killed or surrenders, and should any piece of armor or thong break, it may not be repaired. The armor should be without concealed advantages and of the type common in war.

Whoever smites the shield of Honor must fight on horseback with neither shield nor buckler. His lance must be ten feet long, without hand-guards or other advantages, and should he break or lose it, he may take as many more as he likes until one of the adversaries is slain or surrenders.

Whoever smites the shield of Courage must ride a mount with a bridle, reinforced saddle, and unfastened stirrups, and wear chest and back armor weighing less than twenty pounds. He shall bear one lance ten feet long, including the handle, but as stout as he likes and with multiple jousting points,[4] as well as a sword three feet long, a dagger of his own devising, an ax about a hand's-breadth across, and a light helmet with a beaver, that this battle may promptly reach its desired end. Should the ax slip from his hand, he may recover it as often as he likes, but no one else may return it to him.

"The last lion then did as the others had done, and as soon as the king had taken the note, he had it read aloud:"

·LXXIᵇ·

*T*HE FOURTH KNIGHT'S NOTE

Anyone who smites the shield of Lesserworth must fight on foot with four weapons: a lance, a dagger, a sword, and a double-edged battle-ax. Whoever so wishes may bear a lance with a lead weight at one end and a sword that can be flung in the manner of a javelin. The combatants must fight until one dies or surrenders, and if the vanquished is still alive, he shall serve any lady the victor chooses. Death will be equal among us, and we freely pardon any who may harm us, just as we beg the forgiveness of those we may harm.

"When the king had read these four notes, he granted all their requests, saying the four challenges were very dangerous and they were risking their lives.

"Then the four knights bowed to the monarchs, mounted their horses, and returned to their tents. His Majesty dispatched a king-of-arms to invite them to supper and sent thirty pack mules loaded with food and everything else necessary for human life.

"Seeing their host's generosity, the four knights thanked him heartily and replied that, for the present, they preferred not to accept gifts or reveal their identities—not because they were displeased with His Highness but because they had sworn a vow. The king was most vexed when he saw his pack mules return still loaded.

"That night, my lord, the four knights had their platform richly adorned and hung with four shields, along with a note that read:

Any knight who smites these shields must present a shield with his arms. This shield may be brought by a lady, damsel, king-of-arms, herald, or pursuivant. After smiting the shield of his choice, he must hang his own beside it.

"The next day, a great crowd went to see their magnificent lodgings and retinue. Everyone was served abundant royal dishes, and when their servants went to market they always paid in gold. If there was any change they left it, saying they scorned silver coins.

"On the morrow, clad in long scarlet brocade robes lined with ermine, they walked to the king's lodgings and asked to hear Mass with him.

"Their hoods were of one color and embroidered with large pearls, they wore Turkish-style hats and solid gold belts, and each one held a rosary made of big chalcedonies. Attended by their lions, which held books of hours in their jaws, they waited in the great hall till the king left his chambers.

"When the king beheld them, he was delighted and asked his queen to escort two of the lords. He took the other pair by the hands while those with the queen took her arms, and thus they entered church, where before Mass the king said:

" 'I know not how to honor you, being ignorant of your ranks, and as you refuse to make yourselves known, please take your places according to the station God granted you.'

"They bowed their heads in thanks but refused to reply, whereupon His Majesty had them seated nearer the altar than anyone else. The lions lay down, and the knights took the prayer books from their jaws. When Mass ended, they returned the books and left with the king and queen. Then they visited the wondrous rock, where they took great pleasure in watching the water and wine flow from those ladies' breasts and pubes. They made signs and wrote notes to show they thought it all had been done with the greatest subtlety, yet despite the king's many entreaties, they would not stay to lunch.

"Now, Your Lordship should know that as soon as the four knights had delivered their notes, Tirant slipped into London and purchased four shields. That night he had one painted with his father's arms, one with his mother's, one with his grandfather's, and one with his grandmother's. While the shields were being painted, you could see knights gathering in groups of four. Many from France, Italy, Aragon, Castile, Portugal, and Navarre were eager to show their prowess. The Dukes of Clarence, Exeter, and Bedford and the Prince of Wales also agreed to fight together. In our own group we asked Tirant, since he had risked his life in battle, to choose the four bravest men, though in fact he did no such thing.

"Once the shields had been painted, Tirant gave them to four gallant damsels and we all went before the king with many trumpeters and attendants. Beholding the four shields, he asked whose they were, to which a herald replied: 'Sire, they are from Tirant lo Blanc and his company.'

"Tirant dismounted and approached the king, whose leave he asked to smite the shields. The king was pleased for two reasons: first, because Tirant and his company were doughty knights; and second, because the visitors had found opponents so quickly.

"Tirant had hurried so, lest anyone arrive before him, that he barely had time to have four flags with coats of arms painted for his two kings-of-arms, his herald, and his pursuivant.

"Then our procession set out to visit the challengers, who, upon hearing trumpets and the sound of many people, were astonished to have found what they were looking for so soon. Splendidly attired but with hoods over their faces, the four knights had the platform lowered so our damsels could smite the shields. First Fair Agnes smote the shield of Love, though the others were nearer, because after reading their names she vowed only to have that one. Lady Guiumar, the Count of Flanders's daughter, selected the shield of Courage, while Cassandra, the Duke of Provence's daughter, chose the shield of Lesserworth. The Duke of Anjou's peerlessly beautiful daughter, Bella, contented herself with the shield of Honor. After smiting each shield, the damsels hung one of Tirant's beside it. Everything was now in order, and the triumphant knight would bear away both his shield and his opponent's.

"Then the knights helped our damsels to dismount and led us into the tent with the beds, where one of them penned this note to Fair Agnes:

> On my faith, my lady, if you and your three companions were lying in these beds in your nightshirts some cold winter eve, one might truly call them the finest beds on earth.

" 'My lords, you do not need our company,' said Fair Agnes, 'as I see four gallant ladies who surely keep you warm at night.'

" 'A man chooses the very best,' replied the gallant knight.

"Then their servants brought us abundant refreshments and sweetmeats, and when we left, the first knight gave Fair Agnes a lovely prayer book. The second gave Lady Guiumar a half-gold and half-steel bracelet set with diamonds and other precious stones. The third gave Cassandra a golden bejeweled snake biting its tail, with two big sparkling rubies that served as its eyes. Seeing Peerless Bella's long blond tresses, the fourth knight offered her a golden comb worth as much as any of the other gifts. After giving a thousand nobles apiece to all the kings-of-arms, heralds, pursuivants, criers, and musicians, they escorted the damsels back to Their Majesties, who welcomed them with great honor. The four knights asked the king in writing if they might build new lists near their camp, since so many men had died in the others that they were like a cemetery. Having received His Majesty's approval, they excused themselves and went to have the new lists built.

"Every day they donned rich new vestments, and you may be certain that many great lords cursed Tirant's celerity.

"When the lists were ready and the knights had rested, they left a note at the queen's door saying the knight who had struck the shield of Love should prepare to joust in three days.

"Shortly before the appointed hour, Tirant summoned his company and led us to the lists, where the monarchs were waiting. As Tirant entered, he saw his opponent at the other end. The judges welcomed our knight, positioned him, and closed the gates as the trumpets sounded. The two combatants spurred their horses and fought many splendid passes, during one of which the knight struck Tirant in the ribs. Tirant squirmed to avoid the blow, but the lance hit his rerebrace, tearing it loose along with a lot of cotton from his doublet. On their next pass, the knight smote the hinge on his helmet, and had the blow landed two fingers lower, Tirant would have perished. Instead, the lance stuck there, knocking him to the ground. Unnerved by the two blows, Tirant remounted as quickly as he could. He had also hit the knight twice in his left rerebrace, which is where most blows land in jousts. On the next pass, Tirant struck him again in the same spot, snapping the piece of leather that held his straps in place. The knight's rerebrace was tied to his arm by a thick silk cord, and the straps held firm because they were raw hemp. Though the rerebrace stayed on his arm, it was too loose to protect him, and thus they fought many passes, one with his right rerebrace damaged and the other with his left one.

"Luck was on Tirant's side, however, for he smote the knight again in the same place, and their lances were so heavy that his opponent's arm broke. The poor knight called for a sling, but he was dying from loss of blood. A spasm shook him, he suddenly stiffened, and they had to take him and his saddle off together, while Tirant turned and rode off without removing his helmet.

"The second knight then handed King Henry a note asking to joust immediately, but the judges refused to alter their rules. There could not be two deaths in succession, mortal combats were only allowed on certain days, and if they disliked the rules, they could leave whenever they wished.

" 'Having slain our comrade, they now invite us to leave! We shall either die or avenge his death!' cried the three knights.

"His Majesty gave the vanquished knight an honorable burial, just as he had all the others. The three comrades dressed in crimson to signify revenge, but they neither wept nor showed any sign of grief at the funeral."

· LXXII ·

*H*OW TIRANT TOOK THE FIELD WITH TWO KNIGHTS AND BESTED THEM BOTH

"When the appointed day came, our knight donned his armor as secretly as he could and gave flags and tunics with his grandfather's coat of arms to his kings-of-arms and heralds. Only Tirant's closest relatives and one trusted servant knew of his plans, for in the first joust, he had displayed his grandmother's escutcheon, and on this occasion he had asked me to remain in my chamber.

"This being the bout with the shield of Honor, the combatants had to fight without a cloth barrier or hand-guards on their weapons. On the first few passes they barely clashed, breaking only five lances, but after the tenth encounter Tirant called for a stouter lance. Then he smote his opponent such a mighty blow that the lance transfixed him. Since Tirant's weapon was in its rest, it tore open one of his wounds, but so it had to be, and the second knight fell to the ground screaming in his death throes.

"Tirant dismounted, drew his sword, and approached the knight to stab him if he tried to rise, killing him or making him surrender as is customary in mortal combats. Tirant asked if he wished to keep fighting, but the other knight was more dead than alive.

"The judges descended from the stands and told Tirant he could leave without prejudicing his victory, whereupon Tirant, without removing his helmet, mounted his horse and rode away. No one recognized him, and the king thought he was another knight from our company.

"On the day assigned to the knight with the shield of Courage, Tirant entered the lists in his usual manner. As soon as the trumpet sounded, His Majesty's judges told them to commence. They drew their swords and went for each other like two ravening lions, while their axes hung from rings on their saddlebows. Tirant's horse was much lighter, and everyone thought he was getting the better of it, for as the two charged each other, he wounded his foe under the arm. When Tirant saw him bleeding, he sheathed his sword and drew his ax. Feeling blows rain down upon him, the other knight tried to imitate Tirant, but he could not sheathe his sword because his armor impeded him. Befuddled by our knight's buffets, he stuck his sword under his arm and tried to draw his ax, but the Breton was too close to him and struck too many mortal blows. Tirant chopped away as much of his vambrace and rerebrace as he could reach, for truly, my lord, an ax is the deadliest of weapons. Our knight then smote him three or four times on the head, leaving him so dazed that he never did get the ax out of the ring on his saddlebow. Holding his sword under his arm so as not to lose it, the hapless knight tried in vain to turn his horse. He showed his ignorance of arms and the gentle art of chivalry, and in everyone's opinion, he died a coward's death without defending himself. Tirant struck his arm so often that he could no longer lift it, and at last a mighty blow drove his helmet into his skull, causing his brain to squirt out his eyes and ears as he fell to earth dead.

"Then the judges of the field opened the door for Tirant, whom all the damsels welcomed and escorted to his lodgings, but the Breton did not remove his helmet lest he be recognized. He washed, changed his clothes, and slipped in among the other knights."

"What bad luck that three knights should die like that," said the hermit. "Let us now see what sort of end the fourth came to."

· LXXIII ·

*H*OW TIRANT DEFEATED THE FOURTH KNIGHT

"In this, the fourth battle, the foes entered the lists on foot. Then they ran together fiercely and embraced in the middle of the field. They had to drop their axes and draw their daggers, for they were clutching each other too tightly to draw their swords, and each cut the silk cords on the other's helmet."

"What!" exclaimed the hermit. "Do Tirant and the others know so little that they attempt to secure their helmets with silk?"

"What could be better," asked Diaphebus, "if God grants you long life in this world and Heaven in the next?"

"Son," replied the hermit, "I have never borne arms, but I did pass some time with a skilled and doughty knight. Once I saw him fight to the utterance, and his life was saved by a silk cord, for he had secured his helmet in the following manner. Take some flexible wire, the kind they use to make lanterns, and wind the silk around it like a ribbon. Tie it as tightly as you like, since the cord will bend in any direction, but if someone tries to cut it, he will be unable to do so. He will cut the silk but not the wire, and this is a useful trick for knights to know."

"Now, if you please, my lord, let us see how the battle ended. The opponents stabbed each other many times and both fell to the ground, but they quickly rose again like valiant knights. Having regained their feet, they sheathed their daggers, drew their swords, and returned to the cruel combat. Desperate because his three comrades had been slain, the knight did his utmost, but Tirant also fought hard to preserve his life. They struggled so savagely that the delighted onlookers hoped the battle would last forever but that neither knight would perish. Then the two locked together, throwing away their swords, drawing their daggers, and inflicting head and neck wounds on each other beneath their helmets. At last they both fell to earth, but the other knight was lighter, for he had treacherously donned leg armor made of pasteboard covered with silver foil, while on his bottom he wore ox leather nailed to his breastplate. The two opponents bravely rose and returned to the fray, though they could not strike often because those loose helmets impeded their vision.

"The knight clutched Tirant and threw him to the ground, but the Breton held on tight and they went down together. Tirant fell on his head, whereupon his helmet flew off and landed three paces away. He was lighter than before, and the fear of death made him put all his strength into rising before his foe. It is well that he did so, because upon regaining his feet, he saw the other knight on his hands and knees. Tirant shoved him down again, pinned him to the ground, and tried to remove his helmet. Feeling Tirant's knees on his chest, the other knight rolled over, while Tirant's armor slid against his and the two fell together. They struggled to get up, but luck was on Tirant's side, because without his helmet he was lighter and rose to his feet first.

"My lord, I feel great compassion for those four dead knights. The last one would not surrender but was determined to die a martyr, and Tirant defeated them all because he has more skill than strength. His greatest virtue is his stamina, for he can fight all day without tiring."

"That is the most important virtue a knight can have," replied the hermit. "Let us see what you, who are all young and versed in arms, have to say. Which would you rather be: strong but not skillful, or skillful but not strong?"

There were many opinions among the knights. Then the hermit asked which they would prefer: "To enter battle with a sword but no spurs, or with spurs but no sword, for I can tell you I have witnessed such combats. I even saw one, fought before the Duke of Milan, in which two knights chose to joust with equal armor, but one was on horseback with only a sword, while the other was on foot with a lance and dagger. Who do you think had the advantage? . . . But never mind that," the hermit said to Diaphebus. "Tell me about Tirant's other deeds in those noble festivities."

"My lord," replied Diaphebus, "after those four comrades had died, another brave knight named Bonnytown, a native of Scotland, came to court and spoke these words to Tirant in the king's presence:"

· LXXIV ·

H OW A KNIGHT NAMED BONNYTOWN CHALLENGED TIRANT TO BATTLE

" 'Worthy knight, your fame and renown illumine the world. Apprised of your feats, I have traveled from my native land, leaving my lord and master, the noble King of Scotland. The reason for my journey is that one day when I was taking leave of my beloved, she cruelly announced that she would not speak to me till I had slain or defeated that knight who has won such glory, and since it is to you, Tirant, that my lady sends me, I challenge you by your chivalric oaths to mortal combat on horseback without visors. You may devise the other arms as you like, as I have devised half of them.'

"Tirant quickly replied in the following manner: 'Knight, it seems to me that your request is more voluntary than necessary, and I advise you to shun such battles till they are truly imperative. Mortal combats are strong and hard to digest, and as my wounds have not yet healed, I pray you seek another knight, of which there are many present in this court.'

" 'I would follow your suggestion,' said the knight, 'but what can I do, for my lady will not be satisfied until I vanquish you. If the fear of death dismays you, here before His Majesty the king I offer to renounce one weapon, provided it is not my sword.'

" 'It was out of concern for your safety that I tried to excuse myself,' replied Tirant, 'but I would not want worthy knights to think I had declined out of cowardice. I shall gladly satisfy you and accept your challenge, and since you have named some of the arms, I forfeit my right to name the rest. As for the advantage you offer me, I would never accept it, and I think it ill-advised of you to pour so much vitriol into your speech.'

" 'Having agreed to do battle,' said the knight, 'you, Tirant lo Blanc, must swear before the king, queen, and these worthy knights to accept no other challenge, lest you be disabled.'

"When Tirant had so sworn, the knight returned home and asked his queen to grant the Breton safe-conduct for four months, that his wounds might have time to mend. Then Tirant sent an old and trusted Frisian servant named Illgiven to tell his parents he needed money for a journey, and when the servant reached Dover, he found those four dead knights' retainers. They were waiting for a boat to cross the English Channel.

"Once they were all aboard, Tirant's servant became friendly with the others, and as they talked about the four dead knights, he learned that one was the King of Friesland and another his brother, the King of Poland. Stunned to hear that his natural lord had perished, Tirant's servant began to weep and lament his misfortune. As the tears rolled down his cheeks, he cried in a piteous voice: 'Woe is me! What an evil fate that Tirant, who with my help was knighted, has killed my natural lord! What bad luck that I should have served such a knight! Oh Fortune, why have you led me, the King of Friesland's loyal and innocent vassal, to be an accomplice in my master's demise?'

"Tirant's servant uttered so many and such dolorous words that the elderly knight, who had been the four dead knights' steward and was locked in his cabin weeping, heard about his woeful cries and astonishing lamentations. Distressed though he was, he left his room, drew Tirant's servant aside, and asked the cause of his grief.

" 'My lord,' said the gentleman, 'I am the King of Friesland's vassal and my parents still dwell there, but I left them at a tender age and settled in Brittany. There I entered a knight's service—would that I had never met him!—and helped him make flags, robes, and shields for those unequal battles. That one man should have killed four kings and dukes, including my natural lord, is the cause of my sorrows when I recall that in addition he employed treachery.'

"Hearing the gentleman speak thus, the aged knight led him into his cabin and asked him to recount the whole story. Once he had heard it, he said: 'My friend, if you love your natural lord, come with me and abandon Tirant's service.' The gentleman, out of loyalty and good will toward his native land, granted the old man's request, but before setting out with him, he found a man and paid him to deliver Tirant's letter. Upon their arrival in Friesland, whose citizens were still in mourning, Illgiven told a knight named Kyrieleison of Muntalbà⁵ what had happened. This Kyrieleison, who was as tall as a giant, incomparably bold, and most valiant, said such things could not pass without fit punishment. Having dictated a cartel of defiance, he then engaged a king-of-arms named Flower of Chivalry and a damsel to represent him before the King of England. The two of them set sail with such good weather that they quickly reached their destination, and once they were before the king, the damsel cried in a strident voice:"

· LXXV ·

*H*OW A FRISIAN DAMSEL ACCUSED TIRANT OF TREACHERY

" 'Oh most prudent and worthy king, I come before Your Majesty to cry out against and challenge a false and despicable knight, who goes by the name of Tirant lo Blanc and whose acts are of the blackest. If he is here, let him come forward, for I shall tell him how with foul treachery, false arms, and deceit, he killed four kings and dukes less than a month ago.'

" 'How can that be, damsel?' asked the king. 'Tirant has been at my court almost a year, and I have never heard of his doing such things!'

"Some of Tirant's relatives tried to defend him, but His Majesty silenced them, and, knowing the Breton was nearby, he sent them to fetch him.

"They quickly went in search of Tirant, who was lying in bed, as with all the blood he had lost and his still unhealed wounds, he often slept late to give his body a chance to heal. They told him a damsel had come before the king and queen accusing him of treachery.

" 'Mother of God!' Tirant exclaimed. 'Never in my life did I dream of committing such an act! How can this ignorant damsel accuse me of so foul a crime?'

"He quickly threw on some clothes without even buttoning them and asked for a cape embroidered with pearls and gold, for they told him a king-of-arms was in the damsel's company. Then he hastened to the king, who was waiting outside the church, and with bold knightly spirit began to speak thus:"

· LXXVI ·

*H*OW TIRANT SWORE BEFORE THE KING THAT HE HAD COMMITTED NO ACT OF TREACHERY

" 'My lord, who dares to accuse me of treachery? I am here to defend my right, my honor, and my good name.'

"The damsel approached Tirant and said: 'Oh vile and treacherous knight unworthy of your order, spiller of royal blood, who with false arms and deceit killed two noble dukes and the Kings of Friesland and Poland! Such foul crimes cannot remain unnoticed and unpunished!'

"The king said: 'Damsel, may God spare my life, for I was unaware that any kings had come to my kingdom and still less my court.'

" 'How so, sire?' asked the damsel. 'Does Your Majesty not recall those four knightly comrades-in-arms, who refused to speak and brought four crowned lions with them?'

" 'Yes,' the king replied, 'I remember them well, but on my royal honor, I could not induce them to reveal their names or nationalities. Had I known they were monarchs, I never would have let them fight to the utterance, for the dangers are too great and kings should not risk their lives unnecessarily. Tell me damsel: who were the dukes?'

" 'My lord, the first was the Duke of Burgundy, who once came before Your Majesty as the King of France's ambassador.'

" 'I remember him well,' replied the king, 'and I am very sorry that he died. And the other?'

"The damsel said: 'He was the German emperor's son and the Duke of Bavaria, whom that scoundrel Tirant treacherously killed with his cruel hands!'

"Tirant could abide her words no longer and replied with great fury: 'Damsel, my only regret is that you are a woman, for were you a knight, I would send you home crying and holding your head. I shall try to keep from responding to your slanderous lies, which cannot harm me, for everyone knows a woman's strength is all in her tongue, but if Kyrieleison of Muntalbà is here and would care to repeat what you have said, perhaps God will help me send him off to join the other four. Therefore, hold your tongue and let us knights resolve this matter.'

"Then Tirant turned to everyone and said: 'Having slain those four knights fairly, without tricks or concealed advantages, I appeal to His Majesty's judges, who witnessed our battles.'

"They quickly declared him a just and valiant knight, whereupon Flower of Chivalry offered him Kyrieleison of Muntalbà's letter. Tirant replied: 'King-of-arms, your office obliges you to present challenges, reconciling knights if you are asked to do so, but since not all threats are carried out, I accept this challenge before the king and queen, be it a fight to the death or any other sort of combat.'

"Then Tirant took the letter and had it read aloud:"

· LXXVII ·

K YRIELEISON OF MUNTALBÀ'S CARTEL OF DEFIANCE

To you, Tirant lo Blanc, crueler than a ravening lion, spiller of the royal blood of those worthy Kings of Friesland and Poland, user of false and dissembled arms no honorable knight would bear: since you are a recreant knight, or more exactly a treacherous one, a deceiver in arms and everything concerning honor, I, knowing your wickedness, though I shall be reproached by my peers for entering the lists with a vile and disorderly person who behaves like a freed serf, challenge you to single combat according to the usage and customs of France. I grant you the choice of weapons, and shall await your reply for twenty-five days after you receive this cartel. If you are too cowardly to accept, you may be sure I shall reverse your arms, hanging you head down as a traitor deserves and traveling through all the great lords' courts, informing one and all of your treachery. Written in duplicate, signed with my hand, sealed with my arms, and cut along ABC[6] in Friesland, July second.

Kyrieleison of Muntalbà

· LXXVIII ·

H OW THE KING OF ENGLAND AND HIS KNIGHTS HONORED THE FOUR LORDS

"Having heard the letter, Tirant turned to the king and said: 'My lord, everything has its season. I shall defend myself to the death against this knight's slander, and indeed, I shall gladly die if I ever deceived any man.'

" 'We are certain,' replied the king, 'that your honor is secure, but now that we know their identities, let us honor them as they deserve.'

"The judges approved his words, and so they all went to Saint George's Church, where Tirant said: 'I call on Your Majesty for justice, since I killed those knights fairly without fraud or deceit. If you wish to transfer them from one tomb to another, it seems to me that, according to your rules, I should ride behind them fully armed. I ask you to uphold my right, for justice is on my side.'

"The king consulted his judges and knights, who all praised Tirant's words. Only the Prince of Wales dissented, saying: 'You want to be stuffed with honors, Tirant. Not content with having slain them, you now seek still more glory.'

" 'My lord,' replied Tirant, 'the dangers of arms are such and I have lost so much blood that no matter how I turn, my body aches. If those lords had vanquished me, would they have acted otherwise? Therefore I shall not renounce this honor, to which the rules of chivalry entitle me.'

"Tirant quickly went to don his armor and returned holding his sword aloft, accompanied by many damsels, knights, trumpeters, drummers, kings-of-arms, heralds, and pursuivants.

"Once they had assembled, the king, his queen, and all the companies approached the four knights' tomb. Each was in a sealed coffin, for they interred all slain knights thus, that their relatives might reclaim their bodies if they so desired. Tirant beat on the tomb with his sword, crying: 'Let these sleeping lords come forth!'

"Some bailiffs quickly opened the tomb and removed the two kings' coffins, which they carried to the middle of the church and laid upon two large biers hung with fine brocade. Then they honored them with all the ceremonies that are customary in royal funerals.

"Once the service had ended, the king ordered a cunningly worked tomb of aloe wood. The sovereigns' shields were hung upon the tomb, with Tirant's above them, and there were gold letters that said: *Here lie the Lords of Poland and Friesland, two brothers who died like valiant knights at the hands of brave Tirant lo Blanc.*

"When the tomb was ready, the two kings were placed in it, and after the last rites had been observed, the king and queen departed. Then all the companies escorted Tirant to his lodgings, where he removed his armor and sat down to answer the letter."

· L X X I X ·

*T*IRANT'S REPLY TO KYRIELEISON OF MUNTALBÀ

Kyrieleison of Muntalbà: the king-of-arms Flower of Chivalry has given me a slanderous cartel written in your hand and sealed with your arms. Such words ill behoove a knight, for though with colored language you vaunt your ardor, if you were as fierce as you pretend, you would not have written but rather come, but some knights, alas, would rather seek than find! You say I treacherously killed two kings with false and dissembled arms, and I say you lie and will lie as often as you say so. I slew them fairly with the arms they themselves devised, and though Our Lord gave me victory and I won the prize of honor, death was as near to me as to them. Should you ask anyone present, you will find that in all truth, it was they who used false armor unworthy of a knight, wearing pasteboard, silver foil, and other things I scorn to mention. Calling upon God, the Virgin, and Saint George to uphold my right, honor, and good name, I accept your challenge according to French usage, specifying combat on foot, lest anyone say I triumphed because my horse was better. Our weapons shall be axes four-and-a-half feet long without concealed advantages, swords with forty-inch blades, and daggers two feet long. I pray you not to write again, since I shall accept no more cartels, and to come instead of sending messengers, for I promise that you will not have the trouble of going through the courts reversing my arms or any other foulness that comes from your lying mouth. Signed in my hand, stamped with my seal, and cut along ABC in the city of London, July thirteenth.

Tirant lo Blanc

· LXXX ·

*H*OW FLOWER OF CHIVALRY AND THE DAMSEL DEPARTED WITH TIRANT'S ANSWER

"The day after he delivered Kyrieleison's cartel, the king-of-arms received Tirant's reply and departed with the damsel. Upon their return to Friesland, Kyrieleison hastily gathered everything he needed. Then he bade his family farewell and set out with a large retinue, traveling by land and sea till he reached the King of England's court.

"After paying his respects to the king and queen, Kyrieleison asked for Tirant. Flower of Chivalry, who was wearing the robe that Tirant had given him, replied: 'My lord, there stands the knight who offered me this robe. I delivered your cartel to him and he accepted it.'

"Kyrieleison and Tirant approached each other and embraced, but without good will. Then the knight said: 'Tirant, since we are agreed on this battle, let us ask His Majesty's leave to take the field tonight or tomorrow morning.'

" 'Very well,' replied Tirant, clasping Kyrieleison's left hand to make him walk on his right.

"When they were before the king, they asked his permission to fight that day.

" 'That would not be just,' replied the king, 'as you have just arrived, and if you were defeated, people would attribute it to your arduous journey; but let my judges come and decide.'

"Having arrived, the judges said nothing could be done until the next day assigned to fighting. Kyrieleison replied: 'I would rather have satisfaction now than receive an entire kingdom.'

" 'I wish we were in the lists at this very moment,' said Tirant, 'that I might gratify your wish.'

"The king and those present showed Kyrieleison every honor, but the Prince of Wales favored him especially, in order to avenge his dead mastiff and because Tirant had slain those four knights whom the prince and others had wished to battle.

"On the morrow, His Majesty asked the Prince of Wales to join him in inspecting the two kings' tomb, and the prince, to please his lord, said that he would gladly do so. When they entered the church, they saw Kyrieleison gazing at the knights' shields with Tirant's above them, for after each victory Tirant had sent two shields to Saint George's Church. He entrusted them to the prior, that, upon returning to his native Brittany, he might hang them in his chapel and have that worldly glory. Kyrieleison quickly recognized the dukes' arms and those of the King of Poland and his master, over whom he wept long and bitterly, lamenting his patron's death. So crazed with grief was he that he ran to pull down Tirant's shields, which he was tall enough to reach. Through his tears, he saw the King of Friesland's and Tirant's arms painted upon the tabernacle, and he banged his head against them so hard that he was half dead by the time the prince and the others pulled him away. Having come to his senses, he opened the tomb, and when he saw his dead lord, he felt such grief and fury that he choked on his own bile and died instantly.

"Certainly, my lord, had he not perished thus, it would have been a black day, for when Tirant heard that his shields had been dishonored, he gathered three hundred men. The prince would have been obliged to help Kyrieleison, and many knights would then have perished.

"According to what I have heard, my lord, this Kyrieleison was greatly loved and favored by the former King of Friesland, who had given him much of his wealth and made him viceroy of his kingdom. Kyrieleison had a brother named Thomas who was just as favored by the King of Poland, and one Muntalbà dwelt in Cracow while the other lived in Friesland. As soon as this brother heard of Kyrieleison's cartel, he left Poland in great sorrow and hastened to join him. When he reached Friesland, they told him Kyrieleison had left for England a few days earlier, whereupon Thomas hurriedly set out for the sea.

"He found his brother's servants at the port, bemoaning their master's death, and with great rage, both over the death of the kings and his brother's death, he quickly embarked and made his way to London. Before paying his respects to the king, he visited Saint George's Church, but he found no shields because Tirant had ordered them brought to his lodgings. Once the knight saw that they were gone, he prayed, gazing at the kings' and his brother's tombs, weeping bitterly all the while and lamenting their unlucky ends. Then he went to challenge Tirant, who at that moment was talking with some gentlewomen.

"When Tirant learned that a knight was asking for him, he excused himself and went before the king, where the brother quickly spied him and began to speak thus:"

· LXXXI ·

H OW THOMAS OF MUNTALBÀ SOUGHT TO AVENGE THE KINGS AND HIS BROTHER

" 'Tirant, I have come to avenge that worthy knight Kyrieleison of Muntalbà, and by the chivalric code you may not refuse me. I shall fight you in mortal combat under the conditions he specified, neither adding anything nor taking anything away.'

" 'Knight,' replied Tirant, 'your challenge is not necessary but voluntary, and therefore it should be denied by the judges. Nonetheless, you speak as you should, and I assure you that if it is honor you seek, you will soon be satisfied.'

" 'Tirant, I think I have said all I need to say. Furthermore, I have my brother's cartel and a reply sealed with your arms. Everything in these letters applies to me too.'

" 'Then let us attend to the business at hand,' replied Tirant. 'What you have said is insufficient, for the words must issue from your own lips. Otherwise, I shall have to refuse your challenge.'

" 'I, who have come in Kyrieleison of Muntalbà's stead, having no interest in fairy tales or long-winded speeches, accuse you of treacherously killing my sovereign lord the King of Friesland and his brother, the King of Poland, and for your treachery I challenge you to fight to the utterance, adding also the death of my good brother, whom I so loved.'

"He then ended his speech, to which Tirant replied: 'I accept your challenge and declare that you lie in your teeth. All you need do is give the judges your gage, so that if you fail to appear, I, according to the French usage agreed upon by your brother and myself, may enjoy all the rights of a defender against your slanders.'

"The knight removed his hat, while Tirant unfastened a gold chain, and they both presented their gages to the judges. Then the two knights embraced and kissed to show that the vanquished forgave the victor.

"On the appointed day, Tirant, in order to win God's favor, told the knight in the king's presence as they were entering church: 'I would be happy, if you were willing, to let peace, love, and friendship reign between us, and if you will forgive me, I shall also forgive you and your brother. Do not think these words are spoken in fear, for I am ready to fight whenever the judges wish, but I am also ready to walk barefoot to the Holy Sepulcher, remain there a year and a day, and have thirty Masses said for the souls of those dead lords and your brother, though I had nothing to do with his death.'

"This Thomas of Muntalbà was a knight of great strength, well proportioned, so tall that Tirant barely reached his waist, and far braver than his brother. The knight thought Tirant was frightened, as did many others, but they were mistaken, for the Breton only wished to atone for his adversaries' deaths.

"The gentlewomen urged Tirant to make peace with Thomas of Muntalbà, who was the biggest and strongest man in all Christendom at that time. Tirant replied: 'Ladies, though he were twice as mighty as Samson, we are still both flesh and blood, and I shall still defeat him.'

" 'Listen Tirant,' said the ladies, 'do not underestimate your foe, lest you lose in one moment both Heaven and worldly glory. He seems a very brave knight, and therefore we advise and beg you not to fight this battle. Great would be our solace if it could honorably be avoided.'

" 'Ladies, I have already made a difficult offer, and the matter is now in his hands. May God be with me and the rest come as it may, for though I know that knight's reputation, no one lacks witnesses to his courage, and often those most praised for a virtue possess very little of it. Now you must excuse me, as it is time to don my armor.'

"Then the ladies summoned Thomas and asked him to accept Tirant's offer, but he refused to hear of it and spurned their humble pleas.

"After the king had dined, the combatants proceeded to the lists in the following manner. Thomas of Muntalbà, who was fully armed, walked amid four groups bearing short lances. Before him went the Prince of Wales and many dukes, on his right were his counts and the Marquis of Saint Peter, on his left there were knights, and gentlemen of honor followed him. They all took their leave of him at the door to a big tent.

"Tirant was also accompanied by four groups, but he would not allow knights and instead chose the fairest, noblest, and best-dressed damsels in

London. He rode a splendid white charger, surrounded by trumpeters and other musicians making a joyful noise. Having reached his tent, Tirant thanked the damsels, who knelt and prayed for their knight's life and victory.

"Bearing little fans to indicate the four corners of the field, the judges led Tirant's challenger to a small silk pavilion at one end of the arena. Tirant then entered, bowing to the king and queen and making the sign of the cross over the field. When he had finished and they were both in their pavilions, two Franciscan friars came forth to hear confession and offer the knights bread, since they were in a state of sin and could not take Communion. Once the friars had gone, the royal judges entered and asked the challenger to forgive whatever insults he had suffered. The king also pleaded with him, but Thomas replied: 'Noble lords, this is no time or place to forgive the treachery done to my natural lord, brother, and master. I would not forsake my just cause for all the wealth, glory, and honor on earth.'

" 'Oh knight,' cried the judges, 'place your fate in our hands! We shall honor you above your foe, since you are the challenger and the offense was done to your natural lord, your brother, and the king whom you served.'

" 'This is no time for idle chatter,' replied the haughty knight. 'I have come to fight, so do not speak to me of peace. Asking no man's forgiveness, my cruel hand and trenchant sword will soon give an evil death to that scoundrel Tirant lo Blanc, user of false arms unknown to men of honor.'

" 'Do you think,' asked the judges, 'that battles are won by pride? Be mindful of Lucifer, who lost his seat in Heaven by trying to equal his Maker, whereas Our Lord, who is humble and merciful, forgave those who crucified Him.'

"They had summoned a priest with a reliquary, and holding the Corpus in his hand, he entered the pavilion and said to Thomas: 'Do not spurn your Creator, who made you in His image. Just as He forgave those who killed Him, forgive this knight too.'

"Thomas knelt before Christ's precious body, saying: 'Lord, You forgave those who crucified You. I neither forgive nor wish to forgive that treacherous liar Tirant lo Blanc.'

"The judges went to Tirant's pavilion and asked if he was willing to forgive his opponent. Tirant replied: 'Have you spoken with him?'

"They said yes.

" 'Then I shall speak as the defender,' said Tirant. 'If he desires battle, I shall oblige him, and likewise if he wants peace. Let him choose as he thinks best, for I shall abide by his decision.'

"Having heard Tirant's noble reply, the judges returned to Thomas and said: 'We have just spoken with Tirant, who has agreed to heed our counsel. Therefore, we ask you again to place yourself in our hands, and with Our Lord's help your honor will be preserved.'

" 'Alas, what woe,' cried Thomas, 'that you should augment the misery of one so tormented! You have said enough, and further words will only waste our time.'

"One of the judges said: 'Come, for we shall find no good in this cruel man.'

"Feeling most vexed, the judges then drew six lines on the field, lest one knight have more sun in his face than the other. When this had been done, they mounted their platform. A trumpet sounded and cries went up from the four corners of the lists that no one should dare to talk, cough, or make signals under pain of hanging on three gallows the judges had erected outside.

"When that trumpet blew again, the pavilions were removed and the knights were stationed on two lines. Four judges stood before each contestant, restraining him with a lance held by two on each side lest either adversary gain ground on his foe. The lances are held against the knights' bellies so as not to impede their weapons.

"When they had been on those lines for a while, the trumpet sounded again from above the king's and judges' platform. Hearing the mournful blast, a king-of-arms cried: *'Laissez-les aller pour faire leur devoir,'* whereupon the two combatants stepped forward to the second lines. A short while later, the trumpet sounded again and they stepped forward to the third lines, facing each other. The third time the trumpet blew, a king-of-arms cried: *'Laissez-les aller.'* The judges then raised their lances, but Thomas remained where he was. Seeing his foe immobile, Tirant turned and began walking about. After the knight had thought for a while, he ran toward Tirant and cried: 'Turn, traitor.'

"Tirant replied: 'You lie, villain, and thus do I battle you.'

"It was a most cruel combat, for Thomas was so mighty and smote such terrible blows that every time he swung, Tirant was forced to duck. Just when everyone thought Tirant was getting the worst of it, he began to defend himself. The knight struck his helmet and knocked him to one knee, but while he was kneeling, Tirant wounded his opponent in the groin, for Thomas had no chain mail beneath his armor. Tirant quickly rose, and the battle waxed very fierce. Feeling himself bleeding, the knight sought to end it quickly and hit Tirant's visor with such force that his ax stuck in the beaver. The blade touched Tirant's neck and, wounded though he was, Thomas dragged him across the field and pinned his body against the stands.

"As Your Lordship knows, in French battles if your arm, hand, or foot goes outside the boundaries and the judge is asked to cut it off, in all fairness he must do so, and at that point I would have given little for

Tirant's life. As long as they stayed as they were, the knight could not knock him to the ground, so Thomas shifted the ax to his left hand and lifted Tirant's visor, keeping him pinned with his left hand and body. Then he slapped Tirant's face with his right gauntlet, crying: 'Confess your treachery, rascal!'

"Hearing no reply, Thomas tossed aside his gauntlet and reached into Tirant's helmet. He gripped the Breton's neck and dropped his ax and other gauntlet. When Tirant saw his hands free, though he still could not move his body, he raised his ax and struck the knight's hand twice. Finding himself with neither ax nor gauntlets, Thomas drew his sword, but it availed him little against Tirant's mighty buffets. He drove Thomas across the field until his back was to the stands. When the challenger saw his predicament, he began to speak thus:"

· LXXXII ·

*H*OW TIRANT VANQUISHED THOMAS OF MUNTALBÀ

" 'Alas, woe is me! Cursed be the hour of my birth, for cruel Fortune has snatched away my best arms and armor.'

" 'Now, knight,' replied Tirant, 'you have accused me of treachery. Retract that accusation and I shall restore them to you.'

" 'Tirant,' the knight said, 'if you do me that favor I shall retract whatever you like.'

"Tirant quickly summoned the judges, and in their presence the knight retracted his charge. They restored his ax and gauntlet, though his hands were badly hurt and the wound in his groin had weakened him, while Tirant adjusted his visor and awaited him in the middle of the field.

"Once the knight had recovered his arms, they began to fight far more fiercely, but Tirant has the virtue of never feeling winded. His breath lasts as long as he wants it to, whereas Thomas, who was big and fat, had little stamina. He often had to stop and lean upon his ax, but Tirant beheld his weakness and refused to let him rest, and to make him bleed more, he kept moving about, coming close and pulling away while the poor knight tried to strike a mortal blow. After a while, lost blood and lack of endurance began to tell: Thomas's forces waned until at last his legs buckled beneath him.

"Seeing the knight's weakened state, Tirant raised his ax and brought it crashing down on Thomas's helmet just above the ear. While his head was still spinning, Tirant struck him again and felled him with a blow made all the mightier by the heavy axes they bore. Then Tirant lifted Thomas's visor and put a dagger to his eye to kill him, saying: 'Worthy knight, save your soul from eternal damnation. Surrender, since you have already retracted that slander. Admit that I am blameless, for Omniscient God decides all battles. I defeated those kings and dukes by braving death just as they did. If you agree to do as I say, I shall gladly spare your life.'

" 'As Fortune has allowed or caused things to come to this pass,' replied the knight, 'I shall obey your commands and save my wretched soul from perdition.'

"Tirant quickly summoned the judges and notaries, in whose presence the knight duly retracted his accusations.

"Then Tirant let him go and walked to the center of the field, where he knelt and thanked Our Lord for His aid in obtaining victory."

· LXXXIII ·

TIRANT'S PRAYER AFTER THE BATTLE

" 'Oh most holy and glorious Trinity, I kneel and kiss the ground! You are the One God and One Creator from whom all blessings flow, and thus You should be honored, glorified, and praised forever, amen. Oh Jesus Christ, savior and redeemer of mankind, I beg You, by Your compassion, to shield me from sin, and Lord, I thank You for all the countless honors You have bestowed upon this unworthy sinner. With infinite pity and mercy You have preserved me from all harm, and therefore may it please You to grant me victory over my enemies, that I may defend Your honor and the Holy Catholic Faith. Lord, let me not err but rather lead me to that end for which I was created, and to you, Immaculate Virgin, Queen of Heaven and sinner's advocate, I also offer thanks for my victory on this field of battle. Worthy Virgin, preserve me, that I may praise you and your Son forever! Amen.' "

· LXXXIV ·

*H*OW THE JUDGES HONORED TIRANT AND DEGRADED THE OTHER KNIGHT

"Having finished his prayer, Tirant asked the king and his judges for justice. They quickly had the knight seized, disarmed, and carried backward to the entrance, while Tirant followed them with uplifted sword. Upon reaching the gate, they stopped to strip off Thomas's armor, and each time they removed a piece, they threw it over the stands. Once he was completely disarmed, the judges announced their decision. They declared him a false knight and made him walk backward ahead of everyone to Saint George's Church, while all the young men jeered and Tirant marched behind. At the church, a pursuivant poured a basin of hot water over his head, crying: 'Here stands that recreant, defeated, mendacious knight.'

"Then all the king's guests, ladies, and damsels escorted Tirant to His Majesty's lodgings, where they removed his armor and treated his wounds. The king gave him a sable-lined robe and invited him to supper, after which there was dancing that lasted most of the night.

"As soon as the other knight had recovered, he became a Franciscan friar.

"A few days later, we departed to honor Tirant in Scotland, where the king and queen treated us all very well.

"When the two knights, Tirant and Bonnytown, were in the lists and ready to joust, the queen, who was judge of the field, saw that her knight had donned a better helmet and halted the combat.

"Tell me, lords who are versed in honor: Tirant swore in the king's presence not to bear arms before this battle. Then Kyrieleison of Muntalbà came and accused him of treachery. What should he have done: respected his oath before the king, or defended himself against such slander? Many arguments could be offered on both sides, but I shall leave the decision to worthy and honorable knights. My lord, what else can I say of Tirant? He fought in eleven mortal combats and won every time, without mentioning his other jousts. I hope I have not bored Your Reverence," said Diaphebus, "with such lengthy accounts. I see supper is ready and Tirant is our steward tonight. Afterward, I shall tell you of an order the King of England established. It is similar to King Arthur's Knights of the Round Table in olden days."

"Diaphebus," replied the hermit, "I am comforted by your gentle speech, by how well the style and practice of arms has been maintained, and most especially by that illustrious young knight Tirant lo Blanc, who has performed so many brave and chivalrous deeds. Certainly, I should consider myself the luckiest Christian on earth if I had a son so valiant and versed in the art of war, and if Tirant lives long, men will surely call him the second monarch."

As the old hermit finished these last words, Tirant humbly approached and knelt before him, saying: "Oh hermit worthy of far greater glory, if Your Lordship would be pleased to accept a modest supper with my lords and brothers here, you would honor both them and me greatly."

The virtuous lord, wise in all gentility, rose to his feet and smilingly replied: "Though I really should not, out of love and devotion I shall accept."

Then they crossed to the other side of that clear brook, where they seated themselves at table and received his blessing. Everything was as abundant as in a great city, for Tirant had devised ways to obtain many foods.

They spent a pleasant evening discussing the festivities' gallant deeds, which I could not recount even in ten pages.

On the morrow, as soon as the hermit left his dwelling after saying his hours, Tirant and the others approached him, knelt at his feet, and honored him greatly, while he graciously thanked them.

Then they seated themselves again in the green and flowery meadow. The hermit begged them dearly to describe the new order his lord had founded. The knights very courteously urged each other to speak, but above all they besought Tirant, who refused and asked Diaphebus to finish the story. Finally, Tirant rose and went to fetch their gifts for the reverend hermit, whereupon virtuous Diaphebus removed his hat and began to speak thus:

THE ORDER OF THE GARTER

·LXXXV·

*H*OW THE ORDER OF THE GARTER WAS FOUNDED

"When a year and a day had passed and the festivities had ended, the king asked his guests to wait a few days longer, for he wished to announce the founding of a new order comprised of irreproachable knights. This order's inspiration, as I and all these knights heard it from the king's own lips, came from an incident one day when we were dancing and making merry. Having danced awhile, His Highness was resting at one end of the hall, while the queen was at the other end with her maidens. Many knights were dancing with ladies, and by chance one damsel named Honeysuckle[1] drew near the king. As she whirled, her left garter, which was trimmed with silk, fell off. Those nearest His Majesty beheld it on the floor, and do not imagine, my lord, that she was fairer or more genteel than others. She has a rather flirtatious way of dancing and talking, though she sings reasonably well, yet one might have found three hundred comelier and more gracious damsels present. All the same, there is no accounting for men's tastes and whims. One of the knights near the king said: 'Honeysuckle, you have lost your leg armor. You must have a bad page who failed to fasten it well.'

"She blushed slightly and stooped to pick it up, but another knight rushed over and grabbed it. The king then summoned the knight and said: 'Fasten it to my left stocking below the knee.'

"The king wore this garter for more than four months. His queen never said a word, and the more splendidly he dressed, the more conspicuously he displayed it. No one dared to reproach him except one of his favorite servants, who, feeling the joke had lasted too long, told his master one day: 'My lord, if Your Majesty knew what I know and what all the foreigners, your subjects, your queen, and her ladies are muttering!'

" 'What can it be?' asked the king. 'Tell me quickly.'

" 'Sire, I shall tell you: everyone is amazed that you honor such an insignificant damsel, whose token you have long worn on your person in public view. One would think she was an empress or queen from all the honor you do her. Truly, my lord! Your Highness could surely find damsels in his kingdom of greater lineage, beauty, courtesy, wisdom, and other graces, for determined royal hands always reach their desired goal.'

"The king replied: 'So the queen is disgruntled and my guests are displeased!', and he said in French: *'Puni soit qui mal y pense.*² Now I swear before God that I shall found a new knightly order upon this incident: a fraternity that shall be remembered as long as the world endures.'

"He had the garter removed and would wear it no longer, though he still pined for it in secret.

"Later, my lord, when the festivities ended, he decreed the following: 'First, a chapel shall be built in Windsor Castle dedicated to our worthy lord Saint George, and this chapel shall be like those in a monastery. Two seats shall be placed to the right and left of the entrance, with eleven more on either side, and a knight shall sit in each of them with a gold sword above his seat, sheathed in a crimson brocade scabbard embroidered with pearls or silver, whichever he prefers but as richly as he can afford. Next to each sword shall be a helmet like those worn in jousts, made of shining steel or gilded wood, with whatever insignia or device he wishes, and every seat shall have a knight's gold or silver escutcheon on its back.'

"Now I shall tell you what ceremonies must be performed in the chapel and who was selected. The king chose twenty-three knights, which made twenty-four including His Majesty, who was the first to swear to uphold the order's statutes. Not all those knights who wished to join were admitted. Tirant was the first asked, as he had won the prize of honor. Then came the Prince of Wales, the Duke of Bedford, the Duke of Lancaster, the Duke of Exeter, the Marquis of Suffolk, the Marquis of Saint George, the Marquis of Fairhill, the Grand Constable John of Warwick, the Count of Northumberland, the Count of Salisbury, the Count of Stafford, the Count of Wallston, the Count of the Black Marches, the Count of the Joyous Guard, Lord Scales, Lord Greenhill, Lord Newland, Sir John Stuart, and Sir Albert of Drystream, all of them English. The foreigners were the Duke of Berry, the Duke of Anjou, and the Count of Flanders.³

"My lord, each knight selected was given a sealed copy of the ordinances by an archbishop or bishop, who also offered him a sable-lined robe embroidered with garters and a long ermine-lined cape. The capes were blue damask, tied at the neck with white silk cords, and thus the sides could be flung back to reveal both cape and robe. The hoods were lined with ermine and embroidered with buckled garters, the kind many noble-women use to hold up their stockings. Once they have buckled these garters, they loop them over to make a knot and let them hang almost halfway down their legs. The order's motto was embroidered upon each one: *Puni soit qui mal y pense*. The robes, capes, and hoods were all adorned with garters, and each knight is obliged to wear one every day of his life, both in town and in the country, armed or unarmed. If he forgets or refuses, any king-of-arms, herald, or pursuivant who spies him has the right to confiscate his gold chain or any other item of apparel, even if he is standing before his king in the biggest square on earth. Any knight caught without a garter must pay two gold *escuts* to the king-of-arms, herald, or pursuivant who saw him, who in turn must donate one to Saint George's chapels for candles. The other is his reward for noticing the infraction.

"The bishop or archbishop, representing not His Majesty but the order, must take the knight to one of Saint George's churches, if such can be found, and, placing his hand upon the altar, he must speak the following words:"

· LXXXVI ·

THE OATH SWORN BY KNIGHTS OF THE ORDER OF THE GARTER

" 'Oh knight held irreproachable by his worthy fellows, know that I, an emissary from the noble Order of Saint George, ask whether you will swear to keep all its statutes secret, revealing them to no one directly or indirectly, in speech or writing.'

"Once the knight so swears, they give him a copy of the statutes. If he chooses to accept them, he kneels before Saint George's image or altar, where with great honor and reverence he is received into the order. If he does not wish to join, he has three days to reconsider. Then he must say: 'I am unworthy of so lofty, virtuous, and excellent an order.'

"The book of statutes is closed after he signs his name therein, and the emissary returns it to the order."

· LXXXVII ·

*T*HESE ARE THE STATUTES OF THE ORDER

"First, only knights can be admitted to the Order of the Garter."

· LXXXVIII ·

*M*ORE ON THE SAME MATTER

"Second, no knight may betray his king and natural lord, whatever harm or evil he may do him."

· LXXXIX ·

*M*ORE ON THE SAME MATTER

"Third, all members must champion widows and damsels in distress, risking their worldly goods and fighting armed or unarmed, summoning relatives, friends, and men of good will to attack any town, city, or castle where any lady of honor is held prisoner."

· XC ·

*M*ORE ON THE SAME MATTER

"Fourth, no member of this order shall flee his enemies, however numerous they may be. If he retreats, he must do so facing his pursuers, and if he turns his back on them, he is guilty of falsehood and perjury. He shall then be expelled and degraded, while a scarecrow is dressed in his armor and christened with his name as part of the ceremony."

· XCI ·

M ORE ON THE SAME MATTER

"Fifth, if the King of England sets out to reconquer the Holy Land, all knights in the order, even those wounded or ill, must aid him, for the endeavor is his by right as King of England."

· XCII ·

T HE CEREMONIES KNIGHTS OF THE ORDER OF THE GARTER PERFORM AT SAINT GEORGE'S CHURCH

"When the knight has sworn to uphold these statutes, they offer him a splendid garter adorned with diamonds, rubies, and other jewels. On some day of that week there is a great celebration, in which he dons the order's uniform, mounts a white charger if one can be found, and rides through the city, followed by a crowd on foot. This procession makes its way to Saint George's Church, if such there be, or some other house of God, while the crowd holds two banners aloft: one with the knight's arms and one with his device.

"From that moment on, the king calls him brother-in-arms or count, which means the same thing. Any knight who is in England and able to travel must come to Windsor Castle whenever summoned, and those who do not appear must pay fines of ten gold marks, to be spent on candles.

"The king gave the order an annuity of forty thousand *escuts* to pay for uniforms, food on Saint George's Eve, and a solemn feast on his day.

"Now I shall describe the ceremonies at the church: on Saint George's Eve, those in the order ride to the chapel in their uniforms, while everyone else must follow them on foot. Having dismounted, they kneel at the altar and pray, the king along with all the others. Then they take their seats, and when it is time for the incense, two priests—or bishops, if any can be found—walk on either side of the chapel swinging censers throughout the Mass, the Collection, and the Pax. Once Vespers have been said, everyone leaves just as he came, meeting in a big square where abundant sweets are served, and where afterward a noble feast is offered to all and sundry.

"On the morrow, which will be Saint George's Day, they must hold council before Mass with a king-of-arms of their own selection, whose name shall be Garter. He shall receive an annuity of ten thousand *escuts,* with which he must visit those knights who are abroad, learning of their exploits that he may recount them to the others. If some knight has died, they shall elect another in his place, and if any knight should disgrace himself, disobey the statutes, or flee from battle, they shall hang a wooden effigy of him in public view, baptizing it with the usual ceremonies and expelling him from the order, whereupon, if possible, they shall imprison him for the rest of his days. Having seen to all the order's needs, the knights return to the chapel, where they hear Saint George's sermon and solemn Vespers. On the next day, they follow this same procedure, holding obsequies for those knights who have perished during that year, or for the first among them. If a dead knight must be buried, the four knights acting as treasurers must rise at the Collection. Two of them must take his sword by the tip and pommel, bearing it to the altar and offering it to the priest, while the others offer his helmet, for such is the priest's right. Here the yearly celebration ends, and if perchance any knight of the order, being captured in a just war, has to pay a ransom so great that he can no longer maintain himself as his station warrants, the order must give him an adequate yearly stipend. There are still other statutes, for if any knight not of the order, having lost a limb in battle, can no longer bear arms and wishes to end his days in a monastery, he may attend Mass wearing a red cape with a garter embroidered upon the chest and be supported there with his wife, children, and servants in the abundance his rank merits. It was also decided that twenty ladies of honor would join the order and take three vows."

· XCIII ·

THE VOWS SWORN BY THE LADIES OF HONOR

" 'First, I shall never urge a husband, son, or brother at war to return home.' "

· XCIV ·

*M*ORE ON THE SAME MATTER

" 'Second, if I know any of these is starving in a besieged town, castle, or city, I shall do everything in my power to aid him.' "

· XCV ·

*M*ORE ON THE SAME MATTER

" 'Third, if one of these is taken prisoner, I shall do everything in my power to free him, spending up to half my dowry.' These ladies must always wear garters on their left sleeves."

· XCVI ·

*H*OW A DEVICE WAS FOUND THAT THE KING OF ENGLAND ADOPTED

"My lord, now that I have described the Order of the Garter, I shall tell you how the King of England adopted a new device."

"Please do so," replied the hermit.

"One day, His Majesty, the queen, and their guests went hunting," said Diaphebus. "The king dispatched his chief huntsman to flush game, whereupon a great slaughter ensued, for after driving the beasts through a gate, we slew them with arrows, quarrels, and lances. Then we brought them back to the city on carts and pack mules, and as the cooks were skinning a big deer so old its hair had turned snow-white, they were astonished to find a gold collar beneath its neck. They sent word to the seneschal, who took the collar to his lord. The king was delighted at the message inscribed in the collar, which said that after conquering Britain and populating it with Germans and Basques, Julius Caesar had captured the deer and had the collar sewn under its skin in the hope that some future king would find the collar and take it for his device. According to the calendar, four hundred and ninety-two years had passed since then, and many people said no animal on earth could live so long. The collar was decorated with rounded S's, for in the entire alphabet one can find no letter of loftier significance."

· X C V I I ·

*T*HE DEVICE'S SIGNIFICANCE

"First of all, saintliness, as well as sagacity, sapience, sire, and many other noble words commence with S. After giving a gold copy of the collar to everyone in his new order, the king bestowed identical silver ones upon many English and foreign knights, ladies, damsels, and gentlemen. He offered one to me and to each of these knights here."

"I rejoice in everything you have told me," replied the hermit. "This Order of the Garter pleases me greatly, for it has been founded upon lofty chivalric precepts. Tell me, brave knight: is it not amazing that they found the collar on a wild beast, after so many centuries and everything you have told me? In all my time on this wretched earth, I have never heard of such a magnificent marriage."

As the hermit spoke these words, Tirant approached and said: "Reverend father, we beg you for two favors: come to that clear brook and share a little refreshment with us, and let us stay four or five days longer."

The hermit happily agreed, and they lingered more than ten days, recounting noble feats of chivalry and receiving much sound advice.

As their departure neared, Tirant, seeing that the reverend hermit nourished himself on wild herbs and water, was moved by love and charity to send for food and everything necessary to sustain human life, just as though he were stocking a castle about to be besieged. Every day they had to plead with the hermit before he agreed to share their table.

On the eve of their departure, Tirant and all the others begged the hermit to sleep in one of their tents, as they wished to set out the next morning and could not do so without his blessing. The hermit, thinking that was their purpose, happily consented. They prepared a small bed for him, and while he was sleeping, Tirant brought enough hens, capons, and other food into his hermitage to last more than a year, and even charcoal and wood lest he have to venture out in the rain.

When it was time to go, they bade each other farewell with many courtesies.

Having blessed the young knights, the holy man entered his hermitage to say his hours. He found it full of food and said: "Surely this is brave Tirant's doing. I shall mention him in all my prayers, for though I knew of his virtue, he has rewarded me far beyond my merits."

From this point on the hermit is not mentioned.

TIRANT IN SICILY AND RHODES

· XCVIII ·

*H*OW TIRANT AND HIS COMPANIONS
LEFT THE HERMIT AND RETURNED
TO THEIR NATIVE LAND

Tirant and his companions traveled until they reached the city of Nantes. When the Duke of Brittany learned they were coming, he rode forth to welcome them with his aldermen and knights, for Tirant had won first prize at the festivities in England. The duke honored and rewarded him, and Tirant was much admired by everyone in the land.

One day, as Tirant was taking his ease with the duke and many other noblemen, two French knights arrived from Paris and the duke asked what tidings they bore. One knight replied: "My lord, it is well known that after the Knights Templars were defeated, another order was founded called the Knights of Saint John of Jerusalem, and when Jerusalem was overrun, they abandoned Solomon's temple and moved to the isle of Rhodes. Greeks and men of many other nations then settled the isle, whose city and fortified castle attracted the Sultan of Egypt's notice. Every year the sultan built more warships as he prepared to attack them, and the Genoese soon discovered that he was gathering a mighty fleet. Knowing that the port was good, the land bountiful, and that since their ships often sailed to Alexandria and Beirut, a fortified harbor would be of great use to them, they held council with their duke. The council decided that the city and its castle could easily be taken, and having decided that, they set out to put it into practice. After manning twenty-seven ships with stout soldiers, they sent three of them to Rhodes at the beginning of Lent and five more two weeks later, pretending they wanted to put them in dry dock for repairs. Halfway through Lent they sent more, so that by Palm

Sunday, twenty-seven Genoese ships were near Rhodes, all full of soldiers but with little cargo. Others sailed around the island just out of sight, and when Good Friday approached, they also put into harbor and waited to attack, since on Good Friday many holy relics were displayed in the castle, and whoever hears Mass there wins an indulgence confirmed by many popes. Among the relics is a thorn from Jesus Christ's crown. At the hour when they placed it on His head, the thorn bursts into flower, staying in bloom until the hour of His death. The thorn, from an underwater reed, is among those that touched His brain, and on Good Friday they display it for all to see.

"Those renegade Genoese Christians, knowing the Grand Master of Rhodes's customs, persuaded two of their compatriots in the order to remove the notches on the crossbows, replacing them with others made of soap or cheese, so that when the knights needed them, they would be unable to draw the bowstrings. The master and the other Christians suspected nothing, for had this not been the case, they would surely have killed or imprisoned those two Genoese.

"Sometimes, however, Our Lord permits some great sin for an even greater blessing. There was a fair and gallant lady in the city who had been wooed by many knights of the order, but because of her great virtue, none of them had won her favors. She was especially adored by a Navarrese knight named Simon of Far, who, like everyone else, thought her a most honorable lady. It happened that a scribe from the Genoese captain's ship, having gone ashore on Maundy Thursday, beheld the gentle lady and fell deeply in love with her. He pleaded for her favors, promising great riches in return, and as a token of his esteem, he gave her a diamond and ruby worth twenty-five ducats. Then he reached into a pouch on his belt, pulled out a big handful of ducats, and threw them in her lap. She was very pleased, and after many words had passed between them, he had his wish. The gentle lady made a great display of affection, hoping to obtain much more.

" 'Now,' said the Genoese, 'since you have granted what I desire, tomorrow you shall possess the finest house in this city and all its furnishings.'

" 'Woe is me!' she cried. 'Having had your wicked way, you mock me with empty promises that cannot be fulfilled! Go in God's peace and never return to my house!'

" 'Oh lady,' replied the scribe, 'I thought I had conquered a kingdom and held myself the luckiest man on earth, believing that our lives and bodies would never be parted and that I would make you rich. Do not think I spoke in mockery, for I cherish you more than life itself, and tomorrow you will behold it all with your own eyes.'

" 'If this is true and some good may come to me, you should explain, since you say you love me, but you Genoese are nothing but ignorant fools. You are like those Syrian asses who carry gold on their backs and eat straw, and thus I fear you only wish to mock and deceive me.'

" 'My lady, if you swear to keep it secret, I shall tell you.'

"Once the lady had so sworn, the Genoese told her everything they planned to do.

"When the scribe left, the lady sent a wise and discreet servant to the castle. Finding the grand master and his knights at a Tenebrae Service, the servant asked Simon of Far to leave the chapel and spoke the following words: 'Lord and master, my lady begs you, if you hope to gain what you desire, to put aside everything and go to her even though this is Holy Week. She humbly waits to impart something you will never forget.'

"The knight, who was more lovelorn than pious, left Our Lord's service and made his way to the lady's house, where she embraced him lovingly, took his hand, and sat down with him upon a dais. Then she began to whisper: 'Brave knight, well I know of your devotion and the many travails you have endured to win me, yet I, wishing to guard the honor and good name that should crown all chaste damsels, have never yielded to your pleas. I know your efforts have received no compensation, but do not consider me ungrateful, for now I wish to reward you in two fashions: first, because of your great worthiness, I wish to serve you in every way I can, and second, I have asked you to come today because necessity requires it. I must tell you of my soul's unspeakable agonies, as cold sweat pours down my back when I imagine the terrible scenes that will ensue for the grand master, his order, and the entire populace of this city, all of whom will perish tomorrow as soon as the sermon ends.'

" 'Lady of high esteem,' replied the knight, 'great is the glory you bestow upon me, for it is a magnificent prize considering the little service I have done you, and I cherish your favors more than if you had made me king of the world. Tell me how I can save my order and avert such terrible harm, and for my part, I offer you, though they are already yours, my person, my worldly goods, and my honor.'

"The gentle lady was pleased by the knight's words and repeated everything the scribe had said. When the knight heard her, he was astonished to think Divine Providence had favored him so by having such a great secret revealed to him. He knelt to kiss the hands and feet of his beloved, who refused and raised him up, embracing and kissing him with chaste devotion. The knight, seeing there was no time to lose, graciously took his leave of her. By now, night had fallen and the castle was locked, but indifferent to the dangers that might await him, he approached the gates and knocked loudly. The knights standing guard on the walls asked who was making such a noise. Simon called out his name and asked to be admitted, to which they replied: 'Get away from here, villain! Have you forgotten the punishment in store if the grand master learns you are still outside? Come back tomorrow morning, and you can go in whenever you please.'

" 'No doubt,' said Simon of Far, 'but I must enter the castle tonight, and therefore please ask my lord the master to admit me.'

"One of the guards went to the church, where he found the master praying before an altar. Hearing that Simon of Far was outside, he angrily exclaimed: 'I swear that if God lets me live till daybreak, I shall make an example of him. Oh wicked friar who thus forsakes his order! In all my years as grand master, I have never seen or heard of anyone outside the castle at this hour. Tell him he cannot come in tonight, but tomorrow he will get everything he deserves.'

"The master returned to his prayers, and the guard went away with his answer. When Simon of Far heard these words, he again humbly begged the knights to ask the master to admit him, for it was urgent, and after hearing him out he could punish him as he saw fit. Three times they went to ask the master, who remained adamant until at last an aged knight who was praying with him said:

" 'My lord, why do you not give Simon of Far an audience? Sometimes things can happen in one hour that will not recur in a thousand years. This knight already knows the punishment for what he has done. Do you think him foolish enough to seek admission at this hour without good reason, when tomorrow he could simply walk in? Why would he come now when the gates are locked and there are knights on the battlements with boulders? My lord, remember that Saint Peter's Castle once was nearly captured by a Turkish surprise attack, but they opened the gates at midnight, and in a few hours the master—God rest his soul—saved it from the enemy.'

"The elderly knight's words persuaded the grand master, who ordered the walls and gates carefully guarded and the knight admitted. He entered looking most distressed, while the master angrily cried: 'Oh wicked friar and worse knight, scornful of God and your order, what are you doing outside at an hour so unsuitable to monks? I shall teach you a lesson you will never forget. Come, bailiffs! Lock him in the dungeon and give him six ounces of bread and three of water.'

" 'Your Lordship,' the knight replied, 'is not accustomed to condemning people without a hearing. If my words do not suffice to avert the punishment, I shall patiently bear a double one.'

"The master said: 'I refuse to hear a word of it, and I insist that my commands be obeyed.'

" 'Oh my lord,' replied the knight, 'will you be so cruel as not to hear me? I thought that after listening to my story, you would offer me the command of our forces, for nothing less is at stake than your life, your office, and our entire order. If anything I say is untrue, I want nothing more than to be thrown in the sea with a millstone around my neck, there to perish as a martyr to my order.'

"When the master saw how insistent the knight was, he ordered him released and said: 'Now tell us what you have to say.'

" 'My lord,' said the knight, 'it is not something to be said in public.'

"The grand master sent everyone away, and the knight began to speak thus:"

· XCIX ·

*H*OW SIMON OF FAR SAVED THE GRAND MASTER OF RHODES AND ALL THE CHRISTIANS ON THE ISLE

" 'My lord, God in His infinite mercy has shown us the greatest favor ever granted anyone, for tomorrow we would have been killed and seen our order destroyed, the city sacked, ladies and damsels dishonored, and everything reduced to ruins. For this reason, my lord, I have come at such an hour, indifferent to my fate if I can but save you and our friars. Should I deserve imprisonment for this deed, I shall bear it patiently, for I would sooner die than see our order undone.'

" 'My son,' replied the master, 'please tell me how this is to be accomplished, and I swear on my faith as a friar that your punishment will become honor and glory, as I shall make you my second in command.'

"The knight then knelt, kissed his hand, and said: 'Your Lordship should know that two Genoese friars of our order have betrayed us, for on their advice the villainous Genoese sent all those ships with many soldiers but little cargo. These traitors in our castle have done a foul deed, removing the notches from our crossbows and replacing them with soap and cheese. Tomorrow they will send their bravest soldiers to our castle, bearing a dismantled crossbow they have just invented, where the bow is not tied to the stock with a cord but can be attached to the stirrup with a little screw. They will come in pairs, concealing weapons beneath their capes and pretending they want to worship the cross and hear Mass. When Mass is being said, they plan to slip out of church and, with the help of the two friars who will already control the highest tower, they will admit their other friends and capture us all. Before Your Lordship knows what is afoot, they will control half the castle, and we shall all be either slain or captured.'

" 'In that case,' replied the master, 'let us first go to the armory and see if what you say is true.'

"They found that among more than five hundred crossbows, only three had wooden notches. The master, who was stunned, summoned his council and had the two Genoese friars imprisoned. He threatened them with torture, and they confessed that he and his whole order were doomed. The grand master then ordered them seized and thrown in a dungeon full of snakes, vipers, and other loathsome animals.

"No one slept that night, and, after quietly doubling the guard, the master chose fifty brave young knights to welcome their guests the next morning. All the others donned their armor to help if they were needed. At dawn, they opened the gates and the Genoese began to enter, pretending to pray as they went. They had to pass through three gates, the first of which was wide open with two gatekeepers guarding it. Then they went through a little gate into a courtyard in front of the church, where the fifty armed knights seized them and flung them one by one into a deep pit. They shouted for help, but those outside could not hear them. Nearly fourteen hundred Genoese died in this fashion, and if more had entered, still more would have perished. The captain stood outside, but when he saw so many Genoese go in and none come out, he returned to his ships. Once the master saw they had stopped entering, he ordered most of his knights to pursue them, slaying as many as they could catch, and there was a great slaughter of Genoese on that day.

"As soon as the captain reached his ships, he ordered them to set sail for Beirut, where he told the sultan what had occurred on Rhodes. The Genoese suggested that they take counsel together, and they agreed that the sultan himself should go to Rhodes with all the troops he could muster, making two or three trips with his warships. The sultan gathered twenty-five thousand Mamelukes and sent them to the island.

"When the ships returned, they set sail again with thirty-three thousand Saracens, and the vessels came and went until more than a hundred and fifty thousand soldiers were on the isle. Having pillaged it from one end to the other, they besieged the city, while their ships blockaded the port so no provisions could arrive. Every day they assaulted the fortress three times: once in the morning, once at midday, and once before sundown. Those inside defended themselves like manly knights, but they were worried because they had no food left and were forced to eat horses, cats, and even rats.

"The grand master, seeing their dire need, asked his sailors to send a brig through the blockade. They quickly fitted one out, and the master wrote to the Pope, the emperor, and all Christian kings, telling them of his predicament and requesting their aid.

"The brig, which set sail one night when it was raining and very dark, slipped through unnoticed and delivered the letters. All the princes expressed sympathy but were slow in sending help, and likewise the King of France promised much but gave little."

All this was recounted by the knights who came to Brittany from the King of France's court. Distressed by the Rhodians' plight, the duke spoke many brave words, and in particular he promised to send emissaries to the King of France, saying that if His Majesty chose to help the grand master, he would gladly lead the troops and donate two hundred thousand *escuts* to the expedition.

He held council the next morning, and four emissaries were chosen: an archbishop, a bishop, a viscount, and Tirant, for he was a worthy knight of the Order of the Garter.

Once the emissaries were before the King of France, they explained their mission and were told they would receive a reply four days later. More than a month passed before they heard the king's decision. He told them that, for the present, he had more pressing matters to attend to, whereupon the emissaries departed for Brittany.

When Tirant learned that so many Saracens were threatening Rhodes and no one would help, he spoke with many sailors, asking their advice about how best to aid the Christians. They said he could reach the castle by landing not in the harbor but on the other side.

Tirant, with the duke's and his parents' permission, bought a galleon and had it armed and stocked with food. It happened that Tirant knew the King of France's five sons, the youngest of whom was named Philip. Philip was a bit doltish and had a reputation for vulgarity, and because of this the king felt little love for him and people generally ignored him. A gentleman in his service, knowing Tirant was sailing for Rhodes and wishing to go to Jerusalem himself, spoke the following words to Philip:

· C ·

H OW, AFTER FITTING OUT A GALLEON TO AID THE GRAND MASTER OF RHODES, TIRANT SET SAIL WITH PHILIP, THE KING OF FRANCE'S YOUNGEST SON, WHOSE MARRIAGE HE ARRANGED TO A SICILIAN PRINCESS

"Knights who covet honor, my lord, must not stay at home with their parents when they are young and able to bear arms, and especially if they are the youngest and still more if their fathers ignore them. Were I you, I would sooner eat grass in the mountains than spend one more day at this court. Be mindful of that old saying: 'With a change of age comes a change of fortune,' and consider whether you might not find better fortune elsewhere. Look at that famous knight Tirant lo Blanc, who, after all the honors he won in England, is now fitting out a galleon to sail to Rhodes and then to the Holy Sepulcher in Jerusalem. Ah, what glory you could win if we secretly accompanied him, not telling anyone till we were a hundred miles out at sea, for Tirant is so virtuous that he would obey and honor you as your rank deserves."

"My dear friend Tenebrous, your advice is sound," replied Philip, "and I shall gladly accompany you."

"I think," said the gentleman, "that first I should go to the port in Brittany where Tirant is having the ship fitted out. I shall beg him by our great friendship to let me sail with him to the Holy Land, and then I shall ask what provisions I and two squires might need. When I receive his answer, I shall have everything brought aboard."

Philip approved of this plan and said: "Tenebrous, while you are away, I shall gather all the money, clothes, and jewelry I can find, that I may be presentable wherever we go."

The next day, Tenebrous set out with two squires, and after traveling for some days, he reached the port where Tirant was. Upon hearing why Tenebrous had come, Tirant was delighted, as he knew his friend to be a wise and valiant gentleman. Tirant then said: "Lord and brother Tenebrous, my goods, my person, my ship, and everything I own are at your service. I consider it a stroke of luck that you will accompany me, but I would never allow any knight or gentleman to bring food to my galleon, for everything on board will be as much yours as mine."

When Tenebrous heard Tirant speak thus, he was the happiest man on earth and thanked him profusely for his kindness.

Leaving one of his servants to prepare a cabin where they could eat and sleep and where Philip could hide for a few days, Tenebrous set out on horseback and rode till he reached his master.

Philip rejoiced in Tirant's answer, and Tenebrous told him to prepare for a speedy departure, but the prince replied that he already had everything ready.

The next day, Philip asked his father's leave to go to Paris and see the fair, which was a two-day trip. The king, with a bored look on his face, replied: "Do as you like."

Philip kissed his parents' hands, and early the next morning they set out and traveled until they reached the sea, where Philip hid in their cabin and let no one see him.

When they were two hundred miles from land, Philip revealed himself. Tirant was astonished, but since they were at sea, they had to continue on their course until they reached the city of Lisbon. The King of Portugal, when he heard the French Prince Philip was aboard, sent a knight to invite him ashore, to which Philip replied that he would gladly accept. He and Tirant donned their finest clothes and, accompanied by many splendidly dressed knights and gentlemen wearing gold chains, they left the ship and made their way to the palace, where the king embraced Philip and did them all great honor.

Ten days later, when they were ready to depart, the king had their ship plentifully stocked with everything they might need. Tirant gave one of his gentlemen a letter for the King of France, telling him the truth about Philip's whereabouts. The king rejoiced to hear that his son was in such good company, but the queen was still happier, for it was so long since she had heard from him that she thought he had died or entered a monastery.

Having bidden the King of Portugal farewell, they hoisted sail and rounded Cape St. Vincent, making for the Strait of Gibraltar. There they met many Moorish vessels, which, upon spying Tirant's galleon, gave chase and did their utmost to capture it. The battle raged for half a day with many deaths on both sides, for though Tirant's ship was much bigger than the Moorish ones and was manned by four hundred soldiers, it was also alone, whereas the Saracens had fifteen vessels.

There was a crafty sailor aboard, named Look-what-you-do, who had sailed the seas for years and was both skillful and brave. Seeing how badly things were going, he took all the rope they had and wove a loose net like the ones they use to load straw on donkeys. Then he stretched the net between the castles, climbed the mainmast, and secured the net in the maintop lest it hamper the soldiers. In fact, it saved their lives, for the Moors shot so many big stones that, had it not been for that net, the whole deck would have been covered with rocks and iron bars. What else did this sailor do? After collecting all the mattresses on board, he placed them around the forecastle and along the waist of the ship, so the stones from the bombards would hit the mattresses instead of the hull. More-over, he filled big cauldrons with boiling oil and pitch, and when the Moors tried to pull alongside, the soldiers flung the mixture at them, causing such havoc that their foes had to move away. They sailed through the Strait of Gibraltar, fighting day and night, and so many stones, quarrels, and arrows struck them that the sails were pinned to the masts. When they tried to lower the lateen sail after their foes had abandoned the chase, they could not get it down. They were very close to shore, and it seemed the ship might run aground near Gibraltar, but the good sailors brought the vessel into the wind and lowered sail. Then they pulled out of the straits, made sail, and shaped a course in the Mediterranean.

Since Tirant, Philip, and many others had been hurt, they headed for a deserted island where they could treat the wounded and repair the gal-leon. Then they made their way along the Barbary Coast, fighting off Moorish and Genoese ships, and as they approached Tunis, they decided to sail to Sicily for more provisions. They docked at Palermo, where the king, his queen, and their two sons and daughter dwelt. This daughter, whose name was Ricomana, was a clever and beautiful damsel skilled in many arts. As Tirant was eager to obtain food, he sent the scribe and five or six men ashore, telling them not to mention him or Philip but just to say that they were on their way to Alexandria with some pilgrims to the Holy Land.

Learning that they came from the west, the king summoned Tirant's men, who, while recounting their battles with the Moors and Genoese, forgot their captain's orders and mentioned Philip. His Majesty then ordered a long wooden gangway built and covered with satin, and to honor his royal guest, the king himself went aboard with his two sons. He invited Philip and Tirant to come ashore and rest after their battles, to which they replied that they would gladly oblige him.

The king saw that they were well lodged, served the finest foods, and given everything a man needs after a long sea voyage, but Philip, on Tirant's advice, refused to settle into his chambers until he had paid his respects to the queen. Charmed by his courtesy, the king escorted them to the palace, where both the queen and Princess Ricomana welcomed them graciously, and when they finally saw their lodgings, they found them truly fit for a prince.

From then on, they saw the king every day at morning Mass and at lunch. They saw even more of the princess, whose hospitality was legendary and had caused her virtue to be proclaimed throughout the world. Discoursing every day with the king and each other, she and Philip fell in love, but the prince was too shy to declare himself, and sometimes when she addressed him he was unable to speak. Then Tirant would say:

"Ah, my lady, what a strange thing love is! When Philip and I are in our lodgings, his tongue never wearies of praising your virtues, yet when you are present he can scarcely talk, so enamored is he of Your Highness. I swear that if I were a lady and found someone so genteel, brave, and of such ancient lineage, I would forsake all others and love only him."

"Tirant," replied the princess, "you speak well, but if he is a foolish lout and must be kept out of sight, pent up like a checkmated king, what pleasure or comfort can a damsel find in him? Please do not speak such words, as my pleasure requires a man of wisdom, one of lofty rank and lineage, and one neither loutish nor intemperate."

"My lady," said Tirant, "you speak with natural reason, but this man does not belong on the bench where you have placed him. He is young in years yet old in wisdom, generous, bold above all others, friendly, courteous, and gracious in all things. Pacing to and fro in our chambers, he refuses to let me sleep, for each night seems a year to him and his sole delight is the day. Should I wish to give him pleasure, I need only mention Your Highness, and if that is not true love, please tell me what is. My lady, love the one who loves you, who is a prince and your equal, and who cherishes you more than his own life and person. Should he not speak as much as you might wish, think all the better of him, and beware, my lady, of those who audaciously and brazenly declare their love. Love like theirs is worthless and goes as quickly as it comes, wherefore such men are called pirates, since they seek to rob everyone. My lady, give me a man who comes before his mistress shyly and fearfully, who can scarcely utter a word, and who speaks with fearful heart."

"Tirant," replied the princess, "as you are such good friends with Philip, you do well to place him in the seat of honor. Being yourself of such a noble order, you neither could nor should speak otherwise, but do not think me so gullible, for if something is going on, I want to stick my arms in it up to the elbows, feel around, and find out just what it is and whether it really will comfort my soul. My eyes are pleased with him but my heart says no, for experience shows that this man is loutish and crass, and those are two incurable diseases."

"Oh lady! Those who try to peer most subtly into everything often choose most basely, and especially in chaste and honorable loves. Less than three days ago, your father and I were strolling in the garden, talking about various Christian princes and many other matters. We began to speak of Your Highness, and he told me he wishes to divide his estate before he dies. Out of natural love for his children—and especially you, his obedient daughter—he wishes to give you the duchy of Calabria plus two hundred thousand ducats. I praised his noble purpose, as you deserve great dignity and the highest honor, wherefore I beg Your Highness to give me a few hours' audience, for I see ambassadors from the Pope coming to arrange a marriage with his nephew, who some say is his son,[1] while others arrive from the courts of Naples, Hungary, and Cyprus, and though I have not been empowered to do so by that most noble and Christian King of France, yet I would like to arrange this marriage with your father and yourself.

"It is a great help, my lady, to see with your own eyes whether he is lame, one-eyed, or crippled, young or old, of good or bad grace, brave or cowardly. In these matters and many others where Nature can err, you will have to trust ambassadors who may deceive you. A wise, prudent, and clever damsel like yourself should not think I would lie because I am in Philip's service, since you can easily view his perfections for yourself. You, who are so fair and noble, deserve to sit on an imperial throne, protected by the French monarchy, which is even loftier than the Roman Empire. History proves it, for the King of France's arms were not given to him without great cause. Our Lord sent an angel with three *fleurs-de-lis*, and nowhere can you read of any other king receiving his arms in like fashion.[2] Thus, my lady, you can win both temporal and spiritual glory, as your distinguished person will be blessed by marriage to this prince, and how many ladies can gain glory in this world and Paradise in the next?"

At this point, the queen interrupted their pleasant discourse. After a moment, she said to Tirant: "Brave knight, less than an hour ago the king and I were speaking of you and your noble deeds, and His Majesty wishes to entrust you with a great task dear to both our hearts. I hold you to be such that if you undertake it, you will emerge with all the honor a worthy knight deserves, but to ease my fears, I shall raise as many objections as I can."

"My lady," replied Tirant, "your words are so mysterious that I can hardly reply if you do not explain yourself more clearly, though I shall gladly do what I can, even if I must bear a cross on my back."

The queen thanked him for his good will, and Tirant returned to his lodgings, feeling very despondent because his galleon would not be ready to depart for a while.

Then Tirant saw a vessel approaching shore, and before going to lunch, he decided to learn what tidings it brought. He dispatched an armed brig, which returned with news that the ship was from Alexandria and Beirut. It had called at Cyprus but had been unable to dock at Rhodes, so great was the multitude of Saracens besieging the city by land and sea. There were many Genoese ships blockading the harbor, and the city was hard pressed because they had no bread. It was three months since the grand master and his men had tasted anything but horsemeat, and it was a lucky day when they had that to eat. They doubted that they could hold out for more than a few days, and they would have surrendered already had the sultan not refused to spare them.

Upon hearing this, Tirant became very thoughtful, and after thinking a long time, he decided to load his galleon and set out immediately. He quickly summoned merchants and paid them to load the ship with grain, wine, and salt pork.

When the king heard this, he summoned Tirant and told him his will:

· C I ·

HOW THE KING OF SICILY ASKED TIRANT TO TAKE HIM TO THE HOLY SEPULCHER IN JERUSALEM

"My knowledge of your virtue, Tirant, obliges me to aid you, and I shall be grateful if you will also help me, for nothing in my power to give shall be denied you. I cherish you as a brother or son for your brave knightly deeds, which are such and of such renown that you deserve to be rewarded by God in this world and the next. Your noble expedition is a reproach to those Christian princes who failed the Grand Master of Rhodes in his hour of need, and if God lets me accompany you, in disguise, to receive holy indulgence in Jerusalem, I shall be more grateful than if you had given me a kingdom. Therefore, I beg you dearly: do not deny one who wishes you well, but give me such answer as might be expected from your great virtue."

When the king had finished, Tirant began to speak thus: "Great would be my honor if Your Majesty accepted me as his servant, as I am unworthy to be your brother or son, nor have I served you as such. I thank you infinitely for your good will, and, if need be, shall seek your aid as though Your Highness were my natural lord and I had served you all my life. As far as this voyage is concerned, my ship, my person, and everything I own are at your disposal, since I wish only to serve you and obey your every command, but my primary intention was to succor the Christians on Rhodes, who are about to be destroyed by cruel Genoese who love to prey on the weak, showing neither pity nor clemency toward their Christian brethren."

"Tirant," replied the king, "I see your righteous intent and noble purpose, and you act as a worthy knight and a good Christian should. I am sure your project is just and holy, but for that very reason, I am all the more eager to accompany and help you."

Tirant thanked him profusely, and so they reached an agreement, whereupon Tirant asked the king to come aboard and decide which cabin he would like. After inspecting the ship, he chose the one nearest the mainmast, since if any harm befell them that would be the safest spot.

Every day the king and Tirant discussed many matters, and so it happened that one day they spoke of Philip, whom Tirant wished to see married to the princess with the dowry her father had promised her. The king, who was eager to form an alliance with the French crown, said: "Tirant, I would never settle any of these matters without my daughter's consent, for it is she who must be happy, but if she approves, I for my part consent to the marriage and promise to give her everything I mentioned. I shall discuss it with the queen and my daughter, and if they agree, we can celebrate the wedding before our departure."

The king summoned his queen and daughter, to whom he spoke the following words: "I have called you to me, oh queen and daughter, to inform you of my departure, as with God's help I intend to journey to the Holy Sepulcher in Jerusalem, and lest I be recognized, I shall take only one retainer. Since my fate will be in God's hands, I would like you, my daughter, to marry before I leave, that I may have the comfort of seeing you happy and settled, and if this prince wishes to tie us to the loftiest king in Christendom, I am sure that, between Tirant's help and Philip's good will, the matter can be brought to a happy conclusion."

"It seems to me," replied the princess, "that Your Highness knows it will be another two weeks before they finish loading the ship. With the advice of my uncle the Duke of Messina, you can settle the matter before you leave, for we expect his arrival tonight or tomorrow."

"You speak well, my daughter," said the king, "and so it shall be done."

"Excuse me, Your Highness," replied the princess, "but since you have decided to embark upon this pilgrimage, you should hold a great feast so that once you are at sea, Tirant and his men will serve you all the more devotedly, and furthermore, if the King of France hears of it, he will know you have honored his son. Order a public feast to begin next Sunday and last three days, and keep the tables constantly piled high, that all your guests may find abundant food."

"On my faith," the king said, "you are far wiser than I, and as I am occupied with my departure, setting my kingdom in order, and keeping my journey secret lest I encounter problems in Saracen lands, I would like you, my daughter, to arrange the festivities."

The king quickly summoned his steward and purchasers, whom he told to follow all Ricomana's instructions.

The princess planned everything very well, ordering many dishes to show her ingenuity, but the only reason she had arranged this feast was to study Philip's table manners.

On the day assigned for the solemn festivities, the princess ordered a table placed above the rest for her parents, herself, and Philip, while the Duke of Messina, Tirant, and the counts and barons would eat below. On the eve of the feast, her father had dispatched two knights to invite Tirant and Philip to attend Mass and lunch with him the next day.

The next morning, they donned their best clothes and went to pay homage to the king, who welcomed them with great love and took Philip's hand. The Duke of Messina took Tirant's and they set out for the church, where, upon reaching His Majesty's chapel, they begged his leave to fetch the queen and princess. He gladly consented, and as they were walking with the royal ladies, Philip took Ricomana's arm to be near her, while Tirant never left her other side lest he say something loutish and annoy his beloved.

When Mass had ended, they returned to the palace, and to honor Philip, the king seated him at the head of the table facing Ricomana. Tirant wished to remain standing so he could be near his friend, but the king said: "Tirant, the Duke of Messina will not sit down until you do."

"My lord," replied Tirant, "kindly bid him be seated, for at such a feast it is only right that I should serve a prince."

The princess grew impatient and said angrily: "Tirant, why must you always climb onto Philip's lap? We have many knights who can attend him, and your services are not required."

When Tirant saw how vexed the princess was and realized he had to abandon Philip, he whispered in his ear: "When the king picks up the finger bowl and you see the princess kneel and take it from him, imitate her and try not to behave like a dolt."

Philip said he would do so, and when everyone was seated, they brought the fingerbowl to the king, whereupon the princess knelt and took it while Philip tried to do the same, but His Majesty refused to let him. Then Ricomana offered the bowl to the queen, and when it was her own turn, she took Philip's hand so they could wash together, but although the prince showed his courtesy by trying to kneel and hold the bowl for her, she refused to wash until they both did it together. Then the bread was brought in and placed upon the table, but no one touched it because they were waiting for the other dishes. When Philip saw the bread in front of him, he quickly picked up a knife and cut an entire loaf into twelve big slices. Beholding this pantomime, Ricomana and everyone else roared with laughter, and naturally Tirant noticed, since he had his eyes fixed upon his friend. Our knight quickly rose, thinking: "My God! Philip must have done something loutish and dishonorable."

Tirant approached the king's table and, guessing the cause of their mirth, he picked up the slices, placed a gold ducat on each one, and donated them to the poor. When the king and Ricomana saw what he had done, they stopped laughing and asked what it meant.

"Sire," replied Tirant, "once I have finished I shall tell you."

Tirant distributed all the slices, each with its ducat, and upon reaching the last one, he brought it near his mouth, said a Hail Mary to it, and then gave it away.

The queen said: "I would love to hear what this pantomime means."

Tirant turned to the king and replied:

· CII ·

*H*OW TIRANT REPAIRED A GRAVE ERROR PHILIP HAD COMMITTED AT THE KING OF SICILY'S FEAST

"You are surprised and amused at what Philip has begun and I have finished, and the meaning, since Your Majesty wishes to know, is that the most Christian Kings of France, in thanks for the many blessings God has bestowed upon them, ordained that until the day they are knighted, all their sons must take the first loaf of bread at lunch and cut it into twelve slices. Then they must place a silver *real* on each slice, giving it away as charity in honor of the twelve apostles. After they have been knighted, they must place a gold piece on each slice, and to this day everyone in the French royal house follows this practice. For that reason, my lord, Philip cut the bread into twelve slices, that each apostle might have his just share."

"May God preserve me!" cried the king. "What a splendid act of charity! I am a crowned king myself, yet I do not give away that much charity in a month."

As the food had now arrived, the princess asked Tirant to leave them, while Philip, realizing his error and how discreetly our knight had repaired it, watched the princess and ate only as much as she did.

When they had risen, the princess visited one of her most trusted maids, and with mingled anger and love, she began the following lamentation:

· CIII ·

PRINCESS RICOMANA'S LAMENT AFTER THE FEAST

"Alas, what torments my weary soul must endure, as this Tirant will not let me spend one hour alone with Philip! Were Tirant his brother or natural lord, he would not stick so closely to his side, for I cannot say one word without his interfering. Oh Tirant! Begone in your galleon, and good luck to you in other lands, but leave me Prince Philip for my soul's repose and comfort. If you do not soon depart, my sorrows will be unending, since your great discretion compensates for others' indiscretions. Tell me, Tirant: why do you distress me so? Had you ever been in love, you would know how sweet it is to converse with one's beloved. Until now I had never felt love's sufferings, and though I enjoyed being courted by my father's vassals, I thought their love mere flattery, but now, alas, I cannot sleep at night. Food has lost its sweetness and tastes bitter as gall, my clumsy hands mock me and refuse to help me dress, and my soul finds no peace, for I only wish to be alone. If this is life, I cannot imagine what death must be!"

Thus did the enamored princess give utterance to her grief, while bitter tears flowed from those eyes that had so inflamed Philip's heart. As she stood there, the king and the Duke of Messina, who was to be viceroy and caretaker in his absence, came in.

When they had entered, the king beheld her doleful countenance and asked: "What is it, my daughter? Why do you grieve?"

"But sire, have I no right to?" replied the princess. "Your Highness will soon depart, and then what shall I do, disconsolate? Who will comfort me? In what will my spirit find repose?"

The king turned to his brother and said: "Duke, how my heart aches, and one's own blood cannot turn to water."

Having comforted his daughter as best he could with words of great love, the king summoned his queen, that the four of them might take counsel.

· C I V ·

*H*OW THE KING COMMENDED HIS WIFE AND DAUGHTER TO THE DUKE OF MESSINA AND ASKED HIS OPINION OF THE MARRIAGE

"Since good fortune permits and Divine Providence compels me to undertake this journey, my spirit departs in peace, for my brother, who is my very soul, will remain here in my stead and govern my domains. Before leaving, however, I wish to ask a favor of you, duke: tell me what you think of this marriage to Philip."

"My lord," replied the duke, "as Your Majesty and his queen are pleased to ask my opinion, I shall gladly give it. Often a damsel appears content with a marriage, but when it turns out contrary to her will, she feels deceived and angry. Your Highness and Philip will soon depart together, and therefore I think the marriage should await his parents' consent. Let Tirant write to the King of France and ask if he approves, for otherwise, we may turn concord into discord and peace into war, and he may claim we took advantage of his son's youthful innocence. Were she my daughter, I would sooner give her to a knight with his family's blessing than to a prince against his parents' will."

The king and queen thought the duke's advice good, while Ricomana was too shy to object, and in a sense she was pleased because she could learn more about Philip's character.

They quickly summoned Tirant, whom they told of their decision, and, after praising their wisdom, he wrote to the King of France, telling him about the marriage and requesting his consent. The King of Sicily then sent a brig to Piombino with the letter.

Tirant's ship had now been loaded with grain and other foods, and so when the brig was ready to leave, the king made a show of boarding it. Then he secretly returned to his palace and locked himself in his chambers, while his servants spread a rumor that he had gone to see the Pope in Rome. That night, Tirant fetched the king and Philip, and when everyone was aboard, he went to take his leave of the queen and princess. The queen asked him to take good care of the king, whose health was most delicate.

"My lady," replied Tirant, "never fear, for I shall serve him as though he were my natural lord."

Ricomana also urged Tirant to look after her father and appeared saddened by his departure, though she was mostly thinking about Philip.

At the first watch they hoisted sail, casting off with such good weather that in four days they had passed the Adriatic and were within sight of Rhodes, where they dropped anchor near Saint Peter's Castle and awaited a favorable wind. On the advice of two Breton sailors who were much devoted to him, Tirant set sail one night with a stiff breeze, and the next morning when the sun rose they were near the city.

When the Genoese spied a vessel approaching from the east, they thought it was one of two they had sent to fetch provisions, for they believed no other ship would dare to enter the harbor. Tirant's galleon sailed slowly toward them, and when it was nearby, his men suddenly unfurled every sail they had. Then the Genoese tried to give chase, but Tirant was so close to shore that they had no time to hoist sail and pursue him. The vessel passed safely through their midst with all its canvas billowing, but the Genoese did possess abundant lances, crossbows, bombards, and other arms. Tirant ordered his helmsman and pilot not to turn the ship around but to make straight for land, running her aground on a beach beneath the city walls.

Seeing the galleon strike land and thinking it was Genoese, the Rhodians rushed to the walls and began pelting it with stones, while their foes also attacked the ship from the sea. Tirant's men were hard pressed till a sailor hoisted one of his flags, whereupon the Rhodians stopped, while Tirant sent a messenger to the city.

Learning the ship was loaded with grain from France, the townsfolk hastened to tell their grand master, who knelt along with his knights, offering praise and thanks to Divine Providence for succoring them. Then they went down to the city, sending soldiers ahead with sacks to carry the grain to their storehouses.

Full of eagerness to meet Tirant, whose chivalric deeds were legendary, the master dispatched two of his finest knights to invite the Breton ashore. They boarded the ship and asked for its captain, and Tirant, who was experienced in courtly ways, welcomed them with great honor. The knights said: "Lord captain, our master awaits you in the city and asks you to disembark, as he is most anxious to meet you."

"My lords," Tirant replied, "tell the grand master I shall soon join him. Were I not unloading this ship, I would have already done so, but I fear the vessel may split asunder and its cargo be lost. Tell him to store the grain safely, and grant me two favors: first, take some refreshment with me now, and second, allow two of my gentlemen to speak with the master before I go ashore."

"Lord captain," replied one of the knights, "you request two favors that cannot be denied, and indeed the first is so delightful that we shall be forever in your debt."

Tirant, who had ordered many chickens and other meats prepared the day before, gave them such a good meal that they felt like men reborn. When Tirant's steward had found a big square in the city, he sent food for the entire order, and that is why our knight had refused to disembark.

Once the knights had eaten, Tirant sent two gentlemen to ask the master if the King of Sicily and Philip would be safe on Rhodes. Having heard their, mission, the master replied: "Gentlemen, tell Tirant that I shall gladly keep his secrets and that he need not ask if they will be safe in my city. I hope he will deem this island his own, for so great is our good will toward him that he is master of all we possess. I beg him to take command as though he were grand master himself, and should he want my scepter and keys, they shall be his for the asking."

Having heard the master's reply, Tirant relayed it to the King of Sicily, whereupon the king and Philip disguised themselves and went to their lodgings. Tirant appeared dressed in the following manner: he had donned a scarlet brocade robe, a coat of mail over it, and a jeweled cassock embroidered with big pearls over the mail. His sword hung at his side, his garter encircled his leg, and a red skullcap with a splendid brooch adorned his noble head.

Upon entering the city, escorted by many knights from the order and his own company, Tirant found the master standing in the main square. Ladies and damsels watched from windows, doorways, and rooftops, hoping to glimpse the blessed knight who had saved them from cruel starvation and bitter captivity. When Tirant was before the master, he knelt to kiss his hand, but the master refused, raised him to his feet, and kissed his lips with great love. Then he told Tirant how the sultan and his Christian allies had assaulted them day and night, while they had debated hour by hour whether to surrender because of their extreme hunger. They could not have endured much longer, for they had eaten all the horses and even the cats, and it was a wonder if any were still alive in the city. "Many pregnant women have aborted, and little babes are dying of hunger."

Hearing the master recite their past woes, Tirant replied:

· C V ·

HOW TIRANT SAVED THE RHODIAN CHRISTIANS

"Your just prayers, most reverend lord, and the afflicted populace's bitter tears have moved God to pity you and this blessed order, which He has neither permitted nor will permit to be destroyed by enemies of our holy faith. May Your Lordship rejoice, for with God's help these Saracens will soon quit Rhodes, but since one first must attend to the direst need, I beg you to do me the honor of lunching with our company."

"Brave knight," replied the master, "you request something so agreeable that, as our need is great, I accept with infinite thanks, for I am so weak that I can barely talk, and my sole desire is to repay you with both riches and glory."

Tirant quickly had many tables brought to the square and asked the master, his retinue, and his knights to be seated. The master urged Tirant to sit beside him, but the Breton excused himself, saying that he preferred to oversee the meal. Taking a steward's baton, he had the master given two pairs of peacocks, as well as abundant capons and chickens. Once that had been done, everything necessary was brought to the others.

As soon as they had begun to feast, Tirant ordered the trumpets blown, while criers announced that those who wished to eat but could find no room at the tables should sit on the ground, where they would be given everything necessary to sustain human life. Ladies, damsels, and a multitude of townspeople quickly filled the square, and in less than an hour they all had been served. In addition, he sent food to those guarding the castle, and between Our Lord's grace and Tirant's diligence, everyone ate his fill. When they had eaten, sweets were brought for the master and his knights.

Then Tirant had the barrels of flour piled in the middle of the square and asked the master for two knights to help the city aldermen divide it among the townsfolk, as he had already set some aside for the castle. He also asked the master to have the mills readied, since they had been idle a long time, and to summon anyone who wanted flour to the square. When the flour had been rationed, he had the grain distributed among the houses according to how many mouths they had to feed. After giving between twelve and seventy-two bushels to each household, they followed this same practice with the oil, meat, legumes, and everything else.

One could never repeat all the blessings the townspeople showered upon Tirant, but they would have assured his place in Heaven, though he had never done another good deed in his life. When all the food had been distributed and everyone was happy, the master asked Tirant to take him to the King of Sicily's and Philip's lodgings. Tirant gladly consented, and, after sending word to his friends, he led the master to their lodgings, where he and the king did each other great honor. Then the master embraced Philip and invited them both to stay at the castle, but the king refused, saying he was safer where he was.

"My lord," Tirant said, "night is fast approaching. Let me escort you to your fortress, and tomorrow we shall discuss our strategy and how we may rid your island of these Saracens."

The master said goodbye to the king and Philip, and Tirant walked with him till they were near the castle. When darkness fell, the castle and city blazed with bonfires, while the air rang with the joyous noise of drums, trumpets, and other instruments. The flames burned so brightly that the Turks spied them from the mainland, and a rumor spread among their troops that the sultan had captured the Master of Rhodes and all his subjects.

That night, Tirant and his men kept watch over the harbor. The Genoese ships were very near shore, and the captain's vessel was the nearest. Toward midnight, a sailor approached our knight and said: "My lord, how much would you pay to have that captain's ship burnt tomorrow night?"

"If you can do it," Tirant replied, "I promise you three thousand gold ducats."

"My lord," said the sailor, "if you give me your word, I shall use all my cunning, and if my plan miscarries, I swear to be your slave."

"My friend," replied Tirant, "I desire no pledges or promises, for if you fail, your shame will be punishment enough. I declare as a knight that if you burn that ship tomorrow, I shall give you everything I have promised and still more."

Feeling certain of success because of his prowess on land and sea, the sailor gathered everything he needed the next morning.

When the master had heard Mass, he went to visit the king, with whom he sat for a long time, discussing the war and deciding many things for the good of the city, which I shall omit to avoid prolixity. Then an elderly knight of the order said: "It seems to me, my lords, that as you have provisioned the city for some days, we should send our foes abundant food. Now that the sultan knows a ship has arrived, let us show we are so well provisioned that we can offer him a gift."

All the noble lords praised this elderly knight's suggestion, and they quickly ordered four hundred loaves of bread hot from the oven, wine, honey cakes, half a dozen peacocks, chickens, capons, honey, oil, and everything else Tirant had brought sent to their enemies.

Upon beholding these gifts, the sultan told his comrades: "Burn this food along with the rascal who brought it! This will cost me my honor and throne."

Nonetheless, he accepted and sent his thanks to the master. By the time the master received his answer it was early afternoon, and the king said: "Lord master, you were my friend Tirant's guest yesterday, and therefore please lunch with me today as though we were in the field, for we lack some of the items a mighty lord like you deserves."

The master accepted, and they conversed most graciously, while his knights ate outside lest the king and Philip be seen. When they had eaten, Tirant told Philip to invite the master for the next day.

The master and Tirant went out to reconnoiter the city, because our knight wished to learn where there might be skirmishes with the Saracens. Having seen everything, he decided what the best places were to leave and enter.

Then the master returned to his castle and Tirant went to the king's lodgings. After supper, Tirant and his companions stood watch to see if the sailor would keep his promise.

When it was almost midnight and very dark, the sailor collected everything he needed to burn the captain's ship, which he did in the following manner:

· CVI ·

*H*OW TIRANT HAD THE GENOESE CAPTAIN'S SHIP BURNT AND CAUSED ALL THE SARACENS TO ABANDON THE ISLAND

The sailor, who had set up a stout capstan on the shore, brought a heavy anchor cable and a long hempen line as thick as a finger, both of which he placed in a rowboat manned by two oarsmen. When they neared the ship and could hear the men on watch talking on the forecastle, he told the oarsmen to stop rowing and removed his clothes. Then he tied the line around his waist and stuck a sharp knife under it, in case he needed to cut any ropes on the enemy vessel. He wore the knife behind him lest it hinder his movements, and, after fastening the line well, he told the oarsmen to keep paying it out.

Once everything was ready, he slipped into the water and swam until he was beside the ship and heard the men on watch talking again. Then he dived under, swam to the rudder, and stopped for a moment to listen. All ships have heavy iron rings below their rudders that hold them steady in dry dock while they are being repaired or cleaned and caulked. If the rudder post breaks in a storm, the rudder can be secured to this ring, which is always well below the water line. Having slipped the line through the ring, the sailor fastened it to his waist again and swam back to the boat, where he tied one end of the line to one end of the anchor cable and greased both with suet. Then he swam back to the ring and greased it too, so the ropes would slide smoothly and noiselessly through it. When the oarsmen had pulled in the entire line, they stuck a heavy iron pin through the middle of the cable, and when the pin caught on the ring, the sailor knew both ends of the cable were back in the boat.

Finally, he pulled the pin out, swam back to the rowboat, and returned to shore, where he secured one end of the cable to the capstan and the other to a large whaleboat that was full of dry wood and resinous torches soaked in oil. He set fire to the whaleboat and as soon as it was burning well, a hundred men wound in the cable so quickly that the whaleboat struck the ship almost at once. Nothing on earth could save the Genoese vessel, whose sailors' only thought was to reach their boats. Some dived into the sea to swim to the other ships, but many perished before they could escape, while others were burnt to death in their sleep.

The watchmen on the castle walls hastened to tell their master, who quickly rose and climbed the stairs to the tower. When he saw the flames, he said: "My God, that must be Tirant's doing. He told me last night he was planning to illuminate some of the Genoese ships."

On the morrow, Tirant gave the sailor three thousand ducats, a silk robe lined with sable, and a brocade doublet, for which the worthy mariner thanked him profusely.

Seeing the burnt ship, the sultan asked: "What devils are these, who have no fear of death? After sailing through our fleet and succoring the city, they have now burnt the captain's ship and will serve the others likewise. I am astounded that no one can explain how it happened."

While the ship was blazing, the rope attached to the whaleboat had burnt too, and the sailor's men had wound what was left of it onto the capstan. Having summoned his captains, the sultan described the grand master's lavish gifts and the fire, but no one could understand why the whaleboat had made for that ship and no other. It was the beginning of winter, and the rain and cold were starting to trouble them, so he decided to raise the siege and return in the spring.

He quickly ordered the trumpets and clarions blown, while the ships gathered at one end of the island to evacuate all the soldiers.

Having received their orders, the Saracens hastened to the end of the island in great confusion, fearing that those in the city would attack them as they fled. During this rush a horse broke loose, running joyously through the fields, and since it made for the city, the Saracens let it go.

When Tirant saw the infidels departing, he assembled his soldiers and sallied forth. As they were setting fire to the Turkish sheds so that if they returned, they would have to rebuild them, the horse approached and they captured it, whereupon Tirant felt very pleased.

That night the Saracens encamped by a river, and the next morning after Mass, Tirant had the horse saddled. Armed with a crossbow that could be cocked with a hook, a quiver of poisoned quarrels, and a short lance, our knight went out alone to see what his foes were doing. From the top of a hill, he watched them hurrying toward the sea and, looking around, he spied eighteen Saracens with a loaded pack mule. They had lagged behind because their mule had fallen in the mud.

Seeing them far from the others and hidden by a low hill, Tirant spurred his mount and rode nearer to his foes, who were armed only with lances and swords.

"I can do no less," said Tirant, "than kill one of those Saracen dogs."

He planted his lance in the ground, picked up his crossbow, and nocked a poisoned quarrel in it. Then he rode closer, took aim, and shot one Saracen in the side. Before the man had gone thirty steps, he fell down dead, while Tirant spurred his steed, rode a little further away, and cocked his crossbow again. Once he had slain another Saracen, the infidels chased him, but his horse easily outran them and in this manner he wounded or killed six more. The others tried to flee, and had Tirant brought more quarrels they might have perished too. Then Tirant approached those who remained and ordered them to surrender, but first they took counsel to decide whether to capitulate or die, for they saw they were defenseless and could expect no help. They decided to submit, and Tirant said: "Lay down your arms."

Once they had done so, he ordered them to turn and walk slowly backward till he was between them and their weapons, while he picked up a rope and ordered one of them to tie the others' hands behind their backs.

"If you tie them well, I promise to let you return to your comrades."

Hoping to regain his freedom, the Saracen tied them extremely well.

Then Tirant took the pack mule, which was loaded with money and jewels, and set out for the city.

Having returned with his prisoners, Tirant went to look for the master, whom he found about to dine in the square with all his knights. When the master saw Tirant's ten captives, he was the most astonished man alive, and his men also marveled at the Breton's glorious deed of chivalry.

After lunch, Tirant sent a brig to learn whether all the soldiers were aboard, and having done this, he gave the Saracen a silk robe and freed him as he had promised.

Many soldiers went out to the abandoned Saracen camp, where they killed a few stragglers and collected their arms.

The brig returned that same day with news that the sultan had gathered his troops and horses, whereupon Tirant requested two or three guides who knew the island well. Though many knights tried to dissuade him, he set out with five hundred soldiers, and, after marching all night, they hid behind a mountain. The next morning, they saw the Saracens milling about, pushing and fighting as they tried to get aboard. When there were only about a thousand left, Tirant swooped down from the mountain, attacking them fiercely and slaughtering many infidels. The sultan, who was greatly distressed by this massacre, sent boats to the rescue, but most of those ashore were slain or drowned as they tried to escape.

Having watched this rout, the sultan ordered his men to sail for Egypt, where, once his lords heard the reason for his return, they called upon him and one cadi said:

· C V I I ᵃ ·

H OW THE SULTAN WAS SLAIN BY HIS ENRAGED VASSALS

"Oh you, betrayer of Our Glorious Prophet Mohammed, squanderer of our wealth, imperiler of our noble pagan armies, engenderer of evils, lover of cowardice, vainglorious fool, fleer from battle, destroyer of the public weal! With your left foot, you have vilely harmed and dishonored us, for with cruel black hand and false tongue, you abandoned the isle of Rhodes against the advice of your wise counselors. One ship sufficed to dismay you, oh recreant knight always glancing over your shoulder, and though you commanded twelve crowned kings obedient to you at all times, yet your family plotted with those renegade Genoese who show pity to none, being neither Saracens nor Christians, as though you yourself had been born on Genoa's ignoble shore. Thus do your evil deeds condemn you to a scoundrel's death."

With that, they seized him and flung him into the lions' cage, where he died most woefully. Then they elected another sultan, who, to show his love of the public good, gathered a fleet of Genoese ships and had others built. When it was ready, he set sail for Greece along with the Grand Turk, who had brought a mighty horde of cavalry and infantry. Together, the two armies contained one hundred and seventeen thousand infidels and flew two flags: a red one with the chalice and Host, which are the Genoese and Venetian symbols, and another of thick green silk with gold letters saying: *Avenger of the blood of that blessed knight Sir Hector of Troy*.

Once in Greece, they quickly overran many towns and captured sixteen thousand little boys, whom they sent to Turkey and Egypt to be raised in the Islamic sect. They also enslaved many ladies and damsels.

And the isle of Rhodes was saved from the infidels.

Hearing the sultan's fleet had gone, the Cypriots in Famagusta loaded ships with cattle, sheep, grain, and other provisions for the Rhodians. Help came from many lands, and the island soon became so abundant that the old people said they had never seen or heard of the place being so prosperous.

A few days later, two Venetian galleys docked bearing grain and pilgrims bound for the Holy Sepulcher in Jerusalem. When Tirant heard of their arrival, he went to inform the king, who was delighted at the news and told the grand master: "My lord, since His Divine Goodness has been pleased to send these galleys, we would like to depart with your blessing and complete our holy pilgrimage."

The master replied: "Great would be my glory if you consented to remain here, and you could rule this island as if it were your own. Go or stay as you see fit, for I only wish to obey and serve you."

Then the master summoned his knights and told them that, as Tirant wished to leave, it seemed only just to pay him for the grain and his ship. All the knights approved, saying Tirant should be given whatever he requested, and they decided to make their offer the following day in the great square.

As soon as the sun rose, the master ordered the city gates locked lest anyone leave while he and Tirant were talking. Then he had all his treasure piled in the middle of the square and asked Tirant, the King of Sicily, and Philip to come and see it. When everyone was present, the master began to speak:

· CVII^b ·

*H*OW THE MASTER OF RHODES OFFERED TO PAY FOR TIRANT'S HELP

"Sole hope of an afflicted city, worthy successor to the stalwart knights of old, you, Tirant lo Blanc, should rule all noblemen and the Roman Empire, since your valiant feats of chivalry deserve no lesser prize. You have saved our order and Solomon's temple, redeeming us from hunger, thirst, and other woes and afflictions visited upon us for our sins. Had you not come on that blessed day, our city and order would have perished, and hence to whom but you should triumphal glory be offered? We are beholden to your prowess, for this multitude was doomed, and had the city and its fortress fallen, our subjects would have been condemned to slavery. Blessed the hour in which you came to succor the starving, comforting them with the sweetness of abundant food, when our only hope was to die for Christ's faith!

"Oh unspeakable agony and grief of slavery! Whom, then, should we reward for our liberation? Who will be our protector and certain shield if these infidels return, as the dangers are great and our bones and innards tremble within us? Never was there greater misery, nor did the glorious holy martyrs suffer more, for all must die and a quick death ends all evils. Therefore, brave knight, lay your victorious hand upon our treasure, taking what you like, though it be small reward for your ardent deeds. Your great virtue can never displease us, nor can we repay the honor and pity you have shown. With manly spirit you wielded arms, never tiring or shirking, though you might have evaded battles on land and sea. Thus we call 'knights' those who perform knightly deeds and 'nobles' those who behave nobly, wherefore, Lord Tirant, take all your hands can hold, since the more you take, the greater will be our glory."

Thus he ended his speech, to which Tirant replied in the following manner:

· CVIII ·

TIRANT'S REPLY, AND HOW AFTERWARD HE VISITED THE HOLY SEPULCHER WITH THE KING OF SICILY AND PHILIP

"I recall how that glorious prophet, Saint John the Baptist, came into the world to announce the advent of Jesus Christ. Likewise I, with God's leave, hastened with steadfast faith and firm resolve to succor Your Reverend Lordship and his order. I offer infinite thanks to His Divine Majesty, who allowed me to arrive in your hour of need, thereby winning worldly glory and freeing this blessed company. The honor I have thus acquired is sufficient reward for my travails, and I hope to receive my true prize from God in Heaven. Therefore, to honor, praise, and glorify Our Lord and Master Jesus Christ and Saint John the Baptist, protector and defender of this isle, I ask only that you celebrate a Requiem Mass every day for my soul, and I also pray you to forgive the people their debts for the grain, flour, and any other small items. These favors, my lord, I humbly beg of you."

"Tirant," said the master, "all that you ask shall be done, but you must also open your hands and take what you deserve. If the Saracens return and word spreads that you courageously rescued us, sacrificing your ship and grain yet receiving nothing in return, we shall find no one willing to help us a second time, wherefore I beg you to take what you wish from our treasury."

"Tell me, reverend lord:" asked Tirant, "who can hinder me if I wish to give away my riches to charity, and let Your Lordship not think I am such as to go through the world crying out against your order, for I prefer God's rewards to all the treasure on earth. I would not speak in this fashion were it not so, but to please you and that everyone may witness my satisfaction, I now place my hands on the treasure in public view."

He ordered the criers to say he was content with the grand master's generosity and that he freely forgave the people their debts for the grain, flour, and everything else.

Great were the praises and blessings the townsfolk showered upon Tirant, who then asked the grand master to be his guest at lunch. That night, the king, Philip, and Tirant boarded the Venetian galleys with a handful of men, among whom were Tirant's cousin Diaphebus and Philip's servant Tenebrous.

After three days and nights of stormy seas, a prosperous wind arose and quickly bore them to Jaffa. Their next port of call was Beirut, where, after a calm voyage, the pilgrims went ashore and divided into groups of ten.

Each group hired a guide, and when they reached Jerusalem, they spent two weeks visiting all the holy places. Then they set out for Alexandria, in whose harbor they found the galleys and many Christian ships.

One day, as the king and Tirant were walking through the city, they beheld a weeping Christian slave, to whom our knight addressed these words: "My friend, please tell me what grieves you so, as my pity is such that I would gladly help you."

"Why should I waste my breath?" cried the afflicted slave. "I shall receive no aid or counsel from you or anyone else. I have been a slave for twenty-two years, desiring death more than life, and because I refuse to renounce my Creator, I am fed with beatings and starved for food."

Tirant replied: "By your goodness, please show me the villain who keeps you enslaved."

"You will find him in that house," said the slave, "with a whip in his hand to skin me alive."

Asking the king to await him, Tirant entered the house, where he said the slave was his relative and offered to ransom him. The Saracen agreed, and they settled on fifty-five gold ducats, which Tirant paid immediately. He then asked the Saracen if he knew anyone else with Christian slaves. The news soon spread through Alexandria, and everyone with Christian captives brought them to the inn[3] where Tirant was lodged. In two days Tirant bought four hundred and seventy-three slaves, and however many he had found, he would have happily paid to free them all. After selling all his silver, dishes, and jewels to redeem those slaves, he had them brought aboard the galleys and sailed for Rhodes.

Having learned of his friends' approach, the master had a long wooden gangplank built and covered with silk, and upon their arrival the King of Sicily revealed his identity to everyone. The master then escorted his guests to the castle, where he said: "Lords, in my time of need you brought me provisions. Now, in time of prosperity, I beg you to dine with me."

As soon as Tirant reached Rhodes, he bought many rolls of cloth and had capes, cloaks, doublets, stockings, shoes, and shirts made for the slaves. He collected their yellow shirts and sent them to his chapel in Brittany, where they were kept with the shields of the four knights he had slain. When the master learned what Tirant had done, he told the king, Philip, and everyone else: "On my faith, if Tirant lives much longer he will certainly rule the world. He is generous, brave, blessed with peerless wisdom, and I tell you in all truth that had God endowed me with some kingdom or empire, I would sooner give my daughter to Tirant than to any prince in Christendom."

The king listened carefully to the master's wise words and decided that when they returned to Sicily, he would offer Tirant his daughter.

Once the clothes had been made and the galleys were ready to sail, Tirant summoned the slaves and invited them to dine with him. After they had eaten, he began to speak thus:

· CIX ·

*H*OW TIRANT FREED THE SLAVES AND RETURNED TO SICILY, WHERE PHILIP MARRIED THE PRINCESS

"Friends and brothers in spirit: not long ago you were enslaved by the infidel, yet now, through God's grace and my efforts, you have entered the promised land of freedom. I give you leave to go or stay as you please. If anyone wishes to join my company, I shall gladly have him, while those who prefer to remain on Rhodes may do so, and those who want to go elsewhere need only so advise me, for I shall happily pay their passage."

When the slaves heard Tirant's words, their joy and solace were immeasurable. They threw themselves at his feet and tried to kiss them, but he refused and endowed them so generously that they were more than content.

Once the Venetians were ready to sail, the king, Philip, and Tirant bade the grand master farewell and loaded the galleys with everything they needed. As they were saying goodbye, the master again asked Tirant to accept some payment for the ship and grain, but Tirant politely refused, saying he desired no compensation.

As soon as they were all aboard, the galleys set sail with such good weather that they quickly reached the eastern coast of Sicily. Overjoyed at their lord's return, the Sicilians sent a messenger to the queen. The king asked after her, his children, and his brother the duke, to which they replied that everyone was in good health and that the King of France had sent forty ambassadors, all splendidly dressed and with a noble retinue.

Tirant was very pleased by the ambassadors' arrival—more so, in fact, than the king, who recalled and pondered the grand master's words. After staying there a few days to recover from their voyage, they set out for Palermo, where the queen awaited them.

On the day of their arrival, the duke greeted them with his noblemen, followed by the guilds in their finest robes, the archbishop, the clergy, and the queen attended by all her noblewomen. Soon Princess Ricomana appeared with her maids-in-waiting and the damsels of Palermo, who had dressed so gaily that it was a joy to behold them. Last of all came the French ambassadors, wearing gold chains and crimson velvet gowns that reached their feet.

Once the king had greeted the queen and his daughter had curtsied before him, Philip and Tirant bowed to Her Majesty. Then Philip took the princess's arm that he might escort her to the palace, and while they were walking, the ambassadors approached them. Tirant told Philip: "My lord, first order them to pay homage to the king."

Philip told them to do so, but the ambassadors replied that their master had asked them to salute him first and then deliver a letter to His Majesty. Philip declared that he would not consider speaking with them till they had paid homage to the king.

"Since this is Philip's will," the ambassadors said, "we shall do as he says, though we walked last in this procession that we might pay homage to him first."

When the king and his entourage reached the palace, the French ambassadors presented their credentials, whereupon His Majesty welcomed them warmly and did them great honor. Then they approached Philip and bowed before him as he deserved, for he was their master's son, while the prince feasted them nobly and made great joy of them.

Once the king's welcome feast had ended, the ambassadors explained their mission, which consisted of three parts: first, the King of France was delighted at Philip's betrothal; second, if the King of Sicily had a son, the King of France would give him one of his daughters in marriage, along with a hundred thousand ducats; and third, he had asked the Pope and all Christian princes to join a crusade, and they had agreed to do so. He asked the King of Sicily to help him too, and if His Highness was willing to send a fleet, he begged him to make Prince Philip its captain.

Upon receiving the king's reply that he was pleased with the marriage but had to consider the other matters, the ambassadors gave Philip fifty thousand *escuts* to buy whatever he needed. The King of France sent Ricomana four handsome pieces of brocade, three thousand sable skins, and a richly bejeweled golden necklace from Paris, while Philip's mother sent her silk, brocade, fine satin curtains, and many other gifts.

When the princess heard that the king had consented to her marriage, she thought to herself: "If I see Philip acting loutish or petty, I shall refuse to marry him, and henceforth I shall do all I can to learn the truth."

As the princess was contemplating these painful matters, her most trusted maiden entered the chamber and said: "Tell me your thoughts, my lady, for I see your soul is troubled."

The princess replied: "My father has just consented to my marriage, but I fear that Prince Philip is loutish and stingy. Should he possess either of these qualities, I could not last an hour in bed with him and would have to become a nun and lock myself in a convent. Though I have done everything possible to discover the truth, all has been in vain because of treacherous Tirant. May God roast and boil him in his lady's enamored wrath, for that day with the slices of bread I might have found out had he not thwarted me, but before we marry, I shall test Philip again. I shall summon a great philosopher from Calabria, a man of vast learning who will surely tell me what I wish to know."

Having received the money from his father, Philip purchased floor-length robes of brocade and cloth of gold, as well as many brooches, gold chains, and other valuable jewelry.

On the Day of the Assumption, the king invited Philip, the ambassadors, and all the Sicilian nobility to dine with him. Philip donned a long scarlet brocade robe lined with ermine, and Tirant followed suit but then thought to himself: "Since this feast is for Philip and the French ambassadors, if I dress as richly on such a day, it will not be well received."

He quickly removed the gown and chose another of silver brocade, which he wore over stockings embroidered with big pearls.

During the meal, a thunderstorm began and the delighted princess thought: "Now perhaps I shall have my wish."

Once they had finished, the tables were cleared and the king's musicians and dancers came to entertain his guests. After dessert, the king retired to his chamber, but the princess kept dancing lest Philip attempt to leave.

When it was almost time for Vespers, the sky cleared and the sun shone brightly. The princess asked: "Shall we ride through the city, since it is such a pleasant day?"

Philip quickly replied: "But my lady, do you really want to go riding in this inclement weather? If it starts to rain again, Your Highness will be soaked."

Tirant, seeing the princess's malicious intent, pulled Philip's coat to silence him, but the princess noticed the signal and angrily ordered the horses brought forth. When they arrived, Philip took the princess's arm and led her to a mounting stool. Having mounted, she half turned her back to Philip, though she could still see him out of the corner of her eye. Philip asked Tirant: "Could you bring me another robe to save this one from being ruined?"

"Oh, the devil take the robe! When this one wears out, you can order a new one!"

"At least," said Philip, "see if you can find two pages to keep it from dragging on the ground."

"Who would ever imagine that a prince could be so petty?" replied Tirant. "Hurry; the lady princess awaits you."

Then Philip mounted his steed, though his heart was full of gloom.

Ricomana had been trying all the while to hear what they were saying, but she was unable to make out the words.

As they rode through the city, the princess rejoiced to see poor Philip's robe get drenched. He kept looking down at it, and to augment her pleasure, she suggested that they take some falcons and go quail hunting outside the walls.

"But my lady," replied Philip, "this is no weather for hunting. We shall find nothing out there but mud and water."

"Woe is me!" cried the princess. "This lout still refuses to grant me a little pleasure."

Ignoring his words, she left the city and found a peasant, whom she drew aside and asked if there was some river or big irrigation channel nearby. The peasant replied: "My lady, straight ahead you will find a ditch where the water comes up as high as a mule's belly."

"That is just what I want."

The princess rode ahead, and when they reached the ditch she forded it, but Philip hung back and asked Tirant if there was some servant who could hold up his robe.

"I am tired of hearing about it," Tirant replied, "and sick of your ignoble ways. That robe is already ruined, so think no more about it, and moreover, I promise to give you one of mine. The princess has crossed and is riding away; hurry and overtake her."

Then Tirant laughed loudly to show he and Philip had been joking. When they had forded the channel, the princess asked the cause of their mirth.

"On my faith, my lady," Tirant replied, "I was laughing at something Philip has been asking me all day, first in Your Highness's chambers, then while we were riding, and now at the ditch. He wants to know what love is, where it originates, and where its dwelling place is. On my honor, I am ignorant of love's nature and origins, but I believe the eyes are the heart's emissaries and that through speech, heart and will are reconciled. The soul's many messengers are comforted by hope, the five bodily senses obey the heart and do its bidding, and the hands and feet are the will's submissive subjects. Abounding in words, the tongue cures many ills of soul and body, and thus the vulgar proverb says: 'When the heart's in pain, the tongue will complain,' for my lady, nothing can dampen Philip's true and devoted love."

"Let us return to the city," the princess muttered.

When they reached the ditch, she watched to see if they would start talking again, but Philip saw how drenched his robe was and concentrated on reaching the other side. The princess was greatly comforted and believed everything Tirant had said, but she was still uneasy and told him: "By my royal blood, I am in Fortune's hands, as I would sooner die than take a vulgar, loutish, or stingy husband, and I can tell you in all truth, Tirant, that the Fates have always opposed me. My sole remaining comforts are faith, truth, and justice. If I marry a man who does not fulfill my wishes, it will be the death of me and I shall be forced to take desperate measures, wherefore I would sooner be alone than in bad company. Have you not heard that old saying: 'Whoever hangs a necklace on a mule or gives a dowry to a fool will fare ill in this world'? Since God has made me aware of these perils, I want to avoid them lest something terrible occur."

She ended her discourse, to which Tirant quickly replied:

· CX ·

TIRANT'S SPEECH TO THE PRINCESS, AND HOW SHE TESTED PHILIP MANY TIMES TO DISCOVER HIS TRUE NATURE

"Oh lady endowed with every virtue, you astonish me, for though I know you to be the wisest damsel alive, yet you seek to place Prince Philip on trial in your own mind. With all due respect for your honor, this is neither just nor charitable, as he is among the noblest knights on earth. He is young, peerlessly brave, bold, magnanimous, and sagacious rather than loutish, and thus is he regarded by all knights, ladies, and damsels in the lands we have visited. Even the Saracen ladies loved and wished to serve him, and if you doubt my words, behold his face, feet, hands, and body. Should you wish to see him naked, I can satisfy your desire, for true beauty and chastity have little in common. I know you are enamored of him, and certainly he is such as to make himself loved by all. What a pity Your Highness cannot lie next to him in a bed perfumed with benzoin, civet, and fine musk, for if you spoke ill of it the next morning, I would bear any punishment you might devise."

"Oh Tirant," replied the princess, "great would be my joy if I found a man who pleased me, but what good would it do to lie beside a statue who only offered grief and affliction?"

At this point they reached the palace and saw His Majesty conversing with the French ambassadors. Upon beholding his daughter, he took her hand and asked where she had been, and as supper was ready, Philip and the ambassadors excused themselves.

That evening, the Calabrian philosopher reached Palermo.[4] Knowing the princess was anxious to learn what he thought of Philip, he decided to look for her in church the next morning. He went to an inn, and as he was roasting a piece of mutton for his dinner, a pimp entered with a rabbit and ordered the philosopher to take his meat off the fire.

"My friend," asked the philosopher, "are you unaware that an inn is for everyone and first come is first served?"

"I don't give a damn," replied the pimp. "You can see I have a rabbit, which should take precedence over mutton just as partridge does over rabbit, because of its greater rank and nobility."

They insulted each other until finally the pimp struck the philosopher who, feeling himself mistreated, killed his adversary by plunging the spit into his temple. Two soldiers soon appeared and took the philosopher to prison, where the next morning he demanded an ecclesiastical trial, but the king refused and allotted him four ounces of bread and four of water a day. The princess feared to intercede lest the king discover that she had sent for him.

A few days later, a knight was arrested in the king's court after a brawl in which he had wounded four other lords. He was put in the same cell as the philosopher, and, feeling compassion for the sage, the knight shared the food his friends brought for him. When they had been there two weeks, the philosopher told the knight: "Lord knight, by your gentleness I beg you, when you see the king tomorrow, to ask him to pity me, as you can see how I suffer. Were it not for your charity, I would have starved to death with those four wretched ounces of bread they give me. Tell the princess I am here because she sent for me, and I shall be greatly in your debt."

The knight asked: "How can you say such things? Unless God performs a miracle, I shall spend two more years here."

"You will be free within half an hour," replied the philosopher, "or you will never get out alive."

The knight was awed and dismayed by the philosopher's words, and as they were talking, a warden entered and led the knight away.

Shortly thereafter, a gentleman learned that the king wished to send horses to the Greek emperor, and since this gentleman had the finest charger in Sicily, he decided to take it to the king. When His Majesty beheld the steed, he was astonished at its beauty, for it was tall, strong, light, and four years old. Its only fault was that its ears hung down.

"Your horse," said the king, "would be worth at least a thousand gold ducats without this defect."

As no one could discover the cause of it, the knight who had been in prison said: "My lord, that philosopher will surely know, for while I was with him, he told me many extraordinary things. He said that if I was not freed within half an hour, I would never get out alive."

The king sent a warden to fetch the philosopher, and upon his arrival the king asked why so fine a horse had such ears. The philosopher replied: "My lord, common sense proves that this horse must have been suckled by an ass, and as asses have floppy ears, the horse got its nature from its wet nurse."

"Holy Mary!" cried the king. "Can what this philosopher says be true?"

He summoned the horse's owner and asked what kind of milk it had suckled.

"Sire," the gentleman replied, "this horse was so big that the mare could not give birth to it and we had to cut her open with a knife. The mare died, but I had a she-ass who had just borne a foal, so I had her nurse them both, and they were always together till now."

"Great is this man's wisdom," declared the king.

He ordered him returned to prison and asked how much bread he was receiving. "Four ounces, my lord," replied the warden, "just as Your Highness ordered."

"Give him four more to make eight," the king said, and so it was done.

A lapidary came from Damascus and Cairo with many fine jewels, one of which was an especially big and beautiful balas. He wished to sell it for sixty thousand ducats, whereas the king offered only thirty thousand, and therefore they failed to reach an agreement. The king was eager to buy it, because it was the largest and most splendid stone the world had ever seen, even finer than the ones on the Pala d'Oro at Saint Mark's in Venice or on Saint Thomas's tomb in Canterbury, and since the King of France had told his ambassadors that he would soon come to Sicily, the king wished to dress as his station required. The knight who had been imprisoned said: "How can Your Highness pay so much for this stone when there are three little holes in the underside?"

The king replied: "I have shown it to my jewelers, who say they can mount it so as to hide them."

"My lord," said the knight, "even so, you might ask that philosopher to inspect it and tell you its worth."

"Let us summon him," replied the king.

They sent for the philosopher, who, upon beholding the balas, took it in the palm of his hand and raised it to his ear. He closed his eyes, remained silent for a long time, and finally said: "Sire, there is something alive in this stone."

"What?" cried the lapidary. "Who ever heard of anything living in a stone?"

"If it is not so," replied the philosopher, "I shall give Your Highness three hundred ducats and my life as well."

The lapidary replied: "I stake my life, too, since he has staked his, and I shall give him the stone if there is anything alive in it."

When they had both staked their lives and the king had collected the money, they put the balas on an anvil and broke it open with a hammer, whereupon they discovered a worm inside the stone. Everyone was astonished at the philosopher's wisdom and subtlety, but the lapidary was most distressed, for he was unsure of his place in Heaven.

"My lord, do as you promised," said the philosopher.

After giving him back his money and the balas, the king summoned his executioners to behead the lapidary.

"Now," said the philosopher, "since I have killed a bad man, I wish to spare a good one."

The king allowed him to free the lapidary, and the philosopher gave His Majesty the broken balas.

Having taken it, the king sent the philosopher back to prison and asked how much bread they were giving him. "Eight ounces," said the warden, to which the king replied: "Give him eight more."

As they were returning him to prison, the philosopher said to those escorting him: "Tell the king he cannot be the son of that magnanimous King Robert, who was the boldest and most generous monarch on earth. His deeds show he is not of royal blood but rather a baker's son, and if he wants me to prove it, I shall gladly do so. By right Sicily belongs to the Duke of Messina, for no bastard should be allowed to rule a kingdom and the Holy Scriptures say a bastard tree is cast into the fire."[5]

When the bailiffs heard these words, they hastened to tell their master, who said: "To set my mind at rest, I shall find out what he knows, and since it is night, bring him to me secretly."

When they were alone in the king's chambers, His Majesty asked him if what the bailiffs said was so. With calm demeanor and courageous spirit, the philosopher replied: "Sire, everything they told you is quite true."

"Tell me how you know," the king said, "that I am not Robert's son."

"My lord," replied the philosopher, "common sense is all you need to recognize an ass, and these are my reasons: first, when I explained why that horse had floppy ears, which was something no one in your court could unravel or comprehend, you rewarded me with four more ounces of bread. Then, my lord, the matter of the balas, on which I wagered my life and meager savings. I gave you that balas, though by right it belonged to me, and you would have been tricked out of a large sum had it not been for my help. For any of these favors, you should have pardoned and rewarded me, but all I received in return was more bread. Plain common sense forced me to conclude that Your Highness was the son of a baker, and not of our late King Robert of glorious memory."

"If you will enter my service," said the king, "I shall try to improve myself and heed your counsel, but I would still like to hear more about my parentage."

"My lord, do not ask," replied the philosopher, "for the walls have ears, and you would not want people to learn your secret. As they say in Calabria: 'Do not talk without need, for if you scratch it will bleed.' "

Nevertheless, the distraught king, heedless of the perils that might await him, summoned his mother and with pleas and threats forced her to confess that she had once yielded to a baker in Reggio.

Afterward, when the philosopher had been freed, the princess sent for him and asked his opinion of Philip.

"I would like to see him," said the philosopher, "before I say anything."

"He will soon be here," replied the princess.

She sent a page to invite Philip to come and dance with her, telling the philosopher: "Now you will have a chance to study him."

When the philosopher had looked awhile and Philip had departed, he told the princess: "This gallant, Your Highness, has 'crass dolt' written all over him. Expect nought but woe from such a knight, though he will bravely triumph in battle and die a king."

The princess grew pensive and replied: "I have always heard it said that what you fear most will kill you, and I would sooner become a nun or a shoemaker's wife than marry him, even if he were King of France."

After ordering a beautiful brocade canopy for his daughter's wedding, the king had another white one placed in the room as a model for his weavers, and when the brocade canopy was finished, they placed it on a bed next to the white one. The bed with the brocade canopy had a cover of the same material, fine bridal sheets, and embroidered pillowcases, so that it truly looked fit for a king, whereas the other bed was white and there was a great contrast between them.

One night, the princess kept everyone up dancing into the early morning, and when the king saw it was past midnight, he slipped away without a word lest he interrupt his daughter's merriment. Since it had started to rain, the princess sent a servant to ask her father if Philip might sleep in her brother's room, to which the king gladly gave his consent.

A short while later, they stopped dancing and the prince asked Philip to stay the night. Philip said it was very kind of him, but he would sooner return to his lodgings, whereupon the princess took his sleeve and said: "On my faith, since my brother wants you to sleep here, these shall be your lodgings tonight."

Tirant said: "Since they are so eager, stay to make them happy and I shall also stay to serve you."

"Never fear, Tirant," said Ricomana, "for between my family's servants and mine, we can surely find someone to serve Prince Philip."

Hearing her ill-intentioned words and seeing he was unwanted, Tirant set out with the others in his company. As soon as they had gone, two pages entered with torches and asked Philip to accompany them. Saying he would obey the princess's commands, Philip bowed to her and followed the pages, who led him to the chamber with the two beds.

When Philip saw the splendid bed, he felt so awed that he decided it would be wiser to sleep in the plain one. That night while dancing, he had torn one of his stockings, and he supposed his companions would not return before he rose. The pages had been carefully instructed by their mistress, who was in a place where she could see everything.

Philip told one of the pages: "For love of me, fetch a needle and some white thread."

The page went to the princess, who had seen Philip request something and who gave the page a needle and a spool of thread. Upon his return, he found Philip pacing to and fro while the other page watched him.

Seeing Philip approach the torch and open a pimple on his hand, the princess thought he had requested the needle for this purpose. Then he stuck it in the bed where he intended to sleep and took off all his clothes except a silver tunic, which he sat down on the bed to unbutton. When the pages had removed his shoes, he dismissed them, but first he asked them to leave one torch burning. Once they had gone, Philip got up to look for the needle so he could mend his stocking. He searched the bed from one end to the other, shaking the cover with a gloomy look on his face. Having shaken it so hard that it fell to the floor, he removed the sheets and stripped the bed, but he never did find the needle. He thought of remaking the bed, but seeing how disordered it was, he said: "What? I would sooner sleep in the other than make this one again!"

That was Philip's lucky needle, since as he climbed in the marriage bed, the princess delightedly told her maids-in-waiting: "Look, on your lives, at how well-bred these foreigners are, and especially Philip. I tried to test him again as I had often done before, thinking that if he were crass or loutish, he would shun so fine a bed, but he flung the bedclothes to the floor and slept in the good one as was his due, for his lineage is noble, excellent, and very ancient. Now I know Tirant has always told the truth like a worthy knight and everything he said was for my honor and good. I see this philosopher is not so wise as I thought, nor do I desire more advice from him or anyone else. Tomorrow I shall summon noble Tirant, who, having been the first cause of my good fortune, shall now behold its happy end."

With this resolution, she retired to bed.

Early the next morning, Tenebrous and Philip's pages brought clean clothes to their master. As the princess was lacing her skirt, she suddenly felt she could wait no longer and summoned Tirant, to whom she joyously announced her decision.

· C X I ·

HOW THE SICILIAN PRINCESS SUMMONED TIRANT AND TOLD HIM OF HER DECISION

"The careful plottings of my enamored heart have brought Philip's noble perfections to my attention, for last night I beheld his lofty condition with my own two eyes. Until now I resisted this marriage, as my spirit was troubled by certain doubts, but from this moment on I shall gladly obey my father's orders, and since you initiated our sovereign good fortune, now swiftly end it and free two souls from the same torment."

Hearing the princess's kind words, Tirant joyously replied: "Your Highness knows with what diligence I have labored to unite you with one who offers honor and delight. Though you were often vexed with me for praising Philip's perfections, I am most pleased that you now acknowledge the truth, putting aside past errors to make the wise decision I expected. Therefore, I shall now speak with His Majesty your father, that we may bring this matter to a speedy conclusion."

Having taken his leave of the princess, Tirant went to the king and said: "The French ambassadors' distress is the cause of my coming. Since you agreed to the marriage, please celebrate it or let them depart, and if Your Majesty does not mind my approaching the princess on his behalf, I believe that between God's help and the sound arguments I shall present, she will happily do our bidding."

"May God comfort my soul and body," replied the king. "I would love to see this wedding take place, wherefore I beg you to plead with her on your behalf and mine."

Tirant returned to the princess, whom he found still dressing, and repeated the king's words, to which she replied: "I leave everything in your hands, for whatever you do will please me, and if you wish us to marry this morning, I shall gladly obey you."

Tirant, seeing her good will, noticed that Philip was waiting in the doorway to accompany her to Mass. He asked the princess to dismiss her maids, that he might speak to her and Philip privately, and much to their astonishment, she docilely obeyed him.

When they had departed, Tirant opened the door and asked Philip to enter. "My lady," said Tirant, "here you see Philip, who longs to serve you more than any other princess on earth, wherefore I beg you on my knees to kiss him in sign of troth."

"Tirant!" cried the princess. "I pray to God that your sinful mouth may never taste a crust of bread! Are these the words you so wished to speak? Alas, your face reveals your heart's true nature, but I shall kiss him only when my father tells me to."

Then Tirant motioned to Philip, who quickly took the princess in his arms and carried her to the bed, kissing her five or six times. The princess cried: "Tirant, I had more faith in your gentility! I thought you were my brother, yet you place me at the mercy of one who may be friend or foe!"

"Such cruel words, my lady! How can Philip be a foe, when he loves you more than life and only longs to hold you in that royal bed he slept in, either naked or in your nightshirt? I assure you it would be the greatest blessing he could ever enjoy, and my lady," said Tirant, "you who are so high in dignity and rank: let poor Philip, who pines for you, have a bit of the glory he so desires."

"May God defend and guard me from such errors," replied the princess. "How vile I should hold myself if I consented to such a request."

"My lady," said Tirant, "Philip and I are only here to serve you. Surely Your Highness will show a little forbearance."

Tirant seized her hands while Philip tried to resolve things after his own fashion, whereupon the princess screamed and her maids rushed in and forced them to make peace.

When the princess had her skirt laced up, she donned her finest robes and they escorted her to Mass. She and Philip were betrothed before the service began, and the following Sunday they were married with great solemnity. There was a week of continual feasting, with jousts, tournaments, dancing, and mummers.

The princess was so well courted that she felt very pleased with Tirant, and much more so with Philip, whose good works she never forgot.

EXPEDITION WITH THE KING OF FRANCE

· CXII ·

*H*OW THE KING OF SICILY SENT TEN GALLEYS AND FOUR WARSHIPS TO AID THE KING OF FRANCE

Once the wedding celebration had ended, the King of Sicily resolved to send ten galleys and four warships to the King of France, while Tirant purchased his own galley that he might go where he pleased. When the vessels were armed and provisioned, they learned that the King of France was in Aiguesmortes, where he awaited them with the fleets from Castile, Aragon, Navarre, and Portugal.

Having been chosen captain, Philip set sail with the Prince of Sicily, and at the port of Savona they met the imperial and papal fleets. Together with ships from many Italian cities, they sailed to join their captain in Corsica, and, after taking on food and water, they weighed anchor again and voyaged till one day at dawn they hove in sight of Tripoli. Only the king had known their destination, but when everyone saw his ship halt and his soldiers don their armor, they supposed that the Lebanese city was their goal. Then Tirant got in a skiff and, upon boarding the king's ship, he found His Highness ready for battle and preparing to hear Dry Mass.[1]

As soon as they reached the Gospel, Tirant knelt before the king and asked to make a vow, which request His Majesty happily granted. Then Tirant knelt before the priest, who opened a missal while the Breton placed his hands upon it and swore the following oath:

· CXIII ·

TIRANT'S VOW BEFORE THE KING OF FRANCE AND MANY OTHER KNIGHTS

"Since by God's grace I have been knighted and am free from all submission, being constrained by nothing more than my own desire for honor, I swear before God, His saints, and my lord the Duke of Brittany, admiral of this fleet and the most excellent and Christian King of France's representative, that today I shall be the first ashore and the last to retreat."

Then Diaphebus vowed to inscribe his name on the gates of Tripoli.

Another knight also vowed that if they all reached shore, he would storm the walls and shoot a quarrel into the city.

Another knight rose and vowed to snatch a Saracen maiden from her mother's side and give her to Phillipa, the King of France's daughter.

A fourth knight vowed to plant a flag on the city's highest tower.

There were more than four hundred and fifty knights with golden spurs on the king's ship, and where you find many people in the same profession, you also find envy and resentment, for the sin of envy takes many forms and the spiteful abhor worthy knights.

Many, hoping to make Tirant break his vow, prepared rowboats, brigs, and galleys to try to reach land first.

Having seen the mighty fleet, the Saracens sent up smoke signals, and a multitude gathered to oppose the Christians. Tirant and the others returned to their galleys, which rowed in formation that they might reach shore at the same time, keeping so close together that they nearly collided.

As they neared their foes and were about to lower the rope ladders, the galleys turned and backed water so their poops would strike land first, but Tirant ordered his men to keep rowing. When he felt the prow hit the beach, he leapt into the water, while the Saracens hastened to attack him and his men shot crossbows and muskets. Many soldiers and sailors dived in to aid Tirant, and the other galleys also threw down their ladders, but who dared to land amid so many infidels? Seeing the fray thickest around Tirant, the king and his hardy followers descended like bold knights, and so eager were they to reach their foes that many fell in the water.

Once everyone was ashore, a mighty battle ensued in which many perished.

The Saracens took refuge in the city, which a multitude of Christians also entered, but after capturing five streets they found they could go no further. When all the knights had fulfilled their vows and collected booty in those streets, Saracen reinforcements arrived and the Christians were driven back.

The most dangerous part was the retreat, but on his sailors' advice, the king had the galleys line up with planks lain from one to the other. Once the ladders were lowered, the men boarded as quickly as possible, yet even so, many died before they could reach safety.

Tirant watched as the knights boarded and his men cast off and threw down a ladder, for he was waiting to fulfill his vow. Another brave warrior named Richard the Venturesome, who sought glory and deserved it, had also lingered behind and said: "Everyone has either died or escaped; only you and I remain. You had the honor of being first among these conquerors, when, with noble spirit and knightly courage, you alighted on this heathen shore. Since you know I have defended you, board the galley first, that we two may be equal in fame and brotherhood. Sometimes when a man covets all the glory, he loses it all, wherefore you should grant me my just deserts and heed what I say: I am a man, with feet, hands, and heart. Possessing abundant courage and stamina, I am cruel as a ravening lion. In this fist I clasp anger, pride, and envy, and when I open it, no one can find mercy therein."

"This is no time for speeches," replied Tirant. "You hold life and death in your hand, yet I shall be declared victorious if these infidels kill us both, and God will save our souls if we die with firm faith. When I made that vow, I expected to perish, for though I fear death, it is nothing beside chivalric honor. Dying a worthy knight, I shall win glory in this world and the next, and moreover I made that vow in the presence of my lord, the King of France, but even if I had only thought it, I would sooner die than break my word. Knighthood is nothing more than a vow to act bravely, and therefore, Richard, give me your hand. Let us die fighting and waste no more words."

Richard said: "Very well, give me your hand, and together we shall battle these pagan devils."

Both knights were standing in water up to their chests, while lances, arrows, and stones fell all around and those in the galleys tried to defend them.

When Richard saw Tirant going toward shore, he grabbed his tunic and pulled him back, saying: "You are the most fearless knight on earth, and since I have now beheld your ardor, let us do this: place your foot on the ladder first, and then I shall precede you."

The king feared that he would soon lose two of his best knights, but having decided to share the honor, Tirant placed his foot on the ladder first. Then Richard ascended, making Tirant the last aboard and enabling our knight to fulfill his solemn vow.

There was a great debate about these two knights, for His Majesty and

many others said Tirant had won the prize of honor, whereas Richard
maintained the contrary in this speech before the king:

· CXIV ·

*H*OW RICHARD CHALLENGED TIRANT TO A DUEL BEFORE THE KING OF FRANCE, AND HOW THE KING, AFTER ATTACKING TRIPOLI, THEN RAIDED THE TURKISH COAST

"Men devoid of honor reveal their ignorance through their words, repeating that coarse expression: 'Whatever my godfather says is good enough
for me.' They forget such noble predecessors as King Arthur of Great and
Little Britain, who immortalized the blessed Round Table at which so
many brave knights sat, all of them honorable, courteous, and opposed to
deceit, falsity, and evil. If our dispute were fairly judged by the laws of
chivalry, to whom but me would the honor belong? Tirant shrinks from
battle, though Fortune has often smiled upon him, nor can he deny that I
have proved myself the boldest knight of all, and I, who am now barefoot,
shall never wear shoes until His Majesty and these noble knights decide
the matter. Everyone saw how Tirant and I remained behind when others
fled, lengthily debating who would climb the ladder first. He had made a
vow, yet I wished to brave the greatest perils, and when he saw I would
not precede him, he agreed to place his foot on the ladder first. Therefore,
my lord, I beg you to consider our case, awarding honor to whoever
deserves it, though by right it should be mine, but if Your Majesty
refuses, I declare publicly that I am the better knight and shall fight to
the death to prove it."

The king replied: "Richard, no good judge can reach a verdict without
hearing both parties, and that cannot be done unless Tirant is present."

Having learned of their conversation, Tirant ordered his galley to pull
alongside the king's ship, where they told him the king was sleeping in
his cabin. As soon as Richard spied Tirant aboard, he approached him and
said: "Let men think what they will, for the truth is written in my heart,
and since you dare to deny my superiority, I challenge you to mortal
combat." And with that, he bravely threw down his gauntlet.

Seeing that he wished to fight a duel with so little justification, Tirant raised his hand and slapped Richard's face, whereupon such an uproar ensued that the king awoke and drew his sword. Beholding His Majesty, Tirant climbed onto the forecastle and cried: "Sire, punish this shameless knight who delights in sowing discord. He has never been seen in armor, nor has a sword passed before his eyes, yet now he needlessly seeks to fight me to the utterance. Should he triumph, he will destroy all the glory I have won, and should I best him, I shall have slain a coward who has never borne arms."

When our knight had finished, he signaled to his galley and lowered himself onto it with a rope, but had the king been able to capture him after committing such an outrage, it would have been little wonder if Tirant had lost his head.

The king and his fleet then sailed toward Cyprus, raiding the Turkish coast with fire and sword and loading their ships with spoils. Having reached Famagusta, they bought provisions and set sail for Tunis, where they again disembarked and stormed the city walls. As Tirant and his men were assaulting a moated tower, our knight fell in the water and Richard, who had hoped to avenge himself, instead saw his foe struggling to save his life. Richard jumped in fully armed, pulled the Breton out, and said: "Tirant, here you see your mortal enemy, who holds your life and death in his hands, but may God forbid that you be killed by Saracens if I can prevent it."

He bravely dragged him out of the moat, where Tirant would have surely perished had Richard not rescued him. When they were both safe, Richard said: "Now you are free, but be on your guard, as I shall do everything in my power to slay you."

"Worthy knight," replied Tirant, "having witnessed your courage, I now kneel, beg your pardon, and place my sword in your hand. Should you reject my apologies, I shall not resist you, and if you desire revenge, it is yours for the taking."

Hearing Tirant's humble and submissive words, the knight readily forgave him, and from that day on they remained friends until death parted them.

After the sack of Tunis, Richard decided to join Tirant, and when the king learned of their reconciliation, he praised both knights' courtesy.

Then the king, who longed to meet his daughter-in-law, set sail for Sicily. Learning of his approach, the Sicilian king had a great feast prepared and boarded his guest's ship, where the two monarchs greeted each other joyously. Once ashore, the King of France was welcomed by Princess Ricomana, with whom he spent every day hand in hand. Throughout his stay, the king sent her a rich present every morning. One day he sent brocade, another silk, gold chains, brooches, or other precious jewelry. The King of Sicily feasted his guest lavishly, gave him a hundred splendid chargers, and sent his daughter to inspect the ships and supply whatever was lacking. The King of France admired the princess's diligence and saw how capable she was, for she spent every day on the ships and would not eat till she had finished.

Once the ships were provisioned and the horses aboard, the King of France bade his hosts farewell and set sail with the Prince of Sicily, to whom, when they reached Paris, he gave his daughter in marriage.

The fleet followed the Barbary Coast, and after stopping at Málaga, Oran, and Tlemcen, they sailed through the Strait of Gibraltar and sacked Ceuta, Alcazarquivir, and Tangier. On their return, they raided Cádiz, Tarifa, Gibraltar, and Cartagena, for the entire Andalusian coast was ruled at that time by Moors. Then they called at Iviza and Majorca and continued on to Marseille, where the king dismissed everyone except Philip, whose mother wished to see him. Tirant accompanied them to Paris and then went on to visit his family.

A few days after the French princess and the Sicilian were married, news came that his elder brother was now a monk. The king then urged Philip to return to his wife, whereupon he asked his father to summon Tirant. The king wrote to the Duke of Brittany, who helped him plead his case, and so Tirant returned to Paris, where the king asked him to accompany Philip.

Having reached Marseille, the two friends found their galleys waiting. They put to sea with good weather and soon docked at Palermo, where the king, queen, and princess were much comforted by their arrival.

Less than a week later, as the King of Sicily was holding council, he recalled a woeful letter ambassadors had brought from Constantinople. His Majesty quickly summoned Tirant and had the letter read aloud:

TIRANT IN THE GREEK EMPIRE

· C X V ·

*T*HE EMPEROR OF CONSTANTINOPLE'S LETTER TO THE KING OF SICILY

We, Frederic,[1] by God's grace ruler of the Greek Empire, salute you, king of the noble isle of Sicily, and in accordance with our predecessors' treaties, confirmed and sworn to by ourselves, we inform you that two Saracen renegades—the sultan and Grand Turk—have invaded our empire with a mighty pagan host. Together they have conquered the greater part of our realm, and because of my advanced age, I am unable to resist them. They have taken numerous cities and slain my greatest joy: that heir who was my shield and the champion of our faith. He died bravely, battling the infidel to his great glory and mine, and his passing grieves me all the more as he was killed by men of our own party. On that sad and woeful day, our imperial house was shamed, but I know a valiant knight of the fraternal Order of the Garter resides with you. This knight's illustrious deeds of chivalry have often been recounted, and especially how he rescued the Grand Master of Rhodes and his entire order. I therefore pray you, by the faith, love, and good will you owe God and knighthood, to beseech him on my behalf and yours to enter my service, for I shall reward him with all the riches he desires. If he will not come, I beg Divine Justice to make him share my woes. Oh blessed King of Sicily, may my desperate pleas be answered! You, a crowned king, will surely pity our plight, as we are all ruled by Fortune's wheel, which no man can oppose. May God in His mercy smile upon our holy cause. I now lay aside my pen, but my hand will continue to recite our past, present, and future ills.

When Tirant had read the letter, the king turned to him and said:

· CXVI ·

HOW THE KING OF SICILY URGED TIRANT TO SUCCOR THE EMPEROR

"You owe Almighty God infinite thanks, Tirant my brother, for having endowed you with such perfections that your fame resounds throughout the world. I know my pleas do not deserve your respectful obedience, as you are not beholden to me nor have I done you any favors, yet, trusting in your lofty heart, which can only act in accordance with its nature, I now ask you to succor the Emperor of Constantinople. Should my just pleas fail to move you, pity that sad and afflicted sovereign, who relies on your chivalry to save his imperial crown."

When the king had finished, Tirant replied: "Great is my desire to serve Your Majesty, for love is surely the world's strongest bond. If you order me to serve the emperor, I shall do so for love of you, but as everyone knows, I am only one man, though Fortune has smiled upon me and I have triumphed thus far. I must not presume beyond what the Fates have ordained, and I am amazed that the emperor summons me when many kings and lords could serve him better."

"Tirant," said the king, "I know there are many worthy knights on earth, among them yourself. If by chance their honor were examined, the prize would go to you. Therefore, I beg you as my son to aid the emperor in his hour of need, since I know your prowess and how many Christian towns you will deliver. God will reward you with the highest honors in this world as well as eternal glory in the next, and so, ardent knight, my galleys are armed and at your service."

"Since Your Highness thus advises me, I shall do as you say," replied Tirant.

The king ordered his galleys loaded with everything necessary, and when he told the imperial ambassadors of Tirant's decision, they were the happiest men alive.

Upon their arrival in Sicily, they had set up recruiting tables, at which they offered crossbowmen half a ducat a day and foot soldiers a ducat. Unable to find enough men in Sicily, they had gone on to Rome and Naples, where they recruited a large army and purchased many horses. Tirant's only concern was to procure arms and five chests of trumpets, while the king and Philip gave him chargers, which were brought aboard the galleys.

Tirant then took his leave of the king, the queen, Philip, and the princess. When everything was ready, they set sail with a good wind and calm seas, and early one morning they hove in sight of Constantinople.

The day of Tirant's arrival was one of sovereign joy for the emperor, who said he felt as though his son had been reborn. The eleven galleys made such a joyous noise that the whole city rang with it, and the common folk, who had been mournful, acted like God himself had come, while their lord mounted a big platform to behold the approaching ships. When Tirant learned that he was watching, he brought forth two Sicilian flags and one of his own, which three knights in shining armor then held aloft. Each time they passed the emperor, they lowered the flags until they almost touched the water, and they even dipped Tirant's flag in the sea as an act of homage to His Majesty. The emperor was delighted by this ceremony and still more by Tirant's arrival.

When the galleys had sailed to and fro awhile, they threw down their ladders and Tirant went ashore dressed in a coat of mail with gold-fringed sleeves, over which he had donned a handsome French-style shirt. His sword hung at his side and a scarlet cap crowned his head, adorned with a large brooch studded with pearls and precious stones. Diaphebus dressed similarly, but his shirt was of purple satin, while Richard was attired in a shirt of fine blue damask. All their clothes were embroidered with jewels and pearls, and the others in their retinue were just as magnificently clad.

Tirant was greeted by the Count of Africa and many other lords, who escorted our knight toward the emperor's stand. Upon catching sight of His Majesty, Tirant fell to his knees, and his entire company knelt again once they were halfway across the platform. Finally, Tirant knelt a third time to kiss His Highness's foot, but the blessed lord refused and instead kissed his lips.

After bowing to the emperor, Tirant gave him a letter from the King of Sicily, to which His Majesty replied in words of this tenor:

· C X V I I ·

*T*HE EMPEROR'S WORDS TO TIRANT

"I rejoice in your arrival and thank the King of Sicily for remembering my woes, as knowledge of your valor makes me forget my past ills, and in your handsome countenance I recognize what others have described. Your virtues are revealed by your coming at that noble king's request, and in truth I am more grateful than if you had come for my own sake, wherefore, that one and all may know of my gratitude, I now appoint you imperial captain and chief magistrate."

He offered Tirant his gold staff with the imperial arms at one end, but our knight refused it, knelt before him, and humbly replied: "My lord, take no offense, but I cannot accept this staff, for, speaking with Your Highness's leave and pardon, I have not come to rout the Saracen hordes. We are only one hundred and forty gentlemen and knights, all of one will, and we have no wish to usurp what by right belongs to others. Your Majesty knows there are many reasons not to give me such a lofty title: first, because I lack skill in arms; second, because of my small company; third, because of the great usurpation and insult to the worthy Duke of Macedonia; and finally, because I would sooner be a martyr here than a father confessor."

"In my house," replied the emperor, "no one commands unless I appoint him, and I now order you to be the third to lead my army. Having lost my sole comfort and being too old and sickly to bear arms, I yield my place to you and no one else."

Seeing his master's will, Tirant accepted and kissed His Majesty's hand, while the emperor sent criers to spread the tidings throughout the city.

When this had been done, the emperor led them to his palace. On their way, they passed the handsome quarters prepared for Tirant's company, and the emperor said: "Captain, now that we are here, why do you not rest for a few days and recover from your journey?"

"What, my lord?" cried Tirant. "Do you think me capable of such an act? My repose is with Your Highness, whom I would escort to Hell itself, so why should I not accompany you to the palace?"

The emperor laughed, but Tirant continued: "And my lord, when we arrive, allow me to salute your wife and daughter." The emperor said he would gladly do so.

Having reached the great hall, the emperor took Tirant's hand and led him to the empress's chamber. The room was so dark that they could scarcely see, and the emperor said: "My lady, here is our new captain, who wishes to pay his respects to you."

She replied in a faint voice: "May he be welcome."

Tirant said: "My lady, I shall have to trust that this voice is the empress's."

"Captain," said the emperor, "your office entitles you and I beseech you to open the windows, behold those who address you, and order them to end their mourning for husband, child, or brother."

Tirant called for a burning torch, and once the room was lit, he saw a black pavilion in which a lady sat, shrouded in black from head to toe. Tirant lifted her veil and knelt to kiss her hand and foot, while she kissed the beads on her rosary and made him kiss them too. Then he saw a black canopy covering the bed upon which Princess Carmesina lay, clad in a black satin dress and mantle. At her feet sat a damsel, the Duke of

Macedonia's daughter, as well as a lady, known as the Easygoing Widow, who had nursed the princess at her breast. At the other end of the room stood one hundred and seventy ladies and maids-in-waiting.

Tirant bowed to the princess, kissed her hand, and then went to open the windows. All the ladies felt as though they had been freed from prison, for they had been in the dark since the prince's death.

Tirant said: "Sire, with your leave I shall now disclose my plans, since I see that the inhabitants of this glorious city are sad for two reasons. The first is your loss of that brave knight the prince, whom Your Majesty should mourn no more, as he died in God's service. Instead, you should thank the Lord, who sent him and has taken him away, for only thus will He grant you long life, eternal glory, and victory. The other cause of their sorrow is the Saracen host they see approaching. They fear for their lives and goods or at the very least their liberty, wherefore necessity obliges you and the empress to show more cheer, that your grieving subjects may be comforted and fortified by your example."

"The captain has spoken wisely," said the emperor, "and I order all of you to end your mourning."

· CXVIII ·

*H*OW VENUS WOUNDED TIRANT WITH HER DART AS HE GAZED UPON THE EMPEROR'S DAUGHTER

As Tirant listened to the emperor's words, his eyes were fixed upon the fair princess. It had been so hot with all the windows closed that she had half-unbuttoned her blouse and he could see her breasts, which were like two heavenly crystalline apples. They allowed Tirant's gaze to enter but not to depart, and he remained in her power till the end of his days. I can tell you in all truth that Tirant's eyes had never feasted on such a sight, though he had won many honors in England and Rhodes. Seeing the emperor take his daughter's hand and lead her from the chamber, our knight took the empress's arm, and they entered another room hung with splendid tapestries depicting the noble loves of Florice and Blanchfleur, Pyramus and Thisbe, Aeneas and Dido, Tristan and Isolde, Queen Guinevere and Lancelot and many others.

Tirant said to Richard: "Never would I have thought there were such wonders on earth."

He was primarily referring to the princess's beauty, but Richard misunderstood him.

Tirant took his leave of them and returned to his chamber, where he lay down upon the bed. Soon his companions arrived and asked him to come to lunch, but Tirant said he had a headache, for he had been wounded by that passion which ensnares so many. Noticing how Tirant kept to his chamber, Diaphebus entered and said: "Lord captain, please tell me what ails you, since if I can provide some remedy, I shall gladly do so."

"Cousin," replied Tirant, "I shall tell you the cause of my ailment: the sea air has made me ill."[2]

"Oh captain! Do you wish to conceal things from me? Shall I, who am the archive of all your good and bad fortune, now be excluded from such a small secret? Tell me, I pray you; do not hide whatever ails you."

"Torment me no further!" cried Tirant. "Never have I suffered an illness like this, which will either bring cruel death or sovereign bliss, if Fortune aids me. Love's bitter sorrow is the cause of my pain."

He turned away in shame, unable to meet Diaphebus's gaze or utter another word except: "I love."

Having spoken, Tirant wept bitter tears that mingled with his sighs and sobs, while Diaphebus, beholding the knight's unmanly conduct, understood why he had reproached his companions when they spoke of love, saying: "You are mad. Do you not blush to place your freedom in the hands of an enemy who would sooner slay than spare you?" Thus had Tirant mocked them, but now he was caught in the same trap.

Pondering how such an illness might be cured, Diaphebus gently replied:

· C X I X ·

*H*OW DIAPHEBUS TRIED TO COMFORT HIS LOVELORN COUSIN

"To love is human, for Aristotle says everything is attracted by its like,[3] and if love's yoke oppresses you, know that none may escape it. Therefore, the wiser a man is, the more discreetly he hides his sufferings, as he can only reveal his valor by enduring love's adversities. Now cheerfully descend from that fretful place where you are seated, rejoicing that Fortune has led your thoughts to a lofty abode, and between the two of us we shall find a cure for this new woe."

Upon hearing Diaphebus's words of solace, Tirant felt much better. Awkwardly and shyly he rose and they went to lunch, feeling surprised that the emperor had summoned them, but Tirant ate little food and swallowed many tears, being keenly aware that he loved one above his station. He thought: "My trial began today, but when will God deliver a favorable sentence?"

Seeing Tirant's lack of appetite, everyone thought the sea had made him ill, and finally his anguish became so great that he returned to his quarters. There he sighed deeply, beset by shame and confusion, but when Diaphebus and the others sought to keep him company, he told them he wished to rest.

Diaphebus and another knight then went to the palace, not to see the emperor but to behold the ladies. His Majesty saw them coming and sent a messenger to fetch his guests, who told him their captain was feeling unwell. Hearing this, His Majesty was troubled and sent his doctors to examine Tirant.

Upon their return, they said Tirant was in good spirits but a little seasick, whereupon the emperor asked Diaphebus to describe the festivities in England and tell him which knights had triumphed in battle.

"My lord," replied Diaphebus, "I would be most grateful if Your Highness refrained from such requests, as I would not wish you to think I praise Tirant because he is my relative, and to justify my account, I have all the proclamations here, signed by the king, his judges, and many dukes, counts, marquises, kings-of-arms, heralds, and pursuivants."

The emperor asked him to send for the proclamations, and after showing them to His Majesty, Diaphebus described the feasts and tournaments from beginning to end. The emperor was much comforted, and his ladies were still more pleased, for they had listened devoutly to Tirant's noble deeds of chivalry. Afterward, they asked to hear about the Sicilian princess's wedding and how Tirant had succored the Grand Master of Rhodes.

Once Diaphebus had finished, the emperor went to his council, which met for a half-hour every morning and again for an hour after Vespers. Diaphebus asked to accompany him, but the worthy lord refused, saying: "I know how young knights delight in the company of ladies."

As soon as her father had left, Princess Carmesina asked the empress if they might move to a more spacious room, since they had been so long in mourning. The empress replied: "My daughter, go where you wish. It is all the same to me."

They led Diaphebus into a marvelous hall whose windows, columns, and floors were brilliant rock crystal. The walls were covered with dazzling varicolored jasper and porphyry mosaics, depicting the tales of Boors and Parcival, Galahad's wondrous adventure with the Siege Perilous, and the quest for the Holy Grail. The ceiling was gold and dark blue, with a painted frieze of Christian kings bearing splendid crowns and scepters, and beneath each one's portrait, there was a shield with his coat of arms and his name in Roman letters.

Once they were settled in the room, the princess drew Diaphebus aside and asked him about Tirant, to which he replied: "Ah, what joy, after an arduous journey, to reach our desired port! Truly, God has blessed our eyes with the fairest vision since Mother Eve, for you are endowed with sweetness, comeliness, modesty, infinite wisdom, and every other grace and virtue! I care nothing for all our past and future hardships, as I have found Your Highness, who deserves to rule the world. Please accept my words as those of a devoted servant and store them in your soul's innermost recess, for Tirant came because of your fame, having heard that you possess every virtue with which Nature may endow one mortal body. Do not think we are here because of the king's pleas, the emperor's letter, or longing for glory, as we have already won many battles. Neither did we come to see the countryside and imperial palaces, since every one of our houses would make a splendid church, so grand and handsome are they, and each of us lives like a king. You may well believe we came only to behold and serve you, and all our deeds of chivalry will be for love of Your Highness."

"Alas!" cried the princess. "What are you saying? How can I rejoice in your coming for me and not my father?"

"I swear," replied Diaphebus, "that Tirant only wished to gaze upon the emperor's daughter, and when he first beheld you, his delight was so great that he had to take to his bed."

Great was the princess's consternation at Diaphebus's words. She said nothing, seeming half out of her wits, and the lady's angelic face reddened, for her delicate soul was troubled. She could not speak, so assaulted was she by love and shame, the first of which inflamed those secret wishes that the latter held in check.

At that moment, the emperor entered and led Diaphebus away, and the two of them took counsel until it was time for supper. Having excused himself, the knight sought the princess and asked if she had any commands.

"Yes," she replied. "Take these embraces, keep some for yourself, and give the rest to Tirant." Diaphebus quickly approached and obeyed his lady's order.

When Tirant learned that Diaphebus had gone to speak with the princess, he could scarcely contain his eagerness to learn what she had said. As soon as Diaphebus entered the room, Tirant rose from his bed and asked: "Good brother, what news do you bring from one who holds my soul in thrall?"

Seeing Tirant's great love, Diaphebus embraced him on his beloved's behalf and repeated her words, at which the captain felt happier than if he had received a kingdom. He ate well, regained his cheer, and eagerly awaited the dawn.

After Diaphebus left, the princess grew very pensive and retired to her room. She loved the Duke of Macedonia's daughter Stephanie dearly, for they had been raised together and were of the same age. Seeing the princess leave, Stephanie rose to follow her, and once the two damsels were alone, Carmesina told her everything Diaphebus had said.

"I tell you he has given me more joy than all the knights I have ever seen, for he is a man of grandeur and courage whose every gesture breathes nobility. No lady could help adoring one so peerlessly courteous, and to think he came here more for love of me than of my father! Certainly, my heart inclines to obey his commands, and he shows every sign of being my life and salvation."

Stephanie replied: "Among the good one must choose the best, and any damsel who heard of his triumphs would gladly do his will."

As they were exchanging these intimacies, they beheld the Easygoing Widow, who had suckled Carmesina and was privy to all her secrets. She asked what they were speaking of, and the princess replied: "We were discussing what that knight said, and how splendidly they honored the foreigners in England."

They spent the whole night talking about these and other matters, and the princess slept not a wink.

The next morning, Tirant donned a cape of cloth of gold, whose design showed sheaves of millet with pearl stalks and a motto beneath them: *One is worth a thousand and a thousand are not worth one.*[4] Both his French hood and his stockings bore the same device, and he held the captain's imperial staff in his hand. Once his companions had dressed in fine brocade, silk, and silver, Tirant led his splendidly attired company to the palace.

Upon reaching the main gate, they beheld an amazing sight: gold pine cones as big as men and too heavy for a hundred to lift flanked the entrance to the courtyard. The emperor had commissioned them in more prosperous times for some great public occasion. At the palace doors, they found lions and panthers on silver chains, and after mounting the staircase, they saw a great marble hall.

Learning of his captain's arrival, the emperor invited him into a room where Princess Carmesina was combing His Majesty's hair. When she finished, she knelt and offered him his wash basin, as she did every day. Carmesina wore a gown of cloth of gold embroidered with flowers called love-in-a-mist, above which the motto *But not to me* was embroidered in big pearls. Having finished his toilet, the emperor asked Tirant: "Tell me, captain: what was the nature of your ailment?"

Tirant said: "Your Majesty should know I was seasick, for the winds here are weaker than in the west."

Before the emperor could speak, his daughter replied: "Sire, the sea does not sicken worthy foreigners but brings them health and long life." She looked directly at Tirant, smiling because she knew he understood her.

The emperor led Tirant away, while the princess took Diaphebus's hand and said: "I could not sleep all night, thinking about what you said yesterday."

"My lady, if you want to know the truth, we have had our share of troubles too, but I am much consoled that you understood Tirant."

"What makes you think Greek ladies are less clever than French ones?" asked the princess. "We shall understand your Latin, no matter how obscurely you speak it."

"The more glory for us," said Diaphebus, "if we can converse with ladies of understanding."

"From now on, you will see how much we know about your past feats."

The princess summoned her damsels to keep Diaphebus company, and leaving him well attended, she entered her chamber to finish dressing. Tirant, meanwhile, escorted his lord to the Hagia Sophia, where he left him to say his prayers and returned for the empress and Carmesina. Having reached the great hall, he found his cousin surrounded by maidens to whom he was recounting Philip's courtship with more grace than if he had lived there all his life.

Seeing Tirant enter, the damsels rose to welcome him, and, after asking him to sit down, they plied him with questions.

Soon the empress appeared, dressed in dark grey velvet, and drew Tirant aside to ask after his health. He replied that he was quite well. Then the princess entered, wearing a sable-lined crimson robe open on the sides and with wide sleeves. On her head she bore a little crown studded with diamonds, rubies, and other jewels, while her gracious carriage and indescribable beauty showed she deserved to rule the world.

Being the emperor's captain, Tirant took the empress's arm and led the way. There were many counts and marquises who wished to escort the princess, but she said: "I desire no company but my brother Diaphebus."

They left her with the knight, but God knows Tirant would have sooner been beside his princess. As they were walking, Diaphebus said: "Look how hearts understand each other."

The princess asked: "What do you mean?"

"My lady," replied Diaphebus, "Your Highness is wearing a dress of cloth of gold and pearls, and Tirant's wounded heart has led him to don just what you need over it. Ah, how happy I would be if I could place that cape over this dress!"

Since they were behind the empress, he pulled at his cousin's cape, and Tirant, who felt the pressure, began to walk more slowly. Then Diaphebus placed the cape over Carmesina's shoulders, saying: "My lady, now the stone is in its place."

"Woe is me! Have you taken leave of your senses? How can you say such shameful things in front of everybody?"

"But my lady, no one heard, saw, or smelt it," replied Diaphebus. "If I said a Paternoster backward, nobody would understand."

"You must have attended the school of honor where one studies the works of Ovid, that poet who always sings the praises of true love, and any man who strives to imitate a master does well. If you knew the dwelling place of devotion and also spoke Greek, you would have a blessed future here."

At this point their discussion ended, as they had reached the cathedral. Although the emperor was in a private chapel adorned with tapestries, Carmesina decided to enter the church, where it was cooler and she could watch Tirant. Our knight approached the altar with many counts and dukes, while everyone made way for their newly appointed captain. Seeing him kneel as was his custom during Mass, the princess gave a brocade cushion to one of her damsels. The emperor rejoiced to behold her good deed, and as soon as Tirant saw the damsel bringing the cushion, he stood up, bowed to Carmesina, and doffed his hood.

Do not imagine that the princess said all her prayers that day, for she kept looking at Tirant and his splendidly attired men. The Breton also gazed long upon his lady's peerless beauty, and after recalling every damsel he had known, he judged them all inferior. Such was Carmesina's splendor of lineage, beauty, courtesy, wealth, and wisdom that she truly appeared more angelic than human. Her gracefully proportioned body showed that Nature had done her utmost, for she lacked nothing either in general or in particular. He was dazzled by her shimmering golden tresses, and likewise he marveled at her arching, delicately etched eyebrows. Neither too close nor too dark, they seemed Heaven's own perfection, yet he was more astonished by her eyes, which, shining like twin gemlike stars, did not stare wildly about but moved with grace, delicacy, and serene confidence. Her nose was slender and chiseled, neither too big nor too small, while her face was the color of whitest lilies and roses. Carmesina's lips were red as coral, her teeth were white, small, and even, and her hands were so plump and white that not a bone could be seen. Her fingers were delicate, her round, firm nails were painted with henna, and indeed, everything about her was flawless.[5]

Once Mass had ended and they had returned to the palace, Tirant excused himself and led his men to their quarters, where he retired to his chamber and threw himself upon the bed, for Carmesina's charms had redoubled his sorrows. Entering the room, Diaphebus beheld Tirant's doleful countenance and said: "Lord captain, you are the strangest knight

I ever saw, as anyone else would rejoice after the honor your lady did you by sending that cushion to her suitor in front of everyone. You should be the happiest knight on earth, yet you behave like a madman."

Hearing Diaphebus's soothing words, Tirant replied in a mournful voice:

· CXX ·

TIRANT'S AMOROUS PLAINT

"My spirit burns to know if its love will be requited, and among all my tribulations, this is the cruelest, for my heart freezes in terror at the hopelessness of my suit. You know that in all my jousts, no knight has ever bested me, yet this damsel, with one glance, has vanquished my defenseless soul. If she has caused my ills, what doctor can cure me? Who but she can restore me to life and true health? How can I embolden my tongue to beg for mercy, when she surpasses me in everything: in riches, nobility, and station? If love does not incline her to pity, I shall quickly take my life, since all other paths are barred and I see no other remedy."

Seeing Tirant's anguish, Diaphebus refused to let him continue and uttered these words of comfort:

· CXXI ·

DIAPHEBUS'S WORDS OF COMFORT TO HIS LOVELORN COUSIN

"When the lovers of old wished to leave some remembrance of their glory, they strove with great travails to attain tranquil bliss, and yet I see you pining for wretched death. A love like yours is not easily consummated, and you must struggle earnestly and skillfully to bring it to fruition. I, for my part, shall do my utmost to aid you. Had I a hundred lives instead of one, I would risk them all for your sake, but if this continues, you will win reproaches and infamy, which worthy knights should avoid by restraining their disordered impulses, and if, God forbid, news should reach the emperor's ears, how shall we appear when he learns you were smitten by his daughter and sought to strip her of her rank, indifferent to how others might judge your deeds? Do you think he will understand when you recount love's battles and conquests? Why, then, do you wear your heart on your sleeve, ignoring that vulgar saying: 'Where there's smoke there's fire'? Tirant, show your wisdom, or at least endeavor to hide your sufferings."

Feeling greatly cheered by Diaphebus's wise advice, Tirant thought for a while, rose, and went out to address his men, who had been shocked by his discourteous conduct.

When they had dined, he asked Diaphebus to give the princess a handsome book of hours, which had been made in Paris and whose cover was solid gold. The keyhole was disguised as the head of a tiny screw, so that when the key was removed, no one knew where to open it. The lettering inside was beautiful and the stories wittily told and handsomely illuminated, and everyone who saw it said one could find no more majestic book of hours in that era.

Diaphebus entrusted the book to a gallant page, and upon their arrival at the palace, they found the emperor holding court in his great hall. Diaphebus repeated what Tirant had told him to say: "Holy Majesty, your obedient captain does not know how to serve you, wherefore he asks your leave to reconnoiter the Turkish camp, and he also sends this book of hours, begging you to give it to one of the princess's damsels if you do not want it."

When the emperor saw the book, he was amazed. "This," he said, "should only be given to a damsel of royal blood."

Then he offered it to his daughter, who was delighted both with the book itself and to have something of Tirant's. She rose and said: "My lord, let us invite Tirant and his company to dance with us. We have been in mourning too long, and I wish to see your court recover its gaiety."

"Daughter, you know my only joys are you and Queen Isabel of Hungary, who to punish me for my sins has been banished from my sight. Ever since my son's death, you have been my consolation, and any joy I can offer you will comfort me in my old age."

After telling the page to summon Tirant, the princess asked Diaphebus to sit beside her.

Having received his lady's summons, Tirant set out for the palace, and as soon as he arrived, he asked the emperor's leave to dance with her. They danced until suppertime and Tirant left feeling very happy, for she had spoken many words that he would treasure forever after.

The next day, His Majesty held a great feast, at which all the imperial dukes, counts, and marquises honored Tirant. When their meal had ended, they danced till dessert was served. Then the emperor decided to show his captain the city. Tirant's men were astonished at the magnificent buildings, mighty fortifications, and lofty towers above the gates and walls.

As a sign of his good will, the emperor invited Tirant to sup that evening with him and his daughter, whom everyone called the infanta.

"My lord," said Tirant, "a daughter who will inherit your crown should not be called 'infanta.'⁶ Why does Your Majesty rob her of her proper title: princess? I know you have an elder daughter who is Queen of Hungary, but she renounced her rights in exchange for the great dowry you gave her, wherefore, with all due reverence, Carmesina's title should be changed."

The emperor, heeding Tirant's wise arguments, instructed everyone to call her "princess."

Two days later, His Majesty called a general council and summoned Carmesina, whom he told: "My daughter, you should attend councils and learn to discuss affairs of state, for you will certainly outlive me, and when I die you must rule this land."

The princess consented, both to watch the council and to hear Tirant, and once everyone was present and seated, the emperor spoke these words:

· CXXII ·

THE EMPEROR'S PROPOSAL TO TIRANT

"God has punished us for our sins, letting our greatest knights be slain or captured, while those who remain face a similar fate if not succored by your victorious hand. As our forces dwindle, the empire is invaded by vile rabble from afar, cruel and merciless Saracens who oppose our faith and sovereignty. The day I lost my worthy son, the flower of Greek chivalry, I also lost my honor, which only you can restore, for through divine mercy and your trenchant sword we may yet win glorious victory. Therefore I pray you, brave captain, to rout those wicked Genoese, since the crueler their deaths, the more your glorious fame will resound! Take up arms and lead us to the victory we so desire! We know Genoese warships have docked at Aulis with soldiers, horses, and provisions from Tuscany and Lombardy. Our ships have left the isle of Euboea, and I understand they will soon be here."

Tirant modestly removed his cap and replied:

· CXXIII ·

*T*IRANT'S REPLY

"It ill behooves Your Highness to make such requests, for you should command, having already honored me beyond my deserts. When I accepted the captaincy I swore to serve you, and the day I sailed from Sicily I placed my fate in your hands. Therefore, as I have made you my lord and you have accepted my fealty, ask nothing but rather command me as you would your humblest slave. Order me to attack the Genoese whenever you think fit, but with Your Majesty's leave and pardon, I shall now offer some advice: in war three things are necessary, and those who lack even one will fail."

"I would be happy," replied the emperor, "to hear what these three things are."

"Sire," said Tirant, "I shall tell you: troops, money, and provisions. If any of these is absent, your army will be defeated. Since the pagan hordes are supplied by Genoese, who bring them food, arms, horses, and soldiers, we must do our utmost to give them cruel and harsh battle."

"We possess," the emperor said, "everything you have mentioned. Our swollen treasury can pay two hundred thousand soldiers for twenty or thirty years. We have sixty thousand men posted along the frontier under the Duke of Macedonia, as well as eighty thousand more in this city and the lands we still possess. In those forty ships are twenty-five thousand more, and we are also well supplied with armor, horses, and artillery. At present, we have little grain, but our vessels will soon arrive, and once they unload I shall send them back to Sicily for more. Moreover, I have asked George Castriota Scanderbeg in Slavonia to send provisions."

"I am pleased with everything Your Majesty has said," replied Tirant. "Let us hold no more councils, as we have everything we need and can now devote ourselves to making war."

"First," said the emperor, "you must go to the great courthouse and sit upon the judge's bench, where you shall hear each case and dispense imperial justice."

A councilor named Montsalvat suddenly rose and said: "Your Majesty should look more closely into these matters, for there are three obstacles: first, the Duke of Macedonia should not be deprived of his captaincy, which he inherited through closeness to the imperial throne; second, no foreigner should hold imperial office or enjoy its benefits, and still less if he hails from an unknown land; and third, before our soldiers set out, they should make a pilgrimage, offering sacrifices to the gods on that island where Paris abducted Helen,[7] for thus the ancient Greeks won victory over the Trojans."

The emperor would suffer the knight's rash words no longer and angrily replied:

· CXXIV ·

THE EMPEROR'S REPLY TO THE HERETICAL AND UNCHRISTIAN KNIGHT

"Were it not for my age, which is wearied by wrath, I would quickly have your head chopped off as an offering to God and an example to mankind. My wish and command is that our captain Tirant be placed above all others, for he won his office through resplendent chivalry, whereas that craven Duke of Macedonia has never been victorious. I shall select our captain, and if anyone contradicts me, he shall be punished in a manner the world will never forget. The right to bear arms is earned through valiant emulation of our worthy ancestors, and only those skilled in warfare deserve to lead armies, wherefore we need speak no further of this matter."

He fell silent, for he was old and his wrath had exhausted him, but the princess took up the gauntlet and said: "Oh son of iniquity engendered under Saturn's evil sign, you deserve punishment and reprehension for opposing the emperor's will. You urge sinful idolatry against divine and human law, heretically proposing that we sacrifice to your master the Devil. Are you unaware that all idolatry ceased when Jesus came? The Bible tells us that King Herod, feeling slighted by the three kings, planned to slay the infant Jesus, but then an angel appeared to Joseph in a dream and warned him to flee with the mother and child. As soon as they entered Egypt, all the idols fell from their pedestals,[8] and thus should you be castigated for slandering our captain and fomenting discord. Tell me: if these foreigners are worthier than our knights, more skillful, strong, and experienced in war, what do you have to say? Should you doubt my words, take yourself as an example: being too weak and cowardly to brave the perils of battle, you should blush to show your face here."

Tirant tried to speak, but the princess silenced him lest the situation worsen, saying: "A wise man should not answer fools, for a fool's words reveal his folly. Men should not compete in baseness but in gentility and virtue, and one who speaks rashly should be fittingly punished. Were it not for your clemency, that man would surely lose his head. Blessed indeed is the prince with such a councilor."

The emperor rose, dismissed his council, and dispatched criers to summon those with suits or plaints to court, where they would receive speedy justice.

The next morning, having seated himself on the judge's bench, Tirant dispensed justice for the first time since the war had begun.

On the morrow, he summoned the entire council and the city aldermen, with whom he organized the emperor's forces into groups of fifty, each of which was captained by its highest ranking member. This was done throughout the city, and where they lacked soldiers they quickly recruited them. Tirant posted fifty guards every night outside the emperor's room, and before retiring he told them: "Here is your lord, whom I order you to protect under pain of death and dishonor and to restore to me tomorrow morning."

Then he spoke these same words to the empress's and princess's guards.

Once the emperor was in bed, they shut the outer doors and left those to his chamber slightly ajar, while two guards listened outside in case he should request anything. Every half hour these guards were relieved, and altogether a hundred men watched the great hall till morning. Four hundred more patrolled the palace grounds, and when Tirant came at dawn, they restored the emperor to him with a notarized statement, doing the same with the empress and princess.

The emperor was pleased by these precautions and by Tirant's punctuality, though this was more to see the princess than for His Majesty's sake.

Furthermore, Tirant had heavy chains stretched across the streets and left there until he rang a bell in the palace that could be heard throughout the city. Since there were many thieves in the town, he ordered half the houses on each street to hang lanterns in their windows until midnight and the rest from midnight until dawn. Once the emperor had retired, he rode through the streets till midnight, when Diaphebus, Richard, or another would take his staff and make the rounds till morning, and in this manner the city was preserved from all evil. Moreover, Tirant told the aldermen to search every house, bringing all the wheat, millet, and barley they found to the market square. After letting each family keep as much food as it needed, they distributed the rest at two ducats a cartload. Within a few days the city was well provisioned, whereas before Tirant's arrival the people had been unable to buy bread, wine, or any other food.

The commoners praised Tirant's noble ordinances, for now they could live in safety, peace, and love, and the emperor's spirit was also soothed by his captain's wise administration.

When Tirant had been there two weeks, the emperor's ships arrived with soldiers, grain, and horses. Before they docked, he gave his captain eighty-three splendid chargers and many suits of armor, whereupon Tirant asked Diaphebus to select the mount and harness he liked best. When he had chosen, Richard and the others did likewise, but Tirant refused to accept anything for himself.

Tirant suffered greatly for love of the princess, and his woes increased daily, but he was too shy to reveal his anguish. His departure was drawing near, and he was only waiting for the horses to recover from their voyage.

The princess, whose wise heart knew of Tirant's torments, sent a page to invite him to her chambers at midday, when almost everyone in the palace would be asleep. Rejoicing in his lady's order, Tirant summoned his cousin and showed him the note. Diaphebus said: "Lord captain, I am delighted at the beginning, though the outcome remains uncertain. Now grant me one favor: once you are with her, act as bravely toward a defenseless woman as you would with the fiercest knight. Boldly declare your love, for she will think the better of you, whereas fearful pleas are often denied."

At the appointed hour, our two knights entered the princess's chambers with high hopes of victory. She rose, took Tirant's hand, and seated him beside her, while Diaphebus led Stephanie and the Easygoing Widow away. Then the princess began to whisper:

· C X X V ·

HOW THE PRINCESS WARNED TIRANT AGAINST THE DUKE OF MACEDONIA'S TREACHEROUS SNARES

"Since worthy intentions should banish shame and fear, do not take my words as dishonorable, immoral, or blameworthy if I presume to address you with pure and honest intent, feeling only concern for your great valor and nobility. I have no wish to see you caught in a trap, for you have come in response to the King of Sicily's pleas, confiding in your glorious merits and ignorant of the dangers that may await you. Therefore, I wish to give you some advice for your own safety, and if you trust my words, you will win triumph and glory."

Once the princess had spoken, Tirant replied: "Oh lady of high esteem and peerless excellence, how can I repay your favors? The mere thought of your kindness awes me, and with devoted heart I humbly thank you for pitying my travails. Do not think me ungrateful, as I know this offer comes from the best damsel on earth, and all the more praise is due when a favor is freely granted."

Then Tirant tried to kiss her hand, but Carmesina refused. After begging her many times, he called Stephanie and the Easygoing Widow, who also pleaded with their mistress till she consented in the following manner: Tirant could kiss the palm but not the back of her hand, as kissing the palm is a sign of love, while kissing the back is a sign of fealty.

Then the princess said: "Blessed knight, be consoled by the excellence of your works, which through their splendor and nobility enhance the glory of our empire. If you can drive those Genoese, Italians, Lombards, and Turks from our lands, I and my father will rejoice in your victory, yet I fear that adverse Fortune may seek to thwart our plans, for it has long harassed us and you are our sole remaining hope. If you will champion our cause, I promise to reward you fittingly, granting all your requests in whole or in part. May merciful God protect you from that ravening lion the Duke of Macedonia, a cruel and jealous man of great cunning and treachery. It is known that he only kills by deceit, and thus did he murder my valiant brother, for as they were battling the enemy, the duke crept up behind him, cutting the thong on his helmet and sending him to his death. Such a scoundrel should be greatly feared, as all the seven deadly sins reign in him, wherefore I warn and advise you not to trust him eating or sleeping. If you bear my words in mind you will save your own life, and though everyone claims the guilty should be punished, it is not unusual for the just to suffer while the unjust triumph."

As they spoke, the empress entered, having risen from her nap. She sat down and asked what they had been discussing, to which the princess replied: "My lady, we were talking about how to drive those reinforcements from our empire."

"Who knows?" asked the empress. "To me war is like a disease, for one day a man is well and the next he is sick, and one day his head aches, while the next it is his foot. Battles are just so, for one day you win and the next you lose."

The empress went on so long that Tirant had no chance to reply, and as they were leaving Vespers, Her Majesty said: "Let us show our captain the palace, as he has only seen the main floor and we can take him to your father's treasury."

Tirant took the empress's arm, while Diaphebus escorted the princess, and together they visited many handsome monuments. Upon reaching the treasure tower, Carmesina unlocked the door, for she kept the keys. The walls were covered with white marble on which the story of Paris and Vienne had been depicted, while the ceiling was painted gold and dark blue. The princess ordered seventy-two chests of gold coins brought forth, along with others full of gold, silverware, jewels, and rich vestments. There was an awesome quantity of silver plates, piled so high that they reached the ceiling, and all the vessels in the emperor's kitchen were also made of silver.

Tirant and Diaphebus were astounded at the emperor's wealth, the likes of which they had never seen before.

That night, Tirant pondered the princess's words and what he had seen. When day came, he had two banners made, the first of which showed gold padlocks upon a green field above a motto that read:

> The letter that commences
> This object's name
> Is the key with which cruel Fortune
> Holds the last one in chains[9]

He also presented a red banner with a raven and Roman letters around the bordure, saying: *Avis mea, sequere me, quia de carne mea vel aliena saciabo te.* The emperor and his noble knights and ladies found this device most pleasing.

Learning that the princess and empress were at lunch, Tirant entered the dining hall and served as their steward, for such was his right as imperial captain. When he saw they had almost finished, he turned to the empress and begged her to help resolve a question that was troubling him, to which she replied that she would gladly do so if she could.

"Tell me, my lady," said Tirant, "which is better and more honorable for a knight: to die well or badly, since he must die in either case?"

He fell silent and said no more, whereupon the fair princess cried: "Holy Mary! What kind of question is that to ask my mother, when everyone knows it is better to die well than badly? Though we all must perish, a worthy knight will show his mettle. Men will honor him if he dies bravely, but of a recreant knight they will say: 'He died a vile death.' Such men reap perpetual infamy for themselves and their heirs, whereas the Romans won honor by defending their fatherland. Their glorious deeds will endure forever, and when they returned, the walls were breached that they might enter in triumph, yet those who died badly were never mentioned again, wherefore it is certainly better to die well than badly."

When the princess had finished, Tirant brought his fist down on the table, muttering "Quite so" between his teeth so they could hardly understand him.

Then he turned on his heel and silently strode out, while the ladies stared in distress at the expression on his face.

Soon the emperor appeared, and his wife and daughter told him what had happened. His Majesty replied: "I wonder if this knight is tormented by some sorrow and regrets venturing so far from his friends and family, or perhaps he fears the Turks. Do not repeat this to anyone; I shall learn the truth before nightfall."

The emperor left them and went to sleep for a while.

When he awoke, His Majesty looked out upon the courtyard, and seeing Richard enter on a charger, he decided to summon him. Once the knight was before him, the emperor bowed and said: "I beg you by your beloved to tell me what troubles Tirant."

"My lord," replied Richard, "whoever said that was telling lies, since Tirant is now gaily preparing his banners and armor."

"I am very pleased," said the emperor, "to hear it. Now go and fetch him; say I shall await him here."

Richard hastened to deliver the emperor's summons, which Tirant's common sense told him could have only one cause. Mounting a white horse, he led his company to the palace, where he found the emperor about to ride forth with a large party. All the ladies were gazing down from the windows.

Upon seeing the princess, Tirant bowed deeply, while she returned his greeting. The emperor then asked Tirant what had put him in such a humor: "Please tell me, for I shall offer a remedy that will comfort your soul, but you must tell me quickly, without any shame."

Tirant replied:

· CXXVI ·

*H*OW TIRANT ANSWERED THE EMPEROR'S QUESTION

"There is nothing in this world that I would not reveal to Your Majesty, and cost what it may, I shall obey your orders. As your wife and daughter were dining, I heard the empress sigh and thought she must be mourning her son. My heart was filled with pity and I made a vow, as quietly as she had sighed, that by my honor and fame I would avenge his death, for my soul will know no peace until I slay his murderer."

Seeing tears pour from the benign lord's eyes as he thanked him for his devotion, our knight decided to recount some more cheerful tidings.

They continued to converse until they reached the port of Pera, where the emperor showed Tirant a handsome palace with many splendid gardens and statues.

When they had looked at everything, the emperor said: "Captain, I would like you to know how old this city is, for it was first populated many centuries ago by idolatrous heathens. They were converted to Christianity by my noble grandfather Constantine, whose father had been elected Emperor of Rome and ruled Greece and many other provinces. When Saint Sylvester cured him of a dread disease, he converted and made him Pope, giving the Roman Empire to the Church and retaining only Greece. He was succeeded by my grandfather, the emperor Constantine, who was asked by all nations to be both Pope and emperor. Hearing of his generosity, such a horde of foreigners came to settle that there was no room for them in Pera, so my grandfather had our noble city built, christening it Constantinople, and from then on he was called the Emperor of Constantinople."[10]

It was dark by the time they returned to Constantinople, which is three miles from Pera. Tirant and the emperor went to the empress's chambers, where they spoke of many matters, but the Breton's countenance was not cheerful. When he felt it was time, he said good night and retired to his lodgings.

On the morrow, the princess still felt troubled by Tirant's words, though her father had repeated his captain's explanation. That morning during Mass, our knight entered the church to pray, and when the service ended, he went to the emperor's chapel and said: "My lord, the galleys are ready to sail to Cyprus for provisions. Shall I send them forth?"

The emperor replied: "I wish they were already a hundred miles away."

Tirant hastened to the docks and ordered them to weigh anchor. When the princess saw him leave, she summoned Diaphebus, whom she asked to bring Tirant after lunch, that they might speak and dance together.

When Tirant heard this, he quickly guessed her intentions and found a beautiful mirror, which he hid in his sleeve. At the appointed hour our knights went to the palace, where they found the emperor talking with his daughter. Seeing Tirant, he summoned his musicians that they all might dance, and after watching a short while, the emperor retired to his chambers. The princess quickly stopped, took Tirant's hand, and led him to a window seat. Then she said: "Brave knight, I pity your affliction and beg you to tell me what you feel, be it good or bad. If it is bad, perhaps I can share your burden, and if it is good, I shall rejoice on your behalf."

"My lady," replied Tirant, "though I curse all ailments that assail my felicity, I would never share such an illness, as I wish to keep it all to myself. Let us not discuss such matters but rather speak of joy and mirth, laying aside the woes that torment my weary soul."

"Certainly there is nothing," said the princess, "however private, that I would not disclose to you, yet you refuse to trust me. Therefore, I ask again: by what you love most in this world, tell me."

"My lady," replied Tirant, "I beg you not to persist, for I would gladly share my sorrows did I not fear the emperor's wrath, and if I do not tell you, I shall also die of your displeasure and my grief."

"Do you think, Tirant, that I would repeat your secrets? My colors are not as you perceive them, so cast aside your fears. Tell me what ails you, and I shall keep it locked in my heart."

"My lady, since your kindness forces me to speak, all I can say is that I love."

And he silently lowered his eyes.

· CXXVII ·

*H*OW THE PRINCESS ASKED TIRANT TO NAME HIS BELOVED

"Tell me, Tirant," said the princess, "and may God grant all your wishes: who torments you so, for I shall gladly try to help."

Tirant reached up his sleeve, took out the mirror, and replied: "My lady, the woman whose face you see here holds my life and death in her hands. Beg her to spare me."

The princess bore the mirror to her chamber, expecting to find some woman's face painted on it, but all she beheld was her own fair visage. Then she realized that the party was in her honor and marveled to think a knight could declare his love without speaking. As she was relishing Tirant's stratagem, Stephanie and the Easygoing Widow entered and asked their smiling mistress: "Where did Your Highness obtain such a handsome mirror?"

She described Tirant's ruse and said she had never heard of such a thing: "In all the stories I have read, I never found such a gentle declaration. What marvelous things these foreigners know! I thought all wisdom, virtue, honor, and gentility dwelt among our Greeks, but now I see how much more other nations possess!"

The Easygoing Widow replied: "Alas, my lady! I see you treading perilous pathways, for your left foot cannot keep pace with your right and your eyes yield to others' pleas. Tell me, my lady: is it just or decent to court your father's servant? He welcomed Tirant out of pity when the

King of Sicily had banished him, along with his barbarian Breton rabble in borrowed gold and silk. Do you wish to sacrifice your reputation and maidenly vestments for such a man, letting shame and infamy wound the ears of those who discover you? You scorn chastity, glorying in what you should abhor, though all damsels should shun such threats to their virtue. Many magnates and mighty lords seek to wed you, yet until now you have put them off like a coy innkeeper's wife, deceiving your father and soiling his honor. Better you had died in the womb than that such infamy should reach the ears of worthy folk, for if you enter into illicit union with this knight, your subjects will revile you, and if you marry him, be good enough to tell me his title. Is he a duke, count, marquis, or king? I shall say no more, since I am nothing but a helpless woman who can only defend your honor with words. Do you want to know the truth? You have never known the meaning of chastity, and you would do better, my daughter, to die honorably than live in shame."

Distressed by the widow's words, Carmesina ran from the room in tears, while Stephanie followed behind, comforting her mistress as best she could.

"What a curse," cried the princess, "that I should not only be subject to my parents but also scolded by that wet nurse who gave me suck! What would she do if she really saw me dishonored? I believe she would broadcast it throughout the palace and the whole city. May God punish her for her damned lying tongue!"

"No one," said Stephanie, "could persuade me to stop dancing and courting as befits noble ladies. It is customary for courtly damsels to be loved and wooed, as there are three kinds of love: virtuous, profitable, and sinful. The first kind is when some mighty lord, prince, duke, count, or marquis loves a maiden, for great is her honor when other damsels see him dancing, jousting, or making war in her name, and she should love such a man because his love is virtuous. The profitable kind is when some gentleman or knight of ancient lineage woos a damsel, inducing her through gifts to do his will, though she only loves him for his money. I care little for this kind, because when the gifts end so does the love. The sinful kind is when a damsel loves some gentleman or knight for her pleasure, a man so stuffed with sweet words that she will have enough for a year, but if they go a step further, spending a winter night together in a canopied bed with perfumed sheets, then that is the kind of love I prefer."

Hearing Stephanie speak so wittily, the princess broke into a smile and forgot her sorrows.

"Now my lady," said Stephanie, "I shall tell you the three articles of faith, for God graced women with such natures that if men understood us, they would have far less trouble inducing us to do their bidding. We all possess three inborn qualities which, as I have them myself, I can recognize in others: first, we are greedy; second, we love sweets; and third, we are lustful. The first article is that any man who courts a woman should discover which quality dominates her. If she is greedy, for example, and has another lover, you must give her money, for only thus will she forsake your rival, and once you have her, you can get yours back and hers too. If she has a sweet tooth, send her candy, exotic fruits, or whatever she prefers, and if she is lustful, just tell her how much you need what she likes best. There is something still better, however, which is that when married women fall in love, it is always with men lower than their husbands, though every woman is born with the word *Chastity* engraved on her brow in gold. I would not dare to share this with anyone but you, for I accuse myself more than others, but if you doubt my words, look at that Countess of Underlook, who committed adultery and was punished by her husband. One night, while he was sleeping safe and sound beside her, she smuggled her gentleman lover into the room, and not a very noble gentleman at that. Awakened by strange noises, the count found his wife gone, whereupon he sprang to the floor, began shouting, and seized the sword by his bedside. The countess blew out the candle, but her son, who slept next door, also leapt up, lit a torch, and hurried to aid his father. Seeing her son with that torch, the gentleman beheaded him. Then the count slew the lover and countess, punishing them for their evil ways."

While they were talking, they heard the empress calling Carmesina, who went out into the hall. Upon seeing her daughter, the empress asked why her eyes were red.

"My lady," replied the princess, "my head has ached all day."

The empress made her sit on her lap and kissed her many times.

The next day, Tirant told Diaphebus: "Cousin, I pray you go to the palace and speak with Carmesina to see whether she is vexed with me."

Upon his arrival, Diaphebus found the imperial family at Mass, after which he approached the princess, who asked where Tirant was.

"My lady," replied Diaphebus, "he left our lodgings to dispense justice."

"If you knew," cried the princess, "what a joke he played on me yesterday! He confessed his love with a mirror, but just let me see that knight, for I shall tell him a few things he will not wish to hear."

"Alas, good lady!" replied Diaphebus. "Tirant bore his flame to you but found none burning in your breast."

"Yes he did," said the princess, "but the wood was holly and he drenched it in cold water, yet one can find more in this palace, and it will burn better too! It is a wood called loyalty, which is soft, dry, and comforting to whoever lights it."

"My lady, what do you think of this suggestion?" asked Diaphebus.

"With Your Highness's leave, let us take some of your dry wood and some of ours, which is damp, and pile them together in your image and Tirant's?"

"No," said the princess, "for opposites cannot mix." They continued this banter all the way to her chambers, where Diaphebus left the lady and hastened to tell Tirant of their conversation.

After they had dined and Tirant thought the emperor was probably asleep, he and Diaphebus returned to the palace. Stephanie saw them from the window and hurried to tell her mistress: "My lady, our knights are coming!"

The princess went out to receive Tirant, who bowed deeply before her, but Carmesina's greeting was very cold. Troubled by her manner, the captain humbly whispered: "Lady endowed with all perfections, I beg you to share your thoughts with me, for I have never seen Your Highness act this way."

"My conduct," replied the princess, "may not please God or the world, but since you do such unheard-of things, I shall tell you how your scant honor came to my notice."

· C X X V I I I ·

H OW THE PRINCESS UPBRAIDED TIRANT FOR HIS DECLARATION OF LOVE

"I believe you were born with little wisdom, for had you more, you would not sully your honor. Your shameful deeds show that, fearing neither God nor disgrace, you have scorned my generous father's gifts, though he preferred you to all his lords. When word of your presumption spreads, what will people say: that the emperor's daughter, a woman of high degree, was courted by a captain whom she loved and trusted! You have betrayed the reverence due me, showing bad faith like a dishonest judge and offending the worthy emperor and myself! Were I to tell him, you would lose your honor, fame, worldly glory, the obedience of our soldiers, and the office you now hold, for if you yourself were virtuous and saw some vice or fault in me, you would be obliged to rebuke me in my father's stead. Such is the faith and trust he placed in you, wherefore it would be just and proper for me to kneel at his feet, crying out for justice in the presence of all his barons and knights, lamenting your affront in boldly treating me like a common woman. Then the imperial court would learn of your treachery and victory would be mine, though perhaps gallants and courtiers would not agree, as I would have told my parents in everyone's presence. In all honesty, I can say that you have reversed your cloak of honor, and your great offense will be notorious throughout the world."

Carmesina rose to enter her chamber, but Tirant pursued her, clutched her mantle, and begged her to hear him out, while Stephanie and Diaphebus also pleaded until at last she sat down again. Then Tirant began to speak in the following manner:

· CXXIX ·

*H*OW TIRANT EXPLAINED WHY HE HAD DECLARED HIMSELF AND WOULD NOW KILL HIMSELF FOR LOVE

"Oh most virtuous of mortals: Your Ladyship must know that love's sovereign power can move the heavens. Those philosophers who delight in celestial movements hold love alone to be the prime mover, for just as the planets keep their courses for love of their own natures, so do all elements love those things pertaining to their kind. Having contemplated your nobility, I placed myself in your power, with a heart so troubled that I forgot my own station, and now I see Your Highness condemning me to destruction, placing guards around my soul to shorten my woeful life. Thus did Fortune bring me low—I, who had always concealed my passion, for despite my fear of your wrath, love forced me to disclose my thoughts, and if I have erred, you should forgive me as I am love's humble slave. Accuse love but pity your devoted servant, since were you not endowed with such perfections, my eyes would not rejoice in what they see, and the day they first beheld you, they would not have made you their mistress. Lest I anger Your Highness, I shall only answer your unjust rebuke. You should know that if the saints fashioned a mortal damsel in your likeness, I would feel obliged to worship her, and still more if she were an emperor's daughter! Throughout the world, you will find knights of greater dignity, lineage, riches, honor, fame, grace, gentility, bravery, and ardor (and of these last, you will find more than the hairs on my head), but my lady, in a thousand years you will never see a knight, page, or squire who desires your glory, honor, and prosperity as I do, nor one who thus seeks to pile service upon service, honor upon honor, or delight upon delight. Your Highness will give me peace, if one may speak of peace amid tribulations.

"Therefore, you will learn the extent of my devotion, and as my erring heart roused your ire, I shall cut it in two before the sun passes the Pillars of Hercules, sending one half to Your Highness, who may thus be avenged, and the other to my mother, who bore it nine months in her womb. Oh glorious Phoebus, who calms my troubled thought: extinguish your light, that I may have my wish! Do you recall the day I asked you which was better: to die well or badly? Upon hearing your reply, I knew that if I revealed even part of my sufferings, you would find me dead one night in a corner of my room. This will be the last year, month, day, and hour of my life, though, alas, I hoped to do much for your noble father! For love of you, I labored to strengthen his empire, knowing that some day Your Highness would inherit it, wherefore I kneel and beg one last favor. When I am dead, enshroud my body and have them write on my tomb: *Here lies Tirant lo Blanc, who died of loving too well.*"

With tears and doleful sighs, he then returned to his lodgings.

Seeing him leave so disconsolately, the princess was wracked by love and grief, while bitter tears mingled with sighs and sobs as she cried aloud: "Come, oh faithful damsels, and share my torments! Alas, what shall I do, for I fear to lose Tirant, whose heart is so lofty that he will quickly fulfill his promise. Therefore, Stephanie, beg our captain to forgive me and to do nothing rash. How I rue my words, for my pleasure in speaking them will now make Tirant hate me. My anger has turned to pity, though Tirant seems to have none."

Heeding their tearful mistress, Stephanie and a young damsel hurried to Tirant's lodgings, where they found him removing his cape while Diaphebus tried to comfort him.

When Stephanie saw him in his tunic, she thought he was about to slay himself and threw herself at his feet as though he were her natural lord. Then she spoke the following words: "Lord Tirant, after all your glorious deeds, will you sacrifice their prize for such scant cause? Stay your hand, lest you forfeit both honor and fame, for works of mercy excel those of wrath. Will you damn your soul because my lady scolded you? I swear that she only intended to joke, but you are too quickly moved to fury! Therefore, do not tax Fortune, which has smiled upon you till now."

Seeing Stephanie on her knees, our knight also knelt, as she was the princess's friend and a damsel of high degree, being the emperor's niece and a noble duke's daughter. Moved by her gentle pleas, Tirant then replied: "My woes are such as will brook no delay, for flames of love scorch my heart and torment me beyond endurance. My soul longs to end this wretched world's travails, and if I am not mistaken, my sufferings below will be far lighter. They will not be caused by love, which exceeds all other afflictions, nor does death dismay me, since I shall be reborn in glorious fame and men will say I died for the noblest woman alive, wherefore, my lady, please leave me with my sorrow."

Carmesina's anguish redoubled when Stephanie failed to return, until at last she could bear no more and summoned a maid named Pleasure-of-my-life. Tying a kerchief around her head, the princess led her down to the garden, where they found the gate open and reached Tirant's quarters without being recognized. When Tirant saw them enter, he threw himself on the floor, while his lady knelt and began to speak thus:

· CXXX ·

*H*OW THE PRINCESS BEGGED TIRANT TO FORGIVE HER HARSH WORDS

"Tirant, I know my tongue has offended you yet I beg your forgiveness, for when one's soul is saddened, wrath often casts out pity, but I, recovering my good faith and overcome by compassion, now apologize for my ire and humbly beg your pardon."

Hearing his lady's sweet request, Tirant felt as happy as if she had sworn eternal love, while Stephanie said: "Now that peace has been made, I promised you would let Tirant kiss your hair if he obeyed you."

"I shall be happy," replied the princess, "to let him kiss my eyes and forehead, if he promises as a knight to go no further."

Tirant swore it with a good will, and all his sorrow turned to joy as Carmesina led them into the palace garden.

Then the princess sent Pleasure-of-my-life to fetch her other damsels and the Easygoing Widow, who had seen the entire masque and was troubled for the princess's sake, and still more for her own. Soon the emperor awoke and, seeing Tirant below, he went down and said: "Captain, I had summoned you but you were nowhere to be found."

"Sire," replied Tirant, "I called on Your Majesty but they told me you were sleeping, and lest I disturb you, I brought my knights to dance and sport."

"Evil indeed is our sport today," said the emperor, "for we must quickly summon the council."

He ordered the council bell rung, and when everyone had gathered, an emissary read his letter of credence. The emperor said they should know the bad news, as it could not be hidden, whereupon the emissary gave his report, which was of the following tenor:

· CXXXI ·

*T*HE EMISSARY'S REPORT

"Most excellent lord, I notify Your Serene Majesty that his grand constable and captain have sent me hence. Last Thursday night, more than fourteen thousand enemy soldiers hid among the reeds in a swampy field near our camp, and when the sun rose, we saw about fourteen hundred Turkish cavalry across the river. Then the Duke of Macedonia, a haughty man ignorant of warfare, had the trumpets blown and ordered everyone to arms. The constable and his knights tried to dissuade him, but he spurned their pleas, and, after leading his troops to the river, he ordered them to ford it. The water came up to the horses' saddles, and in some places they had to swim.

"As our horses climbed the other bank, many lost their footing, fell in the water, and were carried away, though if the duke had crossed a mile upstream, everyone might have reached land safely. After giving way slightly that we might clamber ashore, our foes retreated toward a low hill with the duke in hot pursuit. Once your valiant captains had joined the fray, those in hiding sallied forth with great fury and a terrible slaughter ensued, during which the fainthearted duke fled.

"The Grand Turk, the sultan, and their royal allies then besieged the city, along with all the Italian and Lombard dukes, counts, and marquises who had joined them. When the sultan heard of the rout, he had himself crowned Emperor of Greece, and they say he will not desist till he has captured the duke's entire army and stormed Constantinople. I can tell you, my lord, that the duke only has food for a month or two, wherefore Your Highness should take counsel and determine what you wish to do."

Tirant said: "Tell me, knight, by your courage: how many men died in that battle?"

The knight answered: "Lord captain, after reviewing our squadrons, we found that among those killed, drowned, and missing, we lack 11,722 men.

The emperor said: "Tirant, I beg you for the love of God to set out within two or three weeks and relieve those poor souls."

"My lord," replied Tirant, "how can you ask me to wait three weeks, when our foes may storm the city and take it at any moment?" Then Tirant asked the emissary how many troops the enemy had, to which he replied: "On my faith, those Turks are battle-hardened, cruel, and merciless. In our estimate and according to some prisoners' accounts, there are more than eight hundred thousand of them."

"In that case, sire," said Tirant, "I think your criers should first offer money to all those who have been or wish to be in your pay, and then inform them that we shall set out within six days."

The emperor thought it an excellent idea and was pleased by Tirant's courage.

Once the cry had gone out, the great lords outside the city were summoned, and they assembled on the appointed day along with those who had come from Sicily. News of the defeat had spread through Constantinople, and a great multitude of men and women gathered in the central market. Some mourned relatives, some friends, and others the empire's doom, as it seemed about to fall and their sole remaining hope was God. They feared starvation, thirst, and the burning of their homes, while two barons suggested that Carmesina might be safer in Hungary.

When Tirant heard these words, he turned white as a sheet and the emperor asked what had made him lose his color.

"My lord," replied Tirant, "I have had a stomachache all day."

The emperor quickly told his doctors to give him some medicine, and once Tirant had recovered, His Majesty asked Carmesina: "My daughter, what do you think about going to Hungary? It seems a good idea, since if the empire were lost, you would still be safe."

The noble lady replied in this manner:

· CXXXII ·

*T*HE PRINCESS'S REPLY TO HER FATHER

"Oh generous father, why risk my life and your tranquility when you know fickle Fortune can only be conquered by Providence? If you wish to die in peace, keep me in your court, as I would sooner perish here than pine away in some foreign land."

When the emperor heard his daughter's loving words and saw that she wished to die by his side, he was the happiest man on earth.

That evening, Tirant set out with two Greek guides and two hundred soldiers, and after traveling all night they reached a great plain called Goodvale that was full of beasts trying to avoid the enemy. Once Tirant's men had captured all the mares and tied them together, he sent his soldiers toward the enemy camp with orders to seize any others they could find. Having completed his mission, he returned to Constantinople.

The next day, the Christians blessed their banners with a great parade and celebration. All the knights donned their armor and mounted their steeds. First came the emperor's banner, borne by a warrior named Dryfount[11] on a splendid white charger, and after him came a banner with His Majesty's device: a silver Tower of Babylon upon a blue field. A gauntleted hand held a sword that transfixed the tower, and there was a motto in gold letters: *Fortune is mine.* All the emperor's servants marched with this banner, followed by the Dukes of Babylon, Sinope, and Persia. Then came the Dukes of Cassandria and Montesanto, both with the squadrons they had brought from Naples, and after them rode the Marquises of Saint Mark's in Venice and Montferrat. The Marquis of Saint George was next, looking extremely splendid, for his horses bore handsome trappings and his men were armed for battle. Then the Marquises of Pescara, Vasto, Arena, Brindisi, Prota, and Montenegro and the Prince of Taranto's bastard brother rode forth, leading the Counts of Bell-lloc, Plegamans, Àger, Acquaviva, Burgundy, Capaci, Aquino, and Benafrio, as well as Count Carlo di Malatesta and Count Giovanni di Vintimiglia from Sicily, each with his own soldiers.[12] Many other counts, viscounts, and captains were in the emperor's pay, and all told there were forty-eight squadrons with one hundred and eighty-three thousand men.

They all passed before the emperor, while Tirant kept order, wearing armor only upon his limbs and an imperial tunic over his mail. His squadron was last, carrying his banners with padlocks and ravens, but as it passed in review the emperor told him not to depart, as he wished to give him some letters for the Duke of Macedonia and others.

Once everyone had left the city, Tirant went to His Majesty's chambers, where he found him seated in an alcove dictating to his secretary. Seeing Tirant speechless for fear of disturbing his lord, the princess summoned him and said: "Captain, I know your departure is imminent, wherefore I pray God to give you victories, honor, and fame as great as Alexander's."

Tirant thanked her, while he knelt and kissed her hand for good luck. The princess said: "Tirant, tell me if I can help you in any way, for all your wishes will be granted by one who only seeks to be your friend."

"Oh peerless lady," replied Tirant, "Your Highness, like the phoenix, has no equal in degree or virtue. I would like to request, if you were willing to grant it, for truly such a gift would crown me above all the saints in Heaven, and I would never wish for anything else on earth . . . yet fear of refusal will seal my lips until you order me to speak."

"Captain," said the princess, "only a fool confuses right and wrong. Though I have never been to France, I understand your words and see that you wish to take me by force, yet I ask not for domination but for liberty in love. A king trusts whom he likes."

"My lady," replied Tirant, "do not banish me from your presence, for I am not like those Jewesses who invoke the Virgin's aid in giving birth and then go through their houses with white napkins, crying: 'Begone, oh Mary, from this Jewish home."

"God, what a precious fool!" exclaimed the princess. "Though you grant me all the wisdom and claim ignorance yourself, you seem to need no lawyers to help plead your case. Women's words are easily spoken, but I see that if I let you, you would abuse my innocent good will. All I meant was that should you need gold, silver, or jewels, I shall gladly supply them without my father's knowledge."

"My lady," replied Tirant, "as your obedient servant, I thank you infinitely, but I wanted to ask a special favor."

"If it is honorable," said the princess, "I shall grant it, but first I want to hear, since my nature is such that when I make a promise, I always keep it for better or worse. I never break my word, as my damsels will tell you, for when I say yes I mean yes and when I say no I mean no."

"All the greater your virtue," replied Tirant, "and I, my lady, ask only for that tunic you wear next to your skin, and that you let me remove it with my own hands."

"Holy Virgin!" cried the princess. "What are you saying? I would gladly give you the tunic along with all my jewels and clothing, but your hands should not touch where no other man's have."

She hastened to her room, took off the tunic and donned another, and went into the great hall, where Tirant was joking with her maids. She gave him the tunic, and, to make him even happier, she kissed it many times in front of everyone. Tirant accepted it with great joy and told the maids before he left: "If the emperor asks for me, say I shall soon return."

When Tirant reached his quarters, he donned the rest of his armor, while Diaphebus and Richard stood admiring their new coats of arms. Richard's was embroidered with heavy gold thread, and his motto was: *I cannot make head or tail of it.* Diaphebus's was covered with opium poppies, and the motto read: *What puts others to sleep wakes me up.* Once Tirant was fully armed, he looked at the princess's silk tunic, which had broad red stripes embroidered with anchors, as well as two mottos: *Those who feel good are in no hurry* and *Those who sit on the ground have no place to fall.* Tirant slipped the tunic over his armor, but as the sleeves touched the ground, he rolled the right one up to his shoulder and the left one to his elbow. After girding his waist with a gold cord, he hung an image of Saint Christopher and the Christ child around his neck.

Thus attired, the three knights went to bid their lord farewell, and upon reaching the palace, they found him waiting to dine with them. As soon as His Majesty saw Tirant, he asked: "Captain, what coat of arms is that?"

"Sire," said Tirant, "if you knew its powers you would be astonished."

"I should like to know," replied the emperor.

"It has the power," said Tirant, "to make one do good. The damsel who gave it to me when I left home was the fairest and most virtuous on earth, though I do not wish to denigrate your princess or the many other honorable damsels in your court."

The emperor said: "Certainly no great feat of arms was ever done except for love."

"I promise you, my lord," replied Tirant, "that in our first battle, I shall have both friends and foes gaping at this tunic."

The emperor sat down to dine with the empress, his daughter, and Tirant, while the other two knights sat at another table with the ladies and damsels. They all ate with great pleasure, and especially Tirant, since he was sharing his lady's plate[13] and thought himself luckier than he really was. Then the emperor led the empress, Carmesina, and his guests into another room, where he addressed these words to his valiant captain:

· CXXXIII ·

*H*OW THE EMPEROR SENT HIS CAPTAIN TO WAR WITH PLEAS AND EXHORTATIONS

"Adverse Fortune has assaulted our empire, robbing me of my worthy son, and as I myself am too old to bear arms, Divine Providence has now sent you, in whom all our hopes reside. I beg you dearly—knowing that you might display your courage in greater matters, though these are certainly perilous enough—to place your wisdom and valor at the service of our patrimony, and I have ordered my lords to love, honor, and obey you, protecting your life as though it were my own. Give these letters to the Duke of Macedonia, the grand constable, and the others to whom they are addressed."

Tirant replied: "My faith in God, who never forsakes His worshippers, assures me of victory, and Your Majesty should feel likewise, for with His help we shall triumph."

After kneeling to kiss the emperor's hand and bid him farewell, Tirant sought to do the same with Carmesina, but she would not permit it. When he had risen, the emperor gave him a sack of thirty thousand ducats, which Tirant refused, saying: "My lord, you have already given me more than enough armor, horses, jewels, provisions, and other items."

The princess said: "Since this is my lord's pleasure, you must oblige him."

Then Tirant and his friends took their leave of the emperor, but as they were about to depart, Richard suddenly said: "Would it not be noble sport, since the emperor is at his window and the ladies have come out to see us, to don our plumed helmets and fight a mock battle, first with lances and then with swords?"

"A splendid idea," replied Tirant and Diaphebus.

They mounted their steeds, donned their helmets in the courtyard, and jousted with lances, riding hither and yon on Sicilian chargers. Then they drew their swords and attacked, wheeling and encountering as they smote great buffets with the flats of their weapons. In the end, the two knights joined forces against Tirant, and it was glorious to behold them all tilting and turning. After fighting awhile, they bowed to the emperor and rode away.

All the ladies blessed the knights and prayed Our Lord to grant them victory.

The princess's angelic eyes were fixed on Tirant until he disappeared from sight, whereupon her vision was blurred by enamored tears, while her downhearted damsels all wept with their mistress. The emperor declared that he had not felt so lighthearted in many months: "I believe Tirant will prove a good captain and a valiant knight."

Once the knights were outside the city, they gave their war-horses to three pages and mounted other steeds, on which Diaphebus and Richard soon overtook their squadron, but Tirant went from group to group, visiting the men and keeping order.

After marching five leagues, they stopped in a fair meadow with several clear streams. As captain, Tirant never dismounted till his soldiers were peacefully encamped, and once they were settled, he went from tent to tent, inviting all his noblemen to sup with him that evening. They were as well served as if they had been in Constantinople, for he had brought the three finest cooks in France.

When everyone had eaten his fill, Tirant told his company and two thousand others to stand watch, and he also dispatched scouts to listen for any sign of movement. Tirant rode to and fro inspecting the camp until midnight, when he dismissed the guards who were not from his squadron and had another two thousand replace them. No knight could bring a page, and they had to be fully armored.

When Tirant was in the field, he only undressed to change his tunic, and two hours before dawn he would order the trumpets blown. Everyone then saddled his steed, while Tirant went to hear Mass, after which he donned his helmet and rode through the camp, making sure everyone was ready to go. By the time the sun rose, his men were armed and horsed, and they followed this same routine until they reached the city of Pelis, which was about one and a half leagues from the enemy camp. Every night they prepared for an attack, as Tirant feared the Turkish hordes.

Upon beholding Tirant's army, the Christians in Pelis threw open their gates, but our knight waited until nightfall for fear that they would be seen. They could not avoid being heard, however, and the Grand Turk soon learned of their presence. He hastened to inform the sultan, who replied: "How can you tell me an army has come? We know that so-called emperor had only those few wretched troops we routed the other day and who fled not like soldiers but like deer through the woods. Having conquered nine-tenths of the empire, we need only defeat the duke, march twenty-five leagues to Constantinople, take that emperor by the beard and throw him in prison, and make his daughter our chambermaid and the empress an army cook. Then my gold statue will gaze down upon the market square."

The Grand Turk replied: "My lord, all that may be, but you still should be cautious, for it is best not to underestimate your foes like that Trojan monarch, who perished with all his subjects because of such carelessness. One reads of many glorious princes who were destroyed in the same fashion: first they lost the kingdoms they sought to conquer, and then they lost their own."

"Well," said the sultan, "If that is your opinion . . ."

He drew one of his captains aside and said: "Behold that cowardly Turk full of shameful fear. He has been telling me all sorts of nonsense that must have come to him in some dream, but to make him happy, send someone to watch the road to Pelis."

Instead of one, the knight sent four scouts to determine how many soldiers had entered the city.

The day after he arrived in Pelis, Tirant went from house to house urging the townsfolk to shoe their horses and grease their saddles. Having done that, he chose a man who knew the land well, and together they set out to reconnoiter the Turkish camp. They rode up a hill and watched the Turks bombarding the town, whose inhabitants shoveled earth into the outworks to protect their walls from the stones. The whole countryside was so full of Turkish troops that no one could pass through it unnoticed, and the sultan's big painted tent was pitched on one side, while the Grand Turk's was on the other.

On their way back to Pelis, they spied the four Saracen scouts, and as soon as they had dismounted, Tirant went to the main square. There he found most of the townspeople, to whom he addressed these words: "Come closer, my friends. We have just reconnoitered the enemy camp, and as we were returning we saw four of their scouts. Whoever captures them will receive five hundred ducats apiece alive and three hundred dead."

Seven men who knew the countryside well set out together that night, and after walking awhile, one of them said: "Listen, here is what we should do: let us hide in the bushes near that stream, and when it gets hot tomorrow afternoon, the Saracens will come down to drink and we can capture them alive."

Having agreed to this plan, they hid and waited until the sun rose and they saw the scouts on a hill. Around midday, they felt thirsty and came down to drink at the stream, whereupon one Christian told the others: "Keep still and let them drink till they are too bloated to run."

After the scouts had drunk and eaten, the Christians rushed forth with bloodcurdling cries and captured them. One tried to escape, but they quickly cocked their crossbows and felled him. Then they cut off his head, stuck it on a lance, and, having tied up the others, they returned to their captain.

Feeling thoroughly pleased, Tirant placed the three scouts under guard and asked their captors: "How much do I owe you?"

"Lord captain," they replied, "you promised us eighteen hundred ducats, but give whatever you like and we shall be satisfied."

"By God," cried Tirant, "I shall do no such thing! You have done a good job and deserve to be paid."

He invited them to sup at the head of his table, and after the meal, he gave them two thousand ducats and identical silk doublets. All the other townspeople said they had never seen such a generous captain.

That same day, Tirant ordered everyone to eat an early supper, saddle his horse, and be armed and ready at nightfall. As soon as it was dark, he led his men forth, carefully separating the cavalry and infantry, while three thousand men followed them with the mares. As they approached the Turkish camp, he had his cavalry move away so the mares could come through without the Greek stallions smelling them.

Once the mares were near the camp, the three thousand men drove them in, sending half toward the sultan and the other half toward the Grand Turk. The Turkish stallions soon caught the scent. Some broke loose, others snapped their ropes, and still others tore up stakes in their eagerness to mount the mares. Seeing their horses running wild, the Turks dashed out of their tents in nightshirts and doublets, for they always slept unarmed as if they were inside the world's strongest castle.

After this commotion had lasted awhile and the camp was in an uproar, Tirant attacked from one side with half his men, while the Duke of Pera charged from the other, invoking Saint George. In less than an hour, the tents were down and there was a multitude of dead and wounded. Hearing his soldiers' death cries, the Grand Turk rushed out of his tent unarmed and leapt on his jennet. A Christian soldier killed his steed, but a Turkish knight rode up and gave the Grand Turk his horse. As the lord was remounting, his savior was slain by the Christians, who swept all before them in a dreadful slaughter, though they had feared such a horde might prove invincible.

Unarmed and mostly on foot, the Turks imitated their master, who had fled and was having his wound bandaged nearby. He sent a messenger to warn the sultan that the battle was lost, but upon learning that the Egyptian was in danger, the Grand Turk donned a coat of mail. He courageously returned to rescue his hard-pressed ally, and fortunately the two Saracen monarchs were not recognized. Beholding piles of corpses all around them, they decided to retreat, though they still could not fathom the cause of their discomfiture. It was the bloodiest battle ever fought in Greece.

Finally, the Grand Turk, the sultan, and some of their troops withdrew into the mountains, while other Saracens fled across the plain. Tirant and his men pursued them for three leagues, slaying as many as they caught and showing mercy to none. Those who took refuge in the mountains were saved, but those who chose the plain were killed or captured.

The ones who had chosen the mountains halted before a long wooden bridge. When the sultan had crossed with his soldiers, he saw his foes approaching and ordered it cut, whereupon those on the other side were massacred.

Truly, Tirant had won a victory over the victorious that day. He and his soldiers were dazzled by what seemed an act of God, for the ruse had worked perfectly. Upon reaching the bridge, the Christians found four thousand infidels, some of whom tried to swim, though many drowned in the attempt. Those on the other side resolved to withdraw as far up the mountain as they could go. There they fortified themselves. Once Tirant had returned to the plain, he saw the Saracens above and first considered an attack but then decided a siege would be better. He posted troops around the mountain and had his dukes and great lords pitch camp there.

It happened that the Duke of Macedonia, hearing the Christians' blood-curdling battle cries, had ordered all his cavalry and infantry to arms. They thought this was their final battle, for they expected no help and were certain they would either be slain or enslaved. When they heard the shouts continue and saw no one approach the city, they were puzzled. At daybreak, the tumult ceased and the watchmen saw the emperor's banners around the camp, while his troops pursued the fleeing Turks across the plain. The watchmen called to those who had stayed behind to loot or because they were disabled, and thus they learned that Tirant's clever stratagem had given them victory.

Finding that there were no Turks left except the wounded, the Duke of Macedonia sallied forth with his troops and stripped the camp of its gold, silver, clothing, arms, and jewels. Not even in the histories of Rome and Troy can you read of such a rich camp being so quickly despoiled.

Once they had gathered everything, they took it into the city, determined not to let Tirant's company enter. Thus it often happens that good and bad go hand in hand, for the city, which had been half destroyed, was now rich and prosperous. When they had stored the booty, they rode toward the banners on the plain, marveling at all the corpses they passed on the way.

Learning from his scouts that an army was approaching, Tirant ordered everyone to arms and hastily marshaled his troops, since he thought the Turks had regrouped in the towns they still controlled. As he was riding forth to meet them, he recognized the imperial banners and gave his helmet to a page, while all his captains followed suit. Once they were near the duke, Tirant dismounted and approached him, but the lord's only response was to silently place his hand on Tirant's head. The other captains thought this gesture despicable and refused to dismount for him. Then our knight remounted and told the duke about the battle, but he hardly replied, though his men honored Tirant's company. Thus the victors and vanquished mingled as they rode toward the camp.

Tirant told the duke: "My lord, if you wish to stay in this fair meadow, I shall move my men elsewhere."

The duke replied: "I prefer not to be near you and shall find another place."

"Just as you like," said Tirant, "but I said that out of courtesy and respect for your lofty station."

Refusing to let him finish, the duke jerked his horse around and rode off without a word. He and his men pitched camp a mile upstream.

Having dismounted, Tirant dispatched three of his finest knights, one of whom told the duke: "My lord, our captain invites you to dine with him, for though he knows Your Grace has better food, his will be ready sooner."

"How tiresome of him," replied the duke, "to vex me so when I have never harmed him. Tell him that I decline his invitation."

He scornfully turned his back, while the knights silently turned to go, but as they were leaving the duke said: "Tell Tirant I want him to dine with me."

"My lord," replied Diaphebus, "there is not a single fire lit in your camp. What can you offer him? All you have is food for hens and drink for cows."

The duke angrily replied: "I can give him chickens, capons, partridges, and pheasants."

The knights had heard enough and rode away.

When they were gone, one of the duke's vassals said: "My lord, you misunderstood that knight's words, for hens eat bran and cows drink water."

"By my father's bones," cried the duke, "you are right: his meaning escaped me! These foreigners are very arrogant, but had I understood his words, I would have sent him running home holding his head."

Having received the duke's reply, Tirant's only concern was to feed his dukes, counts, and marquises. After lunch, they rode one league downstream to a town called Lookfish, which the Turks had abandoned upon hearing of their rout. As soon as the captain arrived, he was given the keys to the town and its fortress. He ordered its Greek inhabitants to sell food to his men, and that well-provisioned town supplied Tirant's whole camp.

Then Tirant told the aldermen to erect six or seven gibbets near his camp, with a dead body swinging from each one. They spread the word that one man had tried to rape a woman, another had stolen, and still another had taken something and then refused to pay for it. When Tirant returned to his camp, he had the criers announce that anyone who robbed any church, raped any woman of whatever estate, or took anything without payment would be executed. Fear swept through the troops when they heard the cry and saw the corpses, as Tirant was both loved and dreaded by his men.

As night approached, the famished and besieged Turks reached an agreement, for they saw their only alternatives were to die or surrender. They sent a messenger, offering to submit if their foes would spare them, and in that instance Tirant preferred mercy to cruelty. He accepted, sending food and everything else they needed.

The next morning, Tirant had a handsome double tent erected with a bell hanging from the top. This tent, which was used only for Mass and council, stood in a meadow between his camp and the duke's. When it was time for Mass, Tirant invited the duke, who haughtily refused, though his vassals all attended. So courteous was Tirant that he humbled himself before them, giving precedence to the other lords at Mass and at table. After the service, his men held council and decided to send the Marquis of Saint George, the Count of Acquaviva, and two other barons to the duke. When they arrived, the Marquis of Saint George began to speak thus:

· C X X X I V ·

HOW TIRANT SENT THE MARQUIS OF SAINT GEORGE AND THE COUNT OF ACQUAVIVA TO THE DUKE OF MACEDONIA

"Lord duke, you should not be surprised at our arrival, as we were sent by our brave captain and his illustrious dukes, counts, and marquises. May it please you, in accord with divine and human justice, to grant us a share of the spoils you took from our enemies."

"It soothes my ears," replied the duke, "to hear idle chatter from foolish folk. How can you think I would agree to such a thing, when we have battled day and night with sweat and blood to preserve our faith, warring ceaselessly against those infidels and foregoing all bodily pleasures? Instead of perfumed sheets, we smell of hard steel, and instead of playing harps or other instruments, our hands wield swords. Our eyes have grown unused to the sight of ladies in our chambers, while our feet are unacquainted with dancing and sport, for we only gaze upon and run toward our enemies in combat, and since we won these spoils, breaking the siege like worthy knights, how dare you arrogantly demand what is not yours? Tell that captain he would be wiser to depart, for if he stays, I shall make him drink so much water that with half of it, he will have more than enough."[14]

The marquis replied: "I am no herald or pursuivant, but if you write or say this to Tirant, he will certainly satisfy you. We are all Bretons under one leader, and being old friends, each of us knows his fellows' worth. Your courage is mere wind, for you are not feared but scorned. What did you ever do except lose battles, sacrificing thousands of knights through your folly? Innumerable brave men have been killed or enslaved because of you, and now you have looted that camp, not like a captain or prince but like a thief in the night. How could you have been given such an office? Such posts should be reserved for men of proven mettle, whereas you are unschooled in honor but wise in trickery. There is nothing good in you, for you betray His Imperial Majesty and wrap yourself in haughtiness and insults."

"I know," replied the duke, "that these rash words come not from you but from your brother and that new captain. This time I shall forgive you, but the next will not be so easy."

"Forgive yourself and your subordinates," cried the marquis, "but not me or my companions! The Duke of Pera and our captain are not accustomed to affronting others, for their glorious fame will be perpetual and immortal. Now those valiant knights are besieging your besiegers, but I shall waste no more words. Tell me your answer: yes or no."

"Why speak in vain?" asked the duke. "I have told you I shall not share it."

"If you refuse to share it willingly," the marquis said, "we shall resort to force. Marshal your troops, for you will see us within the hour."

The emissaries returned to their camp, where they found the captain and his great lords gathered in the big tent. The marquis told them the duke's reply and shouted: "Everyone to arms! Such insults shall not pass!"

The marquis and the others rushed from the tent, but Tirant forbade them to arm or mount their steeds under pain of death. He went through the camp, reminding his knights of their oaths, begging them not to do such unthinkable things, and warning that if they fought a battle, the Turkish prisoners would mutiny.

"Oh, what shame that we, who are brothers-in-arms, should slay each other!" Speaking gently to some and joking with others, he persuaded them not to blacken their knightly honor with brawls or treason and called the recalcitrant ones to order as knights under his command.

Having soothed everyone, he went to the Duke of Macedonia, whom he found armed and waiting with all his men. Tirant persuaded him to dismount, but the duke refused to let his men disarm or unsaddle their horses.

Once calm had been restored, Tirant sent some men to the abandoned camp with orders to collect all the jubbahs they could find. Some knights asked what he wanted them for, and he replied that they might be useful.

When the battle was over and the Saracens were in flight, Diaphebus, after pondering how to spread Tirant's renown, went before his cousin and requested the captain's ring. Tirant took off his gauntlet, removed the ring, and gave it to Diaphebus, who rode among the hurrying soldiers till he found his trustiest squire. Then he gave him the ring and told him what to say to the emperor and Carmesina.

The squire, following his master's orders, spurred his mount and rode so hard that he reached Constantinople before anyone else. The damsels saw him coming and, recognizing him as Pyramus, they hurried to the princess's chamber and cried: "Your Highness, we shall soon have certain news of our knights! Pyramus has arrived in such a hurry that he must bear either glorious or dreadful tidings!"

Laying aside her embroidery, the princess hurried to the head of the stairs and saw Pyramus's horse so bathed in sweat that it looked like it had just been in a rainstorm. She asked him: "Good friend, what message do you bring?"

"Of the best, my lady," replied Pyramus. "Where is the emperor, for I expect my guerdon as a bringer of glad tidings."

"On his behalf and mine, I promise you shall have it."

She took his hand and led him to the emperor's chamber, where they knocked until he awoke and opened the door. Then Pyramus knelt and said: "Reward me, sire, for I bring joyous news."

Once the emperor had promised to reward him, Pyramus gave him the ring, telling him about the battle and their miraculous victory: "Your captain pursued them, killing and beheading those miscreants, and he gave me this ring that you might know of Our Lord's great blessing."

The emperor replied: "Welcome, my friend. Except for the glory of Paradise, nothing could cheer me more."

He ordered the bells rung throughout the city, whose inhabitants went to the Hagia Sophia to thank God and the Holy Virgin for their triumph.

When the commoners heard the news and beheld their mirthful lord, they turned the day into a great celebration, for the city had regained its power, glory, and ancient freedom.

His Majesty rewarded the squire with two thousand ducats, silk robes, a splendid Sicilian charger, armor, and everything else he might need, while the empress took off her mantle, which was of black velvet lined with sable, and gave it to Pyramus in front of everybody. The princess also contributed a heavy gold chain.

On the morrow, the emperor gave the squire a letter for Tirant.

Having pacified his camp, Tirant set out with sixteen hundred cavalry to reconquer the many nearby towns and castles, which he easily won back.

The day after that, three emissaries arrived, but since the bridge was down they had to cross the river in a fisherman's boat. One of these emissaries was a man of great wisdom, whom the Grand Turk loved as a son and constantly consulted. There was no one in all pagandom of such learning and eloquence, and his words were always both sound and judicious. This Saracen's name was Abdullah, but because of his sagacity he had been given the surname Solomon. He attached a sheet of paper to a pole to show he was requesting safe-conduct.

When the Duke of Macedonia saw the signal, he hoisted a white flag, whereupon the emissaries, who thought he was the captain, made their way to his camp and gave him the letter. After reading it, the duke said it was not for him and sent word to Tirant that some emissaries would await him in the great tent. Tirant summoned his dukes and lords, with whom he went to meet the visitors.

Upon reaching the tent, the Saracens received a cordial welcome and gave Tirant the sultan's letter, which was of the following tenor:

· C X X X V ·

THE SULTAN'S LETTER TO TIRANT LO BLANC[15]

I, Armenius, by Allah's will and leave Sultan of Babylon and ruler of three realms—the Greek Empire, Solomon's temple in Jerusalem, and our holy shrine in Mecca—lord and defender of all Muslims under Heaven, upholder and protector of the Prophet Mohammed's sacred teachings, which give endless comfort and glory to those who accept them, eat of the grass and drink of the water in scorn of Christianity, by right of my noble station and to my greater glory. To you, Tirant lo Blanc, captain of the Greeks and defender of Christianity, we send our respectful greetings and declare, after deliberation with the Grand Turk and five subject kings under my command, as well as ten more in my own land, that if you desire peace or a six-month truce, we shall turn a white face to you,[16] offering the aforesaid with reverence toward Almighty Allah, whom all men should serve, for He created and rules us. Give credence to our emissaries in everything they say. Written in our camp on the eastern beach, the second day of the moon of Our Holy Prophet Mohammed's nativity, etc.

When the letter had been read, Tirant asked the emissaries to explain their mission, whereupon Abdullah Solomon rose, bowed before him, and uttered the following words:

· C X X X V I ·

HOW THE SULTAN'S EMISSARY EXPLAINED HIS MISSION

"We, representing those glorious and magnanimous lords the Grand Turk and the sultan, have been sent to you, brave Tirant lo Blanc, who with victorious hand conquered our blessed camp, thus winning infinite riches for yourself and your companions. After that massacre, you imprisoned a small child who is our sultan's brother-in-law, wherefore we ask you on His Majesty's behalf, by your courtesy, knighthood, and the woman you cherish most—be she lady or damsel, widowed or married, and if you have not consummated your love may you do so shortly, and if you love only God may you be seated with the saints in Heaven—to free this child either for love or in exchange for a just ransom."

When Abdullah Solomon had spoken, Tirant replied:

· CXXXVII ·

TIRANT'S REPLY TO THE SULTAN'S EMISSARIES

"Glory cannot bring grief when men act justly, while the future depends on Fortune, which, being uncertain, should be a little feared, though good judgment is within our reach and its use is praiseworthy. I shall do my utmost to honor the sultan without prejudicing my lord, and since you ask me to free a prisoner in the name of the lady I love best—one who deserves to rule the world, including your land and mine—I shall free him along with forty others. As for your other request, I shall consider it in due course and give you an answer."

Having summoned his bailiffs, Tirant told them to let the emissaries select forty-one prisoners, and so it was done.

Once the emissaries had left, a Greek knight who knew which Turks were of high degree and might be ransomed, said: "Lord captain, I urge you before all these lords to reconsider your promise, for some of these prisoners can pay ransoms of twenty-five or thirty thousand ducats. Give the Turks some paupers, and they will rejoice just to receive the boy."

"I prefer," said Tirant, "to offer gifts worthy of glory, wherefore I shall free these prisoners on my own behalf and in the emperor's name."

Tirant then turned to his great magnates and said: "Most illustrious princes and lords, we have heard our foes' request. What is your advice? Will this truce benefit the emperor?"

First the Duke of Macedonia spoke: "Noble and highborn lords, this matter affects me most, as I am closest to the imperial throne. I suggest that we accept either peace or a truce, whether it helps the emperor or not. If they want a respite of two or three years, we should grant that too, for we shall be able to rest and plead with them to quit the empire or reach some compromise."

The Duke of Pera interrupted him, for the two could not abide each other and both hoped to wed Princess Carmesina. He said: "Fortune favors those who pursue her but scorns the haughty, while virtue's enemy is pride, which admits no equal. Thus was Satan cast out of Heaven, and pride has always gone before a fall, wherefore I believe that we can best serve the emperor by granting neither peace nor truce. We won this battle, and with God's help we shall win many more, but I shall respect these lords' judgment should they decide against me."

Many knights thought they should accept a truce or peace, though still more sided with the Duke of Pera.

"Now," declared Tirant, "since you have all spoken, I have more right than anyone, being the emperor's captain general."

After giving the constable and marshals His Majesty's letters, he said: "Speaking on the emperor's behalf, I believe it would serve no purpose to grant these heathens a truce. They sue for peace because of the great destruction you wrought among them, but you know they expect the Genoese to keep bringing soldiers and horses until they replace their lost army with such a multitude that all Christendom will not suffice to stop them. Though they are desperate now, I shall not accept their offer, and if I can, I shall give them such frequent battles that they will quit the empire and beg us for peace."

The Duke of Macedonia cried: "Tirant, if you refuse to accept a truce, I shall, and I advise everyone under my command to do the same!"

"Lord duke," replied Tirant, "respect the emperor's orders, for otherwise I shall have to send you back to him in chains. I have no wish to do so, as I am not here for personal gain but to serve His Majesty, who has honored me far beyond my deserts. You, my valiant lord, have lost all your lands and would do better to die bravely than to live in shameful poverty. If you disbelieve me, read what wise Titus Livius says in one of his epistles: 'A knight should uphold three things: his honor, his riches, and his life. He should risk his life and riches for his honor, his life for his riches, and his honor and riches to safeguard his life.'[17] Therefore, lord duke, you should urge us to recover your patrimony instead of trying to blunt our courage."

The duke tearfully rose and returned to his camp, while our knight's men also returned to theirs. Once a canopy had been erected near a cool spring by Tirant's camp, he seated the emissaries at one table, his prisoners at another, and his dukes and lords at a third. The emissaries, who were served chickens, capons, pheasants, rice, couscous, and many other dishes and fine wines, praised the handsome ceremony with which the Christians dined, and when the meal ended, a sumptuous dessert of cakes and malmsey was brought forth.

The Marquis of Saint George asked the Turks how many men they had lost, to which they replied that some fifty-three thousand had perished or been captured. Then Tirant led his guests to the great tent, though the duke refused to go.

When everyone was seated, the Breton began to speak thus:

· CXXXVIII ·

*T*IRANT'S REPLY TO THE EMISSARIES' OTHER PROPOSALS

"Though a knight's duty is to seek battle and win glorious victories, you should not forget the ancient Greeks, whose splendor will live as long as Troy's memory endures. Our emperor's grandeur outshines even theirs, for his generosity and dignity entitle him to rule the world, whereas your lords, fearing neither God nor the curses of Christians and Saracens alike, have defied chivalry and tried to usurp his title and throne. I trust, however, that God will help me slay your treacherous masters, who have stolen most of the empire and now seek to steal the rest. Acting with inhuman cruelty, they have blackened their good names, wherefore you may tell them that I shall grant no truces till they swear on the Kaaba before all honorable knights to quit this empire within six months. Do not think me prideful or arrogant, as my purpose is to serve God and justice, knowing that in these matters I shall have many judges and few advocates."

Abdullah Solomon replied: "Oh unjust Fortune, how you favor this newfangled captain, awarding him victory and inflicting great damage on our armies! But to embolden your noble spirit, I wish to show myself as much counselor as foe, telling you how to preserve and augment your honor and fame. The Romans, in their day, would have been satisfied with such good luck, for your name, valor, and noble bearing foreshadow a lofty destiny. Do not think I sue for peace while threatening war, but as you refuse, you may expect us on the fifteenth day of this moon, when you will see such a multitude of Saracens that the earth will tremble beneath them."

Wise Abdullah Solomon turned toward the river Trasimene,[18] crying: "Peaceful Trasimene, your face is white, but soon it will be red with blood as we behold terrible battles that will be famed throughout the world. Though you, brave captain, lament the harm done your emperor, you should not be surprised, for the more excellent, noble, and mighty a realm, the greater its neighbors' malice and envy. Thus have the Greeks always faced cruel enemies, nor could so many kings and great lords justly surrender the greater part of this empire. The best you can do is hold fast to your Christian faith."

Once Abdullah Solomon had spoken, the emissaries returned to the river, where Tirant gave them generous gifts for which they thanked him profusely.

After they had crossed in the little boat, Tirant told Diaphebus to set out for Constantinople that night with a strong escort and the prisoners.

As Diaphebus approached the city, all the commoners, both men and women, flocked to see the prisoners, while the emperor and his ladies stood at the palace windows. Trailing the Saracen banners behind them, Diaphebus's men delivered forty-three hundred captives, whom His Majesty quickly locked in the palace dungeons.

The emperor asked Diaphebus to remove his armor and placed a long robe of state embroidered with jewels upon his shoulders. Then the monarch seated himself upon a stool, with his ladies around him, and urged his guest to recount everything that had happened from the day of Tirant's departure. You may be sure the knight omitted no detail in his captain's praise and honor, and though the emperor was pleased, the princess was still more so. Diaphebus and his retinue were well provided for, and only damsels were allowed to serve them.

After supper, they escorted their guest to a room hung with tapestries, where Diaphebus knelt and thanked them for the honor they had done him. They discussed the war till after midnight, and the emperor asked about Tirant's plans, to which Diaphebus replied that they would certainly fight another cruel battle within a few days. Finally, the emperor and his ladies left Diaphebus to rest, but they asked him to spend the night in that room.

The next day, His Majesty paid Diaphebus fifteen ducats apiece for the prisoners and told him to give the money to Tirant.

As soon as Carmesina heard that Diaphebus was unoccupied, she summoned the knight, who had been anxiously waiting to speak with Stephanie. Upon seeing him, the princess asked: "Dear brother, what news do you bring from one who holds my soul in thrall? When shall I see him safely by my side? You may well believe that such is my fondest wish, for though he may forget me, I shall compensate for his failings through redoubled love."

Diaphebus replied: "If Tirant could hear your words, his heart would fill with joy, while his spirit would soar aloft to seventh heaven. Your grace, beauty, virtue, and lofty station outshine all earthly damsels, nor could I say or do enough to repay your generosity. Therefore, I humbly thank you on Tirant's behalf and place my body, soul, and worldly goods at your command, but your angry words astound me, as Tirant is nothing but pure devotion. He has no faults in love, honor, or anything else concerning Your Highness, who, if you knew how he suffers, would cherish rather than scold him. He wears his armor past midnight, as though he were about to enter battle, and while everyone else is sleeping he wanders through the camp, often with the rain pouring down his back. When he finally reaches our tent, he comes straight to me and begins praising Your Highness. If I want to please and serve him, I need only spend two hours listening, and when we make war, he invokes you alone.

Often I ask him why he does not invoke some saint in your name, but he says those who serve many masters serve none."

Seeing her mistress take comfort from Diaphebus's words, Stephanie said: "Now that you two have spoken, it is my turn, so please hear me out. Tell me, my lady: who deserves the imperial crown more than Tirant? You hold him in your hands and refuse to accept him, yet one day you will rue your cruelty, for you should love the one who loves you. Tirant does not seek your riches or title and only woos you for your noble virtues. Alas, foolish woman, what more do you seek? You will never find his equal in all the world, and your father's only wish is to see you happily married. What better choice than this youth, who is brave, generous, spirited, wise, and skilled in everything? Why did God not make me the emperor's daughter and you Stephanie? I assure you that if he lifted my skirts, I would remove my blouse and satisfy him in great measure, but if you marry some foreign king, he may make you miserable, and should you wed some Greek like my father, who by rank is your most eligible suitor, I shall speak out against it, since when you want to play he will be snoring. Tirant is the one you need to expand your empire, and he will chase you through every nook and cranny in your bedroom, sometimes naked and sometimes in your nightshirt."

The princess roared with laughter at Stephanie's words, to which Diaphebus replied: "Lady Stephanie, tell me the truth by your nobility: if Tirant had the good fortune to win the princess, whom would you select?"

"Diaphebus, my lord," replied Stephanie, "I assure you that if the princess married Tirant, I would choose his closest relative."

"In that case, it would be me, and all the more since I am your servant. Just as Tirant is a worthy match for one of peerless beauty and dignity, may you accept me as your chamberlain and kiss me in sign of troth."

"It would not be right or honorable," replied Stephanie, "for me to act without my lady's leave, as she has raised me from infancy and we are in her presence."

Diaphebus knelt, folded his hands, and begged the princess as devoutly as if she were a saint in Heaven to let him kiss Stephanie, but no matter how much he pleaded, she refused to consent. Finally, Stephanie said: "Oh heart hardened by cruelty! You never bend, however great the supplications! I shall not be happy and gay till I see that glorious Tirant with my own eyes."

"Alas, Diaphebus my brother," cried the princess, "do not tempt me to wickedness, for you shall never blunt my will to act virtuously."

As they were taking their ease, a message came from the emperor asking Diaphebus to set out immediately.

Those standing watch above the sea then spied five vessels and hastened to tell their lord, who, fearing they might be Genoese, asked Diaphebus to stay and dispatched a fleet to escort them.

The ships proved to be full of soldiers sent by the Grand Master of Rhodes.

The good Prior of Saint John disembarked with many knights of the white cross, whom Diaphebus and his men recognized and welcomed with great honor. Then they all went to the palace, where they found the emperor on his throne. Having bowed before him, the Prior of Saint John spoke thus:

· CXXXIX ·

THE PRIOR OF SAINT JOHN'S WORDS TO THE EMPEROR

"Most serene lord: we come from the Grand Master of Rhodes, who, knowing of Tirant lo Blanc's exploits, has dispatched two thousand infantry and cavalry, all paid to serve Your Majesty for fifteen months."

The emperor joyfully embraced the prior and welcomed his men, who were given splendid lodgings and everything necessary to sustain human life.

After resting, they and Diaphebus set out, and when they had gone five leagues, they heard stones from Tirant's bombards crashing against the walls of a fortified town. Once a large breach had been opened, Tirant dismounted and led the charge, but as he reached the wall, one of the stones thrown by the defenders struck his head and felled him. His men dragged him out of the ditch just as Diaphebus and the prior rode up.

The Turks inside were terrified at the sight of such an army. Having seen to Tirant's wounds, Richard attacked again with such zeal that he and his men broke through and entered the town. The cruel and desperate Saracens were determined to perish sword in hand, though they knew truth and justice were on the other side. The Christians, for their part, beheaded every Turk they caught, and the Prior of Saint John's knights also received their share of the spoils.

Then the captains went to Tirant's bedside, where the prior addressed him thus:

· C X L ·

HOW THE PRIOR OF SAINT JOHN EXPLAINED HIS MISSION TO TIRANT

"As one of the chivalric order, I am dazzled by the glory your feats have won throughout the world. Unlike certain cowards who flee the perils that might mend their reputations, you nobly brave the greatest risks for the greatest honors, imitating those knights of old whose fame will never perish. Mindful of his debt to you, the grand master has sent two thousand knights, who all place themselves at your service and are ready to obey you."

Tirant thanked them for their generous aid, but it was hard for him to speak because his head ached. The doctors poulticed it with broth from a sheep's head cooked in wine, and the next morning he felt much better.

They left the town garrisoned by its Greek inhabitants, who rejoiced in their freedom from the Turks' harsh rule. Upon reaching their camp, they rested till the fifteenth of that moon, when the Turks arrived as their emissaries had promised. Keeping the cut bridge between themselves and Tirant, they gathered on the other side of the river, led by the Grand Turk's battalion, which was captained by his son, for the father was still recovering from his wound. Then came the King of Asia with his battalion, followed by the King of Africa, the King of Cappadocia, the King of Armenia, and the valiant King of Egypt with a mighty host. After them came the Duke of Calabria's son, the Duke of Amalfi, the Count of Monturio, the Count of Caserta, the Count of San Valentino, the Count of Burgundy, the Count of Alacri, the Count of Fundi, the Count of Aquino, the Count of Moro, and many other counts and barons in the Grand Turk's and sultan's pay.[19] Every day they paid half a ducat to each horseman and half a florin to each foot soldier, who together comprised two hundred and sixty battalions.

The Saracens began mounting bombards and the next day shot so many missiles that Tirant had to withdraw into the mountains, where he camped in a grassy meadow near the river. Sometimes all the artillery fired at once and then, no matter how bright the day, the sky would darken as before a thunderstorm. The Turks had brought more than six hundred bombards, though they had lost many in the rout.

Seeing such a horde of cavalry and infantry, many Christians wished they were a hundred leagues away, while others sustained their courage by recalling their noble captain's prowess. Diaphebus gave His Majesty's ducats to Tirant, who asked two counts to divide them among the knights. They offered him some, but he replied: "Give me the honor, and keep the profit for yourselves."

In order to attack his foes, the sultan had the bridge repaired, but as soon as Tirant beheld the workmen, he rode to another big stone bridge guarded by mighty boulders with small castles upon them. When, after conquering the province, the sultan had reached that stone bridge, Lord Malveí, who ruled the castles, had refused to submit at any price, as he was loathe to betray God and his natural lord the emperor. Instead he constantly raided nearby Turkish towns and cities. The sultan had then ordered the wooden bridge built a league downstream, that his men might cross the river and continue their conquests.

Having reached the stone bridge, Tirant spoke to the knight, whose valiant son defended one castle, while the father captained the other. Each commanded thirty horsemen, and they had grown rich from the war. Tirant became close friends with the son, whose name was Hippolytus[20] and whom the Breton knighted at his father's request.

Then Tirant had the driest trees in the woods cut, and, after measuring the river's width, they nailed the logs that would nearly span it together with heavy spikes. Then they nailed thick planks across them and caulked everything with pitch. When the raft was finished, they covered it with foliage, equipped it with everything they might need, and chained it to the stone bridge at both ends.

Once the Turks[21] had repaired the bridge, they began to send their infantry across, while keeping their bombards loaded in case the Christians tried to attack. The emperor's men were dismayed when they saw what was occurring, but Tirant raised their spirits and made them feel somewhat better. He mounted his horse, had the trumpets blown, and told them to move their camp nearer the stone bridge, whereupon the infidels began to cross more quickly.

As soon as the Saracens had sent their troops across and marshaled their battalions, they began advancing toward Tirant, who then sent his men back to the other side. Beholding him there, the Turks crossed their bridge and made their way toward Tirant, who again had his men cross the river. This continued for three days.

The Turks held council to debate their course of action, and when the King of Egypt's turn came, he spoke out with bold knightly spirit:

· C X L I ·

HOW THE KING OF EGYPT SWORE A VOW

"Since a just solution to our differences eludes you, I see that resolving one problem may lead to many others. If you continue to show your ignorance, we shall win eternal infamy, but we shall triumph if you cease bickering and follow my advice. Should you seek to block our path to victory—a path open to those with eyes to see it—do not count on my support, as honor without risk does not interest me. Therefore, I request a hundred thousand men, with whom I shall cross the river while you remain on the other side. When I attack, come to my aid, and we shall win the glory we desire, for though the outcome of all endeavors depends on Fortune, our numbers are far greater than theirs."

They all applauded the king's wise suggestion, to which the sultan replied: "Everything in this world is subject to dispute. Let no one think I admire your offer to fight with a hundred thousand men, as they have even fewer, but the hope of victory leaps up in my courageous breast, wherefore you may take half our troops and I shall take the other. Whoever luck favors will attack first, and if the other then aids him, we may yet vanquish our treacherous foes."

And so they ended their council.

The king bravely marshaled his troops, while the sultan led the other half across the bridge. When Tirant saw they had divided their forces, he said: "This is exactly what I wanted."

He called the Christians to arms, storing their tents, mules, and wagons in the castles and keeping his men on the king's side. Just before the sun passed the Pillars of Hercules, he sent them across again, and when his infantry had formed ranks on a hill, he began to bring the cavalry across. Seeing all the squadrons but four in formation, the sultan hastened to attack, while the Christians retreated into the woods, though sixty of them were slain in the skirmish. By this time it was dark, so the Turks pitched camp at the foot of the hill, thinking their foes would quickly surrender and allow themselves to be enslaved, but the sultan also kept some men on horseback lest the Greeks mount another surprise attack.

Having overtaken his knights and lords, Tirant found them wandering hither and yon, cursing and bemoaning what they believed to be their fate. Beholding their shameful conduct, Tirant gathered them and said: "Brave knights! How can you forget your obligations to God and chivalry, for even if you were women, you could not act more cravenly. You, who should encourage the troops, instead lament and betray your vows, thus returning to your old habits of tears and recreance. You would do better to die honorably than entertain such mad assumptions, for an imperial law states that anyone who dares to meet his enemy's gaze will vanquish him in battle. I only wish to urge you, if you can be moved by such pleas, to take courage and fight boldly, as with God's help I shall make you victors within three hours."

Everyone felt comforted except the Duke of Macedonia, for while they were in the field, the duke had sent one of his squires to the emperor. When this squire neared Constantinople, he dismounted, left his horse, and pretended to weep. Beholding his disconsolate countenance, the townsfolk followed him to the palace, where he saw a great crowd and cried: "I seek that hapless wretch who calls himself an emperor!"

He was shown into the great hall, while the emperor was quickly informed that the Duke of Macedonia's squire Albí had arrived. The emperor hastened from his chamber, where he had been talking with the empress, and as soon as Albí saw him he fell to the floor, tearing his hair, beating his breast, and making great moan.

"Certainly," said the emperor, "this man must bring very bad tidings. I beg you, my friend, to torment me no further; tell me what happened."

Raising his hands toward Heaven, the squire replied: "Disposing us to bravery, ardor often brings the grief of failure, but those who lack wisdom are responsible for their misfortunes. You demoted your captain and vassals, replacing them with base foreigners of ill fame and unknown origin. Oh emperor! Since you committed the injustice, it is only right that you should pay the price, and do you know what the price will be? Instead of obsequies, they will recite the psalm of malediction[22] over one who destroyed himself by snatching the imperial succession from my illustrious master and gave it to a vile foreigner who betrayed the duke and fled, thus augmenting the glory of our emperor that was! Surely it would be best, in your short time left on earth, to wander through foreign lands bemoaning your folly. In this manner perhaps you will atone for your sins, for in disdain of God's wrath you caused countless Christian deaths. The Saracens besieged your troops on a mountain where they had neither wine, bread, nor water, and by now our captains have undoubtedly perished. I shall depart with my grief, leaving you, former emperor, with yours."

"Woe is me!" cried the emperor. "How cruel Fortune afflicts me, as sorrow quickly follows upon joy and many evils flow from one! Alas, what can I do but travel through the world begging for alms?"

With these and other lamentations, he entered his chamber, where he flung himself on the bed and exclaimed: "Why rule the Greek Empire if I had to lose it? What help all my riches if I am now dispossessed? What use my good daughter, if she cannot succeed me and we are punished for our sins by perpetual enslavement? What good my wife and maidens, when they all must be dishonored? How my eyes will weep at such a sight! I fear my heart will break for very woe!"

Carmesina comforted her father, as the others were too sorrowful to do so.

Word spread through the city, whose inhabitants mourned their friends and relatives, while mothers beat their breasts and wept, raising their eyes to Heaven and bewailing the city's downfall as though it had already been conquered.

Let us leave them with their grief and return to the Greek army.

After placing guards around the camp, Tirant rode here and there, encouraging his troops and seeking to raise their spirits. Then he stole down the other side of the mountain, removed all his armor, and hastened to Lord Malveí's castle, where, remembering the signal they had agreed upon, he pounded two stones together until the knight admitted him. Finding everything ready, Tirant poured great quantities of oil and resin into wooden troughs, along with pitch, quicklime, and other things that burn easily. Then he spread dry wood on the raft, soaked it with the mixture, and had long ropes tied to chains at both ends. Two men got in a little fishing boat, and seizing two ropes, they cast off behind the raft and let the current carry them downstream, but Tirant told them not to light the fire till they were almost at the bridge. When the raft caught at bends in the river, one man pulled while the other paid out slack, and when they wanted the raft to go sideways, they evened up the ropes.

Terrified by the huge flames, the Saracens hurried from their camp and galloped toward the bridge as fast as they could. The sultan and some of his knights arrived a little before the raft, but if the men in the boat had followed Tirant's orders and waited a little longer to light the fire, all their foes would have been killed or captured. Many Saracens were drowned when the bridge collapsed, leaving twenty-five thousand soldiers trapped on the other side, including the Duke of Calabria's son, the Duke of Andrea, the Duke of Amalfi, the Count of Burgundy, the Count of Monturio, and other captains, who fled in disorder from the dreadful conflagration.

When Tirant saw the fire, he returned to his troops, whom he found horsed and waiting to loot their enemies' camp. Tirant halted them and said: "Now we shall win no glory, but tomorrow we shall have both honor and spoils."

He placed a strong guard around his camp, saying: "They cannot all have crossed, and they may try a desperate attack."

At daybreak, he ordered his trumpets blown, called everyone to arms, and sent men to fetch his pages and wagons. Then they rode down the mountain to their former camp, where, after looking around and seeing no Turks below, some knights said they should descend and seek out the enemy.

Tirant replied: "Since we have attained our desired goal, let us act with prudence, for one lost knight means more to us than a hundred to them, but I promise that within a day you may win all the glory you like."

Beholding the Turks' discomfiture, Diaphebus asked for Tirant's ring, to which our knight replied: "Cousin, what do you plan to do?"

Diaphebus said: "I shall send Pyramus to the emperor, who has had no word from us in such a long time! His Majesty will be comforted, and the princess will delight in your stratagem."

"I beg you," said Tirant, "to have Pyramus ask him for provisions, as ours may soon give out."

When Pyramus reached the city, he saw nothing but woeful countenances and weeping women, but things were still worse at the palace: hair had been torn and garments rent. People averted their faces as soon as they saw him, and he thought the emperor, his wife, or the princess must have died. Then he entered the great hall and spied a group of men he knew, some of whom were praying, while others cursed everything French. He approached one and asked in a whisper if the emperor had died or why they were grieving so, to which the man replied: "Those traitors disguised as knights! Not since Judas has the world seen such treachery! Did my religion not forbid it, I would silence you and all your company, that the world might learn of your devilry and wickedness! Get out of my sight, for if you trouble me further, I swear by all the saints in Heaven to throw you out that window!"

Pyramus hung his head and entered another room, where he recognized the emperor's chamberlain and approached him with a smile. The chamberlain cried: "What is the cause of that foolish smirk? How dare you approach the emperor's chamber?"

"My friend," replied Pyramus, "be not angry, for no one will tell me why the palace is in mourning. Let me speak with the emperor, and I shall quickly cheer him."

The chamberlain silently entered his master's chamber, whose windows were shut, as the whole court was in mourning. The chamberlain said: "My lord, one of those traitors from Tirant lo Blanc's company is at the door. His name is Pyramus and he must have escaped the siege. He says he wishes to speak with Your Majesty."

The emperor replied: "Send him away with my curses and order him to leave my lands, for if I find him or any of his rabble, I shall have them flung from my highest tower."

Imagine how the princess's grief redoubled at these words, since whatever harm Tirant had done, she still could not forget him.

When the chamberlain had repeated His Majesty's orders, Pyramus replied: "On my faith, I shall not go, nor has Tirant or any of his men ever betrayed the emperor. If he will not give me a hearing, ask the princess to come to the door, for I shall tell her something that will make her very happy."

The chamberlain returned to his master, who asked Carmesina to speak with Pyramus. Beholding her distress, he knelt, kissed her hand,

and said: "Excellent lady, my soul is troubled by the faces of everyone in this city, for though I ask the cause of their grief, no one will tell me. I am still more puzzled by the emperor's words. If His Highness wishes Tirant to desist from his glorious exploits, let him say so and we shall promptly quit his empire, thus freeing ourselves from these dangers and travails, wherefore I request some explanation that I may take to my lord."

After listening to Pyramus's words, the princess tearfully repeated everything the duke's squire had said. When Pyramus heard this vile slander, he smote his forehead and cried: "My lady, the man who brought this doleful news should be imprisoned! If Tirant has not just won a battle, put the sultan to flight, burnt a bridge, and trapped more than twenty thousand men, may I be drawn and quartered, and that you may give credence to my account, here is our captain's ring."

The princess's heart leapt up at these words, and she hastened to her father, to whom she repeated what Pyramus had said. The afflicted sovereign was so delighted that he fell in a swoon, and they had to summon his doctors to revive him. After Pyramus had again recounted the good news, His Majesty ordered the church bells rung. Then they went to the cathedral, thanked God for Tirant's victory, and upon their return the emperor had Albí flung into prison.

Having asked His Majesty to resupply their camp, Pyramus set out the next day with many good wishes and congratulations. Tirant was astonished at the Duke of Macedonia's treachery, but since the truth had been revealed, he troubled himself no further.

On the day of Pyramus's departure, the Turks decided they had no choice but to surrender and be taken prisoners.

Since Abdullah Solomon was with the Saracens, they decided to send him again, as they had scarcely tasted food for two days. Toward nightfall he fastened a napkin to a lance, and upon seeing Tirant's response, Abdullah went to his camp, where he bowed before him and spoke these reverent words:

· C X L I I ·

*H*OW ABDULLAH SOLOMON EXPLAINED HIS MISSION

"Knowing your genius, I am amazed that the sultan eluded you, for had you acted with your usual skill, such a plan could not have failed. Until now, all your ventures have been crowned with success, as your wisdom is only matched by your ardor and, though unknown to the multitudes, your virtues will win renown, but to get to the point, I and our famished soldiers cry you mercy. If Your Lordship will spare us, your name will be glorified even by infidels, wherefore may it please you to act in accordance with your nature, pardoning those foes who have so ignorantly abused you."

Tirant led the famished Saracens to his tent and, after offering them food, he gathered his great lords and asked their advice. Having agreed upon a reply, they summoned Abdullah Solomon, to whom Tirant said: "Cidi, though we have triumphed through a ruse, I trust that my valiant men will soon display their mettle, as they have not forgotten those Turks' offenses against our emperor. Since justice is on our side, I am certain that with God's aid I shall soon, as chief judge, duly punish those infidels, who will then see me refrain from doing all the harm I might. Now tell them to come forward a hundred at a time, leading their horses and laying down their arms in that field."

Having taken their leave of the captain, the emissaries returned to their camp and repeated Tirant's orders.

Once the Saracens had lain down their arms, the captain placed them under guard. The Turks were grateful to be alive, for they hoped their friends would ransom them, and since they were disarmed Tirant led them to the foot of the mountain, where they were served abundant food while his foot soldiers kept watch. Then Tirant picked out all the Turks' Christian allies, whom he brought to his camp, lodged in a big tent, and served with everything necessary to sustain human life. Some of Tirant's men were angered to see him honoring renegades, and when the prisoners heard their cries, they felt ashamed and stopped eating.

Tirant kept them there till the ships came, and he never let wise Abdullah Solomon leave his side.

One day after lunch, the lords asked their captain to summon the philosopher, whom Tirant urged to say a few words for everyone's edification.

"How can I, poor soul, comply," the Saracen asked, "without first pondering my words? At least give me until tomorrow, and tonight I shall consider how best to please Your Lordships."

The Duke of Pera replied: "Cidi, that cannot be done, for after a good dinner we need a little dessert."

Tirant had a bench placed upon a silk cloth in the middle of the meadow and stationed a guard around them. When Abdullah saw he could not escape, he said: "Since my lord the captain commands me, I must offer some advice that each of you can take to heart."

And mounting the bench, he began to speak thus:

· CXLIII ·

ABDULLAH SOLOMON'S ADVICE TO TIRANT

"God is great, God is great, God ordains all and should be loved and feared without deception. Noble captain and invincible warriors, do not be surprised that I speak of Christianity, for though my father was a Saracen, my mother was of your creed and taught me to love your God.[23] Magnanimous captain, I now see that faith, generosity, and humility will always conquer faithlessness, greed, and scorn, just as hatred must yield to charity and vain hopes to desperation. Virtue's hammer smashes stubborn falsehood, as with firm intention you best your foes, though fame and envy, like good and evil, will forever be at war. Praise be unto Him who is Lord of Righteousness and King of Glory, for the just have vanquished the wicked and the virtuous have conquered, though all too often we behold the contrary. We have witnessed this empire recover its stolen honor, while sinners and invaders, seeing their jealousy confounded, must now grieve and with cruel anger disclose their inner fury, gnashing their teeth to show their bodily corruption. You, brave and mighty captain, calm and wise beyond all others, will soon return your noble emperor to his throne. Driving out sad clouds and tearful rain, you will bring clear skies to Greece, winning a crown of stars by restoring the empire's lost prosperity, while your prowess will light up the world as it has in the past and present.

"But captain, it is far more praiseworthy to justly rule a kingdom than to conquer it! Certainly, now is the time to summon all your courage, preparing great and glorious endeavors if there is any kingly spirit in you. All your past travails will be as nought if you shun the many you must still endure, for your chivalry compels you to be just in all things. We have seen you nobly struggle against adversity, but beware, as vanquished Fortune often returns with deceptive mildness. Having conquered your enemies, be watchful, since good fortune provokes envy and war. War never is caused by love, nor is hatred by charity, which proceeds from the glory of God's majestic spirit; and do not imagine that Fortune, having changed its weapons, will be more benign or weaker, for it will force you to change as well. Think not that your travails will lighten because the enemy is sweeter, but rather know that war is more treacherous when trust is beguiled by flattery.

"Having witnessed your noble defense of the commonwealth, we now shall see how you respond to plentitude. Many battle desperately against woes and afflictions, and many who were strong in adversity are undone by prosperity. After Hannibal's victory at Cannae, he wintered in Capua, eating delicate foods, sleeping peacefully, and taking his ease at the baths, and because of this idleness Marcellus routed him. Thus the frozen ardor of the River Trebbia, where he first triumphed in Lombardy, was doused in Capua by the warmth of baths and other pleasures. Often peace is more dangerous than war, as peace has undone many stalwart knights, who, once deprived of adversaries, found their valor languishing amid luxuries; and in truth, there is no harsher war than with one's own customs and spirit, for since it is fought within the walls—that is, within the man himself—there can be no truce. This war without battles is fiercer in its robes of peace than when clad in martial armor, and, leaving aside countless other examples, I recall how peace and tranquility softened the Romans, who had never been broken in battle and had bested all their foes, wherefore it has been written that sinful luxury, conquering the Roman conquerers, avenged their subjects. Scipio, that statesman so beloved of the Roman senate, appeared to foresee this when, ignoring wise old Cato's advice, he forbade the final destruction of Carthage. According to Florus, Scipio did so lest Rome, losing its dread of the enemy, abandon itself to idle pleasures. Would that his views had triumphed, for verily the Romans were more plagued by their own vices than by foes, and had Scipio's words been heeded, his countrymen's deeds would have been nobler and their battles fewer.

"I believe many will now tell you it is time to rest, but I declare that you should view such men with suspicion, and I say unto all these lords that a life of travails has but one goal, being a ceaseless struggle with enemies visible and invisible. Looking ahead, I disagree with the common opinion, for in the future you will find your pains redoubled, nor was greater effort ever demanded of any knight. Your spirit must rise above itself, that you may face the harshest combats, and thus the world will behold your greatness in both good and bad fortune, and not only you, but those who follow your counsel. You have an aged lord, whom Fortune had brought low, when by tempting it he fell from his high estate. Show him the steps he mounted to reach this triumph, and how to wisely fortify himself in the future. Rather than striving to rise higher, he should recover what he has lost, holding himself content with the rank God gave him and the scepter he inherited through blood more than courage. Power does not make a man but rather reveals him, just as honors do not change one's character but rather illumine it. Advise him to act like an emperor, knowing merit precedes felicity, and teach him to honor God, love his country, and serve justice, without which no reign, however opulent, can long endure. Likewise, a rule based on violence cannot last. A wise prince makes himself loved rather than feared, and therefore let him wish for nothing but a good heart, good sense, and good thoughts. Let him strive only for fame and fear only dishonor, knowing that the higher he climbs, the less he will be able to conceal his acts, and the greater his power, the less his license to abuse it. Let the prince never slacken in his customs, but rather shun extremes and seek the golden mean. Let him lay aside extravagance without embracing parsimony, for the former destroys riches and the latter fame and glory. Let him love and defend his good name, and still more his honor, while jealously guarding his time and fearing to squander it. Let him be generous with his riches, bearing in mind the words of that wise king who said he desired not gold but to rule those who possessed it.[24] It is better to have rich vassals than bursting coffers, for the prince of a rich kingdom will never be poor. Let him recall the calamities and afflictions this wretched land has lately suffered, and let him hold himself blessed if he fulfills his vow, for a righteous prince is he who bravely vanquishes invaders, repairs the damage they have done, makes peace, spurns tyranny, and returns his land to liberty. Let him fill his heart with love for his subjects, for love grows with loving and nothing is more dangerous than being an unloved king. Let the prince be ever mindful of Sallust's teaching that neither soldiers nor money can defend a king but only friends won by good deeds, merit, and honesty.[25]

"Therefore, a prince should live in concord with his subjects, as concord makes small things flourish whereas discord fells great ones. Marcus Agrippa was one example: a man who strove mightily to achieve concord. A good prince will be every man's brother, comrade, friend, or worthy master. After God and charity, let him hold friendship dearest, never banishing those who merit love from his councils, but rather following Seneca's advice and taking counsel with trusted friends.[26] First, however, let him be certain his friend is truly loyal, for he should shun too many confidants and distinguish between amity and flattery, being pleased only by honest praise and just petitions. Let him fear sycophants more than poison but hold fast to true friends, and if he must abandon a comrade, let him not do so rashly but discreetly. As the proverb says: 'Break not an old friendship, for your friends' champions will be yours.'[27] Neither should he feign pleasure in being loved by those he distrusts: an error great lords all too frequently commit. Love always responds to love perceived in another, wherefore he should not distrust an old ally or condemn him without proof. Let him cast out suspicion and turn a deaf ear to intriguers, who, if they persist, should be duly chastised, for as an emperor once said, he who pardons accusers harms himself.[28]

"Alexander the Great, that young and mighty conqueror, once scorned an accuser while revealing true friendship. The outcome was good, as well it might have been, for when Alexander was ill and had to drink a potion prepared by his doctor Philip, he received a letter from Parmenion warning that Darius had bribed the physician to kill him. Alexander read the letter, hid it, and kept silent until he had consumed the potion, whereupon he gave his friend the letter, too late and uselessly had the accusation been true, yet in good time, since in fact it was slanderous and false.[29] Let the emperor abhor evil tongues or at least reproach and disregard them, recalling the emperor Octavian's letter urging Tiberius to forgive those who spoke ill of him, as it sufficed that they did him no evil.[30] Otherwise, men would show less patience than God, whose name is often cursed, though no mortal can harm or injure Him. Let the emperor fix his thoughts on this, for not only was Octavian's forbearance praised, but also that of the great and solemn Roman citizen Pompey, the King of Parthia, and the Athenean tyrant Pisistratus.

"Let the prince take no heed of others' attempts to learn his secrets, but let him not seek to learn the secrets of others. A brave heart is unperturbed by such matters, while the contrary betrays a lack of confidence. Let the prince strive to truly be as he wishes to appear, for then he need not conceal his actions from friends or foes, nor will he hide anything in council but openly refute his enemies. With such surety as this, Scipio led the Carthaginian spies through his camp, and with similar magnanimity, Caesar freed Pompey's captain Domitius, letting him flee despite the many secrets he had learned, yet once, when Caesar came upon his enemies' secrets, he burned them unread.

"Let no prince believe he received his title by chance, but that his spirit might approach God and rise above vain passions, serenely untroubled by grief, woe, fear, or base desires. Let him know that wrath is ugly and cruelty intolerable and sinful in a prince, who has the means to do more evil than other men, and let him feel the truth of Seneca's words in the second tragedy: 'Every reign must submit to a greater reign.'[31] Freeing his mind from wrath and fear, he will know himself equal to his subjects and see that everything he does for them is for himself and comes from God. Let him abhor pride and envy, which are not princely but vulgar passions, for why should a prince be prideful when God has so favored him, and he owes his rank and powers to his Creator alone? How can one with none above him and all below him be envious? Let the prince comprehend that he must serve truth in good faith, as a liar is never believed and great truths sort ill with petty lies, wherefore, if he would be trusted, he must speak frankly at all times. There is nothing more absurd or harmful than a mendacious prince, and his rule will be uncertain. The word of one on whom the hopes and safety of many peoples depend must be stable and firm. He who must never be deceived must also never deceive others, for what use is flattery to one who fears nothing and seeks no gain, which things seem to me the greatest spurs to flattery?

"Let him also avoid vainglory, showing his worth through his deeds, and neither threaten nor rage, for such acts ill behoove a prince, who can frighten with a glance. He should take revenge calmly or even punish by pardoning, which is the noblest vengeance. Let him avoid excessive merriment and above all guard his subjects' souls, nor should he be sad if he considers his honors and magnificence. Let him be accessible to all, since God created him not only for himself but also for the commonweal, and let him know his duty to aid the downtrodden, tempering justice with equity and cruelty with mercy. Let him seek gaiety in prudence, ripeness in haste, caution in trust, pleasure in temperance, authority in cheer, nourishment in food, moderation in invitations, gentleness in speech, charity in rebukes, loyalty in counsel, freedom in judgment, slowness in laughter, elegance in sitting, and gravity in walking. Let him employ spurs in rewarding and reins in punishing, joyously attacking his foes but sadly punishing his subjects, should they deserve it.

"A great prince regards his vassals' crimes as wounds to be cured by cleansing and care, and as Titus Livius says, he should punish his subjects with moans and tears as if stabbing his own entrails.[32] Let him imitate God's clemency, spurning those philosophers who condemn pity, for magnanimity is a royal virtue and no prince who lacks it should rule. Just as generosity is in man's nature and is more customary than malice, so a king, being his subjects' master, must excel them in liberality. A prince should prize chastity, a quality handsome in all men but of singular beauty in a ruler, in whom nothing is finer than continence nor uglier than lust. Even brute animals feel gratitude for remembered benefits, and vile indeed is the man who lacks this quality, which is a handsome ornament and most useful to princes, whereas ingratitude may destroy a kingdom, as men are loath to help one who forgets their services.

"Finally, let the prince admit that his honor is burdensome and his burden honorable, for once crowned, he loses his freedom, accepting the arduous and noble servitude on which his kingdom's liberty depends. From then on he must be an example to others, since kingdoms are governed by example and the commoners' excesses are often caused by their rulers' vices. A prince should desire nothing but his crown, scepter, and authority, as his realm's peace and prosperity are difficult to maintain, and it resembles a Hydra, from which two heads spring for each one severed. Let him combine the wisdom of experience, the modesty of youth, and the bravery of his lineage and royal station. Despising purple, precious gems, and bodily pleasures, he should fix his gaze upon eternal things alone, mocking those that pass and quickly fade away. Likewise, he should occupy himself with arms and horses, his palace, and war and peace, while in ruling, he should follow the arts and ways of the Romans: to act nobly in peace, to forgive his subjects, and to bring low the proud.[33] Let him recall that this life is full of perils and hardships, wherefore he should care nothing for games of pleasure, idle repose, sin, or anything except to make his way toward eternal glory.

"Thus, let him eagerly read of the ancients' noble deeds, fervently asking not for wealth but for examples of illustrious rulers, and remembering that last African prince and conqueror who, outside the city of Numantia (and this was later an example of military discipline to many Roman princes), forbade sinful pleasures and expelled two thousand prostitutes from his camp. Should your lord not banish lust from his cities, correcting his subjects' ways when they madly pursue pleasure, he will have no hope of victory or even safety. In imitation of that great African prince and others who strove to perfect themselves, he should take the greatest saints as his teachers in this life and guides to eternal glory, for often noble spirits are more stirred by words and statues in memory of the ancients than by gifts. Great is men's pleasure in equaling their noble forefathers, and sweet is the envy of those who inquire into the ancients' deeds, as it is well known that only those who love honor and fear shame can act bravely. Many have profited from imitating the wise and shunning evil, and one who strives after goodness will be reputed good.

"I have spoken many words, though they are few, considering my listeners' majesty, and you, noble captain, who feel the weight of great affairs upon your shoulders, know that nothing daunts love except to lack requital. Such a fate cannot befall you, since your virtues will make you loved throughout the world, just as your judgments and counsels have won the loyalty of those beneath you, nor were Chiron by Achilles, Palinurus by Aeneas, Philoctetes by Hercules or Lelius by Scipio Africanus more prized than you are by your emperor. Therefore, quickly conclude the good you have begun, for charity endures travails and love conquers all.[34] He who wishes to share the glory must bear his share of the burden, as all precious things are dearly obtained: gold must be dug from the bowels of the earth, spices brought from distant lands, incense gathered from the sap of Sabaean trees, and murices caught near Saida, while ivory comes from India and pearls from the ocean. All great prizes require effort, and virtue, which is the noblest, is never won lightly. A good reputation shines brighter than gold, but it can only be won through struggle and maintained through diligence. As a rose is girded by thorns, so are virtue and glory by adversity and effort, and just as the finger must brave perils to pluck the rose, so a man must risk his life to win glory. Therefore, gird your valor with worthy principles, for when you think you have finished, you will have just begun. By protecting your prince and commonwealth, you will increase your good fortune, and when your soul leaves your body, it will fly more lightly to its eternal seat. This was Cicero's opinion, and we know it to be true.[35] Commend your honor and ours to God."

· CXLIV ·

*H*OW TIRANT'S GREAT LORDS OBTAINED ABDULLAH SOLOMON'S FREEDOM

The mighty lords, having heard Abdullah's judicious words, rose at once and asked their captain to reward the wise Saracen. Tirant nobly replied: "Lords and betters, tell me what reward you wish to offer him, and I shall gladly obey you."

They thanked him and, after taking counsel, asked that Abdullah and his son be freed, to which Tirant quickly consented while also freeing twenty others. Cidi Abdullah prostrated himself at Tirant's feet and tried to kiss them, but Tirant raised him up, bade him Godspeed, and then returned to his camp.

Two days later the galleys docked with provisions, and when they had been unloaded, Tirant decided to send the prisoners in those same vessels. He entrusted them to his grand constable, who took their captives to the port. As they boarded the ships, Tirant's men searched them and found more than ten thousand ducats in jewels and coins, which the grand constable sent to his captain, who then divided them among those in the camp.

The constable ordered the sails hoisted, and a good wind speedily bore them to Constantinople, where the emperor and his ladies watched from the windows as they approached. Upon reaching the palace, the constable bowed before His Majesty and, after kissing his hand and foot, delivered Tirant's message and presented the captives.

The magnanimous lord joyously welcomed him, placed the prisoners under guard, and led his constable to a chamber where the empress and princess awaited them. He asked how the war was progressing, how his knights were behaving, and how the captain was treating them, to which the constable modestly replied:

· CXLV ·

*T*HE CONSTABLE'S REPORT TO THE EMPEROR

"The renown, oh blessed emperor, of your brave captain's noble deeds cannot be eclipsed by certain slanderers in your court, and that the truth may be known, I shall recount an argument over the spoils from the Turkish camp. It seemed a black day for everyone, and all because your new captain and his men had delivered us, shedding their blood and risking their lives while we bore away the booty, but Tirant pacified his men and let us keep the plunder, for truly, my lord, you have the noblest captain who ever lived. Do not think Alexander, Scipio, or Hannibal were so wise, brave, and chivalrous, as Tirant knows more about warfare than anyone I have seen or heard of. Just when we think all is lost, he gives us victory."

The emperor asked: "How does he behave?"

The constable replied: "Your Majesty will find him the most solicitous of men. He loves and protects the public weal, champions the helpless, and gives comfort to the sick. When knights are wounded, he has them brought to his tent, where they are treated like kings with abundant food and medicine. There are always doctors at hand, and I believe that if Our Lord wishes him to do good, this virtue alone suffices."

"Tell me, constable:" asked the emperor, "how does he organize the camp and his troops?"

"Sire," said the constable, "first of all, every morning he has two thousand horses saddled, whereupon a thousand men ride through the camp and around it, all armed for battle and accompanied by a thousand infantry. At midday, another thousand replace them, but do you think he lets the first thousand disarm and unsaddle their mounts? No; they must remain in armor lest the enemy attack. At nightfall, he doubles the guard to two thousand lances and two thousand infantry, but the other two thousand remain armed and keep their horses saddled. At midnight, they change the guard again and some go to their tents, while others patrol the camp until daybreak.

"Do not imagine that your captain ever sleeps, for he is constantly with his men, riding here and there and joking now with some, now with others. Often I urge him to let me assume his morning duties, but he refuses and at dawn has the bells rung for Mass, while all who wish to hear it gather in the great tent. Do not think him ceremonious, for he will take my arm or anyone else's and stand in a corner, letting all the magnates precede him. Thus he hears Mass, honoring the others above himself, and after the service, they hold council to report on their provisions. If they need anything, Tirant sends for it immediately, and all we talk about in our morning councils is the state of the camp. Then the captain, after entering his tent or the first one he finds, lies down in his armor on a bench or mule blanket and sleeps two or three hours. Having risen, he has the trumpets blown and his magnates come to lunch, where they are marvelously served with every sort of delicacy. The captain remains standing until they have finished the first course, and I marvel that he can feed more than four hundred men, though thirty pack mules come and go continuously with capons, chickens, and as many other fowl as they can find. I am also amazed that he can work so hard with so little sleep. After lunch and dessert, they hold council again, and if there are nearby towns, castles, or villages to be taken, they decide how many soldiers are needed and who should lead them. If they require bombards or other artillery, he quickly sends for them, and I can tell you we have conquered more than seventy places. The captain has ordered things far better than the duke before him."

"How," asked the emperor, "do his companions behave in battle?"

"Very well, my lord," replied the constable. "Tonight or tomorrow, Diaphebus will arrive with the great lords we captured."

"What?" exclaimed the emperor. "Are there still more prisoners?"

"By Saint Mary there are," replied the constable, "including the Duke of Andrea, the Duke of Amalfi, the Duke of Calabria's son, and many other counts, barons, and knights."

The emperor felt even more cheerful.

"Has he impeded you in the exercise of your duties?" His Highness asked.

"No, sire," replied the constable, "for as soon as he had given me your letter, he told me to carry on as before both in his camp and the duke's. He made his own constable my lieutenant, as I had been there first, and all our victories, my lord, are due to Tirant's prowess."

The next day, Diaphebus marched through the middle of the city with the prisoners and many trumpeters and drummers, while the emperor and his subjects marveled at such a multitude. Upon reaching the palace courtyard and beholding His Majesty at a window, Diaphebus bowed deeply and went upstairs to his chambers, where he kissed the emperor's hand and greeted his wife and daughter. Having embraced the ladies, he told the emperor who the prisoners were and gave him Tirant's blessings, love, and good wishes. Then Diaphebus said:

"My lord, please free me, for anyone who guards prisoners is a prisoner himself, and still more when the captives' rank far exceeds their nobility. Therefore, in view of the perils of such a charge, I ask Your Highness to relieve me, as it is a law of life that each man must preserve his honor, and that people of understanding may know I have accomplished my mission, which will be scrutinized by interested parties calling me just or unjust, and that my wishes and yours may be seen to accord, I ask your notaries to draw up an act that may be consulted in the future. Ask Carmesina, noble Stephanie of Macedonia, the virtuous Easygoing Widow, fair and eloquent Pleasure-of-my-life, and the honorable and blessed empress, fount of all wisdom, to offer true testimony that I have accomplished my mission."

The act was prepared, and after accepting the captives, His Majesty spoke for a long time with Diaphebus, asking what honor Tirant had shown them. Then the emperor had them locked in his strongest keeps.

As soon as Diaphebus could excuse himself, he went to the princess's chambers, where he found her surrounded by all the Greek maidens. Beholding Tirant's cousin, she rose from her dais, whereupon the Breton knelt, kissed her hand, and said: "This kiss is from one whom Your Highness keeps in a stronger prison than those I brought."

The damsels flocked around them and he could say no more for fear of being overheard, but the princess took his hand and led him to a window seat, to which she summoned Stephanie, while Diaphebus said: "If the sea turned to ink and its beaches to paper, they would not suffice to inscribe the love and praise Tirant sends you. Everything must be judged by its results, which reveal a man's worth, rewarding or punishing him according to his merits. For a brave knight, love can only end in death or glory, nor should you cherish life more than your captain's adoration, for, having relinquished his freedom the day he met you, he deserves your favors more than any knight who ever lived."

The princess sweetly replied: "My desires are more transparent than yours, which God alone can see, but since men are judged by their deeds, all noblewomen will condemn you, for ill-purposed acts are always thwarted. Alas, brother Diaphebus! I shall be yours and Tirant's if you remain good, true, and manly knights, whom gentlefolk throughout the world may praise and glorify. In regard to your praises, I am amazed that you can bear such a burden, but I receive them as your humble vassal, sending back twice as many plus one."

As they were conversing, His Majesty entered the room and said: "By my father's bones, how fair it is to see damsels delighting in deeds of chivalry."

He told his daughter to don her finest robes, as he would shortly sentence the prisoners, and after escorting him to the central square, Diaphebus returned for the ladies, whom he led to a big platform covered with silk and gold. Once the emperor's great lords had been seated, he had the captives brought forth and placed on the ground, both Saracens and Christians. They all obeyed except the Duke of Andrea, who cried: "I am accustomed to sitting in state, and now you treat me as a defeated slave, but though you may subjugate my body, you will never subdue my will!"

Seeing this disturbance, the emperor summoned his bailiffs, who bound the duke's hands and feet and forced him to sit down. When everyone was silent, the emperor had his sentence read:

· C X L V I ·

*H*OW THE EMPEROR SENTENCED THE KNIGHTS, DUKES, AND COUNTS WHO WERE HIS PRISONERS

We, Frederic, Emperor of Greece, in accordance with the laws of our glorious ancestors and to maintain the prosperity of our empire, hereby proclaim to all the world that these vile knights and false Christians accepted infidel gold, opposing our Catholic Faith and exalting the Muslim sect. Fearing neither God, dishonor, nor their souls' perdition, they treacherously invaded our realms, and as base and impious knights cursed by Our Holy Mother Church, they deserve to be stripped of their titles and disowned by their families, for their brave ancestors' renown has been blackened by this manifest evil, wherefore, considering the aforesaid facts and many others, we declare, notify, and announce to all and sundry with great bitterness, grief, and compassion, but in the hope of setting an example, that these Christians are guilty of treachery and shall be punished as traitors to God and chivalry.

Once the sentence had been read, twelve knights came forth, who like the emperor were attired in long robes and cowls. The prisoners were forced to rise and mount the platform, where they were disarmed and expelled from the knightly order with all the usual ceremonies described in the first part of this book.

When the Duke of Andrea saw such infamy heaped upon himself and his comrades, his gallbladder burst and he choked to death on his own bile.

Seeing the dead renegade, His Majesty denied him a church burial and ordered his body left in a field to be devoured by dogs and other savage beasts.

Then shields painted with the knights' arms and punishments were sent throughout Christendom, and when the Pope and the German emperor saw the sentences, they deemed them most just. Having received the honors they deserved, the knights were returned to prison, while the emperor said: "Let us act with justice and show pity to none."

He ordered the Duke of Macedonia's squire brought forth with a heavy chain around his neck and sentenced him to be hung head down for the great distress he had caused. Upon hearing this sentence and beholding the squire in chains, Diaphebus knelt at the emperor's feet and begged him for mercy, lest evil tongues say Albí had died for speaking ill of Tirant. The emperor, however, was adamant, and seeing Diaphebus plead in vain, Carmesina rose from her dais and knelt at her father's feet. Then

she and the knight begged for the man's life while the empress and her
ladies joined them, but the emperor stubbornly replied: "No sentence
given by my general council has ever been revoked, nor will this one be
now."

Seizing her father's hands to kiss them, the princess slipped off his ring
and said: "Your Majesty is not accustomed to ordering such cruel execu-
tions."

The emperor replied: "His slanders have angered me, but change the
sentence if you like."

The princess gave the ring to Diaphebus, who leapt on his horse,
galloped to the market square where justice was done, and presented it to
the bailiff. The squire had already mounted the steps and they were about
to turn him upside down. After bringing him to his quarters, Diaphebus
returned to the palace, whereupon Albí fled to a Franciscan monastery and
entered Our Lord's service.

The day after the sentence, the emperor sent those Turks who could not
be ransomed to Venice, Sicily, and Rome, where they were sold into
slavery or traded for arms, horses, and provisions. The emperor ransomed
all the Christians he could, including one duke who was freed for eighty
thousand Venetian ducats, and the Duke of Calabria's son, who cost his
father fifty-five thousand. Those who were destitute but swore fealty were
sent to the Greek camp, while the rest were chained together and put to
work on the towers and palace, which they greatly improved.

When it was time for the constable and Diaphebus to leave, the emperor gave them all the ransom money for Tirant.

On the eve of his departure, Diaphebus learned that the emperor was
asleep and hastened to Carmesina's chamber, where the first person he met
was Stephanie. Tirant's cousin then knelt and said: "Gentle lady, as good
fortune has allowed me to find you alone, please assure me that you have
accepted my proposal. If you take me for your faithful servant, I shall hold
myself the luckiest of mortals, and though I know I cannot equal your
nobility, grace, or station, love often accords wills and makes the unworthy worthy. Do not hide behind the princess but rather sally forth
bravely and give me your hands in sign of victory, as mine will not betray
you. Should you refuse, you will be guilty of shameful cruelty, for which
all noblewomen will curse and punish you, stripping you of your lofty
rank. You will be banished to the isle of Remorse where no one finds
repose, and if my words fail to move you, I shall publish them in the court
of chivalry."

Stephanie gently replied: "Since ignorance deserves no pardon, open
your eyes and behold your guilt, for noblewomen will condemn you to my
greater honor and proclaim that such contraries cannot be reconciled. You
must mend your ways and atone for the past, and still more when knights

and ladies hear those words that besmirch your honor. Seeing how quick you are to take liberties, I fear you will seek to conceal your sins beneath my skirts, but I assure you that I have no wish to raise another Lazarus. Therefore do not despair of my love, which is greater than you think, though you sometimes willfully refuse to acknowledge it."

Diaphebus was about to reply when a chamberlain entered and said the emperor had summoned him, whereupon the knight asked Stephanie to wait, promising to return as soon as he could.

His Highness asked Diaphebus and the constable to accept the ransom money, but after consenting, the Breton pretended he could not count and asked the other knight to take it. Having received orders to set out before daybreak, Diaphebus returned to his lady's chamber, where he found her weeping over his imminent departure. Beholding her distress, he consoled her by displaying his own, and as they were comforting each other, the princess returned from the treasure tower, clad in a white damask gown and with her hair loose because of the heat. When she saw Diaphebus she tried to leave, but he was close enough to stop her.

"If you want to know the truth," said the princess, "I do not mind, because I think of you as a brother."

Pleasure-of-my-life said: "My lady, behold Stephanie's face! She looks like she has just been blowing on a fire, for she is redder than a rose in May. Diaphebus's hands have certainly not been idle while we were in the tower, and indeed, we might have known that he would come! Here she was with the thing she likes best. A pox on them both! If I had a suitor, I would play just as you do, but I am barren, alas, as I have no one to adore. Diaphebus, my lord, do you know whom I love with all my heart? Tirant's page Hippolytus, and if he were a knight I would love him still more."[36]

"I promise you," said Diaphebus, "that the next time we enter battle he shall be knighted."

They continued this banter until at last the princess said: "Do you want to know the truth, brother Diaphebus? I have searched every corner of this palace without finding Tirant, wherefore my heart languishes, though if I saw him it would soon revive. I fear I shall die of longing, and one thought alone consoles me: despite my sufferings, I love a brave knight endowed with every virtue. What I admire most is his liberality, for the grand constable told me he is the most lavish of captains, and thus do all great lords reveal their grandeur and preserve their rank. Since Tirant has neither money nor family here, I hope he will safeguard his honor, and wishing to be his father and mother, sister and daughter, beloved and wife, I ask you, my friend, to take him half the gold a horse can carry. I and Pleasure-of-my-life have just had it weighed, and if your men come at suppertime, they will find it loaded in sacks. Should I not be here, Stephanie or Pleasure-of-my-life will give it to them, and I beg you:

remind your cousin to protect his honor, which is mine as well. When he has spent this gold I shall give him more, and if I could raise his station by spending my days at a spinning wheel or shedding my blood, I would also do so. Though the future depends on Fortune, my rank turns everything to its favor, and thus I have asked my father to make him a count. The Easygoing Widow told me that she knew I planned to give Tirant a title because I was in love with him, and I shall remember her words every day of my life. One of my aunts willed me the county of Sancto Angiolo,[37] which I shall now give to Tirant, for then if people find I am in love with him, I shall say I am enamored of a count."

Astonished to hear the princess speak so lovingly, Diaphebus replied: "By God, my lady, how can I thank you for the honors and riches you bestow upon Tirant, though in truth, he deserves much more for his virtues. Your Highness has spoken with such affection that what you offer should be esteemed far beyond its worth, for as the proverb tell us: 'Gifts come not from those who have but from those accustomed to having.' Favors should be valued according to who gives them, and therefore yours should be prized above all others. Please let me kiss your hands and feet, first on that famous knight's behalf and then for all his relatives."

Stephanie's woe was so great that she could keep silent no longer and cried: "Only shame and fear of dishonor prevent me from leaving with Diaphebus, for good folk would defame you if I did so with your knowledge, yet I envy these gifts to your worthy lord Tirant, and therefore I shall imitate you, offering all I have to Diaphebus."

She rose, went to her chamber, and wrote a declaration, which she slipped between her breasts and bore to the princess's chamber.

Meanwhile, Diaphebus pleaded with the princess to let him kiss Stephanie, but she stubbornly refused till at last the Breton said: "My lady, since our wills are in opposition, it is reasonable that our actions should be so too, for thus do men say that when one is unwilling, the other two need not argue. Until now I have been so faithful that had you bought me as a slave, I could not have obeyed more blindly, and had I a hundred lives instead of one, I would have risked them all for Your Highness, yet you refuse me a taste of freedom's rewards. Seek another brother and unpaid servant, and do not think I shall say another word to Tirant on your behalf or give him that gold. As soon as I see him, I shall say goodbye and return home, and some day you will be sorry that you caused my departure."

As they were talking, the emperor came in and asked Diaphebus why he was not preparing to leave, to which he replied: "Sire, I have just come from our lodgings, and everyone is ready."

The emperor led him from the room, reminding him as they walked of his instructions to Tirant.

"Alas, woe is me!" cried the princess. "Diaphebus is furious and refuses to help me. What bad luck that these Frenchmen are all in such a hurry! Stephanie, go and ask him not to be so angry."

"Very well," replied Stephanie.

Pleasure-of-my-life spoke up and said: "You certainly are a strange one, my lady, for you refuse to keep your knights happy in time of peril! They risk their lives and fortunes to defend you and your empire, yet you are willing to incur their hatred for a kiss! What is wrong with a kiss? In France, it is no more important than a handshake. If Diaphebus wants to kiss you or even stick his hands under your skirt, you should let him, as when peace is restored, you can change vice back to virtue. Ah, good lady, you are a precious fool! No one fights duels in wartime or uses ballistas in peace."

The princess then hastened to Stephanie's chamber and again urged her to fetch Diaphebus: "For I fear he will depart, and should he go, Tirant may well accompany him, but even if he stays for love of me, many others will forsake him, and just when we thought to triumph we shall be conquered and enslaved."

"You complicate things, my lady," said Pleasure-of-my-life. "Instead of sending another, go yourself and pretend you want to see the emperor. Tell Diaphebus you have changed your mind, and he will quickly forget his wrath."

The princess hurried to her father, whom she found speaking with Diaphebus. Once they had finished, she took Diaphebus's hand and asked him not to be angry, to which he replied: "My lady, I have tried everything possible. I thought you realized that with the future so uncertain, the hope of happiness alone sustains us, but you have acted like Saint Peter, who, fleeing Rome to save his life, was forced by another to recognize his errors. I have only two choices: to kiss or to leave. Just or unjust, this is my will and you may command me."

"Were shame earned through villainy honor," said the princess, "by granting your wishes I would win fame and glory, while if honor incurred shame, you would not need to rue—since you are unwilling to wait for Tirant, who holds my soul in thrall—those words that sully your good name: 'kiss, kiss.' "

When the princess had finished and Diaphebus had kissed her hand in thanks, he approached Stephanie, whom he kissed thrice on the lips in honor of the Holy Trinity. Stephanie said: "Since you have striven, pleaded, and finally kissed me at my lady's command, I now ask you to take possession of me, but only from the waist up."

Diaphebus, who was no sluggard, quickly began to caress her breasts, fondling the nipples and everything else he could lay his hands on, and thus he found the declaration, which he thought was a letter from another suitor.

"Read it," said Stephanie, "and stop acting so dismayed, lest these noblewomen think you have gone mad or discovered some just cause for suspicion."

The noble princess took the declaration from Diaphebus's hands and read it:

· C X L V I I ·

STEPHANIE OF MACEDONIA'S MARRIAGE VOW[38]

Every day we see how wisely Nature orders our affairs, and being both free to dispose of myself as I wish and in that virginal state which is every damsel's birthright, I hereby declare that I, Stephanie of Macedonia, daughter of illustrious Duke Robert of Macedonia, with pleasure and certitude, being neither constrained nor forced but with God before my eyes and the Holy Gospels in my hands, promise to take you, Diaphebus of Highmount, as my husband and lord, offering you my body without fraud or deception, and in contemplation of marriage I give you the duchy of Macedonia with all pertinent rights. Furthermore, I offer you one hundred and ten thousand Venetian ducats, three thousand silver marks, jewels and robes worth eighty-three thousand ducats, and finally my own person, which I hold dearest of all.

Should anything I say be disproven, I wish to be accused of deceit and shall appeal to no law of past or present emperors, and likewise I renounce my rights under Caesar's *lex Julia maritandis ordinaribus* in favor of damsels, widows, and heiresses.[39]

Moreover, as I have now renounced my rights of chivalry, let no knight enter the lists on my behalf nor any woman challenge me, for I would sooner have a nail driven through my hand with the customary ceremony of knights and ladies of honor.[40]

And that greater credence may be given to my words, I sign with my own blood.

                                                                Stephanie of Macedonia

· CXLVIII ·

*H*OW DIAPHEBUS, HAVING BIDDEN THE EMPEROR AND HIS LADIES FAREWELL, RETURNED TO TIRANT'S CAMP

In fact, Stephanie was not the present duke's daughter. Her father, a brave knight and a noble and wealthy prince, had been the emperor's first cousin and, since Stephanie was his only child, upon his death he left her his duchy, to be inherited on her thirteenth birthday. Stephanie's mother, a powerful noblewoman, shared the guardianship with the emperor, and in order to have more children she later married the Count of Albí, who thus received the title of Duke of Macedonia. Stephanie was fourteen when Diaphebus met her.[41]

As soon as night fell everyone prepared to set out, while Diaphebus, feeling happier than words can express, sent for the money Carmesina had promised him. He had it brought to his lodgings, and as his men were donning their armor, he went to take his leave of the emperor, his ladies, and especially Stephanie, whom he begged to remember him while he was away.

"Alas, lord Diaphebus!" cried Stephanie. "Everything good requires faith. Have you forgotten what the Gospels say: 'Blessed are they that have not seen, and yet have believed.'[42] You see but do not believe, though you possess more of me than anyone else on earth."

She kissed him many times before the princess and Pleasure-of-my-life, shedding abundant tears as is customary between lovers, whereupon Diaphebus knelt and kissed the princess's hands on his behalf and Tirant's. When he was at the head of the stairs, Stephanie ran to him and said: "Take this as a token of my love."

She removed a heavy gold chain from her neck and gave it to him.

"My lady," replied Diaphebus, "I thank you for this token, and though the day had a thousand hours, I would think of you every one of them."

Then he kissed her again, returned to his lodgings, and had the pack mules loaded. They all mounted their horses and set out at two in the morning, but before leaving, Diaphebus asked the emperor to send more ships with provisions.

Once Tirant had welcomed them, Diaphebus and the constable unloaded the ransom money, while their captain summoned the two counts who had distributed His Majesty's gifts before. Then Diaphebus recounted everything that had happened and brought forth Carmesina's gold, at which Tirant was very pleased, though he was even more delighted by Stephanie's declaration.

Diaphebus asked: "Would you like to know how she did it? She tied a string around her finger, and once it was swollen, she pricked it with a needle to make the blood flow."

"Now," said Tirant, "we are nearer to winning our case with my lady, since gallant Stephanie will be on our side."

Diaphebus asked: "Do you want to weigh the gold?"

They did so, and it weighed two quintals.

"Her Highness," said Diaphebus, "gave me more than she had promised, as half a load is only one and a half quintals, and thus do great-hearted lords always behave, delivering more than they pledge."

Let us leave them now and see what their foes were doing.

The grand constable and Diaphebus had left the Turks in despair, cursing the adverse fortune that had brought them such cruel defeats, for after counting heads they found that a hundred thousand of their men had been killed or captured. In their rage, they held council to discuss how they might slay Tirant and decided to send the King of Egypt, who was their bravest and most dexterous knight. He rode well with bridle and stirrups and wore Italian harness like ours, with a plumed helmet and armor upon his horse.

They sent a messenger who, upon reaching the river, waved a flag of truce to request safe-conduct. The Christians quickly returned his signal, and Tirant told them to ferry him across in a little boat.

When he was before Tirant, he requested safe-conduct for the king and ten others, which the captain readily granted. The monarch arrived on the morrow and was welcomed with all the honor he deserved. He had donned a rich tunic embroidered with gold and pearls over his armor, while Tirant wore the shirt Carmesina had given him. The captain asked two of the emissaries to supervise the slaughter of two hundred capons and hens, from which a splendid feast was prepared with rice, couscous, and other royal dishes. The king spent the next day inspecting Tirant's camp, and asked why there were so many men on horseback, to which our knight replied: "My lord, they are here in your honor."

"Had we acted thus, you would never have routed us, but you shall pay with your life for those you captured and flung in the river without a decent burial. Their deaths fill me with mortal loathing, nor should my just hatred surprise you, as it is neither fair nor reasonable to love one's enemies in war. Conflict never engenders love, wherefore you shall perish by my cruel hand, for you yourself have cruelly slaughtered many innocent victims, who may truly call you the most bloodthirsty, recreant, and shameful knight on earth."

Tirant replied: "Your tongue wags so venomously that it must do so through long custom, but I, with my trenchant sword, shall soon punish your evil sect, and therefore I scorn to argue, and still less in my own tent."

Tirant then walked out as the king began to reply and, upon returning to his camp, the Egyptian summoned his allies to a large field, where he addressed both Christians and Saracens in this manner:

· CXLIX ·

*H*OW THE KING OF EGYPT TOLD HIS ALLIES OF TIRANT'S REPLY

"Some prefer talking to fighting, but I, who am not of such stuff, would sooner send my hands on manly errands, submitting to Fortune as an ardent knight should, wherefore, magnanimous lords, I wish to describe the Christians' wise measures. Men on foot and horseback patrol their camp at all hours, and thus we shall never surprise them as they once did us, for their troops have been well ordered since that captain came."

The sultan asked: "How many do you think they have?"

"My lord," replied the king, "I estimate that there are less than forty-five thousand infantry and ten thousand cavalry, but though few, they are better disciplined than when they were led by the Duke of Macedonia, whose ineptness assured us of constant victories. Had that devil not come from France, we would rule Constantinople, its cathedral would be a mosque, and we would have killed the emperor and enslaved his wife and daughter, but now we shall be thwarted as long as this captain lives. He will only fight with every advantage because he knows we are much stronger, wherefore there is only one way to kill or capture him. With your leave, I shall challenge him to single combat, which he will valiantly accept. If you see me winning, do not intervene, but if he gets the better of me, attack with crossbows, slaying him and all his party."

Everyone thought his suggestion good.

Once the council had ended, the King of Egypt went to his tent and wrote a cartel of defiance.

The sultan had an old and trusted servant who, though born a Christian in the Cypriot city of Famagusta, had been captured at sea by Saracen pirates. Because he was young and innocent they were able to convert him, but upon reaching majority, he recognized the error of his ways and, determined to return to the true faith, he armed himself well and mounted a good horse, on which he rode toward Lord Malveí's bridge. When he was within crossbow range, he fastened his turban to the end of his lance as a flag of truce. Those inside saw he was alone and returned the signal, but as he approached, a crossbowman who had not seen the exchange shot a quarrel and wounded his horse.

"My lords!" cried the Saracen. "Are you so faithless as to kill me and my horse under a flag of truce?"

Lord Malveí, who was most distressed, told the Saracen to dismount and sent his horse to be looked after, promising him a better one if it died. The Saracen said he had come to convert and asked for the captain, whom he wished to be his godfather and to whom he could offer much useful information. They told the Saracen to return on the morrow, and he left feeling very content. After reaching his camp, he brought his mount to the veterinarians, whereupon the sultan asked whence he had come and how his horse had been wounded. The Saracen replied: "Sire, as I was riding toward the bridge, I spied a Christian horseman who stopped to await me. He shot a quarrel when I approached, but I spurred my mount, overtook him, and knocked him to the ground. I was about to kill him but he knelt and begged me to spare his life, and since I am merciful by nature, we became such good friends that he promised to tell me everything that happens in the Christian camp."

"What good news!" exclaimed the sultan. "Now I shall be able to learn their plans! Please ask him tomorrow whether they intend to give battle or withdraw to Constantinople."

The Saracen said he would do so, and the next day he requested permission to speak with his friend. At the appointed hour he mounted one of the sultan's finest steeds, and upon reaching the bridge he was quickly admitted and made welcome. Soon Tirant arrived and greeted Lord Malveí and his son, who led him to a room where Lady Malveí was entertaining their guest. The Saracen then said he had recognized the truth of Christianity and asked Tirant's leave to enter his service.

"And I warn Your Lordship that they plan to send a cartel tomorrow or the next day, but do not accept the challenge under any circumstances, for if you do, great harm will befall you and your men."

Tirant thanked him for the warning, agreed to accept his service, and escorted him to the church, where, after asking Tirant and Hippolytus to be his godfathers and Lady Malveí to be his godmother, the repentant Saracen was christened Cypriot of Paternò. Having been baptized, he said: "By Our Lord's grace, I now hold myself a true Christian, and in this holy faith I hope to live and die. Should you wish me to stay, I shall do so with a good will, but if you want me to return to my camp, I shall report to you every day, as the council meets in our sultan's tent and I take part in it."

Tirant rewarded him with a gold chain he was wearing, while Lord Malveí's son gave him forty ducats, which Cypriot left in Lady Malveí's keeping.

Tirant asked him to return to his camp but to inform Lord Malveí as often as he could of any Turkish plans, to which Cypriot of Paternò replied: "Noble captain and lord, never doubt my loyalty, for as a Christian I swear to serve you as if you had protected me from infancy. I know you have little reason to trust a convert, but in the future you will see my firmness and devotion, and finally, if you have any sweets, please give me some for the sultan, since he loves them and it will help me to come and go without suspicion."

Lord Malveí said: "I can give you some."

He ordered dates and candied fruit brought forth, and after they all had eaten a few, he gave a box of candied fruit and another of dates to the convert.

Upon seeing him, the sultan asked for news of the Christians, to which Cypriot replied that his friend had told him they were planning to stay: "Until Your Majesty departs; and he gave me these sweetmeats."

The sultan was delighted with the gift and made him return frequently, while Cypriot reported to Lord Malveí, who then relayed the information to Tirant.

This Cypriot of Paternò swore never to serve the sultan again.

The King of Egypt summoned a messenger, to whom he gave his cartel of defiance, which contained bellicose threats of this tenor:

· CL ·

T HE KING OF EGYPT'S CARTEL OF DEFIANCE

From Abenamar, vanquisher of three kings by Allah's will and leave—that is, the mighty King of Fez, the brave King of Bougie, and the blessed King of Tlemcen—to Tirant lo Blanc, captain of the Greeks:

I lay aside prolixity, that deeds may bear true witness between us, giving one glorious victory to the other's harm and ignominy. I see you wear a woman's tunic, which shows you are her suitor, and as I swore a solemn vow to my lady, sending it to Our Holy Prophet Mohammed's tomb in Mecca, that I would defy a king, a prince, or the mightiest captain in Christendom, I challenge you to single combat, swearing to slay, defeat, or dishonor you in the lists. With these hands I shall defend my beloved's superior beauty and lineage, sending her your head as a token of my affection. I rely on your good faith, but should you cravenly refuse me, I shall utter that word so abhorred by all who prize their honor. Every knight should shrink from disgrace before his

peers, yet with malice, or more precisely treachery, you attacked our camp to
your eternal infamy. My just cause assures me that I shall slay you in battle, as
Allah will not let such a foul crime go unpunished, wherefore I shall meet you
on foot or horseback as you devise, before a competent judge during as many
days as need be. Should you wish to answer this letter, give your reply to my
messenger Egypt, for thus we may reach an agreement, bringing our contest to
its desired end.

  Written in our camp on the eastern shore, the first day of this moon. I place
here my seal:

King of Egypt

· CLI ·

HOW TIRANT ASKED HIS GREAT LORDS' ADVICE

Having read the letter, Tirant summoned his knights, whom he asked
what they thought he should do and whether he should reply. The Duke
of Macedonia spoke first: "I think you should respond with the same
rhyme, for as the priest chants, so the choirboy answers. His letter makes
two points: the first is the damsel, and the second is the accusation of
treachery. In the first case, the king is enamored of the Great Khan's
daughter, whom everyone claims is wondrously fair and who has been
promised to him as soon as the war ends. Consider whether your beloved
is of nobler lineage and do not fight him unjustly, as Our Lord performs
great miracles in battles."

  "My lord," replied Tirant, "in my land I loved a widow who was also a
virgin. I wished to marry and I believe she did too, for she gave me this
shirt, which I have always worn in combat."

  The Duke of Pera said: "That will not suffice, since the King of Egypt's
lady is the Great Khan's daughter. This khan commands six kings, and
though less mighty than the sultan, he nonetheless rules many lands,
including Karaman. Do you know how much territory his vassal the
Grand Karaman governs?[43] More than all France and Spain, as I know
from experience, because I passed through his realms on my way to
Jerusalem, after which I was moved by devotion to make a pilgrimage to
Saint James's tomb in Galicia, and thus I crossed all of Spain as well. If
you wish to act justly, imagine you are in love with our lady princess,
whereby your cause will be righteous, for she will excel his mistress in
every way."

"I would not want," Tirant said, "the emperor to be troubled by suspicions of me."

The Duke of Sinope asked: "How could the emperor be affronted by something done without fraud or dishonor?"

"Even if he were not," replied Tirant, "what shall we do about the princess, who may be angered at such presumption in a foreigner of little rank and no title?"

The Duke of Cassandria said: "Damsels take pleasure in being wooed by men of every station, and Carmesina's wisdom will glory in your noble zeal."

"Who can change God's designs?" asked the Duke of Montesanto. "It is nothing new for a king to pursue some humble damsel, or a queen some poor gentleman of unknown parentage. This gracious lady will rejoice in your words and deeds."

The Marquis of Saint George said: "Captain, you make ignorance your guide, for it is well known that knights have performed many deeds for damsels of resplendent fame, and he who forgets the past will also forget himself."

The Marquis of Ferrara said: "Women like nothing so much as a man's adoration, and if you removed her clog, she would not feel offended, nor could so virtuous a damsel be displeased by your devotion."

"We are all children of Adam and Eve," said the Marquis of Pescara. "Some of our parents were damned while others were saved, but I say with true conviction: if our captain conquers in the princess's name, he will be among the saved, and even if he sticks his hand under her skirt, he will find nothing but love and honor there."

Tirant had his secretary record their opinions and send them to the emperor, so that if anyone spoke ill of him the blame would be theirs and not his.

When the council ended, he went to his tent and answered the King of Egypt's cartel:

· CLII ·

*T*IRANT'S REPLY TO THE KING OF EGYPT

Truth is in no way harmed among men of understanding when words of deceitful intent unwittingly disclose it, wherefore I, Tirant lo Blanc, conqueror and destroyer of that renowned Sultan of Babylon, the Lord of Turkey, and yourself, the King of Egypt, acknowledge receipt of a cartel in which you say you beheld me in a damsel's tunic, and that in order to fulfill a vow, you wish to battle me to the utterance, declaring your beloved loftier and fairer than mine.

I say first that in making such a vow, you sullied your honor. Better you had sworn to spend ten years in Mecca, doing penance for your sins abominable to God and the world, as everyone knows the damsel I love has no peer in beauty, rank, or splendor, nor is her lineage, grace, or wisdom excelled by any other's. It is known that you love the Great Khan's daughter and I the emperor's; you woo a Saracen and I a Christian. Your mistress has the schism and mine the chrism, and everywhere mine shall be judged better and nobler. Your lady is unworthy to remove my princess's shoe, and though you say you will offer my head to your beloved, I shall not let you since I need it to expel your allies, yet even if you sent it, the head of a corpse is of little value, while I, on the other hand, promised Her Highness that I would rout your hordes in four battles and in the fifth imprison a king, whom I would bring before her with conquering sword. No damsel will esteem a knight who offers dead and defeated things, but to get to the point, you claim I bested your men twice through treachery. The Emperor of Rome once decreed that anyone accused of perfidy should denounce his slanderers, and your words oppose the truth, just as your vile speech dishonors knighthood. Even ladies of honor, should you ask them, will say I have practiced no deceit but followed the gentle style and customs of chivalry. If I triumphed through greater skill, no infamy can be spoken against me, for only if I had tricked you would your calumnies be justified.

Therefore I, Tirant lo Blanc, in the name of Our Lord, the Virgin Mary, and my lady Carmesina, upholding my right, honor, and fame, accept your challenge, and by my prerogatives as defender, affirmed in your letter, I choose to fight on horseback clad in armor of the type customary in warfare but without concealed advantages. Our weapons shall be ten-foot lances with stout points four fingers long, three and a half foot swords from pommel to tip, axes a hand's-breadth wide and daggers two feet long, while our horses shall wear leather or chain mail coverings as each man devises, steel headpieces without spikes or other advantages, and saddles as worn in war with unfastened stirrups. Having agreed on the arms, we must now choose a judge, but whom shall we consider a competent arbiter? You are sworn to serve your king, just as I am sworn to mine, and since you are a Saracen and I a Christian, who will this competent judge be? If you mean we should travel through the world seeking a judge, you may do so but I cannot, for I have many dukes, counts, and marquises under my orders and am indifferent to combats of dubious execution. Should you propose the sultan, I declare that those without faith cannot keep it, nor can he guarantee that, if I slay you, I may return safely to my camp. Neither do I ask that you come to me, as I cannot request what I myself refuse, and should you win, who among my friends and relatives could assure your safety? Nonetheless, I shall offer a solution that I hope will satisfy you: everyone knows that when you besieged the Duke of Macedonia, I sought you out and routed you, and when you later attacked me, I again defeated you, putting to flight those who haughtily and vaingloriously declared themselves conquerors of three kings. Therefore, it is only right that I should go to you this time.

I swear before God and my lady, by my knightly honor, that on August twenty-fourth I shall await you upon the eastern shore, wherefore you will have no cause to accuse me of wrongdoing, writing letters blackened by vile words to which I disdain to reply. I leave you with your glory, and that all worthy knights, ladies, and damsels may behold my innocence, I send you this letter with your messenger Egypt, cut along ABC, written in my hand, and sealed with my arms in Camp Trasimene on August fifth.

Tirant lo Blanc

· CLIII ·

*H*OW THE DUKE OF MACEDONIA DEFAMED TIRANT

Once Tirant had written the letter, he showed it to his lords, who found it good. Then he summoned the messenger, to whom he gave his reply, a silver tunic, and two hundred ducats, saying: "Please inform your lord the sultan that the king-of-arms who will accompany you wishes to speak in my name."

Egypt promised to do so, and the two of them set out together.

When they reached the camp, everyone celebrated their arrival, while Tirant's king-of-arms told the sultan he wished to address him before his vassals and allies. The sultan ordered the trumpets blown, and as soon as they had gathered he said: "Now you may deliver your master's reply."

The king-of-arms said: "The captain of the Greek Empire, representing His Glorious Majesty the emperor, informs and notifies you that as you are aware of the laws and customs of warfare among kings, emperors, and other lords, and as you have lost your flags in two battles, by right you should only bear standards. He demands this of you by the rules of chivalry, for otherwise he will use his rights as conqueror: that is, after painting your arms on a shield and tying it to a horse's tail, he will drag it through his camp and all the cities he visits, wherefore, lest you incur such insult and infamy, he asks you to bear no flags."

"Cursed be the man who discovered such a rule," said the sultan, "but if the knightly code demands it, I am content."

He quickly ordered his and all his subjects' flags furled, and they were left with their standards. Then Tirant's messenger turned to the King of

Egypt and said: "My lord, our captain has responded to your challenge. Tell me how you will dress on the day of battle, that he may recognize you in the crowd."

"My friend," replied the king, "tell him that for his foul deeds I would sooner kill him outside the lists, but to satisfy his request and that justice may be done, say I shall wear a scarlet jubbah that belonged to my virtuous lady. Her portrait will be painted on a little pennant atop my helmet, and if he attacks or I see him, I shall either force him to admit the truth or kill him with my own hands."

The messenger returned to his captain and repeated everything the king had said.

Then the Turks prepared for battle.

The next day the Duke of Macedonia, who was jealous of Tirant's glory, spoke the following words to him before everyone: "Having betrayed your chivalric oaths, you should embrace the Saracen faith, for when reason fails them, they defend their doctrines with the sword. You seek to battle a Turkish army so big it could defeat the entire world, and thus you pretend to display your courage, but how can you expect to win fame through deceit? Instead you should examine your conscience, which will inform you of your treachery. What love of life or fear of death so blinds you that you cannot see your error? We shall not let you wager our lives in hope of drawing an ace, nor shall you fight without cause, for if we lose we shall all be killed, but alas, you care little about our fate! For you the world is wide, and you will always find some brigand rabble to command, yet woe unto us who were born in this land, and woe unto those who have wives and children here and whose future is in the hands of an unknown foreigner!

"You say you have promised to fight the King of Egypt, but that is only a ruse to deliver us to the Turks. Tell me: how much did our adversaries pay you? Will you be a second Judas, betraying Christ for thirty pieces of silver? Are you that infamous Cain who killed his brother Abel? Are you that Prince of Cyprus who lay with his mother and flung his father from the castle walls? Are you perchance Canace, who, having raped his sister Macareus, fled to the Roman army and betrayed his natural lord for money?[44] Oh Tirant, open your eyes, for we know who you are! We even know your noble past: how you fled your land in disgrace and do not dare to return after allying yourself with our enemies, from whom you should protect us. Do you remember your words to the King of Egypt: that those without faith cannot keep it? How can we trust you after the evil you have done us? Knowing your wicked schemes to destroy our empire, we could justly submit you to trial by burning oil, for I never heard of any Christian committing such a sin. The very stones should rise up against you, but still more men of wisdom, as we trust in our faith to bring us heavenly glory, whereas subtle sophists like you will go straight to Hell. You should not be captain except by my consent, and therefore I strip you of your office from this moment on."

A great uproar arose when the duke finished his speech. All the knights donned their armor and seized their weapons, while the most headstrong mounted their horses as if to enter battle. Many were pleased, since one of men's vices is to rejoice in a new leader.

· CLIV ·

*T*IRANT'S REPLY TO THE DUKE OF MACEDONIA

"If you think your acts are too remote to be remembered or that despite your evil ways, you deserve my office, you are mistaken, and to spare you from hearing your glorious deeds recounted, I shall only point to what I have to tolerate every day. Lest I sully my mouth and men think me as loose-tongued as you, I shall only mention a few of your noblest feats. Who cut the thong on the prince's helmet, striking the first blow to send him from this world? Who led all those dukes, counts, marquises, barons, knights, and soldiers to death beneath his banner? Thus do men call you a loser of battles, for you have always been defeated through your own mistakes, nor have you loved your honor, which is a knight's most prized possession. I did not lose the county of Albí or the duchy of Macedonia, which by right is not yours but belongs to Stephanie, nor did I surrender the city of Cappadocia and its entire province, thereby abandoning the greater part of the empire.

"If you had any wit, you would disguise yourself and flee. Do you think the Greeks consider you loyal and patriotic? They harbor no such thought, though they may not dare to tell you; and now you have discarded your usual cowardice, steeling your heart to betray me, for as our ancestors said: 'He who wants to hear evil must speak it first.' Were sin grace and not disloyalty to the emperor and princess, I would bathe my hands in your body's purest blood, but I trust that those you disgraced and killed will cry out to God for justice, thus avenging your slanders and villainous calumnies. I shall say no more and take comfort in one fact: that I speak the truth and shall therefore be believed, whereas you speak with false and detestable malice."

The secretary noted down these words, as he was planning to leave the next day, and later, when they were at council, Tirant announced to one and all: "Noble, illustrious, and magnificent lords: come what may, I intend to fulfill my promise, and I ask you by the powers the emperor gave me to be ready for battle on the appointed day."

The Duke of Macedonia replied: "Tirant, you would do better to sleep than plot such folly, for I can assure you that neither I nor my men will do your bidding. We are not subject to your bitter orders, nor is our disobedience surprising, and to free you from the error in which you are enmeshed, I repeat: had you specified when you received your captaincy that we were under your command, your request would be just, yet to your great discredit, you remain unsatisfied with the powers your lord granted you. Let us, therefore, submit our case to worthy knights, since otherwise my opinions and prophesies will be confirmed."

Tirant replied: "I have no time to plead cases in the midst of war, as my hands are busy with more urgent matters than scribbling and litigation. No one of our house has ever sullied his good name, and with God's help I too shall preserve my own, nor should you imagine that I derive pleasure from my position, having neither sought nor requested such an office. If it has brought me some honors, I did not request them either but received them for my constant trials and tribulations and because these dukes and princes have been safe under my command. When the emperor selected me, he did not ask your consent, nor should that surprise you since you were not with him at the time, but lest anyone think me ambitious, I am willing to share my office. Do you think your vassals will not fight without your consent? They must, for on the appointed day I shall appear before our foes, and though some may cower in fear, I shall go with my own men, who I know will not fail me, nor will my Rhodian friends lag behind. Oh duke, if you fear the sight of blood, so terrifying to cowards, stay here with the pages, the wounded, and the disabled."

The next day, Tirant summoned his great lords after Mass and said: "Most illustrious, noble, and magnificent knights: you all must share the burden of this war. Holding my office by imperial appointment, I have sweated to ensure your safety, but now, at the Duke of Macedonia's instigation, I relinquish my post, comforted by the thought that we have ousted our enemies from this area. The futures of many should never be entrusted to one man, wherefore everyone should share the position I have held, receiving nothing in return and only striving to serve His Majesty. If you elect someone fitter, I shall neither leave nor take offense, as I only wish to live and die in your company. All of you should consider me less than an equal, for I shall gladly obey and serve you until our campaign ends."

Unable to abide such words, The Marquis of Saint George cried: "By God, captain, I shall not fail you in any worthy endeavor, and even in shirtsleeves I would follow you into battle. I solemnly swear by Saint George that if anyone defies the emperor's wishes, I shall kill him with my own hands, for His Majesty appointed Tirant, whom we should obey as though he were our sovereign."

The Duke of Pera said: "Lord captain, your word is our command, and if you wish to execute the Duke of Macedonia, entrust me with the task."

"I shall split whoever dares to accept the captaincy," said the Duke of Sinope, "to the waist with my naked sword."

The Duke of Cassandria declared: "I swear to kill anyone who sows discord, urges Tirant to resign, or offers to replace him."

"I have not spoken," said the Duke of Montesanto, "but after hearing the Duke of Macedonia's slanders, I hold him a confessed liar."

The Marquis of Saint Mark mounted a bench, drew his sword, and cried: "Let anyone who wishes to sow further treason come forth, and I shall battle him to the utterance before you all. Our just, good, and loyal captain has done nothing to warrant the Duke of Macedonia's accusations, and if the duke is not condemned now, he will be in the next world."

The Marquis of Ferrara shouted: "I wish you all to know that when the Duke of Macedonia suffered his last defeat, ladies and damsels at the market in Constantinople cried: 'Where is that recreant Duke of Macedonia, loser of battles and shedder of Greek blood? Where is that inept and ignominious knight? Let us take his life, for he has slain the light of our eyes.' Tearfully cursing you as their foe, they demanded your corpse, and had you perished at that moment you might have been buried with honor, whereas you now live in disgrace, which is far worse than death."

The Count of Acquaviva spoke up: "Since our natural lord has appointed Tirant captain of his empire, what causes you, Duke of Macedonia, to vex our leader and seek to divide us, persevering in your shameful perfidy, whose end you fear so little? You flee the truth and seek that which was not given you, but no man should accept the testimony of his father's foe. Control your tongue, lest Tirant defend his rights. This man, who excels Hector, is a mighty conqueror, a shedder of blood. Our forefathers live on in glorious fame while the defeated die in dull obscurity! If anyone contradicts me, I shall make him confess his error, since God will not allow our captain to be accused of such foul crimes. May worthy Tirant remain unpunished and chastise you as an example."

The Duke of Macedonia turned to answer the Marquis of Saint George: "You do not deserve your name, which is contrary to your deeds, and you may be sure I know what name you do deserve. Should I disparage your honor, let our listeners recall that such is not my custom, for in merely hearing of your treachery, the ears of worthy knights are offended, yet so great are your crimes that I cannot hold my tongue.[45] Why do you exchange such loving words with Tirant, trying all the while to defame me with lies and falsehoods? Where are all your false oaths and promises now? I am not surprised, however, as you are truly your father's son, and your wickedness is known to all knights and ladies of honor, while in Constantinople they amuse themselves by mocking your evil deeds, wherefore I pity your plight and advise you to hold your peace." Having spoken, the duke rose and returned to his camp.

"Oh dukes, counts, and marquises," said Count Plegamans, "now that the Duke of Macedonia has departed, heed my words lest we suffer an irreparable defeat. You are more eager to wrong your betters than to have an honest captain, but the office belongs to the duke and no one else. If you, Tirant, wish to hear that evil word so abhorred by all, I am prepared to utter it, though I fear to damn myself through pride. Relinquish your post and its burdens, for you are watched by many eyes, and recall that glory is only won through valiant deeds."

When he saw that the duke had left, Tirant refused to let anyone else speak. Instead, he ordered them to return to their tents and prepare for battle.

Here the book leaves them and returns to the emperor, who was eagerly awaiting news from the camp.[46] One day he saw seven ships approaching, and upon their arrival, he learned that they bore soldiers and horses from Sicily. The eldest Prince of Sicily had married a French princess, and the French king, cherishing his wisdom and courage, would not let him leave Paris. Much to his father's dismay, this prince fell ill and died, whereupon the other son, who was a friar, renounced his claim to the throne.

The king, his heart broken by the younger son's disobedience, took to his bed, set his soul in order, and abdicated in Philip's favor. Once Philip had been crowned, he recalled Tirant's generosity and decided to help him, but the Sicilians begged their lord not to depart while his queen was pregnant. Yielding to their opposition, Philip sent the Duke of Messina in his stead with five thousand foot and cavalry, while the grateful queen also sent two thousand men under the Lord of Pantelleria.

As soon as the two lords had disembarked, they met the emperor's secretary, who bore the cartels of defiance and the knights' declarations, all arranged in order for His Majesty's perusal. As they were walking toward the palace, the Duke of Messina said: "Sir, may God preserve you and grant your fondest wish. Tell me: in what city does Tirant lo Blanc reside?"

"My lord," replied the secretary, "you will not find that brave knight in any village, town, or city, for I recently left his camp by the river Trasimene."

"What are his companions like?" asked the Lord of Pantelleria. "Are they men of sport and pleasure?"

"By Saint Mary they are!" cried the secretary. "First of all, they always find mercy at his door, and a step higher, he judges men's good and evil deeds. As he knows whom to trust, his judgments are always wise, and this is the quality a captain most needs, for he must not be swayed by pleas, threats, or bribes. Tirant is also magnanimous, dividing everything among his men, and if he has nothing to give he will take the shirt off his back, but even when he cannot help, his intentions are always good. In nobility, courage, and gentility, he has no equal on earth, as may be seen by the victories he has won and wins every day. He gaily entertains his friends with music and dancing, being both courteous to ladies and fearless among knights. In his tents, some wrestle and turn somersaults; others play checkers or chess; others act foolish or solemn; others speak of war or love; others play lutes, guitars, and flutes or sing five-part harmonies, and so anyone who seeks merriment will find it with our captain. I never saw a man of any nation who served God so well, and if six thousand barons came before him, he would know how to please them all. He honors his own men greatly and foreigners still more, for two of those German barons who elect the emperor visited us a few days ago, and they left saying they had never seen such lavish hospitality."

The secretary took his leave of them and, having mounted the palace steps, found the emperor finishing lunch in the imperial dining hall. His Majesty was delighted to see him and asked whether Tirant needed provisions, to which the wise secretary replied: "My lord, what we need at present is not food but love and honor."

He fell silent and said no more. The emperor quickly had the table cleared, while the secretary handed him first the cartels and then the dukes' opinions. After reading them, the emperor turned to his daughter and said: "Carmesina, my knights say Tirant is enamored of you."

She blushed bright red and was speechless for a long time, but at last she regained her composure and replied: "Sire, I am pleased that victorious knights should woo me, but although Tirant is an ardent warrior, a winner of battles, and a mighty conqueror, let Your Majesty not heed the slander of malicious tongues. While I cherish him and his companions as brothers, I have never offered myself to him and it is far from my mind. Should you hear such gossip, do not condemn me without a trial, for God has girded me with chastity and my breasts turn colder than ice at such a thought."

"No, my daughter," replied the emperor, "that was not their meaning. Read this report, and you will see what they said."

Having read it, she felt better and whispered to Stephanie: "Not a drop of blood remained in me, for I thought we had been discovered. The Devil beguiled me into giving Tirant that money, both causing my action and bringing it to light, but my crime was virtuous and should be judged by its charitable end."

Stephanie replied: "My lady, you behaved properly, as I know you wish to be Tirant's wife and I beheld your dismay at the emperor's words."

While they were whispering, the Sicilian barons entered and bowed before the emperor, who welcomed them with great honor. They told him why they had come and gave him their past and present treaties, which he signed. After ordering fine lodgings prepared, the emperor went to council, leaving the ladies with his guests, who were so dazzled by the princess's beauty that the Lord of Pantelleria uttered these words of praise:

· CLV ·

*T*HE LORD OF PANTELLERIA'S WORDS TO THE PRINCESS

"I can see, fair lady, that Nature did her utmost in fashioning you, and now I know how the saints must feel when they behold the glorious Divine Essence, for as the Holy Scriptures tell us in the psalm addressed to Christ: 'A thousand years in thy sight are but as yesterday when it is past.'[47] By God, my lady, if I could spend my life before you, it would not be like yesterday as the psalmist says but like this very moment, since just as time creeps for souls in torment, so it flies for the blessed. Those who seek to be parted from you deserve short lives and ill health, and may such men wander forever without reaching salvation's harbor! Your peerless beauty is renowned in our kingdom, where men say your noble acts have restored the art of chivalry, yet I believe Your Highness's presence far exceeds all those praises, as your infinite grace and wisdom are worthy of a goddess. Unable to recount your perfections, I hold myself blessed merely to have seen you."

At this point His Majesty entered, so the princess had no chance to reply. He stayed with them awhile, discussing the war and other matters.

When the two lords thought it was time, they retired to their lodgings, where they found a splendid supper awaiting them. Once they had gone, the emperor asked: "Have you ever heard or read in chronicles of any captain in another's service whose friends and relatives sent him aid? I am amazed and greatly indebted to Tirant, since ten thousand soldiers paid by others serve me for love of him. I think I should seek to reconcile the duke and our captain, who otherwise may shortly slay one another, for it has almost happened twice and I fear the third occasion. Would that I myself might resolve the matter by beheading the duke!"

Then the emperor ordered his servants to prepare for their departure.

"What, my lord?" asked the empress. "Will you go with so few retainers?"

The emperor replied: "Those Sicilian barons will accompany me."

That night while Carmesina slept, Stephanie entered the room and woke her, saying: "My lady, Diaphebus appeared to me in a dream and declared: 'Upon my life, Stephanie, how Tirant and I long to see you, for only thus shall we vanquish those treacherous Turks.' If you wish, we may quickly turn our absence into presence, and by visiting them in the field we shall prove our devotion."

The princess replied: "Give me my robe, and say no more."

She quickly dressed and went to the emperor's chambers, where she knelt before him and said: "Sire, though damsels tremble at the words 'war' and 'battle,' please let me accompany you, for my reasons are weighty. At your age, you should go nowhere without your daughter, who loves you and knows your condition better than all others. If you fell ill, I could nurse you back to health, and furthermore, since it is a natural law that children outlive their parents, by joining you I shall gain knowledge of warfare, which I may need in the future."

"My daughter," replied the emperor, "I am aware of your good will, but it is neither decent nor customary for damsels to visit battlefields, which are places of great peril and still more for one your age. I love you too much to let you be troubled by our foes."

"My lord," said the princess, "do not fret on my behalf, as it would distress me more to lose sight of you than to be surrounded by enemies. Just as I was your servant in adversity, let me be so now in prosperity, nor shall I ever forsake you until your soul leaves your body, when I shall give you the burial your imperial dignity deserves. I fear that if I do not go with you, my eyes will never see you again."

"My daughter," replied the emperor, "since you insist, I shall say no more, though your zeal is excessive. Ask your mother if she wishes to go, and prepare yourself quickly."

Carmesina hastened to ask the empress, who replied that she would not accompany them for anything on earth, lest upon seeing the Duke of Macedonia or the spot where her son had died, she be overwhelmed by grief and thereby end her wretched life.

Having summoned all the armorers in Constantinople, the princess ordered a coat of mail, vambraces, and gauntlets of gold and silver. She wore the gold on her right side and the silver on her left. She also ordered a small silver helmet, on which she could place her crown, and finally she asked the emperor to lend her some Sicilian soldiers.

On the day of their departure, Carmesina donned a gold mantle with jeweled embroidery over her armor and mounted a fine white charger, from which she could command her troops with a staff. The sixty most gallant and beautiful imperial damsels attended her: Stephanie was grand constable, the Duke of Pera's daughter Saladria was captain general, and Contesina was chief bailiff, while Pleasure-of-my-life bore their standard, which showed a flower called love-in-a-mist and the princess's motto: *But not to me.* Eliseu also carried a big pennant, the Easygoing Widow was their seneschal, and every damsel in Constantinople held some office in the princess's company. Thus they journeyed to the camp, but upon arriving they found no one except the disabled and a few pages.[48]

The Greek army had set out at midnight on the nineteenth of that month, and the emperor arrived at three o'clock the next afternoon. To evade enemy spies, Tirant crossed the bridge under cover of darkness, though the day before he had dispatched soldiers to arrest all the scouts and shepherds they could find. After reaching the other side, the Christians marched a good half a league upstream, where they turned and proceeded till they were two leagues from the Turkish camp. Tirant marshaled his troops at dawn in a place called Thorny Valley, giving each man provisions and fodder for a day.

As soon as the emperor reached the camp, he summoned Lord Malveí, who hastened to salute his master and recount Tirant's exploits to the delighted princess. Lord Malveí invited the emperor to stay at his castle, while the Sicilian barons camped by the river.

One of Lord Malveí's men went to inform Tirant that the emperor, his daughter, and two Sicilian lords had arrived. Tirant kept these tidings secret until the next day, lest anyone try to leave with the excuse of visiting His Majesty or some relative. When just before midnight the cavalry mounted their steeds, only Diaphebus knew that his beloved was nearby.

After placing the infantry under Diaphebus's command with thirty-four horsemen on armored mounts, Tirant begged his cousin dearly to hide behind a cluster of boulders, from which spot he was neither to move nor let any of his men be seen even if he beheld his captain's troops fleeing. Still unsatisfied, Tirant then made Diaphebus swear a solemn oath not to budge until he received orders to do so.

Diaphebus stationed himself in the aforesaid manner, while Tirant advanced with all his cavalry. When they were within bombard range of the Turkish camp, they halted, not in the stockade ringed with trenches that they had constructed earlier but in a flat, open field on their foes' other flank. Upon hearing them, the Saracen watchmen raised a shout, for seventeen thousand infidels had spent the night on horseback to avoid another rout. Since Tirant did not dare to assault such a multitude, the Turkish horsemen all seized their weapons and rode forth.

Both armies then drew up ranks, and Tirant marshaled his troops thus:

he had his cavalry line up even with one another with the emperor's flags in the middle, while the Duke of Sinope commanded one flank and the Duke of Pera the other. Seeing that everyone had obeyed his orders except the Duke of Macedonia, Tirant rode to and fro, urging his knights to stay in formation, for if they did so God would surely give them victory that day, as our knight explained in the following speech:

· CLVI ·

TIRANT'S SPEECH TO ALL HIS KNIGHTS

"Praise won without risk is of little value, and since our cause is just, our hope must be firm. Noble knights, the day we have longed for is at hand, as we shall now triumph and each man will regain his birthright! Covet glory won through courage, scorning danger and fear, and to better express my thoughts, I remind you of Darius. He and his army were massacred through their ineptitude, just as many others have been undone by the sin of envy, wherefore let us boldly prove our mettle and clear a path to our salvation, mindful that God decides all battles and allots honor, fame, and victory.

"Should we triumph, noble lords, the empire's cities, towns, and castles will be ours, but should outrageous Fortune put us to flight, the opposite will occur. Those infidels trust in their swollen multitudes, while we defend our fatherland, our liberty, and our very lives. Valiant knights, do not fear the enemy hordes, as the few have often vanquished the many, and the greater their numbers, the more chaos within their ranks. Good order and discipline have always decided wars, and thus I remind those who prize chivalry that we have bested them twice already. Do not think them braver now or less dismayed by their comrades' deaths, but rather think how woeful and despondent our foes must be. For all these reasons we must now give battle, and their riches will be ours if only we attack them with invincible ardor. Should any coward feel the urge to flee, let him look well at what he does, as it is nobler to perish in battle than to retreat without resistance, and those who take to their heels will be butchered like sheep, whereas by fighting with manly spirit we shall carry the day. Look toward that castle, where the emperor and his ladies wait to behold our victory. Oh suitors who feel true love: great will be your glory if you triumph today, but what infamy, should you approach His Highness as vanquished fugitives! Who will dare to show his face before such a lord? May the earth cover my eyes and wild beasts tear my flesh before I dishonor myself so!"

He could say no more, because he saw the Turks were ready.

· CLVII ·

HOW THE SULTAN MARSHALED HIS TROOPS AND THE BATTLE BEGAN

Once Tirant's men were in position, the sultan quickly arrayed his hordes, which were led by lancers carrying huge shields that almost hid them. Then came his archers and crossbowmen, followed by Christians in the Grand Turk's pay, who rode armored mounts fifteen paces behind the crossbowmen. The rest brought up the rear with more than four hundred bombards that they estimated would alone fell seven hundred men. When the Saracen battalions were in order, the King of Egypt sent a message to Tirant, thanking him for having kept his word and swearing to kill or capture him. The king declared that after taking Constantinople, he would have his gold image placed above the main gate and that the Breton captain would soon taste his bitter lance. Tirant retorted that he would gladly taste it, but he had eaten so much sugar that he would not notice the bitterness, and that the king should expect no quarter, for his wretched blood would flow that day.

Then Tirant again addressed his troops, urging them to steel their hearts and fortify their spirits with hopes of victory, while the Turkish bombards shot a stone that flew over their heads. Tirant held a pennant in one hand and a little ax in the other, with which he signaled to the Duke of Pera, who then had his men turn their mounts till their backs were to the enemy while the Duke of Sinope kept his troops steady. When the Duke of Pera had finished, Tirant signaled with the flag, and the Duke of Sinope had his men turn in the same fashion so that they all ended up facing Diaphebus with their backs to the Saracens. Then they began galloping away, though still in formation.

Seeing this stratagem, the Turks shouted: "They are fleeing! They are fleeing!"

The infantry dropped their shields, lances, and crossbows to pursue the Christians, while the cavalry thought only of winning more spoils, and those with armored mounts threw away their harness to lighten them. Looking back from time to time, Tirant saw them all charging in great disorder, but his sole concern was to keep his own men in line. Some Turks on good horses even prodded them with their lances.

Beholding them from the castle tower, the emperor thought all was lost, as did his damsels, who had kept vigil all the previous night, devoutly praying the Decider of Battles and His Mother to grant them victory.

Having left the Turkish infantry far behind him, Tirant raised his flag, at which everyone halted and the squadrons assembled a stone's throw apart. Then the infidels realized that they had been tricked once again, while Tirant ordered the Duke of Pera to attack first. As the Saracens were forming ranks, Tirant sent the Marquis of Saint George and the Duke of Sinope into battle. Each squadron attacked in order, and a terrible slaughter ensued.

By now, almost half of Tirant's troops were fighting valiantly, but the King of Cappadocia had also slain many Christians. Recognizing the monarch by the gold lion on his helmet, our knight seized a stout lance and hurriedly joined the fray. The king saw him coming but stood his ground, and they clashed with such force that the two knights and their mounts were felled, whereupon they rose, drew their swords, and dealt each other mighty buffets, though in the midst of such a melee they could not fight well. Each man's troops helped him, and after a great effort, the Turks rehorsed their king despite the Christian army, while Pyramus rode in front of Tirant that he might also remount. They went on fighting until Count Plegamans's squadron came to their aid, and Lord Agramunt lifted Tirant onto his horse, thus rescuing him from the press. The Christians captured a riderless steed and gave it to their captain, who quickly returned to battle, smiting many mortal blows. He fought in another's name but risked his own life, knowing that if he triumphed he would win honor and glory.

The Breton ordered all his remaining squadrons to attack, some on the left and some on the right, though on both sides the ground was so littered with dead and wounded that it was truly a wonder to behold. Tirant charged wherever the fighting was thickest.

Seeing how fiercely Tirant battled, the King of Egypt drew the Kings of Africa and Cappodocia aside and asked them to forget everything but slaying the Greek captain. Having made a pact, the three kings returned to the fray, but before they could reach Tirant, the Duke of Macedonia rode up behind him, stabbing him beneath his helmet so the sword-point pierced his neck. Hippolytus and Pyramus saw this treachery and shouted: "Oh perfidious duke! Why do you assault so brave a captain?"

Thus they bore witness to their lord's betrayal, while the three monarchs opened a path with their lances and rushed at Tirant, though only the Kings of Egypt and Cappadocia won through. So fierce was the clash that Tirant and his horse were felled, for the mount had already received six grievous wounds.

The King of Africa charged the Duke of Macedonia, who was nearby, with such force that the lance transfixed and slew him, whereby the duke paid for his evil ways.

Tirant, whose horse had fallen across his leg, struggled mightily to rise and at last regained his feet. One of the lances had struck his helmet and knocked off the visor, while the other had hurt his left arm, and only his men's courage saved him.

Beholding him on the ground, the King of Egypt tried to dismount, but as he was lifting his leg over the saddle, Lord Agramunt stabbed him in the thigh. The wound caused the king such pain that he fell to earth, where Tirant tried to reach him, but the fighting was too thick. The king rose, seized a lance, and slowly made his way toward his foe, and since Tirant had no visor, the Saracen smote his jaw and dislodged four teeth. Though our knight lost a great deal of blood, he did not leave the fray, and Hippolytus, seeing his captain in danger, slowly edged toward him. Once he was close enough, he dismounted and said: "My lord, I beg you to take my horse."

Tirant, who was making his way toward one flank and trying to escape the press, mounted the horse and asked Hippolytus: "Now what will you do?"

Hippolytus answered: "My lord, save yourself, for even if they kill me, I shall hold my death in your service useful."

Tirant returned to the struggle and sought the King of Egypt, whose wound was so painful that he had withdrawn from battle. Finding him nowhere, our knight attacked wherever he could, and some time later he again spied the King of Cappadocia. The infidel lunged at Tirant, wounding his ax hand, yet nothing daunted, the Breton brought his ax down and smashed the king's helmet into his skull. As he lay on the ground, Tirant dismounted and cut the thongs on his helmet.

A knight rode up, crying out in a piteous voice: "My lord, spare this monarch, who is mortally wounded, and allow him a little time, for you have already bested him."

Tirant asked: "What makes you seek to help our public enemy, who has cruelly done his utmost to slay my companions? It is only fair that he be served as he sought to serve me, nor is this the time for mercy, as only courage can win the day."

He removed the king's helmet and cut off his head with an ax so bathed in blood that it stood out among the others, while the ground beneath him was covered with corpses and red with gore. Tirant mounted his steed again, but at the sight of their dead lord, a multitude of Turks rushed our knight, wounding him badly and knocking him from his horse. Undismayed by his fall and aided by his friends, he quickly rose and rejoined the cruel combat.

This harsh and bitter battle continued until evening, but the harsher it waxed, the greater Tirant's glory.

Diaphebus cursed Tirant for stationing him in that place and said: "He always wants all the honor and thus he left me here to rot, but by God, I demand my share of the glory! To arms!" he cried. "Have at them, and fear nothing!"

He left his ambush and bravely attacked the Turks, who had not known there were more troops and were dismayed at the sight of Diaphebus's squadron.

The wounded sultan left the fray for a moment and told his men: "It appears that we have lost the day, and I think we should retreat before they slay us."

Once Tirant saw the sultan's troops fleeing with their banners, he rode after them, while his men seized the pennants and killed many Saracens. This battle lasted from dawn until three hours past midday, and so huge was the infidel horde that the Christians wearied of killing them. Most noble and gracious were the Greeks' deeds that day as, flushed with victory, they pursued their foes for three leagues. Truly, Tirant could be called an invincible king of battles, for just as Fortune had favored the Saracens, so Divine Providence now crowned him with glory, but night was falling and the Christians were exhausted.

The captain and most of his men made their way toward a fortified city that had been ruled by the Marquis of Saint George and had given him his title. After it fell to the Turks, they entrusted it to the King of Egypt, who kept it well provisioned and made his headquarters there. This monarch fled with the others, but he was in such pain from his wound that he had to stop in Saint George, while the sultan continued on to the port of Bellpuig. As it was almost nightfall when Tirant and his men reached Saint George, they camped in the fields, where the wounded were cared for, though many Greek soldiers perished before sunrise. Never had there been such a fierce battle on that eastern shore, nor had so many ladies been widowed and so many damsels orphaned, but their hopes of deliverance also increased.

The next day, Tirant called his men to arms and stormed the city, whose rulers defended themselves with wondrous bravery. After four fruitless assaults, the Marquis of Saint George walked around the walls and, when he reached the gate to the Jewish ghetto, he called out to a Jew named Jacob. Recognizing his master's voice, the Jew hastened to admit him, and by the time their foes realized what was afoot Christians had occupied most of the city, whereupon the marquis sent word to Tirant that he need attack no more. Upon entering the ghetto gate, our knight found that the marquis had captured the king, who had fought on, defending a tower despite his grievous wounds. The marquis then asked Tirant to come and behead his enemy, but after receiving our knight's reply that he would never kill a prisoner, he seized the king's hair and slit his throat without further ado.

Having inspected the city and found it well provisioned, the marquis said: "Lord captain, from now on we can take refuge here if need be, as by raising the sluices on the irrigation channels we can flood the fields and thus rout our foes. Had they been able to do so, we never would have bested them, and since I know the city well, I sent most of my men to guard the channels."

The captain said: "Tell me, lord marquis: how did you lose so strong a city?"

"My lord, I entrusted it to a man of scant mettle, whom I knighted and gave money, jewels, a wife, and a fine house, but when he learned that the Turks had captured Bellpuig—which is four leagues hence—he promptly surrendered the city and its ancient privileges."

Though Tirant had triumphed, he forbade all feasting or merriment and, tempering joy with his enemies' grief, he only said before everyone: "Had Diaphebus obeyed my orders, I would have killed the sultan and ended this war."

Let us now return to the emperor, whose grief at Tirant's flight changed to solace when Lord Malveí sent one of his men to learn what he could about the battle. Upon his return, the emperor knelt and turned his gaze Heavenward, offering infinite thanks to Jesus Christ and Our Lady and praying for Tirant's life in words of this tenor: "Were it not for that Breton's courage, we would never have won the day, for though our knights knew only defeat before he came, now the Turks await their destruction, while his glorious deeds fill those around him with admiration."

Then His Majesty, the Sicilian barons, Carmesina, and Stephanie rode to the Saracen camp, where they found many splendidly furnished tents. The soldiers asked permission to start looting, but the emperor refused, ordering the Lord of Pantelleria and Lord Malveí to guard the camp till Tirant sent instructions.

While the emperor was in the Saracen camp, the princess saw a little black boy in the distance. She rode toward him, dismounted, and, after entering the tent where he had hidden, she seized his hair and brought him before her father, to whom she said: "My lord, now I can glory in my valiant knighthood, for I have boldly captured a Turk in the enemy camp."

The emperor was charmed by his daughter's wit.

Beholding Tirant's ire, Diaphebus felt ashamed to appear before him and neglected to send word to the emperor as he had before. His Majesty told the princess: "I fear Diaphebus may be dead, since I have heard nothing from him about the battle."

Stephanie overheard these words and burst into sobs, whereupon the princess led her away lest her grief betray her. Once they had returned to Malveí Castle, Stephanie gave her most trusted squire the following letter to Diaphebus:

· CLVIII ·

STEPHANIE'S LETTER TO DIAPHEBUS

If there is any steadfastness in your devotion, I, defeated Stephanie, beg you to send word, as you have offended me mortally by not hastening to my side. Certainly love always brings worry and distress, but I once had higher hopes, having seen you behave more nobly. Since I cannot speak, I pray my tears upon this paper will move you, yet I fear they fall in vain, and though I meant to struggle against my passion, when I heard that mighty old man declare you dead I could not restrain my sobs. Shame left its marks upon my face, wherefore I beg you to come quickly, for if you cannot, I too shall perish and they will inscribe upon my tomb: *causa odiosa*. Thus will the world discover that I died of a broken heart.

· CLIX ·

HOW STEPHANIE'S LETTER MADE PEACE BETWEEN TIRANT AND DIAPHEBUS

Filled with joy at Stephanie's words, Diaphebus quickly bore her missive to his cousin, who then summoned the squire and asked for news of the emperor and Carmesina. The squire recounted the princess's exploits and described her prisoner: "Whom she hopes to present to you as soon as she can."

Delighted by the squire's words, Tirant sent Diaphebus to Malveí Castle.

Upon his arrival, the knight went straight to His Majesty, while news of his coming spread and the damsels prepared to welcome him, but especially Stephanie, whose face clearly showed her sufferings. They went to the emperor's chamber, where, after hearing of Tirant's wounds, his beloved turned pale but then calmed herself and asked: "Tell me, Diaphebus: are our captain's wounds mortal?"

"No, my lady," replied Diaphebus, "the doctors say he will live."

"But he must be in pain," said the princess, unable to restrain her sobs, nor could the damsels and her father keep from bursting into tears as well. This lasted for quite some time, though Diaphebus sought to comfort them, until at last the emperor regained his composure and asked how many had perished in both armies.

"On my faith, sire," replied Diaphebus, "I could not estimate the Turkish casualties, but you cannot journey from here to Saint George on the royal road, so littered is it with corpses, and instead you must go a mile out of your way. I can also tell you about our own dead, because the captain had 1,234 bodies collected for burial: we found the Duke of Macedonia slain by a lance wound, plus the Marquis of Ferrara, the Duke of Babylon, the Marquis of Vasto, and Count Plegamans. These were our most notable losses, but there were many others too, including our grand constable, who was much mourned as a good and valiant knight. The captain has given them all honorable burials, though the Duke of Macedonia did not deserve one, for Lord Agramunt and Hippolytus say they saw him stab our captain in the neck, but Tirant is so benign that he never speaks ill of anyone."

The aged lord scarcely knew how to reward his worthy captain. Diaphebus pretended he was ill in order to stay longer, and the emperor ordered his doctors to look after him as they would his own daughter.

Having asked the Sicilian barons to remain till he divided the spoils, His Majesty dispatched two knights to learn Tirant's wishes. He replied that he had nothing to say and left everything to the emperor, who then divided the booty among his knights.

Tirant was well enough by now to inspect the city and the camp, for all his troops could not fit inside the walls. The sultan remained in Bellpuig, where he felt safe from attack, and spent more than two weeks in his room, mourning their defeat and the dead King of Cappadocia, though he still knew nothing about the King of Egypt. Cypriot of Paternò asked: "My lord, would you like me to ride to Saint George? Perhaps I can speak with my friend and learn what he knows."

The sultan jumped up and cried: "Hurry! Mount your horse and go!"

After donning a white damask tunic with Saint George's cross beneath his scarlet jubbah, Cypriot leapt on one of the sultan's finest steeds. As soon as he was out of sight, he took the jubbah off, laid it across his saddle, and tied a white cloth to his lance. When the Christian scouts saw him, they thought he was one of them, and so he soon reached the city, where he asked for Tirant. The captain was delighted to behold him and requested news of the Turks, to which Cypriot replied that the sultan and the King of Africa were slightly wounded, while the Grand Turk's son had a head wound like his father's. Having recounted the great lamentations caused by their defeat, he said he had come for his own pleasure, to see his lord, and to find out if the King of Egypt was alive.

"Tell me:" asked Tirant, "how many soldiers do they think they lost?"

"My lord," replied Cypriot, "their captains have counted 103,700 men between those killed and captured, nor can anyone recall such a terrible slaughter. Their mounts were so weary that, had you gone a little further, you might have captured them all, for between their exhaustion and the wounded they were forced to camp on the road to Bellpuig, where many died for lack of doctors to treat them. They had the King of Africa slung across a horse."

"Can you give me any other news?" asked Tirant.

"Yes, my lord," replied Cypriot of Paternò. "Seven big ships have docked with grain, fodder, and other foods, and they say the Grand Karaman is coming with fifty thousand foot and cavalry. He is bringing his daughter to marry the sultan, and the King of Armenia is with him."

"Have they unloaded those seven ships?" asked Tirant.

"No, my lord," replied Cypriot, "they are awaiting a favorable wind to enter the harbor."

As they spoke of these matters, Tirant embraced him frequently and gave him candied fruit and other sweets for the sultan.

Before leaving, Cypriot asked for a safe-conduct, which he showed to the sultan as soon as he reached Bellpuig, saying his friend had obtained it with great pleas and supplications. Cypriot told him the King of Egypt was dead, at which the sultan's grief redoubled, for he had loved the king dearly.

By now Tirant's wounds had nearly healed, and one day he set out with a man who knew the countryside, its hidden passes, and how to avoid populated places. Upon reaching the sea, they beheld the city of Bellpuig atop a great hill, while ships sailed aimlessly to and fro outside its harbor. The captain then returned to Saint George, where he learned that the emperor would soon set out with the Sicilian barons to reconquer nearby towns and castles, of which they quickly recaptured many.

The Sicilian barons then asked to see Tirant before continuing their campaign, but Diaphebus begged them to obey the emperor's orders.

Having heard of His Majesty's exploits, Tirant rode forth with the Duke of Pera and part of their army, leaving the rest under the Marquis of Saint George's command. When they were outside Malveí Castle, our knight gave Hippolytus a message for his lady.

As soon as Hippolytus spied her, he bowed humbly and said: "My lord asks Your Highness to let him enter and leave without harm or loss of liberty."

"Oh newfangled knight," replied the princess, "what is this bizarre request? Does the captain not know we are under his orders and that he can arrest and imprison, absolve or condemn, according to each man's merits? Why, then, should he have occasion to ask me for safe-conduct? Tell him I have no power or need to issue such documents, for neither I nor the emperor know of any crime he has committed, and I am surprised at his timidity, which he should have lost battling the Turks."

Hippolytus rose to embrace the damsels, and you may be sure Pleasure-of-my-life was pleased to see him.

Then he returned with the princess's reply, but Tirant refused to budge and sent him back. When Hippolytus was before the princess again, he said: "My lord begs Your Highness not to deny him, as he will neither enter this castle nor approach you without a safe-conduct written in your hand."

"I cannot understand this captain," replied the princess. "He has done nothing to offend us, so why should he ask for safe-conduct?"

Stephanie said: "My lady, what can you lose by granting his request?"

The princess called for ink and paper and wrote the following safe-conduct:

· CLX ·

*T*HE PRINCESS'S SAFE-CONDUCT

Our hope and trust have turned to fear and doubt, for you cling like a madman to the frailest of branches, and I cannot understand why you request safe-conduct. Dismayed to hear my captain speak so foolishly and vainly, I nonetheless, with sound mind, shall now sign this document. I shall in no way limit your freedom to come and go as you please, nor should brave knights cravenly seek such assurances. Signed in Malveí Castle, September tenth.

· C L X I ·

*H*OW TIRANT RECEIVED THE SAFE-CONDUCT AND WENT TO PAY HOMAGE TO THE PRINCESS

Once Tirant had the safe-conduct in hand, he entered the castle, where he found the princess in a large hall. She rose to her feet, while her suitor shouted for all to hear: "Honor the safe-conduct, my lady, why do you not honor the safe-conduct? Why do you enchain me so cruelly, as it ill behooves a damsel of such noble lineage to incarcerate her servant! Respect the safe-conduct and restore my freedom."

"Oh lord captain," replied the princess, "I shall gladly honor it, but as far as I can see, no one has touched or imprisoned you on my behalf or the emperor's."

"Honor the safe-conduct and set me free," cried Tirant, "for never have I been in so cruel and strong a dungeon."

The Easygoing Widow said: "Alas, my lady, this dungeon of yours is love, its gown is grief embroidered with hope, and the shirt he wears as his device reveals his wish to be with you."

Then the princess understood Tirant's request and declared: "Captain, though Fortune has fettered you, in time you will regain your liberty . . ." She took the safe-conduct from his hand, tore it up, and said: "You were wrong, captain, to ask for safe-conduct, but although I was fated to err in granting it, my mistake was honest and my guilt will exceed my punishment. I gave you that safe-conduct on the emperor's behalf, lest you turn against him."

Taking the Duke of Pera by one hand and Tirant by the other, she sat down between them and asked about the many noble lords who had died in battle, whereupon Tirant lamented the loss of the Duke of Macedonia, Pyramus, and Richard.[49] Then they discussed the emperor's campaign, and the two knights decided to join him in the morning, as he had assaulted a city for three days without success. The princess said: "May God honor my lord the emperor, and if you go to his aid I promise to accompany you." Then she sent for her prisoner and said: "You may well believe I have seen harsh battles and captured cruel enemies too."

With these words they rose and went to supper, but the princess ate little, for her only joy was watching Tirant. The duke spoke with the mistress of the castle and the Easygoing Widow, whom he told about Tirant's noble victories over the infidel. The Easygoing Widow was also enamored of Tirant but disguised her passion lest her honor be sullied, though often she grew faint at the mere thought of her beloved. The princess invited the duke to sit with them, to which he replied that he would when he had finished talking with the other ladies.

Only Stephanie overheard the princess speak these words to Tirant: "Fortune brought me here, not because battles amuse me, but to see my lord and master. Finding no other way to relieve my sufferings, I committed a great sin and deceived my father, but do not imagine that the observant have been deceived. I renounced my claim to exemplary virtue, that my mournful soul might find some peace, yet my hope exceeds my fear of sin and the sight of you has dispelled my worries. If I have erred, love will absolve me, just as it gave me leave to visit you."

"My past ills," replied Tirant, "cannot compare to my present torments, for when I behold your peerless beauty I fear I shall go mad. I had no choice but to adore you, and knowing you possess all virtues, I am surprised that you have one fault (speaking, of course, with your leave and pardon): that your heart is cold and cruel. Had I served God as I have you, I would be able to perform miracles by now, yet I, the unluckiest of men, do not know if I shall be rewarded. Your tongue utters sweet words, but where shall I find the deeds to prove them? My lady, have you really forgotten your promise? When I left, you said before Stephanie: 'Tirant, return quickly to one who awaits you, and if God grants my wish I shall quickly grant yours.' It ill behooves noble damsels to break their promises, but my lady, let us present our case before others. In part, I merely repeat what the Easygoing Widow said when I arrived, for she told me your words were nought but pretty fictions, wherefore I beg you not to slight your honor and my good opinion. Stephanie will speak for me, and Your Highness might choose Pleasure-of-my-life or Diaphebus."

"I have always heard it said," replied the princess, "that when your father is the judge, you can take your ease in court—not that our case is of that kind, but you wish it were so. You want to be sentenced by your own lawyers, though everyone who knows the meaning of love will condemn you, and should you persist in such perfidy, you will die a traitor to yourself and God, who fashioned you of such stuff that you wish to stain my honor and good name."

As they spoke, Pleasure-of-my-life entered the room, sat down at Tirant's feet, and said: "Lord captain, I am the only one who loves and pities you. None of these ladies has asked you to remove your armor, though your shirt is full of holes and no seamstress could mend it better than I. I used to watch the princess put it on, perfumed with civet, whereas now I see it in shreds and stinking of iron and steel."

The princess said to Tirant: "Give me that hand so cruel to enemy kings."

Stephanie took Tirant's hand and placed it on Carmesina's knee, whereupon the noble lady bent over and kissed it.

"For me honor, far from stinking," Tirant said, "is the highest grace and blessing. Your Highness did first what I should have done myself, but how great would be my joy if you allowed me to kiss your hands whenever I liked, and still greater if you included your feet and legs!"

The princess took his hand again and said: "Henceforth, lord captain, I wish these hands to do as they like with me, for such is your right."

Then she rose, as the hour was late, and to ward off any suspicions, they escorted the princess to her chamber while the duke and Tirant slept together in one bed.

At dawn the trumpets blew, they mounted their horses, and Tirant sent for some scaling ladders he had left in the castle. Then they set out and rode until they sighted the emperor, who was assaulting a fortified town bravely defended by the sultan's troops. Having left the princess with Diaphebus, just out of bombard range, Tirant stopped behind the Sicilians and had his ladders brought forth. He was the first to scale the walls, and as he was climbing, a Saracen flung a boulder, thus forcing our knight to duck. The stone hit the ladder and knocked it over, but although Tirant fell with it, he was not harmed. He quickly sent for three more and began scaling the wall again, while the many crossbowmen above them shot at every arm and leg they could see.

The emperor, who had gone to welcome his daughter, asked who had fallen off the ladder and, upon learning that it was his captain, sent orders that he not scale the walls under any circumstances. Tirant ignored them, however, and when all the ladders were in place, the Christians attacked so boldly that they fought their way into the town and killed or captured all the Saracens.

Once their foes had surrendered, the Sicilian lords went before Tirant and gave him letters from their king and queen, at which Tirant rejoiced and honored his guests greatly, thanking Philip, Ricomana, and the barons for their good will. Then they left the town and walked to where the emperor and his daughter were. Tirant bowed before His Majesty, who said: "Captain, do not scale walls in that fashion lest you be gravely injured, for only God's divine mercy and justice enabled us to recapture this town. Confiding in your right and expecting constant victories, you risk your life for those who live in safety, but I beg you not to endanger yourself so. If you wish to triumph, do not spurn my counsel."

The captain replied: "Sire, I must do such deeds to encourage the troops, and what else should I do if I wish to behave well? It is not right for Your Majesty to involve himself in such affairs, as your age and position oblige you to defend yourself with virtue, and the outcome of battles is always uncertain."

The emperor marveled at the zealous words spoken by his captain, who then escorted him and Carmesina into the town.

The next morning, His Majesty held council to decide what to do and in which direction to march, for some lords said they should go one way and others another. The captain spoke last: "My lord, I have asked Your Majesty not to advance further but to escort these Sicilian barons to your noble city. Take the prisoners, who are costly to feed and whose guards are growing restive, since the duke and I can reconquer any nearby towns and cities. This war has lasted so long that the peasants have no grain, wherefore you must send provisions by sea."

"Last night," replied the emperor, "I learned that five cargo ships have reached the port of Kaffa."

"I am very pleased," said the captain, "by this news."

Tirant had the flour mills along the Trasimene readied for use, while the prisoners in Saint George and his camp were brought to Malveí Castle the next day. The Sicilian barons pitched their tents near the river, the Duke of Pera kept the rest of the soldiers, and Tirant asked the Marquis of Saint George to send more. When the emperor reached the castle, he summoned Carmesina, her damsels, and Tirant, to whom he addressed the following words: "Captain, since Fortune has slain our grand constable, the Count of Bithynia, whom would you like to take his place?"

Tirant knelt and replied: "My lord, if Your Majesty were pleased to give the office to Diaphebus, I would be most grateful."

"I shall not depart from your will," declared the emperor. "For love of you and worthy Diaphebus, I appoint him grand constable, and now I take the county of Sancto Angiolo from my daughter, offering it to you with all its rights, pertinences, and emoluments, in addition to which I shall give you the town of Altafoglia.[50] Together, the two places produce an annuity of seventy-five thousand ducats, though with God's help I shall soon reward you far more lavishly. Tomorrow, we shall hold a feast at which I shall make you a count. I would sooner make you a count than a marquis, though marquis is a higher rank, for 'count' means brother-in-arms, wherefore you will be more closely tied to me."

Tirant replied: "My lord, I thank Your Majesty for so honoring me, and I prize the annuity as though it were four hundred thousand ducats, but I must decline your offer for two reasons: first, I have spent too little time in Your Majesty's service to deserve such a reward; and second, if my father who engendered me learned that I held some title, he would despair of ever seeing me again, as would my poor mother who suffered for nine months before she bore me. Their grief might be such as to shorten their lives, and then I would be called a parricide, for I am their only son. At the very least they would curse me, though I wish to cause them no grief."

"Under no circumstances," said the emperor, "shall I allow you to refuse this county, and if you spurn the title, take the rule and annuity."

"I fear the princess may be offended," replied Tirant, "if you give away her county."

"This county," said the princess, "was generously left to me by an aunt. Everything I own is also my father's, and he may command my person and possessions, giving or throwing them away as he sees fit. Do not hesitate to receive what he graciously offers, for I confirm his gift to you and your descendants."

The emperor again pleaded with Tirant and insisted that he accept, to which our knight replied: "My lord, I shall never do so."

"With reason men will disbelieve your words," said the emperor, "but affirm the truth of mine, and you should gladly accept my offer as I am the giver and you the recipient. I offer you what all men seek in this world: honor and gain, wherefore, should you speak sincerely, you will welcome it without feigned distaste. If perchance you want people to think I am rewarding your services, do not commit such an error, since the opinions of commoners, ladies, and damsels are nothing to me. Your refusal to accept makes me think you plan to leave."

"God forbid," said Tirant, "that I should abandon Your Majesty in his hour of need, and if you insist, I shall accept the county and swear fealty to you, but as Diaphebus is my cousin and we hold all things in common, he shall have the title of count."

"What can I do?" asked the emperor. "Once you have accepted it, you can sell it or give it away as you please."

Tirant threw himself at the emperor's feet and kissed his hand in thanks, while His Highness said: "Tomorrow we shall hold a feast for our grand constable and count."

"In that case, my lord, I beg Your Majesty, the princess, and these ladies to be our guests."

Having left the emperor, Tirant asked Lord Malveí to ready peacocks, capons, partridges, and chickens for the next day. They also baked many loaves of bread and prepared everything else. As Diaphebus, who was ignorant of all this, walked toward the castle with some other knights, he saw Tirant running and asked: "Cousin, why this haste? Have you heard something about our enemies?"

"No," said Tirant, "but go to the emperor's chamber and kiss his hand and foot, as he has given you the county of Sancto Angiolo and the office of grand constable, wherefore I shall organize a great feast for tomorrow."

After thanking the emperor, Diaphebus sought out Stephanie and the other ladies, who all jokingly requested posts in his county or the army, gaily laughing and taking their ease till Carmesina appeared.

Diaphebus quickly knelt to kiss her hand, while she gave him ten thousand ducats wrapped in a cloth and said: "Brother, promise not to open this till you reach your chamber."

She also made him swear to obey the instructions inside, but although Diaphebus felt how heavy the bundle was, he failed to guess what it contained.

He went to Tirant and said: "Now that I have kissed the emperor's foot and hand and the princess's hand, it seems right that, as you gave me the county . . ."

He knelt and seized Tirant's hand, but our knight quickly raised him up, kissing him thrice on the lips in sign of love. The two spoke for a long time, and Tirant told him to think no more about it, since the county was nothing compared to what he planned to do for him: "And I trust God will let me offer you things of far greater worth."

Diaphebus thanked him profusely and said: "Now, captain, shall we see what that virtuous lady gave me?"

He placed the bundle in Tirant's hands, and they found a note inside it that read:

> I ask my brother, our grand constable and Count of Sancto Angiolo, to accept this modest contribution to his feast, for though I know it is insufficient, his virtue will excuse me, considering where we are, and I confess my fault in giving so little to one of such courage.

When they saw it they both grew thoughtful, and to try Tirant's patience, Diaphebus asked: "Do you think we should return it?"

"No!" cried Tirant. "For both father and daughter have such lofty and generous hearts that they would be greatly offended."

When everything was ready for the next day, they went to the emperor's chamber, where they spoke for a long time about the war and Diaphebus again thanked the princess.

The emperor walked to the river, on whose banks soldiers were setting up tables and benches, and when he asked what they were doing Lord Malveí replied that it was for the feast.

Meanwhile, Tirant strolled arm in arm along the water with his lady, who said: "Tell me, Tirant: why did you spurn that county? I tried to speak three times but my tongue refused to obey me. I wanted to say: 'Take it; I meant it for you,' yet I feared to disclose my ailment, as shame is often mixed with love, and though I approve of your other actions, you should not reject what I offer."

"May I never see God," replied Tirant, "if such a thought crossed my mind. I am more grateful for that county than if it were ten duchies, precisely because it was yours, and lest you misconstrue my intentions, let me say that I shall only accept one title: that of emperor. Do you know how you slay me? With your extreme beauty, for ever since I first beheld you in that black satin dress and saw your breasts, your golden tresses, and your skin like roses and lilies, my heart has been yours alone. How cruel to make one who loves you suffer so! My grief is unending, while your callousness remains unpunished, but right is on my side and my cries of 'Justice!' echo before God. When the time comes, you will say: 'Alas, that I did not love faithful Tirant,' and that my pleas as an enamored vassal may soften your stony heart, I kneel and make the sign of the cross on the ground, worshipping it as I worship you and begging a favor."

Tirant felt so sorry for himself that he nearly burst into tears, but the princess quickly rebuked him in this manner:

· CLXII ·

THE PRINCESS'S REPLY TO TIRANT

"Tears are sometimes shed honestly and sometimes deceitfully. Your request is hard and bitter, for what you ask should not be granted, nor do bad beginnings lead to happy endings. If you truly cherished my honor, you would not strive to disgrace me. Why this hasty harvest, when the crop is just sprouting? You are a fool to sacrifice what you may count on in time."

Her father then approached, so she could say no more, and gaily conversing, they all returned to the castle.

The next morning, Mass was celebrated in the middle of a field. Diaphebus stood between Carmesina and the emperor, who, once the service had ended, placed a ring on his finger and then kissed his lips. All the trumpets blared, while a king-of-arms shouted: "Behold this noble and courageous knight: the Count of Sancto Angiolo and Grand Constable of the Greek Empire!"

Then the feasting began, and only Carmesina danced with the grand constable that day. At lunch, the emperor placed Diaphebus on his right, opposite the princess, while Tirant acted as steward, since he had organized the feast. The damsels were served at other tables, with knights and barons facing them, after which the soldiers and then the prisoners were given food. Tirant even had bread mixed with the horses' oats.

When lunch was half over, Tirant gave every king-of-arms, herald, and pursuivant a thousand ducats, whereupon the trumpets sounded again as they cried: "Largesse, largesse!"[51]

Once they had finished, sweetmeats were brought forth and the knights rode past His Highness, bearing lances and the constable's banners. After performing many handsome feats of arms, they galloped as far as the sultan's old camp, from which they returned with great joy and merriment.

In that same spot they ate supper: a wondrous feast composed of many dishes. Our knight, however, looked so sad during the meal that Carmesina called him over and whispered in his ear: "Tirant, tell me what ails you, as your face reveals your woe. Tell me, I cry you mercy!"

"My lady, so many are my ills that they cannot be counted, and I hold my life worthless, since Your Highness will leave tomorrow while I, alas, must remain here with my grief."

"He who commits the crime," said the princess, "deserves the punishment. Why did you send my father back to Constantinople? I never saw a man in love give such foolish advice, but if you want me to feign illness for two or three weeks, I shall do so for love of you and the emperor will surely stay."

"But how can we," asked Tirant, "with so many prisoners? Alas, I fear that my sorrows are incurable and often I feel like poisoning myself, cutting my throat, or dying suddenly in battle."

"Do no such thing, Tirant," replied the princess. "Take counsel with Stephanie, for perhaps the two of you can find some solution that will not disgrace me."

Tirant quickly told Stephanie and Diaphebus of his despair, whereupon they decided that when everyone was asleep, the knights would steal into their damsels' chamber and seek a remedy for their ills.

At last the hour struck, and the knights set out to visit their beloveds. All the damsels were lodged with the Easygoing Widow, except five who slept in a room the suitors had to pass through. Pleasure-of-my-life noticed that Carmesina had dismissed her without undressing, and smelling her mistress's perfume, she guessed a secret marriage was in the offing.

At the appointed hour, Stephanie bore a little candle to the five damsels' beds and peered at them one by one to ensure that they were sleeping, but Pleasure-of-my-life, who had remained awake because she wanted to see and hear everything, only pretended to be asleep when Diaphebus's lady entered. Then the enamored duchess quietly opened a door, behind which she found the two knights waiting more devoutly than Jews for their Messiah.

Once they were inside, she snuffed out the candle and, taking the constable's hand while Tirant walked behind him, she led them to the chamber where Carmesina awaited them.

Now I shall describe Her Highness's attire: she wore a long green gown embroidered with large pearls, a necklace of enameled gold leaves from which diamonds and rubies hung, and a splendid gold chaplet that glittered in the candlelight.

Beholding his mistress, Tirant bowed before her and then knelt, kissed her hands, and uttered many amorous words. When they thought it was time, the knights returned to their quarters; between love and grief, who could sleep that night?

Everyone rose at dawn, for that was the day of His Majesty's departure, and as soon as Pleasure-of-my-life awoke, she entered Carmesina's chamber, where she found her mistress dressing while Stephanie sat on the floor, trying to tie her coif. She looked very cheerful and seemed in no mood to be disturbed, though her eyes were so sleepy that she could scarcely see.

"Alas, Saint Mary help us!" cried Pleasure-of-my-life. "What ails you, my lady? I shall fetch the doctors, that they may examine you."

"There is no need," replied Stephanie, "as I shall soon recover. That breeze from the river last night gave me a headache."

"Mind your words," said Pleasure-of-my-life, "lest you forfeit your life, and beware of pain in your heels,[52] for I have heard doctors say that the trouble starts in women's feet and spreads to their knees, thighs, and sometimes even that secret place, after which it afflicts our heads, rattling our brains and toppling us over. Do not think this malady strikes often, as that great philosopher and subtle doctor Galen tells us it comes only once in a lifetime, but though incurable, it is not fatal, and there are many ways to ease it. This epistle of mine is good and true, and you should not be surprised that I can diagnose illnesses, for if you stick out your tongue, I shall identify yours."

Stephanie stuck out her tongue, and after examining it, the damsel said: "I shall repudiate my father's teachings if you have not been bleeding."

Stephanie replied: "Yes, I had a nosebleed."

"I cannot decide if it was your nose or your heel," said Pleasure-of-my-life, "but you have certainly lost blood, and henceforth you can testify to my veracity and wisdom. Now, with the princess's leave, I shall recount a dream I had last night, but only if she promises not to be offended."

The princess, who had roared with laughter at Pleasure-of-my-life's diagnosis, told her to continue and absolved her of all guilt by apostolic authority, whereupon the maiden began to describe her dream:

· CLXIII ·

*P*LEASURE-OF-MY-LIFE'S DREAM

"I dreamt that as I lay in a sumptuous room with four other damsels, Stephanie entered with a little candle and approached my bed. My eyes were shut and my mind drifted between waking and sleeping, but I thought I saw her open the door very carefully. Tirant and the constable stood outside, dressed in capes and doublets, with swords in their hands and wool slippers on their feet. Once they had entered, she snuffed out the candle, taking the constable's hand like a blind man's guide while Tirant followed them into this room. Seeing you perfumed with civet and not at all badly dressed, the knight then carried you about the chamber in his arms and covered you with kisses, but Your Highness whispered: 'Put me down, Tirant! Put me down!' Finally he obeyed, placing you upon the bed."

Then Pleasure-of-my-life approached the bed and cried: "Alas, sir bed! To think of those who saw you then and those who see you now, alone, abandoned, and of no further use! Where is that knight I imagined was here? In my dream, I rose in my nightgown and watched everything through the keyhole."

The princess laughed again and gaily asked: "Did you dream anything else?"

"By Saint Mary I did," replied Pleasure-of-my-life, "and I shall tell you all about it, for you picked up a book of hours and said: 'Tirant, I offered you a little solace to prove my devotion!' As Tirant still hesitated, you urgently implored him: 'If you loved me, you would try to quell my fears. Having obtained this amorous favor through Stephanie's intercession, you should not seek to torment me in return, wherefore I beg you to be satisfied with what you won through her weakness.' 'I see your error is extreme,' replied Tirant, 'and all true lovers will condemn you for restraining your own desires. Nonetheless, I do not want you to think I would break my word, as I believed you would freely consent to my wishes. Since you resist and struggle, I shall do as you command.' 'Be quiet, Tirant,' Your Highness said, 'and do not grieve, for my honor and good name depend upon your love.' You made him swear to do nothing against your will: 'And if you do, I shall lament all the days of my life.' Then I dreamt that he kissed you again and again, unbuttoning your blouse and caressing your breasts. Once he had kissed them, he put his hand under your skirt, but at that point you became angry and defended your virginity. Your Highness said: 'A time will come when you shall have all your wishes, and my maidenhead will be intact because of your chivalry.' Then he pressed his face against yours with his arms around your neck, while yours twined around his like vines upon a tree.

"Afterward I dreamt that Stephanie was on that bed, where I could see her white legs as she shouted: 'Oh my lord, do not hurt me! Show a little pity and spare your beloved's life!' Tirant said: 'Sister Stephanie, why do you endanger your honor with such cries? Have you forgotten that walls have ears?' She took a sheet, stuck it in her mouth, and bit it to keep from screaming, but a little later she exclaimed: 'Alas, what shall I do? My pain forces me to speak, for it seems you seek to slay me.' Then the constable closed her mouth, and when I heard that sweet complaint, I cursed my bad luck not to be the third. Though my idea of love may be vulgar, my heart always knew this was its final goal, and my passion for noble Hippolytus redoubled. The more I thought about it, the sadder I became until finally I washed my neck, breasts, and belly to calm myself.

"As I looked through the hole, I saw Stephanie spread her arms in surrender, saying: 'Begone, cruel loveless knight who shows no pity to chaste damsels! Oh, treacherous knave! What punishment will you not deserve if I refuse to pardon you, yet even as I complain my love grows ever stronger. Where is your promised faith? Where is your right hand that clasped mine? Where are the saints by whom you swore not to trick or harm me? How ardently you have fought to rob me of my virginity, you who have such authority, and that my suit may be fairly judged . . .' Then she summoned Tirant and Your Highness, to whom she showed her nightgown, saying: 'This blood must be paid for in love.' With tears in her eyes, she asked: 'Who will trust or respect one who cannot protect herself? How can I safeguard another damsel's honor? I have only one consolation: that I have done nothing against my husband's honor, but rather at his command and against my own will. No courtiers or priests attended my wedding, nor did my mother and relatives have the trouble of dressing me in my bridal gown and forcing me into bed, which I did myself. No musicians had to bother about playing or singing, as mine was a silent wedding, though everything I did was for my husband's pleasure.'

"Stephanie said many other things of this nature, and toward daybreak, when it was all over, you and Tirant comforted her as best you could. Shortly thereafter, the cocks crowed again, and Your Highness asked the knights to leave before anyone saw them. Tirant begged Your Highness to free him from his vow, that he might equal his cousin's glorious triumph, but you stubbornly refused. Once they had departed, I awoke and saw nothing. I scarcely knew what to think, but my breasts and belly were still wet, and that made me believe my dream was indeed true. I felt so bad that I started tossing and turning in my bed, like someone about to die who cannot find the way to do so, wherefore I have decided to love Hippolytus with true devotion, spending my wretched life like worthy Stephanie. Why should I lie there with my eyes shut and no one to help me? Love has so addled my brain that I shall die if he does not save me. Would that I might sleep my life away, for sad is the sleeper who awakes from a pleasant dream!"

Having risen, the other damsels came to help their ladies dress. After Mass, the emperor and the Duke of Pera set out with the Sicilian barons and the prisoners, whom Tirant and his grand constable also accompanied for a league. Then the emperor asked them to return, and when he had said it twice they had to obey. Having taken his leave of the emperor, Tirant approached Carmesina and asked if she had any orders, at which she raised her veil but could only tearfully stammer: "It will be . . ." Her voice failed her, dissolving in sobs and deep sighs, and she lowered the veil again lest her father and the others notice.

Something then happened to Tirant that no one could remember seeing before: as he was riding away, he felt so distraught that he fell to earth. He picked himself up immediately, felt the horse's hoof, and said it was hurt, but the emperor and many others had seen him and hastened to the spot, while Tirant pretended he was inspecting the hoof.

The emperor asked: "Captain, how is it that you fell?"

Tirant replied: "Your Highness, thinking my horse was injured, I leaned over and my stirrup strap broke, but there is no reason to be surprised when a man falls, for even horses fall, though they have four legs instead of two."

He quickly remounted, and they all went their ways. The princess was afraid to look back because she was weeping, but she asked Stephanie what had happened to Tirant, whereupon the damsel repeated His Majesty's words.

"Surely it was on account of me," said the sorrowful princess, "for as soon as I was alone, I also felt dizzy."

They rode along talking, while Tirant returned to Malveí Castle, from which he dispatched the constable with half their foot and cavalry to guard the camp.

"Now," said Tirant, "I shall see whether the ships have been unloaded, and should we lack sufficient food, I shall send them back to Constantinople or to Rhodes, where men say there was an excellent harvest. If they cannot buy enough there, they can go on to Cyprus."

Upon reaching the port that evening, Tirant found the ships almost completely unloaded. The captain and sailors rejoiced to see him, for the seven Genoese ships had docked at Bellpuig.

"And we fear they may try to attack us."

Tirant replied: "Thus far, they have shown more dread than eagerness for battle. Would you like to frighten them a bit more?"

That night, they sent a small boat to learn how strong the enemy was, and meanwhile they hastily finished discharging the grain. Upon their return the next morning, the crew announced that as the soldiers and horses were ashore, their foes were starting to discharge grain and other provisions.

"By God who sustains the world," said Tirant, "I shall do my utmost to steal those horses' fodder!"

He quickly manned five ships with soldiers and crossbowmen, for though he also had three galleys, they were in dry dock for repairs. Tirant's vessels set sail that evening and quickly covered the thirty miles between one port and the other. At dawn the Turks spied Tirant's little fleet and thought it was bringing the Grand Karaman till, having quietly entered the harbor, each ship pulled alongside a Genoese vessel, and suddenly all Tirant's men jumped aboard. Then they seized the two others, for there were so few soldiers on the enemy ships that the Christians captured them all without a single casualty. They sailed away with the foe's wheat, oats, salt beef, and Cypriot wine—all things the Greeks needed badly, for the countryside had been ravaged. Tirant gave some of the grain to Lord Malveí and sent the rest to Saint George.

On his return voyage, Tirant questioned the Turkish sailors to see if they gave the same answers as Cypriot of Paternò. They said the Grand Karaman was bringing the King of Armenia and a big army, as well as his fair daughter, whom he had promised to the sultan.

"He is bringing many other damsels of high degree, including the Grand Turk's betrothed, and they are all richly clad in brocade jubbahs embroidered with precious stones."

Another sailor named Galançó said: "I saw the Grand Karaman's daughter one Friday after prayers, and she wore a jubbah embroidered with jewels said to be worth a whole city. There are twenty-five betrothed damsels, each of whom has a dowry, and they are being escorted by the King of Cappadocia's widow. When we arrived, they told us that the Greeks are captained by some French devil who has won all his battles and whose name is Tirant. On my faith, he may have done everything they say, but his name is base and ugly, since 'tyrant' means usurper of others' goods, or to put it more bluntly, a thief. As his name is so are his deeds, for they say he refused to fight the King of Egypt in single combat and claimed to be in love with the emperor's daughter. When he has completed his campaign he will get the daughter with child and the mother too, after which he will slay the father, for thus do Frenchmen behave. Nasty folk! You shall see: if the Turks and Christians spare him, the next thing you know he will be Emperor of Constantinople."

"On my faith," said Tirant, "what you say is true: those Frenchmen are wicked, but that Tirant is even worse than you say, for he is nothing more than a thief and a highwayman. Once he has deflowered the emperor's daughter and had himself crowned, who will be able to stop him from raping all the other damsels?"

"May God send you a good Easter," replied Galançó, "for I see you know all about his past and future treacheries."

Hippolytus drew his sword to cut off the sailor's head, but Tirant leapt up, snatched it away, and went on insulting himself. Galançó said: "I swear by the fount I was baptized in that if I capture that scoundrel, I shall hang him from the highest mast I can find."

Tirant roared with laughter at Galançó's words, for which someone else might have struck him or even taken his life, but our knight gave him a silk doublet, fifty ducats, and his freedom when they docked. Imagine how that poor sailor felt upon learning his benefactor's name! He knelt to apologize, but Tirant cheerfully forgave him, saying: "Give to the evil that they may speak well; give to the good that they may speak no evil."

Tirant called a council of sailors and served them lunch, after which he said: "Gentlemen, you already know that the Grand Karaman and the King of Armenia are coming with a mighty fleet, many betrothed damsels, and three hundred thousand ducats. This vast treasure was gathered from good Saracens everywhere, all of whom contributed something to defeat the emperor. They amassed seventy thousand ducats in the kingdom of Tunis alone, and think what riches will be ours if you devise a way to defeat them. Now let each man speak his mind."

· CLXIV ·

THE SAILORS' ADVICE TO TIRANT

"It is well known, lord captain, that as the Genoese charge two ducats for every Turk' and three for every horse they transport, those renegades would sooner be hacked to pieces than forfeit their profits. There are so many Turkish soldiers that we would need half the power in Christendom to attack them, yet we have only twelve ships and three galleys, while they have the twenty-three biggest and best galleons in all Genoa. Furthermore, they have four other vessels and two lateeners, wherefore we all advise you not to beat your head against the wall, since there is no comparison between land and sea battles. Once the hatches are shut, you cannot escape."

Brave Galançó, who was from Slavonia, then rose to his feet and said: "Lord captain, do not be surprised at what I said earlier, since I fought your countrymen for many years, but Your Lordship's generosity has cured me of my anger. Now that you have freed me, I want to give you some advice: I have sailed the seas all my life, and if you trust my words I shall give you victory. Should you dislike my suggestions, you can still do as the others say, for it is always best to choose the lesser evil. Inasmuch as they have twenty-three big warships and almost thirty vessels in all, anyone who wishes to capture those thirty must follow my advice. Lighten your twelve ships and three galleys as much as possible, whereby the Turks, with all their cargo, will be slower than you. You can accept or refuse the battle, but your glory will be great if you challenge the Genoese and Turkish fleet with only twelve big ships. By attacking together, your vessels will win an easy victory, for those terrified infidels know you have bested them in every battle, and at night they awake with the name 'Tirant' on their lips. Think also of the spoils you can win in this engagement, as they will waste all their stones in the first assault, and after shooting a few quarrels they will lose heart and surrender. I know this because for eleven years I have commanded my own ships in their service."

"Very well," replied Tirant, "I have heard enough. Unload and ready the ships."

As soon as Tirant had given this order, he went to Malveí Castle, from which he rode forth on the morrow to visit his camp. Everyone rejoiced in their captain's arrival and told him seven thousand Turkish cavalry had appeared early one morning. Without waiting for the others, the Marquis of Procita had bravely attacked them, certain that his companions would come to the rescue: "But the opposite occurred: the Turks saw we were outnumbered and cut his men to shreds, whereupon they stormed the walls while we fled into the city. Some hundred and eighty men died."

"Holy Mary!" cried Tirant. "What disorder! You fell right into their trap! You know they would not dare to show their faces without a mighty horde, and you, Marquis of Saint George: having lost your teeth once, you should have known better the next time. If they were right outside the city, why did you not raise the sluices? You could have captured them all! Let me tell you something: renown comes not from wealth but from boldness of spirit." Rueing his absence, Tirant then exclaimed: "Remember the ancient freedom we regained so recently and the persecutions you all suffered!"

After speaking of many other things, Tirant sent his grand constable to select the two thousand ablest soldiers in the camp. When Diaphebus was already on his way, he suddenly wondered what his cousin had meant. He returned to him and said: "That is truly a hard request. How can I tell if they are good or bad, brave or cowardly?"

"If you have not yet learned, I shall tell you," replied Tirant. "Sound the alarm as if the enemy were coming, and once you reach the camp, touch everyone's spurs. Choose only those men who have fastened them well, for they will be brave and dexterous in arms."

Diaphebus left but soon came back again: "And how can I tell with foot soldiers, who do not wear spurs?"

"In the same fashion," replied Tirant. "Have the sergeants feel their clothes to see if they are loose or tight, and henceforth you will know how to separate the wheat from the chaff."

As the captain was setting out with his two thousand soldiers, the Prior of Saint John said: "Lord captain, knowing you are unsatisfied with those seven ships and wish to return to sea, I beg you to let me aid you in this endeavor."

Tirant gladly consented.

Upon reaching the port, Tirant had everything prepared for their departure.

"Lord captain," said Galançó, "I think you should dispatch two galleys now, and when they spy the fleet have one return while the other follows the Grand Karaman's ship, whose capture will bring you great riches and still greater glory."

"How will they recognize his ship?" the captain asked.

"By its sails, my lord, which are red and show his arms. His rigging is silk and the poop is covered with double brocade, whereby he hopes to show his magnificence, since his daughter has never been to sea before."

The captain quickly sent two galleys forth, telling one of them to trail the fleet and to hang a lantern on its stern every night.

On the morrow, the emperor reached Constantinople, and after resting two days, the Sicilians returned to Malveí Castle, where they found many wagons loaded with bombards for the fleet. The barons hastened to the port and begged Tirant to take them along, which request he gladly granted, as they were islanders and used to sailing. Then he appointed captains and loaded the ships with brave soldiers and crossbowmen. Though the vessels were small, they were manned by ardent warriors.

At the sight of a galley approaching with both sails and oars, Tirant guessed that his foes were near and had the bombards loaded. They spied their foes' ships late that afternoon, and the captain's vessel was the first to weigh anchor. When the Turks saw it, they were delighted by what seemed an easy prey, while the Grand Karaman summoned his daughter and damsels to watch the capture. A little later, the Duke of Pantelleria's ship put to sea, followed by the Duke of Messina's, at which the Turks and Genoese rejoiced still more.

The Grand Karaman told his daughter: "Choose the ship you like best, and I shall give it to you."

She chose the one she had seen first, and he promised it would be hers. Meanwhile, Lord Agramunt and Hippolytus both set sail, followed by the Prior of Saint John, who left port when it was almost dark.

As the astonished Genoese puzzled over those twelve warships, all Tirant's whaleboats and skiffs appeared, followed by a fleet of fishing boats. The boats without sails set up long poles or oars, which they secured firmly and bedecked with lanterns. First the captain's ship lit a lantern on its poop, as they had arranged, whereupon all the other craft, great and small, did likewise. Seeing all those lanterns, the Genoese cried: "The Venetians must have warned the Rhodians and Sicilians, who have sent their fleets."[53]

They decided to flee: "For it is better to save our lives than battle seventy-four warships."

The Genoese captain's ship blinked a lantern three times, and they all put about and fled as fast as they could. Some turned east and some west, some north and some south, but the galley kept after the Grand Karaman, who ordered his captain to sail toward Cyprus and then Alexandria. Tirant kept his eye on the galley and followed it, while both ships set every fore and mizzen sail they had and put on many extra ones.

When morning came, Tirant had lost sight of his ships, but he could still see the Grand Karaman, whom he overtook at midday. Men from each ship then leapt onto the other, while the Turks shot so many stones that Tirant's soldiers could hardly move. Many Christians were slain or wounded in that first encounter, from which the galley kept its distance as best it could. Both vessels had thrown out grappling hooks, so they could not have separated even had one wanted to. Tirant's men had an advantage because most of them wore steel armor with cuirasses and helmets, which as soon as one man was disabled, another would don. They also flung iron bars from the crow's-nest.

After that first encounter, they rested for half an hour and then the battle recommenced most fiercely, as the Turks threw lime and vats of boiling oil at their foes. Both ships heaved boiling pitch at each other and fought without pause until there were so many lances, shields, and quarrels floating in the sea that the corpses could not sink.

Let us leave them to their battle and see what the other knights and barons were doing.

The eleven other warships lost sight of Tirant, who had doused his lantern, but they spotted ten enemy vessels within bombard range. The Christians then pulled alongside their foes, while Hippolytus kept his distance, sailing windward to observe the battle. Beholding more Turks than Christians on the Lord of Pantelleria's ship, the knight hastened to assault the Sicilian's attackers, and having defeated the few Saracens who remained on their own vessel, Hippolytus flung all the dead and wounded Turks and Genoese into the sea. Thus he saved the Lord of Pantelleria, who felt as happy as a man cured of a fatal disease, and everyone thought it was most courageously done. Hippolytus then went to help others in need.

Seeing that no one remained on the Turkish ship, the Lord of Pantelleria divided his men and seized another vessel. The eleven warships fought so well that they captured fourteen Turkish craft and sank two others.

Now let us return to Tirant, who battled from midday through the night and till sundown the next day. There were twenty-seven fierce encounters, but he knew he could expect no aid and ruthlessly returned blow for blow. "Come what may," he said, "I shall capture you or die trying."

During the fray Tirant's arm was wounded by a quarrel, and as he was climbing onto the forecastle another pierced his thigh. Encouraged by this success, three Turks leapt aboard his vessel to slay him, but as soon as they landed they were thrown into the sea.

Believing all was lost, the Grand Karaman sent for a chest of money, jewels, and clothes, and made his daughter don a gold brocade jubbah with a silk cord around her neck. Then he tied her to the chest, flung it overboard, and, after serving the other ladies in like manner, he and the King of Armenia hid in the daughter's cabin, where they lay down, covered themselves, and awaited their deaths.

Once the ship had been captured, Tirant went aboard, wounded though he was, and asked what had become of the Grand Karaman.

"Lord captain," replied a Christian who had been the first aboard, "the fear of battle is worse than battle itself. He is hiding under the covers and awaiting his end."

"Is the King of Armenia with him?" asked Tirant.

"Certainly, my lord; they are both here."

"Bring them up," said Tirant, "for I wish to address them."

The gentleman quickly obeyed, but the Grand Karaman refused to budge and said he would sooner perish in his daughter's cabin than on deck.

"Do not speak so," cried the king, "but let us die like worthy knights!"

Nonetheless, the obstinate Grand Karaman obliged the gentleman to use force. When they were on deck, Tirant, who wished to honor them as kings, rose to his feet and asked them to be seated, but with his thigh wound he could not remain standing. After calling for a chair, he began to speak thus:

· CLXV ·

TIRANT'S SPEECH TO THE GRAND KARAMAN AND THE KING OF ARMENIA

"Noble kings and valiant knights: God has granted us victory, not through any lack of courage on your part, for you have fought to the last like ardent captains, but because your cause is unjust. Beholding your iniquitous plan to destroy the Greek Empire, God has allowed us to subdue and capture Your Majesties. Despite your cruelty, which cries out for vengeance—and especially in your case, Grand Karaman, as you inhumanly killed your daughter and those other Saracen ladies, who would have been set free had they fallen into my hands—so great is our emperor's clemency that he will spare your lives, not because you deserve it but to prove his virtue."

The Grand Karaman replied:

· CLXVI ·

*T*HE GRAND KARAMAN'S REPLY

"I would sooner die than be enslaved and suffer your arrogance, knowing that Allah caused my undoing to augment your glory and try my patience, wherefore I beg you to free me from my sufferings, as the fear of death is more terrible than death itself. You say I murdered my daughter, but I need not justify my acts before you or anyone else, and better she should perish than endure dishonor before my eyes, nor do I wish anyone else to enjoy my treasure and jewels. Though your men forced me to come before you, by rights you should have bowed to me, and do not think the knights in my service less valiant than yours, for if I ever regain my freedom, I shall quickly be avenged."

Tirant did not bother to reply and instead invited them to board his ship, where he divided his few remaining men and set sail. When he unplugged the scupper holes, a torrent of blood poured forth, and the older sailors said they had never heard or read in chronicles of such a gory sea battle. There was not a soul alive on the Turkish vessel except the two kings, while of four hundred and eighty men on the Christian ship, forty-four were unscathed, sixteen wounded, and the rest dead. Tirant had shown his mettle both on land and sea, and his fame increased amid triumphant praises.

Upon approaching the harbor on the Trasimene, they sighted a few Saracen boats making for Bellpuig, where they arrived amid cries of woe and dismay. Those on board described the lost battle with its innumerable casualties, which the astonished sultan lamented bitterly, weeping and bemoaning his latest setback. Cursing the evil fortune that had so favored their foes, the Saracens resolved to attack Tirant's camp.

After routing the Christians twice and capturing the Count of Burgundy and Count Malatesta, the infidels offered a truce or peace, for fear that Tirant would again defeat them.

Tirant was warmly welcomed by his men, who said the Prior of Saint John had put to sea in search of him and, finding him nowhere, had returned two days later. The only one now missing was Hippolytus.

Thinking Tirant must have sailed east, Hippolytus decided to follow him, but although he saw no sign of his captain, he did meet another Turkish warship. At his approach the ship fled, but the wind was against it and, since they were near a deserted island, the soldiers rowed ashore. Hippolytus then seized the rich vessel and continued on his way.

Seeing everyone there but Hippolytus, Tirant dispatched three ships that met him as he returned with his prey.

This Hippolytus, who proved to be a most brave and generous knight, performed many noble deeds as he strove to imitate his master. Thus do men say you should know a knight before entrusting your son to him, for a brave knight will create a thousand warriors, but a corrupt one will spread his vices.

Upon hearing of Tirant's victory, Lord Malveí went to see him, but before setting out, he sent messengers to the emperor and the camp, where the good news was received with joyous celebrations. The emperor ordered all the bells rung and held a great feast, at which everyone celebrated Tirant's amazing feats of chivalry, while Carmesina and the other ladies all praised him highly.

Lord Malveí advised Tirant to take the captured ships before His Majesty, to which our knight readily agreed, being eager to see the princess. As soon as a favorable wind arose, he told his men to set sail.

When the watchmen in Constantinople caught sight of Tirant's ships, they told the emperor his captain was coming with an entire fleet. Scarcely knowing how to celebrate his arrival, the emperor ordered a long satin-covered gangway that would reach more than thirty paces from shore. He also had a large platform covered with silk and brocade erected in the middle of the market square for himself and his ladies. A long, red velvet carpet was laid from the platform to the gangway, and since once Tirant had passed, anyone could take a piece, many people's hands were cut by swords and knives as they tried to grab their shares.

Tirant appeared with the Grand Karaman on his right, the King of Armenia on his left, and all his barons before him. A great crowd of commoners came to welcome their savior, at whom they gaped as though he had been sent from Heaven, treating him more like a god than a mortal captain. To worship him all the more, the clergy brought their relics, for they wished to place him as high as they could in Paradise. The procession stopped at the market, where the emperor and his ladies awaited them.

Upon reaching the platform, Tirant knelt to kiss the emperor's hand and told the Grand Karaman to do likewise, but as the infidel refused, our knight slapped him with his gauntlet, saying: "Dog, son of a dog, kiss His Majesty's hand and foot."

"I shall do so by force and against my will," replied the Grand Karaman, "and if you and I were alone, I would quickly teach you to respect a sovereign. You still do not know how long my arm is, but I swear by our prophet and my beard that if I ever regain my freedom, I shall make you kiss one of my black slaves' feet."

And he said no more. To avoid a second slap, his companion knelt and kissed the emperor's hand and foot, whereupon Tirant began to speak thus:

· CLXVII ·

*T*IRANT'S REPLY TO THE GRAND KARAMAN

"The noble King of Armenia here can bear true witness that before we came you did not dare to try my patience so; what, therefore, makes you now speak so outrageously before His Majesty? I shall not deign to return your insults, but every time you wish to act like a woman, you should remember that I subdued not only your body but your soul. It is you who chose life over death with honor, kneeling before me, crossing your arms, and uttering those words abhorred by worthy knights: 'I am your prisoner and you my master.' At that moment, I chivalrously spared the life you bought so dearly, and you will also recall the words this noble sovereign spoke, nor indeed, have I ever beheld such baseness in a monarch. He resembles that King of Poland, who, when the German emperor challenged him to a duel, shamefully fled on the appointed day, leaving his opponent alone in the field."

Tirant fell silent, while the emperor had the two kings seized and placed under guard.

Then the emperor and his ladies made their way to the Hagia Sophia, where they thanked Our Lord for their glorious victory. Tirant walked with the empress, who said: "Captain, your nobility is unequaled on earth, as you vanquished those two kings to win fame and help the emperor. If only you had visited Germany when my father was emperor! Though I had a thousand suitors, I would have quickly dismissed them all, but now, alas, I am old and married, wherefore my hope has come too late."

They spoke of such matters until they reached the palace, where, having overheard their conversation, the princess whispered to Tirant: "That old lady pities herself and wants to join the game, for her heart aches when she beholds you and thinks of her former beauty. Had you come in her youth, she feels certain she could have won you. Oh, what folly to crave what one cannot possess, or to regret a virtuous life and seek to end it in sin!"

"Oh reproacher of amorous crimes," cried Tirant, "you deserve great punishment for spurning my enamored pleas. I have no wish to incur your wrath, but ladies who quarrel with worthy gentlemen come to bad ends, nor do your words befit a noble damsel and still less one of such lofty station."

At this point the emperor approached them and asked Tirant about his wounds, to which he replied that he still had a slight fever: "And I think this voyage has made it worse." The imperial doctors then escorted him to his lodgings, where, after examining our knight, they told him to stay in bed if he wanted to recover the full use of his arm. Tirant gladly followed their advice, while the emperor visited him once a day and sent his wife and daughter every morning and evening. The Easygoing Widow, moved more by love than pity, was also constantly at his side.

Let us now see what transpired between the Turks and their foes. Upon learning that Tirant had captured the Grand Karaman, the infidels began attacking Saint George more often. They spared few who fell into their hands, and the Greeks feared to enter battle without Tirant, Diaphebus, or Lord Agramunt to lead them. In desperation, the Christians called upon Tirant as though he were a saint, for all their former boldness had vanished with his departure. They prayed God to restore their captain, who was their only hope.

Finally, they asked the emperor to send their messiah and wrote a second letter to Tirant that contained words of this tenor:

· CLXVIII ·

*T*HE LETTER TIRANT RECEIVED

Oh sword of virtue, most noble in the world, whose courage is manifest to God and men: we ask you to succor your humble servants, who shamefully confess their fear of battle without you. Prizing our lives above our honor, we shall fight no more until you come, and just as we beg you to hear our pleas, so may your beloved grant all your wishes.

· CLXIX ·

*H*OW THE EMPEROR HAD HIS DAUGHTER TAKE THE LETTER TO TIRANT

Having read the letter and beheld his men's dismay, the emperor wondered whether to give it to Tirant or wait till he was better. After pondering the matter for three days, he decided to have Carmesina deliver it and ask the captain to return to his camp as soon as possible.

Upon entering Tirant's chamber, the princess approached his bed and sweetly cried: "Oh flower of chivalry, hear your starving soldiers' cries: 'Where is that brave knight who won such honor? Where is that valiant winner of battles? All hope is lost if that conqueror does not come!' They have sent this letter, addressed 'to the best of all knights,' and if that is not you, who could it be?"

Once Tirant had read the letter and showed it to the empress, Carmesina said: "If you are willing, noble captain, to depart for those cruel battlefields, your deeds will live on in glorious memory, for your mere presence will so terrify the Turks that they will fear to oppose you. Thus you will bravely complete your mission and do us all a great service, but if you will not go for love, do so out of courage and virtue."

Tirant replied: "Your Highness need not plead, as the emperor's wishes are my commands. You know how much I long to serve you even if it means my certain death, and you may tell your parents that all my life I shall be their servant."

And seizing her hands, half against her will, he covered them with kisses.

Then the empress went to one end of the room with a psalter and started praying, while her daughter remained with Stephanie, the Easygoing Widow, Pleasure-of-my-life, and Tirant, who kept clasping his lady's hands and kissing them until at last she protested:

· CLXX ·

HOW THE PRINCESS SCOLDED TIRANT

"I see clearly, generous captain, that my resistance only inflames you, wherefore I rejoice, as things too easily won soon lose their value, and if I let them, your avid hands would disobey me. Should the empress behold your presumption, what will she think of you? She will forbid you to woo her daughter and will hamper your freedom. Why, then, do you forget to shield yourself from infamy? What will your conscience say if you choose treachery as your paramour? You act as though you had drunk at the fountain where fair Narcissus died, having already lost both memory and honor, and if by chance love makes you hesitate to heed the emperor's pleas, I now humble myself before you as you so often have before me, kneeling at your feet that my father may be served."

· C L X X I ·

*T*IRANT'S REPLY TO THE PRINCESS

"Cruel Fortune has so emboldened the Turks that I must be parted from my greatest treasure, nor have I yet learned to bear love's trials and tribulations. What could endanger my life more than separation from Your Highness, who should grant me some compensation, seeking your enemies' deaths instead of mine, for though many former and present knights were undone by love, someone must compensate for their woes and afflictions. Who is worthy of such a blessing? I, Tirant, who deserve to touch and possess Carmesina's perfections, and should you ask me how I know, I shall reply: because I want it, but if you are angry, force the one who lives for you to die for you. I already feel the strength draining from my limbs, and if I lose the hope that sustains my life, what sister will then comfort me? I declare that I would sooner stay and see you every day than depart, since if I stay I shall be blessed, whereas if I go I shall be damned."

The princess quickly replied in the following manner:

· C L X X I I ·

*T*HE PRINCESS'S REPLY TO TIRANT

"I cannot believe you wish to confess such shameful sentiments, for your words ill behoove a valiant warrior. Those who break their promises are always disgraced, and I know the difference between mustard greens and parsley. Why, then, do you let me bedevil you so? I have always heard it said that honor and delight cannot fit in the same box, wherefore you should imitate noble Alexander, who, after defeating and killing Darius, entered the city where the Persian's wife and three daughters dwelt. Apprised of the monarch's death, they knelt before the first captain who entered, begging him to spare them till their father was buried, and, awed by their peerless beauty, the captain readily agreed, while all those sensitive to pulchritude gladly stopped to gaze upon them. Once this captain had escorted them to their palace, he and many knights urged Alexander to visit the ladies, and moved by natural love, Alexander decided to go, but when he was within sight of their abode he changed his mind and turned back. His knights asked him why, to which he replied: 'I fear to be seduced by the sight of those damsels, for if at my age I allow my senses to be flattered, I may sacrifice my honor and martial spirit, nor do I wish to be enslaved by a foreign damsel.'

"That knight made courage his device; I hope you will do the same, as your body must suffer wounds and hardships if you wish to win glory. Men have been driven mad by envy of our good fortune, but now that it has changed to sorrow we are little respected, and should you sully your honor, both you and I shall be blamed. Consider all those knights of old who began well but came to bad ends: Samson, for example, surpassed all men in strength, but his force lay in his hair and a woman tricked him into revealing his secret, whereupon she promptly cut his locks and betrayed him. Think of our father Adam, whom a woman beguiled into renouncing God, and contemplate that great poet Virgil, whom a damsel deceived in like fashion, hanging him in a pannier for all the world to see. His revenge was terrible, but nonetheless his shame remained; and look also at those great philosophers Aristotle and Hippocrates, who were undone by women, as well as many others whom I shall omit to avoid prolixity.[54]

"How do you know I am less astute than those women of old? Perhaps I only feign love, hoping to rob you of your good judgment and ensure that you restore our empire once you have liberated it. Lord Tirant, look well at what you do, and do not let love so confound you that you risk your triumphant fame. You should not sacrifice so much for one damsel, and I can tell you there is nothing so mysterious as a woman, whose tongue always says the opposite of what she feels. If men knew of our duplicity, they would only love us out of pity, but lust blinds them to our faults, for to love is in man's nature. I beg you: be on your guard and recall wise Solomon's words: 'There are three things which are too wonderful for me, yea, four which I know not: the way of an eagle in the air; the way of a serpent upon a rock; the way of a ship in the midst of the sea; and the way of a young man when he grows older.'[55] And in verse it reads thus:

> When a snake's way
> upon a rock you behold
> then you may say
> what dwells in a woman's soul
> No man can state
> where a bird in flight will land
> nor whether a young man's fate
> will be evil or grand.

"Therefore I advise you, Tirant, to set aside love, not forsaking it altogether, for in peace it can bring great joy, but mindful that in war men must endure hardships and travails. Look at the Romans, who ruled the world and whose courage derived from wisdom, wherefore their glorious fame will endure forever. Though I send you forth, my heart is troubled by war's perils. Almighty God made man the master of earthly things, as man is the loftiest of all His creations, and likewise I want you to be victorious waking or sleeping, for I feel as though I had been present at the Creation and said: 'Lord, make Tirant thus, as such is my desire.' "

When the princess finished, Tirant quickly replied:

· CLXXIII ·

*T*IRANT'S REPLY TO THE PRINCESS

"Immortal lady, though our cunning enemy always strives to confound his adversaries, my desire to serve you makes me feel like a god, for my thoughts rise to such heights that earthly matters appear petty. I shall not bother to enumerate Your Highness's perfections, but I insist that my pleas for your amorous kisses are just. If someday I win them, I shall be called more than glorious, wherefore I am forced to contest your claim that men are of greater dignity, as all ancient and modern sages attribute greater excellence to women.

"I shall prove my point by citing nothing less than the Gospels, whose authors could not lie because they were illumined by the Holy Ghost. When Christ was resurrected, He appeared first to His Mother and Mary Magdalene, whereby we are shown that women are superior, as God honored them so in recognition of their virtue. In regard to your dignity, one need only mention that God made man from dust and woman from man's rib, which is a nobler substance.[56] Beyond the Holy Scriptures, common sense will support me, since if a woman washes her hands twice, the water will flow off clean and pure the second time, whereas if a man does the same, the water will remain dirty. Here we see that man cannot surpass the stuff of which he was made, and I could offer many more proofs, which I shall leave for another day."

At this point they saw the doctors, whom the empress was asking when Tirant would be able to walk.

"Your Highness," they replied, "within three or four days."

The empress left with her ladies, while Tirant stayed behind, and God knows how his heart ached when the princess had gone!

Once Carmesina reached her chamber, the memory of Tirant's words filled her heart with such love that she fell in a faint. Her damsels' screams quickly drew the emperor, who rushed in thinking his daughter had perished.

Beholding her prostrate body, he flung himself upon it, while the empress placed Carmesina's head in her lap, weeping so dolefully all the while that her face and clothes were bathed in tears. A knight was sent to fetch the doctors, and upon reaching Tirant's lodgings, he cried: "Hurry, my lords, for our princess is in such a state that you will have to run to find her alive.

They left Tirant's supper and hastened to the princess, while our knight's wise heart quickly guessed what had occurred.

He rose, ill though he was, and followed the doctors to her room, where he found that she had recovered and was lying on the bed.

They told him the doctors had used all their skills to revive her. Seeing his daughter out of danger, the emperor returned to his chamber, escorted by the doctors, who saw that he was exhausted. Tirant then approached his lady and began to speak in a tremulous voice:

· CLXXIV ·

*H*OW TIRANT ASKED THE PRINCESS WHAT HAD CAUSED HER TO SWOON

"Never did my lovelorn spirit feel such grief! Tell me what caused your suffering, for if illnesses bore arms, I swear by my baptism that I would soon punish this one. Despite my sins, God has pitied me and saved my soul, as I would sooner slay myself than live without you. When I heard those screams, I turned white as a sheet, but then I thought: 'If she is ill, she will certainly summon me!' If Your Highness must perish, I pray God not to let me see it but rather to kill me first, lest I be damned forever. My eyes are rightfully affronted by your indisposition, and I shall never be happy till you quiet my fears."

The princess quickly replied:

· CLXXV ·

*T*HE PRINCESS'S REPLY TO TIRANT

"Tirant, do not disappoint my hopes, as you caused my illness, which was due to love. I am more enamored than I should be, but I cannot hide my feelings, for alas, who can light a fire without smoke? My words are the messengers of my heart and soul, wherefore I beg you: hasten to the emperor lest he discover that you visited me first."

Then she pulled the covers over her and told Tirant to put his head under them, saying: "Kiss my breasts for your consolation and my repose."

Tirant readily obeyed, and having kissed her breasts, his lips began on her eyes and face while she said: "My lord, a day's pay is better than a day's work. In such matters fear often exceeds danger, and the fearful are abashed when they rue their cowardice."

Tirant had no time to reply but he felt greatly cheered, and when he reached His Majesty's room, the doctors scolded him for leaving his bed. Tirant replied: "Though I knew it would cost me my life, nothing could keep me from the emperor's side, and when I saw you hasten from my chamber in such distress, I could only suppose he was in grave danger."

The emperor replied:

· CLXXVI ·

*T*HE EMPEROR'S REPLY TO TIRANT

"Now that Carmesina has recovered, I can tell you my grief was almost unbearable, as I would have been like a man with one and a half eyes who loses one. My eldest daughter is half-lost, for I have neither seen nor spoken with her since she married the King of Hungary, and knowing that Carmesina is all I have, I nearly perished when I saw her. May Almighty God be praised for saving her life, and now that the danger has passed and I also have recovered, I beg you to visit her, as the sight of you will cheer her greatly."

They spoke of many other things, but the doctors kept insisting that Tirant return to his lodgings. "It is my pleasure," replied Tirant, "to stay by the emperor's side."

The emperor urged him to obey the doctors once he had seen Carmesina, and Tirant readily consented, being more eager to see his lady than to remain with her father.

Upon reaching her chamber, he beheld the empress, who was very pleased to see him and spoke for a long time about the princess's attack. Once Tirant saw that he could not speak with his beloved alone, he left lest the doctors tell the emperor he had tarried so long. Gallant Stephanie escorted our sighing knight to the head of the stairs and said: "Lord

Tirant, either help me or bury my tear-stained corpse beneath some path the grand constable will tread, that he may say: 'Here lies a woman who loved me in extreme degree.' At least pity me and give me this satisfaction, for I tremble like a leaf in a gentle breeze. My blood turns to water, my body grows cold, and I am blamed for what should earn me praise, but I regret nothing, even though the relentless Fates pursue me. What have I done? Why should I be parted from my husband? My only solace lies in dreams and imaginings at night. Tell me, lord captain: when shall I be freed from this torment?"

Tirant replied in the following manner:

· CLXXVII ·

HOW TIRANT COMFORTED THE DUCHESS OF MACEDONIA

"Your words, my lady, deserve to be heeded, but every warrior also needs good sense, and if Diaphebus forsakes his calling, he will be scorned by worthy knights. I wish you could see his prowess and wise organization, as then you would be more patient and rejoice in his glory. I shall tell you my intentions, though sometimes silence is better than speech, for you saw how the princess ordered me to return to battle, but when I reach Saint George, even if Diaphebus has been swallowed by a fish, I promise to pull him out and send him to his lady."

Leaving the duchess to ponder these comforting words, Tirant then returned to his lodgings, where he found the doctors waiting. They put him to bed and examined his wounds, which love and fear for his lady had inflamed and deepened. The long treatment was more dangerous than the injuries themselves, as the soldiers in his camp now despaired of victory.

The sultan sent emissaries to Tirant's camp, and upon learning of his absence, they decided to visit the emperor, who quickly granted them safe-conduct, since no prince should ever refuse to receive his foes.

By the time they reached Constantinople, Tirant was feeling much better and could walk to the palace, where he spoke with the emperor every day.

Having learned that emissaries were coming, the emperor asked Tirant to stay until the day of their arrival, when all the greatest Christian lords rode forth to welcome them. Though he was the sultan's representative, Abdullah Solomon dismounted and knelt before Tirant, thanking him profusely for having freed him from captivity. The captain made him remount, and they all approached the emperor, who saluted his guests most affably and did them great honor, for the chief emissary was the Grand Karaman's brother and the King of Lesser Armenia. Then they asked Abdullah Solomon to speak, since he was the wisest.

· CLXXVIII ·

*H*OW ABDULLAH SOLOMON EXPLAINED HIS MISSION

"We have been sent hither, my lord, by that dreadful, excellent, and peerless king of Muslim kings, the Grand Sultan of Babylon, as well as by the Grand Turk, the Lord of India, and the other sovereigns in our camp. Apart from Their Majesties' desire to ask after your health, life, and honor, we have come to your court for the following three reasons: first, the aforesaid monarchs wish to propose a three-month truce on land and sea; second, knowing that your brave captain subdued the Grand Karaman and the King of Armenia with his trenchant sword, they offer the Grand Karaman's weight in jewels, three times his weight in gold, and one and a half times the King of Armenia's weight in gold as ransom; and third, the sultan proposes a peace treaty and alliance, promising to regard you as a father and to behave like a devoted son. To seal this alliance, he offers to marry your daughter Carmesina on condition that their sons be raised as Muslims and their daughters as Christians, though he will respect the princess's religion and allow her to follow its laws. Thus we may put an end to all hostilities, and in exchange for this marriage, the sultan will restore all the cities, towns, and castles he has conquered. Furthermore, he will give you two million doubloons, sign a final peace treaty with you and your descendants, and aid you against all attackers."

Having heard the proposals, His Majesty retired to another chamber with his councilors, who decided that in view of Tirant's wound, it would be best to accept the truce. The emperor then announced that for love of the sultan and Grand Turk, he would sign a three-month truce, but he would have to consider the other proposals more carefully.

The truce was duly signed and broadcast by imperial and Turkish criers, while the emperor held many councils to consider the other proposals. So many lords urged him to seal the peace treaty with his daughter's marriage that Tirant started to fret, and one day when he was in the princess's chamber, he suddenly cried: "I curse the day I came here, for two contraries unite against me! Oh Tirant, how can you bear to see father and council united against daughter or to think that she may be subjugated to an enemy of our holy faith, and that such beauty, virtue, grace, and noble lineage may be sullied and trampled? Alas, I imagine what my eyes cannot yet see! Oh cruelest of messengers whom men call Abdullah Solomon: had I known you planned to harm me, I never would have freed you, for your actions show you are ignorant of love. Blessed the death that will end my ills! I, damsels, do not know which is the greater grief: to be near or far from one's beloved, as when I am near, flames of hope torment me, while those who are far, though their hopes be great, are not so badly burned. If Your Highness leaves, I shall be like Tantalus, from whose desirous mouth the apples and water fled, but I shall soon prove my love by taking my own life, whereupon everyone will behold the depth of my devotion."

The princess quickly replied:

· CLXXIX ·

*H*OW THE PRINCESS COMFORTED TIRANT

"Since Fortune has made you lord of my destiny, you should be pleased with your powers and accept me as your reward. How can you think I would marry an infidel? My noble spirit could never live with a Saracen dog, who can have all the women he wishes, yet none is truly his wife, for he can divorce every one of them whenever he likes. Though many kings have sought to wed me, I have refused them all, and really, you go too far in entertaining such a notion! I would have to lose my wits before such a thought could cross my mind, and if you are worried that my father may yield to his councilors, have no fear, as he will abide by my tongue whether it says yes or no. Your love and hope are made of frail stuff, and bad luck always afflicts wretches who distrust their worthy lovers. Do not waver, brave knight, but trust your Carmesina, who will defend your rights just as you have defended hers."

At this point, the empress came in and asked what they had been discussing, to which Tirant replied: "Since Your Majesty wishes to know, we were speaking of those emissaries who so madly and presumptuously asked the princess to marry a renegade dog. What if he denies his wife as he has his God? Surely he will do so, and who then will save her? To whom will she turn for help? To her father? He is too old, nor will her mother be of any use, for like all women everywhere, you will tremble at the thought of a perilous sea voyage. On the other hand, were you to go, who could stop some Turk from forcing you to do his bidding, thus robbing us of two ladies instead of one? At the very thought, my soul weeps blood and cold sweat trickles down my back, while the mere mention of such proposals makes me long to die. Shame prevents me from saying more, and I only wish that my soul were in Heaven and my body in its grave."

The empress quickly tried to comfort Tirant:

· CLXXX ·

THE EMPRESS'S WORDS OF SOLACE

"These emissaries come with ill will and hope for quick success, but a false and unjust sentence is quickly revoked. Let the emperor hold council; my daughter and I are here too, and anyone who forgets his guest is obliged to count twice. Since you know right from wrong, champion our worthy cause, for if they try my patience I promise to punish those givers of bad counsel, and should the marriage take place I know a thousand ways to kill myself painlessly, having learned to fear foreigners when my other daughter married one. All I can do now is weep to ease my sorrow, and at night my eyes shed bitter tears instead of resting, but let us put aside sad thoughts lest they increase my woe. Valiant captain, your chivalry deserves great praise, and I would sooner give my daughter to a brave pauper than to the loftiest coward alive. Let no one think I shall permit Carmesina to leave my side, nor shall I accept a suitor of impure love or tarnished past."

"My lady," asked the princess, "what good is an ardent fool? It is true that nobility, courage, and wisdom usually go together, but of these wisdom is the most useful and highly esteemed."

At this point the emperor came in and asked what they were discussing, to which the captain replied: "Sire, here you have a most amusing debate. The empress says that if she had a son, she would subject him to Lord Courage, for valor is the finest gift Nature can bestow upon us, while the princess maintains that though Courage is a mighty lord and should be much revered, Wisdom is of greater degree, since no one can perform noble deeds without it. This is their quarrel; may it please Your Majesty to decide the issue."

The emperor replied: "I can deliver no judgment without hearing both sides, wherefore I ask you, my daughter, to make your thoughts known."

"My lord, it ill behooves me to precede my worthy mother."

"Speak," said the empress, "if such is his command, and display your wisdom, for which I promise to love you all the more."

The two ladies went on exchanging courtesies and refusing to speak until finally Carmesina gave in and uttered the following words:

· CLXXXI ·

*H*OW THE PRINCESS SPOKE IN FAVOR OF WISDOM[57]

"Varied opinions on this subject were held by the ancients, many of whom favored riches, which may bring a man honor. Virgil, who was one of these, wrote treatises on amassing wealth, while Caesar also maintained that happiness lay in opulence. Others advocated knighthood, as valiant knights win glorious fame, and among these was Lucan, who wrote tales of chivalry and conquered most of the world. Still others sought health, which prolongs a man's life, and one such was Galen, who composed works on how to heal the sick, nor did our ancestor Constantine hesitate to sacrifice his empire for his health. Some preferred love, which makes men glad and joyful, inducing them to perform noble deeds of glorious memory. Among these were Ovid, who celebrated love, and Paris, who performed so many worthy feats for Helen. Others said good customs raised men from baseness, and one of these was Cato, who wrote books about proper conduct.

"Still others defended wisdom, which helps us know God and ourselves. Such a one was Aristotle, who wrote books of great sagacity, and another was Solomon, to whom God showed unequaled grace, sending an angel to offer him three gifts: peerless wisdom, riches, or victory over his foes. Solomon chose wisdom, and the angel said he had chosen well, since with this gift he also had gained the others. He was not only the wisest but the richest man alive, and having learned the secret of the philosophers' stone, he used his treasure to defeat his enemies. Then Your Majesty can look at the Romans, who, though small in number, conquered the world through wisdom, nor could any fool, however brave, be a Roman consul or senator. Their empire lasted as long as they maintained this custom, but once they ceased to choose wise emperors, they were quickly vanquished. Wisdom decides battles, makes lovers generous, amasses money, and promotes virtue, wherefore everyone wants a wise man as his alderman, duke, king, or lord, and those who are bold but lack wisdom are considered foolhardy. We all should fear death, which is the *ultimum terribilium,* as the body is nothing once the soul has forsaken it, and thus I conclude that wisdom rules all other qualities."

When the princess had finished praising wisdom, the empress began to speak:

· CLXXXII ·

*T*HE EMPRESS'S REBUTTAL

"Just opinions are too often dismissed because of clumsy expression, and as I, unlike my daughter, have never studied the liberal arts, I cannot support my views with the sayings of philosophers. Nonetheless, I shall appeal to common sense in such manner that His Majesty will award me the prize of honor, and first I declare that wisdom is not for knights, for a wise knight will never perform noble deeds but will shrink from the pursuit of honor lest some harm befall him, wherefore I declare wisdom and courage incompatible. Do you know who needs wisdom? Burghers and magistrates, who have to run cities, administer justice, and protect the commoners from war.

"Honor, however, makes great lords of small men, as in the case of Alexander, who though small in stature bravely conquered the world, or Julius Caesar, who through his prowess became Emperor of Rome, and have you forgotten, my daughter, how Hector and Troilus kept the Greeks at bay for ten years? What of King Arthur, Lancelot, Tristram, and above all Galahad, who, together with Boors and Percival, boldly retrieved the Holy Grail? These knights are not remembered for wisdom but valor, and thus does courage excel wisdom, for a wise man flees danger. Satisfied with the little within his grasp, he shuns glory and its attendant perils, whereas a knight-errant must endure hunger, thirst, cold, and heat, risking death in cities, towns, and castles. A wise man does no such thing but avoids the sun in summer and the cold night air in winter, while if he sees a town or city burning, he laments the loss of property. Deriving no pleasure from war, he chooses good over evil, yet a bold knight seeks nothing but his enemies' destruction, and the more he can harm them the happier he is. Brave Tirant is a good example: look how dauntlessly he slays his foes, striving through his gallant deeds to restore our freedom and imperial dignity, whereby one sees that courage is king and wisdom its counselor.

"Moreover, I declare that bravery alone caused Christ to die for our sins, spurning wisdom, though had He wished to He might have avoided death. Whoever seeks the glory of Heaven must battle this world, the flesh, and the Devil's temptations like the many valiant martyrs who have preferred death to apostasy. I believe I have said enough if you are willing to be swayed, for courage is the strength of spirit with which Christ imbued his disciples, that they might go forth to spread God's word as one reads in Acts of the Apostles, and therefore I ask His Majesty to declare me victorious."

The princess quickly replied:

· CLXXXIII ·

*T*HE PRINCESS'S REPLY TO HER MOTHER

"Since natural right and reason oblige me to obey Your Majesty, I shall seek to respond in my awkward fashion, begging my mother's pardon should I contradict her gentle words. Lest I weary your ears with useless repetition, I shall merely touch upon the deeds of noble Alexander, whom Your Highness cited, claiming he was small but conquered the world through bravery. With all due respect, this was not the case, as it was wise Aristotle who enabled that knight to triumph, advising him to burn his spoils lest his troops weary of battle. Caesar was certainly a mighty warrior, but he also won his power through wisdom, though at the pinnacle of his career he became cruel and his companions killed him. I shall not speak of the others.

"Your Majesty has said the wise are content with little, because God helps them to distinguish good from evil. Our Lord does indeed forbid us to win anything unjustly, and a wise man will certainly avoid such acts, but wisdom has two aspects: temporal and spiritual. The spiritual aspect only warns us to shun wickedness, obey the Ten Commandments, observe the articles of our faith, and atone for our sins. The temporal aspect is to know oneself and one's duty, studying and imitating the deeds of sage and stalwart heroes. A wise man deserves to rule the world, whereas a brave fool can only die in sin, and in truth, only a fool would think Christ saved us to prove his mettle. All theologians agree that He was moved solely by wisdom, and since a woman was the cause of our perdition, God chose a woman to repair the damage: one free of all mortal, venial, and original sin. Having assumed human form in her virgin womb, He died on the cross to give us eternal life, nor could courage alone have done such a deed. Wisdom resides in the immortal soul, whereas courage is in the heart, which, being mortal, cannot outlast the body. Since wisdom alone can truly shield us from harm, those who live by courage will not long endure, being slaves to this world's grief and delusion. Let Your Highness recall that no one can enter Heaven except through wisdom, wherefore I ask you to overlook my clumsy arguments, considering only the manifest truth of my words."

The emperor was delighted by his daughter's understanding and the graceful turns of phrase that adorned her speech.

The empress, however, did not hesitate to reply:

· CLXXXIV ·

*T*HE EMPRESS'S REBUTTAL

"Contemplating the wide world, we see that courage alone preserves it, whereby this quality is clearly of greater excellence than wisdom, yet you persist in defending a hopeless cause. Wisdom is in the head while courage is in the heart, wherefore philosophers proclaim the heart our noblest organ and the others its docile servants, as all the body's powers derive from the heart. The countenance quickly reveals an unhappy heart, and when the heart is asleep, our other members lie still. As the heart rules the body so does courage rule wisdom, and thus did Divine Providence place a man's heart in the center of his frame, just as a king rides into battle surrounded by his troops. Hence commoners call courage the chief among virtues, since no man can hope to be respected without it. I think I have said enough to prove my point, for without courage one can neither enter Heaven nor vanquish one's foes, and so I rest my case, asking the emperor to pronounce his judgment."

The emperor quickly replied:

· CLXXXV ·

*T*HE EMPEROR'S REPLY TO HIS WIFE AND DAUGHTER

"Those who obscure the truth defy both God and man, and although I see that neither of you needs a lawyer, for your eloquence is manifest, tomorrow, after consulting with knights and sages, I shall pronounce my impartial sentence."

The emperor then entered another room, to which he summoned his lords and jurists, whereupon a second great debate ensued between the proponents of courage and wisdom.

Finally the emperor called for a vote, and the next day at the appointed hour, he seated himself upon his throne. His wife sat at his side, with their daughter before them, while the entire Greek nobility waited to hear their lord's sentence.

When they were all seated and quiet, the emperor ordered his lord chancellor to speak, at which the chancellor rose, knelt, and uttered these words:

· CLXXXVI ·

*T*HE EMPEROR'S SENTENCE

In the name of the Father, Son, and Holy Ghost, one God in perfect Trinity, we, Henry,[58] Emperor of Constantinople by God's grace, having heard the debate between our beloved wife and daughter, with God before our eyes and in accord with the majority of our holy council, pronounce wisdom the greatest gift God and Nature can bestow upon us, as the other virtues are nothing without it and, just as planets and stars take their light from the sun, so does noble wisdom illumine the universe, but men also require courage, without which no one can win honor, wherefore, though courage is second, the two virtues must be inseparable. A knight both wise and valiant merits glory and a royal throne, for generous of spirit is the captain who loves ardor, and thus did Pompey bravely vanquish his foes. Therefore we order the empress, who favored courage, to praise wisdom from this moment on, and whenever she hears wisdom and courage spoken of she must give precedence to the former, which she herself possesses, doing so cheerfully and without ill will. Let there be no bitterness between mother and daughter, but rather true maternal and filial love.

Both ladies praised the sentence, which all those present also applauded, repeating that vulgar proverb: "As a worthy seed makes a good tree, so a worthy knight makes a good judge."

The Grand Karaman, the King of Armenia, and the sultan's emissaries were also in attendance. They waited while the emperor took counsel with his knights and captain, who urged him to hold a great feast and reply to the Saracens. His Majesty then told Tirant to organize feats of arms, dances, and other entertainments, whereupon our knight quickly dispatched criers to announce a feast in two weeks.

Failing to see Diaphebus among the lords gathered in Constantinople, Stephanie summoned a squire, to whom she gave the following letter:

· CLXXXVII ·

*S*TEPHANIE'S LETTER TO THE GRAND CONSTABLE

A knight who breaks faith will be punished for treachery, and you have betrayed my love by not returning to my side. You deserve no pardon, being unrepentent, and I can see you are of lesser weight than a grain of wheat. Do you fear that I am unworthy to be your wife? If you have found some new love, may my life quickly end, and I pray God to slay me before I witness such adultery! I do not say this because of any rumor, yet I tremble at such thoughts, for all lovers doubt and every cruel error stirs new anxieties. Torment your enemies but not your spouse, lest our pleasure come to light, for already the jealous Fates pursue me. My hope of good and dread of evil make me believe first one thing and then another, and my hand, wearied by writing, now rests in my lap.

· CLXXXVIII ·

THE CONSTABLE'S REPLY

Would that I were dead and free from poisonous slanders, for how can I reward one who deserves not only love but worship? Though you may think I have been idle, I hoped my deeds would bring you joy, nor will my own life last long if you choose to take yours, wherefore I hasten to reply that my devotion is unshakeable. How well I remember that night we spent together! A ray of moonlight entered the room, but you thought it was the dawn and cried: "Oh sun, pity poor Stephanie's moans and sighs! Let me repose a little longer with my Diaphebus!" Then you said: "Alas, would that by some spell I might stay the morning's light."[59] Happy with virtue's sweet reward and disposed to obey you, I close quickly lest your noble person be imperiled.

· CLXXXIX ·

THE EMPEROR'S SPLENDID FEAST FOR THE SARACEN EMISSARIES

When Diaphebus finished the letter, he gave it to Stephanie's squire and said: "Friend, tell your mistress that I cannot abandon my post without orders, but once the feast is over I shall do everything in my power to visit her. Kiss the princess's hands on my behalf, for she is endowed with every virtue, and then kiss my lady's."

Upon reaching the palace, the squire saw Carmesina talking with Stephanie, who as soon as she spied him leapt up and cried: "What news do you bring from one who holds my heart in thrall?"

The squire silently approached the ladies, kissed their hands, and handed Stephanie the missive, which she raised aloft as an offering to Heaven. After reading it, she spoke with Carmesina for a long while, and both damsels lamented the constable's absence from their feast.

Shortly before the festivities, Diaphebus set out for the city, but he stopped a league away and camped there overnight. At first Stephanie refused to attend, since her beloved would not be present, though when the princess threatened not to go either, her friend at last relented.

After hearing Mass with great pomp and ceremony, they all made their way to the central market, where they found the ground and roof covered with green, white, and purple woolen cloth, while French silk tapestries adorned the walls and splendid tables had been placed all around. The emperor sat beneath a rich brocade canopy in the middle of the market, with the emissaries around him, his wife and daughter at the head of another table, and the Grand Karaman and the King of Armenia seated on the ground. His Majesty had invited the noblest ladies in Constantinople, many of whom feasted with Stephanie at yet another large table, and there were also twenty-four platforms piled high with gold and silver. The first held the city's relics; the second had all the gold from its churches; ten more were heaped with big straw baskets and panniers in which all the gold coins in the Greek treasury could be seen; and still others displayed His Majesty's drinking cups, plates, salt-cellars, jewels, and silver pitchers. Around each platform stood three stalwart knights, attired in long brocade robes and holding splendid silver staffs, while in the middle of the market there were some lists for jousting.

Tirant, the Duke of Pera, and the Duke of Sinope, who were the appointed champions, then rode forth to tilt for His Majesty's pleasure. First the Duke of Pera appeared on a horse with blue and gold brocade trappings, followed by the Duke of Sinope, whose mount was clad in green and grey brocade. Tirant's steed was covered with green velvet bedecked with huge ducats, each one of which was worth thirty ordinary ducats.

A few days before the feast, as Tirant walked toward the princess's chamber, he had met Pleasure-of-my-life and asked what his lady was doing. The damsel had replied: "Alas, good fool, why should you inquire into my mistress's affairs? Had you come earlier, you might have found her in bed, whereupon your soul would surely have attained eternal bliss, since looking is far more pleasant than mere imagining. Come in if you wish, but she has already donned her skirt and is scratching her head and heels, for we shall soon have our wishes, yet I cannot understand my Hippolytus's absence, as in my sad imaginings I often behold him, and no one should defer pleasure or accept pain in its place."

"Oh damsel," replied Tirant, "please tell me if the empress is inside. I humbly request your aid, which you should not deny me."

"I would never deceive Your Lordship," said Pleasure-of-my-life, "for our guilt would be equal: yours for entering and mine for letting you. I know the princess does not wish your love to go unrewarded, and therefore I shall help you fulfill your desires, since nothing is more lightly lost than what no woman can regain."

Then Tirant entered the chamber, where he found the princess combing her golden tresses. Upon seeing him, she asked: "Who gave you permission to come in? You must not visit me without my leave, lest my father accuse you of treachery. Please go, for my breasts tremble with fear and distress."

Ignoring Carmesina's words, Tirant clasped her in his arms and kissed her breasts, eyes, and mouth again and again. The damsels merely watched as he caressed their mistress, but when he slipped his hand under her skirt, they quickly intervened. They played and joked so much that they did not hear the empress's footsteps until she was right outside the door.

Tirant flung himself on the floor, they tossed some clothes on top of him, and Carmesina seated herself upon the clothes, where she began combing her hair. The empress sat down beside her, very close to Tirant's head, and God knows how frightened our knight was of being discovered! His misery lasted for a considerable while, as mother and daughter spoke of the coming celebrations.

Finally a damsel brought a book of hours to the empress, who then rose, went to the other end of the room, and began her devotions. Carmesina remained motionless lest her mother spy Tirant, and having combed her hair, she slipped her comb under the clothes and began combing his, while from time to time he kissed her hand or grabbed the comb. The damsels, who had become uneasy, managed to block the empress's view, whereupon Tirant rose as quietly as he could and left with his lady's comb.

Just as he stepped outside, however, he spied the emperor and a chamberlain, who were crossing the great hall, making straight for the princess's chamber. Tirant scarcely knew where to turn, but since there was no other solution, he slipped back into the room, whispering: "My lady, save me, for the emperor will soon be here!"

"Alas!" said the princess. "We escape one predicament only to encounter another. I warned you not to come at times like this!"

Having told her damsels to keep the empress occupied, she and Tirant tiptoed into another room, where she told him to lie down and covered him with many mattresses, as the emperor often entered that chamber when he was visiting his daughter.

Upon his arrival, the emperor found her pinning up her hair, and once she had finished, they left with her damsels, but as they reached the door, the princess suddenly remembered her gloves and said: "I put them in a place that none of you knows."

She and her damsels returned to the room where our knight was hiding. As soon as they had uncovered him, he leapt up and took the princess in his arms, dancing about the room with her, kissing her many times, and crying: "Never did I see such perfection in a mortal damsel! Your Highness surpasses all others in wisdom and discretion, and I am in no way surprised that the sultan longs to embrace you."

"You are deceived by appearances," replied the princess, "and I am not so perfect as you claim, though your good will makes you say so, since the more one loves something the more one wishes to. Were you content with the sight of my black garments and hair tied beneath chastity's veil, I would willingly give you both honor and glory, but if not, you will be considered madder and crueler than Nero. Now kiss me and let me go, lest the emperor discover us."

Tirant had no time to reply, and the damsels seized his hands, but when he saw his lady leaving he slipped his leg between her thighs.[60] The princess ran from the room, while the Easygoing Widow showed him out through the garden.

As soon as Tirant reached his lodgings, he removed one shoe and stocking, which he had embroidered with pearls, rubies, and diamonds worth more than twenty thousand ducats.

On the feast day he donned his richly bejeweled apparel, at which everyone marveled, for only his left leg was armored, and atop his helmet, four gold rods sustained a copy of the Holy Grail, on which the princess's comb rested, inscribed with the motto: *She possesses all virtues.*[61]

There was a platform covered with brocade in the center of the lists, and upon it stood a splendid chair that could turn in all directions. There sat wise Sibyl, gazing now here and now there, while other masked goddesses sat at her feet, since in the past the pagans had thought them heavenly bodies. Those ladies who had loved most truly waited upon them: Queen Guinevere, Isolde, Briseis, Queen Penelope, Medea, Dido, Deianira, Ariadne, Phaedra, and so many others that one would weary of naming them. Many had been deceived, as when Jason tricked gentle Medea or when Theseus seduced Ariadne, enticing her from her father's house only to abandon her on a desert isle. There were many other betrayed damsels, each holding a scourge to punish the defeated and felled knights who were brought before their platform. Sibyl sentenced them to die for defrauding love, but then the goddesses and damsels knelt and begged her to reduce the sentence to scourging. Once she had yielded to their pleas, they stripped off the knight's armor, scourged him in public view, and dragged him from the platform. Such was the reward of those knights who were vanquished.

His Majesty's champions entered the lists first, allowing only knights whose horses wore silk, brocade, or beaten gold trappings to challenge them.

As soon as Diaphebus learned that the feast had begun, he entered the city, attired in scarlet double brocade and purple damask. The damask was embroidered with golden-stalked sheaves of wheat, each grain of which was a magnificent pearl, and his helmet was also covered by this same material. The felt hat he wore over it was adorned with pearls and gold, while his sword hung at his side, whereby everyone could see that he had just arrived. He was attended by thirty gentlemen dressed in scarlet capes, some of which were lined with sable and others with ermine. In addition, ten knights in brocade robes escorted Diaphebus, all wearing hoods that covered their faces. A gallant damsel led him by a silver chain, and behind them walked twelve pack mules, each with a scarlet saddle and silk harness. One mule bore his bed, another carried six stout lances, and the rest were loaded with Diaphebus's clothing. The knights circled around the lists until they reached His Majesty and bowed to him, whereupon he sent his chamberlain to ask who their master was, but Diaphebus's men would only reply: "A most favored knight."

The emperor said: "He may not wish to reveal his name, but that damsel with the chain shows he is love's prisoner. Ask her who enslaved him and read those words on his shield, for perhaps our mysterious guest's name is inscribed there."

The chamberlain quickly obeyed, and the damsel replied: "A virgin imprisoned this knight when by yielding to his will, she subjected him."

The chamberlain returned to his master, who said: "Alas, the love of worthy knights is often unrequited. Though I long for my youth, I shall never again know joy, and indeed, I scarcely remember anything except my afflictions. Tell me: what did you find written on his shield?"

"My lord," replied the chamberlain, "I read it many times. It is inscribed in Spanish or French and says:

> Cursed be Love, who made her so fair,
> If my sorrows she refuses to share.

By now the constable was at one end of the lists with his lance at the ready. Upon asking his opponent's name, he was told: "The Duke of Sinope."

They charged each other and fought many splendid encounters. On the fifth pass our constable unhorsed his foe, who was brought before wise Sibyl's platform, where the forsaken ladies disarmed and scourged him.

When this ceremony had been performed, Diaphebus jousted with the Duke of Pera, and on their tenth pass the Breton smote his visor, felling both him and his mount.

"Who is this cursed fellow," asked Tirant, "who thus defeats my friends?"

He quickly donned his helmet, mounted his steed, and positioned himself at one end of the lists. While Tirant was arming, they brought the duke before wise Sibyl, who treated him as she had the other. The constable, realizing that Tirant was his opponent, asked to leave the lists, but the judges said he was obliged to fight twelve encounters. The ladies and everyone there laughed heartily to see an unknown knight defeat two dukes.

The emperor said: "Wait a bit, for only a miracle can save our captain."

"Never!" cried the princess. "The Holy Trinity will shield Tirant from such misfortune, but if that knight does win, he may truly be deemed favored."

The emperor replied: "By God, never in all my days have I seen a knight defeat two dukes in fifteen passes or come before me thus, leading pack mules with silk and brocade trappings. This man must be a mighty foreign king or a prince. I wish I knew his name, as I fear he may depart to escape his opponents' wrath."

He sent two noble and indescribably fair damsels to ask the knight on Carmesina's behalf if he would not reveal his name.

The constable replied: "Let Her Highness not be distressed but remember that great prizes are never lightly won, and lest my words appear scornful, tell her I hail from the Westernmost Shore."[62]

The damsels returned with his reply, and the constable was forced to joust with Tirant. They ran at each other, but the constable kept his lance upright in its rest, at the sight of which Tirant raised his lance too and sadly asked why he was treating him with such courtesy. He begged Diaphebus not to defer to him but rather to do his utmost.

As the herald who delivered this message repeated Tirant's words in a scornful tone, the constable replied: "Tell your lord I only wished to honor him, but let him watch his step, for I shall now treat him like the others."

He called for his stoutest lance, yet when they were about to encounter Diaphebus again refused, whereupon Tirant flung his weapon to the ground, cursing his inability to avenge the dukes. The emperor's servants quickly took Diaphebus's mount by the reins lest he escape, and the judges brought him before wise Sibyl, where they removed his helmet while the goddesses welcomed him and gloried in his victories.

Having discovered his identity, they seated him on Sibyl's throne and brought him food, sweetmeats, and everything else he desired. One combed his hair, another wiped his brow, and each one served him as best she could.

Thus did they honor the other triumphant knights, each of whom remained enthroned until some braver knight displaced him.

The emperor and all his ladies were comforted to learn the mysterious knight's name, but especially Stephanie, who fainted for sheer joy and had to be revived by the emperor's doctors. Thus does Aristotle declare that excessive love can harm a damsel as much as excessive grief.

The emperor asked Stephanie why she had fainted, to which she replied: "My gown is too tight at the waist."

The constable spent the whole day on Sibyl's throne, from which no one could displace him.

When night fell, they went on jousting by torchlight, and after supper there were dances, mummery, and many noble masques. The entertainment lasted until midnight, and to augment their pleasure, the emperor ordered lodgings prepared in the market, that they might feast day and night for a week without returning to the palace.

The next day, all the knights tried to dethrone Diaphebus. One Greek lord named the Grand Noble entered the ring in wondrous style, for a damsel rode behind him, standing with her hands on his shoulders and her head above his helmet. These words were inscribed on his shield in gold letters:

> True lovers, rejoice in her sight,
> For nowhere on earth will you find such delight.

Another knight bore a maiden on his shoulders, just as Saint Christopher had carried Christ. His beloved was named Leonore, and these words were written on his horse's trappings:

> Honor her, oh lovers,
> For she surpasses all others.

Tirant tilted with the Grand Noble and in the end almost killed him, as our knight smote the edge of his foe's shield, driving it into his helmet and unhorsing him. He was so big and heavy that he broke two ribs in his fall, but not before landing a mighty blow under his opponent's shield. After staggering three paces backward, Tirant's horse dropped to its knees, and though the Breton pulled his feet out of the stirrups, he had to touch the ground with his right hand to keep from falling. The steed quickly expired, while they brought the Grand Noble to Sibyl's platform, where they scourged him but not as hard because of his broken ribs. Since Tirant's hand had touched the ground, the judges told him to joust without a right spur, a right gauntlet, or trappings on his horse.

Seeing himself thus shamed by his mount, Tirant vowed never to tilt again except with kings and princes.

Then the constable stepped down from Sibyl's throne, on which another knight replaced him that he might become the champion and joust with all comers. The last day of that week was as noble as the first, abounding in adventure, merriment, and splendid dishes.

The day after his vow, Tirant appeared in a black velvet cape embroidered with gold and silver sycamores, a tree that bears a small white nut used to make rosary beads.[63] He wore those same stockings, one embroidered and the other not, and likewise the shoe that had touched the object of his desires. Before setting out, he had the best horse in his stables saddled, caparisoned, and sent with his armor and helmet to the Grand Noble, who thanked him profusely, for the gift was worth more than forty thousand ducats.

Tirant sat with the court every day, chatting and taking his ease with the emperor and still more with the ladies, but although he changed his clothes daily, he always wore those jeweled stockings. Finally, the princess asked him in jest: "Tell me, Tirant, and may God grant you honor: is this festive custom of wearing one embroidered stocking and one plain one a French fashion, or where is it from?"

This was the day after the feast ended, and they were on their way to Pera with Stephanie and the Easygoing Widow. Tirant replied: "What, my lady? Do you not recall the day your mother surprised us, and, when your father arrived, you hid me beneath some mattresses? After they left, I was playing with Your Highness and, as I could not use my hand, I slipped my leg between your thighs. My foot nearly touched the spot where I hope to attain bliss, but I fear that for my sins such glory will be denied me."

"Ah, Tirant," said the princess, "how well I remember, for my body also bears love's imprint, but in time you will wear two embroidered stockings instead of one and be free to place them wherever you like."

Hearing these amorous words, Tirant dropped his gloves and dismounted to retrieve them. He kissed his lady's leg and said: "Grateful kisses should be bestowed where the favor was granted."

Upon reaching Pera, they saw nine galleys in the distance, and though the emperor had announced a glorious mock battle, he postponed it till he could learn where they were from. Within less than an hour, the ships entered the harbor amid great rejoicing, for they were captained by Tirant's first cousin, the Viscount of Branches, who had been a page at the King of France's court.[64] Knowing of Tirant's noble exploits and how eager his parents were for news of him, the viscount had yielded both to their pleas and to his own wish to bear arms. He and his company had sailed to Greece with five thousand royal French archers,[65] each of whom was accompanied by a squire and a page. The King of France had also granted Tirant's cousin the viscountcy of Branches, money for six months, and those well-provisioned galleys. On the way they stopped in Sicily, where King Philip gave them many horses.

When Tirant and Diaphebus learned that their cousin Sir Amer had come, they boarded a skiff and rowed out to the galleys. After greeting one another, they went ashore to salute the emperor, who rejoiced at the archers' coming and that the emissaries could see them. Then they went to pay their respects to the ladies, who did them great honor for Tirant's sake, while His Majesty postponed the mock battle till the following day.

The next morning, His Majesty asked Tirant to take part, as he could do so without breaking his vow, to which Tirant gladly consented since there would be no single combats.

Sir Amer asked Tirant to lend him a charger, and though the emperor sought to dissuade him, saying he must be weary after such a long voyage, he gallantly swore that such hardships were his greatest pleasure. When Tirant saw his determination, he sent him the ten best horses in his stable, to which His Highness added fifteen splendid mounts, the empress fifteen more, and the princess ten more at her father's request. The constable gave him seven, and all the dukes and counts sent chargers, so that in the end he had eighty-three of the city's finest steeds.

His men rode forth with the trappings the King of France had given them, embroidered with lions *couchants* wearing big gold bells and cubs with tiny ones that tinkled sweetly as their horses moved.

Eight hundred lords took the field, on which only knights with silk, brocade, or gold caparisons were allowed to fight, and many gentlemen were knighted that they might participate.

When the viscount, who was not a knight, learned of this rule, he dismounted, approached the empress's stand, and begged her to knight him.

The princess asked: "But why? Would you not sooner be knighted by the emperor?"

"My lady," replied the viscount, "I vowed never to be knighted by a man, since I am a woman's son and a woman's suitor, for love of a woman I am here, and through women I have always attained great honor, wherefore it is only just that I be knighted by a woman."

The empress summoned the emperor, who came with the emissaries and told her to knight him. Then Carmesina girded him with a beautiful sword that had been her father's and whose pommel and guard were gold. The empress gave him a pair of gold spurs with diamonds, rubies, sapphires, and balases on every rowel and ordered the damsels whose fathers were dukes to fasten them on him, but the emperor forbade it, for those who wish to be knighted by ladies must wear half gold and half silver. It is customary for the lady who has knighted a gentleman to kiss him, and the empress did so.

Then the viscount returned to the field, where the Duke of Pera captained half the knights and Tirant the rest. To avoid confusion, one group wore white pennants on their heads and the other green ones. Tirant and the duke each sent ten knights into battle, followed then by groups of twenty or thirty who took the field and slowly mingled, all doing their best to display their mettle. Tirant kept to one side, but when he saw his men faltering, he charged into the press and transfixed a knight's shield with his lance. Then our knight drew his sword and smote his foe like a raging lion, while all the Greeks marveled at his might and ardor.

The emperor rejoiced to behold such splendid feats of arms, but after almost three hours he mounted his horse and halted the battle, for he had seen some treachery and many knights were wounded. Once everyone was disarmed, they went to the palace, where they spoke of similar mock battles and all the foreigners said they had never seen knights so valiant, finely dressed, well armed, and nobly horsed. After seating himself at table, the emperor invited those who had fought to lunch with him, and when the meal was over, they told him a black ship without masts or sails had docked.[66]

As this news was being reported, four damsels of indescribable beauty entered the hall. They were all dressed in mourning and their names were most strange: one was called Honor, and her every gesture breathed nobility; the second was called Chastity, in celebration of courtly love; the third had been baptized in the river Jordan and therefore was called Hope; and the fourth had inherited the name Beauty. They curtsied before the emperor, and since Hope was their leader, she began to speak:

· CXC ·

*H*OPE'S SPEECH

"We come to ask a favor of Your Transcendent Majesty, as vindictive Fortune, that enemy of all repose, has cursed our loves and frustrated our desires, sentencing us to eternal exile and spurning our pleas. Deprived of Nature's gifts, for the evilest things rarely give delight, and aware that Fortune's dictates cannot limit our lady's powers, we left the sheltered harbor of our peaceful life, unfurled our pure sails, and braved adversity's stormy seas, where those who venture often come to grief. We have entered your glorious port in search of King Arthur of England, whose sister Morgan le Fay we have consoled these four years. Here you see King Arthur's ladies and damsels, who, having come to you in a vessel sorely afflicted, will now tearfully recount their woes and travails."

The emperor waited to hear no more from the gracious damsel, and, knowing that King Arthur's wise sister Morgan was nearby, he led his knights to the ship, where they found her dressed in black velvet and lying upon a bed, while her entire vessel was adorned in like manner. One hundred and thirty maidens of peerless beauty, all between sixteen and eighteen years of age, welcomed the worthy emperor and seated him on a throne, whereupon His Majesty uttered these words:

·CXCI·

THE EMPEROR'S WORDS

"Oh noble queen, abandon these sad tears that can be of little use in your quest, and behold my joy at your coming, for thus I can honor you as you deserve. Four damsels have requested tidings of your illustrious brother, and your ancient authority obliges me to reveal what I know. A mighty lord whose name I have been unable to learn is in my power. He possesses a wondrous sword called Excalibur, which seems to have great powers, and he is attended by an aged knight named Breunis Saunce Pité."

When Morgan le Fay heard the emperor's words, she rose, knelt before him, and asked to see the knight, upon which the emperor raised her up, took her hand, and led her to his palace.

His Majesty showed her a fair cage with silver bars wherein King Arthur sat with his sword across his knees, hanging his head and staring dully at the weapon. Though Queen Morgan addressed him, he chose to keep silence, but Breunis Saunce Pité quickly recognized his mistress and hurried to the bars, where he bowed and kissed her hand. As he was doing so, King Arthur suddenly began to speak:

·CXCII·

KING ARTHUR'S WORDS

"Royalty must encourage righteousness in others, for vice can drive wisdom from men's souls, engendering fear and chaos, whereas virtue is the hope of good and fosters faith in the life to come. Nobility, wealth, and power should be deemed blessings if well used, but they are not always found together, as some inherit nobility but are poor. Poverty cannot negate greatheartedness, and those who act otherwise should not be called noble, since some are rich but of little lineage yet, being virtuous, cherish worthy customs. Having risen above their origins, such men should be esteemed. Theologians and philosophers agree that all virtues are linked; he who has one has all, and he who lacks one lacks all, wherefore in reason's abode you will also find love of God. Why do I speak thus? Because I see this wretched world sliding from bad to worse: wickedness and deception prosper, virtue and loyalty are scorned, and damsels who in the past loved truly can now be bought with silver."

"No one loves purely," added Breunis Saunce Pité. "Tell me, sire, you who can see such things in this sword: what are a damsel's passions?"

He asked this question at the princess's behest, and the king quickly replied: "Let me gaze into it and I shall tell you."

Having looked, he declared: "Love, hatred, desire, loathing, hope, despair, shame, fear of discovery, audacity, anger, delight, and sadness. The greatest gift a lady of honor can possess is chastity."

"I beg Your Majesty," said Breunis Saunce Pité, "to tell me what a man should abhor."

"Wisdom without good deeds, age without honor, youth without obedience, riches without charity, a negligent bishop, an unjust king, a haughty pauper, a lying nobleman, a scornful captive, an unruly populace, and a lawless kingdom."[67]

The emperor said: "Ask him what Nature's gifts are."

The king replied that they were eight:

· CXCIII ·

NATURE'S GIFTS

"First, high lineage; second, a strong and handsome body; third, great might; fourth, agility; fifth, good health; sixth, good eyesight; seventh, a clear and loud voice; and eighth, youth and gaiety."

The emperor said: "Ask him what a monarch should swear to uphold when he is crowned."

King Arthur replied:

· CXCIV ·

WHAT A KING SHOULD SWEAR WHEN HE IS CROWNED

"First, to maintain love and peace in his kingdom; second, to shun wrongdoing; third, to serve justice; fourth, to be merciful; fifth, to detest tyranny; sixth, to be a good Christian in word and deed; seventh, to defend the populace and love them as his children; eighth, to always serve the public weal; ninth, to declare himself a son of our Holy Mother

Church, neither abusing, taxing, nor distressing it in any fashion; tenth, to be good, true, and honest with his subjects; eleventh, to imprison and punish the wicked; twelfth, to be a father and protector to the poor and wretched; and finally, to love, honor, and fear God."

They asked him many other questions, to which he replied with great wisdom. Then they opened the doors, those who wished to enter did so, and when everyone was inside his cage, they took away his sword and he fell in a swoon. Having restored it to him, the emperor asked the meaning of honor, as he had never found any sage or knight who could explain it. The king gazed at his sword and replied in this manner:

· CXCV ·

*T*HE ORIGINS OF HONOR

"It is both necessary and expedient that mighty lords should prize honor, for though men of good sense naturally seek this quality, those who cannot recognize it will never acquire it. Therefore I declare, with God before my eyes, that while honor is the reverence accorded virtue, glory and fame differ from honor, as the former can only proceed from the latter. An honorable king fears what he should fear and braves those dangers that must be braved, whereby his majesty remains untarnished, being enhanced through worthy deeds. Men are wont to seek honor that they may be held wise and righteous, yet the outward sign merely reveals the inner truth, and since reverence indicates its giver's righteousness, honor is the external sign of such goodness, wherefore it is nobler and more honorable to defer than to be deferred to."

The emperor then urged Breunis Saunce Pité to ask what a man of arms needs, to which the king replied:

· CXCVI ·

*W*HAT A KNIGHT REQUIRES

"The first and principal thing a knight requires is to support the weight of his armor;[68] the second is to practice arms constantly; the third is to withstand hunger; the fourth is to be able to sleep badly and live uncomfortably; the fifth is to fearlessly risk his life for justice and the common good, thus saving his soul as though he had been pious and chaste all his life; the sixth is not to fear the sight of blood; the seventh is to skillfully defend himself and slay his enemies; and the eighth is to be ashamed of craven flight."

Then Breunis Saunce Pité asked how wisdom could be attained, to which the king replied:

·CXCVII·

*H*OW WISDOM IS ATTAINED

"Wisdom may be attained in five manners: the first is through prayer, the second is through study, the third is through wise teachings, the fourth is through generous explanations, and the fifth is through constant discourse."

Then the emperor asked what Fortune's gifts were, to which the king replied:

·CXCVIII·

*F*ORTUNE'S GIFTS

"Fortune's gifts are five: the first is great riches, the second is high rank, the third is a fair wife, the fourth is many children, and the fifth is grace in company."

Then the emperor asked what nobility was, to which the king replied:

·CXCIX·

*T*HE VIRTUES OF NOBILITY

"Nobility has four aspects: first, a knight must win glory; second, he must be truthful; third, he must be stalwart; and fourth, he must be learned, for God abhors ignorance. Nobility means honoring one's vassals and acknowledging one's debt to God."

Then the emperor asked what a knight defeated in battle should think, to which the king replied:

· C C ·

WHAT A DEFEATED KNIGHT SHOULD THINK

"A defeated knight should harbor six thoughts: the first is that only God can grant victory; the second is that God, who favored his opponent, may yet favor him; the third is that he should be humble before his Creator and fellow men; the fourth is that some of the world's noblest princes have been vanquished; the fifth is that, for his sins, he deserves discomfiture and even worse; and the sixth is that Fortune's wheel has been pleased to turn against him."

Then the king was asked what a prince owes his vassals, to which he replied:

· C C I ·

WHAT A PRINCE OWES HIS VASSALS

"A virtuous prince owes five things to his vassals: the first is to uphold their rights and privileges; the second is to give them whatever he has promised; the third is to love and honor them according to their rank; the fourth is to defend them; and the fifth is to respect their goods, taking nothing by force."

They asked the king many other questions until finally the emperor, loath to weary him further, took away his sword. At first King Arthur neither saw nor recognized anyone, but then his sister took a ruby off her finger and passed it before his eyes. The king suddenly regained his senses, rose from his seat, and embraced her with great love, while the gentle lady said: "Brother, thank the emperor and his wife and daughter."

Once he had done so, the knights kissed his hand and led him into the great hall, where they feasted and made merry. The emperor asked Queen Morgan to dance, since her fondest wish had been granted, and in obedience to his pleas she sent for gayer apparel, which she and all her maidens took into another chamber. They reappeared dressed in white damask skirts and ermine-lined mantles, while their mistress wore a grey satin dress adorned with big pearls and a green damask mantle embroidered with gold and silver waterwheels. The buckets on the wheels had holes in them, and the ropes were of enameled gold with a motto in large pearls: *Unrecognized faults lead to wasted efforts.* Together, Queen Morgan and her brother approached the emperor, to whom she said: "What glory to find a spring after long thirst but then defer to another, for truly generous is that lord who shares his treasures."

Saying no more, she immediately began to dance with Tirant, whom she deemed the knight of greatest authority. Then King Arthur rose and asked the princess to be his partner. When the dancing ended, Queen Morgan asked the emperor to honor King Arthur by escorting him to her ship, where they would offer him and his knights a modest supper. Her Majesty said that every virtue should be enhanced by noble manners and declared the emperor the finest prince on earth, since he rewarded everyone according to his deserts.

Refusing to hear himself praised further, the emperor replied:

· CCII ·

THE EMPEROR'S REPLY TO QUEEN MORGAN

"Your nobility, gentle queen, bespeaks royal perfection, for you are truly the beginning and end of all good. Your Highness valiantly defied the salt seas for many years, seeking your lost brother and showing the grandeur of your ancestry. Such merits oblige me to please and honor you, and since you have invited me to your ship, I shall gladly accept."

They all rose to go, and seeing the emperor take Queen Morgan's arm, King Arthur did likewise with the empress, as did Breunis Saunce Pité with Carmesina. Upon their arrival, they found the black cloth replaced by brocade, and the stench of bilge had given way to delightful odors. An abundant supper was served, of which all the knights and damsels partook.

Afterward the emperor's retinue left feeling dazzled by what they had seen, as everything seemed to have been done by magic.

The emperor then seated himself on a throne with his ladies around him, while Tirant and his company remained on board. Once Queen Morgan was ready to sail, Tirant climbed into a skiff. The empress saw him coming and asked her daughter and the others: "How would you like to play a joke on Tirant? We can send a Saracen slave to carry him ashore on his back and then stumble, wetting that embroidered shoe he has worn throughout the festivities. Though I am ignorant of its significance, I should love to find out, and if that shoe alone is soaked, he will surely betray himself."

Everyone thought it an excellent idea, and the Saracen hastened to obey his mistress. He waded toward the boat, and the captain climbed on his back, but when they were close to land he pretended to stumble under Tirant's weight. He only meant to wet that shoe, but they both fell in the water.

Soaked from head to foot, our knight approached the ladies, and seeing them roar with laughter, he realized that it was a joke. He gently took the Saracen by the hair, asked him to lie on the ground, and, placing his embroidered shoe on the slave's head, he swore a solemn vow:

· CCIII ·

*T*IRANT'S VOW

"I vow to God and my lady that I shall neither sleep in a bed nor wear a shirt until I have killed or captured a king or prince."

Then he placed his foot on the Saracen's right hand and said: "You, a Saracen, have shamed me, but I do not hold myself affronted, for though you have done me a private wrong, I shall avenge myself in battle."

The Viscount of Branches placed his foot on the Saracen's back, saying:

· CCIV ·

*T*HE VISCOUNT'S VOW

"Since you have lost all nobility and, as a slave, your crime was civil, you deserve no punishment, for you were only obeying orders. Therefore, I swear to God and His saints never to return home until I have faced at least forty thousand infidels and defeated them, either as captain or beneath Tirant's banner."

Then the constable came forth, placed his foot on the Saracen's head, and said:

· CCV ·

*T*HE CONSTABLE'S VOW

"Though with soft words I seek to restrain my ardor, love of Tirant inflames my heart with fresh zeal, wherefore I swear before God and the lady who holds my soul in thrall not to shave my beard, eat meat, or sit until I have captured the sultan's flag in battle—that is, the red one with the Host and chalice on it. Only then shall I be freed from my vow."

Having come forward, Hippolytus placed his foot on the Saracen's head and said:

· CCVI ·

*H*IPPOLYTUS'S VOW

"Gladly shall I risk my life for future glories, as I have often withstood the Turkish might in my lord's service. To test my prowess and please my fair lady, whose love I desire above all else on earth, I vow to eat only kneeling, swallow neither bread nor salt, and sleep in no bed until I have killed thirty Saracens with my own hands." Seizing the Saracen's hair, he stepped on his back and cried: "I pray for long life and quick fulfillment of my vow."

· CCVII ·

*T*IRANT'S GIFT TO THE SARACEN

Hearing his comrades' vows for his sake, Tirant tore the jewels from his stocking and shoe and gave them to the Saracen, along with a rich cape he was wearing. He later sent him the other clothes he had on, including his shirt, though he refused to part with the shoe and stocking. The Saracen thought himself most fortunate, as he was now free, rich, and safe from the poverty that had always plagued him. The emperor declared Tirant a truly generous knight, for he gave without fretting about how to obtain more.

The sultan's emissaries were awed by the sumptuous festivities, and, having heard the Bretons' vows, they lost all hope of peace. Abdullah Solomon told the emperor that they had come as emissaries and would depart as soon as he granted them safe-conduct.

That night, the emperor and his retinue returned to Constantinople, where the next morning after Mass, they gathered in the market square, which was as splendidly decorated as it had been the first day.

Once the emissaries had arrived, the emperor addressed them before all his subjects.

· CCVIII ·

T HE EMPEROR'S REPLY TO THE EMISSARIES

"Although nothing grieves us more than deeds offensive to God, to safeguard my tongue's honor I shall refrain from reproaching you, but it is only meet that I, who make laws and enforce them, should uphold them myself in accord with reason and justice. I shall never betray our faith by giving my daughter to an infidel, and moreover, I declare that however much treasure the Grand Karaman and the King of Armenia offer, they will never be freed until they make peace and quit my empire."

Having heard his words, the emissaries rose and departed.

In the following days, His Majesty often held council, while Tirant pressed his suit and stayed close to his lady, for the truce was nearly over and the emperor expected him to leave. Every day Tirant urged his companions to prepare for their departure and proclaimed his eagerness to face the Turks.

Our knight begged the princess to reward his services and swore that all his happiness lay in reaching love's goal: "Since the greater a man's former poverty, the more pleasing he finds wealth. Your cruelty and delays have not quenched my ardor, and should Your Highness grant my suit, you will see how true my love is, as one woman shall be my mistress both in life and death. I do not hesitate to plead my case before your damsels, who I hope will pity my enamored woes. If you are so ruthless to yourself, how will you grieve for me? It is always better to choose the lesser evil, but what will the greater be if I prefer death? Let Your Highness not hesitate to give me an answer."

Beholding Tirant's affliction, the princess sweetly replied:

· CCIX ·

*T*HE PRINCESS'S REPLY

"Tirant, your words deserve an answer, for I know you wish to sully my good reputation, which until now has been untarnished by any hint of scandal. Tell me: what word of mine made you hope to share my bed, when the very suggestion stains a damsel's honor? Others may sin and many scorn chastity, but who can forbid me to be among the few? If I yield to you, nothing will hide my wrongdoing, wherefore I beg you: safeguard my good name. Your love does not displease me but I hesitate to requite it, knowing the treachery of foreigners, who go more quickly than they come. Consider how Jason (and many others I could name) betrayed worthy Medea and caused her to perish.

"Henceforth I shall think no more about the present, as my sole wish is to profit from the past and serve God. When a damsel desires something, however wicked it may be, she often strives to veil or color it with good. Scorning marriages with great kings, I chose to stay by my father, though he often tells me: 'Carmesina, before I leave this world let me behold you in some knight's arms, whereby we both shall have our desires, be he foreign or Greek.' Often his kind words make me burst into tears, and, thinking I weep for fear of that more pleasant than dangerous battle, he praises my chastity and affirms his faith in my honor, yet he fears for my beauty, and when I hear you all praise me before him, I am angered by your words, though I would like to be as you describe me. Alas, Tirant, now I must show my wisdom! I would be deemed fortunate if I did not love you, for then I would not suffer, and recalling that night at Malveí Castle, I must sadly say: 'He who lacks pity should find none in others.' "

Tirant frowned as he pondered the princess's cruel words, since he had thought himself close to victory and now found it was quite the opposite, but at last he conquered his grief and bravely replied:

· CCX ·

*T*IRANT'S REPLY TO THE PRINCESS

"Many things remain hidden from one too foolish to perceive them, and at first I was blind to my lady's heartlessness. I have battled to preserve my life, to succor you, and to augment your prosperity, but now I would sooner die than serve such an ingrate. Alas, cruel Fates! Why did you save me from Lord Barrentowns, knowing that I would soon face such a woeful death? My tearful pleas cannot move you to pity, and I shall never again rely on a lady's words, for if such a lofty damsel can break faith, why should I trust another?"

"What is faith?" asked the princess. "Please tell me, that I may use it in the right time and place."

"I am amused," replied Tirant, "that you feign ignorance to hide your failings, but I shall tell you what little I know, begging your pardon should I offend you. I once read that faith and truth are united, faith being the trust in things unseen, which concern God and should be believed as the Church believes them, since reason is insufficient to explain Christianity's divine mysteries. We can only be saved through the Holy Scriptures, and as God is truth, everything that issues from His blessed lips must be accepted. Thus are faith and truth linked, yet Your Highness scorns both, breaking faith and spurning truth, though God abhors mendacity.

"Much to my amazement, for I thought you always kept your promises, you seek to excuse yourself and deliver me to despair. All the ladies here will testify to your words; can I be so unlucky that your generosity fails me alone, when I have served and obeyed you above all others on earth? I cannot credit such perjury in one who should be mindful that the nobler a sinner's station, the more he offends God. I sought to test Fortune, which often favors the brave, and one day I shall show you how little I prize my life. Now I can only lament my undoing and the evils that may befall you after my demise, when I shall be far from your resplendent sight and you will little remember how you deceived me. Had our ancestors spoken thus, they would have won eternal infamy, yet I am satisfied with what you have seen to my honor and your shame and, with your leave and pardon, I suggest that you stop trying to turn black into white. Not long ago, aggrieved by Your Highness's cruelty, I told the Easygoing Widow and Stephanie how little I seemed to please you. If some doubt has crossed your mind because I am a foreigner, remember that just as I enter battle with your name upon my lips, thus have I entered your chamber, thinking my trials might at last be over."

The princess impatiently replied:

· CCXI ·

THE PRINCESS'S REPLY TO TIRANT

"Oh foolish knight, by strength alone you hope to triumph, yet fame can only be won through hazardous deeds. Confiding in your might, you audaciously demand your reward, but know that just as you bravely slander me, so I shall bravely endure your words."

As she was speaking, the emperor came in and asked what they were discussing, to which the princess replied: "My lord, we asked the captain, since he gives such good sermons, what faith is, and he has told us."

Before the emperor could reply, Tirant said: "Your Majesty, Jesus Christ ordered us to accept His holy teachings, wherefore those who disobey Him shall be deemed heretics and apostates. Thus all ladies and damsels must avoid breaking faith, for should they do so, they will be excommunicated and denied a church burial."

The emperor quickly took his captain's side, saying that it was indeed a great sin to lie, but had he known the cause of the argument he would have praised Tirant less.

Then he took Carmesina's hand and led her to the treasure tower, while Tirant remained with the imperial ladies. Knowing that the Easygoing Widow had heard their quarrel and hoping to win her over by promises, he uttered the following affable and loving words:

· CCXII ·

*T*IRANT'S SPEECH TO THE EASYGOING WIDOW AND CARMESINA'S OTHER DAMSELS

"It is painful to imagine the ills that may befall us, for if God deprives a sage of his wits, what will he then have left? The greatest woe that can afflict the wretched is to recall their former bliss, and thus does my lady torment me by revealing her indifference. My sufferings will be believed when I prove my words, but if she comforted my soul, I would soon show my devotion. I also wish to see every one of you happily married, and though my friend Stephanie possesses great riches, I plan to give her as much again or more. I shall make the Easygoing Widow mistress of my soul, marrying her to a mighty lord with a dowry that will make her family wealthy, and likewise, I hope to reward Pleasure-of-my-life and the rest of you."

Stephanie thanked Tirant profusely, but the Easygoing Widow said: "Thank him on your own behalf, as I am quite capable of doing so on mine."

Then she turned to Tirant and uttered these sweet words:

· CCXIII ·

THE EASYGOING WIDOW'S WORDS OF THANKS

"Instead of proffering gifts tardily, you make them the start of love, for a gift quickly given is both pleasing and gracious. He who gives what he cannot withhold does well, yet though his offering may be generous it has little merit. I thank Your Lordship, but I want no husband, however great he may be, except one: a knight whom I worship as a god and who is ever in my thoughts, even when we are apart. Though he has not killed me, he has given me cause to die, and I would sooner perish than reveal his name, as this is neither the time nor the place to do so."

When the Easygoing Widow had finished, Pleasure-of-my-life said:

· CCXIV ·

PLEASURE-OF-MY-LIFE'S WORDS

"Lord captain, how your patience has been tried, but remember that repentance follows sin and do not despair. How can you be dismayed by a few harmless words? You, who fight like a lion and always vanquish your foes, should not fear a damsel over whom we shall give you victory, yet you urge on your soldiers and hold us in check, letting pity and fear constrain your ardor. Do you recall that sweet night I dreamt of in Malveí Castle and how mercifully you then behaved? There is a Greek proverb that says: 'He who shows mercy and then repents is not merciful at all.' Your last resort is to use a bit of force, as whenever women are courted they dread to utter that terrible word: 'Yes.' Ah, what a shameful syllable for a lady, but I shall not forsake you even if the blame falls on my head, and lest my labors go unrewarded, see that Hippolytus keeps me in his heart. I know where his crooked steps lead him and am most displeased, for being a good swordsman, he will strike at the head and not the legs."

Feeling cheered by Pleasure-of-my-life's pleasantries, Tirant rose to his feet and said: "Damsel, as far as I can see, you wish everyone to know your secrets."

"Why should I mind," replied Pleasure-of-my-life, "if the whole world knows, since God has given me both the appetite and the hope? Often you men foolishly try to hide your guilt with words, thinking we damsels will not dare to accuse you. You are like the sea, which is calm near shore yet treacherous further out, and thus you are soft and virtuous when love begins but cruel and terrible later."

As they were talking, the emperor came in and led his captain away. They discussed the war till it was time for supper, whereupon Tirant and his men returned to their lodgings.

That night as the princess was preparing for bed, the Easygoing Widow exclaimed: "If you knew what poor Tirant told us all, Your Highness would be amazed, and later he drew me aside and said some disgusting things! He showed by his vulgar speech how little he respects you, for the truth will out and sinners are always punished."

Stunned by the Easygoing Widow's words and eager to learn more, Carmesina hastily donned her robe and they retired to a little alcove where no one could hear them. After repeating Tirant's promises, the wicked widow began to speak thus:

· CCXV ·

*T*HE EASYGOING WIDOW'S WICKED WARNING AGAINST TIRANT

"Manifest experience shows that people of judgment heed good sense, and the higher a woman's station, the more perfect she must be. Men like Tirant may be skilled in warfare, but they still tend to speak badly and act worse with women. Knowing this to be true, we must be ever watchful, for no one can rule or maintain a kingdom without sagacity, and Your Highness knows how many wise and able knights seek the same thing as Tirant. He mistakenly thinks those around him are blind and, though foolish, he is bolder and more shameless than others. If Your Highness knew the way he talks about you, he would never find a place in your heart."

"Tell me quickly," cried the princess, "and do not torture me so!"

"He told me in great secrecy," said the Easygoing Widow, "and made me swear on the Gospels not to breathe a word to anyone, but since you are my lady, such an oath means nothing. First of all, he, Stephanie, and Pleasure-of-my-life have decided that willingly or by force, he will possess you. If you refuse, he will cut off your head and your father's too, whereupon his men will steal the palace treasure, load it on their galleys, and return to their own land. With all that money, clothing, and jewelry they will find more beautiful damsels than Your Highness, whom he accuses of acting like an innkeeper's wench and shamelessly offering it to anyone who wants it. Look, my lady, at how that treacherous scoundrel insults you, and the faithless rascal says more: that although he did not come to fight, he has been wounded many times and it was a black day when he met you. What do you think of a knight who speaks thus? Look how he scorns your honor and the emperor's, after you gave him such riches and glory! May all who speak such words roast in eternal fire! He also said that he only loves women for their money and would never spend another night like that one at Malveí Castle, for though he swears a thousand oaths he will not keep one of them. He will take you willingly or by force, and when he has had his way, he will thumb his nose at you three times and cry: 'Expect no thanks, vile harlot, now that I have had my will.'

"Alas, dear lady, my heart weeps blood when I recall his words, and therefore I must warn you, though you have not asked my opinion. Only your parents cherish you as much as I do, and ever since I gave you my breast I have sought your honor and delight, yet Your Highness shuns me, courts Tirant, and trusts Stephanie and Pleasure-of-my-life, who alas, poor child, have sold and betrayed you! Tirant has already defamed you and plans to do so even more, while Stephanie has behaved nobly and wants company in her sin. Spurn such friendships now that you know the truth, and promise not to repeat a word of this to anyone, as I fear that if Tirant finds out, he will have me killed and then sail away. Pretend to know nothing and end your friendship slowly lest he forsake your father, since if you suddenly push him away, he will realize that I have warned you. Beware those treacherous women, who should be chastised in the future. Do you not see how Stephanie's belly has grown? I marvel that the emperor has not noticed, and the same thing will happen to Pleasure-of-my-life."

Overcome by grief and rage at these words, the princess wept bitterly, lamenting thus:

· CCXVI ·

*T*HE PRINCESS'S LAMENT

"When I think of your motherly reproaches, my soul yearns to leave my body and I wish to spend my days bemoaning this misfortune, but as I must account for my sorrow, I shall coldly dry these tears. If you ask who caused my grief, I shall say only man's fallen nature, which parts me from one I thought deserved my love and gratitude. Oh God! Where is Your justice? Why does lightning not strike cruel Tirant, whom I thought one day would be mine?[69] He was the first knight to win my heart and I hoped he would bring me joy, but alas, I see that the opposite has occurred. I thought he would rule both me and the empire, and that I would serve him as a father and brother, a husband and a worthy lord.

"But why do I lament in his absence, when it would be far better if he were here? Ah, woe is me! My heart is broken and my love is mixed with rage! The four passions besiege my weary heart: joy, grief, hope, and fear, without which no one can endure, yet the virtuous love only God. Oh, who would have thought such words could be spoken by one so brave? What harm have I done him, that he should seek to kill my parents and their wretched daughter? Lady widow, Tirant could as easily turn back the sun as rob me of my honor. Oh Tirant! Where is the loyalty we swore to one another? What have I done that you should find me so vile and hateful? Your trifling love and scant devotion: whither have they fled so quickly? I, wretched Carmesina, who was once your slave, beg you to spare me as you did the Master of Rhodes. Will you be so much crueler to us than him? Because I celebrated your virtue and knew of your valor, will you now speak shameful words, saying you court women for their money? What bloodshed such perfidious utterances deserve! I want people to think me kind to foreigners, but were I cruel by nature, I would flood your chambers with Breton blood as soon as the sun rises."

Hearing the bells strike midnight, the princess then said: "Widow, we must go to bed, though I fear I shall sleep little with the anger I feel toward Tirant, whom I once loved so dearly."

The widow replied: "I beg you, my lady, not to breathe a word to anyone, and also please do not think me a bearer of bad tidings."

"Fear not," said the princess, "for I shall preserve you from harm and myself from blame."

As they entered the princess's chamber, Stephanie saw them and said: "You must have enjoyed the widow's words, since you have been so long conversing. I would love to hear your thoughts."

The princess silently climbed into bed, pulled the covers over her head, and began to weep.

When the widow had gone, Stephanie asked her friend why she was crying so. The princess replied: "Stephanie, leave me alone and be on guard lest this evil come home to roost, for it could happen far sooner than you imagine."

Stephanie, who was stunned and scarcely knew what to think, quietly got into bed beside the princess, as the two ladies slept together.

The princess spent a sleepless night weeping and lamenting, and the next morning, though she felt ill, she forced herself to attend Mass.

Upon learning from Stephanie that the sad princess had wept all night, Tirant approached his lady with humble gesture and began to speak thus:

· CCXVII ·

*H*OW TIRANT ASKED THE PRINCESS TO REASSURE HIM

"Pitiful words sadden those who hear them, and especially one as true and steadfast as I, who feel as if your sufferings weighed upon my shoulders, though if Your Highness deigned to share her ills with me, my soul would be in Heaven. I say this because I behold your sad countenance, yet I am certain that you have done no wrong. If you wish me to stay alive, you must tell me what distresses you, for though I may not resolve the problem, I can surely be of use, and leaving aside most of the words I wish to utter, I shall say only that it saddens my heart not to be able to contemplate your beauty all my life. Great was my solace when the emperor postponed my departure."

Tirant, who was now in tears, beheld his mistress's anger and said: "My lady, I shall strive to control my feelings lest they vex Your Highness, whose malevolence I shall seek to alter with loving service, since you seem pleased by my woes and refuse to even let me touch your garment. Is this the reward I deserve for my concern? If so, I shall prove my virtue by ending my life once you are crowned, and my unrewarded exploits will live on in men's memories."

Seeing Tirant in such agony that he could say no more, the princess whispered:

· CCXVIII ·

THE PRINCESS'S REPLY TO TIRANT

"I would answer your pleas while incurring no blame, for my tongue finds it hard to speak of shameful matters, nor will my face, which is frightened instead of fair, give you reason not to remove such foul treachery from my presence. I wish you to see my patience and humility, and therefore I shall dispute with you no more. Hardships and ills oppress my weary heart, and I shall spend my life concealing my great sorrow. Do not think such grief is easily hidden, as those in torment find relief in sharing their tears with trusted friends, wherefore I crave now what you perhaps will crave in the future."

She could say no more, since the doctors and the empress had come in, whereupon Tirant took his leave of them and returned to his quarters, pondering the princess's words as he went. Plunged into thought, he locked himself in his room and refused to eat until finally the constable went to the palace, where he spoke for a long time with Stephanie and Pleasure-of-my-life, telling them how the princess's words had affected Tirant.

"How can we cure his grief," asked Stephanie, "when whatever we heal by day the widow inflames by night? Before, all Carmesina wanted to talk about was Tirant and love, but if I mention him now, she wraps herself in chastity. Her heart is too fearful and her mind too vulgar for love, while the widow, who knows how enamored she is, controls her like a mistress of the art. Were that widow not here, I would have brought Tirant not once but a hundred times to her chamber whether she wanted him or not, but since I cannot do so, I shall speak of him with kindness and friendship."

The two damsels then entered a room where Carmesina was speaking with the Easygoing Widow, but Stephanie saw that it was no time to plead Tirant's case. The emperor, having learnt that the constable was nearby, summoned Tirant, and when it was almost time to hold council, His Majesty said: "Let us go to Carmesina's room and see how she is faring, for she has been ill all day."

Diaphebus, who led the way, followed by the emperor, Tirant, and many councilors, found the princess sitting in a corner playing cards with the widow. His Highness sat down beside her and asked if she was feeling better, to which she replied: "Sire, when I see Your Majesty, all my ills disappear . . . ," and she looked at Tirant and smiled.

Rejoicing at his daughter's words and still more at how much better she looked, the emperor then spoke to her of many matters, while Carmesina replied cheerfully to everything Tirant said. The Easygoing Widow had urged her to be friendlier with him—not as much as before, but the same as with everyone else.

The widow, who did not want Tirant to depart, hoped he would despair of winning the princess's love and woo her instead, which was why she had slandered him and caused such grief.

Shortly before nightfall, Tirant's men retired to their quarters, and the next day His Majesty asked them to return to battle, whereupon Tirant and everyone else hastened to make ready. That evening, Stephanie told the princess how her knight was feeling, but she replied: "Shut up, Stephanie, and do not inflame my wrath, for the lofty saints in Heaven are little troubled by our sorrows, and we must strive through good deeds to win those rewards reserved for the virtuous. Not all those who glitter with love are gold. That metal pleases everyone, great and small, rich and poor, but some men prefer words and are full of hot air. If you asked me to recite Tirant's noble deeds, all I could say is that I have never seen him except in time of truce. Though I am aware of your treachery, I shall keep silent until Fortune lets me speak, but let us now sleep before I suffer more."

Stephanie tried to reply, but her mistress would not let her and departed, leaving the damsel mortally wounded.

Two or three days passed in this fashion, and the princess was friendly toward everyone, including Tirant, whom she knew would leave soon. She told her father: "My lord, I am certain that your brave captain will quickly serve the sultan as he has the Grand Karaman, the King of Armenia, and the King of Egypt, for if all the world gave battle, he alone would win immortal fame. He is a mighty warrior who merits great rewards, having fought with loyal and honest heart to defend Your Majesty."

The emperor said: "Valiant captain, I thank you for the honors you have given me, and I urge you to battle at least as bravely in the future. All my hopes rest on you, and may God permit me to reward you as you deserve."

Hearing such vain words and the princess's mocking tone, Tirant could only reply: "So be it."

To return to his lodgings, Tirant had to descend a staircase and walk through a room. There he found the constable, Stephanie, and Pleasure-of-my-life in conversation. He approached them and asked: "Good friends, of what do you speak?"

"My lord," replied Stephanie, "of how little love the princess has shown you recently. Knowing you will soon depart, she should court you all the more amorously, even if she loses a bit of her honor. Then we started talking about what will become of me when you go, as the empress told me last night: 'Stephanie, you have a lover.' I blushed and lowered my eyes, but my silence was a confession, since I had not known love until that night at Malveí Castle. Now you will leave me in sorrow, with only my grief to keep me company. Alas, what a cruel fate to be thus punished for your sins!"

"My lady," said Tirant, "have I not told you that the day we leave, I shall ask the emperor to celebrate your marriage? The viscount will take Diaphebus's place, and the two of you will be wed."

"How can I marry," asked Stephanie, "if you have departed, for in your absence there will be no feasts or dancing."

"Why do you need a wedding feast when you were betrothed without one?" asked Tirant. "Leave the feasting for when you are in bed without apprehensions."

The emperor then came down the stairs hand in hand with his daughter, and, thinking it was a good moment to ask him, Tirant knelt at his feet and said:

· CCXIX ·

*T*IRANT'S SUPPLICATION

"What glory, Your Majesty, to watch you seek fame and Heaven's favors, which you deserve for your virtuous and clement ways. You have enjoyed many years of worldly triumph, giving light to mankind as a most Christian lord, and since Your Majesty knows that life is short and only good deeds live on, I humbly beg you, the empress, and the princess here to consent to the marriage of Stephanie of Macedonia and my brother, your constable and the Count of Sancto Angiolo. Such marriages are bonds of love and still more when they produce sons, who will be imperial vassals and servants along with their friends and relatives. Life being short, men are naturally consoled when they can bequeath fortunes to their offspring. We all must brave many dangers, but especially those who make war, wherefore we are comforted by the thought that our sons will live on after us, as happiness does not lie in transient things but in virtue."

The emperor quickly replied:

· CCXX ·

*T*HE EMPEROR'S REPLY TO TIRANT

"Seneca, in one of his treatises, declared that a thing much begged for is too dearly bought.[70] Therefore, captain, I wish to hear no more pleas and yield all my rights to my daughter here, who may do as she likes if her mother consents."

Seeing him leave without another word, Stephanie thought he disapproved of her marriage and ran into an empty room, where she began to weep and lament.

Tirant took the princess's arm and they all called upon the empress, whom they persuaded to bless the marriage since the emperor had done so. Then they summoned the entire court to witness Stephanie's betrothal. Everyone assembled in a large hall before a cardinal, but when the damsels went in search of Stephanie, they found her still crying. She had not realized they were awaiting her, while the ladies had thought she was changing clothes.

After the couple had been triumphantly betrothed with dancing and delicious foods, the emperor told them to marry the next day, that Tirant might depart. There was a great feast ennobled by such splendid jousts, dancing, mummers, and other entertainments that everyone felt happy except poor Tirant.

On Diaphebus's and Stephanie's wedding night, Pleasure-of-my-life left five kittens on the windowsill above their bed, where they spent the entire night meowing. Then the damsel went to His Majesty's door and said: "My lord, come quickly to the bride's chamber, for I just heard some bloodcurdling screams and fear your niece may have died or been mortally wounded. You, her doting uncle, must rush to her aid."

Amused by Pleasure-of-my-life's words, the emperor donned his clothes and followed her to Stephanie's chamber, where they listened for a while outside the door.

Hearing nothing, Pleasure-of-my-life cried: "Lady bride, why are you silent? Has the battle's pain and fury ended? May you feel it in your heels!^{71} Could you not utter that delightful 'Aaah!' once more, for truly, nothing is sweeter than a maiden's cries. I can tell by your silence that our constable has shot his bolt, but much good may it do you if he fails to reload! The emperor himself is here, as he feared you were in pain."

The emperor told her to be quiet.

"On my faith, I shall do no such thing," retorted Pleasure-of-my-life. "I want them to know of Your Majesty's presence!"

Hearing the bride scream and protest for their benefit, Pleasure-of-my-life said: "Sire, her words are feigned, and that is not to my liking."

The emperor could not help laughing at Pleasure-of-my-life's spicy jests, whereupon the bride asked: "Who put those damned cats in here? Please take them away! They refuse to let me sleep!"

Pleasure-of-my-life replied: "On my faith I shall do no such thing, so help me God! Have you forgotten that I can get live kittens out of a dead cat?"

"Really, this girl knows too much," said the emperor. "How it comforts my soul to hear the things she says! I swear to God that were I unmarried, I would promptly propose to you."

The empress went to the emperor's chambers but found no one there except a page who said his master was outside the bride's door. The empress found him surrounded by three damsels and Pleasure-of-my-life, who saw her coming and cried: "Die quickly, my lady, for my lord the emperor has sworn that were he unmarried, he would propose to me. Therefore offend me no longer but die as soon as you can."

"Ah, daughter of a rogue," replied the empress, "how dare you speak such words to me?" Then she turned to the emperor and said: "And as for you, idiot, what do you want another wife for? Your weapon is better for slapping than stabbing, and remember: no damsel was ever killed by a slap."

Laughing and joking, they all returned to their rooms.

On the morrow, everyone joyously led Diaphebus and his bride to the cathedral, where they heard Mass with great honor. After the reading from Scripture, a preacher mounted the pulpit and, having delivered a solemn sermon about virtues and vices, made a most edifying speech at the emperor's command:

· CCXXI ·

*T*HE FRIAR'S SPEECH

"My unschooled tongue is unworthy to recite this serene and mighty lord's memorable deeds, for he has favored, endowed, and promoted his servants and vassals and will surely do so as long as he lives. I permit myself to enumerate his perfections, because it is a delight to behold great princes who increase their vassals' rank, as he has done with this noble foreigner Tirant lo Blanc of France. Likewise, the emperor's gracious and clement hand has given Stephanie, daughter of that illustrious and mighty lord the Duke of Macedonia, to Diaphebus, Count of Sancto Angiolo and our grand constable, along with all her goods, jewelry, and clothing, and His Serene Highness hereby offers the aforesaid Stephanie a hundred thousand ducats out of his own treasury to do with as she likes. It is good to serve a man who knows how to love his servants and who embraces honor and never releases it from his clasp, as honor comes from munificence and is adorned with all other virtues, wherefore Seneca declares that a generous-spirited man's every act is virtuous, since magnanimous princes are also wise, brave, and honorable.

"There are three things excellent above all others on earth: the first is to scorn transient honors and good fortune; the second is to seek eternal bliss; and the third is enlightenment in thought and deed. You knights are sometimes defeated in arms because of five sins: the worst of these is to fight without just cause; the second is to break faith or kill by treachery; the third is to court or have carnal knowledge of any lady or nun in God's service; the fourth is to maliciously pursue churchmen and seize their property; and the fifth is to speak irreverently of God and His saints. Now I wish to tell you what habits a worthy knight's sons should acquire: the first is to attend Mass and pray every day; the second is to learn to read and write, studying grammar and other learned sciences; the third is not to take God's name in vain; the fourth is to shun pride and be humble toward all men; the fifth is to be ashamed of any base act; the sixth is to fear God and obey our Holy Mother Church; the seventh is to cheerfully bow and pay homage to one's superiors; the eighth is to associate only with knights and people of virtue; the ninth is never to speak too much or maliciously; the tenth is not to judge or condemn others lightly; the eleventh is not to lie or speak ill of one's fellows; the twelfth is to learn to ride, serve, and welcome graciously; the thirteenth is to be moderate in food and drink; the fourteenth is to be loyal and honest; the fifteenth is not to gamble; the sixteenth is to be clean; the seventeenth is to hunt; and the eighteenth is to know how to fight with sword, lance, battle—ax, or bare hands.

"Now, lest they be offended, I shall speak of the qualities damsels need: first, they should learn to read; second, they should be devout and prayerful; third, they should observe all fast days; fourth, they should be chaste and modest; fifth, they should speak little and calmly; sixth, all their behavior should be founded on honor; seventh, they should be humble; eighth, they should be moderate in eating and drinking; ninth, they should be meek and obedient; tenth, they should spurn laziness; eleventh, they should not be haughty; twelfth, they should be simple and humble; and thirteenth, they should cultivate womanly skills and abhor sloth. This is how they should be but in fact they are quite the opposite, as may be seen from their virtues, which I shall now ennumerate: first, they are willful; second, they chatter and stroll about too much; and third, they are fickle both in love and in judgment.

"Ovid calls love the highest good and the Holy Scriptures confirm it,[72] for just as Christ died for love while pardoning the repentant thief, so man can only win eternal life by loving God and his neighbor. The fruit of worldly love is pleasure, and the fruits of conjugal love are sons and daughters. The following virtues proceed from love: frankness, which every knight should possess; ardor; courtesy; humility; genteel eloquence; gaiety; self-control; modesty; prowess; patience; wisdom; discretion; good judgment; and bold spirit. Every knight should swear three oaths: first, to courageously obey his lord's commands; second, to never forsake his order;

and third, to brave death defending ladies and damsels, the state, and our Holy Mother Church. A knight's virtues should be these: first, to be truthful; second, to be loyal; third, to be bold; fourth, to be generous; and fifth, to love justice, for Saint John says the just correct the unjust, who are hateful to God and lose grace in this world and the next."

· CCXXII ·

HOW THE EMPEROR MADE HIS CONSTABLE DUKE OF MACEDONIA

When the Mass and sermon were over, His Majesty sent for the hundred thousand ducats and all the clothes, jewels, and other riches Stephanie's father had bequeathed her. Then they had the constable don his coat of arms, which they replaced with the Duke of Macedonia's, while unfurling the duke's banners and placing a silver crown on his head, as was the custom with all those given titles. They gave leather crowns to counts, steel crowns to marquises, silver crowns to dukes, gold crowns to kings, and emperors' crowns had seven gold points. Diaphebus, therefore, was given a silver crown inlaid with jewels, and they crowned Stephanie in this fashion too.

They proceeded through Constantinople with fluttering banners and rode out into the countryside till they reached a clear spring called Holyfount. Whenever anyone was given a title, his banners were blessed at this fount and he was declared a duke, count, marquis, king, or emperor. Once the banners had been blessed, they baptized the Duke and Duchess of Macedonia with musk-scented water, and asked if he wished to appoint a herald or king-of-arms, offering him his duchy's name and giving him generous gifts. Only gentlemen's sons may be heralds or kings-of-arms, for they are more trusted and obeyed than other men.

Having appointed a king-of-arms, the duke returned to Holyfount, where the emperor christened him Duke of Macedonia again. Then the trumpets blared and the heralds and kings-of-arms shouted: "Behold His Illustrious Lordship: the Duke of Macedonia of Saltrock lineage."

Three hundred knights with gold spurs and shining armor came forth. They bowed before the emperor and honored Diaphebus, who was never again called constable and whose office was given to a knight named Sir Adedoro. These three hundred knights split into two parties, one of which took the fairest damsels' horses by the reins. Having chosen in order of rank and estate, they rode into the woods, and when those without damsels met those with them, they jousted for the maidens.

The emperor and empress went to watch the jousts, but Carmesina, Diaphebus, and Stephanie stayed behind, as did Tirant, who had vowed only to tilt with kings and princes. Then the emperor went to Pera, where a great feast had been prepared, and since it was past midday and his knights had not returned, he climbed one of the towers to see if they were coming and ordered a big horn blown that could be heard more than a league away. As the knights approached, they fought before His Majesty, but three hundred other knights dressed in the same color soon rode forth and barred their way. A splendid tourney ensued, which gave the emperor great pleasure, and while it was in progress, the damsels fled into the city.

Having fought for a while with lances, the knights drew their swords, but at last, after two hours, His Majesty ordered the trumpets blown. All the knights came together, dismounted, and stormed the palace while the ladies defended it. In the end they forced their way in, but upon reaching the central courtyard they split up again and the first party sent a king-of-arms to the other, asking them to depart without the damsels. The others replied that they would not do so for anything on earth, as they had risked their lives and deserved a share of the bounty. They began to fight again on foot inside the palace, and it was wondrous to behold them falling on all sides as they smote mighty blows with their axes. Anyone who lost his ax or touched the ground had to retire to the sidelines, and at last, seeing only ten left on each side, the emperor told them to disarm and come to lunch in the great hall. Afterward, they danced until a half-hour before sunset, when the knights and ladies joined hands with Carmesina and returned to Constantinople, dancing as they went.

After supper, Tirant summoned his thirty-five knights and gentlemen, who were called the men of Saltrock because Brittany had been conquered by two brothers, the younger of whom was the English captain Uther Pendragon, King Arthur's father.[73] With great bloodshed these knights had captured a mighty fortress built upon a huge salt rock, and since it was their first conquest, they abandoned their old name and took that of the castle, where the elder brother was crowned Duke of Brittany. When the King of France dispatched emissaries to offer him his daughter in marriage, the duke sent Uther Pendragon to arrange the betrothal, but upon beholding the fair princess, he said his brother had not given him leave to do so, for the duke wished to espouse her on Breton soil. Uther Pendragon had false letters of credence written, which the king gladly accepted, giving him his daughter and two hundred thousand *escuts* on the condition that his lord be crowned King of Brittany within three years. Uther Pendragon agreed to everything and took the princess back to Saltrock Castle, where he married her immediately.

Upon learning what his beloved brother had done, the Duke of Brittany gave his consent to the marriage, while the knights who had escorted the damsel returned to France and informed their king, who flew into a rage, gathered a mighty host, and hastened to besiege Saltrock Castle. When the Duke of Brittany heard the king was coming, he wrote a letter begging him to spare Uther Pendragon, and at the same time he sent his brother soldiers, food, and everything necessary to withstand a siege. The king camped outside the castle for a year and two months, but with all his assaults he could not subdue it. The duke, who was with the king, pleaded with him to forgive his brother, and as he could not vanquish the castle, the king agreed to lift the siege and to give the duke a bastard daughter with no dowry. All Tirant's companions came from this ancient lineage, which had produced nothing but brave knights and honorable ladies.

Tirant and his men kissed the emperor's hand and foot, thanking him profusely for his kindness to Diaphebus, to which His Majesty replied:

· CCXXIII ·

THE EMPEROR'S REPLY TO TIRANT BEFORE ALL HIS MEN

"As this world's glory lies not in appearances but in good deeds, my love of you, Tirant, is infinite, for I know your great courage. I loathe the thought of acquiring relatives not from the Saltrock line, and my great joy in your feats has made me forget all other families. Thus did I plan to offer you my niece Stephanie, through whom I hoped to tie you more closely to our empire, but as the proverb says, no one should love another so much that he harms himself. Diaphebus should have been content as grand constable, yet you refused the county of Sancto Angiolo and gave it to him, and now you have done the same with the duchy and my worthy niece. Do not think I shall give you my empire, which I need myself, and I fear your generosity will ruin me before I make you rich. Any knight in foreign parts should first see to his own fortune and then reward his relatives, distinguishing vice from virtue and placing virtue first, since the most dangerous spies are those one takes for loyal servants."

Tirant quickly replied in the following manner:

· CCXXIV ·

TIRANT'S REPLY TO THE EMPEROR

"Happiness is the greatest treasure, and my happiness lies not in wealth but in serving Your Majesty and striving to restore the Greek Empire to its former glory. Though my heart may be generous, it does not lust after money or power, and if I can win honor I consider myself well rewarded. I rejoice to see my friends and relatives well provided for and desire no riches beyond my horse and armor, wherefore Your Highness need not fret over my fortune. Since I also serve God and the Holy Catholic Faith, He will show me the grace that has never failed me yet. My lord, I kiss your hands and feet in thanks for your gift to Diaphebus, which I consider as great a boon as if you had made me lord of all pagandom, for I am more eager to see him and my other relatives endowed with goods and honors than to have them myself."

Tirant's noble words pleased the emperor, who turned to Carmesina and said: "Never have I beheld a knight so virtuous as Tirant! His goodness astounds me, and if God lets me live I shall make him a crowned king."

When the celebrations ended, Diaphebus moved to the palace, where he invited his companions to lunch with him the next day. The emperor had eaten earlier, so he sent his daughter to join Stephanie and the Bretons: "For the duke wishes to honor them, and such feasts are dull without damsels."

The princess replied: "Sire, your wish is my command."

As Carmesina was on her way with many ladies and damsels, the Easygoing Widow maliciously approached her and said: "Oh, my lady! Why does Your Highness visit those foreigners? You and your father think they will be pleased but instead you will annoy them, for they prefer the sight of a partridge wing to all the maidens on earth. A princess should not go about so freely but should respect herself if she wants others to respect her, yet to my amazement, you still seek out that scoundrel Tirant. Love forces me to speak, since I, who care for you more than anyone, now see your father rashly send you into a room full of men."

"Should I disobey my father's commands?" asked the princess. "No one should scold me for heeding his orders, but alas, cruel Fortune afflicts me and with harsh words you augment my sorrows. My friend is also my mistress, whether I desire one or not!"

She returned to her chamber instead of visiting Stephanie. After everyone had eaten, Pleasure-of-my-life went to see how Tirant was faring and to speak with the duchess. Seeing him seated pensively by a window, she approached and spoke these words: "Lord captain, my soul grieves to behold your mournful countenance. Think whether I can help, for if God gives me Paradise I promise to serve you even after death."

When Tirant had thanked her, the duchess asked why Carmesina had not come, to which Pleasure-of-my-life replied that the widow had scolded her. Though she did not repeat the conversation lest Tirant be angered, the duchess quickly guessed what had been said and exclaimed:

· CCXXV ·

THE DUCHESS OF MACEDONIA'S AND PLEASURE-OF-MY-LIFE'S ADVICE TO TIRANT

"I am my own mistress while the princess is not, and thus does she tarry in making her decision, but I swear to Our Lady that by this time tomorrow I shall know the truth!"

"Alas, woe is me! How my heart grieves!" cried Pleasure-of-my-life. "Now that you are full, fasting does not trouble you, yet you will learn nothing as long as that widow is present, for your lady will act as though her ears were stuffed with cotton. I dare not repeat the bad things she says about Tirant."

"How happy I should be," replied the captain, "if she were a man! Then I would make her eat her wicked words!"

"Do you know what we should do?" asked Pleasure-of-my-life. "We should forget about her, proceed with our own plans, and fret about the consequences later, lest we fail for want of a little brute force. Carmesina told me to draw her bath the day after tomorrow, and while everyone is at supper I can slip you into the alcove where her tub is. No one will see you, and when she comes out and gets into bed you can climb in beside her. Consider this a new and exciting adventure, for you must act as bravely in bed as you do in battle, and this is the shortest path to what you desire, though if anyone knows a better one I shall gladly defer to him."

The duchess said: "Let me talk to her first and as she chants, so I shall respond, since your suggestion should be our last resort."

Tirant said: "I do not wish to triumph through deceit, and I would sooner die a thousand deaths than affront Her Highness."

"By the faith I owe to God, I find that a bad sign," said Pleasure-of-my-life. "If you truly want success, you should not flee love's narrow straits. Here I am trying to help you as much as I can and still more, yet you stubbornly head down a blind alley. Look for someone else to help cure your so-called illness, as I shall trouble myself no further."

"Damsel," replied Tirant, "I beg you to forgive me. Let us all take counsel and determine what is best, since if you forsake me now I shall surely despair, nor can the duchess be with her as often as I would like."

"An angel could not give you better advice," said Pleasure-of-my-life, "than I have, but to be more precise, you have not seen the delights I offer you. Had you done so, one way or another you would have enjoyed them, for those who never taste sugar do not know what sweetness is."

The two damsels decided to go to the princess's chamber, where they found her dressing in an alcove. Then another clever feminine ruse occurred to the duchess, who knelt at the foot of the bed with her head between her knees. Carmesina invited her into the alcove, but the newly wed duchess refused and Pleasure-of-my-life said: "Leave her alone; she cannot come. I do not know what troubles her, but she is feeling most unhappy."

Once the princess had finished her toilet, she came out and saw the woeful duchess, to whom she addressed these words:

· CCXXVI ·

HOW CARMESINA ASKED THE DUCHESS WHAT WAS AILING HER

"What ails you, dear sister? Please tell me quickly! I hate to see you suffer, and if I can help I shall gladly do so."

The duchess replied: "My soul is in torment, for you disappoint my hopes. Weary of speech, I wish only to be alone on a mountaintop or in some deep forest, but instead I have come to rest by this sad and woeful bed. I shall tell you what grieves me: I fear my life will end, as I cannot retract what I promised Tirant at Malveí Castle. After we returned to court, I was forced to confirm what I might justly have refused, had I not already granted it. Tormented by grief and fear, I beg you not to make me a liar or disgrace me, since you will gain nothing by it and I freely confess my error."

As she spoke, the duchess wept bitterly and showed signs of great suffering. Moved to compassion, the princess gently replied: "Duchess, you should realize that I am as sad as you, but lady cousin, do not strive to increase my woes. You know I have loved and love you above all others, and God willing I shall do so in the future. For love of you I shall speak with Tirant as you request, yet I have little reason to help him, for you would marvel at the way he defames me. Knowing there is a time to suffer in silence and another to laugh and cry, I shall keep quiet because we need him, though otherwise I would soon dismiss him. Who could credit such baseness in so brave a knight, whom I loved so dearly and wished to reward? May our justice shine so brightly that men will have to cover their eyes not to see it."

The duchess replied: "My lady, I am amazed that you defame a worthy knight who would slay the entire world if he heard your name slandered. Do not believe everything you hear, for some scoundrel has been lying to you."

Pleasure-of-my-life spoke up and said: "My lady, cast ill will from your mind, since if anyone is virtuous, it is noble Tirant. What wretch could persuade you that the best knight alive might compete with him in honor and courage or that Tirant speaks of anything but your virtues? Pay no heed to evil tongues, and love the man you should love, as it is glorious to possess such a brave and gentle knight. May he rule your bed as you will rule his person, which cannot be corrupted by gold or silver. Love the one who loves you and ignore that devilish widow, who is the cause of this evil, and I pray God to punish her. My only wish is to see her dragged naked through the town, while they beat her ribs, eyes, and face with cow's lungs."

"Be quiet," replied the princess. "You think the widow is behind this but you are mistaken, as I accuse Tirant, having seen how much harm he may do. Nonetheless, I am willing to follow your advice."

"Trust me," said Pleasure-of-my-life, "and I shall safeguard your happiness."

And so they parted.

The duchess returned to her chambers and repeated their conversation to Tirant, who joyously went into the great hall, where he found the emperor and his ladies. They danced for a long time, and the princess seemed very friendly.

When the music ended and the princess was on her way to supper, the Easygoing Widow approached her and whispered these words:

·CCXXVII·

HOW THE EASYGOING WIDOW SCOLDED THE PRINCESS

"Your words augment my sorrows, as you rob me of my honor by willfully entering the pit of infamy. I live in despair, cursing the wretched day of your birth, for many people look first at you and then at me, saying three times: 'Oh widow, Easygoing Widow! How can you let a foreigner steal

Carmesina's maidenhead?' Imagine how I feel upon hearing such words and whether I am right to mourn and think of death, which alone could free me from unjust accusations. Do you really think you can have your way without bishops and archbishops hearing of it, after recklessly declaring before many that you would marry no foreign sovereign, brave or cowardly, that you needed no riches beyond what Our Lord and your father had given you, and that you would have Tirant lo Blanc and no one else? Should you behave dishonorably because you plan to wed him, when you are his wife he will say: 'You are nothing but a whore, for what you did with me you could do with someone else.' Who can assure you that he will never be jealous, and God knows, he would have good reason to keep you locked up the rest of your life. If you act virtuously, you will be thought noble and good, but should you do the opposite, men will call you vile and fallen. May I perish before my eyes behold or my ears hear such infamy."

She said no more and awaited the princess's reply, but Carmesina was unable to answer the widow's venomous words, since the emperor was at table and had summoned her twice.

The princess said: "Lady widow, I would enjoy this supper far more if I could respond to what you have said."

She entered the dining hall, where Stephanie, who had gone to ask if she wanted Tirant to come that night, saw how red her lady's face was and did not dare to speak. Pleasure-of-my-life had seen the princess with the Easygoing Widow and said: "My lady, a red sky is a sure sign of storm."

"Shut up, you fool!" cried the princess. "You always talk nonsense!"

When the emperor saw what a state Carmesina was in, he asked if anyone had offended her, to which she replied: "No, sire, my heart has been aching ever since I left your presence and I had to lie down, but by Our Lord's grace the ache has vanished."

The emperor asked his doctors what she ought to eat, and they ordered a pheasant, which is the best meat for the heart. The duchess sat down beside her, and, once the meal had ended, she leaned over and whispered in Carmesina's ear:

· CCXXVIII ·

THE DUCHESS OF MACEDONIA'S WORDS TO THE PRINCESS

"If noble lineage and generous spirit caused you to make that promise, then let it quickly be kept, for honesty is shown by good deeds while secret plotting reveals malice. A vassal should not rob or cheat her lady, and since the widow is my vassal, I hope she meets the death she deserves."

"Duchess," replied the princess, "I love you dearly and would do more for you than for any sister. Forget the widow, who has not wronged you even if she is your vassal, and calm yourself, as I shall give you everything you deserve. What troubles me is my heart, which is full of mortal doubt and fear, wherefore you should not take from me what you cannot return. Give the widow clothes, jewelry, and money for her expenses. You, who are so kind, should leave such courtesies for Maundy Thursday."

The duchess said: "Answer my question about Tirant, who has been waiting so eagerly: do you want him to come tonight? By the life you hold so dear, do not deny him."

"I shall gladly see him tonight," replied the princess, "and I shall await him right here. We can dance, and if he has anything to say, I shall listen with a good will."

"Idiot!" cried the duchess. "How can you be so faithless? With unequaled cunning, you now seek to change the rules. Listen, my lady: one who misses often but hits the mark once cannot be said to err all the time. I ask if you want Tirant to visit you as he did at Malveí Castle, for without him you will be neither honored nor happy. Now do you understand me?"

"When you spoke of Tirant," replied the princess, "I thought he wanted to tell me his woes, which I am already forced to behold every day. Sad is the damsel who wearies herself with useless tears. Tell Tirant I beg him to stop trying my soul, which has been weeping blood for days, but if he comes I shall agree to more than he imagines."

"Oh my lady," said the duchess, "no one should weep except for his sins. If Tirant were dead and buried, you would not forget him so quickly. Should you wish to resist, pin his arms to his sides with promises and oaths as you did at Malveí Castle, for then you can tell everyone about your noble feats of valor. Your imperial virtue and gentility have no equal in Christendom or pagandom, and since you do not lack beauty, neither should you lack honor."

"Shall I tell you something, sister?" asked the princess. "I wish to guard my good name, which a damsel should cherish above all else, and so shall I act with God's leave."

The duchess left feeling very annoyed, and upon seeing Tirant, she told him what his beloved had said. Tirant's grief then knew no bounds.

Once the emperor had supped, he summoned Tirant from the duchess's chambers and told his daughter: "Fetch my musicians so these knights can make merry, for they will soon depart."

"No, my lord," replied the princess, "I would rather sleep than dance."

She quickly left to avoid Tirant.

The Easygoing Widow felt very pleased by this conversation, while

Pleasure-of-my-life went to the duchess's chambers and told Tirant: "Lord captain, you have no hope unless we rid ourselves of that widow, who is now sitting in the princess's room discussing your affairs. Tomorrow after her bath I shall put her to bed, where you will find your noble princess naked. It will be especially easy because I now sleep with her, and I assure you that shame will seal your lady's lips."

"Damsel," replied Tirant, "I thank you for your kind words, but you know I would never force, anger, or act basely toward any lady, even if it meant losing the Greek or Roman imperial crown. How can you think I would disobey such a damsel when I would sooner surrender to my enemies than cause her a speck of harm? If I were on the battlefield and saw an adversary on the ground begging for mercy, I would generously spare his life, though as my mortal foe he would not spare me. How, then, could I betray my lady, whom I should protect? I swear never to offend Her Highness, nor would my conscience permit it, as I prefer to spend my whole life mourning my noble hopes, serving her day and night on foot and horseback, begging her on my knees to pity me. I do not wish to be called a traitor, vainglorious, or lustful, for Nature and honor oblige me to mercy, and one who disinherits another unjustly cannot sleep peacefully at night. Likewise, a servant who deceives his master deserves infamy and punishment, wherefore I shall go on pleading for her angelic favors."

Pleasure-of-my-life then lost her temper and began to speak thus:

· CCXXIX ·

HOW PLEASURE-OF-MY-LIFE ENCOURAGED TIRANT

"Tirant, Tirant, never will you be feared in battle if you refuse to use a little force with reluctant damsels! Since your wishes are honorable and your beloved is worthy, go to her bed when she is naked or in her nightshirt and attack bravely, for you can invite a friend to dinner even if you lack clean tablecloths. Should you refuse, I shall quit your bailiwick, as I have known many knights whose hands were quick and courageous enough to win honor, glory, and fame from their ladies. Oh God, what a wonderful thing it is to hold a soft, naked, fourteen-year-old damsel in one's arms, and still better if she is of royal blood! Oh God, how glorious to be an emperor's son-in-law, and how splendid to have a rich and generous mistress untainted by infamy!"

It was late now and they were about to lock the palace gates, so Tirant took his leave of Stephanie, but as he was on his way out, Pleasure-of-my-life said: "Lord captain, I could never find anyone to help me the way I help you. Go and sleep, but do not roll over and forget my admonitions."

Tirant laughingly replied: "Only an angel could give such good advice."

Whoever offers counsel," said Pleasure-of-my-life, "should help carry it out."

"Tell me, damsel:" asked Tirant, "have you forgotten that those who take bad advice come to dishonorable ends?"

And so they parted.

That night Tirant pondered her words, and the next morning His Majesty summoned him. Our knight found him dressing, attended by his daughter, who wore a dress that left her breasts half uncovered, while her hair hung loose almost to her feet. Unaware of Tirant's astonishment at so perfect a human body, the emperor said: "Captain, I beg you in God's name to quickly depart."

Tirant was dumbstruck at the sight of his fair lady, but after a while he came to his senses and replied: "I was thinking about the Turks and did not hear what Your Majesty said. Would you mind repeating your command?"

The emperor was surprised to see Tirant acting so absent-mindedly, for he had spent half an hour in a daze, but His Majesty believed him and repeated his words. Tirant replied: "My lord, I have sent criers through the city to announce our departure next Monday. Today is Friday, so we shall set sail very soon and almost everyone is ready."

Then Tirant covered his eyes, and though the emperor could not see him, the princess and her maidens burst out laughing at the sight of his pantomime. Pleasure-of-my-life told the emperor: "Any lord must have the right to give or take back his loved ones and vassals, since lordship is nothing without sovereign power."

She took the emperor's arm, made him turn toward her, and said: "All your noble deeds have been Tirant's doing, as he routed the sultan and foiled his plans. Those infidels thought they could defeat our aged emperor, but instead the Turkish kings had to retreat to Bellpuig—not calmly, but as fast as their terrified legs could carry them. Tirant deserves a reward for his courage, and if I held the royal scepter I know what I would do, but we damsels foolishly strive for honors, rank, and dignity, whereby many of us come to bad ends. What good would it do me to be King David's daughter, if I lost it all for want of a good knight? Arm your soul, my lord, since you have not risked your body in battle, and do not think of giving her to another . . . Shall I say it? I must: bestow her upon Tirant. Enjoy a little solace in your old age and do not leave it till you are dead, for by yielding to God's and Nature's decrees, you will win glory in this world and the next. I shall say nothing of myself, as damsels should not reveal their desires but wait for men to speak first, yet I do not wish to diminish the reward I deserve. Listen, mighty lord and most Christian emperor: do not emulate that King of Provence, whose fair daughter was wooed by the King of Spain. Her father loved her so much that he refused to let her marry in his lifetime, wherefore she grew old in his palace and when he finally died no one wanted her. They seized her lands and banished her to a hospital in Avignon, where she perished miserably because she had obeyed her father."[74]

Then she turned to the princess and said: "You, who are of noble blood: find a husband now, and if your father will not help you, I shall do it myself. I shall give you Tirant, who is truly a great prize, for how often has one knight done such outstanding deeds or turned so many defeats into glorious triumphs? Should Your Highness disbelieve me, look at the disorder that reigned here before he came."

"Damsel, I beg you to be silent," said Tirant, "and not to exaggerate so."

"Worry about your battles," said Pleasure-of-my-life, "and leave this to me."

The emperor replied: "By my father Albert's bones, you are the most remarkable damsel I have ever known, and the more I see you the better I like you. I shall grant you fifty thousand fresh-minted ducats from my treasury."

Stephanie knelt and kissed his hand, while the princess fretted over what she had heard and Tirant also felt a little embarrassed. When His Majesty had finished dressing, Tirant escorted him to Mass and then returned for the ladies. As they were leaving the church, he had a chance to address his mistress:

· CCXXX ·

THE WORDS SPOKEN BY TIRANT, CARMESINA, AND PLEASURE-OF-MY-LIFE

"A promise made, a debt to be paid."

"The promise," replied the princess, "was not made before a notary."

Pleasure-of-my-life, who was nearby, retorted: "No sir, a promise of love requited needs neither witnesses nor notaries. What would become of us if it had to be in writing every time? All the paper on earth would not suffice. Do you know how it is done: in the dark, where there are no witnesses, and even so men always find the right door."

"You are mad!" cried the princess. "Why must you always speak so crudely?"

No matter what Tirant said or how much he pleaded, she would not consent.

When they reached the palace, the emperor summoned Carmesina and asked: "Tell me, dear child: when Pleasure-of-my-life said all that, did anyone in particular put her up to it?"

"I am sure I do not know, sire," replied the princess, "nor did I ever speak to her of such matters, but being wild and brazen in speech, she says whatever comes into her head."

"You err," said the emperor, "for she is the most sensible girl in my court and always gives good advice. Have you not noticed that I make her speak in council? Would you like to marry our captain?"

The princess blushed demurely and remained silent, but after a moment she collected herself and replied: "My lord, once your captain has vanquished the Turks, I shall gladly do anything Your Majesty orders."

Tirant went to the duchess's chamber and summoned Pleasure-of-my-life, to whom he said: "Oh gentle lady! I know not what to do, for my soul is at war with my body, and I shall die if you do not ease my sufferings."

"I shall ease them this very night," replied Pleasure-of-my-life, "if you will trust me."

"Tell me damsel," said Tirant, "and may God increase your honor— those words you spoke to the emperor about the princess and myself: who asked you to say them? You have troubled me greatly, and I am anxious to know."

"You are not the only one," replied Pleasure-of-my-life. "My lady was troubled and so was her father, who asked me about it afterward, and I gave him more reasons why you deserve the princess. Whom would he be better off giving her to than you? If the world has no beginning, neither does it have an end, and I shall tell you why he agrees to everything I say. He would like to get under my skirts and is so enamored that he swore on the Gospels to marry me when the empress dies, saying: 'Let us seal our troth with a kiss, which, though it may not be much, will at least be better than nothing at all.' I replied: 'If you are so lecherous in your old age, what were you like in your youth?' Just a few hours ago he gave me this string of heavy pearls, and now he is asking Carmesina if she would like to marry you. I spoke thus so that if you are caught in her bedroom and they try to blame me for it, I shall be able to say: 'I warned Your Majesty, but the princess ordered me to let him in,' whereby everyone in the palace will have to keep quiet."

Tirant said: "Tell me how it can be done, for I greatly desire to know." Pleasure-of-my-life quickly replied:

· CCXXXI ·

HOW PLEASURE-OF-MY-LIFE PLACED TIRANT IN THE PRINCESS'S BED

"My desire to please you obliges me to do your bidding, for though my guilt will be great, I know you deserve such a prize, and now you shall see how much I wish to serve Your Lordship. When the emperor goes to supper, await me here, setting aside all sad thoughts, as I shall lead you to my lady's chamber. In the still of the night lovers find consolation, which fights with redoubled power against somber misgivings."

While they were talking, the emperor, who knew Tirant was in the duchess's room, sent for him and interrupted their conversation.

Then our knight took counsel with His Majesty for a long time about the war and the Greek army's provisions, since Tirant's men were now armed and ready to set out.

Once it was dark, Tirant went to the duchess's room and, while the emperor was eating with his noblewomen, Pleasure-of-my-life greeted our knight, who had donned a red satin cloak and doublet and held his naked sword aloft. She took his hand and led him to the princess's chamber, where there was a big chest with a hole cut in it to admit the air, in front of which stood Carmesina's bathtub.

After supper the ladies danced with the gallant knights, but as Tirant was absent, they soon stopped and the emperor retired. The damsels escorted Carmesina to her chambers, where they bade her goodnight, leaving her alone with her servants. Pleasure-of-my-life, with the excuse of taking out a fine linen wash cloth, opened the chest and left it slightly ajar. Then she put some clothes on top lest anyone notice, and while her mistress was disrobing, the damsel arranged things so that she was standing right in front of Tirant. Once she was naked, Pleasure-of-my-life picked up a candle, that he might enjoy himself still more, and looking the princess up and down, she said: "On my faith, my lady, if Tirant were caressing you now in my stead, I believe he would be happier than if they had crowned him King of France."

"Certainly not," replied the princess, "he would sooner be King of France."

"Oh lord Tirant, where are you now? Why are you not touching what you prize most in this world? Look, Tirant: do you see my lady's hair? I kiss it in your name, you who are the best knight on earth. See her eyes and mouth? I kiss them for you. See her delicate breasts, one in each hand? I kiss them for you. Look how small, firm, white, and smooth they are. Look, Tirant, behold her belly, her thighs, and her sex. Ah, woe is me, if only I were a man! Oh Tirant, where are you now? Why do you not come when I call you so piteously? Only Tirant's hands deserve to touch what mine are touching, as any man would happily gulp down such a morsel."

Tirant, who saw everything, was delighted by these jests, while a great temptation crept over him to open the chest and get out.

After they had joked awhile, Carmesina got into her bath and asked Pleasure-of-my-life to undress and join her.

"I shall do so, but only on one condition."

"What is that?" asked the princess.

"That you allow Tirant to lie in bed with you for an hour," the damsel replied.

"Shut up; you must be mad!"

"My lady, grant me this favor: tell me what you would say if Tirant came one night unbeknownst to anyone and you found him beside you."

"What would I say?" the princess replied. "I would ask him to leave, but if he refused, I would sooner keep mum than risk disgrace."

"Upon my faith, my lady," said Pleasure-of-my-life, "thus would I also behave."

While they were talking, the Easygoing Widow entered, and the princess invited her into the tub. Then the widow stripped down to her red stockings and linen cap, and although she had a fair and well-proportioned figure, the stockings and cap suited her so ill that she looked like a devil, and certainly any lady or damsel you see so dressed will seem ugly, however genteel and noble she may be.

When the bath was finished, they brought the princess a pair of partridges cooked in malmsey and a dozen eggs with sugar and cinnamon. Then she got into bed.

The widow retired to her room, as did the other maidens except two who slept near the princess's chamber. Once they were asleep, Pleasure-of-my-life rose in her nightdress, helped Tirant out of the chest, and told him to undress, but his heart, hands, and feet were shaking.

"How now?" asked Pleasure-of-my-life. "No man alive is brave in arms but afraid of women. In battle you are not daunted by all the knights in creation, and here you tremble at the sight of a mere damsel. Have no fear, for I shall remain by your side."

"By the faith I owe to God, I would sooner enter the lists for a joust to the utterance with ten knights than commit such an act."

Nonetheless, with her constant encouragement he finally roused his spirits, whereupon the damsel took his hand and he followed her, protesting: "Dear maiden, as my fear derives from shame caused by the great love I bear my lady, I would sooner turn back now before she hears us. Upon beholding such presumption, she may very well change her mind, and I would rather die than live after offending Her Highness. I want to win her through love, not force, and when I see such impropriety caused by my devotion, my will ceases to accord with yours. For pity's sake, let us turn back lest I lose what I most cherish, as it seems a serious enough crime to have come here without erring further. For such a misdeed I ought to take my own life, and do not think, my lady, that I am stopping out of fear. When she learns I was so near her and yet refrained from doing harm, she will understand the depth of my chaste devotion."

Pleasure-of-my-life was most vexed by Tirant's words, and feeling thoroughly fed up, she replied in the following manner:

· CCXXXII ·

*H*OW PLEASURE-OF-MY-LIFE SCOLDED TIRANT

"You are chief in vices and first in mortal sins. Do you think this is a time for idle chatter? If you falter now, my woeful life will soon end, and as a witness to your deceitful words I shall speak out clearly, revealing your evil deeds and moving my listeners to pity. You dash the hopes you engendered by requesting my help with piteous words that the duchess, whom you changed from a damsel into a lady, also heard. You know I did not hesitate but quickly brought you to this delightful chamber, yet your faint heart is incapable of knightly victory. I want to bring this matter to an end and am tired of waiting for your battle challenge, for I see you prefer words to deeds and would sooner seek than find, wherefore, since I must, I inform you that after waiting so long and seeing you so satisfied with vain words, I shall now shout for the emperor and everyone will think you forced your way in. Oh knight of little valor, are you too frightened of this damsel to approach her? Alas, ill-fated captain! Are you so craven that you dare to speak such words? Make an effort! When the emperor comes, what story will you tell him? Before God and the world, I promise to unmask your shameful lies, but should you do as I say, I shall give you happiness and the imperial crown. The hour has come; I can say no more. Hurry to the princess's side, where you will win another battle and add luster to your glory."

Tirant, hearing Pleasure-of-my-life's plain speech, began to whisper:

· CCXXXIII ·

TIRANT'S REPLY TO PLEASURE-OF-MY-LIFE

"Though fear of disgrace bars me from winning bliss in this world and the next, I shall tell you what I think: that hard times often turn friends into enemies. My innocent desire is to serve my lady all my days, and for this article of faith I am ready to live and die. If our wills accorded, my soul would rejoice, but all I see is the dark night of shameful fear. I cannot gaze upon what I desire and must have faith in Her Highness's presence, yet I shall cast off fear and shame, dressing myself in love and pity, wherefore I beg you to lead me to my beloved without delay. Show me that glorious body, which, since there is no light, I shall view with my mind's eye alone."

"I have used all my cunning," replied Pleasure-of-my-life, "to safeguard my honor and your delight. May you now be seen for what you are!"

She released his hand, and Tirant scarcely knew what to do, for the room was pitch black and he was afraid to move. She left him standing there, barefoot and in his shirtsleeves, for almost half an hour, while he called out to her as softly as he could. At first the damsel would not answer, but then she began to pity him and took his hand again, saying: "May all false lovers be punished thus! Are you unaware that every lady, great or humble, always longs to find love and gives the prize to whoever can find the most honorable—that is, the most discreet—path to her by night or day through windows, doors, or rooftops? Do you think I would be angry if Hippolytus acted thus? I would love him forty times more and hope he would seize my hair if I resisted, dragging me across the room till I shut up and obeyed him. May he act like a man and not like you, who fear to displease the princess, for elsewhere you should certainly love, honor, and protect her, but when the two of you are alone, you need not fret about formalities. Have you forgotten that psalm about 'the hand of the diligent'?[75] The gloss is that if you want a lady or damsel, you should feel no shame or fear lest she think the worse of you."

"On my faith," said Tirant, "you have enlightened me more than any confessor, however steeped in theology he might be, wherefore I beg you: please lead me to my lady's bed."

Pleasure-of-my-life quickly obeyed, making our knight lie down beside his princess. When Tirant was comfortable, the damsel told him not to move, while she knelt at the head of the bed and bent over that her head might lie between his and Carmesina's. She rolled up her sleeves and placed the Breton's hand upon his princess, whose nipples, belly, and sex he began to caress. The princess awoke and cried: "God Almighty, what a nuisance you are! Go away and let me sleep!"

Pleasure-of-my-life replied: "What a way to talk! Here you have just bathed and your skin feels so smooth and soft. How I love to touch it!"

"Touch me where you like, but not so far down!"

"Go back to sleep, and let me caress this body of mine," said Pleasure-of-my-life, "for I am here in Tirant's stead. Oh treacherous Tirant, where are you now? Were your hand where mine is, how happy you would feel!"

Tirant's hand was on his lady's belly, and Pleasure-of-my-life's was on his head. When she saw her mistress dozing off, she relaxed her grip and Tirant felt where he liked, but when the princess moved, Pleasure-of-my-life gripped his head and he kept still. This game lasted for more than an hour.

Once Pleasure-of-my-life saw Carmesina sound asleep, she relaxed her grip entirely and sought to try Tirant's patience. The princess stirred and asked: "What do you want, wicked woman? Let me sleep! Have you gone mad, trying to do what is against nature?"

Carmesina suddenly realized that this was no woman and let out a scream, but Pleasure-of-my-life clapped her hand over her lady's mouth, whispering: "Be quiet, Your Highness, lest you sully your reputation, for this is your knight who would gladly die for you."

"Oh, damn you!" cried the princess. "You fear neither me nor your own dishonor! You have secretly brought me danger and infamy!"

"The worst has already occurred, my lady," replied Pleasure-of-my-life. "Save yourself and me, as silence is the best policy in such situations."

Tirant also softly pleaded with his lady, who saw herself trapped between love and fear, but fear triumphed and she resolved to scream no more.

Hearing that cry, the Easygoing Widow guessed what had occurred and knew that if Tirant had his way, she would never have hers. Everything was silent as Carmesina defended herself in whispers, urging our knight not to bring the pleasant battle to its conclusion, but then the widow sat up in bed and shouted: "What ails you, my daughter?"

The widow's shout roused the empress and her maidens, who sprang out of bed, some naked and some in their nightgowns, and hastened to the princess's door. They found it locked and called for light, but as they were knocking, Pleasure-of-my-life grabbed Tirant's hair and pulled him away from where he wished to die. She made him jump onto the roof and threw him a rope, that he might climb down into the garden and escape through the gate. She had planned to let him out before daybreak, but the uproar and the damsels' screams made such a plan impossible. She quickly shut the window and returned to her lady.

Tirant fastened the rope to the roof, yet he was so fearful of being seen that he forgot to consider whether it was long enough to reach the ground. After sliding down it, he found a twelve-yard drop at the bottom, and unable to keep his grip, he fell so hard that he broke his leg.

Let us now leave our knight on the ground and return to the ladies.

Once Tirant had escaped, Pleasure-of-my-life admitted the empress and her maidens, who were holding torches and asking the princess why she had screamed.

"My lady," replied the princess, "a big rat leapt on the bed and crawled onto my face, frightening me half out of my wits. It scratched me, but fortunately it did not hurt my eye."

Pleasure-of-my-life had made that scratch when she shut the princess's mouth.

The emperor, who had also risen, entered his daughter's chamber sword in hand. When he heard about the rat, he searched all the nearby rooms, but Pleasure-of-my-life was on her toes and, as the empress was talking with her daughter, the damsel jumped onto the roof and pulled in the rope. Hearing Tirant's groans, she quickly guessed that he had fallen, while the whole palace was in such turmoil that it was terrifying to behold. Had the Turks attacked at that moment, they could not have chosen a better time, yet the wise emperor thought it was nothing but a rat. He even looked inside the chests and had the windows opened, and if the damsel had waited to hide that rope, he surely would have found it.

Diaphebus, who knew what was afoot, heard the commotion, and, fearing for his cousin's safety, he donned his armor and told Stephanie: "Today I shall lose my title if Tirant is in peril."

"What shall I do," she asked, "for my hands are too weak even to put on a skirt?"

As soon as the duke was armed, he set out to find Tirant, and on his way he met the emperor, who was returning to his chamber. The duke asked him: "What is it, sire? Why all this commotion?"

The emperor replied: "Those foolish damsels are upset by trifles and claim a rat jumped onto my daughter's face and scratched her. Go back to sleep; there is no cause for alarm."

Diaphebus returned to his chamber and, after reassuring the duchess, said: "By Our Lady, had they arrested our captain, I was ready to kill His

Majesty and those in his service, whereupon I or Tirant would have been crowned emperor."

"It is better this way," replied the duchess.

She got out of bed and hastened to the princess's chamber, where Pleasure-of-my-life saw her and whispered: "My lady, please stay here and see that no one speaks ill of Tirant, while I go and find out how he fares."

When she got to the roof, she was afraid to call out lest someone notice her, but then she heard Tirant moaning and lamenting thus:

· CCXXXIV ·

*T*IRANT'S LAMENT

"How misery longs for company, for I have no hope left and wish only to descend into death's sad and tenebrous palaces. Since sighs cannot restore my life, I would sooner perish, and that the cause of my death may be manifest to all, I pray God to take my soul, which can find no solace in this vale of tears. Oh, God, who are so merciful: let me die in Carmesina's arms, that my soul may depart in peace from this world!"

Meanwhile, Hippolytus and the viscount had heard the uproar in the palace and city, and though they knew nothing of Tirant's exploits except that he was going to spend the night with the duke, they nonetheless decided to call their men to arms. Lord Agramunt said: "The only thing I can imagine is that Tirant slipped into Carmesina's chamber and the emperor discovered him. Let us arm ourselves and attend the wedding, where he may require our help, for though nothing ever happened when he was sleeping here, as soon as he gets out strange things begin to occur."

Hippolytus said: "While you are donning your armor, I shall go to the palace gates."

"Hurry!" cried the others.

The viscount accompanied him.

"My lord," said Hippolytus, "go to the main gate, and I shall go to the garden. Whoever learns something first will look for the other."

When Hippolytus reached the garden gate, he assumed that it was locked and stood outside listening, but although he heard a voice moaning and grieving, he thought it was some lady and said: "Alas, how I would love to hear Tirant's voice instead of that damsel's!"

After trying without success to climb over the wall, he went back to the gate still thinking it was some damsel.

"Cry as much as you like," said Hippolytus, "since you are not my captain."

Then he set out for the square, where he met the viscount and others who were trying to learn what had happened. By now the tumult was abating, and Hippolytus said that although the garden gate was locked, he had heard what sounded like a damsel in distress, whom he supposed must be the cause of the disturbance.

"By God, we must get in," replied the viscount, "for if some damsel has been wronged, our vows oblige us to aid her."

They all returned to the garden gate and heard Tirant's lamentations, but they could not make out the words or tell who it was, as our knight was in such pain that his voice was not his own. The viscount said: "If we break down this gate while it is still dark, no one will ever know we did it."

The gate, which Pleasure-of-my-life had unfastened so Tirant could escape, was unlocked the whole time.

The two of them slammed into the gate as hard as they could, where-upon it flew open and the viscount entered, making his way toward the strange voice, to which he said: "Whoever you may be, I beg you in God's name to tell me if you are a dead soul in torment or some mortal in distress."

Thinking they were the emperor's men, Tirant disguised his voice to be rid of them, though his pain had already disguised it enough, and said: "I, a baptized Christian in life, have been punished for my sins by being made a ghost. I am invisible unless I choose to take shape. The devils down here hack my flesh and bones to pieces, which they throw in the air, and if you remain you will share the cruel torments I suffer."

Terrified by their captain's words, the two knights crossed themselves and began reciting the Gospel of St. John. The viscount said loudly enough so Tirant could hear him: "Hippolytus, let us return to our lodgings, where we can gather soldiers, a crucifix, and holy water, for there is something diabolical in this garden."

"No," replied Hippolytus, "there is no need to go back for anything, as our swords will serve as crosses. Let me go closer."

Hippolytus drew his sword, held it before him, and crossed himself, saying: "I, a true Christian, believe in the articles of the Holy Catholic Faith and our Holy Roman Church, in whose blessed doctrines I wish to live and die."

He approached Tirant with great fear, leaving the viscount too fright-ened to move, while Tirant called out softly: "Come here; I am Tirant."

Upon hearing him, the viscount felt even more dismayed and was about to flee when Tirant shouted: "Oh recreant knight! Even if I were dead, why should that frighten you?"

Hippolytus recognized the voice and hastened to his master's side. "My lord," he asked, "is that you? What misfortune has occurred? I see you in such a state that you must be wounded and unable to move."

"Do not make so much noise," replied Tirant. "Who is with you? If he is of Breton lineage, tell him to approach."

"My lord," replied Hippolytus, "it is the viscount."

Hippolytus summoned him, and when the viscount saw his master, he was amazed that they had not recognized his voice.

"Let us waste no more time," said Tirant. "Get me hence quickly."

They lifted him in their arms, carried him from the garden, and closed the gate. Once they were near their lodgings, they left him under a colonnade.

"I never felt such pain," said Tirant, "in all the times I was gravely wounded. I need to see a doctor, but without the emperor's knowledge."

"My lord," asked Hippolytus, "do you want some good advice? Your ailment is not the kind that can be concealed, and still less with so much talk. Mount your steed if you can and ride to your stables in Bellestar, while we spread the word that your horse fell and you broke your leg."

The viscount said: "Hippolytus is right, and if you ignore his advice the emperor will certainly hear about it. No one can expect anything but travails and grief from His Majesty Love, who inflicts a hundred torments for every pleasure. I would thank and praise you if after you are cured and we have fulfilled our vows, we could peacefully return to our native land."

"Lord viscount," replied Tirant, "let us not speak of such matters, for no one can free his heart once it is enchained, nor is this the time for such idle discussion. Hippolytus, bring me the mount you think will ride most smoothly."

Now let us return to Pleasure-of-my-life, who stayed on the roof till she saw them take Tirant away and then hastened to her mistress, the duchess, and the empress. Still marveling that a rat could cause such turmoil, the empress sat down on the bed and said: "Do you know what I think, damsels? Since calm has been restored, let us go back to sleep."

The princess summoned Pleasure-of-my-life and whispered: "Where is Tirant?"

"He has gone, my lady," she replied, "but he was in great pain."

She did not dare to mention his broken leg and was glad no one had discovered him. The empress rose and everyone prepared to retire, but then the Easygoing Widow said: "It would be wise, my lady, to let the princess sleep with you, as she will be still more frightened if that rat returns."

The empress replied: "The widow is right. Come, my daughter; you will sleep better with me than by yourself."

"No, my lady, go and leave me with the duchess, for I would not want you to have a bad night because of me."

The widow said: "Though I am old, the fire of my Roman blood still burns brightly. I was the first to try to save you and catch that rat, who fled with evil feet from my cursed chambers."

The empress told her daughter: "Come; I am getting cold."

"My lady, since you insist," replied Carmesina, "go, and I shall join you shortly."

The empress left after telling Carmesina to hurry, whereupon Tirant's beloved turned to the Easygoing Widow and spoke these wrathful words:

· CCXXXV ·

*H*OW CARMESINA REBUKED THE EASYGOING WIDOW

"Now that I see what you have been plotting, with woeful cries I shall rend my garments, for you vaingloriously seek to bind me with your lies. Who gave you the right to tell my mother I should sleep with her? You steal my pleasure and give me grief in return, serving not virtue but envy and spite, and thus it is written that no deceitful woman can be called honest. You wish to rule your betters, but instead you shall be chastised like that Roman senator's son who, seeking to rule a prince's house, risked his life so often in battle that at last he was slain. He hoped to command but the prince made an example of him, ordering his death lest others presumptuously seek to rule their betters' homes."

The Easygoing Widow replied:

· CCXXXVI ·

*T*HE EASYGOING WIDOW'S REPLY, IN WHICH SHE INFORMED CARMESINA OF TIRANT'S UNFORTUNATE FALL

"Alas, I am beset by woes and misgivings! My intentions are shown by deeds and not by tricks, lies, or pimping, for I believe in faith, love, and charity, humility and forbearance, honesty and good doctrine, alms, contrition, and penance. I cast pride, vainglory, envy, wrath, hatred, malice, lust, and all other vices from me, and thus you should not be vexed if my eyes are open. I prize your honor above my soul, and though I see you would defame me, I shall now tell you in what manner I have failed: I love you more than you wish, wherefore I shall pine away, never enjoying a good day or a merry feast. Do not seek to turn me into a butcher's lantern, which gives light to others but burns its owner. Do you think I am not sorry for Tirant, my lady? I saw that rope break as he slid down it and heard him fall with such a thud that he must have broken his ribs or legs."

She burst into tears and threw herself on the floor, tearing her hair and wailing: "Dead is the best of knights!"

Hearing such words, the princess exclaimed: "Jesus, Jesus, Jesus!" and swooned.

She had screamed so loudly that the empress heard it and hastened to Carmesina's chamber, where she found her on the floor. Unable to revive her, they summoned the emperor and his doctors, who spent three hours restoring the princess to consciousness. The emperor asked what had happened, and his ladies replied: "Sire, she saw a little mouse, but she still was so terrified of that rat that it gave her a dreadful fright."

"Alas, sad and embittered old emperor! Must I suffer such grief in my few remaining days? Ah, cruel death! Why do you not hasten to one who longs for you?"

Then he swooned too, falling on top of his daughter, whereupon the cries were so great that it was a wonder to hear them, as they were far louder than on the first occasion.

Tirant, who was still waiting by that colonnade, heard screams that seemed to come from the palace. Despite his grief and pain, he mounted his steed, though he feared that his lady might also be in danger. Hippolytus wrapped a piece of sable lining around Tirant's leg to protect his wound, and when they reached the city gates, the guards asked where they were going at such an hour, to which Tirant replied that he was bound for Bellestar to inspect his horses. The gates were quickly opened and they continued on their way, but when they had ridden half a league Tirant said: "I fear the emperor may harm his daughter because of me, and therefore I must return and see if she needs help."

The viscount replied: "On my faith, you are in fine shape to help anyone!"

"But lord viscount," said Tirant, "I feel no pain, as the greater ill obscures the lesser, wherefore I beg you: let us ride to her aid."

"You must be mad!" cried the viscount. "You cannot even stand up, and now you want the emperor to discover you. We shall have enough trouble concealing your wrongdoing, and I guarantee that if we return, you will be slain or wounded."

"Is it not right," asked Tirant, "that I, who did the damage, should also pay the price? If I die for such a lady, I shall consider my life well sacrificed."

"May God forsake me," replied the viscount, "if you return with my help. Really! Is the duke not able to help defend her honor? Now you can see what these wretched loves come to! Let us waste no more time, for the longer we stay here the more danger you are in."

"Then do me one favor," said Tirant, "since you will not let me return: go yourself, and if someone tries to harm her, slay him without mercy."

Tirant pleaded so piteously that the viscount finally yielded, but as he turned his horse, he whispered so that Hippolytus alone could hear him: "Would that I never had to succor damsels but only fetch doctors for my lord."

Tirant rode off with Hippolytus.

When the viscount reached the city gates, the guards refused to let him enter till he said his captain had fallen and he had come to fetch the doctors. He had some trouble finding them, as they were with the emperor and his daughter, but once His Majesty had recovered, they prepared to set out for Bellestar. Meanwhile, the viscount tried to see Carmesina.

Upon opening her eyes, she asked: "Is the lord of my soul dead? Tell me quickly, I beg you, for if he has perished I wish to join him."

The tearful empress asked Carmesina to repeat what she had said, and Stephanie, who was holding the princess's head in her lap, replied: "My lady, your daughter asks if they have killed the rat."

Carmesina, whose eyes were closed, said: "That is not what I asked. I asked if my life's hope is still alive."

The duchess shouted: "He is not dead! They never caught him!" Then she turned to the empress and said: "Her mind is wandering, as this illness causes even the wisest men to rant."

As soon as Carmesina had recovered, two doctors set out with the viscount and Diaphebus. The princess grieved to see them go, crying: "Lord Tirant, flower of chivalry, you are dead, dead! Lost is the Saltrock lineage! The Breton house is undone, for no one who falls from such a height can expect to live long! Alas, would that it were I, since the blame was all mine."

The duchess was most distressed by the princess's woe and Tirant's broken leg, but she feared to speak in front of all the maidens. The doctors left without telling the emperor, lest his condition worsen.

They found Tirant lying on his bed in great pain, as his leg was so badly broken that the bones stuck out through his skin. He fainted three times during the examination and, after reviving him with rose water, they bandaged him as best they could, warning him to stay in bed if he valued his life. Upon their return to the palace, the emperor asked where they had been.

"Sire, we were at Bellestar with your captain, who is badly hurt."

"What ails him?"

"Your Majesty," replied one doctor, "he says he left early this morning to inspect his horses. He mounted a Sicilian charger and was galloping along cheerfully, when his horse fell in a ditch and he broke his leg."

"Holy Mary!" exclaimed the emperor. "Tirant never lacks ills and hardships! I shall hasten to his side and tell him that a good life is spent bravely, whereas a life of vice is death, and no man should forsake glory except for greater virtue."

Despite his determination, the doctors persuaded him to wait till the next day, whereupon he went to see how his daughter was faring and to tell her the sad tidings. What grief the princess felt, though she feared to weep before her father, and her own sufferings appeared trivial beside Tirant's tragic mishap.

The emperor remained with his daughter until suppertime. On the morrow, he saw his doctors ride past and, telling them to await him, he mounted his horse and accompanied them on their second visit to Tirant. Seeing that many days would pass before his captain could return to battle, once they had finished treating the Breton His Majesty began to speak thus:

· CCXXXVII ·

*H*OW THE EMPEROR COMFORTED TIRANT

"No man should take umbrage at what Providence ordains and Fortune executes, for the human mind is not all-seeing, and brave knights are known by their forbearance. In this case, it is I who have been punished for my sins, since your accident will hasten the Turkish triumph and my downfall. The hope that you would hasten to oppose those pagan hordes gave me strength, old and weak though I am, to put aside sad thoughts and resist my foes. I shall refrain from reciting my doubts and fears, though when I first learned of your accident, I felt all was lost. I had placed all my hopes in your noble chivalry, believing your brave arm and manly spirit would shed the blood of our cruel enemies, but now, alas, they will quickly subdue us, defiling my honor in word and deed. I pray for your health above all else on earth, as without it my empire will never regain its freedom, and so I ask you, captain, to be comforted if you cherish your life and mine. I trust that God will pity you and this

Christian nation, so plagued by infidels that only you can save it, wherefore you should weep no more over what cannot be altered."

· CCXXXVIII ·

*T*IRANT'S REPLY TO THE EMPEROR

"Oh most afflicted of mortals! I see myself in great pain and believe my hour is at hand, but what grieves me most is to behold your sufferings, for I have lost all hope and wish only to die quickly."

With many sighs our knight turned to face the emperor, from whom he concealed the cause of his woe by saying: "Sire, you have no need of my sword and captaincy, as you command many bold knights who can battle the Turks, but should you insist, I shall obey your commands. On the appointed day, you will find me ready."

The emperor returned to the city, feeling very pleased with his captain's spirit, and upon seeing her husband the empress said: "My lord, may God grant you long life in this world and Heaven in the next. Tell me the truth about our captain: is his life in danger?"

The emperor replied before the princess and her maidens: "My lady, he will surely live, though his leg is painful to behold. The bones stick out and you can see the marrow inside them, but he swears that tomorrow he will depart for his camp."

"Holy Mary!" cried the princess. "What madness is this? Do you want him to perish on the way? What will you gain by risking his life and your crown? No, my lord, battles are not won in this fashion! Better he should live than die, since as long as he endures our foes will fear him. If he is lame, let him enter some religious order, yet I am sure that if he can he will bravely defend his honor. To send him away now is the act of a wicked, cruel, and pitiless prince."

The emperor entered his council chamber, where his knights all agreed that Tirant should not be moved from his bed at Bellestar.

As soon as the emperor had gone, Tirant ordered a strong chest built to carry him. Only Hippolytus knew about it, and once Tirant's visitors had left, he dismissed the viscount and Lord Agramunt lest they try to impede him. He told them to prepare for their departure, but they never dreamed Tirant would be mad enough to go himself. Having bribed one doctor to accompany him, since the other refused to cooperate, Tirant climbed into the chest at midnight and had it placed upon a litter, which four men lifted onto their shoulders and bore to Saint George. Before leaving,

Tirant told his servants to hang heavy silver curtains across the door to his room and to say that he was resting after a difficult night. Hearing this the next morning, some of his men returned to the city, while others waited for their lord to awaken. After waiting all morning, the duke and the viscount decided to enter, for they said no wounded man could possibly sleep so long, but upon forcing their way in, they found their cousin gone. Then they quickly mounted their horses and rode away, sending word to the emperor that his orders had been obeyed, while they cursed him and all his ancestors. When His Majesty heard this news, he exclaimed: "My God, he certainly keeps his promises!"

Once the duke and viscount had overtaken Tirant, they learned that he had fainted five times on the way. Diaphebus accused Hippolytus and the doctor of trying to murder him: "And you, Hippolytus, of Saltrock lineage and Breton stock: how could you let our captain set out? The day he dies, we shall be lost and never heard of again. Were it not for my fear of God and disgrace among men, I would slay you with this sword as Cain did Abel. Oh wretched knight, heartless and cruel! Begone from my sight, lest honor oblige me to chastise you!"

Then the duke turned to the doctor, whom he berated thus:

· CCXXXIX ·

HOW THE DUKE SLEW THE DOCTOR AND PLEASURE-OF-MY-LIFE FLED THE COURT

"How dare this insolent and stupid doctor imperil our lineage? Flames of anger, pride, sorrow, fury, and grief burn within me, and I shall now teach you a lesson men will never forget!"

Unsheathing his sword, Diaphebus lunged at the doctor, who sought in vain to flee, but the duke split his head to the shoulders and his brain spurted out.

When the emperor learned that one of his best doctors had perished, he rode after our knight, whom he found in a place called the Devout Hermitage where the duke had left him to rest and recover. Moved to pity by Tirant's condition, the emperor summoned his doctors and even examined the bed to see whether it was comfortable. The physicians said that if Tirant had gone another league, he would have died or lost his leg.

The emperor and his greatest barons visited the hermitage, where they held council and decided that as their captain could not move, those in His Highness's pay would depart the next morning. Tirant told His

Majesty: "My lord, I think you should give your soldiers two months' pay for the next month and a half, for thus they will feel grateful and fight with more spirit."

After promising to do so immediately, the emperor said: "This very night I received a letter from the Marquis of Saint George, who says such a horde of Saracens has come that the earth trembles beneath them. They have gone to conquer Lebanon, which borders on my empire, and when the truce ends they plan to rescue the Grand Karaman and the King of Armenia. The marquis reports that the King of Jerusalem has arrived with his wife, his children, and sixty thousand soldiers. He is the Grand Karaman's cousin and rules the fertile province of Enedast, where as soon as a male child is born the king takes charge of his training. Once the boy is ten years old, they teach him to ride and use a sword, and after he has mastered these skills they place him in a forge, that his arms may grow strong and good for smiting Christians. Having taught him to wrestle, throw a lance, and wield all other weapons, they place him in a slaughter-house where he becomes accustomed to hacking flesh. This king's cruel and hardened knights quarter Christians without pity,[76] and twice a year he makes them drink cow's or sheep's blood. They are the bravest warriors in pagandom, and ten of them are worth forty of the others. The wealthy King of Lesser Armenia, who is the King of Armenia's brother, has also come with forty-five thousand soldiers. In addition, King Menador has brought thirty-five thousand men, the King of Damascus forty-five thousand and King Verumtamen forty-two thousand. Many other kings have arrived as well."

Tirant replied: "Let them come, for I have faith in Our Lord, whose clemency will give us victory though they were ten times more."

Once they had finished talking, the emperor commended Tirant to God and ordered the doctors not to leave his side or let him rise from his bed.

On Monday morning, the emperor and his ladies watched as Tirant's soldiers set out, ably captained by the Dukes of Pera and Macedonia. When they reached Saint George, the marquis welcomed them with great joy. Knowing there was a month of truce left, Tirant planned to stay in the hermitage till he was cured. He enjoyed his convalescence, in which Lord Agramunt kept him company, declaring that he had left home for love of our knight and would never forsake him in adversity. Hippolytus, who had also remained, went to the city every day for supplies and news of the princess, as Tirant's hopes were still high and whenever the doctors wanted him to eat or do anything else, they told him his lady had ordered it and he obeyed them immediately. During those days, the princess frequently reprimanded Pleasure-of-my-life, threatening to lock her in a dark, windowless room. The damsel defended herself with sweet words and merrily replied: "If your father finds out, he will say you put me up to it so Tirant could deflower you. His Majesty wants me to be your step-mother, and when I am, I promise to punish you so that next time our captain comes you will not dare to scream or budge."

The princess flew into a rage and ordered her to abandon such wicked schemes.

"My lady, since I have lost your favor, I shall return to my father's house."

She stormed out of the room, gathered her clothes and jewels, and left them with the widow Montsanto, who was staying at the court. Then she and five squires quietly set out for the Devout Hermitage.

Upon learning of her damsel's departure, Carmesina sent soldiers in all directions to fetch her back willingly or by force.

Pleasure-of-my-life followed the back roads till she reached the hermitage, where the sight of her made Tirant forget two-thirds of his pain. Upon beholding his pale visage, the damsel burst into tears, as with faint voice and piteous gesture she uttered these words:

· CCXL ·

HOW PLEASURE-OF-MY-LIFE APOLOGIZED TO TIRANT

"Oh knight afflicted beyond all others, infinite woes besiege my heart at the sight of you, for though I come in shame, knowing I caused this harm, the love I bear you has brought me to your side. You always show mercy to both friend and foe, and thus is your virtue celebrated in all mighty courts. Now I, saddened beyond compare by the travails I see you suffer, must beg you to testify to my worthy intentions. I sought to defend you from the Easygoing Widow's malicious slanders, but, defeated at last, I must now cry you mercy. My life and death are in your hands, since I and Fortune caused your ills, wherefore I ask Your Lordship to forgive me."

A sigh issued from Tirant's heart as he gently replied: "Damsel, one who has always served virtue need not apologize, but had you wronged me, I would gladly pardon you a thousand times, as I owe more to you than anyone on earth. Speak no more of such matters but rather tell me about our princess, who I fear will now forbid me to approach her. I have often been wounded and about to give up the ghost, yet the thought of her wrath afflicts me far more, and so I ask you, damsel, if you wish me well, to tell me everything both good and bad, thus ending my doubts."

Pleasure-of-my-life sweetly consented and began to whisper these words:

· CCXLI ·

*H*OW PLEASURE-OF-MY-LIFE TOLD TIRANT EVERYTHING THAT HAD OCCURRED SINCE HIS FALL

"Iniquitous Fortune assailed you that night, and after you left cries and tumult filled our rooms. The old emperor, forced to rise from his bed, furiously searched the palace sword in hand, saying be it rat or man he would slay it without pity. The empress, wearied by such uproar, retired to her bed, whereupon all the guards returned to their posts. Then the lovelorn widow approached our princess with grief and wickedness. That old witch always returns evil for good, though one might expect the opposite after all your gifts to her. With feigned pity, wails, and screams, she said: 'My lady, I saw the rope break as Tirant slid down it. He fell so far that he must have broken all his bones.' Hearing these words, Carmesina could only cry: 'Jesus, Jesus, Jesus!' Then she fell in a swoon that lasted for three hours, while the emperor's doctors vainly sought to revive her. It seemed she would lose all the gifts Nature and Fortune had bestowed upon her, and this time the cries and tumult were still greater."

Then she told Tirant about her conversations with the princess: "Words cannot express her longing to see you, and had shame not restrained her, she would have come already. She scarcely knows how to act when she first beholds you: whether to grieve or rejoice, as these two feelings war within her breast. She claims that if she shows her love, you will wish to return, yet if she does the opposite you will be vexed with Her Highness."

· CCXLII ·

*T*IRANT'S REPLY TO PLEASURE-OF-MY-LIFE

"All mortals depend upon those they love, and if the princess forsakes me, she will cause my demise. Neither death nor disgrace can alter my will, and though I admit that I was the cause of my own misfortune, if she wishes me to live, she must lay aside cruelty. What crime have I committed except adoring Her Highness? Therefore I beg her not to condemn me but to mercifully let me behold her visage, as I am certain her unjust anger would then pass."

Pleasure-of-my-life replied: "My lord, if you write a letter, I shall do my utmost to obtain an answer, whereby you will know her will and disposition."

As they were talking, the soldiers sent to fetch Pleasure-of-my-life entered, and at the sight of our damsel they repeated their mistress's orders. Pleasure-of-my-life replied: "Tell my lady she cannot force me to serve her, and that I shall return to my father's house."

"Had I found you elsewhere," said the knight in command, "I would bring you back by force, but I trust that our captain will not displease his lady and will virtuously see that her wishes are carried out."

"Never fear," replied Tirant. "Her Highness will be served, for I shall plead with this damsel till she agrees to accompany you."

Then Tirant called for pen and paper, though the pain in his leg made it difficult for him to write, and inscribed these amorous words to his lady:

· CCXLIII ·

*T*IRANT'S LETTER TO THE PRINCESS

Had fear of giving offense restrained my eager hands, my hopes would still reside in Your Highness, but I was too foolish to see that only your generosity could redeem me. No one else has beheld your many perfections, whose glory is the greatest blessing any mortal can possess, yet fear that you no longer love me redoubles my grief, since if I lose you I shall lose everything I cherish. What pleasure it gave me to hear your words in my hour of woe, and though I despair at your high station, all my forces will obey you. My hand will never weary of writing to Your Highness, who I hope will excuse my clumsy style, for I wish to leave nothing to chance, that enemy of all joy. To err is human.

· CCXLIV ·

*H*OW PLEASURE-OF-MY-LIFE RETURNED TO THE PRINCESS

Then Pleasure-of-my-life returned to the palace where, upon learning of her arrival, Carmesina ran to the head of the stairs and cried: "Dear sister! Who made you so angry that you sought to leave me?"

"What, my lady?" asked Pleasure-of-my-life. "Your Highness spurned my advice and banished me from her presence."

Carmesina took the damsel's hand and, after leading her into a chamber, turned to those who had brought her and thanked them for their help. Once the two damsels were alone, the princess said: "Have you forgotten, Pleasure-of-my-life, that sisters often quarrel? Though some words passed between us, you should not have been so hasty, as you are my favorite damsel and privy to all my secrets."

"Your words are sweet," replied Pleasure-of-my-life, "but your deeds are bitter, for you heed the Easygoing Widow's wicked lies, which time shall yet unmask. She was the cause of my troubles, and I fear she will harm you too as she did on that cruel night when Tirant broke his leg and you fainted, much to everyone's dismay except the delighted widow's. Your Highness does not lack virtues but you do lack good sense, and cursed is the noblewoman who shames herself by crying out."

"Let us leave such words," said the princess, "and speak of Tirant. How does he fare, and when may I see him? I think of him all too often, and his suffering grieves me more than death. Courtship brings such perils that my poor mind cannot encompass them, yet I am overwhelmed by a passion that I have never felt before. I would have followed our ancestors' noble customs had Tirant truly perished, wherefore I beg you, sister, to describe his condition, for should he die, I swear men will never forget my devotion. I shall be cited as an example of true love and shall do the deed in public, that it may be remembered as long as the world endures. God can grant me no greater favor than to let me see him in good health."

Pleasure-of-my-life replied:

· CCXLV ·

PLEASURE-OF-MY-LIFE'S REPLY

"May Our Lord soon heal his wounds and return him to your side, for he would then consider himself the most blessed of knights, but should you refuse him, I curse the day he met you. In your absence, he does nothing but pine and sigh, dreaming of your beauty and how happy you could make him. You know he deserves this honor, yet your actions belie your words and though I do not wish to offend Your Highness, I must declare you two mismatched. You have no reason to think him importunate, as love is blind to rank and riches. In diverse ways it conquers some more than others, and lack of love is one of your distinctions. Brave Tirant sends you this letter."

The princess took the missive, read it, and dictated her reply:

·CCXLVI·

*T*HE PRINCESS'S REPLY TO TIRANT

I feared to take pen in hand, for, while writing with friendship, I felt obliged to show my indignation. Though my grief has redoubled, I shall bear it patiently all my life, knowing that such cruelty and love were never seen together. This thought alone forces me to reply: to make you see that your hands, which learned a new trade and pitilessly seized pleasure, now deserve no pardon from the lady you wronged. How often have I urged you not to steal my honor, and if my words never moved you my tears and sad countenance should have, yet, crueler than a raging lion, you trampled upon my innocence, nor would they let me die nobly but repeated my last words to the Easygoing Widow. Then the empress came, and my face revealed the shame that often battles love, as my woeful sighs disclosed what my words sought to conceal. So great was my distress that I cried out: "Jesus, Jesus, Jesus!" thus confessing my grief . . . He who errs deserves no pardon, and your punishment will be such that you will think of me no more, nor shall I of you.

Having finished her reply, she commended it to Hippolytus.

Upon reaching the hermitage, he gave Carmesina's letter to his captain, who read it with great delight and was pleased by everything except the end. Calling for pen and paper, he then wrote the following reply:

·CCXLVII·

*T*IRANT'S REPLY TO THE PRINCESS

At the hour when all beings repose, I alone lie awake recalling your sad words: "Think of me no more, nor shall I of you." Overwhelmed by love's torments, I take pen in hand to correct your ignorance, for though you hope to obliterate my years of service, I know your worth too well,[77] and while some may mock such devotion, I alone deserve your beauty. Your reply, should you grant one, will give me life or death, as I shall humbly obey all Your Highness's commands.

· CCXLVIII ·

HOW HIPPOLYTUS'S LOVE AFFAIR WITH THE EMPRESS BEGAN

Having finished his reply, Tirant entrusted it to Hippolytus and sent him back to Carmesina, who took the missive with great joy. She could not read it immediately because the empress was there, but when she saw her discussing Tirant's health with Hippolytus, she led Pleasure-of-my-life into another chamber.

After talking for a long time about their captain, the empress said: "Hippolytus, your face is pale and gaunt but not without reason, for Tirant's misfortune must grieve his companions. I myself often lie awake at night, feeling as anguished as if he were my husband, son, or brother. Gradually I calm my fears and drift back to sleep."

Hippolytus quickly replied: "Were I lying next to some lady in her bed, I would never let her rest, however great a sleeper she might be, yet in your case I am not surprised, since you sleep alone. This, my lady, and not Tirant's wound, has made my face so gaunt. Every day I pray God with all my heart to free me from those torments known only to steadfast lovers."

The empress had already guessed that Hippolytus must be enamored of some damsel, for his sad countenance could be due to nothing else. Suspecting Pleasure-of-my-life, who had declared her love for him in everyone's presence, Her Majesty began questioning the knight to learn what cruel lady had caused his grief.

· CCXLIX ·

HOW THE EMPRESS ASKED HIPPOLYTUS WHO HAD CAUSED HIS ANGUISH

"Tell me, and may God grant you happiness in this world and Heaven in the next: who torments you so?"

"Misfortune," replied Hippolytus, "has parted me from God and His saints, nor should Your Majesty think my life safer than Tirant's."

"If you wish to act well," said the empress, "you should feel no shame in recounting your exploits. Tell me; I promise never to betray you."

"Who would dare to share his woes," replied Hippolytus, "with one so exalted that her perfection lacks nothing but a saint's bright halo? Te Deums should be sung and the Scriptures read for you in all our churches, where you should be worshipped as an earthly goddess."

"No one," said the empress, "should refuse to hear good or evil, for Our Lord has granted mankind free will, and the higher one's station, the more humbly one should listen."

"I would happily obey you," replied Hippolytus, "were my words as pure as gold—that is, just and lawful—but I have neither vassals, wealth, nor lineage to offer Your Majesty, yet since you insist, it is love that torments me."

"I already knew that," said the empress, "but everything requires its own words and measure. You say you are in love, and I ask: with whom?"

"My five senses fail me," replied Hippolytus, "when I think of telling you."

"Oh foolish man!" cried the empress. "Why do you not share your woes?"

"There are four things," replied Hippolytus, "of peerless excellence, and the fifth is to know the truth. Heaven commands me to serve and love Your Majesty all my life . . ."

Having declared himself, Hippolytus feared to meet her gaze and fled without a word, while the empress called after him. She asked where he was going, but he was too mortified to return and decided that if she questioned him, he would say he had not heard her. He then retired to his lodgings, feeling that he had spoken badly and acted worse.

The empress, whose heart had never beaten so for anyone, pondered Hippolytus's amorous declaration.

The young knight, for his part, was overcome by shame and wished to leave immediately lest he meet her again, but he had to go back for Carmesina's answer. Finding her with her head in Pleasure-of-my-life's lap and surrounded by damsels devoted to Tirant, Hippolytus asked for her reply, whereupon the princess spoke these words:

· CCL ·

THE PRINCESS'S WORDS TO HIPPOLYTUS

"Would that I might spend my lovelorn days reading Tirant's sweet missives, to which I shall now respond, since his hand never tires of writing, and though our bodies may be parted our souls remain together. Were I wise enough to answer him, I would gladly do so, but I know I have a faithful messenger to whom all things may be entrusted, wherefore I beg you to spare me the trouble of writing and to say I shall visit him with my father one day this week. Please ask nothing else, for I almost fainted when I read his letter, and, finding all companionship odious, I prefer to be alone."

"My lady," replied Hippolytus, "I see your heart is made of stone, but may your eyes show the pity that alone sustains our captain. Should you not realize how Tirant suffers and prays for your well-being, his gaunt face will quickly convince you of his affliction. You can end his life or save it as you see fit, but remember: Tirant is not your enemy but your humble servant. Your reply will bring him death with bitter tears or be sealed with promised joy, as I know he longs for a sheet of paper with amorous words inscribed upon it. He has faith in your wisdom, and I speak as your devoted vassal."

The princess quickly replied in the following manner:

· CCLI ·

THE PRINCESS'S REPLY TO HIPPOLYTUS

"I shall keep silent and conceal my ignorance, though your slippery words deserve a rebuttal, yet I hope these damsels will not think Tirant wishes you to accuse me, since I am fully aware of the harm you did him. Pleasure-of-my-life, pull out three of my hairs and give them to Hippolytus for his master. As I cannot write, he should take them as his reply."

"May God punish me," replied Hippolytus, "if I take them unless you tell me the significance of their being three instead of four, ten, or twenty. Really, my lady! Does Your Highness think these are the old days, when people followed the laws of grace and a damsel who loved some suitor in extreme degree would give him a well-perfumed bouquet of flowers or a hair or two from her head, whereupon he considered himself exceedingly fortunate? No, my lady, no. That time is past. I know quite well what my lord Tirant desires: to see you in bed, either naked or in your nightdress, and if the bed is not perfumed, he will be just as pleased. Offer me no hairs, as I am unaccustomed to bearing such gifts, or else tell me why you have pulled them from your head."

"I shall be happy," said the princess, "to tell you the truth: the first hair means I love him more than anyone alive, with such devotion that I forget my parents and very nearly God Himself. I hoped to offer Tirant not only my body but my riches, and though I meant to save my soul for

God, had he asked I would have given it. The second hair signifies the suffering he has caused me and those great lords who envy him, for neither my tongue nor my honor can bear to speak of his affronts. The third means I know how little he loves me. Alas, what sadness my weary soul must endure! He, who was once so merciful, has damaged my health, and only fear for my honor keeps me from crying aloud how he imperils my life. I keep my eyes lowered lest people behold my shame, yet knowing what the hairs mean, you are still too wicked to take them."

She snatched them from his hand and furiously flung them to the floor, weeping bitter tears that rolled down her breasts. When Hippolytus saw how his meek words had offended Carmesina, with piteous voice and humble gesture he began to speak thus:

· CCLII ·

HIPPOLYTUS'S REPLY TO THE PRINCESS

"Your Highness, claiming that violence was done you, seeks to hide her sins and condemn poor Tirant, but the truth is that you were not raped by our captain. Tell me, my lady: how can he be blamed for so noble an exploit? You have banished beauty, grace, good sense, wisdom, and every other virtue from your heart, yet instead of spurning one who longs to serve you, you should be mindful of his devotion. Do not strive to kill his hopes with cruel and callous words but put aside such doubts and consider the desolation you have caused. Should you slay the best knight alive, you will be punished here and in Heaven, for when Tirant is happy his wounds begin to heal, whereas if you make him suffer you will curse yourself and our Breton company, and should he die, you will lose over ten thousand knights. Look how many warriors the King of Sicily, the Master of Rhodes, and the Viscount of Branches sent and brought you. After Tirant's death they will depart, leaving you to learn whether the Easygoing Widow is ready to fight your battles. Your Highness is like a doctor without medicine, for though a worthy physician cures both bodies and souls, Tirant will find no health in such a vixen."

Pleasure-of-my-life, who wished to help Hippolytus plead his case, then said:

· CCLIII ·

PLEASURE-OF-MY-LIFE'S WORDS TO THE PRINCESS

"Would that I had never met you and been forced to serve one so pitiless, for while in arms Tirant is the luckiest of mortals, in love he is the most wretched. I cannot believe a damsel endowed with so many virtues could lack Nature's greatest gift: love, as you scorn your most devoted vassal. How can I cheerfully obey one who shows such ingratitude? Had you suffered as I have or felt the glory others know, if God permitted me to make you see and feel those amorous delights prized by many, you would be blessed and praised eternally like all other true lovers, yet Your Highness is like one who smells food but never eats it. Were you to taste its sweetness, you would live forever in glorious fame, but, my lady, in spurning Tirant you also spurn his companions. One day you will weep, beating your breast and cursing the day and night, since as soon as Tirant can ride he will flee from your displeasure. The others will also abandon your empire, and when you knock at Heaven's gate, God will condemn you in the following manner:"

· CCLIV ·

PLEASURE-OF-MY-LIFE'S IMAGINARY CONDEMNATION

" 'I made man in my image and woman from his rib, saying: be fruitful, multiply, and replenish the earth. Tell me, Carmesina: how did you behave after your brother's death? Did you marry? Did you leave sons to defend the Catholic Church?' Alas, good lady, finding no suitable response, you will instead be forced to cry: 'Oh Lord of Mercy! Forgive me, clement Lord!' Then the guardian angel will make you say: 'It is true, Lord, that I loved a brave knight whom Your Majesty sent to free us from the infidel and whom I adored above all others and hoped someday to wed, yet I scorned the sage counsel of my damsel Pleasure-of-my-life. When he came to my bed, I foolishly cried out, and though I soon regained my senses and decided to keep quiet, a widow heard my scream and roused the palace to my great distress. Afterward they begged me to yield to this knight's desires, yet I stubbornly refused to grant his humble pleas.' Then Saint Peter, who keeps the keys to Heaven, will say: 'Lord, this woman does not deserve to dwell in glory, for she disobeyed Your most holy commandment.' They will cast you into Hell along with the Easygoing Widow, but when I die they will make great joy of me in Paradise, where I shall be seated in the highest circle and crowned as an obedient daughter."

At this point His Majesty entered, and after greeting Carmesina, he took Hippolytus's hand and asked how their captain fared. While they were talking the empress came in, whereupon Hippolytus would have liked nothing better than to be a day's ride away. She smiled sweetly at her suitor, and the three of them discussed many things, but especially how cruel Fortune had spirited their son away in his youth. Upon re- calling his death, the empress burst into tears.

Many elderly knights from the council sought to comfort her and told Hippolytus how bravely the emperor had borne the news of his heir's demise. His Benign Majesty told the cardinal and those who had informed him: "I am not surprised, for I knew he was born to die and it is a law of Nature that anyone given life must relinquish it."

When he heard that his son had perished (it was the first of January, on which day the emperor always held a feast and wore his crown), he removed the crown and asked how it had happened. Upon learning that the prince had died in battle like a worthy knight, the emperor donned his crown again, swearing that pleasure in his son's courage had dispelled the sadness of his death.

The emperor then drew some of his councilors aside, while the empress, seeing her knight so silent, thought he must be embarrassed and said:

· CCLV ·

H OW THE EMPRESS DECLARED HERSELF TO HIPPOLYTUS

"Though scant learning impedes my eloquence, you will certainly under- stand what my tongue cannot express. Perhaps eagerness or foolishness made me misconstrue your words, as the errors of my age make me question their meaning, wherefore I beg you to tell me what emboldened you to speak. Did Tirant ask you to do so, that he might gain more power? Answer me quickly, for I am anxious to know."

Hippolytus whispered: "Who would dare to bare his soul before Your Majesty? Whose body would not quake at a mere disapproving look from Your Highness? Just one such glance would make me long to be dead and buried, and when you entered this room, I sank to my knees. Surely the emperor noticed how fear and shame battled within me, but then I breathed a deep sigh, having seen your smiling countenance. Therefore, my lady, instead of asking further questions, send me on perilous quests that will test my devotion, since your power over me is such that though you tear my hair and claw my face, I shall patiently bear it and even fret about your hand. In regard to Tirant, I swear that neither he nor my confessor knows, and indeed who would suspect it at this late hour? My heart can say no more, as love holds it in thrall."

· CCLVI ·

*H*OW THE EMPRESS REPLIED

"I hoped, Hippolytus, that you would state your intentions clearly, and so you should, for love is indifferent to nobility, lineage, and station. Whoever bears love's arms in secret deserves no punishment, as it is natural to woo with discretion and devotion. Tell me: do you think that knight lucky who is loved by a great lady, one who forsakes her husband and children for his sake? Look how steadfast he must be to preserve her honor once he has seen if she is beautiful, ugly, or cursed with some hidden defect. I do not speak thus to conceal some blemish but to show that a man must protect his mistress, and so I say again how much your speech pleased me. You boldly declared yourself, and I am delighted at your words, though however base they might have been, I would never have repeated them. Your embarrassment also pleases me, since such requests should be made with shame and awkwardness, and a love easily won is too easily lost."

The empress talked so much that Hippolytus regained his courage and replied in a hoarse whisper:

· CCLVII ·

*H*OW HIPPOLYTUS ASKED FOR THE EMPRESS'S LOVE

"My delight in your company has often tempted me to declare myself, though your high station and my fears made me hesitate till now. If God made you mine, what other knight could feel such joy? Since I am young and my clumsy tongue cannot express all my heart's desires, Your Majesty must help me to master this new trade. Your sweet words cheer my spirit, for without you I am nothing, whereas by your side I make such profits that any other business would be a loss, and should you requite my love, all will be easy. I hope you will see how wise I hold my virtuous lady, who, had she lived in Paris's time, would have borne away the apple. If love confuses my speech, I beg you to be patient with one who kneels at your feet and awaits your commands."

The empress quickly replied:

· CCLVIII ·

THE EMPRESS'S REPLY TO HIPPOLYTUS

"Your kind words deserve an answer, but not the one you desire, for you have troubled my spirit. What leads you to court a woman so much older than yourself? If this becomes known, people will say that I am enamored of one who could be my grandson! I also know that foreigners are neither true nor steadfast lovers, and blessed is that woman who has no husband to impede her! I am so unused to love that I would have trouble satisfying your appetites, wherefore your hopes are tardy and vain, as another possesses what you desire, though if I wished to cuckold him I could do so. Your youth and sweet disposition make me forgive your audacity, and any damsel would rejoice in your devotion, but I would rather see another win this prize than perish myself for love of a foreigner."

The empress could say no more, since the emperor, who had returned, then approached his wife, took her hand, and led her away to supper.

Hippolytus had no chance to see the princess that evening, but he spoke with Pleasure-of-my-life, who asked: "What are those secrets you whisper to the empress? It must be important if you speak to her so often."

"She only asks when our captain will be able to walk," replied Hippolytus. "She wishes he were in Saint George, as letters arrive daily and the troops long for Tirant more than Jews for their Messiah."

The next morning, Hippolytus departed without an answer. Upon beholding him, Tirant said: "I have not seen you in five days."

"My lord," replied Hippolytus, "the emperor's daughter detained me, that she might accompany me to the city gates and talk about Your Lordship, but since they all plan to visit you she gave me no written reply."

Tirant said: "This news comforts me greatly."

Then he asked the doctors if he might return to Constantinople, saying: "I swear I shall mend more in a day there than two weeks here, as I was born and raised near the coast and am accustomed to sea air. I have been wounded many times, and after the first five treatments I always had them move me to the shore, where I knew I would heal more quickly."

After praising his words and granting his request, two doctors went to tell His Majesty, who visited Tirant with a great retinue. They placed him on a litter, and four days later he was in Constantinople.

Once he had settled into his lodgings, the imperial ladies went to see him and rejoiced to behold their captain's recovery. The empress, having heard a rumor from her favorite chambermaid, scarcely left Carmesina's side when they were in Tirant's chamber. This, however, did not stop them from speaking of love, since Pleasure-of-my-life went back and forth every day, striving to bring the battle to its conclusion.

Let us now leave Tirant and return to Saint George, where fierce fighting again erupted as soon as the truce ended. Every day the Turks assaulted their adversaries, performing noble feats of arms and slaying many Christians. One day the Saracens marshaled their troops for an attack on the city's irrigation system, but the Christians vanquished them by raising the sluices, whereby more than three thousand Turks drowned and the surrounding fields were flooded. Though the infidels were eager for battle, their outnumbered foes chose to wait and prayed for Tirant's health as much as for their own.

To encourage them, the emperor wrote daily reports in which he told them how Tirant got out of bed every morning to exercise his leg. Everyone was cheered by this news, and especially Diaphebus.

Tirant was feeling healthier by the day and could now walk around his chamber with a crutch. The ladies attended him and kept him company while out of both love and self-interest, Carmesina honored him greatly, but no one should think our knight was eager to recover, for he saw that he would not be lamed and had no desire to leave his mistress. Having forgotten about the war, he only wished to have his way with her, while someone else fretted about military matters. Thus does excessive love often turn wise knights into fools.

Tirant, who could not address his lady when the emperor and empress were present, summoned Hippolytus one day and whispered: "Go out but come back quickly and then talk to the empress about anything you think will distract her, while I inform Carmesina of my woes and afflictions."

Hippolytus quickly obeyed, and upon his return he approached the empress, to whom he began to whisper:

· CCLIX ·

H OW THE EMPRESS YIELDED TO HIPPOLYTUS'S PLEAS

"Your great wisdom and nobility redouble my sorrows, for so great is my love that I cannot leave your side, and when I do, I feel as though I were in a second Purgatory. Just as the torments of the damned are lightened when they recall their former lives, likewise I, being unsure of your love, take solace from the thought of your lofty station, for the more virtuous a lady, the more reverence she deserves. Should you requite my love, I promise to adore and serve you both waking and sleeping all the days of my life, and you will make me the happiest of mortals."

The empress smiled sweetly and replied:

· CCLX ·

T HE EMPRESS'S REPLY

"Such kindness obliges me to lay aside chastity, for I see that your virtue deserves my love. If you swear to keep silent, you shall have your wish, but you must fear no peril lest your beloved be defamed, wherefore I expect you to bravely follow my instructions and in the still of the night, when all God's creatures are at rest, to await me on the roof outside my chamber. Never doubt that I shall be there, as only death could prevent me."

Hippolytus tried to object, but the empress replied that if he truly loved her, he would brave any danger.

"Do as I tell you, and forget about the rest."

Hippolytus replied: "My lady, I shall obey your commands."

Then he assuaged her doubts and fears.

Once they had finished talking, the empress left Tirant, and upon reaching the palace, she told her ladies: "Let us visit the emperor."

After taking her ease with him for some time, the empress rose, feeling anxious about her assignation, and told Carmesina: "Remain here and keep your father company."

She gladly obeyed.

As soon as the empress was in her rooms, she summoned her chamberlains, whom she told to replace the heavy silk curtains with embroidered ones. Then she said: "His Highness will come to me tonight, and I wish to celebrate a little, for it has been such a long time."

Once the whole chamber had been adorned with silk and brocade, she had the room and her bed well perfumed.

After supper the empress retired, complaining of a headache. One of her chambermaids named Eliseu asked: "My lady, does Your Highness wish to see the doctors?"

"Do as you like," replied the empress, "but do not tell the emperor lest he change his mind."

The doctors came and took her pulse, which they found to be fast, since she was about to enter the lists with a young and doughty knight.

The doctors said: "If Your Highness will eat a few candied marijuana seeds and drink a glass of malmsey, they will rid you of your headache and help you sleep."

The empress replied: "My illness is such that I do not think I shall get much sleep or even rest, since the way I feel now, I shall be tossing and turning all night."

"Your Highness," said the doctors, "if this proves to be the case, send for us at once, or if you prefer, we shall spend the night here or outside your door and observe you every hour."

"That will not be necessary," replied the empress, "as I want my bed all to myself and prefer not to be observed when I am making merry, nor is my ailment one that can bear too much scrutiny. This woman will show you out, for I wish to go to bed."

When the doctors were at the door, they told her to wash the seeds down with wine, whereby they would soothe her stomach all the more. After eating a big box of seeds and washing them down with abundant wine, the empress had civet placed in all the pillowcases. Once everything was ready, she perfumed herself, dismissed her maids, and closed the chamber door.

There was an alcove in the empress's chamber where she dressed, and this alcove had a door that opened onto the rooftop. When the empress rose to let Hippolytus in, Eliseu heard the noise and hastened to see if her mistress was in pain. Upon reaching the chamber, she asked: "Why did Your Highness get up? Are you feeling worse?"

"No," replied the empress. "I feel well, but I forgot to say my bedtime prayers."

Eliseu said: "My lady, please tell me what they are."

"With pleasure," replied the empress. "When you see the first star, you kneel and recite three Paternosters and three Hail Marys for the three Magi, that they may intercede for you with Christ and His Holy Mother. You beg them to shield you from disgrace, just as they were shielded from King Herod, and then you ask them to safeguard your prosperity. Such prayers will surely be granted in full. Now go back to bed and let me finish my devotions."

The damsel returned to bed while the empress entered the alcove, where once Eliseu was quiet and the appointed hour had struck, she threw a sable-lined green velvet mantle over her nightgown. She opened the door and, seeing Hippolytus lying on the roof, she thought how well and discreetly he would protect her honor. After kneeling on the roof and kissing her hands, the knight tried to kiss her feet, but the valiant lady refused and instead kissed him many times on the lips in sign of true devotion. Then she told him to follow her, to which Hippolytus replied: "My lady, you must forgive me, but I shall never enter your chamber until I have tasted my future glory."

He took her in his arms, whereupon they lay down and consummated their love.

Then they happily entered the alcove, where Hippolytus uttered these joyous words:

· CCLXI ·

HOW HIPPOLYTUS SHOWED HIS HAPPINESS

"If I sought to reveal my soul's delight in your perfections, my tongue would be unable to describe such gentility, for I cannot express my love and how it grows from hour to hour, nor indeed, could I ever tell even its smallest part, and yet I cannot bear to think of Your Majesty hearing it from another, as my woes would then redouble just when I thought myself happy."

The empress sweetly replied:

· CCLXII ·

HOW THE EMPRESS ANSWERED HIPPOLYTUS

"Though you have troubled my soul, I know your worth, and lest I offend such a noble knight, I shall complain neither of you, God, nor myself."

"My lady," replied Hippolytus, "this is no time for idle chatter. Lead me to your bed, where we shall find both solace and delight."

Having spoken, Hippolytus undressed and removed the old gentlewoman's mantle. Anyone who beheld her would have recognized her peerless beauty, for while Carmesina resembled her in many respects, you could see that in her time the mother had excelled the daughter. Our young gallant took her arm and led her to the bed, in which they spent a long time talking and joking as lovers are wont to do. Some time after midnight, the lady heaved a deep sigh.

"Why do you sigh," asked Hippolytus, "if God has granted all your wishes? Tell me, I beg you: are you displeased with me?"

"No, it is quite the opposite," replied the empress. "My desire has increased, and though I liked you before, I now think you infinitely braver and better, yet I sigh because I fear men will deem you a heretic."

"How so, my lady?" asked Hippolytus. "Have I done something heretical?"

"I shall tell you," replied the empress. "You have dared to court your mother."

"My lady," said Hippolytus, "only I know your worth, as I alone gaze upon your noble and flawless beauty."

They spoke of many matters, as is customary between lovers, and the empress had been right to say she would not sleep a wink. They finally dozed off toward daybreak, just as the sun was rising.

A few hours later, Eliseu awoke and entered her mistress's chamber to see how she felt and whether she wanted anything. Upon approaching the bed, the damsel saw a man lying beside the empress with his arm outstretched and her nipple in his mouth.

"Holy Mary!" cried Eliseu. "What renegade traitor has thus deceived my lady?" She was tempted to shout: "Kill this scoundrel who crept into my lady's bed of bliss!"

Then she realized that no one would dare to come without an invitation and she remembered that her mistress had ordered the room redecorated. Eliseu tried to see who it was, but Hippolytus's head was half-covered, and, afraid that the other maidens might also enter, she went to the room where they slept and cried: "My lady orders you to stay here and keep silent lest you awaken her."

When the doctors arrived a half-hour later, Eliseu went to the door and told them her lady was resting after a hard night.

"We shall stay here until she wakes," they replied, "for such are the emperor's orders."

Scarcely knowing what to do or whether to wake her mistress, Eliseu stood there trying to decide until the emperor knocked at the door. The damsel, who lacked both patience and wit, then rushed to the bed and whispered: "Get up, my lady, get up, as your death is at hand! Your husband is at the door and knows that you have betrayed him. Who is this cruel and wretched man by your side? Is he an unknown king? May God crown him with fire. If he is a duke, may he end his days in prison! If he is a marquis, may I see his hands and feet eaten by wild beasts! If he is a count, may he be slain in battle! If he is a viscount, may a Turk slit him from head to navel! If he is a knight, may he drown in a pitiless sea! Were I as brave as Queen Penthesilea, I would make him rue his deeds, but our sad custom is only to weep and mourn."

Awakened by this din, which was worse than a trumpet blast, the empress could not even move her tongue. Hippolytus, who heard Eliseu's voice but could not understand her words, pulled the blankets over his head to avoid recognition. Then he pulled the empress under the covers and asked what was wrong.

"Alas, my son," cried his lady, "one can find no joy in this world! Get up; the emperor is at the door. Forgive me for saying no more, but if we talk we shall lose our lives. Though I hoped to bathe your tomb in my enamored tears, I shall never throw myself upon your body, covering your lips with sad and bitter kisses."

Hippolytus felt very sorry for himself when he heard these words, and being inexperienced in such matters, he offered more tears than advice, but then he screwed up his courage and told the damsel to fetch his sword, crying: "If I must be martyred and give up the ghost, I shall be proud to die defending my beloved."

The empress, after listening but hearing nothing outside, told Hippolytus: "Go, my son, and hide in that alcove. I shall keep them occupied while you escape, for I wish you to live in honor and dignity."

"Though they gave me the Greek Empire and four others, I would sooner sacrifice my life and everything I own than betray Your Majesty, whom I beg to kiss me in sign of troth."

The empress's enamored grief redoubled at these words, and, still unable to hear anything, she went to the door and listened. Upon peering through the keyhole, she saw the emperor and his doctors arguing about her illness, whereby she knew there was no cause for alarm. She hurried back to Hippolytus, pulled his ears, and gave him a big kiss, saying: "My son, please go into that alcove and stay there till I can dispose of the emperor and his doctors."

"My lady," replied Hippolytus, "I shall be more obedient than a slave, but do not dismiss me until I see if they wish to harm you."

"Have no fear," said the empress, "for if that were the case, our whole palace would be in an uproar, but I can see Eliseu was mistaken."

Hippolytus quickly hid in the alcove, while the empress returned to bed and ordered the doors opened.

The emperor and his doctors asked how she fared, to which the empress replied that between her headache and her stomach, she had not fallen asleep until the stars had vanished. "Finally, unable to keep my weary eyes open, I dozed off and now I feel infinitely better. Had I slept a little longer, it would have been the sweetest night of my life, but one cannot spend a happy day or night in this world, for Eliseu cruelly woke me and filled my soul with sorrow. If only I could again hold what I love best in my arms, earthly paradise would surely be mine, and you may be certain, my lords, that could I regain that glorious repose, I would be both happy and quickly cured."

The emperor said: "Tell me, my lady, what you held in your arms."

The empress replied: "My lord, it was my greatest joy. I dreamt that, clad in my nightgown with a green velvet mantle over it, I went onto the roof and prayed to the three Magi, and as I finished my prayers I heard a voice saying: 'Stay where you are; you shall now have your wish.' Then my son appeared, attended by many knights in shining armor. He was holding Hippolytus's hand, and they both tried to kiss my feet, but I would not permit it and instead bade them be seated. We talked for a long time, and I shall always keep their words in my heart. Then my son took my hand and led me inside, where we got into bed and I embraced him while he kissed my breasts. Never did I have such a pleasant dream, and he said: 'My lady, as I shall never return to this wretched world, take my brother Hippolytus as your son, since I love him as much as Carmesina.' Meanwhile Hippolytus knelt on the floor. Then I asked my son to tell me his abode, and he said he dwelt in Heaven with those knights martyred by the infidel. I could ask no more questions, because Eliseu woke me with a blast worse than a bugle."

"Did I not tell you," asked the emperor, "that all she talks about is the prince?"

"Alas, my lord," cried the empress, "what a rude awakening! I held him in these very arms and felt his sweet mouth on my breasts. Many early morning dreams come true, and he will surely return if I go back to sleep."

"Please," replied the emperor, "put aside such follies and get up if you feel well, since the more you carry on the worse you will feel."

"Sire," said the empress, "let me rest a little longer for my health and delight, as my eyes are still bleary from lack of sleep."

"Your Majesty," said the doctors, "should go and let her repose, lest by depriving her of this pleasure we aggravate her condition."

The emperor left with all the damsels except Eliseu.

Once the doors were shut, the empress summoned Hippolytus and told Eliseu: "Now that by chance you have discovered us, I order you to serve this knight faithfully and to wait in that alcove till we have slept awhile. I shall favor you above the others and find you a better husband, and Hippolytus will endow you so generously that you will be well satisfied."

"May God forsake me," replied Eliseu, "if I wish to love, serve, or

honor Hippolytus. I shall obey your commands, but otherwise I would
not pick up a pin he dropped, for ever since I saw him lying beside you I
have loathed him more than any man alive. May starving lions devour his
eyes, face, and body."

Hippolytus said: "Damsel, far from seeking to offend you, I only wish
to love and reward you above all other maidens."

"Help them," replied Eliseu, "and do not fret about me, since I shall
never accept anything from you."

Then she went into the alcove and began to sob.

The two lovers stayed in bed till it was almost time for Vespers, and
upon arising, they found the poor damsel still in tears. Fearful that she
might betray them, the empress sought to comfort her.

"My lady," replied Eliseu, "I would sooner die than breathe a word
against your orders. I can see that you would be martyred more cruelly
than the apostles, nor should you trouble about Hippolytus, whom I shall
serve with all my might."

Leaving Hippolytus in the alcove, the reassured empress returned to
bed and had the doors opened, whereupon Carmesina, the emperor, and
his doctors quickly entered and she again described her delightful dream.

Once they had left, lunch was served, and the empress ate like someone
who had been walking all day. The damsel took care to serve Hippolytus
well, bringing him a pair of pheasants and delicious sweetmeats. When he
would not eat, she asked him to on her lady's behalf, but although he
tried to joke and make friends with her, she refused to say a word beyond
what was necessary.

The empress stayed in bed until the next day after lunch, when she
dressed and went to chapel to hear Mass, thus provoking a great dispute
among the priests as to whether services could be held at such an hour.

Hippolytus spent an entire week in that alcove, and when his lady felt
him begin to flag, she told him to recuperate, but first she opened a jewel
case and took out a gold necklace made of half-moons, each of which was
adorned with pearls at either end and a big diamond in the center. The
necklace's steel chain was fastened with an enameled gold pine cone that
was half open, and inside it were big ruby pine nuts. Such exquisite pine
nuts had never been seen before, and having tasted them himself, Hippolytus knew of their sweetness. The cone was studded with diamonds,
rubies, emeralds, and sapphires, and the necklace was worth more than a
hundred thousand ducats. The empress hung it on her lover's neck,
saying: "Mention me in your prayers, Hippolytus, as it would not surprise
me if you soon were emperor. Now wear this in my honor, and when you
see it recall my love."

Hippolytus knelt and thanked her profusely, kissing her hands and
lips. Then he asked: "My lady, does Your Majesty really wish to part with

such a precious necklace? If it were mine, I would offer it to you, for no one would display it better, wherefore I beg you to take it back."

The empress replied: "Never refuse a gift from a lover, since when two people make friends, the loftier one should offer a gift, which the lesser should not refuse."

"Then what is your command? What does Your Highness wish?"

"I beg you to depart, lest the emperor come tomorrow and find you here. Go now; I promise you will be able to return often."

Hippolytus burst into laughter and gently replied:

· CCLXIII ·

*H*IPPOLYTUS'S PARABLE OF THE VINEYARD

"Being far below you in station, I despair at your coldness, for how little I must please Your Highness if you dismiss me thus! A terrible grief wells up within me at the thought of our being parted, but to get to the point, Your Majesty is like that man who, dying of hunger as I am of love, lost his way one night in a deep and thick forest. Emerging at daybreak, he looked around for some town, but as there was none in sight, he walked on without seeing a soul. Weak from hunger, he had to spend the next night on the ground, and once the sun rose, he resolved to climb a great mountain, from whose peak he saw a castle that he then approached, more dead than alive. When he was nearby, the knight of the castle spied him from his window, while the weary traveler beheld a vineyard laden with grapes. He left the path and plunged into it, whereupon the knight told a servant: 'If you go to that vineyard, you will find a man whom I order you not to disturb but merely to watch, that you may come back and tell me what he is doing.'

"The servant returned and said: 'My lord, he is lying on the ground, eating your grapes off the stem without looking to see if they are green or ripe.' 'Then they must please him,' replied the knight. 'Go and see what he is doing now.' The servant came back and told his master: 'He is swallowing whole bunches!' 'Leave him alone, for they must taste good to him. Now go back again.' The next time the servant said: 'My lord, he is eating more calmly now and only takes four or five at a time.' 'Let him continue, since he is enjoying them.' The next time the servant said: 'My lord, now he is searching for the ripest ones and peeling them.' Then the knight shouted: 'Hurry and throw him out of my vineyard before he ruins me!' Your Majesty is like that knight, as when at first I grabbed whole handfuls and then ate four or five at a time, Your Highness did not dismiss me. Now that I eat them one by one, you order me to leave."

When Eliseu heard this parable, she roared with laughter, much to Hippolytus's astonishment, for she had not smiled since his arrival. Then she said: "Lord Hippolytus, I take great pleasure in your words, which show your appreciation of my mistress's perfections. I promise as a gentlewoman to serve you at least as loyally as Pleasure-of-my-life does the princess, and I shall defend you against all comers, since good luck has brought you to us."

She turned to the empress and begged her to let Hippolytus stay as long as he liked, and to please her the lady granted this request. Hippolytus then rose from his beloved's side and approached Eliseu, whom he kissed, embraced, and thanked for her help, whereby the two of them made peace and became friends.

One day when Hippolytus was in the alcove, the empress and Eliseu began talking about him. The damsel asked: "My lady, why do you let this knight dwell with Tirant when if Your Majesty helped him he would need no one else? I am only a poor wretched damsel, but if I had a lover I would help him every way I could, even if I were forced to pawn all my clothes. You, who are so rich and mighty, ought to do far more."

The empress replied: "I shall heed your advice, though ladies who love foreigners and give them money are always scorned and forsaken."

"No, my lady," said Eliseu, "Hippolytus is not so, for you have seen him in your court ever since he was a child."

"Then take the credit yourself," replied the empress, "and may he love you all the more for it."

Hippolytus stayed in that alcove for another week, and on the eve of his departure, as he was lying with his head in the empress's lap, he asked her to sing a song in her flawless voice. She softly began to intone the ballad in which Tristram laments his wound from King Mark's lance, but she changed the refrain to: "Woman, your Hippolytus will soon forsake you." The music was so sweet that tears rolled down his cheeks, and to spare them more grief, Eliseu made them follow her into the alcove, where she took the key to the jewel chest and hastily unlocked it. The empress then placed her hand on top to keep it shut, while she uttered the following words:

· CCLXIV ·

H OW THE EMPRESS REORGANIZED HIPPOLYTUS'S LIFE

"Your knightly vows should forbid you to serve another, and if you have not trusted me I beg you to do so now, as I shall maintain you all my life in accord with your deserts, and I offer you three hundred servants."

Hippolytus knelt and thanked the empress for her gift, but he asked her not to make him leave Tirant too abruptly lest people talk. He promised that within a short while he would obey all her commands.

The damsel opened the chest, taking out a sack of ducats so big that Hippolytus could scarcely lift it, but although the empress offered them to her lover, he nobly refused. Then Eliseu brought forth fourteen hundred big pearls and begged him to have a pair of stockings embroidered with grapevines, each grape of which would be a pearl since they had become friends through his story.

Hippolytus slipped away that evening when the emperor was at supper and went to see a tailor named Bartholomew Spikenard, from whom he ordered a sable-lined green brocade mantle along with the stockings Eliseu had asked him to wear.

Once Hippolytus had arranged everything, he secretly rode to Bellestar, while sending word to Tirant that he had been sick for the past ten days. Hippolytus's messenger told his story so cleverly that the captain and everyone else believed him.

Having learned that his clothes were ready, Hippolytus returned to the city, where he donned his new mantle and those handsome stockings. The empress and her daughter were visiting Tirant, and when Hippolytus beheld them at the palace windows, he spurred his horse and turned many times. Then he went upstairs and bowed to the empress, her maidens, and Tirant, who asked after his health, to which he replied that he had attended Mass for the last two days.

The delighted empress exclaimed: "My son, please tell me if you were with my firstborn that morning when I dreamt of him."

As she spoke, tears streamed down her cheeks, while Tirant and the others sought to comfort her. Then the emperor came in and said: "Tell me, my lady: is this how you soothe our captain? Why do you not amuse him with some other sport than tears?"

"Sire," replied the empress, "grief lacerates my anguished soul and my woes redouble as I recall that fair morning when Your Majesty and those doctors robbed me of my glory. If only I could die so sweetly, for it is best to perish in the arms of one's beloved, but since I cannot have him back"—and she took Hippolytus's hand—"this knight shall replace him. I now take you as my son, and I, as your mother, shall help and love you in my firstborn's stead."

Everyone thought she was mourning her dead son, but she was really addressing Hippolytus. After she had described her dream again, they all departed and the empress asked Hippolytus to take her arm.

Now let us leave her gifts to Hippolytus, without whom she refused to eat lunch or supper, and return to Tirant's love. He never missed a chance to press his suit in speech or writing, nor did Pleasure-of-my-life forsake him or forget to plead his case.

When Tirant's leg had healed, he often walked to the palace with no one but the doctors, who still would not let him go about unattended. The emperor frequently asked them how soon he would be able to ride, and Tirant began to fear that he might not have his wish.

The Easygoing Widow had kept her passion secret, but when she overheard the emperor saying that Tirant would soon depart, she began to fret and wrack her brain for some scheme to accompany him. Determined to sow as much discord as possible, she asked the princess: "Did you see how, as we were leaving Mass, Tirant said he wished to speak to me about something to my advantage? I told him I would gladly do so with your leave, for I suspect that he is plotting some further treachery and thinks that if he has his way, so much the better, but if it ends like the other night he will soon forget you. Thus did he speak, roaring with laughter all the while. You should not admire a man who is capable of any baseness, and should you disbelieve me, think of his impudence the other day. May God's wrath descend upon the scoundrel, who says even more: that no man should either take up arms or lay them down for the fairest lady on earth. He talks like a captain but not like an enamored knight, though all or most glorious feats of arms have been done for women."

"Then talk with him," said the princess, "and see if there is perfidy in his heart. Advise me well, as I shall be on my guard against him."

"My lady," replied the widow, "if you truly want to find out everything, you must remain in this room until I return."

The Easygoing Widow then found a page and told him: "Inform Tirant that his princess eagerly awaits him in the great hall. If he appears, she will be delighted, but if not, he may abandon hope."

The page quickly obeyed, and when Tirant heard that his lady was asking for him, he did not look around for someone to go with. Once he had entered the hall, the widow pretended to come from Carmesina's chamber and, after approaching the captain, she curtsied and said: "The malicious empress is with your lady, whom I told to summon you, for as Jesus Christ lit up the world, so you illumine this palace. When you leave, we shall all feel sad and mournful, nor should God grant me solace if when I see you I do not rejoice, as the mere sight of you banishes wrath and sorrow. My lady ordered me to keep you company until her mother leaves. Please sit down, since I would not want your leg to worsen because of me."

They sat down upon a dais, and Tirant began to speak:

· CCLXV ·

*T*IRANT'S WORDS TO THE EASYGOING WIDOW

"My lady, thank you for saying I illuminate my goddess's dark palace, whose third step I know I am unworthy to climb. Had I won your good will, I would have honored and enriched you, as after Our Lord it is you I should pray to. My sufferings, which I thought were over, have sadly increased, yet if I could win your help I would gladly befriend you, and to illustrate my point I shall tell you a story about a merchant named Gaubedí.[78] Having invested all his wealth in a barrel of valuable playing cards, he set out from the city of Pisa and boarded a ship bound for Spain, but when they had passed the Rhone and were near Aiguesmortes, the ship hit a rock and split asunder. Fearing all was lost, the sailors dived into the sea, while this wretched merchant, who cherished his barrel more than his life, went to the storeroom, which was now half full of water. With great risk and effort, he brought the barrel up on deck and threw it overboard. Then he dived in after it and, though he tried to steer it toward shore, the current was so strong that after losing it two or three times and almost drowning, he finally had to abandon it despite all his efforts. As he swam along, he spied a big wooden crate that he clutched in his weariness, and soon both man and crate hit shore.

"Then the afflicted merchant sat down and began to lament, for, being devoid of both hope and clothing, he only wished to die. After bemoaning his fate for a long time, he rose and walked along the beach, but when he was more than two crossbow shots away, he decided to make the best of things and see if there were any clothes in the crate. He broke it open and found many silk and brocade robes, doublets, and stockings, while the bottom was covered with ducats, brooches, and priceless jewels. Perhaps, my lady, this all seems of little moment, yet I am like that crate and you resemble the merchant. If you let go of the barrel, you will be prosperous and happy, and before you reply please take this chain for love of me, that when you see it you may remember one who wishes to be your friend."

The widow quickly replied:

· CCLXVI ·

*T*HE WIDOW'S REPLY TO TIRANT

"Lest you take my silence for approval, I shall reply to your words, as I know what you seek and my tongue must protect my honor. If you value your reputation, remove your foot from this perilous threshold. Everyone knows how you broke your leg, and though necessity now obliges them to humor their captain, were we at peace, Carmesina would be the first to throw you into sorrow's stable. Are you too deaf to hear the vile rumors in this palace? I am disliked because I declare such talk distasteful, for alas, noble Tirant, you are not loved as you should be! If you want a true lover, seek one steadfast, chaste, and wise, but above all choose a lady who is not proud of her lofty station, since they say a good couple should fit together snugly. Would it not be better to court one skilled and experienced in the art of love? Such a woman would follow you in war and peace, thinking only of your happiness."

"Tell me, my lady," asked Tirant, "and may God reward you: what woman is this who will serve me so well?"

"Alas!" exclaimed the widow. "Have I not said enough? Why do you wish to augment my grief? Do not strive to hide what you already understand. I tried so hard to find an opportunity to reveal my woes, which I have kept hidden since the sad day of your arrival. I have said quite enough, and you should consider yourself lucky."

Tirant quickly replied:

· CCLXVII ·

*H*OW TIRANT REPLIED TO THE EASYGOING WIDOW'S DECLARATION OF LOVE

"Though I shall reply to your gracious words of love, I cannot satisfy them as my heart is pledged to another. Even if I tried, my five senses would betray me, since if I leave her for a moment they torment my grieving heart. I did not know what love was but now I have learned, and anyone who parts me from my lady will rob me of all my joy, wherefore, lest I suffer more, I beg you to consider other knights, of whom you will find an infinite number who are braver, better, and nobler. I speak the truth, for had I set my heart on you I would never betray your faith, and you should thank me, since if I were a different sort I would promise much but give little, turning black into white to enjoy your perfections. Think how angry you would be if someone loved and then abandoned you, but I know your great virtue and how much praise you deserve."

The widow quickly collected her wits and replied:

· CCLXVIII ·

*T*HE WIDOW'S REPLY

"Though I do not seek to equate divine and human law, I cannot hold my tongue after beholding your foolishness. My words were meant to test your loyalty and to show my wish to serve you, as I see you are deceived by the cunning princess, who is pitiless and indifferent to both her own and her parents' honor. She knows brave and worthy knights like you and her other suitors, with any one of whom she might honorably satisfy her desires, but the heavens, earth, sea, and sands cry out against the sins she commits every day. Why does Our Lord let her fornication go unpunished? If you knew what I know, you would spit in her face and those of other women.

"Why, however, should I waste my words on such filth, whose deeds provoke even more horror than amazement? No one who hears of them can eat or sleep in peace, and after all these years in her service, my weary heart is dressed in mourning, nor can I hide my thoughts, seeing her feign honor but live in sin while wicked women rejoice in her scandalous wrongdoing. It is true that there are many varieties of sin; some are venial, others mortal, but hers is so great that my tongue dare not speak its name. You know our religion constrains women to guard their chastity, yet if a woman must sin, let it not be with some heathen, as such sins are abominable to God and Christian damsels. The princess cannot plead ignorance, for her wrongdoing is public knowledge, and while virtuous damsels deserve honor, the wicked must be chastised. Though we all are born innocent, our vices are soon revealed, wherefore I beg you to quickly end your courtship, since she is in love with a black Moorish slave named Lauseta.

"If you promise to keep mum, I shall show you everything. Long ago she renounced her virtue, scorning the company of kings, dukes, and lords. My tongue recoils from her crimes but her sins force me to speak, as no matter what I tell her she persists in doing evil. The other day she found something alive under her belt. What can I say of such a sordid affair? She scarcely ate or slept, and each night seemed like a year. Then she started getting cramps, and my heart wept for our princess, whose face lost its color and whose limbs grew frail and thin. How often I had to gather herbs to end her pregnancy! Alas, that unborn child was punished for my cowardice when his little body was cruelly thrown in the river! How else could I keep the emperor from seeing his grandson? She gets the pleasure and I take the blame, wherefore I warn you: do not drown in a black pool of stinking oil. I shall omit her other sins to avoid prolixity, but I hope that you, who hold the scepter of justice, will punish her as she deserves. Often I tell her: 'My daughter, now is the time to resist temptation, shun corrupt loves, and cherish your lineage, reputation, and the flower of your beauty. Will you spurn Tirant's services and pursue a black gardener who should please no chaste or honorable damsel? Ponder my words and cast foul pleasures from you.' I can tell you, lord Tirant, that it does no good, as only a miracle can save one indifferent to noble thoughts."

Though filled with despair, our knight hastened to reply:

· CCLXIX ·

H OW TIRANT, UNAWARE OF THE WIDOW'S EVIL SCHEMES, REPLIED

"Alas, dark blindness of sinful lovers, who audaciously and persistently damn their souls and lose their lives! How virtuous the holy fear of those who shun vice, for they shall rise to Heaven with uncorrupted souls! Your words, lady widow, which have pierced my heart, now imperil my very life, and if I survive I shall live in mourning. At this moment, a thousand thoughts beset my weary mind, but they all join in one: if she loves another, I shall leap from this tower. Therefore I beg you, virtuous lady, to let me see my undoing, as I cannot trust words so contrary to human reason. Surely she would not give her body to a black savage, making her beauty odious to all who love righteousness! Alas, lady princess! Where are your thoughts now? Come, and with aching heart you shall hear how people slander you, but may God forbid me to credit such gossip! Oh, lady princess, you alone are my joy!"

A gentle sigh rose from Tirant's breast, accompanied by these words: "Oh pious faith! Oh holy shame! Oh chaste and modest damsels! Who can adore you as I do? You are wrong if you believe anyone's love can equal mine, and as I love you best, I deserve the most pity."

While they were talking, the emperor appeared and led our knight away. The widow remained alone, angrily thinking to herself: "If Tirant disbelieves me, my ruse will be foiled, but I shall have my way even if I must sell my soul, as otherwise I shall blush to go before him. I fear he may tell the princess, in which case I shall bear the blame. . . . I shall wait here till he returns." Then she exclaimed: "Alas, old fury, I shall relentlessly pursue you to the bitter end! Then why do I hesitate? I must not falter! I am capable of such wicked deeds and even greater ones! My only regret is that I did not start long ago!"

Pretending to laugh and displaying the chain Tirant had given her, the widow entered Carmesina's chambers and said: "My lady, your captain's plans would astonish you, for he wants to abduct you one night and take you back to his land. He is like a man blowing on a fire with his mouth full of water," and she went on lying and pretending to joke.

Offended by the widow's mockeries, Carmesina retired to her bedchamber, where she began to count the splendid gifts Tirant had given her damsels. As she pondered his great love, regrets filled her heart till at last she decided to dress and to comfort him before his departure.

The Easygoing Widow waited for Tirant to emerge from the council chamber, and upon seeing him, she said: "Lord captain, promise not to repeat what I said even in jest, as you shall see everything within twenty-four hours."

"Lady widow," replied Tirant, "I would be most grateful. Have no fear; I swear by my patron Saint George to repeat nothing."

The emperor turned around, saw the widow, and said: "Please fetch my wife and daughter, whom I shall await in the garden."

When they arrived, the emperor told them he had summoned two thousand knights to escort Tirant. The princess paled at this news, and after complaining of a headache, she said: "I shall not stand on ceremony before our captain."

She unpinned her golden tresses, which were the fairest in all the world, and at the sight of their splendor, Tirant's desires redoubled. His lady wore a white damask skirt with wide gold bands along the seams, while over it she had donned a shawl of French cloth. Seeing her hands struggle to loosen her skirt as she paced about in great distress, the emperor asked if she was ill or wanted to see a doctor, but she shook her head and replied: "My illness cannot be cured by medicine."

The widow led a damsel and two squires to the house of a master painter, whom she told: "I know you are the best artist in Constantinople. Can you fashion a mask covered with black leather that will look like our gardener Lauseta's face? Some of his hair is black and some white. Glue the hairs on, for Corpus Christi is near and I want to dress up like him, with black gloves on my hands so everything will appear genuine."

"My lady," replied the painter, "though it can easily be done, I have a great deal of work at present, but if you pay me well, I shall attend to you first."

The Easygoing Widow reached into her purse and gave him thirty gold ducats, in exchange for which he made a mask that looked exactly like Lauseta.

As Carmesina strolled about the garden, she saw Lauseta pruning an orange tree and stopped to talk with him, while the Easygoing Widow, who had returned, signaled to our knight. He turned around, saw them chatting, and thought to himself: "Ah, that wicked widow! She still hopes to trick me, but no matter what she says or does, she will never convince me of such evil, nor shall I believe her until I see it with my own eyes."

At this point, the emperor summoned a maiden and said: "Praxidis, tell my daughter to ask our captain when he will depart, for young knights often heed damsels more than their fathers."

The princess replied that she would obey his orders, and, after talking with Lauseta about the orange trees and myrtle, she continued her walk through the imperial garden. When she was near Tirant, she told him she felt tired, whereupon he took her arm and they strolled about together. God knows how comforted the poor knight felt, and as soon as they were out of hearing he began to speak thus:

· CCLXX ·

*T*IRANT'S AMOROUS WORDS

"You could make me the happiest knight alive by keeping faith, but Fortune's wheel has turned and I find no steadfastness in Your Highness, who mocks me with sweet lies and robs me of my just deserts. If the Fates only pitied me and granted part of my desires, I would be the most glorious knight ever born, yet now, alas, I am sustained only by a last scrap of hope. If you heard my laments, they would surely move you to compassion, since those of noble lineage should not imitate the wicked."

Restraining her tears, the virtuous lady replied:

· CCLXXI ·

*T*HE PRINCESS'S REPLY TO TIRANT

"Indescribable agonies afflict my heart, since the end of one ill is the beginning of another, and though some consider me fortunate in love, they do not know of my enamored sufferings. Never have I been so tormented by passion, but to give my spirit repose I shall now grant your request, wherefore I ask you to take my right hand." Once Tirant had clasped her hand, the princess continued: "That this may be a true marriage, I declare that I, Carmesina, offer you, Tirant, my body as a faithful wife, and I take you as my faithful husband."[79]

When Tirant, as is customary, had repeated these same words or similar ones, the princess said: "Let us kiss in sign of troth, as Saint Peter and Saint Paul require. They shall be our only witnesses, and in the name of the Holy Trinity I give you full powers over my goods and person, swearing before those two saintly judges, Saint Peter and Saint Paul, that I come to you unblemished and shall be yours all my life. Tirant, never doubt my word, for though I have sometimes been cruel, my spirit is always with you, whom I worship as a god. As my age increases so does my love, yet fear of disgrace has made me guard my virginity, which I hoped to bring intact to our blessed marriage bed. Henceforth, however, I shall give you love's rewards, so be of good cheer and cherish my honor as your life. The worst of my woes is to know that you must soon leave me, and for this reason alone I have withheld the joy you deserve, but soon I shall place my very life in your hands."

Tirant, showing his solace, then smiled at his beloved.

· CCLXXII ·

*H*OW TIRANT SWORE TO BE FAITHFUL TO HIS PRINCESS

Tirant's heart leapt up when he saw he would soon rule the Greek Empire and heard how sweetly his lady had declared her love, for in his happiness he felt certain that he could conquer the world. He was especially eager to tell his cousin Diaphebus, since he thought that everyone would rejoice in his good fortune, but to be absolutely certain, he took out a holy relic with a splinter of *lignum crucis,* on which that chaste damsel's Son had placed His precious shoulder. He gave it to his princess, asking her to swear that she had spoken with pure devotion. Once she had done so, he said: "My lady, knowing that Your Highness would like me to swear the same oath, I promise to serve you faithfully all the days of my life."

In reply, the princess renounced any rights under imperial law that might be to her benefit or to Tirant's detriment.

When all this had been done, Tirant knelt on the hard ground and tried to kiss her hands, as he revered her more than any saint in Heaven. She refused to let him, and after receiving his thanks, the virtuous damsel continued in the following manner:

· CCLXXIII ·

THE PRINCESS'S REPLY TO TIRANT

"Youth and fear of scandal have kept me silent, and despite my great devotion I withheld part of your guerdon, but once your conquests are complete you shall harvest love's fruits in holy matrimony, ruling both me and the empire you bravely succored. Do not grow impatient, for this world's glories must be won through travails and my heart's greatest joy is to love and serve you. Who could separate two wills so united unless you choose to sunder them yourself? The greatest harm that can befall me is to leave your side, though I take comfort in the thought of your quick and victorious return. Command me as my lord, and I shall do your bidding."

In a voice trembling with joy, Tirant replied:

· CCLXXIV ·

TIRANT'S REPLY TO THE PRINCESS

"Never have I felt such sovereign bliss, for I see that Your Highness has yielded to my pleas. Had I served you all my life, I would not merit the favors of one who, though young in years, is old in royal wisdom. Thus have you shown yourself by rewarding my feeble efforts, as a princess should only offer gifts of great value, but much as I cherish your vows, an hour without you seems infinite, and I fear that for my sins what I seek will be denied me. Therefore, if you will but let me taste that promised glory, I swear to do nothing against your will, since you are my deity whom I worship like God."

The princess sweetly replied:

· CCLXXV ·

*H*OW THE EMPEROR ORDERED A GREAT FEAST IN TIRANT'S HONOR

"No other mortal is so full of love as you, and your merits will triumph in this world and the next, just as your efforts to augment the Church will live forever in men's memories. I cannot entirely reject your supplications, for I do not wish to offend such a lord, yet shame and fear oblige me to guard my chastity. I have almost lost my wits, as I dread to vex my father, and how often have I thought: 'This man has no scruples.' Therefore, though I should flee you, blushing at my own desires and begging you to postpone such matters lest my reputation suffer, I now give you leave to speak with Pleasure-of-my-life, by whose arrangements I promise to abide."

Then they kissed many times behind an orange grove that concealed them.

Upon returning to her father, the princess saw that he was pensive and asked: "My lord, what are you pondering?"

The emperor replied: "Daughter, I plan to hold a feast tomorrow in honor of Tirant's triumphs, and for each of them, a flag with his arms shall adorn the main altar in our cathedral. His love of the public weal has been this empire's salvation."

Once His Majesty's words had been written down as an example to all present and future knights, he summoned his council, to whom he disclosed his plans. They all praised him, saying it was nobly done, and after counting, they found that in four and a half years, Tirant had reconquered three hundred and seventy-two towns, cities, and castles.

Upon learning why the imperial council had been convened, Tirant hastily returned to his lodgings. He refused to attend lest he hear himself praised, and also because there are always disputes in councils of great lords and he did not wish to hear His Highness contradicted. When the council had ended, the emperor sent for his drapers, and the next morning Tirant's flags were all ready.

Tirant found Hippolytus and said: "Summon Pleasure-of-my-life to the great hall, where I shall await her."

Hippolytus carried out his mission, and at the sight of his friend, Tirant embraced her and took her hand. Then they sat down by one of the windows, and he began to speak thus:

· CCLXXVI ·

TIRANT'S PLEAS TO PLEASURE-OF-MY-LIFE

"I commend all my hopes, gracious damsel, to your wisdom, for I am nothing without your aid and counsel. My weary mind knows no peace and I dream with open eyes, wishing to sleep my life away like Saint John the Baptist,[80] on whose feast day Christians, Saracens, and Jews all rejoice. They say his soul sleeps, lest by entering Heaven he forfeit some of his glory, and I, like him, love one of peerless virtue. As I adore and contemplate her, I recite this prayer: 'Oh merciful earthly goddess who began my sorrows! Fortify my soul, ease my sufferings, and cure my tribulations!' Sister, look how I strive to serve my lady and how often I have braved cruel battle for her sake. Does my steadfast devotion deserve such torments? I was ignorant of her perfect love, but now we have spoken words of peace and she has sworn to do whatever you and I devise. We decided that I should tell you my present and future woes, in the hope that you might enable me to speak with her tonight. Then she clasped my hand, vowing to take me as her servant, husband, and lord and promising to let me share her bed of bliss. You hold the key to my joy and sorrow, wherefore I implore you to cure my affliction."

Hearing Tirant's laments, Pleasure-of-my-life thought for a moment and then replied:

· CCLXXVII ·

PLEASURE-OF-MY-LIFE'S REPLY TO TIRANT

"Words reveal our intentions, which otherwise would be known only to God. My mother was born in Rome, and my ancestors were noble Roman warriors who wore crowns of triumphant victory and were linked by blood with the Greek Empire. I shall not glory in my lineage, for there is no need, but as a helper of true lovers I say: Tirant, lord of the world, why have you spoken so fearfully? Are you unaware that my heart, will, and wits are at your service? Rest assured that I shall do everything in my power to help you, whom I loved in my cradle and shall adore in my grave. Many women surpass me in wisdom and beauty but none in steadfast devotion. I shall detain you no longer, as a knight about to enter battle should not be wearied, and when the emperor is at supper I shall tell you what to do."

After joyously kissing her, Tirant departed while Pleasure-of-my-life returned to the garden, where she found Carmesina and her father talking about the flags.

Once the drapers had left, the emperor went upstairs and the two damsels stayed behind to determine when Tirant should come. The princess repeated everything she and our knight had said, and Pleasure-of-my-life was pleased to see her mistress so happy.

As soon as it was time for supper, Tirant hurried to the palace, where he found Pleasure-of-my-life waiting at the head of the stairs. She told him when to return and exactly what to do.

When everyone was fast asleep, the princess rose from her bed and donned a bridal gown the emperor had given her. It was the richest gown in Christendom at that time, for the cloth was crimson satin, embroidered with so many pearls that between the mantle and skirt, there must have been two bushels of them. Carmesina's mantle was lined with ermine, and she wore a dazzling imperial crown that glittered in the light shed by Pleasure-of-my-life's torch. When the clock struck eleven, Tirant hurried to the garden gate, and as he was climbing the stairs he met the princess's confidant Damsel Montblanc, who knelt and said: "The best knight on earth and lord of the fairest lady."

Tirant replied: "May you have all your wishes, damsel."

Then they entered an alcove, where they waited for Pleasure-of-my-life, who arrived feeling happier than Paris the day he abducted Helen and led them into another room, which the princess entered through a separate door. After embracing joyfully, the lovers knelt and shared such a long and pleasant kiss that one could have walked a mile before it ended. Pleasure-of-my-life, who was feeling uneasy, approached them and said: "I declare you good and steadfast lovers, but I shall not quit this battle-field till I see you bedded, nor shall I consider you a knight if you leave without shedding blood."

They rose, and after placing her crown upon Tirant's head, Carmesina knelt before him and began to speak thus:

· CCLXXVIII ·

THE PRINCESS'S PRAYER FOR TIRANT

"Oh Lord Jesus Christ, omnipotent and compassionate, who pitied mankind, descended to earth, and assumed human form, dying on the true cross to be resurrected the third day: true God and true man! When my father dies, may it please Your Holy Majesty to give Tirant his crown and empire, for just as he saved us from the infidel's power, so may his reign augment Your glory and the Holy Catholic Faith."

Having finished her prayer, the princess picked up a pair of scales her father used to weigh gold and said: "Lord Tirant, Fortune has been pleased to subject my will to yours without my parents' consent or that of the Greek people. Behold these scales: on the right you see love, honor, and chastity, while on the left you will find only shame, infamy, and grief. Which do you choose?"

Tirant, who always sought to serve honor, touched the pan on the right and said: "Before I met you, I heard your name on wise men's lips as they told me of your virtues, which my eyes have now beheld. To uphold my faith, I shall always shun error and sin, wherefore I choose what accords with my will."

He took the right pan, saying: "I hold love and honor dearer than this crown. Your Highness knows how I long to see your perfections, and if I can trust your promises and my supplications move you, let us now consummate our marriage."

The princess replied:

· CCLXXIX ·

*T*HE PRINCESS'S REPLY TO TIRANT

"You betray your chivalry, for worthy knights shun sinful loves, and I thought you would protect me from undeserved scandal, wherefore I ask you, who have embraced the scale of love, not to forsake your accustomed nobility. Should you disobey your beloved, my parents and the Greek people will say that no one should trust me, whereupon I shall be disinherited and unable to give you money, jewels, or clothing. After you are banished, who will champion my good name, and if I become pregnant, what shall I do? I tell you, my lord: I have gone too far to turn back, and if I yield to you now, I cannot hide from God. As your wife I have sworn obedience, but remember: all that glitters is not gold. Think of the harm that will befall us when, locked in a tower, I call out to one who will no longer hear me, while my offenses make me odious to God and man. Tirant, you will be my master until I die, and though I received my soul from God, my body and goods are yours. Should you contravene my will, you will be both culprit and judge, and when I think how everyone will stare at me, I am overcome by shame!"

Unable to tolerate further lamentations, Tirant laughed and replied in the following manner:

· CCLXXX ·

TIRANT'S REPLY TO THE PRINCESS

"My lady, long have I waited to see you in your nightgown or naked. I desire not your sovereignty but my rights as the Church commands: 'Any man who honorably marries a damsel and does not copulate with her when he may commits a mortal sin.' It seems to me that if you cherish my body you should forbid me to damn my soul, as those who bear arms are already cursed."

As he spoke, Tirant began to remove his lady's skirt, kissing her many times and saying: "An hour's delay is like a year, and I fear to lose what God has so generously granted me."

Pleasure-of-my-life said: "Alas, my lord! Why wait to be in bed? Do it on her robes, that they may bear witness. We shall close our eyes and say we saw nothing, whereas if you wait for her to undress you will be waiting all night! Afterward, Our Lord will punish you as a recalcitrant lover, taking away this morsel and never granting you another, for any real man would swallow it whole even if it choked him."

The princess replied: "Be quiet, enemy of virtue! I never imagined you were so cruel! Until today I loved you as a daughter or sister, but now you seek my ruin like a wicked stepmother."

By this time, Tirant had undressed Carmesina and placed her on the bed, where she found herself in a tight pass, since her knight, who had disrobed and lain down beside her, now brought out his artillery and tried to storm the castle. Unable to defend herself by force of arms, she thought her feminine wiles might save the day, and with tears streaming down her cheeks she began to speak thus:

· CCLXXXI ·

THE PRINCESS'S LAMENT AS SHE LAY IN TIRANT'S ARMS

"With trembling hand I shall dry my sad eyes, for alas, how many sorrowful pleas you have rejected! Pity my weakness and fear of disgrace, as my love will sour if you take me by force, and you will feel more confounded than Lucifer when he fell from Heaven. I seek to shield you from so monstrous an error, nor do I wish to think you prefer your pleasure to my honor. May God forbid so little love to dwell in a French soul of Breton lineage! Tirant, imagine what misfortunes await you, abide by reason, restrain your lustful appetites, and chasten unwise desires with noble deeds. Since love conquers all, including friendship and God's commandments, you should not make me hate you but resist sinful inclinations."

As the princess uttered these laments, her eyes wept abundant tears.

Seeing his lady's distress and hearing her wise and piteous words, Tirant decided to prove his devotion and yield to her will. Even so, the two lovers slept little that night as they played and made merry, sometimes at the head of the bed and sometimes at the foot. They caressed each other often and both felt very happy, but when the palace began to stir, Carmesina sadly said: "Alas, that the sun should rise so soon! Would that our pleasure might last a year or never end. Arise, lord of the Greek Empire; tomorrow you may return to the same place."

Tirant rose and sadly said: "I shall do as you command, but I fear my heart will find no solace."

Having covered her face with kisses as they said goodbye, our knight slipped away feeling very downcast, and when he had gone, Pleasure-of-my-life could scarcely contain her wrath. The princess quickly summoned her and Damsel Montblanc, whom she told what had happened, to which Pleasure-of-my-life replied: "May God curse you both! You have the pleasure while I am left with the blame, yet what grieves me most is that nothing happened! Let me see that recreant, vanquished knight and I shall tell him what I think of him, nor should he seek my help henceforth, as I shall harm him however I can."

"On my faith," said Damsel Montblanc, "he has shown his virtue as befits a brave and courteous captain, sacrificing his pleasure lest his lady be offended."

They went on talking till the sun had risen and the emperor summoned the empress, his daughter, and their ladies to the feast. Likewise, he invited all the gentlefolk in the city, and though God knows the princess would have sooner slept than left her chamber, for love of Tirant she donned her finest robes. Then they entered the great hall, where her father awaited them, and after forming a procession they bore their two hundred and seventy-two flags to the cathedral.

Tirant approached his lady, who sweetly welcomed him with these words: "Tirant, my lord, I give you everything I possess."

Tirant did not dare to reply because the empress was nearby.

A solemn Mass began, and as the worshippers were crossing themselves at the fount, the first of Tirant's flags was hung upon the altar. During Confession they put up another and another after each psalm and antiphon, so that by the time the service ended, all the flags were in place. Tirant stood neither in his usual spot nor near the emperor but took his prayer book into a chapel that had a good view of his lady, and in fact our knight prayed very little during that Mass. I do not know about Carmesina, but throughout the divine rites she kept her eyes so fixed on the Breton that people started whispering.

When Mass was over, everyone went to a square near the palace, which they found covered with red carpets and full of tables heaped with food, for their generous lord always sought to honor worthy knights. The emperor decreed a week of feasting during which everyone could eat at his tables, but misfortune, that enemy of every virtue, refused to grant his wishes.

After the lords and ladies had dined, there were dances in the square, while Carmesina quietly made her way to the palace. She ordered her room locked, undressed down to her skirt, and led her two damsels to the treasure tower, where they weighed out a mule-load of ducats that Pleasure-of-my-life then bore to Tirant's lodgings. Once the princess had dressed again, she returned to her father's side, and seeing Tirant nearby, she whispered in his ear: "Your hands have touched all my riches."

Tirant replied: "Great is my glory that they have learned this new trade."

The emperor asked: "What are you two whispering about?"

"My lord," replied the princess, "I was asking Tirant if there would be tournaments and jousts at these glorious festivities, but he said no, for he expected to hold them with the Turks."

"This is the best news I could hope to hear!" exclaimed the emperor. "And do you feel well enough to depart?"

"Yes, by Saint Mary!" cried Tirant. "When the feasts are over, I shall set out with the doctors."

As they were talking, Pleasure-of-my-life beckoned Tirant.

As soon as Tirant saw His Majesty chatting with some others, he made his way to Pleasure-of-my-life and asked what she wanted, to which she replied in the following manner:

· CCLXXXII ·

H OW PLEASURE-OF-MY-LIFE ASSAULTED TIRANT WITH WORDS

"By rights, my lord, you should lose the prize of your travails, as your negligence and clumsiness deserve no further rewards. You were defeated through your own fault, and may you never have a second chance! You need the Easygoing Widow, who will certainly treat you as you deserve, nor should I ever have helped you, the most reprobate lover ever born. Were I a man, I would challenge you to a duel, for you were in bed with the fairest and loftiest damsel on earth, yet you cravenly yielded to her tears and supplications. If she lay down a virgin, she got up one too, much to your shame and eternal discredit. No gentlewoman who knows your history will ever befriend you, but rather they will all hold you vile and common. I shall speak no more of such scandalous outrages and only wish to say that His Majesty awaits you. I have just come from your lodgings; here is the key to your chamber. I asked them to give it to me lest anyone read what you will find there."

Tirant would have liked to answer Pleasure-of-my-life, but he could not because the emperor then ordered him to be seated, while His Highness, the empress, Carmesina, and their damsels served him. For three hours the other guests listened to an old knight experienced in arms, an eloquent jurist who began to recount Tirant's deeds, which were so wondrous that the lords and ladies forgot about their food. Once Tirant had finished eating, the elderly knight stopped his recital.

Then the others ate, each seated according to his station, and after lunch they went to the market square, which they found splendidly adorned with rich silk hangings. There they watched a fight between wild bulls, a most delightful entertainment, and thus they devoted the entire day to mirth and revelry.

That night, there was an abundant supper as sumptuous as the lunch, followed by dances, masques, and mummery as such a glorious feast warranted. The entertainment lasted most of the night, since the emperor refused to leave till just before dawn. The princess rejoiced in her beloved's sight, and though they could speak but little for fear of her father, nonetheless Tirant did whisper: "My lady, last night was certainly more pleasant and honorable than this."

Pleasure-of-my-life quickly retorted: "Your Lordship speaks brave words, but your deeds belie them."

When the emperor beheld the first signs of dawn, he rose and urged everyone to escort their captain to his lodgings. Tirant thanked him for the honor and then offered to accompany him to the palace, but His Valiant Majesty nobly refused.

Tirant, who expected to find an angry letter from Pleasure-of-my-life in his chamber, instead beheld the sacks full of gold. Amazed at the princess's kindness and devotion, he told Hippolytus to store her gift in a safe place.

When it was time for Mass, the lords assembled to continue their feasting, but Tirant had no chance to thank his beloved till after lunch. If there had been merriment the first day, there was so much more the second that one could never describe it all. Once the meal had ended, they urged the emperor to sleep a little and everyone agreed to meet again after His Majesty had rested. As the ladies were setting out for the palace, Tirant whispered in his princess's ear: "My soul cannot encompass nor my tongue express all the love and honor Your Highness shows me."

She did not dare to say much, seeing her father nearby, and therefore only replied: "You are my lord, and I am your servant. If I do not help my master, whom shall I help? What I have done is nothing beside what I plan to do, yet if you want more, our treasury doors are as open to you as they are shut to all others."

While our knight was thanking her, they entered His Majesty's chamber. Only the Easygoing Widow stayed outside, waiting for Tirant at the head of the stairs. She had marshaled all her wiles to commit an unheard-of crime, and upon seeing the Breton, she smiled and sweetly said:

· CCLXXXIII ·

THE WICKED WIDOW'S LIE

"I am not surprised that you seek to subdue the world, as you have certainly vanquished my heart. Fortune, that enemy of mankind's peace, has overwhelmed my frail spirit with pity, and thus I must speak, seeing that of your own free will you foolishly prepare to drown in a calm sea. You wander blindly over a precipice from which I alone wish to save you, wherefore if you seek happiness, you must pray for my soul. Only madmen brave God's fury and that of their fellow men, and in two hours, Lord Tirant, you shall see everything I described to you."

Tirant said he was ready whenever she wished.

The widow quickly made her way to an old woman's cottage at one end of the garden, where she hung rich tapestries around a splendid bed. The princess, who was very tired, had taken off her clothes to sleep.

When the rabid widow saw that the appointed hour had come, she went to meet Tirant and made him swear mighty oaths. He disguised himself and together they went to the borrowed cottage, which had a small window that looked out upon the entire garden, but the window was so high that one needed a ladder to reach it. Having found two big mirrors, the widow placed one opposite the window and the other below it, or to explain her device more clearly: if a man's back is hurt, how can he inspect his wound? He must take two mirrors, hang one on the wall, and hold the other in his hand. The wound will be reflected in the first mirror and then in the second.

Once the widow had finished, she hurried to the palace, where she found the princess in bed and cried: "Arise, my lady! Your father forbids you to sleep, for you slept little last night and if you nap in this hot weather, many illnesses could harm your body."

She flung open the shutters to keep the princess from sleeping, and Carmesina let her do so in deference to His Majesty. Then she rose, donned a skirt, and stood there half-dressed, with her breasts uncovered and her tresses unpinned. The widow said: "Your doctors advise you to admire the flowers in the palace garden, where we shall play some games to help rouse you from your lethargy. I have a costume for Corpus Christi that looks like our gardener's clothes, and Pleasure-of-my-life, who is so witty, will put it on to amuse you."

The widow, Carmesina, and her two damsels went down to the garden, where Tirant, who was looking in the mirror, saw his beloved seat herself by a stream. Having sent the black to Pera lest he interrupt their merriment, the widow helped Pleasure-of-my-life dress and gave her the mask. Then the damsel entered the garden attired in Lauseta's clothes, and when Tirant saw her, he truly believed she was the Moor. Over one shoulder she carried a spade with which she started to dig, and after a short while she sat down beside the princess. Having kissed Carmesina's hands, she began to caress her breasts, fondling the nipples and speaking sweet words of love. The princess laughed so hard that she forgot her weariness, while the damsel edged closer and felt beneath her mistress's skirt. Everyone was delighted by Pleasure-of-my-life's pleasantries, but the widow turned toward the cottage, wrung her hands, and spat in disgust.

Think of poor Tirant! The day before he had been proud to possess such a lofty wife, and now his eyes were forced to behold his undoing. He wondered if the mirrors might be false or fashioned by black magic, yet upon breaking them open, he found nothing of the kind. Then he decided to look out the window and see how it all would end. Having cut a draw cord from the curtain, thrown it over a beam, and hoisted himself up, he saw the gardener lead Carmesina into the hut where he slept and kept his tools. The damsels found his chest and, after examining its contents, they emerged and started strolling about near the cottage. To ensure that everyone kept laughing, the widow gave the damsel a kerchief and said: "Now tie this cloth under the princess's skirt."

Kneeling before Carmesina, Pleasure-of-my-life tied it between her legs, whereby the princess's ignorance abetted the widow's malice.[81]

Tormented by such foul sights, Tirant began to lament thus: "Oh Fortune, enemy of those who wish to live virtuously! Why do you force me to gaze upon what no mortal has yet imagined, though women are certainly capable of any sin? Alas, cruel Fates, what have I done that you should curse me so in love? First you granted me a marriage far above my station—one I gained through my travails and your generosity—and now you defile me all the more, allowing a man of the lowest type to shame me. Oh lady princess! How can you foolishly think that after binding me with oaths, you can abuse not only God but your parents and husband? I never dreamt that one so young could commit such audacious crimes! Oh Fortune, ease my lamentations lest I do something I shall regret. Unlucky servant, I am spurned by my mistress and hateful to myself!"

At this point, the Easygoing Widow entered and beheld Tirant's tears. She had heard his speech and thought: "Now my schemes are on the right path."

The widow then sat down beside him, ready to profit from his grief, and upon hearing his moans continue she comforted him in the following manner:

· CCLXXXIV ·

HOW THE EASYGOING WIDOW COMFORTED TIRANT

"Moved by that love of virtue to which Nature inclines us, I behold your lost honor and can find no solace. Having performed such noble feats of arms, you deserve better of your beloved, who prefers lead to gold and merits condemnation. Neither pleas nor threats can move her, for she exults in her desires. Alas, woe is me! Whatever shall I do? With these breasts"—and she showed them to Tirant—"I nursed that cruel lady."

She left her breasts exposed for a long time, pretending to be so carried away by grief that she had forgotten they were visible. Meanwhile, she continued: "Lord Tirant, take whatever comfort I can give you. God Almighty, Holy Trinity! I too have wept blood! Thus did I show with what fury, tears, and anguish such thoughts assailed my soul. My yellow countenance filled my sad chambers with melancholy! Bitter regrets inflamed my grief, and I raved deliriously! At night I found myself alone, wearied by sorrow and drying my tearful eyes with sackcloth to augment my torments."

Tirant quickly replied:

· CCLXXXV ·

*T*IRANT'S REPLY TO THE EASYGOING WIDOW

"The wretched are comforted when someone shares their tribulations, but your love, lady widow, cannot equal mine, since yours descends and diminishes while mine ascends and grows. Mine will only stop when it becomes celestial bliss, and truly, no knight ever felt such enamored sorrow! Yesterday I stood on love's highest peak, yet now I am the most confounded suitor alive, for my eyes have seen a black Moor gain what has always been denied me, though I have often risked my life in that lady's service. One so ill-fated should cease to be, as only thus shall I be freed."

He rose to go, but the widow said: "My lord, stay a moment lest those outside behold you. I shall keep watch at the window and tell you when it is safe to leave."

Tirant returned to the bed, lamenting his sorrows, while the widow entered the old lady's bedroom. There she donned a perfumed blouse and black velvet skirt as boldly as any knight about to enter battle, and without buttoning her clothes she approached Tirant and addressed him thus:

· CCLXXXVI ·

*T*HE EASYGOING WIDOW'S DECLARATION OF LOVE

"Were you cognizant of the afflictions my weary soul sustains, you would pity me, knowing there is nothing as strong as love. Oh brave knight, how often have I prayed and lit candles for your sake! How many alms and fasts have I offered, lacerating my body that yours might be preserved! Mine were the sacrifices, but the princess hoped to reap the rewards, for never did any woman love virtue as much as I. My only excess is loving you too dearly, wherefore, if you wish to triumph, let me serve you in your tents and lodgings and spurn that deceitful damsel, who is subject to a black slave. She has betrayed her father; how can she honor her husband? She has tricked her mother; how much more so her lover! Ladies of honor will never say the Easygoing Widow served any man unworthy of a royal crown, nor indeed have I ever betrayed my husband's memory. What will brave knights think when they hear of her conduct, and how will they judge Your Lordship if you should marry her? Having been forewarned, you will deserve whatever harm may befall you. Lord Tirant, love the one who loves you, forget those who wish you ill, and, though it is improper for me to say so, take me as your slave. True lovers care nothing for riches or lineage but only for honor, chastity, loyalty, and devotion."

"My lady," replied Tirant, "trouble my soul no further, as it longs to forsake my body and I understand nothing of what you say. Waste no more words, for I could no more forget Her Highness than renounce my faith."

The widow said: "Then if you refuse to have me, let me sit awhile by your side."

She pulled off her skirt, which she had left unfastened. Seeing her half naked, Tirant leapt to his feet, flung open the door, and returned to his lodgings feeling as miserable as the widow.

He arrived in such distress that he scarcely knew what to do. Tears streamed down his cheeks as he paced to and fro, and thus, pacing and lying down and getting up, his torment lasted three hours.

Finally Tirant disguised himself, slipped out of his quarters, and made his way to the garden, where he beheld Lauseta, who had just returned and was donning some red breeches. Our knight seized his hair, dragged him into the hut, and quickly beheaded him, nor did anyone witness his crime, since they were all at the feast. Having returned to his lodgings, Tirant cried out in fury: "Oh just and true God who corrects our errors, I demand not justice but vengeance from my depraved lady! Tell me, pitiless damsel: did my appearance please you less than that black gardener's? Had you loved me as I believed, you would still be mine today, but now I see that you never cherished me at all."

Let us now leave Tirant to his doleful laments and return to the emperor, who was preparing to attend the feast. A messenger arrived with news of a most unfortunate quarrel that had broken out three days earlier in the camp.

The Dukes of Macedonia and Pera, who shared the captaincy, had often sallied forth together. A multitude had died on both sides but for every dead Christian there were thirty Saracen casualties, for as soon as their foes approached, the Greeks flooded the river and irrigation channels, and thus many infidels had perished upon the slippery clayish soil.

One unlucky day the Turks sent four thousand workmen who, equipped with shovels, panniers, pickaxes, and fire, began to cut through a mountain so that the water from Saint George would flow into a dry river bed on the other side. About a league away, there was a deserted village with a stretch of broken wall where the Saracen infantry encamped one night, while the cavalry hid in a nearby wood. On the morrow, the Greek scouts reported these movements, and after holding council, the Christians decided to attack.

First they dispatched more scouts, who upon their return said the enemy was trying to cut through the mountain. The Christians set out to meet them, and a fierce skirmish ensued, which lasted for quite a while with many deaths on both sides. Finally, late that morning, the Turks began to feel hard-pressed and, abandoning their tools, they fled toward a marshy pass half a league away. The pass was difficult to ride through, but once the Turkish horsemen reached the other side they had a great advantage and galloped away as fast as they could, leaving their workmen to the advancing Christians. The Saracen cavalry then regrouped in that deserted village, which turned out to be less deserted than their enemies thought. The invaders fortified themselves behind the broken wall, while the Duke of Macedonia said: "My lords, I think we should venture no further, as we do not know what traps these infidels have laid."

The Duke of Pera, moved by jealousy, began a malicious speech:

· CCLXXXVII ·

THE DUKE OF PERA'S VICIOUS ATTACK ON THE DUKE OF MACEDONIA

"Oh Breton, you show your inexperience by predicting your own defeat," and heaving a deep sigh, the duke furiously cried: "Your body should not be buried but burned for such infamy, and all knights should blush in shame at your memory. Now is the time to show your courage, if indeed you possess any. Follow reason's dictates and return to the city, for you will feel happier among ladies than in battle, from which you shrink so cravenly."

The Duke of Macedonia decided to hold his peace lest he divide the knights and set them fighting among themselves, but all the same he could not resist uttering these words:

· CCLXXXVIII ·

*T*HE DUKE OF MACEDONIA'S REPLY

"Duke of Pera, instead of speaking you should make the sign of the cross, since everyone here knows which of us has won more honors. I, the Duke of Macedonia, have always been victorious and you, the Duke of Pera, have been vanquished and humiliated. Do not seek to persuade others of your valor when you are nought but an errant knave, for your guilt and perpetual infamy will be all the greater. A worthy knight will risk his life a hundred times rather than be accused of cowardice, and I declare that if you outlive me—however I may die—my ghost will haunt you relentlessly forevermore."

At this point, the other knights intervened and calmed them. Some thought they should return to the city while others wished to give battle, as is always the case when you have more than one captain. Thus does Aristotle say a captain should be both valiant and old, because old knights possess more wisdom and experience. Likewise, Caesar says a captain must treat his enemies as doctors treat illnesses, vanquishing some with starvation and others with iron. In the end they had to advance because the Duke of Pera said: "You can follow me or turn back as you please," and he rode off without a word.

Once they reached the deserted village, the Turks atop the broken wall attacked them fiercely, and as there was a ditch in front of it, the Christians had to dismount. They fought bravely with lances, having no other weapons, but then the sultan sallied forth from one gate and the Grand Turk from another, trapping their unfortunate foes between them. A great slaughter ensued, in which many men were taken prisoner, and indeed everyone who dismounted was killed or captured and only one knight escaped to tell the tale.

The Turks then returned to Bellpuig with their prisoners.

The emperor heard this news in the great hall as he awaited his ladies, who then shed bitter tears over their vanquished fathers, sons, husbands, and brothers. The emperor told them: "Oh grieving widows, tear your hair, beat your breasts, and dress in mourning, for the flower of Greek chivalry is lost forever! Oh Greece, I see you orphaned, widowed, and forsaken! Now I fear you will have a new master."

A great weeping and wailing arose in the palace, while doleful cries spread through the city, growing as they went. The emperor summoned Tirant to tell him the evil tidings, but upon reaching our knight's door, the chamberlain heard him lamenting thus: "Alas, woe is me! Ah, cruel Fortune! Would that you had killed me before letting me behold so foul a crime! Men will cover their ears lest they hear of such wickedness: that

Her Highness bestowed her favors upon a black Moorish infidel. Would that God had blinded me before I witnessed such an outrage, for had I died or lost my sight, my woes would be lessened. Oh evil widow, enemy of my happiness, would that I had never met you, as you will surely cause my destruction!"

The chamberlain, who heard Tirant's laments but could not make out his words from behind the door, cried: "Lord captain, be not dismayed, as it ill behooves a knight to complain of God's acts, and though we are in a sorry pass, we shall yet defeat our enemies. Do you not know the sun always rises after the cold and bitter night? To seek your own death shows more wrath than wisdom."

Tirant asked: "Who thus seeks to assuage my grief?"

The other replied: "I am one of His Majesty's chamberlains, whom he has sent to summon you."

With tears in his eyes, Tirant opened the door and said: "My friend, do not fret over my troubles or say a word to anyone. Tell your master I shall hasten to his side."

When the chamberlain was before the emperor, he said: "Sire, our captain already knows what happened, for his eyes betray him and I heard him lamenting bitterly."

He thought Tirant's anguish was caused by the bad news.

Tirant dressed in black, took his sword, and made his way to the palace, where he found everyone too distraught to speak.

Upon entering the great hall and seeing his lady on the floor surrounded by doctors, our knight exclaimed: "How can you let this pitiless lady die, when her guilt is great and her hope of Heaven small? I shall always fear for her life and pray God she may outlive me. Woe is me! I hold my life as nothing and blush to tell what I recall."

The doctors thought he was distressed by the bad news, while Tirant believed everyone was weeping on the princess's behalf. Turning around, he saw that the empress had torn her veils, skirt, and blouse. Both her breasts were visible, and she was clawing them and her face, crying out with all her damsels: "We shall be slaves! Who will pity us?"

On his other side, he beheld the emperor sitting on the floor like a statue, for he wanted to bewail his misfortune but could not. He gave the letter to Tirant, who read it and exclaimed: "This is worse than I thought!"

Then he comforted the emperor, saying: "Your Majesty should not be surprised, as such reverses always occur in war, where one is sometimes defeated, killed, or imprisoned. Being a knight, you should not let such events dismay you but take them calmly, since with God's help another day we shall triumph."

At this point the princess opened her eyes and summoned Tirant, whom she began to address in this fashion:

· CCLXXXIX ·

H OW THE PRINCESS SHARED HER WOES WITH TIRANT

"Oh, my soul's last hope, if words can move you and your love is true, let us not leave this world until those noblemen have been rescued. Only half an hour ago, my soul sought to flee, and surely it would have done so had I not seen my beloved."

As they were talking, two messengers arrived with news of the quarrel and their rout, in which five hundred knights had been killed or captured.

When they finished their sad tale, the court's grief redoubled, while tears flowed from the emperor's eyes and, though his tongue could barely speak, in a hoarse voice he began to bemoan his sorrows:

· CCXC ·

T HE EMPEROR'S LAMENT

"I grieve, though not for death, which no man can escape, yet how much worse when it comes in some base manner! May my heart be freed from shame, which makes me walk with troubled mien. Oh hapless captains, your suffering would afflict me more had I not warned you, but you, more willful than wise, preferred to follow your own whims. Having stained your reputations and emboldened spiteful tongues, you should now comfort each other and never think to see my face. Temper your grief, which you must endure, and rue your errors and previous sins, as those knights who do not share your guilt must bear a double burden, and I mourn both your broken faith and my unheeded commands."

His Majesty left the room, weeping bitterly and clutching his head, while the princess, who saw his anguish, then fainted again. The wisest doctor said: "I believe this lady is dead, for she has swooned three times and I cannot find her pulse."

Hearing these words, Tirant quickly cried: "Oh cruel and callous Death, why do you plague those who shun you and flee those who seek you? Would it not have been better to visit me before Her Highness? Though she has offended me, yet I wish to keep her company."

His sorrow was so great that he fainted too, falling on his leg and breaking it again worse than the first time. Blood poured from his nose and ears but still more from his wound, and according to the doctors it was a miracle that he survived. They quickly went to inform the emperor, who said with great sorrow: "I am not surprised, since all his companions are dead or captured, and this alone gives me hope that he will perform great deeds to free them."

The grieving emperor left his room and went to Tirant, but then he saw his daughter half dead and cried: "God help me; I scarcely know which one to aid first!"

He had the princess placed upon her bed, while Tirant was brought to a handsome chamber where they quickly undressed him, treated his wound, and tried to straighten his leg. He felt nothing, and it was thirty-six hours before he regained his senses.

Upon awakening, he asked who had brought him there, to which Hippolytus replied: "What, my lord? For two days you have tortured us, neither opening your eyes nor taking any nourishment, wherefore I beg you to eat what the doctors prescribe."

"I desire no restoratives," said Tirant, "as my sole wish is to die."

They quickly went to tell the emperor and his daughter. Then Tirant said: "Tell me how Her Highness fares."

Hippolytus replied: "My lord, she is much better."

"I can well believe," said Tirant, "that her pain is slight, since only a few days ago she had her wish. She is neither the first nor the last to defy God's commandments, but however sinful my death may be, let it pass without scandal. Not even wretched Ixion on his turning wheel can suffer as I do, and alas for the knight who cannot openly bewail his grief!"

At this point the emperor came in followed by the empress and her ladies, who all asked if Tirant could speak, but instead of greeting them he cried:

· CCXCI ·

TIRANT'S LAMENT

"Sad and wretched above all others, I shall soon grieve no more, for my misfortunes multiply and the cruel Fates ordain my downfall! Surely I do not deserve to end my life so woefully, but what torments me most is to think of those Turks being declared victors, for I know destruction awaits the Greeks, who will be punished for my sins."

Then he called for a crucifix, speaking with such sobs and sighs that it was hard to understand him: "Oh Merciful Lord, I, a wretched sinner, confess my failings and beg Your Holy Majesty to pardon my wicked deeds! I plead for mercy, recalling Your death to redeem all sinners, and Eternal God: when You pronounce Your last judgment, place me among the elect!"

Then he humbly embraced the cross, crying: "Oh Son of God, Almighty Jesus, I die for love as You died to save mankind! For love You endured beatings, wounds, and torture, just as I endured the sorrow of beholding that black Moor. Only You have suffered like me, and as Your Holy Mother endured infinite grief at the foot of the cross, so I endured mine with two mirrors and a cord in my hand, nor do I believe any Christian ever suffered more. Who can compare his sorrow with mine? Please excuse my clumsy words; grief has made me delirious, and forgive my sins as You forgave that thief and Mary Magdalene."

The emperor and his ladies, who were present along with the cardinal and many other ecclesiastics, all marveled at Tirant's words, for they had considered him a good Christian. Nonetheless, the cardinal absolved our knight of his sins, whereupon Tirant raised his head and cried: "Pitying listeners, heed my words and turn your thoughts to me in grief and sorrow. Friends, console each other, for your captain's death is near."

Then he turned to the princess, saying: "In sorrow I leave my body; my soul belongs to God. Never before did a knight die of woe, nor can anyone's sorrows compare with mine."

The emperor and the others all mourned his death, weeping copiously both for Tirant and for their plight. Then our knight turned to the emperor and tried to comfort him, saying with gentle mien and piteous voice: "Oh Lord God, save my soul! Alas, my eyes fail me! Let me behold Your splendor once I leave this vale of tears, for though my wound is not mortal, sorrow makes it so. Tell me, lord emperor: who will now champion you, when your knights are imprisoned and your humble servant is dead? My only regret is that I did not complete my conquests, and may God pardon the lady who caused me such woe! I did you no disservice but rather sought to exalt Your Highness, whose forgiveness I beg if I failed in any way, and you, my lady, the north wind before which sailors yield: all my life I would have aided you against those who did you wrong, yet now I can only lament what my eyes beheld. Alas! Who ever felt such grief as mine?"

Then he turned to the ladies and said: "Though misfortune has prevented me from rewarding you, please pray for my soul."

He lay down and told Hippolytus: "My son, behold how this wretched life ends. Look how changed my face is."

Seeing that Hippolytus's grief was such that he could not reply, Tirant told him: "Do not cry, for I have commended you all to my lord the emperor and I shall do so again. Lord emperor, if ever you saw my wish to serve you, I beg you now to retain my friends, relatives, and servants as your vassals."

The benign lord's anguish was so great that he could only reply: "It shall be done."

At that point Tirant's head dropped back on the pillow and his eyes closed. Everyone thought he was dead, and Hippolytus cried: "Oh Death, what now awaits me in my sorrow and misfortune?"

He wept bitterly over Tirant, whom he truly loved, and all our knight's servants thought he was on the brink of death. Hippolytus said: "If this knight dies, all chivalry will perish with him," and he shouted: "Oh lord Tirant, why do you refuse to hear your servants?"

Tirant replied: "Who calls me?"

"It is I, unlucky Hippolytus whom you cause such affliction, since all the ladies curse my abundant tears, saying: 'Blessed is the man who does no evil.' Do not pass away in misery, for death is the *ultimum terribilium.* Here is Lord Agramunt, who wishes to speak with you."

Hearing these words, Tirant opened his eyes and said: "You are most welcome, knights, to witness my last hours, and as it grieves me doubly to think of dying without rewarding you, I beg you to divide all my present and future wealth."

With a great effort, he raised his hand and reached out to those around him, while in a faltering voice he began to pray and kiss the crucifix: "Oh Almighty God, I thank Your Holy Majesty for letting me die in my friends' arms before the emperor. Though I have wronged You, forgive my sins and save my soul from perdition. Take vengeance on my flesh, but place me among Your saints."

Then he turned to his companions and asked: "Where is the flower of Breton chivalry? I bid you a sad farewell, unable even to raise my head, for the next world calls me and I must depart. Oh Diaphebus, Duke of Macedonia! Oh Viscount of Branches! For love of me you languish in Turkish dungeons. Who will free you now that the Fates have torn us asunder? Oh Diaphebus, what will you say when you learn of my lady's treachery? You who are here: serve the emperor in my stead and send my embalmed corpse to the worthy knights of Brittany, who should forbid my aged parents to gaze upon it. May the helmet, sword, and coat of arms I wore in battle be hung above my tomb, beside those four shields I won jousting with the lords of Poland, Friesland, Burgundy, and Bavaria. May a black Moorish head adorn my sepulcher, with these words inscribed around it: *The hateful cause of Tirant lo Blanc's demise.*"

The dying knight then asked everyone to be silent. None of the doctors knew how to save him, while the others could only weep, lament, and beat their breasts. They neither ate nor slept, knowing slavery's yoke awaited them, and certain that all was lost, they left the chamber in great sorrow.

The physicians tried many remedies but everything was in vain until an old Jewess heard of Tirant's illness and went before the emperor, whom she audaciously addressed in the following manner:

· CCXCII ·

*H*OW THE JEWESS SAID TIRANT COULD BE SAVED

"Natural love brings me before Your Majesty, whom pity moves me to save from destruction in his old age. All our hopes rest on that noble knight Tirant lo Blanc, for as Aristotle said, fear makes the coward tremble in time of peace, while a brave man fights on, preferring death to disgrace. This is well known among philosophers and sages. Look at Hector of Troy, who in such a case asked: 'What will the Greek Captain Palomides think of me? What will Agamemnon and Diomedes say?', but to get to the point, you see your captain on his deathbed. Your doctors have forsaken him, and I alone can help. If I fail, take my life or punish me as you please, but Tirant's courage will yet save him if you do as I say. First, have many knights enter his chamber, shouting and brandishing swords, lances, and shields with a mighty clash and tumult. When he awakes and beholds them, he will ask the cause of such turmoil, to which they should reply that the Turks are at the city gates, as courage will then vanquish grief and fear of shame will cure your captain."

Once the emperor's counselors had approved the Jewess's plan, such a mighty tumult arose that Tirant heard it long before anyone reached his room. The Jewess stood beside his bed, saying: "Arise, lord captain, and fear no evil, for your foes are at the city gates and have come for their revenge."

When Tirant heard the old woman's words, he asked: "Are the Turks really so near?"

"If you rise," the Jewess replied, "you will see they are much nearer than you think. Go to the window and behold what awaits you."

Once his leg had been bandaged, Tirant donned his finest armor and prepared for battle. So great was his ardor that he forgot most of his pain, but since he was weak, at the doctors' urging he took a restorative and ate some stew.

When he realized it was all a ruse, he said: "May God be praised, for He saved me from death when a woman had nearly killed me. The emperor and his physicians have done me a great service."

While Tirant was still in bed, Carmesina knelt before an image of the Virgin and, ignorant of the Jewess's schemes, she kissed the floor and prayed: "Oh merciful Queen of Heaven, hear my humble pleas! Pity me, for if my husband dies I shall have no choice but to kill myself." Then she took a knife and hid it under her skirts, thinking: "Better to die than be dishonored by Saracens. Oh Sinners' Advocate, save my body and soul!"

Beholding Tirant dressed and about to don his armor, Hippolytus hurried to the princess's chamber and cried: "My lady, grieve no more! Change your sad thoughts to sovereign bliss, as I bring the best tidings you could hope to hear."

The princess, for sheer excess of joy, remained seated and speechless for some time. Finally she asked: "Can this be true? I have wept so much that my eyes no longer see."

Hippolytus swore it was true, and the delighted princess kissed his forehead while tears of sovereign joy streamed down her cheeks. Then Hippolytus said: "My lady, no one should weep except for his sins, which are best forgotten."

With that, Hippolytus left and Carmesina went to her mother's chambers, where they stood at the windows watching the emperor return with their captain. As soon as Tirant saw them, he covered his face with his hands, and the empress asked why he had done so, for it is a sign of disappointment in love. The princess replied that she certainly did not know.

After dismounting at the palace gate, His Majesty asked Tirant to stay, but although the emperor promised to serve him well, our knight preferred to return to his lodgings. The princess wondered why he had spurned her father's pleas, since he had always striven to be near her, nor could she understand why he had covered his face.

When Tirant reached his chambers, he told Lord Agramunt and Hippolytus to arm and provision ten galleys. They said they would gladly do so and quickly had the vessels loaded.

Once lunch had ended, Tirant arranged everything necessary for his departure and sent his men overland to Malveí Castle, saying he would go by sea to join them. Toward evening, the doctors said Tirant was better, whereupon the princess, who longed to see him, sent her two damsels to his lodgings. As they approached, one of the captain's pages beheld them and gaily entered Tirant's chamber, saying: "My lord, rejoice, for two gallant damsels have come to visit you."

"Hurry to the door," replied Tirant, "and announce that I am sleeping peacefully."

The page did as he was told and excused his master, but as soon as she heard what had happened, the princess led her parents to our knight's lodgings. He learned that they were coming and gave his pages careful instructions, so that when the emperor was at the door, the wisest of them said: "Your Majesty will understand that no one can enter at this moment, for your captain is unwell and has had no rest for many days. His body is now recovering, and he is covered with sweat. It would be better if a doctor could go in without waking him."

Tirant climbed into bed, wrung a wet cloth out over his face, and pretended to be asleep. The doctor examined him and told the emperor: "My lord, it would be dangerous to awaken him now, wherefore we advise Your Highness to return tomorrow morning."

The princess felt too impatient to wait, but she also had to leave. After having his clothes packed and taken to a galley, Tirant himself slipped out toward midnight and would have sailed immediately had his friends been with him.

At dawn the trumpets called Tirant's men to their vessels, while he sent Lord Agramunt to His Majesty with the following message:

· CCXCIII ·

*H*OW TIRANT SENT LORD AGRAMUNT TO INFORM THE EMPEROR OF HIS DEPARTURE

"Fortune's mysterious whims often foil those who seek glory, as such knights are ignorant of the perils that may await them. New adventures are more boldly undertaken than those often seen, since men prize what they lack and long use can dull anything, but to come to my point, your captain is aboard his galley. Because of his wound, he will sail to the mouth of the Trasimene and then to Malveí Castle while his men ride overland, and he has sent me to inform you of his departure."

The emperor replied: "Knight, I am comforted by this news and thank God's grace for Tirant's recovery, which after Heaven was my fondest hope. My faith in his courage makes me indifferent to past woes, and to soothe my aging soul I shall regard him as a son. Tell him that although his deeds have always been splendid, in the future they should be far better, for his reward will be such as to fill him with joy."

After kissing the emperor's hand and bidding him farewell, Lord Agramunt went to the empress's chamber and took his leave of her and Carmesina.

When the royal ladies heard that their champions were about to leave, they lamented sorely and wept over their misfortune, but especially the princess, whom our knight had not bidden farewell. They hastened to ask the emperor if it was so, and upon learning of Tirant's plans, they persuaded His Majesty to meet them at the port. He arrived first and his boatmen rowed to the galley, where he commended his entire empire to noble Tirant, who welcomed him with great kindness and promised to do his utmost.

The sailors warned His Highness not to tarry, for a mighty thunderstorm was gathering, whereupon he departed, leaving his daughter in despair. The sea was too rough for any woman to brave it, and her father forbade her to set foot upon the boat. Carmesina, who saw no other solution, asked Pleasure-of-my-life to go to the galley and learn why Tirant had covered his face, refused to stay at the palace, and then slipped away without a word.

Pleasure-of-my-life understood her mistress's wishes and hid in a boat with Hippolytus and his company.

The empress's grief was indescribable when she saw Hippolytus board the galley.

Upon seeing Pleasure-of-my-life, Tirant sought to avoid her, but she insisted that he listen and began to speak thus:

· CCXCIV ·

PLEASURE-OF-MY-LIFE'S MISSION TO TIRANT

"Oh most praiseworthy knight, to whom Nature has given all, I have come to terminate my sad existence, yet I cannot forsake you nor do I deserve such punishment, for though my travails have been great, my wish to please you has caused my grief. Fortune, ever jealous of pleasures that last too long, has poisoned your love, which once took discreet and decorous paths, wherefore I shall no longer praise a captain who scorns my words and defames me. Oh pitiless knight, most valiant and noble! Who has thus befuddled your thoughts? Where are your sighing pleas? Where are your sad eyes filled with tears and the love you confessed so sweetly, and where are my trials and tribulations in your service? How can you forsake so virtuous a lady, the loftiest on earth? Cain did not spurn Abel as you do your beloved! If you want to slay her, depart in silence, but if you wish to save her, let her behold your countenance."

Having spoken, the damsel could no longer restrain her sobs and drew her cape over her face with deep sighs and moans.

Tirant replied in a voice so soft that no one else could hear him:

· CCXCV ·

*T*IRANT'S REPLY TO PLEASURE-OF-MY-LIFE

"Where shall I find the poison to end my bitter woe? Only death can cure me, for in losing life I shall lose the memory of an affliction greater than Pyrrus's largesse, Medea's anguish, Darius's might, Ariadne's misfortune, Jugurtha's cruelty, Canace's infamy,[82] and Dionysius's tyranny. I shall not recite the many ancient sorrows, which, being similar to mine, often console me in my doleful sepulture. I pity the lady who makes me suffer and dare not show my distress, yet if I spoke, all those who grieve would be comforted. Oh woman of evil seed, accomplice in my downfall! We foreigners should trust no one, as everything conspires against us, and though my hope of Heaven is bright and hers is pitch black, so supreme are her beauty and wisdom that only a madman would praise another.

"She feigned pleasure in my services and sought sweet words to reward my pains, but who can speak of such scandalous wrongdoing? In the end, she repaid me with the sight of herself and Lauseta sharing a lustful kiss that pierced me to the quick. Then they entered his hut, uttering amorous endearments, and when the widow appeared with a silk veil, he fastened it between my lady's thighs. What agonies assailed my soul at the sight of such behavior! I know not how I kept my hand from murdering—I shall not say whom—but that wretched wall forbade it, more their friend than mine, while the trees blushed for very shame at such a sight."

Then Tirant furiously continued: "Expect nothing from me, Pleasure-of-my-life, for had I seen you with the Easygoing Widow, I would fling you into the sea, yet as I did not, I beg you to leave me in peace, since you too are certainly privy to my lady's sins. After what I saw, I could not keep my sword from beheading him. Oh princess, enemy of honor! Death is your only hope! You want to know my sorrows but they cannot be told, as the air weeps to hear them and your ears would be appalled. Better you should die and live in glory than live and die in infamy! Alas, how cruel were your promises to me! To save myself from black despair, in which only my life was safe, I threw myself at your feet and told you my sorrows. The afflicted love to share their troubles with trusted friends, but you, damsel, should expect nothing from me. To forgive is my duty in death's retreat, which welcomes equally all who knock upon its door.

"Maddened by grief, I returned to my lodgings, pretending I wished to sleep and desired no company. I threw myself on my bed, uncertain whether to live or die, but I decided that to take my life would earn me perpetual guilt and infamy. Thus I pray God—for when the princess held me in her arms to her discredit and my scant delight, she excused herself with pleas and tears lest I discover her sin—to drown me and let my corpse drift upon the waves until it reaches my beloved."

When Pleasure-of-my-life heard the cause of Tirant's distress, she recalled the black gardener's mysterious demise. Though shaken, she nonetheless forced herself to continue, and with carefree gesture and cheerful mien she told Tirant and Hippolytus:

· CCXCVI ·

PLEASURE-OF-MY-LIFE'S REPLY

"How dare you slander my lady with cunning lies? You strive to stain her honor while feigning devotion, but do not think you will convince me with such deplorable words, for you could as easily empty the sea with a broken cup. You, who decided to fall in and out of love, should consider all this a dream, since only a recreant and foolish knight would believe such wicked falsehoods. What you saw was nothing but a game in which, to delight Carmesina, the widow lent me her Corpus Christi costume and I dressed up as Lauseta."

Then she told Tirant everything that had happened.

Tirant, who was amazed, then asked to see some proof, to which the damsel laughingly replied: "My lord, send Hippolytus to my chamber, where he will find a black mask under the bed. If I am not telling the truth, you may throw me overboard head first."

Tirant told Hippolytus to fetch the clothes quickly, as the waves were now high and the storm was fast approaching. By the time he returned, the sea was so rough that he could not board the galley, nor could Pleasure-of-my-life leave it. They threw a rope down to the boat and hoisted up the costume, at the sight of which the scales at last fell from Tirant's eyes. Swearing that if he could go ashore he would burn or slay the widow like that gardener, he begged Pleasure-of-my-life to forgive his base suspicions and apologize on his behalf. The damsel sweetly agreed, whereby friendship was restored between them.

The sea was so choppy that they prayed for Hippolytus and his crew, who reached shore soaked and with their boat half flooded. Fierce winds snapped the galleys' anchor cables, and the vessels drifted loose. Two of them ran aground and though their crews were saved, the ships were lost. Three more were driven into the tempest with broken masts and torn sails, while another was forced windward and ran aground on a small island. Tirant's galley and the other three were blown leeward with broken rudders, and still another ship split asunder and sank in the cruel sea. Everyone was drowned, and not one man escaped alive.

As Tirant's galley drifted toward Barbary, his sailors lost their bearings. Weeping and lamenting, they knelt and sang the *Salve Regina,* after which they confessed their sins and begged each other for absolution. Pleasure-of-my-life lay in bed more dead than alive, while Tirant comforted her as best he could and devoutly prayed to God:

TIRANT IN
NORTH AFRICA

· CCXCVII ·

*T*IRANT'S PRAYER IN THE MIDST OF THE STORM

"Oh Lord, true merciful and omnipotent God, what sad fate has brought me such hardship and misfortune? Alas, why do You drown me in these pitiless waters? After surviving such fierce battles, must I now die defenseless? Why did Lord Barrentowns not slay me if I am thus doomed to perish? Praise be unto God, who chastises my sins, as I do not grieve for my own demise but for this poor helpless damsel! Ah Tirant, what a sad and ill-fated day! Oh lady princess, phoenix of the world, if only I could see you before I die! Then I would apologize for my wrongs, though they were caused by the widow's lies. Oh wicked and deceitful widow! Would that I might punish your treachery, for you fear neither God nor disgrace in this world. We shall die for your sins, which will destroy the Greek Empire! Oh benign lord emperor, how you will mourn my passing! Oh knights of my company, who will rescue you from prison? Oh noble princess and wife, you were my sole consolation! May God preserve you from your enemies, increase your honor and esteem, and send another Tirant just as eager to serve you."

Pleasure-of-my-life could not help reproaching Tirant for complaining of his misfortunes:

·CCXCVIII·

PLEASURE-OF-MY-LIFE'S REPLY

"You are like a farmer who instead of wheat reaps empty husks, as you should curse yourself rather than Fortune, which has no power over your free will. Do you know what made you err? Your own ignorance of reason's dictates. Fortune allots things like wealth, rank, and power, but the decision to love or hate, to behave well or badly, to seek or shun is in each man's power."

Tirant quickly replied:

·CCXCIX·

TIRANT'S REPLY TO PLEASURE-OF-MY-LIFE'S WORDS, AND HOW THEIR VESSEL WAS WRECKED ON THE BARBARY COAST

"If your words are true, I shall not mourn my demise, but it grieves me to think you might die through my fault. Having lost Carmesina's favor, I am plagued by bad luck, as I know not what torments me most: love or misfortune. Let us discourse no further but pray for our souls, devoutly begging Jesus Christ to spare us both."

Turning away, our knight heard his men's cries of woe and saw his best sailor, the boatswain, lying crushed beneath the block of a great tackle. A galley slave approached Tirant and cried: "My lord, order the men to bail her out! Take this staff and start giving orders, for all your men are terrified. If we can round that cape we may yet be saved, and it is better to be captured by Moors than to lose our very lives."

Tirant looked up and asked: "Where are we?"

"My lord," replied the slave, "Sicily is that way, and we are not far from Tunis. Knowing your valor, I grieve more for you than for myself, since this storm may shortly wreck us on the cursed Barbary Coast."

Tirant rose, though he was so seasick that he could barely stand, and did what he could, but the cabins and storeroom were already flooded. Then he donned his noblest clothes and wrote out a note, which he placed inside a bag with a thousand ducats:

I beg and beseech any man who finds my body to give me a decent burial for love and pity, as I am Tirant lo Blanc of Breton Saltrock lineage, Captain General of the Greek Empire.

Night was approaching and water poured into the galley, while the sailors lamented their impending destruction.

As they drew near land, some Moors spied the ship, and Tirant, knowing they would either die or be captured, again appealed to the Virgin Mary: "Compassionate Mother, I truly believe that you were a virgin before, during, and after Christ's birth, wherefore I beg you to spare my sinful soul!"

Once they were close to shore, everyone leapt overboard and swam except Tirant, who remained on the galley, which had neither rowboats, ropes, nor oars. He pleaded with two Breton sailors to help save the damsel, and in deference to his urgings they at last agreed to do so. They stripped her naked just as the ship was about to go under, and one of them cut a long cork board that was fastened to a hook. He then prepared to lash Pleasure-of-my-life to the board, which the damsel embraced and the other man held upright, but at that moment a big wave washed them all overboard, whereupon the one with the board and rope drowned trying to disentangle himself and save her life. The other sailor helped as much as he could but finally had to abandon her, though luckily it was now dark and they were very near shore. The damsel felt land beneath her feet and walked along in the shallows, where from time to time, a mighty wave would break over her as she sought to avoid the fighting. She feared she would be killed by the Moors, whom she heard squabbling over their prisoners, and occasionally a bolt of lightning would reveal their flashing swords. Whenever she heard people coming, she hid in the water till they had passed.

Poor Pleasure-of-my-life, who was dying of cold, prayed the Holy Virgin to send her some champion. About half a league further on, she found some fishermen's boats on the beach. The damsel then entered a hut where she spied two sheepskins, and after tying them together, one in front and one behind, she felt a little warmer and lay down to sleep.

As soon as Pleasure-of-my-life awoke, she began to lament, and though her eyes hurt and her voice grew hoarse, she went on cursing cruel Fortune. The hapless damsel cried: "Oh pitiless Fortune, why do you treat me so? What more could you do than make me a slave to Moors? Would that I had drowned and been entombed in a fish's belly, but from now on I shall seek nothing, since what is little prized cannot be missed. I only wish to die, yet I fear that by invoking death I shall prolong my life, as all the saints oppose me and oblige me to damn my soul. May death end my woes and bring me chastity's reward! Oh lady princess, though you mourn my absence and await Tirant's reply, seek comfort elsewhere, for you will never see me again."

As she lamented, the sun began to rise. A Moor came down the path singing, and she hid lest he see her, but as he passed she saw his white beard and thought perhaps he might succor her. Pleasure-of-my-life then approached the old man and told him what had happened. His pity roused by her gentility, he speedily replied: "Damsel, I see Fortune has brought you to this pass. I spent many years as a slave to Christians in the town of Cádiz, where one day my mistress's enemies came to kill her son, and they surely would have done so had I not thwarted them. I seized the child, slew two of the rascals, and drove the rest away, in thanks for which my mistress freed me, bought me new clothes, and paid my passage to Granada. Now I shall return her favor, and my widowed daughter will care for you."

Pleasure-of-my-life knelt on the hard ground and thanked the old Moor, who gave her his burnoose and led her to the village of Rafal near Tunis.

Upon beholding our gentle damsel, the daughter was filled with compassion. Her father said: "You should know, my child, that this is the daughter of that lady who freed me, and I now wish to repay her generosity and kindness."

The old man's devoted daughter welcomed Pleasure-of-my-life, to whom she gave a skirt, jubbah, and veil so everyone would think her Moorish.[1]

Let us now return to Tirant who, after Pleasure-of-my-life was swept overboard, remained on the galley with only one sailor. When it sank, they swam for their lives, though Tirant was sure he would die on land or sea, since after learning his identity the Moors would not spare him for any ransom. The two men clambered ashore under cover of darkness, crept away from the fighting, and, once they were out of range, decided to turn inland. There they found a vineyard laden with grapes, and the sailor said: "My lord, let us spend the night here and look around in the morning, for tomorrow I shall go wherever you lead me."

Having filled their bellies with grapes, they entered a cave and fell asleep. The next morning, they awoke chilled to the bone and started moving big rocks around to get warm, but our knight's leg ached terribly and he was filled with despair.

It happened that not long before Tirant's arrival, the King of Tlemcen had dispatched his bravest warrior to Tunis. This ambassador, who was known as the Bey of Beys,[2] spent three months there with his retinue, residing on an estate that abounded in wild game. By chance he went hunting that morning with his falcons and greyhounds, which spotted a hare and chased it into Tirant's cave. Seeing it run in, a hunter followed it and saw our knight lying on the ground. When he had captured it with the sailor's help, the Moor returned to his captain and exclaimed: "My lord, I do not believe Nature could have fashioned or any painter depicted a more beautiful mortal body. Alas, cruel Fortune, why have you abused him so, for if my eyes do not deceive me he looks more dead than alive. His face is pale but handsome, his eyes glow like twin rubies, and I have never beheld such a perfectly formed body, yet the poor wretch seems burdened by grief and sorrow."

The bey asked where this man was, to which the Moor replied: "My lord, come with me; he is in a little cave near that vineyard."

The ambassador followed him with great pleasure, while the sailor slipped away as quietly as he could.

Once the bey had reached the cave he gazed long upon Tirant, and, overwhelmed by compassion, he uttered these words:

· CCC ·

*H*OW THE AMBASSADOR COMFORTED TIRANT

"Your noble aspect rouses my compassion, as great lords are often shipwrecked or taken prisoner, wherefore if you are brave you will not despair. Though Fortune brought you to this pass, you should trust in Almighty Allah, and I swear by Our Prophet Mohammed, who placed you in my hands, that so fair a body must also be full of courage. I have three sons; you shall be the fourth." Then he summoned his second son and said: "Treat this man as your brother," and he told Tirant: "If you wish to please me, you will now recite your story. I still must help my eldest son, whom they seek to rob of his betrothed, the virtuous Princess of Tlemcen,[3] but Mohammed willing, the matter will soon be resolved. Do not mourn your losses, however great they may be, as when we return to my estates I shall make you rich. I cannot leave yet, for the sinister Fates oppose their marriage. Oh Christian whom I hear grieve and sigh most sadly, tell me why and have no more fears for the future."

When the ambassador had finished, Tirant rose and began to speak:

· CCCI ·

THE STORY TIRANT CONCOCTED FOR THE AMBASSADOR

"To pity the forlorn is a sign of true humanity,[4] wherefore I rejoice to have fallen into your hands, since you generously restore what Fortune snatched away. If Your Lordship wishes to share my sorrows, I shall gladly recount them, as the wretched find solace in describing their woes. I am no prince or great lord but, having been born a gentleman, in my youth I roamed the world seeking fame and honor. Once, in the Levant, I foolishly heeded a mendacious widow, who forced me to behold the worst evil my soul could suffer. So great was my agony that I took vengeance instantly, and still tormented by grief, I boarded a ship bound for Syria. Then I went to confess my sins at Christ's Holy Sepulcher, and as I was returning in that same galley, a mighty storm arose. Thus you see my misfortune, how God saved my life, and my hope that Your Lordship will accept me as his humble servant."

The ambassador replied: "Too late do men learn that a mad course makes for a perilous voyage. Be comforted, as I rule many lands and upon our return to my rich estates, you shall be given everything you desire. If you will tell me your name, I swear to make you my son."

"My lord," said Tirant, "I thank you infinitely and pray God to let me serve you. Should you wish to know who I am, I shall tell you the truth: my name is Blanc."

The bey kindly replied: "Blessed be the mother who named you in accord with your perfection."

The son took off his jubbah and gave it to Tirant, who rode behind him until they reached the bey's lodgings, where they dressed their captive in Moorish style.

Lest the King of Tunis discover Tirant, the bey sent our knight to one of his castles with instructions to guard him well.

Comforted by his new clothes and the Bey of Beys's words, Tirant turned toward the sea, raised his eyes to Heaven, and prayed Our Lady to change the cruel winds and tides.

On the night of his departure, the sky was blue and the full moon shone with midday brilliance. As Tirant left the house, he tripped and fell with his arms outstretched, whereupon all the Moors said: "After such an evil omen, this Christian's life cannot last long."

Tirant quickly rose and replied: "You misunderstand, for my name is Blanc and the moon, which is white, bright, and fair, shines to show me the way. My hands stretch toward the moon, and thus with God's help I shall conquer Barbary."[5]

Roaring with laughter at what they thought was a joke, the Moors mounted their horses, rode on their way, and three days later reached a mighty castle. The king had sent word to his son (the Princess of Tlemcen's betrothed) that a handsome and noble Christian slave would shortly arrive, but upon seeing Tirant, the son ordered him chained and shackled, at which our knight felt much aggrieved and resumed his gloomy ponderings.

Two months later, the Bey of Beys received his reply and returned to Tlemcen, where he found the royal family in great distress, as King Escariano was marching toward them with his army, accompanied by many other kings and their troops. This King Escariano, a powerful black much taller than other men,[6] possessed a great treasure, ruled many vassals, and was allied with the King of Tunis, who had detained the bey.

King Escariano's realm bordered the King of Tlemcen's and, hoping to inherit his neighbor's crown, the black had asked for his daughter, but the cowardly King of Tlemcen had replied that she was betrothed to the Bey of Beys's son. Her father said she was pregnant, and surely King Escariano would not want to raise another man's child, but if greed was his motive he could have half his wealth. King Escariano refused to accept anything less than both the daughter and the treasure and vowed to lock the King of Tlemcen's sons in a dungeon.

In the end they could not agree, and King Escariano set out with fifty-five thousand foot and cavalry.

The King of Tlemcen, who had only twenty thousand men, decided to await his foes in the mountains. Many of King Escariano's soldiers died fording a mighty torrent, but those who reached the other side continued their advance and besieged the King of Tlemcen in a fertile river valley the Moors called Fairdale. It contained three castles surrounded by large, fortified towns, and in one of these castles the King of Tlemcen's entire court and family were lodged.

There were two castles on one side of the river and one on the other, with a big stone bridge between them. King Escariano conquered one castle and, though the King of Tlemcen was in a much stronger one, he considered himself doomed, as only an act of God could save him.

The Bey of Beys, who had been defeated in the first assault, fled to the castle where Tirant was being held. There the Moor told his son: "You should die before letting King Escariano steal your noble bride. Hasten to our king and prove yourself worthy of your forefathers, who preferred battling the enemy to quarreling with kin. Remember how he honored you in offering his daughter and that glory comes to those who can seize it, wherefore, if you covet fame, you should hurry to her side while I seek other allies to help raise the siege."

His son replied: "My lord, I shall gladly go to our king, by whose side I shall triumph or die."

After bidding his father farewell and kissing his hands and lips, the son began to speak in the following manner:

· CCCII ·

*T*HE BEY'S SON'S FAREWELL

"Hardships should not daunt the brave but foster courage and wisdom, and thus, lord and father, I kiss your hands in thanks. You have shown me the right path, and I would sooner die than lose my lady. May Our Prophet Mohammed increase my wisdom and shield me from disgrace, helping me to emulate my father, whose fame will always be a beacon. I shall now hasten to my king and the lady who rules my heart."

He then set out for the king's castle.

As the bey's son approached, he heard the clash of arms and feared for his beloved's life, but after looking down from a hill and seeing the other castle under attack, he and fifteen other horsemen quickly entered the king's castle.

His father, who had stayed behind, asked what had become of the Christian. Upon learning that Tirant was in chains, the bey was furious, for he had often pondered our knight's words after his fall, and furthermore, he believed that all Christian warriors were dexterous in arms. He therefore greeted his prisoner with a smile and uttered the following words:

· CCCIII ·

*H*OW THE BEY COMFORTED TIRANT

"Valiant Christian, I beg you to forgive my son's abuses, which, alas, were inflicted without my consent. My intention was always to treat you as a son, and I now beg you to pardon me and help our afflicted king. Do not be surprised that I ask you to aid my lord, as I know you are able and experienced in warfare. Your words when you fell convinced me of your prowess, but there is also another reason: your body looked like Saint Sebastian's after his martyrdom. Whoever gave you all those wounds possessed very little pity, nor do I believe you received them sleeping or with folded hands. Do not seek another father or surrender to despair, since death visits those who fear it and shuns those who invoke it. Lay aside sad thoughts and comfort me instead, for when I think of our rout I long to return to nothingness. I ask you as my son to console me in my distress, knowing your honor will increase when the world learns of your kindness."

Tirant quickly replied in a gentle voice:

· CCCIV ·

*T*IRANT'S REPLY

"I recognized your great worth when you freed me—not for my deserts but in accord with your noble spirit. My adversities make me pity yours, and I thank you for your words of comfort, but no captain should despair lest he dismay his troops, for all knights are sometimes defeated and sometimes victorious. Be mindful of your virtues and rely on the aid of one who has long borne arms in Spain and can advise you as well as any man alive. Excuse me for speaking thus, but my deeds will bear me out, nor should you be surprised if that king besieges yours, as all sovereigns behave thus in battle. If you fear King Escariano's bombards, I shall destroy them for your pleasure."

Feeling calmed by Tirant's words, the bey asked him to gather what he needed and set out as soon as possible. Our knight replied: "My lord, our ancestors were right: any commoner who would prove his mettle must also be wealthy, for paupers rarely perform valiant deeds of chivalry. Thus does Solomon call poverty a blessing in disguise, since a poor man must only satisfy nature's needs."[7]

The bey gave Tirant his finest steed, armor, and all the money he required.

After buying some old whale bile, Tirant mixed it with quicksilver, saltpeter, iron sulfate and other ingredients to make an ointment, which he put in a box and gave to his lord of the moment. Then the two knights secretly crossed the river and slipped into the king's other castle. The next morning, Tirant reconnoitered Fairdale and noticed the big stone bridge, on which their foes were so positioned that no one could cross it without falling into their hands. Having asked the bey for a Moor who would not be recognized and two hundred sheep, our knight dressed in a shepherd's cloak to look like the Moor's servant.

King Escariano knew his enemies were trapped, and his first victory had emboldened him, while his thirty-seven bombards, which fired three times a day, had destroyed most of the king's castle. All those who provisioned King Escariano's camp were escorted coming, going, and during their stay there.

Setting out with their flock, Tirant and the Moor crossed the bridge and headed straight for the camp, where they found so many buyers that they could charge what they liked, and they raised their prices further to avoid selling the sheep too quickly. They spent three days pasturing their flock near the artillery, and, pretending he was curious to see the bombards, Tirant smeared them with the ointment, whose ingredients turned any metal brittle within three hours.

When the bombards fired at the king's castle the next morning, they cracked and not one was left whole. King Escariano was dismayed and thought it a very bad omen, while Tirant and the Moor returned to the fortress where the bey awaited them.

Then Tirant ordered one of the arches on the bridge cut and replaced with a wooden drawbridge flanked by a stockade. Once the stockade was ready, Tirant donned his armor, mounted his steed, and rode toward the enemy with a stout lance in his hand. Seeing five Moors lying in the sun, our knight headed for them, and since he was alone they assumed he was from their camp. Tirant killed the five of them, whereupon a great hue and cry arose as the infidels rushed to arms and the Breton slew them right and left. When still more attacked, he retreated to the stockade, fighting as he went, and dismounted outside it while the enemy crowded around him and those in the bey's castle hastened to his defense. A splendid encounter followed, in which many knights were felled, but such a crowd assailed Tirant that he was forced to withdraw and order the bridge raised. Though King Escariano's soldiers destroyed the stockade, Tirant's men rebuilt it during the night, and thus they battled every day with many casualties on both sides. Knowing the bey possessed two bombards, Tirant had them brought to the bridge and aimed at the enemy camp, where they wrought great havoc.

One day Tirant asked the bey: "My lord, would you like me to rescue the king and bring him here or to some other fortress?"

The bey replied: "If you saved my son and his betrothed, I would give you everything I own, and if you forgot the king I would be but little troubled."

"Now, my lord," said Tirant, "select a page whom your son will recognize, and tell him to await me with three horses by that pine tree about half a league from here."

It was quickly done, and as soon as the sun rose, Tirant mounted his horse, took a hundred soldiers, and led them forth from the stockade, while those behind it fired the bombards as fast as they could. The

Saracens, who feared that Tirant would assault their camp again, donned their armor and rode out to meet him, whereupon such a fierce battle ensued that the Breton's men had to withdraw, for King Escariano had decided to storm the drawbridge and attack the bey. Seeing almost no one left in the enemy camp, our knight then told his master: "My lord, hold them off as best you can while I go and do my duty."

He spurred his steed and galloped so hard to where the page was waiting that by the time he arrived, his horse was exhausted. He dismounted, tied it to a tree, and took a fresh mount from the page, with whom he then skirted the enemy camp and tried to keep out of sight. Tirant sent the page ahead, since those in the castle knew him, and as they neared it the bey's son spied the lad, who was his youngest brother, and ordered no one to fire at either him or his companion.

Once they were inside, the king entered the hall and made great joy of his saviors. "My lord," said Tirant, "take your daughter and follow me, for I shall lead you to a safer place."

The king took the page's horse, on which the bey's son rode behind him, and the fair princess also mounted behind Tirant. They galloped until they were a league from the enemy camp, but then night fell and they slowed their pace while the king led them to his strongest city: Tlemcen.

As they rode, the grateful monarch asked Tirant what luck had brought him there.

· CCCV ·

H OW THE KING OF TLEMCEN SHARED HIS WOES WITH TIRANT

"If the cruel Fates resent my longevity, let them snatch away my life, which has been a vale of tears ever since I lost that battle, for thus all men may behold my sad demise. Tell me why you braved death for a hapless king like me, who with weary heart left the castle where I expected to die and where my woes multiplied as I sat among the wretched. Oh unlucky stars, why do you envy my happiness and poison my old age? Yet what use are complaints when Mohammed has sent such a brave warrior, whose noble deeds of chivalry I soon shall reward?"

Tirant replied:

· CCCVI ·

TIRANT'S REPLY TO THE KING OF TLEMCEN

"Your Highness will soon see how your afflicted subjects sigh for you, and their tearful countenances moved me to end your cruel sufferings, for my own grief was renewed when I heard how your foes abused you. My present master, the Bey of Beys, sent me to your castle, and if I have helped you I desire no further reward. Forgive me, sire, for not better resisting your enemies, but I hope to do such deeds that Your Majesty will praise me. I placed my life in Fortune's hands to save your fair and gracious daughter."

The king replied, heaving deep sighs all the while:

· CCCVII ·

THE KING OF TLEMCEN'S REPLY TO TIRANT

"A man whose deeds match his words is worthy of respect. I can see that Nature endowed you with every virtue, since you are not only fearless but sagacious and skillful, wherefore I beg you to pity me and my daughter. Prudently guard your life, for ardor combined with wisdom deserves the highest praise. The name 'Escariano' fills me with such hatred that I wish to die. Oh Mohammed! Why have you dashed all my hopes?"

As they were talking they reached the city of Tlemcen, where they were welcomed with great honor by the king's joyous subjects. His Majesty offered Tirant good lodgings and showered gifts upon him, while his knights visited the Breton, who behaved so graciously that everyone became his friend.

One day our knight asked the king's leave to rejoin the bey as he had promised, to which His Majesty replied: "Brave Christian, please stay a while longer, for I have summoned your lord and he will be here in ten days. Organize my city as you think best, and I promise as a crowned though unlucky king to free you."

The princess, who beheld Tirant's beauty and delighted in his flatteries, hoped her betrothed would die that she might marry the Breton. One day when they were alone together, she said: "Blessed Christian, by Mohammed and your gentility, please tell me where you hail from, for I greatly desire to know."

Tirant replied: "Lady worthy of honor, since Your Highness inquires, I am a knight who lost everything in a storm at sea. I was once a captain, and many kings died beneath my banners, but now I am merely a humble slave. I, who had servants, now must serve others."

The gentle lady lowered her eyes in pity and said: "Tell me clearly, and may Mohammed bless your soul, where you were born, who your parents are, and where your ancestors lie buried."

Tirant replied: "Oh most splendid of ladies, your grace and beauty stir men's souls, and Christians vie with Saracens to win your peerless virtue. I would sooner die than reveal my origins, but since you insist I shall tell the truth: I was born in Nether Spain,[8] and my father is a brave knight of ancient lineage. My mother is just as rich and generous and I am their only son, yet by now they must have given me up for dead, as they know nothing of my fate."

While they were talking, some people entered and interrupted their pleasant discourse. The gentle lady was charmed by the way Tirant praised her each time they conversed, as none of the Moors knew how to speak so courteously, and she declared that she had never seen such a genteel knight.

A few days later the Bey of Beys arrived, feeling very happy that the king, the princess, and his son were out of danger. After paying homage to his lord, who asked him to free Tirant, the bey, both out of deference and out of gratitude for his friend's services, absolved our knight of his vow not to leave him until he had said "Go!" three times and then seized him by the hair and said "You are free!" thrice more. After kissing the king's hands and feet, Tirant replied: "My lord, I promise on my faith as a Christian not to depart until I have killed, captured, or expelled King Escariano from this kingdom."

The monarch and everyone else felt most content.

When King Escariano learned of the King of Tlemcen's escape, he was dumbfounded and enraged, but since he could not capture the king he decided to conquer his lands.

So mighty were the black's forces that no city, castle, or town could withstand them, and those that resisted were taken by force and their inhabitants beheaded.

Knowing all this, the King of Tlemcen improved his city's fortifications, which were already very strong, and stored enough provisions for five years, yet everyone still despaired of victory.

One day in council, Tirant told His Majesty: "My lord, if you will send me on a mission to King Escariano, I shall see how his forces are armed and try to devise some way to rout them." Though the councilors praised his suggestion, many feared he would defect as others had, for everyone loves a victor and men are quick to change masters.

Tirant collected a large retinue and went to King Escariano, before whom he boldly explained his mission in words of this tenor:

· CCCVIII ·

*H*OW TIRANT EXPLAINED HIS MISSION TO KING ESCARIANO

"Do not be surprised that we fail to honor you, as you are our greatest enemy and no man need flatter his foe. I come from the King of Tlemcen, who, having heard your wisdom praised, is amazed that so magnanimous a prince should embrace tyranny. If you examine your motives, you will see that you have behaved disgracefully, soiling your escutcheon with eternal shame and infamy. Who can call you upright? All men hold you wicked and greedy, since without faith, cause, or reason you seek to dispossess another. You have no right, nor does any law compel you, and if you or any of your knights denies the truth of my words, I shall joust with him in single combat until one of us is killed or bested. Do not think the king sent me because he fears you or your armies, for I promise your deeds shall receive their just rebuke. My lord is well prepared, and with God's help he will triumph, while your invasion will prove to be the cause of your undoing. My king only wishes to know why you have come, that it may be written down as an example of presumption."

The king quickly replied:

· CCCIX ·

*K*ING ESCARIANO'S REPLY TO TIRANT

"Knight, whoever you may be, how dare you insult me? Were you not an emissary, I would make you pay for your words, as all the world knows your king promised me his daughter and then sought to trick me. How can you say my cause is unjust? I shall never be happy till cruel death undoes him, humbling his pride and chastising his treachery, nor shall I seek to excuse Fortune if she punishes him thus, as the Fates have also done me great harm. I demand that lady, who is mine by right and whose very name, Emeraldine, reveals her peerless gentility. Since I know you are a Christian, I shall describe her virtues, and though we spoke for a year I would never weary. If you have ever wooed a maiden, your love will help you imagine mine. When I was young, three Franciscan friars were my tutors, and, being learned theologians, they often sought to convert me. Convinced of their doctrine's superiority, I would have followed their counsel had my mother not wept until she drove them from our palace, but I can tell you one thing: this damsel's beauty has so won my heart that I shall never rest till I win her or perish, while you, who have beheld her splendor, should share my wrath at your perfidious master.

"I have read of many brave and ancient women[9] like the Amazon Queen Hippolyte, to whom King Eurysteus sent Hercules, knowing all the while she was too valiant to conquer. Likewise one reads of the Assyrian Queen Semiramis, who not only reigned but subdued the Medes and founded Babylon. One day when she was combing her hair in her chamber, they told her the Babylonians had risen in rebellion. She combed one half, left the rest, and took up arms against the city, which she won back in less time than it would have taken to finish her hair. A copper statue of this queen was placed above Babylon, with half her hair combed and the other half uncombed.

"One also reads of the Scythian Queen Tomyris, whose courage was just as great and who, to avenge her sons, killed King Cyrus of Asia after defeating his army of two hundred thousand Persians. Then she had his head cut off and soaked in a wineskin full of blood, which she declared a fit tomb for such a bloodthirsty man, and what shall I say of stalwart Zenobia, Queen of the Orient? Though her story is too long to tell, her deeds are so worthy of glorious memory that when Cornelius bested her, he was as proud as if he had vanquished the mightiest prince alive. Neither am I unaware of the Amazon Queen Penthesilea's amazing feats in the battle of Troy or of stalwart Camilla's ardent deeds in Italy. Who can deny the arts Minerva taught us, or how she surpassed all Greeks in wisdom and ingenuity? Who can describe King Mithradates of Pontus's devoted wife? Not only did she follow her husband in his long war with Rome, but even in defeat she followed him armed and on horseback, laying aside her womanly garb and delicate nature.

"What of Cato's daughter Portia? When she heard of her husband's death and could find no sword to slay herself, she swallowed burning coals, nor was Julius Caesar's daughter Julia less brave. Seeing her husband Pompey's bloody clothes and finding him nowhere at home, she chose to kill herself and her unborn child. Even more heartfelt and memorable was Queen Artemisia's love for her husband Mausolus, whose ashes she had pulverized after his solemn last rites and then drank the powder, saying she wished to be his tomb, and what of Emilia, Scipio Africanus's wife? When her husband committed adultery with a slave girl, she shielded him from disgrace, and as soon as he was dead she freed his former mistress. You will recall that after the knight Mirilla killed a man in Saint John Lateran and was condemned to death by starvation,[10] his wife visited him every day in prison, and though the guards searched her carefully, she gave him her breast to suck, thus keeping him alive without his captors' knowledge. Once her good deed was discovered, they commuted her husband's sentence, and all the aforesaid ladies were braver than any man who ever lived. They deserve still more glorious fame, since through diligence they overcame their weaknesses, yet I recall their deeds only to show how my beloved outshines them all. For her this war began and for her it must end; this is my answer."

The king, who then turned and walked away without awaiting Tirant's reply, had his guest well lodged and that night decided to test his gentility. He invited Tirant to lunch the next day and offered him many dishes, some of which were more delicious and better prepared than others. The king sat at the head of the table and Tirant near the foot, but our knight, who was skilled in everything and knew as much as the king, ate only the most exquisite ones and left the others. After they had finished, dessert was brought in: glazed citron, pine nut paste, candied almonds, and pine nuts heaped upon a golden platter, from which Tirant selected only the biggest and best of each. Then the king led him to a tent where they saw piles of gold doubloons, ducats, and silver coins, as well as silver vessels, clothing, armor, and horses with fine trappings. At one end, three hunting falcons were perched upon a bar, and the king said: "Knight, it is my custom to offer all royal emissaries their choice of gifts. Take as much as you like, for the more you take the happier I shall be."

Tirant yielded to the king's will, since it was no loss to his master, and chose the finest falcon, whereat the king was most impressed. He decided his guest must be a brave and noble lord, as his every action revealed a lofty lineage. He also saw how well proportioned the Christian was and declared that he had never beheld such a handsome knight. Though he would have liked to keep Tirant at his court, he said nothing, supposing that our knight would never forsake his lord.

The Breton then returned to Tlemcen and reported to the king, who asked about the size of his enemies' forces.

"On my faith, sire," replied Tirant, "their hordes swell with each passing day, and though I did not see them all I beheld eighty thousand men."

They held council and decided that Tirant and the bey should command their ten thousand remaining soldiers, as the rest were dead or had fled to the enemy. The two captains set out to defend the city of Alinac, without which the entire kingdom would be lost, but upon learning of the enemy's approach, they brought their troops into the city, where Tirant fortified the walls and had ditches dug around them. They also tunneled under the weakest side so they could slip in and out when the gates were shut, and these tunnels ended in some orchards not far from the city.

The bey was astonished at Tirant's subtlety and skill, for he had never seen anyone so experienced in warfare.

The king stayed in Tlemcen, where he was well provisioned, and King Escariano continued his conquests.

It happened that one day, the richest Jew in Tlemcen crept out of the city and made his way to King Escariano, whom he slyly and maliciously addressed in this manner: "My lord, why do you persist in plowing the sand? All will be for nought unless you capture the king, yet once you have him you will rule this entire land and, far from stumbling along cautious byways, you will come and go as you like. If we can reach an agreement, I shall give you victory and the princess."

King Escariano thought the Jew was joking and asked: "How could I harm them so? If you render me this service, I promise to make you the greatest lord in Tlemcen, but I do not believe you can do as you say. Get out of my sight lest in seeking to harm them you enrage me, as I fear that your advice will be my downfall and my foes' delight."

When the Jew heard him speak thus, he quickly replied:

· CCCX ·

*T*HE JEW'S REPLY TO KING ESCARIANO

"Fortune often thwarts men's fondest desires, and Your Highness knows how often wars are won by chance, for no one can foresee all dangers and mishaps. The few may vanquish the many and the weak the strong, while Adonai, who gives victory to those whose cause is just, never grants fame to cautious knights or victory to petty-minded princes. Heed my words: this is no dream but an infallible plan, and to prove it, I shall place my three sons in your custody. If I do not fulfill my promise, you have my leave to kill them, and all I ask in return is to honorably marry my daughter (who will have a dowry of twelve thousand ducats) to a young Jewish oil vendor who dwells with your chief watchman. In return for this favor, I shall give you all Tlemcen, as one of the city gates is near my house and a hundred thousand soldiers can pass through it."

Having heard this offer, the king pondered it and asked: "How can you deliver the King of Tlemcen and his daughter, when they are in a mighty fortress that can withstand the whole world?"

The Jew replied: "Had you listened well, you would understand that I do not offer the castle but the city, king, and court. His Majesty only sleeps in the castle in times of need, wherefore I assure you that I can do everything I promised."

So they agreed, and the Jew promised to reward King Escariano well if the marriage took place. The monarch then summoned his chief watchman, whom they called the mustafa, and when the man arrived, he asked: "What can you tell me about a Jew of yours who sells oil?"

"My lord," replied the watchman, "he wanders about plying his trade, and sometimes he also mends shoes."

"Go and fetch him," said the king.

When the Jew arrived, King Escariano asked where he hailed from.

"My lord," the Jew answered, "according to my father we have always been your vassals, and I consider myself one too."

"Then mark my words," said the king. "I already knew you were my vassal, and, wishing to advance, love, and honor those who faithfully serve me, I have decided to help you wed Jemima, the daughter of Don Jacob, whom I have persuaded to give you ten thousand ducats as well as two thousand for me. You should thank me for thus remembering you."

The Jew's face turned red and he angrily replied: "Sire, I know how generously you reward your servants, and great is my glory that you recall one so lowly. Therefore I kiss your hands and thank you infinitely, but you must excuse me, as I would not consent to this match though he gave me ten times what he has. He has been scheming for many years, but however great my poverty, it shall not be, since I would sooner die than commit such a misdeed."

"What do you mean, misdeed?" asked the king. "You are poor and downtrodden, while he is the richest and most favored Jewish merchant in Barbary. What harm or dishonor could come from such a match? All the great lords love this man, who is virtuous both in public and private, wherefore if you consider his power you will kneel and kiss his feet."

"May the great God of Liberty," replied the Jew, "shield my heart from such baseness, and when I explain why this marriage cannot take place, you will certainly excuse me. Ever since Jesus Christ was crucified, all Jews have been of three lineages, the first of which consists of those who called for His death. Their restlessness reveals them, as they are forever fidgeting and their souls know no peace, nor have they much sense of shame. The second lineage is those who took part in His crucifixion: those who whipped and bound Him, nailed Him to the cross, and, after placing a crown of thorns upon His head, slapped that Righteous Man, gambled for His clothes, and spat in His face. You can recognize them by the fact that, unable to meet your gaze, they look down or to one side and can barely turn their eyes Heavenward. The Jew who wants to be my father-in-law is of this type. The third lineage, descended from David, was in

Jerusalem too, but they opposed Christ's execution and, moved by compassion, took refuge in Solomon's temple lest they see that Holy Man so cruelly abused. These kind and generous Jews, who did their utmost to save Christ, treat their neighbors with love and can look in all directions. Being of this type, I do not wish to taint my blood with perpetual grief, since my children's lineage would be eternally corrupted. I fear such Jews more than death and feel ashamed to speak with them."

King Escariano accepted the Jew's explanation but asked him to remain silent for the moment. Then he summoned Don Jacob, whom he assured that the wedding would take place shortly, and as the young Jew said nothing, the merchant thought he had consented. The two conspirators agreed to meet outside Tlemcen at midnight on the seventeenth of that month, when Don Jacob would admit the black under cover of darkness.

The king arrived at the appointed hour, and the Jew, true to his word, opened the ghetto gate, which the Ethiopian's armies quickly entered. They stormed the palace, slew everyone except their lord's beloved, and assaulted the fortress but were unable to take it. Feeling unsafe in Tlemcen, King Escariano left most of his troops there and set out with his lady, who was still mourning her loved ones. He took her to an impregnable castle, garrisoned the town below it, and sent the rest of his escort back to Tlemcen.

When these sad tidings reached Tirant and the bey, their soldiers wept bitterly, and many urged their captains to surrender, since most of Tlemcen had been conquered, their lord was dead, and if they laid down arms King Escariano might spare them.

Tirant told the bey: "My lord, this is bad advice. It would be a great mistake to capitulate, for you now command ten thousand soldiers and control this well-fortified city, as well as several other towns and castles. If all else fails, you can negotiate better terms, as the king will return your lands or enlarge them in exchange for the strongholds still in your power."

The bey thought his friend's advice good, but he still mourned his lord and son. Meanwhile, Tirant sent a spy to find out what had occurred in Tlemcen, which he had left well defended by brave and able captains. No one understood why it had fallen so quickly. They only found out later, when a fugitive described how seven of his sons had been killed, his house looted, and his wife and other children enslaved. He said that after the Jew's treason, King Escariano had seized his goods and ordered him stripped, bound, covered with honey, and pilloried. The next day he quartered him and fed his body to the dogs, saying no one could trust such a traitor, who might serve him as he had his previous lord.

Thus Tirant and the bey learned how the enemy had entered the city, which towns they were billeted in, and that King Escariano was holding his beloved in the mighty fortress of Mount Tuber. Then Tirant and ten men who knew the countryside well rode until they were near the castle.

They spent the night in a house called the Old Mosque, and just before daybreak, they captured two Saracens, whom Tirant forced to reveal the king's whereabouts and strength. They said he was protected by sixty knights and some paid watchmen, while another thousand soldiers guarded the town below. Having learned what he wished to know, Tirant released them and went to reconnoiter the fortress.

Upon his return to Alinac, our knight sent a hundred men with pickaxes and shovels to a bridge they were to cut if they spied King Escariano's soldiers, who would thus have an extra day's ride to avoid all the towns and villages not in their power. Then Tirant and the bey set out for Mount Tuber, which was three days from Tlemcen and nine leagues from Alinac. As soon as the king saw them, he marshaled his troops and sallied forth, but instead of giving battle, Tirant and the bey captured all the livestock they could find and drove them toward Alinac.

Tirant often camped near the castle for two or three days, and when his men ran out of food, he led them back to the city. One morning as he rode forth, grieving over Carmesina, Pleasure-of-my-life, and his imprisoned relatives, he beheld a clever Christian slave from Albania who was weeping and lamenting, for his master had beaten him with switches and sent him to dig in a nearby orchard. Tirant recognized the slave, with whom he had spoken many times, and moved by pity, he summoned him and uttered these words:

· CCCXI ·

*H*OW TIRANT PROMISED TO FREE THE SLAVE

"Cruel Fortune always torments the wretched, and especially those too weak to bear their grief, but if you like, you can now win both your liberty and my gratitude. Your countenance shows that you must be a brave man suffering more afflictions than you admit. Who would not sacrifice what he has to gain what he hopes for? Long separation from my beloved has brought me close to death, while slavery's woes make you sad and mournful. Alas, my poor heart weeps with pity for your sufferings! Though you may not die, your life will be worse than death, yet if you do as I say you will soon regain your freedom. The only conditions are that you let us drive you through the camp, beat you with a leather strap that will hurt but little, and slit your ears. If all goes well you may become a great lord, but even if my plan fails, I promise to free you."

The Christian slave quickly replied:

· CCCXII ·

*T*HE CHRISTIAN SLAVE'S REPLY

"Only God knows how your compassionate words have comforted me, and my gratitude is such that I shall gladly obey you, both to repay your kindness and to regain my freedom. Were it not for love's delights, I would never have been enslaved, wherefore I cry out against love, which brought me grief, tears, and sorrow, but whatever my past, I am now at your command. Your Lordship's courage inspires me to brave death in your service, nor do I fear for my ears or any other part of my body."

Tirant thanked him and replied: "On my faith as a knight, I promise not to eat until I free you."

He left the slave and hastened to the bey, with whom he arranged to buy the Albanian's freedom for a hundred doubloons. On the morrow they all set out again for Mount Tuber, where they encamped near the fortress, whose guards were little troubled, for the bey had no artillery and if he stayed long all the king's forces would come. Knights from the town parleyed with them every day on the king's behalf.

That day, as on many others, the king sent two knights to offer generous gifts and favors if the bey would capitulate, but he and Tirant replied that their sole desire was to avenge his son and the king. When they had finished talking, Tirant offered the knights some refreshment, while he waited for the Albanian to carry out their plan.

After they had eaten, the Albanian crept up to a table heaped with drinking vessels, from which he stole a big silver pitcher inlaid with gold. One of the guards saw him and immediately raised a shout, whereupon Tirant, who was talking with the knights, asked what had occurred. Then they beheld a big crowd chasing the Albanian, whom they caught and brought before their captains, while a guard who was holding the slave's hair cried: "I demand justice from this thief who stole your silver pitcher!"

Tirant said: "Lord bey, this is no time to kill except in battle. I beg you to commute the sentence to beating and having his ears slit."

And so it was done in the emissaries' presence. Having slit the slave's ears, they tied the pitcher to his neck and drove him around the camp, beating him as they went, but as they neared the town their captive suddenly wrenched his hands free and ran. The bailiff who was chasing him pretended to trip and fall, whereby the Albanian was able to enter the nearest gate while the guards on the walls covered him with their crossbows. Then everyone in the town went before their lord and lady, who, moved to pity by the sight of that naked slave soaked in blood and with his ears slit, offered him a shirt and some other clothes. The black kept the pitcher and accepted the Albanian as his servant.[11]

Pretending to be enraged by the Albanian's escape, Tirant warned the emissaries that if their king did not return him, he would kill all his prisoners or cut off their hands, feet, noses, and ears. The king refused, swearing that if his foes wanted war he would serve them worse than they had served the slave. Without bothering to reply, our knight marshaled his troops and returned to Alinac, while to excuse himself the Albanian spoke these words to King Escariano:

· CCCXIII ·

THE ALBANIAN'S WORDS TO KING ESCARIANO

"Distress has so hardened my heart that I no longer fear death, but I do dread shame over my tarnished reputation and damaged ears, wherefore I, cruelly slandered, demand vengeance from that wicked captain who sought to starve us. Though I committed a crime, it was solely out of need, and if Your Highness gives me leave to come and go, I shall keep you informed of all your enemies' plans, that you may serve them as you did the famous King of Tlemcen."

The king replied: "I shall gladly let you come and go as you please."

Having told his guards to let the slave pass, the king consulted his knights, who said: "Lord, this man has been sorely abused and craves revenge, but even so, it would be wise to watch him closely."

Unbeknownst to anyone, the Albanian left Mount Tuber through a false door and made his way to Alinac, where he told Tirant everything that had occurred. The Breton gave him seven doubloons and three and a half *reals,* as well as some smaller coins, a sword, and a basket of peaches, for all the orchards and fields around Mount Tuber had been destroyed. Then our knight said: "That the king may trust you more, tell him I am having lots of bread baked and therefore must be planning to stay a while."

Upon the Albanian's return, King Escariano welcomed him cordially and gave the peaches to his queen, feeling happier than if he had offered her a town, as he could see she was content for the first time since her capture, though he had often striven to comfort her in the following manner:

· C C C X I V ·

*H*OW KING ESCARIANO COMFORTED HIS LADY

"My great devotion, noble lady, is caused by your beauty and wisdom, for the first time I beheld you, your priceless worth enslaved me. I beg you by your virtue to torment yourself no more but to rejoice in ruling a young and mighty king. Do not mourn your family and betrothed, who were destined to die, nor are you any the poorer, since I shall be your father, brother, husband, and slave. All these tears and lamentations can only harm your health, wherefore, my heart and soul, be calmed and comforted, as I shall give you everything within my power."

He said no more and hopefully awaited his lady's answer, but the disconsolate queen replied in this fashion:

· C C C X V ·

*T*HE QUEEN'S SORROWFUL REPLY

"What cruel agony to hear words of comfort when one has no hope of joy, for alas, my honor deserves more faith than you possess! You may well believe my tearful plaints are justified, as I could only please you by forsaking my greatest pleasure: to mourn my father's death that so troubles my soul. My afflictions will not subside until my tears turn to blood, and I would be praised if like Ariadne, Phaedra, Hypsipyle, or Oenone, I slew myself to end my woes. I would also offend you and thus avenge my father, yet although my sorrows are unequaled, I do not wish to be an example to a world that has beheld too many ill-fated ladies! Grief so consumes me that I scarcely know how to end my torments, but if I thought it might revive my father, I would quickly take my life. Oh unlucky brothers, devoured by cruel death: in my anguish I still see you and for your sake I am abused. I address my lamentations to love's humble servants, and, furiously renouncing all worthy intentions, I declare that my grief does not diminish but grows day by day. The fear of death grips me when I contemplate your power, nor could any woman resist such a mighty tyrant. Pity for the wretched pleases Allah and the world."

The queen then left the room, sighing and weeping bitterly as she went.

After giving his lord the peaches, the Albanian showed him the money and said: "Master, look at these coins I stole from one of your foes. If I go often I shall bring back many things, since I have a close relative who informs me of all their doings and who told me they are baking bread and gathering supplies. You have time to plan an ambush, for by acting astutely you may conquer them."

The king was pleased by his servant's words and said: "Now we shall see if your relative told the truth."

Three days later, Tirant arrived and camped in his usual place. The king now trusted the Albanian enough to make him one of his chief watchmen, and to keep him company, he placed six trusty men under his orders. The Albanian had bought some sweets that he shared with his companions, and together they stood watch every five days.

Tirant spent three days negotiating with the king and then departed, but he returned soon thereafter, and all this continued for nearly two months. The Breton came and went so frequently that people hardly noticed him, and King Escariano often sent the Albanian to fetch fruit and sweets from his foes' camp. One day he returned leading a pack mule loaded with wine and brandishing a bloody sword. When he was before his master, he said: "My lord, I heard the captain had sent for wine, and seeing that one of his packers had lagged behind, I felled him with a rock. Then I beat him to death, taking his sword and this mule laden with the best wine I have tasted in a long time, wherefore I beg you to let me open a tavern, and when this wine has been drunk, I shall endeavor to steal or buy more."

The king agreed, and many Saracens drank there every day. Whenever the Albanian's watch came, he took a big jug of wine up to the tower and passed it around, thus winning his fellow guards' affection.

Tirant had spoken many times with his foes' emissaries and had often come and gone with all his troops. Knowing that King Escariano trusted the Albanian, our knight gave him a perforated metal box, which when his turn came to stand watch, he filled with live coals, wrapped in a piece of leather, and hid under his shirt. While his mates were drinking and playing some big kettledrums on the tower, he hid the box in a corner lest the fire go out. The Albanian had mixed some potions with the wine to drug his companions, who by midnight had fallen so fast asleep that they never awoke. After a patrol had passed, the Albanian hid the box under his cape and lit a piece of straw, which he stuck three times in a crack in the wall facing Tirant's camp.

Recognizing the signal, Tirant rode forth with a small band of soldiers, while everyone else stayed behind, ready to attack at the bey's command. To avoid a stream, Tirant's men had to ride past another tower, and though the Albanian beat the kettledrums as hard as he could, it was only by luck that no one noticed them. When they heard the guards yelling "Good watch to you! Good watch!" they hastened forward, and when there was silence they stopped to listen. This went on until they reached the Albanian's tower and found a thick cord, whose other end was tied to his leg so that if he fell asleep it would wake him. As soon as he felt a tug, he pulled in the cord, to which Tirant had attached a rope ladder that the Albanian then tied to the wall and threw down along with another one. Tirant, who climbed up first, beheld the sleeping guards and asked: "What shall we do with these men?"

"My lord," the man replied, "leave them alone, for they can do no harm."

Still feeling uneasy, Tirant went to look at the guards, whose throats were all slit and whose clothes were drenched in blood. Then he brought up his men, one of whom he told to keep beating the drums while another one hundred and fifty-nine manned the tower very well. The Albanian led them to the sleeping kaid, who leapt out of bed naked and seized his sword to defend himself, but Tirant split his head with a halberd and his brains spilled onto the floor. His wife began to scream, but the Albanian served her in like manner, whereupon they went through the castle, bolting all the doors from the outside, and the noise from the kettledrums was so loud that no one noticed.

When they reached the towers, the guards believed they were a patrol until Tirant's men seized them and threw them off the battlements. One guard fell onto a barbican and bounced into the moat. More startled than hurt, he ran through the town giving the alarm, and as the news spread people began to awaken. The first one in the castle to know was a man on one of the lower floors, who was fishing in the moat when he heard a splash and opened his door. Beholding Tirant's soldiers, he shouted and woke the castle, but when the king's men tried to leave their rooms they found the doors bolted. The black, who slept in the highest tower, barricaded himself therein with his queen and a chambermaid.

By daybreak Tirant's men had hoisted flags and lit bonfires with great rejoicing, while those who sought to flee were captured by the bey, who sent some of his men into town and stationed others in the fields or on the barbicans. Upon reaching the castle and finding that none of his soldiers had been hurt, he marveled at Tirant's more angelic than human deeds, for nothing he set out to do proved impossible. Then the bey spoke these words:

·CCCXVI·

*H*OW THE BEY FLATTERED TIRANT, THROUGH WHOM HE HOPED TO BE AVENGED

"How just to proclaim the loftiness of one in virtues unequaled! With what words shall I tell my listeners of your noble chivalry? Oh celestial warrior whose courageous deeds reveal his worth: through you I hope at last to avenge my lord's betrayal, and I trust that you will comfort me by sending his soul to Hell. Once I have killed his queen, my erstwhile daughter-in-law to be, I shall be lord and master of all Tlemcen, wherefore, knight of glorious lineage, I apologize for the little honor I did you, as I now recall your prophesies on the night of your fall, and since the beginning has been good, I trust the end will be still better. Let us consolidate your victory while Fortune favors us."

Tirant quickly replied:

·CCCXVII·

*T*IRANT'S REPLY TO THE BEY

"No warrior, however villainous, should return evil for evil, nor do virtuous lords betray the chivalric code, which tells us to spare rather than kill our enemies. You should not be surprised that this blameless king slew your lord, since I knew his cause was just as soon as we spoke together. Now that this young knight is in our power, we should let him live out his days, striving thus to set an example for posterity. Neither, my lord, should you think of killing this royal lady, for all women are exempt from cruelty in warfare and no one who wishes to triumph may harm them, as only adulteresses deserve death even under Jewish law. You know she merits no punishment, and our honor would be sullied by such a sin. How can you, the Bey of Beys, wish to act so cruelly? It is unworthy of your virtue, whereas if you show pity your fame will grow."

In the end, the bey recognized his error and the harm he did both himself and knighthood. Then Tirant said: "Now force them to surrender and join our other captives."

They went to the highest tower, but the black, who considered himself as good as dead after killing the King of Tlemcen, refused to capitulate unless they spared his life.

"If we leave him alone," said Tirant, "hunger will quickly change his mind, and meanwhile we can lock up those other knights."

They searched the castle, which they found stocked with enough wheat, millet, and sorghum for seven years, while a clear fountain flowed from one of the rocks.

That night the king, who felt very sorry for his beloved, leaned out a window and shouted: "Since I see you are merciless, I offer to embrace virtue. Is there no knight among you to whom I can surrender?"

"My lord," replied Tirant, "the valiant Bey of Beys is here."

"I do not want him," cried the king, "but if you assure my safety, I shall both knight you and place myself in your custody."

"Sire," replied Tirant, "I was knighted by the worthiest prince in Christendom: the peerlessly valiant King of England who, just as the moon outshines the stars, outshines all others in ardor and virtue."

Recognizing the emissary with whom he had spoken at such length, the king asked: "Will you, who came to me as an ambassador, guarantee my life and royal dignity?"

Tirant replied: "I promise on my faith that a month after you surrender, you will still be alive."

Feeling as happy as if they had set him free, the king descended the tower steps and opened the door. Standing on the threshold, he then uttered these bold words:

· CCCXVIII ·

*H*OW KING ESCARIANO SURRENDERED TO THE BEY

"Having caused my own downfall, I do not blame misfortune, but I do claim that youthful ignorance led me to kill an innocent man. What true knight would not die bravely, knowing his fame will outlive him? Since you refuse to let me knight you, please bring me that little boy," and he pointed to the five-year-old son of a woman who baked bread.

The child approached the black, who knighted him, kissed his lips, and gave him his sword in sign of surrender.

"Now," said the king, "you may do what you please with me."

The bey said: "Seize him, Christian captain, and throw him into prison."

"God forbid," replied Tirant, "that I should take a king from a virgin's hands, as worthy knights would then rebuke me and I prefer subduing kings to imprisoning them."

"Come, come!" cried the bey. "I said that out of courtesy and to grant you the honor."

"No," replied Tirant. "Give it to your son, whereby the two of you can share it."

Without further ado the bey seized his foe, had him shackled, and threw him in a dungeon, at which Tirant felt very angry but kept silent lest he vex his lord. Then they entered the tower in search of the grieving queen, who felt such joy when she saw them that for a while she could not speak. Upon regaining her wits, the lady began to lament thus:

· CCCXIX ·

THE QUEEN'S LAMENT UPON SEEING TIRANT AND THE BEY

"Just as the wind fans a flame, so the sight of you augments my sorrows, bringing to mind my beloved family and valiant betrothed. Woe is me! Why do I long to see my father when he would only have to die again, for this world's afflictions surely surpass those of the next. What, then, should I crave but death, which ends all ills and will reunite us? Perhaps I curse myself in desiring their return, whereby greater evils might ensue for both you and them. On their last woeful day, I could neither cry out nor lament, so I wept in the hope that they would hear my tears. What else could my eyes do, being denied their only solace? The grief my sobs could not express was revealed by cries and breast beating, while my hair was loosened in sign of mourning, my garments were so drenched in tears that the drops ran off them, and my body trembled like a grain of wheat in a gentle breeze. I ask only one favor: for pity's sake do not prolong my sufferings but kill me quickly that I may join them, as I am the unluckiest of damsels and the last farewell I heard was a woeful 'Alas!' "

She fell silent, while the captains comforted her as best they could.

Upon weighing the king's treasure, they found one hundred and four thousand pounds of doubloons, for he was very rich and had grown wealthier through his conquests.

Tirant chose the noblest women in Mount Tuber and ordered them to serve the queen.

After summoning his captors and the little boy he had knighted, the king said: "My lords, I have but one wish. Inasmuch as this lad, to whom I surrendered, possesses no inheritance, with your leave I shall grant him an annuity of twenty thousand doubloons."

Then he wrote it down on a sheet of paper, which he entrusted to two cadis, while at the same time he willed all his lands to Queen Emeraldine.

"Now," said the king, "you may do as you please with me. I am ready to die whenever you like and to be buried in disgrace, but first please summon that cunning rascal who betrayed me, that I may forgive him."

Once the Albanian was before him, King Escariano said: "Gallant gentleman, I can see what your word is worth, for you wickedly robbed a king of his life and possessions. What did I do to deserve such treachery? Tell me: where is the fealty you falsely swore as a bad Christian? Who would have imagined you had such recreance in you? Your captain should mistrust you, since if you can you will betray him too, and though I forgive you, as my death is at hand, I am certain that Mohammed will punish such perfidy."

Refusing to let him continue, Tirant replied: "My lord, calm yourself and do not expect to die. Remember that we were at war, in which all knights must endure setbacks, but still more those mighty princes who prey upon the helpless. Sometimes they make war justly and sometimes unjustly, yet Our Lord, who is just, gives victory to the righteous, wherefore if Fortune has imprisoned you, remember that you are neither the first nor the last."

The Albanian said: "Lord captain, do not fret, since what he accuses me of others will consider a virtue. He should have known that, as a Christian, I would seek his ruin and my freedom, and as for you, good king who greedily hoarded all your spoils, look how much money you amassed by robbing towns and castles your father never left you! They belonged to the virtuous King of Tlemcen, whose lands you cruelly stole, while sacking his villages, raping his women, and mercilessly slaying those who resisted. Hear my words, oh king: such acts are odious to Our Creator, and if you do not mend your ways, your life will soon be over. God placed these words in my heart to chastise your sins, just as He made me the first cause of your undoing, and if He wishes, I am ready to finish the job, for my sword has been sharpened on the whetstone of thieves and murderers. Tell me: who can count the treasure you stole from your vassals, whom you forced to massacre peasants and pay a hundred doubloons for every house they pillaged? You rewarded your troops with wind, saying: 'Rob what you can, as I shall give you nothing.' Were our Christian captain not so merciful, you would have been burnt by now."

Tirant pitied the king, who had to bear such insults, and seeing the bey too surprised to speak, he told the Albanian to hold his tongue.

"What, lord captain?" exclaimed the Albanian. "Do you not wish me to speak the truth? This king is guilty of three mortal sins, for any one of which he should die."

"What are they?" asked Tirant.

"Lord captain," replied the Albanian, "I shall tell you: the first is lust, for he abducted the queen against her will; the second is avarice, as he is the greediest king alive; and the third is envy. In Old Testament times he would have quickly lost his head, but our faith is merciful, and thus he is still alive."

Our knight ordered him to be silent and torment the king no further. Then the Albanian turned to Tirant, whom he addressed in this fashion:

· CCCXX ·

*H*OW THE ALBANIAN ASKED TIRANT TO KNIGHT HIM

"All the world's glory derives from chivalry, as knights not only win honor, respect, and victory over their enemies but also gain power, subdue kingdoms, and make the earth tremble as Alexander did. Though I recognize my unworthiness, I beg Your Lordship to knight me, for with God's help I shall do such deeds that my wrongs will be forgotten. Should any shameful thought cross your mind, let the blame fall on me and plead my case, recalling the words of that wise philosopher who said: 'A knight who does not help, a priest who does not give, a Jew who does not lend, and a peasant who does not serve are worthless.' Therefore, place yourself among the blessed."

Tirant quickly replied:

· CCCXXI ·

*T*IRANT'S REPLY TO THE ALBANIAN

"Old sins will come to light, shameful misdeeds have caused your troubles, and though I do not wish to offend you, your bloody hand has often erred. To grant such a request would sully your honor, wherefore I must refuse you. I shall say no more."

The Albanian replied: "My lord, please tell me why."

Tirant said: "Albanian, you have served me well and I am in your debt, yet I would sooner pay than knight you lest kings, dukes, counts, marquises and other noble lords reproach me. Your base instincts are unworthy of the genteel chivalric order, while worthy knights would condemn you for slandering this noble king and would condemn me as well for betraying my vows. Once knighted, you would be hard put to atone for your miscreancy, and you would do better to become a good squire than a bad knight, for thus the envious will rage at your good fortune. Take these fifty thousand doubloons with my thanks, as you have acted most valiantly."

The man pocketed the doubloons and returned to Albania.

Then Tirant sent two hundred thousand doubloons to one of the bey's cousins who was among the King of Tunis's governors, asking him to ransom Lord Agramunt and his other companions. For love of his cousin, the governor secretly purchased them and sent them to our knight. Seeing they were being taken inland, the slaves lost all hope of freedom, but to their amazement and delight they soon beheld their captain's face.

Tirant asked Lord Agramunt if he had seen Pleasure-of-my-life, to which he replied: "Lord cousin, since our sad shipwreck I have heard no news of her and I suppose she must have perished in the stormy sea."

Poor Tirant then cried: "Would that I might sacrifice my life for hers, and if I had two and a half basins of blood in my body, I would offer her two of them!"

After giving them all fine clothes, arms, horses, and so many doubloons that they felt like men reborn, Tirant and the bey dispatched merchants to buy armor and horses in Christian lands, for the king's armies were only six leagues from Mount Tuber. Aware that King Escariano had sent messengers to ask his relatives for help, Tirant stocked the castle with still more provisions.

One day, King Escariano's troops appeared at dawn and assailed the town. Leaving the bey and Lord Agramunt in the castle, Tirant had a bulwark built just beyond one of the town gates, which he told his soldiers to keep open day and night. On the first assault, their foes saw the open gate and galloped toward it, but so many of them were killed on the bulwark that those behind them could not climb over the corpses. Many of those inside were wounded, yet only a few were slain.

This onslaught lasted till dusk, as when one squadron wearied another would take its place. That night Tirant had the bulwark and trenches repaired wherever necessary, while the attackers, seeing they could do no harm and that many of their men had perished, decided to stop and send for all the bombards that could be found. Tirant had been wounded twice: once in the leg, which was his weak point, and once by an arrow that had grazed his head.

A month then passed with so little fighting that Tirant returned to the castle, leaving Lord Agramunt in charge of the town. When the enemy had collected more than a hundred bombards, they began to fire, and though the stones did great damage, Tirant was powerless to stop them. Then he had an idea and ordered his prisoners lashed to heavy stakes atop the walls. Many of those outside had close relatives among the captives and forbade the bombards to fire, whereupon violent arguments arose and several men were slain. In a pitiful voice, the king begged his captains not to fire for the love of Mohammed, and, deciding not to risk their master's life until his brother the King of Bougie arrived with a mighty host, they hoisted a white flag and declared a two-month truce.[12] Tirant then ordered the prisoners taken down.

Once the truce began, many of the king's relatives and vassals asked to visit him. Tirant and the bey admitted five knights, who after spending each day with their lord would return to their camp, where they awaited the following monarchs: the King of Bougie, whose sister was Queen of Tunis; the King of Fez; King Menador of Persia; the King of Tana;[13] the King of Lesser Armenia; the King of Damascus; King Geber; the King of Granada; and the King of Africa. All were related to King Escariano, and the weakest commanded forty-five thousand soldiers. The King of Belamerin had joined the King of Tunis with eighty thousand men, and both of them were riding toward the besieged castle.

One day the queen summoned Tirant, who, wondering what she wanted, hastened to her chambers though his leg still caused him pain. When Her Majesty saw him, she smiled, bade him be seated, and whispered these words:

· CCCXXII ·

THE QUEEN'S DECLARATION OF LOVE

"My eyes have regained their sight and my uplifted gaze beholds your glory, for Heaven, earth, and all Allah's creatures do the bidding of one who deserves to rule those who cherish honor. Tell me, oh blessed Christian of eternal fame: what robbed your fair countenance of its ruddy hue? Your eyes, which were like twin stars, have now lost their luster, yet they burned most brightly the night you rescued us. Then your beauty so charmed me that I despised my betrothed, and once he died my heart turned to your resplendent chivalry. I know well, lord captain, that I can never repay you, but I beg Our Prophet Mohammed to give you what I cannot. My greatest treasure is this body, though it be scant reward for your services, wherefore I beg you to take me and this land as your guerdon, since I would sooner be your servant than queen of all creation. Were I free and fearless, I would have joined you already, but should you forsake me, death will be my only solace."

Amazed by her declaration, Tirant quickly replied:

· CCCXXIII ·

*T*IRANT'S REPLY

"Were I free, I would willingly grant your request, whose gracious words constrain me to help and champion you, but I cannot offer what is not in my power. My wish to serve you obliges me to confess my sins: I and a noble lady have long since plighted our troth, and as she has always been faithful, I would err if I betrayed her. I prefer death to such baseness, and should the thought cross my mind, I pray God to open the earth and bury me in sorrow. You, my lady, who understand love, should not wish upon another what you would not want yourself. Do not hold yourself affronted, for no other can excel you, nor is any prince so brave that he would not feel blessed to win your beauty. Your words disperse the clouds of ignorance that darkened my mind, while the bright sun of true doctrine warms my will to aid you, and since I have now confessed my sins, your absolution should be more generous.[14] My soul weeps blood and will never rejoice till I behold my lady, yet I assure you of my good will and desire to honor you. Fear of error restrains me from reciting my sorrows, but although my weariness is great, it will never dim my love. There is another reason too that I must not omit: you are a Saracen and I am a Christian, but you may rest assured that I shall never fail you."

With tears in her eyes, the queen replied thus:

· CCCXXIV ·

*T*HE QUEEN'S REPLY TO TIRANT

"Never would I have imagined that so noble a knight could display such cruelty, for if you knew how I have suffered, you would quickly cure me. Do not spurn my pleas lest I die hoping to see you in Heaven or Hell, and though I worship you as a god, my adoration has one flaw: that while I love you for your virtues, you do not love me for mine. You say we cannot marry because I am a Saracen and you are a Christian, but that can easily be resolved by your conversion, and if you claim your faith is better, I shall believe you and embrace it. Therefore, brave knight, open your eyes and look into your heart, since I shall carry out my promises more readily than you suppose. As for that damsel you say you love, I believe you invented her as an excuse, yet I thank you for offering to champion my cause. Although such is your knightly duty, I prefer to consider it the act of a father or lord."

Rejoicing in the queen's offer to embrace Christianity, Tirant decided to show her all the love he could without betraying his princess, and to encourage her good intentions, he then smiled and replied:

· CCCXXV ·

TIRANT'S REPLY TO THE QUEEN

"Words reveal our hopes, which otherwise would be known only to God. Virtuous lady, I wish to serve you not with carnal love but true charity, for what tastes sweet to others is bitter as gall to me, and natural reason compels me to keep faith with my beloved. You cannot be mistress of my person but you can rule my will, as I shall honor you with brave deeds, combining valor and prudence. Anything that will improve its owner is well worth desiring, nor should one wish to die except for something nobler than life, wherefore I beg you to be baptized and join God's company. With His help and mine you will regain your kingdom, and I shall find you a young and stalwart king, since as I said I am already married. Were you and I to wed, I would call you not spouse but mistress, yet your peerless beauty deserves better and any lord would rejoice to win you. Trust my words: if I died in war, your grief would be unbearable. Choose someone who will outlive me, for any man who often enters battle will leave his skin there, and though you weep now for love, you will soon smile at some gentle knight."

When Tirant had ended his speech, the queen dried her tears, sighed, and responded in this fashion:

· CCCXXVI ·

THE QUEEN'S REPLY TO TIRANT

"Your youthful glory makes me long to be your slave, for thus my enamored gaze might always rest upon your noble person. Knowing that you prize fame and spurn worldly riches, I submit to your words and shall do as you say. Since one can often forsake a course not clearly charted, whereas afterward it can only be relinquished with great shame, I ask you, the flower of the baptized, to quickly baptize me."

Beholding the queen's good will, Tirant sent for a golden basin and pitcher. Then he asked the lady to uncover her hair, which shone as dazzlingly as any angel's, and to kneel while he sprinkled her head with water, saying: "Emeraldine, I baptize you in the name of the Father, the Son, and the Holy Ghost."

From that moment on, she deemed herself a good Christian. Four damsels in her service also received Christ that day, and they all led honorable and holy lives thereafter.

When King Escariano learned of his queen's conversion, he summoned Tirant and addressed him thus:

· CCCXXVII ·

*H*OW KING ESCARIANO ASKED TIRANT TO MAKE HIM A CHRISTIAN

"Just as adversity often tests a man's mettle, so has God brought me low to augment my honor. Battles fought for love embolden worthy knights, nor would this world long endure if enamored kings found no champions, wherefore I declare, brave defender of your faith, that as my wife has become a Christian I shall follow her example. Baptize me and be my comrade as long as we live, helping my friends and chastening my enemies. Should you consent, I shall be eternally grateful, but first I wish to study Christian doctrine and the Trinity, that I may receive Christ's precious body more devoutly. If you can instruct me, I beg you to do so, yet from what my eyes have seen, I imagine you know more of war than theology."

Tirant replied: "My lord, though I know but little, I shall share what I learned as a boy: Christian doctrine tells us to believe not by reason but by faith, for these matters are so lofty that the more you delve into them, the less you understand, and only God's grace can illumine a sinner. Though I bear arms, I know something of spiritual matters, but even if I were learned enough to discuss the Holy Trinity, you would still have to elevate your understanding to fathom it."

Then Tirant told him everything a Christian knight should know about his faith, and so great was the king's devotion that with the Holy Ghost's help, he came to understand Christianity as though he had practiced it all his life. Then he joyously exclaimed: "Brave captain, I never would have thought any knight could explain the Trinity so well, as you alone have taught me more than all those friars in my court. Now that through God's grace I understand this holy mystery, please tell me what the greatest blessing is in life."

Seeing the king's good will, Tirant replied in the following manner:

· CCCXXVIII ·

*L*IFE'S GREATEST BLESSING[15]

"Varied opinions on this subject were held by the ancients, many of whom favored riches, which may bring a man honor. Virgil, who was one of these, wrote treatises on amassing wealth, while Caesar also strove to gain worldly prizes. Others advocated knighthood, as knights win many victories, and among these was Lucan, who wrote tales of chivalry. Still others sought health, which prolongs a man's life. One such was Galen, who composed works on how to heal the sick, nor did Constantine hesitate to sacrifice his empire for his health. Some preferred love, which makes men glad and joyful, and among these were Ovid and Boccaccio, who celebrated Troilus, Cressida, and fair Helen.[16] Others said good customs raised men from baseness, and one of these was Cato, who wrote books about proper conduct. Still others defended wisdom, which helps us know ourselves, God, and God's creatures. Such a one was Aristotle, who wrote books of great sagacity, and another was Solomon, to whom God granted unequaled sapience and who said: 'I cherish wisdom, which is enlightenment of the soul. For wisdom I shall be honored by elders and youths. I shall possess keenness of judgment in the sight of rulers, and thus my government of nations will always be remembered.'[17]

"Men should heed his words, for wisdom is more precious than gold or silver, and though many pursue knowledge, they are not all truly wise. Those who flaunt their learning are guilty of pride and their wisdom is mere wind, while others who use it to gain riches, thus committing the sin of avarice, would do better to study medicine, through which they might become wealthy. Others seek wisdom in order to win praise, but such men are vainglorious and learn only what suits them: the nature and movements of the planets, the properties of elements, and such matters. Still others strive to know themselves, being inspired by God's virtue, and their understanding is sound, for by living well and serving their Maker, such men win celestial glory and become known as sages. My lord, now that I have answered your question as best I can, I ask you to be baptized that we may live as comrades-in-arms."

The king said he was ready and that his greatest desire was to become a Christian, to which Tirant replied: "Sire, I beg you to swear to our brotherhood, first on the Kaaba as a Saracen and then as a Christian after your baptism."

The king said he would gladly do so, and to test him, Tirant asked: "My lord, do you wish to be baptized publicly or privately?"

"What?" cried the king. "Do you think I wish to deceive God? I want everyone to witness my baptism and conversion, which I hope will inspire my knights to do likewise. Please send for them right away."

Expecting great benefits for his holy faith, Tirant sent a Moor to summon King Escariano's captains and their troops, whom their lord urged to come peacefully and unarmed.

· CCCXXIX ·

HOW KING ESCARIANO WAS BAPTIZED

After baptizing the queen, Tirant freed her suitor and brought him to the town, where a platform hung with silk brocade had been erected in a square. The king seated himself upon it in his royal robes, while our knight placed a silver basin of water beside him and sent for a broad stairway, that those who wished to convert might ascend.

King Escariano's men set out on foot, as they had camped close to town, and upon reaching the gates, his knights, captains, and soldiers all entered. Seeing their lord on the platform, they bowed and awaited his orders, whereupon His Majesty boldly addressed them thus: "Faithful vassals, comrades, and brothers, God has blessed us with His grace, for this virtuous Christian captain has done me two great favors: first, he set me free; and second, he taught me Christian doctrine, exposing the falsehood of Mohammed's sect and the damnation of its wicked followers, wherefore I ask you to be baptized here today, that your souls may be saved from Hell and damnation. Those who wish to embrace the truth should remain where they are, while those who do not should leave the square, that others may enter it."

When the king had uttered these words and stripped down to his shirt, Tirant led him to the basin, poured water over his head, and said: "King Escariano, I baptize you in the name of the Father, the Son, and the Holy Ghost."

Tirant then baptized most of the other prisoners, almost all of whom were the king's close companions, including two captains and their families, one of which was called Ibn al-Sarray and the other Capsan. Altogether, more than six thousand Saracens converted, and this same procedure was followed every day thereafter, though a few of the vilest scoundrels refused and left the square.

Then Tirant told the king: "Sire, when you were a Saracen you promised to be my brother-in-arms, and I ask you now to repeat your oath as a Christian."

The king said he would gladly do so, and after writing the names of the four Gospels on a piece of paper, Tirant placed it before his friend, who swore the following oath:

· CCCXXX ·

KING ESCARIANO'S OATH

"I, King Escariano of Greater Ethiopia by God's grace, place my hands on the Gospels and swear as a true Christian to be a loyal brother-in-arms to you, Tirant lo Blanc, as long as we live, succoring your friends and chastising your enemies. Likewise, I place my riches at your disposal, and should you be imprisoned, I shall risk my life to save you."

Tirant repeated the same oath, as he had before when the king was a Saracen, whereupon they embraced, and from that day on all brothers-in-arms spoke those words.

Then Tirant continued his baptisms, but the flood of Saracen converts threatened to halt his campaign until one lucky day they spied a friar who had come on a merchant ship to ransom Christian slaves.

The friar was from Valencia, a most blessed and noble Spanish port endowed with valiant knights and abundant in everything but spices. This city, which exports more merchandise than any other, is inhabited by virtuous, peaceful, and well-spoken men. Though its women are not very fair, they are wittier than elsewhere and captivate men's fancies with their charming ways and sweet discourse. In the future, Valencia's wickedness will be the cause of its downfall, for it will be populated by nations of cursed seed and men will come to distrust their own fathers and brothers. According to Elias, it will have to bear three scourges: Jews, Saracens, and Moorish converts. He also calls the city blessed because it lies beneath the sun's sphere.[18]

But to return to our story, this friar, who knew that a Christian captain had captured King Escariano and freed the slaves from a shipwrecked galley, came to ask Tirant for a donation to help redeem Valencians. After welcoming him with great joy, Tirant asked him to complete the baptisms, and in the following days he set 44,327 infidels on the path to salvation.

Those who clung to their faith departed, leaving only the Christians.

The news spread through Barbary until it reached the lords on their way to rescue King Escariano, and in their rage they invaded Ethiopia, which they entrusted to the Prince of Persia.

During this time, King Escariano received reports every day about the conquest of his realm, and at last, when there were only three castles left, his foes marshaled their troops to storm them.

After King Escariano was baptized, Tirant asked him to restore the Queen of Tlemcen's captured cities and towns, to which the king generously agreed but begged our knight to help him win her hand.

"Sire," replied Tirant, "leave it to me; I shall plead with her till she consents, as under Christian law marriage by force is invalid."

Then they rode forth, leaving Lord Agramunt in charge of the castle. Seeing the converts' love of Tirant, whose eloquence and generosity had won their hearts, the bey asked to continue in his faith until such time as he felt moved to renounce it. Tirant readily agreed, for he deferred to the bey as much as possible and would only speak in council once he and the king had finished.

The king and his knights went to Tlemcen, which he restored to Queen Emeraldine along with her other towns and castles. Almost all her subjects had converted, and the friar instructed them in true Christian doctrine.

One day the queen, having regained her sovereignty, proposed to Tirant again in the following manner:

· CCCXXXI ·

*T*HE NEW QUEEN OF TLEMCEN'S PROPOSAL TO TIRANT

"I must tell you what powers love has given you, for my tears reveal the grief that afflicts my weary soul, and though I swear I shall die if you do not save me, yet fear of refusal augments my torments. Lord Tirant, grant me life or speedy death but do not prolong my anguish, as my pleas are just and holy. Have no fear of the king, since victors always excel the vanquished, and love's laws outweigh not only friendship but even God. Nothing can rival love, which makes the wise foolish, the old young, the rich poor, the stingy generous, the sad happy, and the happy pensive. Many fathers have adored their daughters, as have brothers their sisters, yet it is proven that steadfast love only thrives among the wise, whereas the vulgar are like asses and love whatever they see. Therefore, brave knight, let your devotion match your wisdom, and pity one whose sole desire is to honor and serve you."

After thinking awhile, Tirant replied:

· CCCXXXII ·

*T*IRANT'S REPLY TO THE QUEEN

"No one can build a mighty fortress upon sand, and I speak thus, my lady, to remind you of my words, since I cannot grant what is in another's power and Your Highness knows true love is indivisible. Therefore open your eyes, forbidding grief to blind you with vain hopes, and heed my advice to turn your thoughts elsewhere, as my deeds will show I cherish you as a daughter or sister. Please take brave King Escariano as your husband, for you already know how he adores you, and by living peacefully in your kingdom, you will please me and serve His Majesty, who will be most grateful."

Beholding Tirant's will and how little choice she had, the afflicted queen replied in this fashion:

· CCCXXXIII ·

*T*HE QUEEN'S REPLY TO TIRANT

"My grief turns to joy at your steadfast devotion, and I know you should be canonized for your noble love. Do not think I can be comforted, as I shall always worship your gentility, but if I cannot wed you I shall serve you as a daughter. I pray God to grant you prosperity, which you refuse from my hand, allowing you to save the world as you rescued me from perdition, and I promise to obey your every command."

Hearing the queen's gentle speech, Tirant knelt to thank her and then summoned the friar, who married her and King Escariano. Their wedding was solemn, as befitted a royal couple, and on the morrow Tirant made them attend Mass like good Catholics. The king, who now also ruled Tlemcen, cherished our knight above all men and would have done anything for him, and Tirant, for his part, also loved the king and queen.

While the couple was feasting and celebrating the marriage, news came every day of an impending attack, since once the Saracens took those castles they planned to massacre the Christians. Knowing this, Tirant said: "My lords, we must defend our lives. How many men are ready for battle?"

"What?" cried the bey. "Do you think you rule the world? Having captured the king, you should depart and let us live in our faith, for if these newfangled Christians renounce their so-called baptism, our foes may yet spare us."

King Escariano drew his sword and, turning to the bey in great fury, split his head so that his brains spilled onto the floor. Then the black cried: "Oh dog, son of dogs, seed of an evil sect! This is the reward your vile person deserves!"

Tirant, though furious, held his peace lest some greater evil ensue. The bey's death pleased some and displeased others, but it served as an example to all those on Mount Tuber.

Then Tirant counted their troops, which numbered 18,230 cavalry and 45,000 infantry. He told the king to pay them and said: "Sire, let us offer privileges to attract more men."

The king, who now rued his crime, replied in this fashion:

· CCCXXXIV ·

*H*OW KING ESCARIANO APOLOGIZED TO TIRANT AND THEY MADE FRIENDS AGAIN

"Alas, what grief to think my wrongdoing has enraged you, and I shall slay myself if your virtue does not pardon me! Have pity, as excess of wrath made me kill him and I could not stay my hand."

After weeping and showing his contrition, King Escariano said: "Lord and brother, command me, for all your orders shall be obeyed."

Tirant, who felt much happier when he heard the king speak so humbly, quickly approached His Majesty and kissed him many times. Thus their comradeship grew, since Tirant loved him truly, while the king both loved and feared his Breton friend.

Once they had made peace, Tirant proclaimed the following privileges: any man with a horse and armor could become a gentleman, anyone with two horses could be a peer, and those with three horses were dubbed knights of noble lineage and exempted from taxes on their farms and villages. Through this proclamation, Tirant gathered twenty-five thousand of the bravest men in Barbary, who fiercely defended their new rights and helped conquer many kingdoms but who also were quarrelsome and often killed each other.

When Tirant saw them brawling, he issued another proclamation: any gentleman, peer, or knight who slew, wounded, or abused another would be beheaded, and if he could not be captured, his family would become commoners again. To retain their privileges, the new recruits made peace, and when quarrels arose they no longer fought but appealed to their captain. Everyone praised Tirant's judgments, and, wishing he were their king, they greeted him with shouts of: "Long live our generous captain!"

When this had been done, four hundred and forty Sicilian chargers arrived with such splendid trappings and armor that our knight would have sent them against three thousand cavalry.

Tirant's men set out to meet the Saracens, and upon reaching a town perched on a mountaintop, they spied their foes in the distance. Some groups were encamped only three leagues away, while messengers hurried to and fro, angrily warning King Escariano that unless his troops converted they would be slaughtered. Tirant merely laughed at this empty threat, and once the messengers had departed, he told his comrade: "My lord, they should arrive tomorrow, so let us await them here. Guard this town with half our troops. I shall take the rest, and if they are badly arrayed, I promise to make short work of them."

"Brother Tirant, I would sooner accompany you and leave Lord Agramunt in charge, as I wish to live or die by your side."

Seeing the king's will, Tirant made Lord Agramunt captain and said: "Keep the horses saddled, forbid your men to remove their armor, and when you see a red flag, attack their right flank. They will camp near that river, in whose deep waters many will perish, but do not leave the town until you behold my flag."

To reach their enemies, the Saracens had to ride up a mountain, and Tirant circled around its base until he caught sight of them in the distance. Then he told his troops to dismount in a thick wood where they could rest, and after climbing a tall pine, he watched the infidels pitching camp. It had taken them all day to advance two leagues, and it was another league from their camp to the town.

When the rearguard reached the mountain and spied the others above them, they decided to camp in a fair meadow near a wide canal. There were only about forty thousand of them, but they felt safe with help nearby.

Once half their foes had dismounted, Tirant and the king attacked. They killed an astonishing number of Saracens and would have slain more had night not fallen. Those on the mountain heard the cries but never imagined what had occurred.

At dawn King Menador descended, and, thinking Tirant's men were a small raiding party, he sent a messenger to demand their surrender, as otherwise he swore by Mohammed to hang every one of them. Tirant replied: "Tell your master I shall not answer his foolish words, but if he is brave enough to attack, he will learn whom he threatens and will drink from grief's bitter cup all the days of his life!"

The messenger took the reply back to his master, who furiously spurred his mount while all his soldiers followed him. A most cruel battle ensued, and after many Saracens had perished, King Menador retreated with the survivors and summoned his brother, the King of Lesser Armenia. When he arrived, King Menador said: "Lord and brother, those baptized Christians are the bravest soldiers alive, for though we fought them all day, instead of retreating they routed us. I shall not consider myself a knight if I do not slay their recreant captain, who wears a damask coat of arms with three silver stars on one side and three gold ones on the other. An image of his Mohammed hangs from his neck: a bearded man crossing a river with a child on his shoulder.[19] I suppose that child must be his son, to whom the captain appeals for help."

The King of Lesser Armenia replied scornfully: "Let me have at him and I shall soon be avenged, though ten Mohammeds dwelt in his belly."

Then he turned to his men and addressed them thus:

· CCCXXXV ·

*T*HE KING OF LESSER ARMENIA'S SPEECH TO HIS COMRADES

"Friends, brothers, and noble knights who cherish honor, I beg you to help avenge my brother's shame. May your cries be so loud that our foes will flee in disarray as you bear away the ones I fell, though you will be hard put to collect them."

Clad in brilliant gold jubbahs and uttering bloodcurdling screams, his men mounted their steeds and charged with such ferocity that many horses were soon riderless. When Tirant's lance broke he seized his ax, harming someone with every stroke. Once the two kings were near our knight, one stabbed him with his sword, whereupon the Breton cried: "Oh king, you have slain me, but before going to Hell, I shall send you to announce me and open the door!"

He brought his ax down on the king's head, splitting it in two, and the monarch fell beneath his horse's hoofs while the Saracens fought to retrieve his body. This was the King of Lesser Armenia, who had spoken with such braggadocio.

Seeing his brother's corpse, King Menador fought even more desperately, but it was Tirant's wound that saved many Saracens from death or injury. When they spied their dead leader, they hurried to inform the King of Bougie, who ordered everyone to break camp and follow him down the mountain. It was night by the time they reached the bottom and pitched their tents.

At the sight of such a horde, the Christians hurriedly took counsel, and, after learning that their captain was in great pain, they decided to retreat under cover of darkness. The infidels planned an assault the next morning, but finding no one there, they followed their foes' tracks to the town.

Tirant then sent Lord Agramunt forth with their remaining troops. He valiantly attacked, and many died on both sides, but at last the Saracens broke through the Christian ranks and pushed them toward the walls. They retreated as best they could, fighting till they were inside the town, while their enemies pursued them and battered the gates with their lance butts.

King Escariano, who was in charge of the defense, led his men forth on the morrow, but after a long and bloody battle, the Christians had to withdraw again. Tirant, whose heart ached to behold such carnage, said: "My lord, you should stop these sorties, as we are only wasting soldiers."

And so they stayed in the town till Tirant recovered.

When Tirant was almost well, he wished to ride forth and give battle, but King Escariano reprimanded him in the following manner:

· CCCXXXVI ·

HOW KING ESCARIANO FONDLY REBUKED TIRANT

"You must think you have already won the battle, as I see you burning with desire to have at our foes. Do you not see those grey skies threatening death by snow, rain, thunder, and lightning? Who values his life so little that he would attack in such inauspicious weather? Therefore please wait till you are cured and the storm has passed, at which time you may display your mettle with far less risk. I shall not restrain you, since my place is only to beg, but should you come to any harm, I would sooner die than live in grief."

Tirant quickly replied:

· CCCXXXVII ·

TIRANT'S REPLY TO KING ESCARIANO

"I shall not speak long or recount my deeds, as warriors should never praise their own victories, but neither do I wish to lessen my reward. God in Heaven cares little for us or our sufferings, but He will forgive us if we behave like worthy knights."

Tirant quickly called for his armor, mounted a fine steed, and led most of their forces against one side of the enemy camp. The Saracens rushed to ward off the attack, and Tirant got the worst not only of that battle but of many others that followed it. Instead of rallying his troops, he was forced to watch them flee, and one day in his despair he rode to the river, where he was spied by the King of Africa, who wore a gold bejeweled crown over his helmet. His saddle was silver, his stirrups were gold, and he had donned a crimson jubbah embroidered with oriental pearls.

Seeing Tirant, he called out: "Are you the Christian captain?"

Instead of replying, Tirant gazed after his fleeing troops. The ground was strewn with corpses piled amid their flags and standards, for that day his men had barely resisted. Then he exclaimed: "Oh wretched soldiers, why do you bear arms? Sad and recreant knights, you have disgraced yourselves and died shameful deaths, wherefore your memory will be scorned and bemoaned forever!"

Then he turned to the East, raising his eyes Heavenward and clasping his hands, while he cried: "Oh eternal God of Mercy, for what sin do You thus forsake me when my sole desire is to augment Your holy faith? Here I am alone, abandoned by all my men, wondering what will become of me if I have caused this evil. Let me die before my ears must endure such infamy, for if I lose Your grace, death or slavery await me."

The King of Africa heard these laments and told his men: "I shall ford the river and kill or capture that Christian dog. Do not help me unless I need you."

Upon reaching the other side, the king charged Tirant, whom he struck so fiercely that the Breton's horse fell to its knees. The monarch's lance pierced his breastplate and nearly killed him, for in his dejection Tirant had not noticed the king's approach. The infidel then drew his sword, as his lance was broken, but despite his valor and prowess, our knight landed a blow that would have been mortal had his adversary's horse not stumbled at that moment. Tirant's sword split the animal's head, whereupon mount and rider fell to earth, while the king's men hastened to his defense and rehorsed him despite his foe's best efforts.

Seeing that the king had eluded him, Tirant grabbed a Saracen's lance, with which he quickly knocked six others from their saddles. His lance broke, but he seized his ax and smote one enemy with such force that he split the infidel's head to the breastbone.

Beholding such destruction, the Saracens cried out in consternation: "Oh Mohammed, what Christian is this who routs our entire army? Woe unto the man his ax strikes next!"

Lord Agramunt, who was in the castle, looked out a window and spied Tirant, whom he recognized by his coat of arms. He was fighting all alone, and Lord Agramunt shouted: "My lords, hurry to your captain's aid, as his life is in peril!"

The king sallied forth with his few remaining men, yet they nearly arrived too late, for Tirant was bleeding in three places and his horse was covered with wounds. He had to retreat, not as he would have liked to but fleeing for his very life.

The hapless Christians lost every battle they fought, while the Saracens rejoiced at their foes' misfortune and poor Tirant cried: "When I see them glory in our discomfiture, I wish that I had perished when no one succored me!"

Beholding his friend's distress, King Escariano comforted him thus:

· CCCXXXVIII ·

*H*OW KING ESCARIANO COMFORTED TIRANT

"No one can forsee the future, which is known only to God. Cowards may weep over tomorrow's misfortunes, but you know better than I that though battles be lost and soldiers slain, brave knights may still win victory's crown of glory. Trust in God, who, having allowed you to exalt His holy faith, will now also heal your wounds, for He never forsakes His servants. All of us, even the enemy, know your courage and nobility will triumph, as your deeds deserve nothing less than an empire. Let your valor be an example, since you are the sun from which we take our light."

Feeling comforted by King Escariano's spirited words, Tirant replied:

· CCCXXXIX ·

*T*IRANT'S REPLY TO KING ESCARIANO

"Oh most noble of mortals, my laments should not surprise you, as it is not fear that daunts me but these wounds, which delay my vengeance. Your kind words and brave spirit have restored my will to live, wherefore I, who shall now be even more your servant, celebrate the coming victories that will augment your power and glory."

As Tirant was speaking, the king's doctors entered and removed his armor, beneath which they found many wounds, including three serious ones.

Once their foes' sorties had stopped, the Saracens tightened the siege and crossed the river with such enormous herds of cattle and camels that the Christians could barely ride in or out.

By now the king and everyone else considered themselves as good as dead. Tirant, who feared the Saracens would tunnel under the walls, ordered a countermine dug and filled with brass bowls that would rattle at every blow of their pickaxes. [20]

A few days after Tirant's wounds had healed, a servant girl in the castle bakery heard the bowls rattling and hastened to her mistress, to whom she said: "I do not know why, but those bowls are clanging like a bloody battle."

Her mistress, who was the keeper of the castle's wife, quickly sent her husband to inform Tirant and the king.

They crept into the countermine and, finding that the girl had spoken truly, fetched their weapons and waited in a nearby chamber. Within an hour light began to appear. Thinking no one had spied them, the infidels widened their tunnel, from which the first men soon emerged, and when there were about sixty, Tirant and his soldiers fell upon the intruders. Many were hacked to pieces while others tried to escape, but the Christians fired bombards into the tunnel and slew them all.

Knowing that his troops fretted about their dwindling provisions, Tirant told the king: "Sire, give me half our remaining soldiers, whom I shall hide in that grove till you set out from the Tlemcen gate. Once you have circled the town and launched a frontal assault, I shall attack from the rear, and by trapping them between us, we may yet rout our foes and capture their camp. Our greatest problem will be those cattle, which often gore our horses."

A wise Genoese named Almedixer, who had been a slave on Tirant's galley, asked: "Lord captain, would you like me to stampede the cattle? While the Saracens are chasing them, you can mount your attack."

"If you do that," replied Tirant, "I promise by my lady Carmesina to give you so many towns and castles that you will be more than satisfied."

The king told Tirant: "Lord brother, please let me hide in that grove. When I see a flag on the highest tower, I shall ride into battle."

Tirant agreed and then ordered his men to have their horses well shod and saddled.

After gathering great quantities of goat's hair and mutton fat, the Genoese chopped it all up fine and placed it in sixty large pans. Before anyone set out, Tirant summoned their troops to the main square, where he mounted a platform and delivered the following speech:

· CCCXL ·

TIRANT'S SPEECH TO HIS MEN

"Noble knights and barons, tomorrow we may win great honor, for our glory will resound if so few can rout so many! Fret no more about their conscripts, who are here against their wills, but be mindful that God aids champions whose cause is just and holy. It is better to die with honor than to live in shameful slavery, and if you bravely risk death, He will crown you before His angels."

Hearing Tirant's words, the soldiers wept tears of joy and resolved to either triumph or die like good Christians.

At midnight the king led his men to the grove, while Almedixer placed the pans outside the walls. He lit them at daybreak and fanned the smoke toward the cattle, which stampeded through the camp, ripping up tents and wounding men and horses. They butted and gored each other until there was scarcely a single unwounded camel or ox left, and though many soldiers pursued them, no one knew what had caused such turmoil.[21] Tirant and his men, who had neither seen nor heard of such a thing, also marveled at the stampede of more than five thousand oxen, cattle, and camels.

Once the cattle had been disposed of, Tirant hoisted a green and white flag, which the king saw and shouted: "Have at them, valiant Christians!"

Tirant then attacked from the other side and a cruel battle ensued, in which a multitude of worthy knights were either slain or wounded. The tumult was so terrifying that it sounded like the earth was giving way, while Tirant rode to and fro, knocking helmets off heads and shields out of hands, killing and maiming with inexhaustible fury. King Escariano also fought like a ravening lion, but there were many dauntless knights among the Saracens too, and especially the King of Africa, who battled fiercely to avenge his brother. Neither side gave any quarter, and Lord Agramunt sowed terror among his foes.

It happened that the King of Africa spied our knight's arms and charged him so furiously that both captains were unhorsed, but Tirant, who was the more spirited, regained his feet first and went to sever the thongs on his adversary's helmet. The press was so great that he could barely move and it was a wonder he did not perish, for twice his foes dragged him off the king. When Lord Agramunt saw the captain of the enemy camp doing his best to kill Tirant, he spurred his mount and each smote the other mortal blows: the Christian to defend his cousin and the Saracen to slay him. Both Bretons were near death when Almedixer, who was also badly wounded, rode up and shouted: "Will this noble captain, the flower of chivalry, die today?"

One of those baptized peers who was mortally wounded hastened to King Escariano and cried: "My lord, rescue your captain and brother-in-arms! He is surrounded by infidels, and it will be a miracle if he escapes alive! Help him, for if he perishes we all shall be lost!"

King Escariano attacked with all his forces just as the King of Bougie was about to behead Tirant. Recognizing the king, who was his brother, by his arms and the gold bejeweled monkey on his helmet, the black charged with such fury that he transfixed the monarch's heart. The infidel fell and his allies did their best to rescue his body, while many knights who had been unhorsed found other mounts and the battle raged even more fiercely than before. The fighting lasted until nightfall, when the Christians entered the town in triumph, since they had carried the day and slain three kings: King Geber, and the rulers of Bougie and Granada. They had also wounded the Kings of Damascus and Tana.

Tirant's men and their horses rested so well that by sunrise they were ready for battle, to the great astonishment of their enemies, who had not yet buried their dead. The second day was bloody too, but as neither the Saracens nor their horses were well armored, a hundred infidels died for every Christian casualty. After five more days of fighting, the heathens could bear the stench of corpses no longer and sent messengers to request a truce, which the Christians quickly granted.

Every day Tirant attended Mass with the king and all his men. Once the truce had been declared, our knight prayed Christ and His Mother to show which corpses were Christian, that they might be buried as holy martyrs to their faith. The Lord heard his just pleas and answered them in this fashion: all the Christians gazed Heavenward, their hands were clasped, and they smelled sweet, whereas the Saracens lay face down and stank like dogs.[22] Upon beholding this miracle, Tirant asked the friar to record it lest men forget that those who die for God go straight to Heaven. The Christians buried their dead with great honor, and a church was later dedicated to Saint John where the fighting had been thickest.

The Saracens threw their dead in the river, with each man's name written on a piece of leather so that his relatives downstream might identify his body, but the corpses dammed up the river so much that it changed course.

The infidels withdrew into the mountains while their foes remained in the town, and during this truce, the Marquis of Liçana arrived from France. Disguising himself as a merchant, he had sailed in a galley from Aiguesmortes to Majorca and thence in a ship to Tunis, where he heard of Tirant's exploits and hastened to join him. As he approached, wondering whether the truce had already ended, he stopped in a town called Safra and wrote a note to Tirant, whom he informed of his whereabouts and asked for an escort.

As soon as Tirant received the message, he dispatched Almedixer with a thousand soldiers, but the Saracens witnessed their departure and sent ten thousand cavalry to ambush them. The King of Africa, who was now captain, hid his men in a wood, and when they saw the returning Christians, they attacked and killed or captured most of the party. A few escaped and brought the news to Tirant, who then swore the following vow:

· CCCXLI ·

TIRANT'S VOW TO ACCEPT NEITHER PEACE NOR TRUCE

"I curse my youthful ignorance for accepting a truce when victory was in our hands! How blind I was not to foresee our foes' treachery! I mourn the imprisoned marquis, yet I granted that truce for their sake, knowing it would harm us while they received reinforcements. I would not be surprised if we ended where we began, since every man we lose is like a thousand for them. Therefore I vow to accept neither truce nor peace until this war ends, and if any more are declared, I shall depart immediately."

Distressed by Tirant's words and feeling responsible for his dejection, King Escariano humbly replied in this manner:

· CCCXLII ·

KING ESCARIANO'S REPLY

"Death, which no man can escape, does not dismay me, but I grieve to think my errors caused our defeat. Your anger torments me, as I know I am to blame, and therefore I beg you to pardon my wrongdoing. Henceforth I shall heed your counsel, since we shall quickly be vanquished if Your Lordship forsakes us."

Moved by the king's pleas, Tirant replied in a gentle voice:

· CCCXLIII ·

TIRANT'S REPLY TO KING ESCARIANO

"Never shall I deny a friend who shows contrition, and since I forgive my enemies, I should be much quicker with those I love. Trust me, for I shall never abandon you, and if I had a hundred lives I would risk them all for you. Though we have lost many soldiers and are outnumbered ten to one, I shall plot some clever ruse to preserve our knightly honor."

Consoled by Tirant's kind words, King Escariano swore to obey him.

"If such is the case," replied Tirant, "set out this evening with fourteen thousand cavalry, and when you reach Tlemcen, collect all the asses, mules, and donkeys you can find and conscript every man, woman, and child in the city. Leave only those who are useless, like the aged, crippled, or women who have just given birth, and after gathering everyone else between seven and eighty-five years of age, give each a steed covered with white trappings. Should you not find enough mounts, leave the weakest folk behind, and if they lack white cloth make them use sheets and blankets. They should all be wearing white gowns over their jubbahs, while the women and children should hold calabashes covered with white cloth upon their heads."[23]

Tirant also advised the king to take his queen, in whose presence the women of Tlemcen would obey him more readily.

The king quickly mustered his troops and set out as secretly as he could. Once he had gone, Tirant sent an emissary to demand the release of the marquis and the other knights: "All of them. Otherwise, prepare for battle in ten days."

While he waited, Tirant had a deep moat dug around the town. King Escariano returned on the appointed day, leading more than forty thousand men and women who entered in broad daylight that the Saracens might behold them.

The enemy attacked at midnight as the last day of truce ended, but Tirant, who was wise in warfare, always slept in his armor. He quickly dispatched four hundred men to defend the walls facing the Saracens, while the king and his troops sallied forth, circled the town, and attacked their foes from the rear. All the Christians were dressed in white, including the women, who stood in the moat with two hundred men guarding them. Each lady held a thick staff, and they clustered together.

In this battle, which was harsh and indescribably bloody, our knight carried a short, thick lance reinforced with leather thongs. Woe unto those infidels who felt its bitter sting, for their souls poured into the blackest pits of Hell! Tirant had left the five hundred best Christian knights behind, and seeing that his cause would triumph, he abandoned the press and fetched the reserves, with whom he entered the Saracen camp, crying: "Marquis of Liçana, shout if you are here, as Tirant lo Blanc has come to free you!"

When Almedixer and the marquis heard those heavenly voices, they approached our knight, who told them to mount behind his men. Once they were out of the camp, he smashed their chains, armed them, and set the enemy tents ablaze. Then they returned to the battlefield, where Tirant dealt such mortal blows that none could face him, but his foes also fought fiercely and did all the harm they could. The longer the fray lasted, the crueler it became, as there were so many corpses that the soldiers could hardly move. Seeing his defeated army, his burning camp, and those motionless women whom he had not noticed, the King of Tunis cried:

"My lords, I cannot believe these are Christians, for either they are baptized devils or Mohammed has converted. That king has bested us and destroyed our camp with a handful of men, nor have all our multitudes been able to resist them! Those soldiers in the moat, moreover, have not even begun to fight, but once we are weary they will hack us to pieces. I think we should retreat, not to our camp but to that mountain, since I fear those white-clad devils more than our present adversaries. Never have I seen such tall and mighty warriors!" This was because of the calabashes the women bore on their heads.

Then the King of Africa boldly began to speak:

· CCCXLIV ·

HOW THE KING OF AFRICA SPOKE HIS MIND

"On my faith, King of Tunis, a hundred miseries beset my soul, and though I also fear death, I cannot forget my brother. My heart cries out for vengeance, which I shall take with my own hands, nor should you be timid or hesitant in aiding me. Put aside your fears, which are unworthy of our dead comrades, for ever since my brother died grief has obliged me to follow his banner. I expect no victories, since bad luck has always been my lot, but I prefer to die in battle and live on in glorious fame."

Without another word he charged into the fray and by chance met the Marquis of Liçana, whom he struck so fiercely that man and horse both fell to earth, where the marquis would have perished had Lord Agramunt not saved him. The Christian flag bearer then hurled himself into the press, which was witness to some of the noblest feats of arms in history, as the Saracens also showed their mettle with ceaseless cries of "Mohammed!" There were many riderless horses, while a multitude of dead and wounded littered the ground.

The battle lasted until two hours past midday, but no one knew which army was winning. The King of Tunis, who bore a little statue of Mohammed on his gold helmet, recognized Tirant's starry tunic and asked his fellow monarchs: "Do you want to carry the day? If we can slay that brave knight, all those Christians will be our slaves."

Clad in shining armor and rich attire, they galloped toward Tirant, who, as soon as he saw them coming plunged into their midst like a raging lion. The first to taste his lance was the King of Tana, whose harness availed him little, for he fell to earth dead. Then Tirant charged the King of Tunis, whom he smote on the arm, and seeing himself unhorsed, the hapless sovereign cried: "Oh King of Africa, now I see what your folly will cost us, as we shall lose not only this battle but our lives as well!"

King Escariano and Almedixer hurried to aid Tirant and bravely wounded the King of Tunis, whom they brought into the city. A Saracen contrived to steal our knight's lance, but, seizing the ax that always hung from his saddlebow, he smote the foe so hard that the blow split his head to the breastbone. Never had Hercules, Achilles, Troilus, Hector, Paris, Samson, Judas Maccabaeus, Galahan, Lancelot, Tristram, or ardent Theseus landed such a splendid buffet. The Saracens were confounded and, seeing their lances broken, they sounded the retreat and fled toward the mountain. The Christians were glad to see them go, for they needed a rest, but they pursued them all the same to make their victory more glorious, while Tirant rode wherever the danger was greatest.

Once their foes were out of reach, the Christians returned to the town, whose inhabitants shouted: "Hurrah for noble Tirant! Blessed the day he baptized us! May God make him King of Barbary!"

Upon reaching the castle amid great rejoicing, they found the King of Tunis watching the queen and all her ladies enter astride mules and donkeys, still holding those calabashes wrapped in sheets on their heads. Filled with despair at Tirant's deception, the king tore the bandages from his wounds and refused to let them heal, whereby he caused his own death, though not before uttering this lament:

· CCCXLV ·

*T*HE KING OF TUNIS'S LAMENT

"Tirant's fame grows ever greater and all Moorish kings should bow before him, as his valiant deeds will surely win an imperial crown, yet he vanquished us not by force but through that trick with the women. Though in the first battle we lost some kings, our troops carried the day, but on this occasion our own stupidity defeated us, wherefore my sole desire is to be buried in disgrace, since my ignorance of war cost many ladies their sons and husbands. I would sooner end my life than witness further cruelty, nor can we hope to conquer such disciplined and skillful warriors. His captains are seasoned veterans, and his soldiers never flee but place their hopes in their right arms rather than in their feet as we have done. We are mocked and discomfited by this brilliant captain, who always offers wise counsel, instructing others in warfare. He burned our camp and defeated our hordes with those women, at whose sight we cravenly abandoned the field, and I swear, glorious captain, that until today I was undefeated."

Tirant begged the king to let his wounds be treated, for they were not serious, but the monarch replied: "Trouble me no further. If I conquer my rage tonight, I shall let myself be cured, but if it vanquishes me, I shall instead descend to Hell, where I expect to find Mohammed who availed us so little."

Then the king collected the blood from his wounds and drank it at midnight, saying: "As my tomb should be either gold or blood, with this blood I shall shortly end my bitter life."

He lay down on the floor to die, and God bore away his soul.

As soon as he was dead, Almedixer asked Tirant for his corpse, which he invited their foes to come and collect. Upon hearing these tidings, the infidels mourned him as no prince had ever been mourned before and sent fifty of their noblest knights to retrieve his body. They found it covered with cloth of gold and lying upon a bed with many mattresses where a hundred knights with drawn swords guarded the Moor, whose comrades pulled off the cover and, after recognizing their lord, the eldest among them began to speak thus:

· CCCXLVI ·

THE SARACEN'S SPEECH TO TIRANT

"Inherited fame is easily maintained but the truest glory derives from mens' praise, which is inspired by bravery and unsullied by sin. Oh lord captain, flower of chivalry, heed an old man's words! Your sovereign virtue has converted these new Christians, and if you pursue what you have begun your nobility will never fail you. The more you honor this lord, the more you show your own goodness, as honor adheres to those who give it and augments their honor too. This valiant king, who ceased to live lest others glory in his downfall, deserved to conquer the world, placing popes in Rome and sultans in Babylon, and had his life lasted longer he would have risen to great heights. Alas, cruel and indifferent Death, why have you felled this gallant monarch? His downfall will be ours as well, wherefore, brothers and companions, I ask you to join me in bemoaning our natural lord's demise."

They knelt on the floor, kissed the king's feet, and wept bitter tears. Then another elderly Moorish knight rose and began to lament:

· CCCXLVII ·

$\mathcal{T}$HE MOORISH KNIGHT'S LAMENT

"Oh Almighty Allah, Creator of Heaven and earth: how could you let this lord, who might have conquered the world, die defending Our Holy Prophet's faith? How could one man, with treachery and cunning, pervert so many peoples and slay so many kings and knights? Help me, oh comrades, with sad words and anguished cries, protesting in harsh voices against our champion's woeful death. Oh Mohammed, is it not enough that Fortune should slay a multitude in battle, without removing the pillar that sustained all Barbary? King of Tunis, may Allah forgive you and hold you to the true path, making you first in that garden where you and all your followers shall dwell!"

Then he turned to Tirant and cried: "Lord captain, we dress in mourning, for piles of corpses surround our tents and their spilt blood cries out to this worthy king. All we hear is: 'This one is dead' or 'that monarch has lost a limb,' and wherever we turn, our ears are beset by plaints and mourning. Oh wicked Christian who fears neither Allah nor the world: cursed be the day you came and cursed the galley that brought you! Alas, that you and all your men did not drown in the Gulf of Adalia!"

Hearing these rash words, Tirant laughingly replied: "Knight, I thank you for your insults, to which I shall not reply. For speaking thus in my castle you and your companions should be flung off the walls, but as I see anger has destroyed your reason, I shall safeguard my honor. Quit this castle at once lest some greater evil befall you."

Tirant left the room without another word, while the Saracens requested their lord's body, to which Almedixer replied that they had forfeited it through their insults and that the king would be fed to wild beasts unless they paid twenty thousand doubloons. The infidels quickly paid them and bore the corpse back to their camp, where their comrades furiously seized their weapons and mounted their steeds. Then they rode toward the city, crying: "Death to that Christian dog who seeks to ravage our kingdoms!" for concord strengthens nations just as discord weakens them, and a community in concord is strong and dreadful to its enemies.

The King of Damascus then said:

· CCCXLVIII ·

THE KING OF DAMASCUS'S WORDS

"My lords, I have always heard it said that man inclines more to folly than wisdom, though reason preserves sages from many impending perils. Are you unaware that rashness can cost a king his crown? Knowing that this cruel captain and his renegade allies have slain more than eighty thousand believers, we should calmly plot our strategy instead of rushing into battle, for those who attack in haste and rage usually end up in flight. If we organize our troops well, we shall triumph and be praised, but if we do the opposite we shall be vilified and cursed."

Everyone condemned the King of Damascus's words and refused to hear him out, while the new Saracen King of Tlemcen, who had been elected upon his uncle's death, began to speak in the following manner:

· CCCXLIX ·

THE KING OF TLEMCEN'S WORDS

"What we consider so difficult is actually easy, and what we think mysterious is clear and manifest, for if we assault that town, we shall certainly triumph, first slaying that wicked heretic King Escariano who forsook our blessed faith and embraced Christianity and then giving his crafty captain the punishment he deserves: to be beaten with iron rods till he kisses our province's fertile soil."

He turned toward the town and cried: "Oh tyrannical city swollen with pride, now your pleasures shall end and you shall become a desert! Think of the harm that awaits you today!"

They boldly attacked like devils out of Hell, while Tirant marshaled his troops and inspected the fortifications.

The ladies mounted their mules and donkeys, forming ranks as they had before. Then King Escariano sallied forth, showing mercy to none who crossed his path and charging ahead so fiercely that he found himself surrounded. The Saracens slew his horse and he fell to earth, where he began to pray: "Oh humble Virgin, Mother of Jesus, whom you sheltered in your chaste tabernacle and bore without pain or taint! I commend myself unto you, who are the sinner's advocate, that your Son may preserve one who loves and seeks to serve Him. Oh Jesus, pity those who were baptized with pure hearts and save us that we may augment Your Holy Catholic Faith!"

Lord Agramunt and Almedixer, who were nearby, saw a squadron attack King Escariano beneath a blue banner with a swarm of golden bees upon it. Thinking the king was Tirant, the two warriors hurried to his aid, and had they not done so the black would surely have perished. Almedixer performed many noble deeds that day, running his lance through five Saracens' cuirasses and leaving them for dead. As Tirant battled on the other side of the camp, one of the king's men approached him and cried: "Lord captain, hasten to rescue your friend, for our foes have encircled him and will shortly take his life!"

Tirant immediately gathered his troops and rode to succor the king, whom they found on foot, as the Saracens had kept him from remounting. Tirant and his knights set upon the infidels, and woe unto the mother whose son crossed their path.

Seeing another sixty thousand Saracens attack beneath a red banner adorned with eagles, Tirant ordered his soldiers at the city gates to join the fray. Meanwhile the Saracen King of Tlemcen tilted at a valiant Christian knight, and when the King of Persia spied them, he hurried to aid his friend, but the Christian, whose name was Melquisedec, plunged his sword through the Persian's left eye. The monarch fell from his horse in agony, crying: "Alas, King of Tlemcen who proudly aspired to rule the world, Allah's will and not yours has been done! Woe is me! Was there ever such an ill-fated prince as I, who have seen my father, son, brother, and innumerable knights slain in battle. I am filled with despair, yet I find no one to help me."

The cruel battle lasted from morning till night, and only the darkness made them desist at last. On the morrow, Tirant's scouts scoured the field, where they found 35,072 bodies, most of whom had commended their souls to Christ or Mohammed.

When the Saracens fled, Tirant restrained his soldiers from pursuing them. Knowing how many men they had lost, for their troubles increased by the hour, the kings held council and decided to request a thirty-day truce. Though Tirant was opposed, King Escariano accepted for the sake of the wounded, and once the truce had been declared, many women searched the battlefield, collecting the Christian corpses for solemn burial. The Saracen King of Tlemcen spied them from his tent and asked: "What are those women doing among so many dead bodies? The Christians must have abandoned their old ways to mistreat them so cruelly."

Having decided to depart before the truce ended, the Saracens set out one evening for the Atlas Mountains, where they hoped to be better protected from their foes.

Later that night, Tirant's scouts knocked on the gates and announced that his foes were fleeing, whereupon he ordered everyone to arms and led them forth at daybreak. Their advance guard overtook the baggage train and killed a few men, but the fleeing kings sent messengers to demand compensation for the casualties and pillaging, since Tirant had accepted a thirty-day truce. If he refused, they threatened to appeal to Mohammed and inform all emperors, kings, counts, and marquises that Tirant and King Escariano had broken their words.

When Tirant heard this, he decided to honor the truce rather than tarnish his good name, though there were arguments on both sides, as the infidels had also broken faith by fleeing. The Breton paid for what had been taken and freed ten captives for every casualty, while his enemies declared him the noblest Christian alive, for he had acted with mercy and bad beginnings seldom lead to good ends.

After the Saracens had disappeared into the rugged mountains, Tirant began conquering the lands they had abandoned, and some days later Lord Agramunt told him: "Perhaps I should follow them and subdue the cities on their side, whereby all Barbary will be yours once you finish here."

Tirant sent him forth with ten thousand cavalry and eighteen thousand foot, but upon reaching the other side, they found that the Saracen army had disbanded. Lord Agramunt then bravely captured many cities, towns, and castles, conquering those that resisted and increasing his captain's glory.

In the course of their campaign, they approached a city called Montagata that was ruled by the King of Belamerin's daughter (he had been killed at the beginning of the war) and her betrothed. Fearing an attack, they and their counselors offered the city's keys to Lord Agramunt, who benignly granted all their requests, but as his men approached, the city elders changed their minds and decided to fight to the death.

Seeing himself thus mocked, Lord Agramunt assaulted the city, and as he rode toward the walls an arrow transfixed his jaw. His soldiers beheld him on the ground, and, thinking he was dead, they carried him back to his tent on a stretcher and fought no more that day. Then Lord Agramunt vowed that, to avenge the infidels' treachery and his wound, he would slay every man, woman, and child in the city, and he sent a messenger to ask Tirant for his heaviest artillery.

Upon hearing of his cousin's wound, Tirant set out with all his forces, whom he ordered to attack the moment they reached Montagata. So fierce was the onslaught that they captured a minaret on the walls, but then night fell and Tirant was obliged to withdraw. On the morrow, the queen's elders offered to capitulate, pay thirty thousand gold crowns, and free their prisoners if the Christians let them keep their faith. Tirant replied that since they had affronted his cousin, they would have to obtain his consent, yet although the elders begged and pleaded, Lord Agramunt was adamant. Then they resolved to send the queen and her retinue, as maidens' pleas often receive a friendlier hearing.

Now the book recounts Pleasure-of-my-life's adventures.

· CCCL ·

H OW PLEASURE-OF-MY-LIFE LEARNED OF TIRANT'S EXPLOITS[24]

As has been previously recounted, God spared Pleasure-of-my-life and brought her to the fisherman's daughter's house near Tunis. When, two years later, this daughter married a neighbor, our damsel became their honest slave and spent her days weaving gold and silk in the French style. One morning her mistress went to Montagata, where she made a few purchases and then visited the princess, whom she addressed in the following manner: "My lady, I understand that Your Highness plans to marry and wishes to buy embroidered gold and silk slips, nightgowns, and other items pertaining to damsels. I have a skilled young slave whom I taught to do fine embroidery when she was a child, and you can see from this sample that her work is exquisite, yet in exchange for a hundred doubloons I shall sacrifice all the time I spent training her."

Once the princess had agreed, Pleasure-of-my-life's mistress continued: "Then I shall sell her, but only on one condition: that you pretend I lent her to you for three months, as her devotion is such that if she learned I had sold her, she would quickly perish of grief and rage."

Pleasure-of-my-life came to cherish her new mistress, whose city was attacked shortly thereafter, and one of the Christians taken prisoner was an oarsman from Tirant's galley. Pleasure-of-my-life recognized him and asked: "Were you on a galley that sank near Tunis?"

"My lady," replied the man, "after suffering terribly and barely reaching shore alive, I got a good beating and was sold into slavery."

"What do you know about Tirant?" asked Pleasure-of-my-life. "Where did he die?"

"Holy Mary!" cried the prisoner. "He is still alive and doing his utmost to take your city."

He said Lord Agramunt was wounded, whereupon the damsel asked: "What became of Pleasure-of-my-life?"

"They say she drowned," replied the prisoner, "and our poor captain was heartbroken."

Pleasure-of-my-life then told the prisoners how to escape and wondered whether to flee with them, for she now realized that the mighty Christian conqueror was our knight. The damsel knelt and thanked God for Tirant's converts, who were battling so valiantly against Christ's enemies, and the knowledge that she would soon be freed banished all her previous woes.

On the day her mistress was to plead with the Christians, Pleasure-of-my-life accompanied her in disguise, but Tirant refused to listen and sent the fifty-one damsels to Lord Agramunt, who, if he had been hard on the men, was worse with the ladies. They returned home in despair, weeping and lamenting, and all the townspeople spent a night filled with doleful sighs.

The next morning, Pleasure-of-my-life told the queen's elders that if they sent her, she would tell the captain such things that he would quickly do their bidding. She spoke so eloquently that at last they agreed, and after dressing in her finest Moorish clothes, the damsel disguised her eyes with galena. She and several maidens left the city at noon and walked to the camp, where they found Tirant standing at the entrance to his tent. Upon seeing them, he sent a chamberlain to say they should speak with Lord Agramunt, but Pleasure-of-my-life replied: "Tell your captain he should not refuse to hear us, for if he does so men will call him pitiless and unjust, and moreover, his knightly vows oblige him to aid and counsel damsels."

The chamberlain quickly returned to Tirant and said: "On my word, my lord, there is a fair damsel among those infidels who speaks very good Christian.[25] If Your Lordship wishes to reward me, he will baptize her when we conquer this city and give her to me in marriage."

"Go," said the captain, "and bring them before me."

All the damsels curtsied when they saw him, and Pleasure-of-my-life began to speak thus:

· CCCLI ·

HOW PLEASURE-OF-MY-LIFE PLEADED WITH TIRANT

"Your heart, lord captain, will surely not forsake its accustomed kindness but will pardon this afflicted city's inhabitants, who wish only to kiss your hands and feet. You know better than I that God's arms are always open to sinners, and being here in His stead, you should not spurn our pleas, for the greatest revenge a knight can take is to spare an enemy who kneels before him. Do not be surprised that I, who know of your triumphs in Greece, your shipwreck on the Barbary Coast, and how you and King Escariano have pursued those fleeing kings, should implore you by your beloved to spare our noble queen, nor can I believe your generous heart will let her be slain and dispossessed. If you aspire to be a magnanimous monarch, order Lord Agramunt to make peace, as I can see your power is such that you will be obeyed both on earth and in Heaven."

Refusing to let her continue, Tirant frowned and replied:

· CCCLII ·

T IRANT'S REPLY TO PLEASURE-OF-MY-LIFE

"Fortune inclines men's hearts more to cruelty than pity, but those who do not serve God's truth should at least keep faith. Our men's sufferings are unforgivable, for they languish in their beds, while my cousin Lord Agramunt was tricked and grievously wounded and your fields are strewn with the corpses of our valiant warriors. How can you Saracens beg for mercy when you show none yourselves? You are doomed, and I assure you that no one under ninety-five or over three will be spared. Now depart from my sight; this is no time for pity but vengeance, which will punish you, serve as an example, and cleanse your city of its dishonor."

Enraged by Tirant's inhumanity, the damsel replied:

· CCCLIII ·

P LEASURE-OF-MY-LIFE'S REPLY TO TIRANT

"Both Hannibal and Alexander hungered for power, and both died of poison. Though Nebuchadnezzar had been born out of wedlock, he became King of Babylon, and just as you seek to destroy our city so he laid waste Jerusalem, burning Solomon's temple, massacring the Jews, and doing as much evil as you intend to do. Suddenly he fell from power, and such will be your fate if you persevere, yet unlike you, who persist in sin, he saw the light and repented, spending seven years in the desert where he atoned for his wickedness. You vainly strive to conquer the entire world, but tell me, pitiless captain: what right have you to the city of Montagata? Did you inherit it from your ancestors? Our queen's father won it from the Moors and restored its greatness, whereas you hope to usurp what has never been yours.

"Do not think because I am a Saracen that I know nothing of a knight's duties, or have forgotten Our Lord's words: 'Blessed are the peacemakers, for they shall be called the children of God,' and on Christmas Eve when Christ was born all the heavenly angels sang: 'Glory unto God on high and peace on earth to men of good will.' If you are a Christian, why do you disobey God's commandments? All we desire is peace, which is precious to all women, and though our city is full of brave knights prepared to die in its defense, we wish to do you and your men no more harm. Think carefully, for no captain should murderously shed blood, yet you rashly prefer worldly to spiritual glory. Remember that while life's electuary is composed of many tastes, its final purpose is to save one's immortal soul, and heed the words of Saint Augustine whom you Christians so esteem: 'He who acquiesces in another's sin is not far from sin himself.' Peace and friendship please the Lord and all men of good will, nor should you forget Saint James's words: 'A knight's heart should incline more to mercy than cruelty.'[26] Think of what Seneca says: 'Civil authority should be acquired through virtue,' and virtuously grant our humble pleas, banishing greed from your heart. This city has been sorely tried; do not bear away its riches. Fortune has so often smiled upon you that you imperil your very soul, wherefore by your hope of victory I beg you to cease this hatred, and the wisest counsel I can offer is to make peace immediately. Should present dangers not daunt you, think of those that lie in wait, as no worthy knight should spurn a damsel's entreaties. If you desist your fame will grow, but unblemished honor needs constant attention."

Tirant quickly replied:

· CCCLIV ·

TIRANT'S REPLY TO PLEASURE-OF-MY-LIFE

"Damsel, you are like someone who steals a cow and then gives its rump to charity, for though you are a faithless Saracen you try to teach me how to behave. How can you appeal to the saints without knowing who they are, being ignorant of our holy sacraments and the articles of our faith? If you want instruction, I can help you, but for the moment I shall merely cite Saint Bernard's words: 'Anyone who sins voluntarily while confiding in God's mercy will be damned.' At times I sin myself, but then I humbly pray for absolution, and since I uphold God's commandments and accept all the Church's teachings, my guerdon will be eternal life whereas you all will be cursed. Our noble faith maintains that Christ died to redeem us from Adam's sin, and one drop of His precious blood sufficed to save a thousand worlds. Such is the lesson of Saint Peter who denied Our Lord, Saint Paul who persecuted Christians, Saint Matthew the usurer, and a multitude of others who were saved through sincere contrition.

"You too can enter Heaven by embracing Christianity, with whose true and holy doctrines you are already acquainted. Be mindful of Judas's treachery and Lucifer's rebellion against God, for by spurning His mercy they condemned themselves to eternal darkness; and my lady, one day a year I confess my sins and give alms for my Creator, who I trust will reward me while you infidels burn in Hell. My purpose in conquering Barbary is to save you from perdition, as God condemns no Christian without due cause, and do you know why? Because reason and justice derive from God, whose will is always just. You are not troubled by your sins but by the punishment that awaits you, nor do I, who prize glory, crave tributes or riches. Being no merchant but a knight, I would sooner give than receive, wherefore, if you want your prisoners you need only ask me, and you may tell your masters I shall free them out of generosity rather than friendship. I do not delight in your adversities but seek to conquer my enemies, and I fight damsels only in their bedrooms, preferably perfumed and decorated ones. Without Lord Agramunt's consent I cannot make peace, since he is our captain and has decided to attack tomorrow. Prepare to defend yourselves, for though you desire peace, your evil deeds deserve no reward or honor. God, whom you so scorn, gives each man his due, nor will the outcome of this battle differ from our previous ones."

Pleasure-of-my-life quickly replied:

· CCCLV ·

PLEASURE-OF-MY-LIFE'S REPLY TO TIRANT

"It is only human to pity the forlorn, and especially those who formerly had friends to comfort them.[27] I am of this sort, and as a knight you should aid me, but instead I see you poised to destroy the work of many years in a single day. Neither should you let your triumphs befuddle you, as Fortune is hard to please and if you loosen the reins she will drag you over a cliff. Do not think me unable to refute your arguments, since I persuaded my lady and these damsels to plead for mercy, but should you refuse us, I pray God to blacken your name, denying you and your men the glory of Paradise, and should you do us violence, I shall denounce your cruelty throughout Italy, Spain, France, and Germany. Christians should be humble and make no one suffer, yet while the mightiest oriental kings fight just wars and win battles, you, in your haughtiness, seek to do the opposite.

"Heed the words of our poet Geber, who tells us that Pompey once set out with a mighty host and, had he not asked too much of Fortune, might have returned in glory, but alas, that noble captain was routed and disgraced.[28] Be mindful likewise of the prophet Isaiah, who called Barbary a charmed land. A wise man frees himself from Fortune and is wary of her charms, as was Aristotle, who warned against trusting Fortune's wheel. Not only is Fortune blind, but she blinds those she favors, exalting men only to later bring them low. Solomon declared that poison is often sweetened with honey, and since death is a cup from which everyone must drink, I beg you: purchase a virtuous death with a virtuous life, for death is truth whereas life is illusion, nor should you forget death, which will not forget you. Virgil says men should love life, fear death, and shun fame won by force. Generous lord, you can see that I wish to save your soul from the fate suffered by Hector, Alexander, Hannibal and other brave captains, yet I fear you will blindly persist in your ignorance. Do you recall that psalm: 'Wicked is the knight who gives no rewards, and wickeder still if he forgets past honors and services?' Thus have you behaved in your ignorance and folly! Alas, I can only appeal to King Escariano, who has shown his queen more love than you have your princess.

"Listen, brave captain, to one who knows all: do you remember the day you were knighted at the English court? Do you recall your noble jousts with those four kings and dukes, how you honorably slew Lord Barrentowns in single combat, and the Muntalbà brothers, whose deaths helped you win the prize of honor? What of Prince Philip, who with your help became King of Sicily, and the Knights of Saint John, whom you saved from starvation? Oh Lord Tirant, may God bless you and prolong your days, covering you with glory both in this world and the next! Your fame led the Emperor of Constantinople to request your aid, and as his captain you often vanquished the Turks. Tell me, my lord: do you remember your fair princess or your cousin Diaphebus, whom you made Count of Sancto Angiolo and Duke of Macedonia? Oh noble Saltrock lineage, where are you now? Sad and ill-starred, you languish in Turkish dungeons, while your captain and former friend is untroubled by your travails. Who will free you now? Death is your sole escape. Though I am a Saracen and speak in riddles, my heart bleeds for those worthy knights. Weep and lament, for Tirant has forgotten you, nor am I surprised, since to conquer this evil land you forgot the noblest damsel in Christendom!"

Astounded and dismayed by Pleasure-of-my-life's words, Tirant gently asked how she knew so much about him.

· CCCLVI ·

TIRANT'S PLEA TO PLEASURE-OF-MY-LIFE

"Damsel, your words have pierced my heart. I cannot believe that you are human, for you either keep some familiar spirit or are yourself a devil sent to thwart my pious intentions. When I have conquered this evil city, I shall repopulate it with Christians, and I would consider myself a fool if some maiden dissuaded me by citing philosophers, poets, and theologians. You have reopened my wounds by speaking of my comrades, who, though you claim I have forgotten them, torment me day and night. I pray God to grant me victory that I may hasten to their rescue, but this is no time or place to recite my enamored woes. Oh damsel, so great is your knowledge of Christian doctrine that you need only be baptized! By the One God, please tell me how you learned so much about my past."

Pleasure-of-my-life's face, which had been clouded with anger, suddenly cleared and with a smile she spoke these words:

· CCCLVII ·

*P*LEASURE-OF-MY-LIFE'S REPLY TO TIRANT'S REQUEST

"Alas, Tirant, you love justice more than mercy! Pursue those fleeing kings, whose defeat will bring us peace, and do not vex God, who sees your wickedness and cruelty. I assure you that, being no devil but one of His creatures, I only recite your errors to show my wish to serve you. There will be no more wars between us if you forsake your swollen pride, but should you refuse, I shall fill men's ears with your recreance. Was it not you who battled Carmesina at Malveí Castle? If I am not mad, I believe I heard you tempt her with supplications and seek to affront her parents by stealing into her chamber, crowning yourself emperor with the help of a sad damsel named Pleasure-of-my-life, yet now you act as though you had never met them, while Her Highness languishes in a Franciscan convent.[29] Oh Tirant, what has become of your kindness? The Turks have subdued Greece and will soon take Constantinople, imprisoning the emperor and your beloved wife. Oh hapless knight, will you let your lady be captured? While you conquer this sinful land, infidels will enslave her.

"Do you know what Titus Livius says? That a knight should uphold four things: his life, his riches, his honor, and his wife.[30] He should risk his life and riches for his honor; his wife, honor, and life for his riches; his riches for his life; and his riches, life, and honor for his wife. Beware, wretched knight, lest Saracens take her virginity and empire, which, though you do not deserve them, she was saving for you, spurning countless kings for a lowly knight who would be nothing without his captaincy. Imitate your worthy ancestors, who preferred honor to worldly riches, and turn from Africa toward the East, where you shall behold your happiness. If you are wise, you will see that your solace may soon turn to sorrow, for you conquer a land that you yourself would scorn to rule, yet what glory will you win by humbling our defeated city? No damsel should expect joy from so cruel a knight or hope to share his bed, wherefore I invoke the wrath of father, mother, and Pharoah upon you! Go; rescue your comrades, father-in-law, and wife, all of whom are dying of sorrow and starvation."

These words so kindled Tirant's amorous zeal that he heaved a great sigh, and as he thought of his beloved, he was stricken by grief and fainted. Everyone feared that their captain had given up the ghost.

Feeling not at all amused, King Escariano wept bitterly and cried:

· CCCLVIII ·

*H*OW KING ESCARIANO REBUKED PLEASURE-OF-MY-LIFE

"Oh damsel, you deserve to be cruelly chastised and will curse the day you came, for should this knight die, I promise to massacre all of you without pity! Oh merciless lady, you entered this tent with poisoned tongue, glorying in harsh insults and scorning gentle pleas, yet your crime will be duly punished, as you are like the blacksmith who, if he does not burn your clothes, afflicts you with his smoke. Tell me, damsel: can you really have conquered us without a blow? Truly, you must be among the world's greatest poisoners!"

The doctors then said: "Our captain's hour has come."

King Escariano quickly had the maiden seized and bound, while she condemned his misdeeds in the following fashion:

· CCCLIX ·

*H*OW PLEASURE-OF-MY-LIFE REBUKED KING ESCARIANO

"Kings should be merciful, but you are cruel and wicked, though all knights are obliged to champion and pity damsels. Let me help this captain, whom I loved before you knew his name, since I see that these ignorant doctors cannot save him. I do not fear your vengeance, however terrible it may be, if I have killed the world's best knight with my simple words. The Grand Turk and sultan can attest to what I say, for he slaughtered innumerable thousands of their men on the battlefield, and I know something you do not: that he is heir to the Greek throne."

Having seated herself, the damsel tore open her jubbah so that everyone could see her breasts, and, placing Tirant's head between them, she began to speak thus:

· CCCLX ·

*P*LEASURE-OF-MY-LIFE'S PLEA TO TIRANT

"Oh inexorable Fates who ordain all our actions, why do you plague my grieving heart with further woes when my sole wish is to die, as I cannot save this afflicted city? Generous captain and invincible knight, open your eyes and hear the last pleas of one who humbly begs you not to forsake your virtue and would sooner die at your hands than be saved by another."

A bone in our knight's ear had been injured in his combat with Lord Barrentowns, and if Tirant fainted he could be revived by tapping that bone, which caused him excruciating pain whenever it was touched. Seeing his eyes open and hearing his sighs, the damsel gently whispered: "Lord captain, I know you dwell on the isle of Sorrows, but please do not forsake your accustomed generosity. If revenge is your desire, you may begin with me, bathing your well-sharpened sword in the blood of one who only wishes to serve you. Ovid says that love, being fickle, can rarely be rekindled, and likewise the poet Tobias pronounces a virtuous fool superior to a wicked sage. Though I am but a frivolous maiden and often speak ignorantly, I know your generous heart will forgive my errors."

Tirant replied:

· CCCLXI ·

*T*IRANT'S REPLY TO PLEASURE-OF-MY-LIFE

"Damsel, you are like a bee with honey in its mouth and a stinger in its tail. Your words have wounded me, but if you will disclose the source of your knowledge, I promise to perform such deeds that you will be well satisfied."

Feeling pleased by the captain's reply, Pleasure-of-my-life decided to reveal herself and said:

· CCCLXII ·

PLEASURE-OF-MY-LIFE'S REPLY TO TIRANT

"The great philosopher Aristotle declared it nobler to shed enemy blood than shameful tears, and likewise Saint John of Damascus said: 'True devotion is proven in time of need.' We know we are loved when our friends suffer with us, and therefore, captain, let us rejoice and ease our woes. If you wish to understand Cupid's power, remember those who braved God's wrath by dying for love, oftentimes not only choosing death but inflicting it upon themselves. Lord Tirant, I beg you to pity this afflicted city and aid the Greeks, who recall your past feats and look to you for salvation. By the lady you cherish, do not spurn our humble pleas."

As they spoke, Lord Agramunt stormed into the tent brandishing a sword. Seeing his master's head in the damsel's lap, the knight scowled furiously and cried:

· CCCLXIII ·

HOW LORD AGRAMUNT TRIED TO KILL PLEASURE-OF-MY-LIFE

"What is this witch in league with Satan doing in our camp? How can Tirant's false friends let her bedevil him thus? If they cherished his life, they would behead her on the spot, since no punishment could compensate for so villainous a crime, but as you all hesitate, I shall do the deed myself, though I have never struck a damsel for fear of betraying my chivalric vows."

Then he seized her hair, wrenched her head back, and held a sword to her throat, but our knight saw her predicament and grabbed the blade with his hands. Lord Agramunt thought the pressure was from her neck and pulled his weapon toward him, cutting Tirant's hands so badly that the doctors said it was a miracle he kept them.

Seeing how little his cousin honored and respected him, our knight furiously cried:

· CCCLXIV ·

*T*IRANT'S WORDS TO LORD AGRAMUNT WHEN HE SAW HE WAS WOUNDED

"Oh recreant knight, you should lose all your honor, for your pride and cruelty are only equaled by your folly. Seeing me in this damsel's lap, you seek to harm us both, but you shall know my wrath if you do not mend your ways. I shall speak no more lest I sully my mouth with insults, though I curse the day the worst of all our lineage was born. If disgrace were honor you would be the most blessed knight alive, and if honor won disgrace you would have no cause for shame."

King Escariano sent Lord Agramunt to his tent, and, staring humbly at the ground, the lord bowed to the two captains, thus rousing Tirant's compassion and assuaging his fury.

Hoping to make peace, King Escariano then uttered these words:

· CCCLXV ·

*H*OW KING ESCARIANO ASKED TIRANT TO FORGIVE HIS COUSIN

"Brother, forgive Lord Agramunt, whom rage deprived of his reason and who nearly fainted when he realized what evil he had done, nor do I believe he will soon dare to meet your gaze. Pardon him for the sake of one who only wishes to augment your glory, as I consider your wounds my own and should therefore be the most aggrieved."

To satisfy King Escariano, Tirant calmed his wrath and, after pardoning Lord Agramunt's ignorance, turned to the damsel, whom he asked whether she had been a slave in Constantinople or how she had learned so much about his princess. Pleasure-of-my-life quickly replied:

· CCCLXVI ·

*H*OW THE MOORISH DAMSEL REVEALED HER IDENTITY

"Sinister Fortune will soon end my days, and should you wish to slay me, you may easily do so, but why utter vain words when I only long to please Your Lordship?"

She rose, knelt before Tirant, and asked: "What, lord captain, have you lost your natural wits or can it be true that love destroys men's memories? Really! Do you not recognize Pleasure-of-my-life, who endured so many hardships and was enslaved for your sake?"

The scales fell from Tirant's eyes and, refusing to let her continue, he knelt before the damsel, whom he kissed many times in sign of love.

When they had made merry for a while, our knight placed a high wooden platform covered with silk brocade outside his tent. On the highest step of a staircase leading up to it sat Pleasure-of-my-life, wearing an ermine-lined scarlet brocade mantle that Tirant had given her. He placed the queen on the lowest step with her damsels all around her, and that day Pleasure-of-my-life's royal nature was manifest to all.

After removing her veil that everyone might see her hair, Tirant honored his friend so much that people thought she was his bride, for he sent criers through the camp summoning everyone to kiss her hand on pain of death and then dispatched messengers to tell the townspeople they had not only been spared but that everyone could follow his faith without fear of reprisal. Finally, Tirant decreed a week of feasting with food for all, and held the noblest celebration ever seen in a camp.

Realizing that he had nearly killed Pleasure-of-my-life, poor Lord Agramunt asked King Escariano and his queen, who never left our maiden's side, to help him plead for Tirant's forgiveness. Once they had promised to do so, they all went to the captain's tent, where with humble voice and piteous gesture Lord Agramunt spoke these words:

· CCCLXVII ·

H OW LORD AGRAMUNT APOLOGIZED TO TIRANT

"Were it not a sin, I would slay myself to restore my honor, since death is far sweeter than to live with disgraceful memories. I beg you: either forgive me or let me depart, for though I know I deserve no pity and my rewards will be shame and sorrow, you should not spurn the devotion my repentance reveals. Remember that I am your cousin and blood cannot turn to water, wherefore I humbly implore you to forgive or dismiss me."

When Tirant heard these words, he pitied Lord Agramunt and replied:

· CCCLXVIII ·

*H*OW TIRANT AND LORD AGRAMUNT MADE PEACE

"God absolves all sinners who sincerely repent, and I, who have sinned greatly, should certainly do likewise, since if I do not forgive you how can I beg Him for mercy? Cousin, I declare that I would risk my life for yours, and though our ties of love might have weakened if you were less contrite, let no one think such thoughts, as I shall quickly prove the contrary. Therefore open your eyes, heed reason, and restrain your wish to see foreign lands. Do not flee the knightly deeds that will augment your fame, nor could you justly depart even if a great inheritance awaited you. Honor our bonds of friendship; to ignore them will bring perdition."

King Escariano and his queen then asked Tirant and Lord Agramunt to make peace. Having sworn to do so, they set out for the platform where Pleasure-of-my-life awaited them, and as soon as they arrived, Lord Agramunt addressed her thus:

· CCCLXIX ·

*H*OW LORD AGRAMUNT APOLOGIZED TO PLEASURE-OF-MY-LIFE

"If Almighty God beholds our every act, no sin can remain unpunished or good deed go unrewarded. Chastisement may be slow in coming but is never undeserved, and though adverse Fortune blinded me to your identity, my cause was not unjust. Should you spurn my pleas, I shall wander the earth crying out for mercy, and when at last I die of woe, men will call you a murderess. I, who only seek to please you, have braved Mars's cruel battles and stained many an African field with my knightly blood, nor have I ever stooped to trickery like this city's inhabitants. Spare me, just as you implored me to spare them, for I surrender to one who defeated our captain without arms."

Pleasure-of-my-life quickly replied:

· CCCLXX ·

PLEASURE-OF-MY-LIFE'S REPLY

"Ladies of honor should not be cruel or vengeful, nor would God be pleased by such qualities in a Greek damsel, for though your offense was great, you were ignorant of my identity. You only slighted our captain, who had guaranteed my safety, but even if you had killed me I would not grieve to be slain by one so valiant. You need not apologize, as I do not consider myself wronged, and if I did I would gladly pardon you in return for sparing this city. I beg you to live in joy and the hope that God will grant you love."

They were unable to discourse further because King Escariano and Tirant then appeared, whereupon everyone made merry and danced to Moorish tunes.

On the tenth day of feasting, the queen offered Tirant the keys to her city, which he gave to Pleasure-of-my-life, declaring her mistress of Montagata. Then everyone formed a triumphal procession and escorted her to the palace. Pleasure-of-my-life rode on horseback, surrounded by musicians, while Tirant banished the former queen and gave maids and servants to his friend, who for a week ruled the city and all the towns and castles around it.

When the week was over, she summoned the former queen and restored the city to her with these words:

· CCCLXXI ·

HOW PLEASURE-OF-MY-LIFE RESTORED THE CITY AND EVERYTHING ELSE TO HER FORMER MISTRESS

"Your great virtue, my lady, has placed me in your debt, and I would gladly risk my life again to save you and your subjects. I am honored to have served one of such peerless nobility, but do not imagine that I wanted to be queen. What Fortune gave me it stole from you, and my sole joy is in returning it, wherefore I beg you to take these keys from one who, though your slave, is of like condition. Now we shall see who is the more virtuous: I, who restore your birthright, or you, whom I now ask to embrace Christianity. Should you grant my pleas, I shall be happier than if they had offered me all Barbary."

Then she handed the keys to her former mistress.

When the lady beheld Pleasure-of-my-life's generosity, she knelt at her feet, weeping for very joy as she tried to kiss them. The damsel, however, quickly knelt before Her Majesty, who said: "You need not prove your nobility, which is revealed by your every gesture. Therefore, my lady, I must gratefully decline your offer, since I know you are worthier to rule than I. To repay you for saving my life, I should serve you as long as you served in my court, where I hope to attend you the rest of my days, and as for becoming a Christian, I shall be baptized whenever you say."

Pleasure-of-my-life quickly replied: "My lady, take these keys, which by right are yours alone, and consider me your sister from this moment on. Accept what belongs to you, as your refusal will only offend me, and, in the end you will be obliged to accept in any case."

The lady humbly took them to please Pleasure-of-my-life, who returned to the camp where Tirant awaited her. Pleasure-of-my-life told him she had restored everything to the queen, and since she seemed pleased he was content as well.

Then Lord Agramunt asked: "Should you not have consulted me? What of that solemn vow I swore?"

Pleasure-of-my-life quickly replied:

· CCCLXXII ·

P LEASURE-OF-MY-LIFE'S REPLY TO LORD AGRAMUNT

"You must conclude your father's glorious efforts to oust the cruel English from France.[31] By their nature, past misdeeds can be condemned but not undone, and if I remember well, you agreed not to harm this city. What, then, do you want: to replace mirth with persecution? Such an act ill behooves a knight like yourself, and indeed, it would be worse than your previous misdeeds. Remember Aristotle's words: 'The noblest ties are those of love and charity, which reveal both men's honor and women's goodness.' Rage no more at your humble servants but ponder King David's wise saying: 'Wicked is the man who forsakes his friends, since a good friend is like a spice merchant: though he may not give you spices, he will at least give you pleasant smells.' You say you swore to make this city's inhabitants pass beneath your sword, and if you follow my advice they will soon free you from your wretched vow. Let King Escariano hold the pommel and our captain the point, while all those who dwell in Montagata pass beneath your weapon, whereby you will fulfill your vow and I shall bless you and sing a Mass."

They all laughed heartily, and so it was done. When everyone had passed beneath the sword, Pleasure-of-my-life asked the queen to keep her word and she happily agreed, receiving holy baptism with three hundred of her subjects. After everyone in the province had followed her example, Tirant asked the Pope to make the Mercedarian friar his legate in Barbary, and from that day on the converts called him "Father of Christians."

Before his departure, Tirant asked the queen, whose Saracen name had been Justa but who had changed it after her baptism, to marry his worthy knight Melquisedec. Pleasure-of-my-life added her pleas to our knight's, and once Her Majesty had consented, Tirant ordered a splendid feast prepared, for Justa was a lady of unblemished honor and most devoted to the Virgin Mary. Her piety led her to build many monasteries and convents, and likewise she sought to help the poor and clothe the naked.

After the wedding feast, our knight, King Escariano, and Pleasure-of-my-life set out to conquer a province ruled by the King of Tlemcen's brother, whose lands Tirant then entrusted to a valiant knight named Lord Antioch. This mighty battler was a great friend of Melquisedec's, and since their cities were three leagues apart, the two kings often visited each other.

Tirant frequently took his ease with Pleasure-of-my-life, who one day scolded him for abandoning his beloved. The captain replied that first he wished to learn what had transpired in his absence and asked his friend to tell him everything she had done. Recalling her hardships and woes, the damsel wept bitter tears, but after a time she wiped her eyes and began to speak thus:

· CCCLXXIII ·

*H*OW PLEASURE-OF-MY-LIFE TOLD TIRANT WHAT HAD BECOME OF HER

"I cannot speak calmly of the torments I endured after finding myself naked and alone on a foreign shore, for although I prayed to the Holy Virgin who never forsakes those who trust her, yet I feared my corpse would be devoured by ravens or vultures, and had the night not hidden me, my fate might have been far worse. In my search for some hiding place I discovered a fishing boat, within which I took shelter, warmed by two sheepskins I tied together. Alas, I spent a sleepless night lamenting my misfortune, but I beg you, my lord, not to make me recount my woes. When I think of what I suffered for you, my sole wish is to die, and remember: anger inclines men to ruthlessness just as love does to pity, while patience alone can temper cruel wrath. Better I should hold my tongue than recall past afflictions."

Hearing the damsel speak so woefully, Tirant refused to let her continue and tried to raise her spirits, since her tribulations had been his fault. After comforting her awhile, he began to speak thus:

· CCCLXXIV

*H*OW TIRANT COMFORTED PLEASURE-OF-MY-LIFE

"Could we foresee the sorrows that besiege our hearts, our spirits might find repose, but vain hopes often cause despair and provoke our damnation. Let rage not overwhelm you with hatred, which is caused by coveting what only Fortune can bestow, for it is dangerous to possess riches, whose owners are enslaved by fear, and thus the ancient philosophers spurned them lest their freedom be hampered. The Fates lull and flatter us while plotting our downfall, never permitting the quiet enjoyment of their gifts, and though Nature endows the soul with inner riches, fickle Fortune determines our outward wealth, wherefore Seneca declares in his epistles that anything striven for is illusory, since what is alien to our nature cannot long endure. Our only shelter is virtue, through which we may win bliss, as Boethius teaches us in his *Consolation of Philosophy,* and in like manner Ecclesiastes pronounces all Fortune's gifts mere vanity.[32]

"Dear sister, everything you lost was merely lent you by Fortune, nor will others fare better, as Fortune treats sages and fools alike. If your anger cannot be mollified, make forgetfulness your medicine, whereby you will see the truth, as wise Cato once remarked, and by drying your tears and striving for redemption, conquering malice with forbearance, fearing God and keeping faith, you will triumph over despair. Saint Gregory and Saint Symeon the New Theologian exhort us to cheerfully endure misfortune, and likewise King David said that though God may vex us with many ills, He will also reward those who suffer them patiently. Remember that everyone must bear hardships and tribulations, including popes, kings, and all great men and women. Be patient, for a brave soul will surmount its natural weaknesses, and though God made you a frail woman, be of manly spirit like your noble ancestors. Adversity reveals valor, and as a poet once remarked, Fortune favors the brave but scorns the fainthearted. Job called our life a constant battle,[33] and Saint Paul concurred, saying: 'I see the perils of our present life: perils of waters, perils of land, and perils among false brethren.'[34] If the stormy sea almost drowned you, I suffered the same fate, being captured, shackled, and later nearly killed. Look, I beg you, at all the wounds I have suffered, yet they are easier to bear than separation from my beloved, whose peerless beauty my soul burns to behold. Though I weep for your sorrows, I also promise compensation, swearing before God, Jesus Christ, and the cross given to me when I was knighted that I shall repay you doubly for everything you lost. Let my love be your pledge that I shall conquer iniquitous Fortune."

Pleasure-of-my-life, whose eyes were still wet, then softly uttered these words:

· CCCLXXV ·

PLEASURE-OF-MY-LIFE'S REPLY TO TIRANT

"Alas, that the cruel Fates should torment me with tears and moans! Pitiless Pluto, Megaera, Persephone, and the other Furies could never persecute me as blind Fortune does, yet to whom shall I complain, for though I served that lady loyally, instead of being rewarded I am now cruelly punished. I, who would have died before losing my honor and station, am exiled among barbarians and parted from my loved ones, while ferocious infidels of insatiable savagery seize my towns and castles. Oh Death who terrifies many, I beg you to pity me! You, who end all ills: end my unbearable afflictions! Who could be so cruel as not to pity my sad youth?"

As she spoke, the damsel's sighs betrayed her failing heart, whereupon Tirant embraced her, splashed water on her face, and rubbed her arms till she recovered. Then she lay her head upon his breast, though her face was still white as snow, while our knight tearfully began to speak in the following manner:

· CCCLXXVI ·

TIRANT'S REPLY TO PLEASURE-OF-MY-LIFE

"The complaints of the wretched incline their listeners to pity, as it is natural to weep with the tearful and feel compassion for the sad; yet by venting our grief we surrender to our basest instincts, which infect the mind and torment the heart, causing men to sin and betray their honor. Our superior faculties must reign supreme, for chaos ensues when servants command their masters, and were our souls rightly ordered, we would perceive Fortune's impotence, wherefore Cato derides those who blame their sufferings on the Fates. Mindful that God ordains all, we must accord our wills with His, disdaining Fortune and the earthly mishaps that may befall us, since that which exists by God's leave cannot be evil, and like it or not, we must submit to Divine Providence.

"Oh madness and vanity! Oh foolish chafing at God's will! Fortune is merely our acts ruled by the movements of heavenly bodies, which the *primum mobile* provokes and thus determines our characters as the changes of season likewise govern our destinies, but free will, being independent of astral influences, can control mad cogitations and surmount adversity. If the Fates treat you cruelly, do not complain but submit like Alexander the Great, who declared that he welcomed Fortune's every gift and thus conquered not only Asia but many other kingdoms as well. By tempering diligence with prudence one acquires good fortune, and just as a gambler's luck may turn his losses into gains, so God exiled you in order to give you two kingdoms, for you will now regain your birthright and marry a Breton knight who will rout your infidel foes and win back your patrimony, while I promise to aid him with money, troops, and my person. Therefore, calm your troubled spirit and banish rage from your heart, as after the harsh storm you will find a safe harbor."

Upon hearing these words, Pleasure-of-my-life quickly replied:

· CCCLXXVII ·

PLEASURE-OF-MY-LIFE'S REPLY TO TIRANT

"My troubled heart allows me no peace, for insatiable appetites perturb my understanding, and when reason is enfeebled, the sinful soul spurns virtue, giving way to those lusts that befuddle us from adolescence. Unable to see God's truth, we become slaves to vice and folly, while lack of wisdom proves to be the cause of many ills, yet if brave knights sin, it is not surprising that I do, as women are weak and inconstant by nature. My tears shall now cease and I shall conquer my despair, not through courage but because of your generous gifts, for which I thank you with all my heart and acknowledge your magnanimity, since to spurn such an offering would affront the noblest knight on earth."

Having spoken these words, Pleasure-of-my-life knelt at Tirant's feet and tried to kiss his hands, but he quickly raised her up and kissed her on the lips. Then he sat down beside her and replied in this fashion:

· CCCLXXVIII ·

*T*IRANT'S REPLY TO PLEASURE-OF-MY-LIFE

"Love is the source of virtue, being the child of understanding, and since God is cherished above all things, we should love our neighbor for His sake. Friendship is a cause of love, and he who finds a friend finds a treasure, nor should any friend be refused, as unity of wills is a sign of amity.[35] The Lord loves a cheerful giver, for He gives generously and freely, and Saint Paul declares in Romans that love can conquer death, enabling men to endure great hardships without suffering or complaint.[36] Virtuous damsel, I beg you to accept the kingdoms of Fez and Bougie, which, having recently been conquered, will require a stout defender, wherefore I also urge you to wed some stalwart knight. Accept my offerings cheerfully, for as Solomon said: 'To every thing there is a season,'[37] and if the Fates exalt you, welcome their gifts lest you vex them through ingratitude."

When Tirant had finished his gracious speech, Pleasure-of-my-life threw herself at his feet, which she tried to kiss, but he lifted her up and swore never to fail her.

Pleasure-of-my-life then said:

· CCCLXXIX ·

PLEASURE-OF-MY-LIFE'S SPEECH TO TIRANT

"Generosity is the noblest virtue one can find in a prince, as it conquers fears and reverses misfortunes. Lord Tirant, my untutored tongue cannot describe your wisdom, which has dissipated my vain and sinful thoughts. In the Gospels it is written: 'Every good tree bringeth forth good fruit; a good tree cannot bring forth evil fruit, neither can a corrupt tree bring forth good fruit.'[38] Good deeds reveal a radiant soul just as a sage refutes pernicious doctrines, wherefore I ask Your Lordship to forgive one whose sole desire is to serve you."

Tirant quickly replied:

· CCCLXXX ·

TIRANT'S REPLY TO PLEASURE-OF-MY-LIFE

"Hell's torments cannot equal those of love, which they exceed only in duration, and though you believed that your hardships would multiply, you should now forget them till their memory may enhance your joy. Tirant lives because God, who always rewards merit, has permitted me to prosper and change your sadness to delight. After darkness comes the dawn, after a storm the sun shines, and after three years of slavery you have regained your freedom. Do not mourn your losses, for you might have been Queen of Montagata, yet instead you nobly offered the crown to your former mistress. You have lost relatives, whom Fortune gave you and then snatched away, but they died defending our faith and their martyrdom will endure forever. Be of good cheer, oh worthy damsel, as I, who caused your hardships, now promise to reward you with love, wealth, and power. You will be first among Breton ladies, and my life, goods, strength, soul, and honor will accompany you, just as you have never forsaken me in my tribulations."

Tirant could not finish his speech because Pleasure-of-my-life knelt before him and, after tearfully trying to kiss his hand, began to speak thus:

· CCCLXXXI ·

PLEASURE-OF-MY-LIFE'S REPLY TO TIRANT

"Your kindness and gentility make me wish to die for one who deserves not a kingdom or empire but to rule the entire world. My woes can never equal yours, yet you have treated me with love, wherefore I beg you to let me kiss your hand in gratitude. You say my blood will now be joined with the Saltrock lineage, but do not force me to wed another, as my sole desire is to obey and serve you."

Tirant then cited many holy authorities, and although the damsel tried her best to refute him, in the end she was forced to yield in the following manner:

· CCCLXXXII ·

HOW PLEASURE-OF-MY-LIFE AND LORD AGRAMUNT AGREED TO MARRY

"Begone, chastity, shame, and fear, for I cannot betray my honor and prosperity! I await your orders; may your will be done."

As the damsel spoke, Tirant removed a rich chain from his neck and, after placing it on hers in token of her betrothal, sent for brocade robes that she might dress as befitted a queen.

When all this had been done, he summoned Lord Agramunt and asked if he would accept the match, to which the knight replied: "Lord captain, I am amazed that you plead with me, for such requests are out of order and your word is my command."

Tirant said: "Cousin, I have decided to give you Fez, Bougie, and Pleasure-of-my-life in holy matrimony, as you know we are in her debt for her sufferings and the love she bears us, and your great friendship will surely lead to a happy marriage."

Lord Agramunt knelt and replied: "Cousin, I had not planned to take a wife, and you honor me too much in asking something I should request."

Tirant quickly lifted him up and kissed his lips, while Lord Agramunt thanked him profusely for both the kingdom and the damsel.

· CCCLXXXIII ·

O F PLEASURE-OF-MY-LIFE'S AND LORD AGRAMUNT'S ENGAGEMENT

Feeling more delighted by this match than by all his conquests in Barbary, Tirant adorned the palace in Montagata with gold and silk, summoned the best musicians in the land, and ordered sweets and splendid wines for his friends' betrothal. Pleasure-of-my-life, whose every gesture showed she deserved to be a queen, was escorted to the great hall, where Tirant, King Escariano, and his wife awaited her. There she pledged her faith with great rejoicing, triumphant dances, and exquisite meals. The feast lasted a week, during which all and sundry ate at Tirant's expense.

Once the festivities had ended, Tirant armed and loaded a big ship, which he entrusted to Melquisedec, who now ruled Montagata. Having asked him to learn everything he could about the emperor, Carmesina, and the empire, our knight gave him instructions, letters of credence, fine clothes, and good companions. Melquisedec then set sail for Constantinople with a cargo of wheat.

· CCCLXXXIV ·

H OW TIRANT AND HIS ARMY BESIEGED THREE KINGS IN A CITY WHERE THEY HAD TAKEN REFUGE

Once valiant Tirant had seen the ship depart, he reviewed all his cavalry, infantry, supply wagons, and artillery. Between what the kings had left behind and what King Escariano had brought, they were strong enough to conquer the entire land. He and his troops then set out for the city of Caramen, which lies on the frontier between Barbary and the black kingdom of Bornu.[39] Aware that three of the defeated kings had taken refuge therein, our knights made their way south, assaulting any towns that offered resistance. Most, however, begged for mercy and delivered their keys, in exchange for which Tirant spared their inhabitants' lives and property. He and King Escariano accorded the towns such generous privileges that their army grew as it advanced, and though many Saracens converted, those who clung to their faith were not harmed.

Upon reaching Caramen, they encamped about two crossbow shots from the city, which was strongly fortified, moated, and well supplied with food and horses.

When all his men had pitched camp, Tirant summoned King Escariano, Lord Agramunt, the Marquis of Liçana,[40] the Viscount of Branches, and many other knights and barons to council. Having decided to send an emissary to their foes, they chose a Spaniard named Lord Rocafort from the town of Oriola. This knight was exceedingly clever and ingenious, for he had spent many years roaming the seas as a pirate and later had been made a galley slave by Moors from Oran, whom Tirant had defeated, thus restoring his freedom. His mission was to count the infidel host and determine how it was arrayed, and they gave him numerous other instructions.

· CCCLXXXV ·

HOW TIRANT'S EMISSARY EXPLAINED HIS MISSION TO THE KINGS

The emissary set out unarmed with a large and splendidly attired retinue. After sending a messenger ahead to request safe-conduct, which was quickly granted, Lord Rocafort entered the city and made his way to the castle, where he was welcomed by King Menador of Persia, the King of Fez, and the new Saracen King of Tlemcen.

Once Lord Rocafort was before the kings, he began to speak without first saluting them: "I come to you, once-powerful kings, on behalf of King Escariano and Tirant lo Blanc, who demand that you quit not only this city but all Barbary. Either prepare for a battle in three days that will be our triumph and your ruin or, if you wish to be known as wise, follow our captain's suggestion. Remember the name 'Tirant,' so terrifying to all infidels, for thus you may yet save your lives and spare your subjects."

· CCCLXXXVI ·

THE KINGS' REPLY TO THE EMISSARY

Once Tirant's emissary had finished, King Menador replied: "Do not imagine that past defeats have daunted our martial spirit, for though

Mohammed has not helped us yet, he will show his might in our hour of need. Tell that renegade black and his henchman that, far from quitting Barbary for their sake, with Allah's help we shall make them pay dearly for their stolen kingdoms. If they wish to know our might, let them prepare to fight tomorrow, when we shall sally forth and vanquish them upon the field of battle."

As soon as the king had finished, Lord Rocafort left without a word and rode back to his camp, where he repeated the Persian's threats to his masters. Tirant immediately gathered his barons, knights, captains, and soldiers, whom he told to prepare for combat on the morrow, and lest they be taken by surprise he had the camp well guarded.

After feeding his horsemen and their mounts shortly before sunrise, Tirant appointed Lord Rocafort captain of the vanguard with six thousand riders at his command. The worthy knight Almedixer captained the second battalion with eight thousand warriors, followed by the Marquis of Liçana, Lord Agramunt, and the Viscount of Branches with ten thousand each. King Escariano led the sixth battalion with fifteen thousand cavalry, and Tirant brought up the rear with twenty thousand more.

Having organized his infantry in like manner, our knight then made the following speech:

· CCCLXXXVII ·

*T*IRANT'S SPEECH TO HIS TROOPS

"Triumphal crowns await us, garlanded with laurel for our coming victory. Oh valiant knights armed with swords so deadly that their mere sight will dismay our enemies: let us all rejoice in a single faith and a common cause, recalling past feats and banishing fear from our hearts! We have nothing but our lives, which we should risk in worthy deeds, for if we are engulfed in the sea of recreance, our fame will reach no worthy harbor. Elevate your thoughts and you will see that beyond our precious honor, we fight for riches, freedom, glory, and above all God, who exalts those who exalt Him and champions those who champion Him. Let this short night be long in your ardent desire for victory, since although our foes may weary of battle, arms are our sole delight."

Soon the Saracen vanguard sallied forth, led by the doughty King of Tlemcen's ten thousand cavalry, who were followed by seven squadrons, each captained by a brave warrior with ten thousand horse. King Menador commanded the rear guard with twenty thousand knights, and each battalion was divided into centuries and decades.

After marshaling their troops outside the city, the infidels made their way toward our captains, while one of Tirant's scouts hastened to inform his master, whose men quickly mounted their steeds lest the enemy find them still encamped.

When the armies spied each other, some blew trumpets and clarions, others uttered war cries so loud that it sounded like the sky was falling, and the two vanguards attacked with wondrous ferocity.

The King of Tlemcen, who led the Saracens, entered battle as bravely as any knight alive, forcing the Christians to give way before his mighty buffets, one of which landed on Lord Rocafort's head and knocked him from his steed. The king rode on, while the lord's men strove to rehorse him, but he surely would have perished had the second battalion not attacked. When Tirant saw his men faltering, he dispatched Almedixer, who bravely assailed the infidels and forced them to retreat. Then the second enemy battalion joined the press, and you could see lances breaking, knights falling, and a battlefield strewn with corpses, for the Kings of Fez and Tlemcen were truly valiant warriors.

Once Tirant saw his men getting the worst of it, he ordered all the remaining squadrons except his to attack, and they charged so fiercely that before the Saracens realized what was happening, many of their souls had entered Pluto's kingdom.

King Escariano and the King of Fez clashed with such fury that their lances broke and they fell to earth, but they quickly rose, drew their swords, and rushed each other like raging lions while men from both armies hastened to aid their kings. After a bloody encounter with many casualties on both sides, Lord Agramunt and the Marquis of Liçana rehorsed King Escariano despite their foes, who, upon rescuing the King of Fez, saw how badly their host had fared and sent their remaining squadrons into battle.

Then our knight joined the fray with his men, and you could hear the Saracens' cries of woe. King Menador, who fought like a rabid dog in his flashing gold jubbah, dealt Tirant a blow to the head that knocked him forward in his saddle. The Breton almost lost his balance, but he righted himself and cried: "I owe my life to my helmet, which you shall never smite again."

Raising his sword, he struck the king so hard on the shoulder that his arm was severed and he fell to earth dead.

The Saracens fought even more desperately once they saw what had occurred, but their casualties multiplied, for everyone Tirant struck was slain or wounded.

During the battle, Tirant encountered with the King of Tlemcen, smiting him on the head and knocking him from his steed. He was saved by his good helmet, but Tirant did not turn back, and after dragging their lord away, the Saracens took him into the city.

The combat lasted many hours, but at last the heathens could stand no more and fled while Tirant cried: "Victory is ours, valiant knights! Slay them all!"

Everyone pursued them as they raced toward the city, but the infidels could not ride fast enough to keep forty thousand from dying. Once the rest had escaped, Tirant had his men withdraw out of range of the enemy bombards.

Praising God for their victory, the Christians returned in triumph to their camp, where they mounted strong guards lest they be taken by surprise and sent scouts to ensure that no one left the city. Their foes built barricades outside the walls and performed noble feats every day, while our knight had catapults built and bombards assembled to fire at them continuously.

As soon as the battle had been won, Tirant had a galley fitted out in the port of al-Hoceina and entrusted it to a knight named Espercius from Tlemcen. Knowing that he was a good Christian and most diligent in all matters, Tirant told him to sail to Genoa, Pisa, and Majorca (which at that time was a great trading center) and hire every ship or galley big enough to carry troops. Having received orders to rent them for a year and send them to the port of Constantine in the kingdom of Tunis,[41] Espercius quickly boarded the galley and set sail.

Now the book leaves Tirant's chivalric deeds and turns to Melquisedec's adventures in Constantinople.

· CCCLXXXVIII ·

*H*OW TIRANT'S EMISSARY ARRIVED IN CONSTANTINOPLE

A favorable wind quickly bore Melquisedec's galley to Constantinople, where His Majesty dispatched a knight to welcome him. Upon his return, the knight announced that Tirant had sent a shipload of grain from Barbary.

The emperor was delighted, as his need had been dire, and after praising and thanking God for remembering them in their distress, he sent his knights and aldermen to welcome Tirant's emissary, whom they honored greatly on their lord's behalf.

Clad in a double brocade sable-lined robe, a brocade doublet, and a heavy gold chain, Melquisedec led his large and handsomely dressed retinue ashore. They were greeted with cries of joy, for the emperor's knights longed to behold their savior again, and once they reached the palace, the emissary bowed before the emperor and empress, kissing their hands and feet while Their Highnesses smiled upon him. Then he presented his letter of credence to the emperor, who handed it to his secretary to read:

· CCCLXXXIX ·

*T*HE LETTER OF CREDENCE

Holy Majesty: the emissary who bears this letter will compensate for my brevity. May it please you to give him credence, for he is a worthy knight of great fame and virtue.

Having read the letter, the emperor ordered fine lodgings prepared for Melquisedec, and on the morrow His Majesty summoned his counselors, aldermen, and nobles to the great hall. When everyone had arrived, he sent for the emissary, who had donned another ermine-lined brocade robe of a different color and wore a heavy gold necklace with fine enameling. This eloquent warrior, the master of many languages, then bowed before His Highness, who asked him to sit nearby that he might hear him better.[42] Once everyone was silent, the emperor ordered Melquisedec to speak, whereupon he rose, bowed deeply, and uttered the following words:

· CCCXC ·

*H*OW MELQUISEDEC EXPLAINED HIS MISSION

"Your Highness will recall that Tirant set out to rescue the knights held prisoner, but iniquitous Fortune tore his galleys from their moorings. After being driven hither and yon for six days and six nights, they all sank except Tirant's vessel, which ran aground near Tunis. Those who survived were captured and enslaved, but luckily for Tirant, he was discovered by the Bey of Beys, whom the King of Tlemcen had sent on a mission to the

King of Tunis. One day as this knight was hunting, he spied Tirant in a cave, and so struck was he by our captain's beauty that he treated him as his son, while the Breton fought by his side against King Escariano's hordes. In the end Tirant was freed for his bravery and captured the invader, who later converted, became his brother-in-arms, and married the King of Tlemcen's daughter. This Christian king now rules both Tunis and Tlemcen, and Your Majesty should know that Tirant has conquered all Barbary except one city. Once he completes his campaign, he will bring two hundred and fifty thousand men to Constantinople, where King Philip of Sicily will join him with all his forces. Tirant is already loading ships with food for Your Highness and will soon perform such deeds that you will be well satisfied, wherefore he asks you to forgive this delay, which was not his fault."

· CCCXCI ·

*H*OW MELQUISEDEC OBTAINED THE EMPEROR'S LEAVE TO SALUTE CARMESINA

The emperor and his counselors, who were astonished that their captain had risen from being a slave to ruling Barbary, praised Tirant's noble deeds and pronounced him the bravest knight on earth, while their fears of the Turks were greatly allayed.

Then Melquisedec knelt before the emperor and asked his leave to salute Carmesina. The noble lord told Hippolytus to escort him, for Carmesina had entered a convent where she pined for her husband, and though she had not yet taken the veil, she dressed in dark grey and followed the same rules as the nuns.

As soon as the knights arrived, Melquisedec asked to see Carmesina, whom the nuns hastened to inform of our emissary's request. Seeing her at the door, Melquisedec bowed to kiss her hand, but the princess was so overjoyed that she burst into tears.

Once the lady had recovered, she asked after Tirant, to which Melquisedec replied that he commended himself to her, was in good health, and longed to see Her Highness: "And he sends you this letter."

The princess then read her knight's missive, which was of the following tenor:

·CCCXCII·

*T*IRANT'S LETTER TO THE PRINCESS

Absence, that adversary of enamored hearts, is my mightiest foe, for your Tirant has borne such tribulations that only your constant prayers have saved him. I thank you for my honors, which I know are due to you alone, and I curse cruel Fortune for separating us, as your image is ever with me and my tongue can only pronounce your angelic name. How many perils have menaced my weary gaze, yet I have overcome them all and only your love eludes me. Forgive me for not writing sooner, since I was never free to do so, but I promise that your just prayers will soon be answered.

Great was the princess's solace when she read this letter, and she asked the emissary how close Tirant was to victory. Upon hearing of his noble exploits, she felt certain that he would succor them, and, comforted by his impending return, she asked what had become of Pleasure-of-my-life. In reply, Melquisedec recited the damsel's adventures and told how Tirant had sworn to make her his cousin's queen.

The princess felt very pleased and declared that all Tirant's deeds revealed his peerless virtue, whereupon Melquisedec told her how Pleasure-of-my-life had been his wife's slave and had saved Montagata.

After delivering his messages, the emissary returned to his lodgings.

·CCCXCIII·

*H*OW THE EMISSARY DEPARTED WITH THE EMPEROR'S AND CARMESINA'S REPLIES

A few days later, His Highness decided to let Tirant's emissary depart with a letter describing the empire's predicament.

He summoned Melquisedec and gave him his reply, in which he urged Tirant to pity his old age, those nations facing perdition, and the ladies and damsels who would be dishonored if he did not save them.

Having bidden the emperor farewell, Melquisedec visited Carmesina, who said that she was pleased by his prompt departure, for she knew he would urge Tirant to quickly succor them. She begged him by his chivalric vows to do his utmost, and she gave him a letter addressed to her knight.

When they had finished talking, Melquisedec kissed the princess's hand, and so, having accomplished his mission, he embarked and set sail for Barbary.

Here the book leaves the emperor and returns to Tirant.

· CCCXCIV ·

HOW TIRANT CAPTURED THE CITY OF CARAMEN

After Melquisedec's departure, Tirant pondered how to take the city, for though his bombards and catapults fired constantly, whatever they demolished was soon rebuilt. The Christians attacked day and night, yet all their efforts were for nought, while the kings and their cavalry made as many sorties as they liked. Being outnumbered two to one, they avoided pitched battles, and this situation lasted for an entire year.

One day Tirant summoned his knights and said: "Lords and brothers, our shame is great, as after a year we still cannot take this city, and in my opinion we should either conquer it or die trying."

Everyone agreed, but Tirant still felt very melancholy, since he longed to finish his conquests and rescue his beloved, whom Pleasure-of-my-life often accused him of forsaking in her hour of need.

During the siege, Tirant's men had started work on a tunnel that took a long time to complete because Caramen was built upon hard rock. When the tunnel had been dug, Tirant placed Lord Rocafort in charge of his thousand best men and divided his remaining troops into ten large battalions.

An hour before dawn, the Christians stormed Caramen at ten different points, setting up ladders to scale the walls, whose defenders resisted furiously, but meanwhile Lord Rocafort led his soldiers through the tunnel and, once they were inside, ran to the nearest gate and flung it open. Tirant and his battalion poured into Caramen as soon as they saw Lord Rocafort, who then hurried to the next gate, where King Escariano entered with all his soldiers.

A great hue and cry arose when their enemies realized what had occurred, and the two armies clashed while the infidel kings mounted their steeds, but Lord Rocafort's men continued from one gate to the next till their entire army was inside.

Beholding the Moors' discomfiture, the valiant King of Tlemcen charged into the press, not to aid his friends but to put an end to his miseries. He was slain by Almedixer, who, after removing the despot's crown, adorned his sword with the hapless monarch's head.

The Saracens fought like raging lions, though they had no hope of victory and their sole desire was to do as much harm as possible. They killed or wounded many soldiers in Tirant's squadrons, who galloped through the streets dodging stones thrown from towers and rooftops.

Lord Rocafort climbed a tower along a stretch of damaged wall where he planted a flag with King Escariano's and Tirant's arms, but the King of Fez spied him and sought to preserve his eyes from such an affront. As the Saracen was scaling the wall, the Marquis of Liçana knocked him off, whereupon a great cry went up among the infidels, who fought more ardently to avenge their captain, but Tirant, King Escariano, and their proud company mercilessly slew those who resisted.

The Viscount of Branches left the battle, not out of fear but to enhance their victory, and occupied all the towers, on which he lit bonfires and hoisted banners while his men cried: "Long live our captain, the king, and our noble soldiers! Long live Christianity! May God exalt our victorious faith!"

· CCCXCV ·

*H*OW TIRANT'S EMISSARY RETURNED FROM CONSTANTINOPLE

Having captured the city and slain his royal foes, Tirant joyously thanked God for his glorious victory. Then he organized Caramen and brought his men inside, since it was very big and well stocked with everything they might require. All the nearby towns, villages, and castles sent him their keys, promising to embrace Christianity and obey his commands. Once he had spared their lives, he gave them so many privileges that everyone praised his great generosity.

One day as he was taking his ease, word came that Melquisedec had docked in the port of Stora. A few days later the emissary reached Caramen, where he was welcomed with great joy, and after bowing before Tirant, the knight gave him His Majesty's letter, which contained words of the following tenor:

· CCCXCVI ·

*T*HE EMPEROR'S LETTER TO TIRANT

Until your emissary arrived, fear and perplexity assailed my heart, though I sought to recall your chivalry and ignore our woes and losses. Your absence has been our enemies' safe-conduct, since the thought that you were dead seemed to imperil our very lives. Divine Providence has not yet permitted such a disaster, but we are truly in great danger and lose ground every day as the Turks fatten upon our empire, which has been reduced to Constantinople, Pera, and a few castles. It would take too long to list all the knights who have died, while those who remain are half crippled by fear and expect to end their lives in slavery. Confound our enemies and avenge our dead, oh blessed captain, whom we love as a son and have never forgotten. How, in our sorrow, can we induce you to aid us? Your relatives cry out, as do the imprisoned knights from Sicily and Rhodes, nor will subjugated Africa forbid you to free our empire, for such an enterprise would be equal to the one you have just completed. To conquer the world is too small a task for a knight whose very name fills the Grand Turk and sultan with dread. Act in accordance with your nature, and come quickly if any love dwells within you.

· CCCXCVII ·

*M*ELQUISEDEC'S REPORT TO TIRANT

Upon reading the letter, Tirant was overcome by pity and his eyes filled with tears at the thought of his imprisoned relatives. Then he remembered all the towns he had conquered in Greece. How quickly they had been lost, and even more besides!

He questioned Melquisedec about Carmesina's state, and the emissary replied that in his absence she had retired to one of Saint Clara's convents. "She asked me to recount your exploits, to tell her how you have fared, and to urge you again and again to preserve them from slavery. If she has ever affronted you, she pleads for the same mercy you show your enemies, for she is of your own flesh, which you should never forsake."

After saying many other things, Melquisedec gave Tirant the princess's missive, which contained words of the following tenor:

· C C C X C V I I I ·

*T*HE PRINCESS'S LETTER TO TIRANT

So great was my sovereign joy upon reading your letter that I lost my senses, while enamored tears rolled down my cheeks. To protect my weak heart, the blood drained from my limbs, and a long time passed before I regained consciousness. Then I heaved a deep sigh that showed I was still alive, for your words are the first solace I have had since your departure, and I thank you for your travails, which I know are caused not by my pleas but by your courage. A happy end should be praised, and blessed are those ills that lead to joy, yet my name, Tirant, is the least of your advantages, nor can I believe it was the occasion for your noble victories. If love has conquered the conqueror, I forgive your false suspicions, but on one condition: that you quit Africa immediately. Let us rejoice in your presence, and remember the crown that awaits you, since the flower of my virginity, which you so coveted, is now threatened by infidels of insatiable cruelty! Likewise, you should recall the honors my father and I bestowed upon you, as you will be guilty of ingratitude should you refuse to succor us. May your clement, good, and loving heart be moved to rescue those threatened with perdition and apostasy and to succor your relatives, who languish in prison because they served you. I scarcely know what more to say! Until now, my sole pleasure has been to behold, kiss, and worship the jewels and other tokens you gave me. Then I would pace about my room, saying: "Tirant sat here, he held me here, here he kissed me, here we lay together naked." Thus during the night and much of the day I allayed my grief, but may such thoughts cease with your coming, which will end my woes and redeem this Christian people.

· C C C X C I X ·

*H*OW TIRANT WAS OVERWHELMED BY LOVE AND GRIEF

When Tirant finished the letter, his agony was so great that he fainted for very pity of the emperor and his daughter. As he imagined their bitter sorrow and his friends languishing in prison, our knight lost his senses and fell in a swoon.

Hearing the resultant uproar, Pleasure-of-my-life hastened to his lodgings, where she splashed rice water in his face and touched the wound on his ear. Tirant then opened his eyes, but grief kept him from speaking, for he truly loved the princess and his companions. Only after a long while did he sit up and utter these enamored words:

· CD ·

*T*IRANT'S EXCLAMATION

"Oh you who tread love's thorny pathways: stop and tell me if such sufferings can be found within your breasts![43] The only doctor who can cure me is far away and in danger, yet Fortune parts me from her glory and imperils my very life. Oh emperor, whom I love and worship as God! Oh empress, who bore my life's fruit in her womb! Oh Carmesina, in whose image Divine Wisdom shines! Oh angelic lady who holds my heart in thrall! Chamber of my soul's repose, you were my hardships' sole reward, but who will defend you now from shame and affliction? Oh Tirant, who will lend you wings to fly to her side? Descend, celestial clouds, and take me to my love, and you, immortal gods whom I poetically invoke, help me to champion my beloved princess! Oh True God and Redeemer, I kneel and raise my hands to Heaven, invoking Your eternal might against those who defy Your glory. Guide and help Your humble servant to save that Christian empire, for I shall bless You and perform countless good works in Your name."

· CDI ·

*H*OW TIRANT GAVE THE KINGDOMS OF FEZ AND BOUGIE TO LORD AGRAMUNT AND PLEASURE-OF-MY-LIFE

Once Tirant had finished his lamentations, he urged King Escariano to accompany him to Tunis and take possession of his kingdom, but before departing, our knight gave Lord Agramunt Fez and Bougie. Then he gathered his troops and they all set out together.

Learning that a Christian host was nearby, the Tunisians sent a messenger to beg Tirant to spare them, for their previous king was dead and they promised to submit. Having agreed, our two captains triumphantly entered Tunis, which Tirant gave to King Escariano along with all the nearby towns and castles.

As they were taking their ease, news arrived that six Genoese vessels had docked at Constantine,[44] whereupon Tirant gave Melquisedec enough doubloons to load them with grain and send them to the emperor.

A few days later, when all the ships were seaborne, Tirant asked King

Escariano to help free the Greek Empire from its attackers, and the monarch graciously replied that he was at his friend's command.

Tirant urged Lord Agramunt to gather as many troops as he could, and he set out immediately while King Escariano also summoned his knights, who armed themselves for battle and within three months arrived in Constantine. Forty-four thousand cavalry and a hundred thousand infantry came from Tunis and Tlemcen, and Lord Agramunt brought twenty thousand horse and fifty thousand foot from Fez and Bougie.

Once everything was in order, Espercius arrived with a fleet of ships and galleys he had hired from Spaniards, Genoese, Pisans, and Venetians. Upon disembarking, he told Tirant that everything was ready, for there were three hundred big ships along with two hundred galleys and many smaller vessels.

Then Tirant sent Espercius to King Philip of Sicily, and so the knight boarded a galley and set sail again.

A few days later, still more ships reached Constantine, and after hiring them for a year, Tirant had thirty vessels loaded with grain and other foodstuffs. When they were ready, he summoned his soldiers and the townsfolk to a plain outside the city, where he, King Escariano, the King of Fez, and many other knights stood upon a platform around which everyone else gathered, waiting for our knight to speak.

· CDII ·

*T*IRANT'S SPEECH TO HIS TROOPS

"The prow of my desires points toward honor's harbor as I sail love's stormy seas, whose hardships are my only joy and solace. We should all behave thus, for as mighty kings, valiant knights, and worthy soldiers, we must now raise anchor and commence our glorious voyage, in which your shining deeds will enhance lineages already adorned by feats of valor. If hope of victory is your standard, your hands can only conquer, as your courage, hard as diamonds, will neither flag nor falter. Let us all take comfort in a single will and spirit, knowing that we shall find a safe harbor at the end of our travails. My purpose is to remind you of our urgent mission, since if we defend Christ's imperiled faith in accordance with our knightly vows, our reward will be infinite, as the reverend here will tell you."

When Tirant had finished his speech, he asked the Mercedarian friar to sit upon a throne. He was a Catalan from Lleida named Joan Ferrer, whom the Pope had made his legate because he spoke fluent Arabic.[45] This friar, who was a master of theology, then gave a most eloquent sermon, as you shall hear:

· CDIII ·

*T*HE PAPAL LEGATE'S SERMON

"When I contemplate the Christian faith, oh excellent kings, lords, and barons, I see that no rational being can live without it, for just as God created man to enjoy Heaven's glory, so one can only enter Paradise in the Church's nuptial gowns. Faith alone can save man from death and original sin, as learned Saint Augustine tells us in his epistle *Ad Obtatum: 'Nemo, inquit, liberatur a damnatione que facta est per Adam nisi per fide Jesu Christi,'* which means: 'Only faith in Jesus Christ can save us from damnation for Adam's sin.' Both ancients and moderns have found salvation in our creed, and even before Christ's birth, men of good will foresaw His incarnation, crucifixion, and resurrection, as well as many other things that have since come to pass. Do not renounce Heaven's glory, which no human eye can perceive, nor can our ears hear or our minds fathom such sovereign splendor.

"Oh you who were raised in Mohammed's wicked sect: open your hearts to God's promise of eternal life and abjure filth and dishonor, than which nothing is more shameful! Such is the creed of that vile pig Mohammed, yet lust and gluttony befit only ignorant beasts, whereas true felicity derives from acts suitable to men of reason, as Aristotle says in *primo et decimo Eticorum* and Lactantius in *libro tercio Divinarum Institutionum, cap. decimo,* and since lust and gluttony make brutes of men, it follows that beatitude cannot be found therein. Thus do we behold the folly of Mohammed's teachings, but Christianity, whose captain is Jesus Christ, preaches obedience to God's word. As King David said: *'Viam mandatorum tuorum cocurri,'* which means: 'I, oh Lord, have walked the path of Christianity, which is my salvation and the way of thy commandments.'[46] Likewise, we read in Ecclesiasticus 23: *'Nihil dulcius quam respicere in mandata Domini,'* which means: 'There is nothing sweeter than to heed the Lord's commandments.'[47] Oh soul, what could be sweeter than these words of Christian doctrine: 'Thou shalt love God with all thy heart and thy neighbor as thyself.' They distill all the perfection of our holy faith, whose charity should burn like fire in our hearts, as we learn from Jesus's words in John 12: *'Ignem veni mittere in terram, et quid volo nisi ut ardeat,'* which means: 'I am come to send fire on the earth, and would that it were already kindled!'[48] wherefore a Christian should always burn with love of

God and his neighbor, but since Saracens spurn God's commandments, it follows that they shall roast in Hell.

"Christianity is called the light of understanding for three reasons: first, because it radiates from the sun of God's glory, and just as material light issues from the sun, so does faith issue from Jesus Christ, for as Saint Paul says in 1 Corinthians: '*Fides nostra non est in sapientia hominum, sed in virtute Dei,*' which means: 'Our faith should not stand in the wisdom of men, but in the power of God.'[49] Secondly, Christianity is the light of human understanding that casts out sin, as Solomon says in Proverbs 6: '*Per fidem et penitentiam purgantur peccata,*' which means: 'Faith and repentance cast out sin.'[50] If you, who are now infidels, embrace our noble creed, the baptismal waters will purge your souls of sin, and if thus fortified, you help Tirant succor the Greek Empire, only two fates can await you: to die in battle and go to Heaven, or to live and win both earthly and celestial glory. Finally, as Christianity illuminates what is hidden, elucidating our articles of faith and many other divine mysteries, we should all make Christ our captain and enter battle beneath His banner, whereby He will give us victory over the Grand Turk and sultan. We shall reconquer the Greek Empire, which they have tyrannically occupied, just as we subdued the kingdoms of Tunis, Tlemcen, Fez, and Bougie, whereupon God will reward us in Heaven and all men will praise our exploits."

· CDIV ·

*H*OW THREE HUNDRED AND FORTY THOUSAND INFIDELS WERE BAPTIZED

When the friar's sermon ended, all the hitherto unrepentant Moors begged to be christened, while Tirant sent for every basin, bowl, and big pot that could be found. Then he summoned the friars and priests in Barbary, for he had founded churches and monasteries and brought clergy from many other Christian lands. Both those about to sail and those who stayed behind were baptized, and within three days, three hundred and forty thousand men, women, and children had converted.

After this had been done, Tirant told King Escariano: "Sire, do not sail with us but gather your foot and cavalry from Ethiopia. If you march overland to Constantinople and I go by sea, we shall trap the Turks between us, thereby defeating them once and for all."

King Escariano said that although it distressed him to leave Tirant, if he could be of more use with a larger army, he was willing to obey.

King Escariano, a tall, handsome black and a most valiant warrior, ruled the inhabitants of Ethiopia, who called him King Jamjam. He was rich, powerful, and adored by his vassals. His cavalry was mighty, and his kingdom was so big that it bordered not only on Tlemcen but on Prester John of the Indies' lands, through which the river Tigris runs.[51]

Seeing Tirant's will, King Escariano and his queen took their leave of the Christian knights and set out for his kingdom with five hundred horsemen. Tirant accompanied them for a league and then returned to Constantine.

Here we leave Tirant and turn to Espercius, who had gone to Sicily.

· CDV ·

*H*OW ESPERCIUS ARRIVED IN SICILY

A favorable wind quickly bore Espercius to Sicily, and upon hearing that King Philip was in Messina, he sailed to that port, where, clad in a splendid brocade robe, he led his noble retinue to the palace.

Once there, he bowed before the king, who asked why he had come. The emissary replied: "Most excellent lord, Tirant lo Blanc has sent me," and without further ado he presented his letter of credence, which His Majesty read with abundant joy. He had Espercius and his men well lodged and sent beef, pork, and fresh bread to their galley.

The next morning after Mass, the monarch summoned his council to hear Tirant's message. Espercius then rose and bowed, but His Majesty told him to remain seated, whereupon the worthy emissary began to speak in this fashion:

· CDVI ·

*E*SPERCIUS'S MESSAGE

"Most excellent lords, you will recall that when Tirant was about to set sail for Saint George, a mighty tempest arose and drove his galleys toward Barbary, where they all sank except his own, which was wrecked near Tunis. Then he was captured by one of the King of Tlemcen's beys, but the monarch later freed him for his bravery and appointed him captain. Since that day, Tirant has conquered all Barbary, slain eight Saracen sovereigns, and vanquished another named Escariano who rules the black kingdom of Ethiopia and who subsequently converted and is now Tirant's brother-in-arms. Knowing that the Turks have undone his conquests, our captain has decided to relieve Constantinople. Barbary is with him and ready to sail, wherefore he asks you to help deliver the Greek Empire, being so certain of your aid that he will be here shortly."

King Philip replied: "Knight, I am much comforted by my brother Tirant's triumphs, and I shall gladly place both my person and riches at his disposal."

The emissary rose and thanked the king profusely. When the council was over, King Philip dictated letters to all the barons, knights, cities, and free towns in Sicily, asking them to send representatives to Palermo on a certain day when he wished to hold a general parliament.

The representatives gathered on the appointed day, and after opening the parliament, Philip asked the whole kingdom in general and everyone in particular to help Tirant. They all gladly consented, and many decided to go along. Once the parliament had ended, they prepared to set out, while the king collected food, vessels, and four thousand handsome chargers.

Here the book leaves the king loading his horses, arms, and provisions, and returns to the six vessels Tirant had sent to Constantinople.

· CDVII ·

*H*OW TIRANT'S SIX VESSELS ARRIVED IN VLONË

The six vessels sailed with such propitious winds that they soon approached Constantinople and docked at the Greek port of Vlonë,[52] where the captains learned that their foes had sailed through the Bosporus with a mighty fleet. To the emperor's great distress, they had blockaded and besieged the capital, whose inhabitants implored God to quickly send Tirant.

Carmesina returned to the palace and sought to raise her father's spirits, while the Greek soldiers defended themselves as best they could.

Hippolytus, who had replaced our knight, performed valiant deeds of chivalry every day, and had it not been for him the city would have already fallen.

Upon learning of the Turkish blockade, Tirant's captains dared not venture further and sent a message to His Majesty that they feared to leave Vlonë, but that Tirant had sailed from Constantine and was on his way to help him. They also sent a brig to inform their captain that the sultan and Grand Turk were besieging Constantinople.

The brig had such good weather that it soon reached Palermo.

· CDVIII ·

H OW TIRANT SAILED FROM CONSTANTINE WITH A MIGHTY FLEET

As soon as King Escariano departed, our knight loaded his ships with arms, horses, provisions, and soldiers. Then he, the King of Fez, Pleasure-of-my-life, and his other lords sailed for Sicily.

When the captain of the brig from Vlonë sighted Tirant's fleet, he made for it and, after asking which ship was the captain's, pulled alongside the vessel and quickly went aboard. Upon hearing that they had feared to run the blockade, the Breton was sorely vexed but continued on to Palermo, where they were welcomed by the royal fleet's trumpets and bombards, while Tirant's replied in kind with such a mighty din that it sounded like the very earth was collapsing.

Once the fleet had docked, the king boarded Tirant's ship and embraced his Breton friend with great joy and affection. After greeting the King of Fez and the others in like manner, Philip led them ashore, though Tirant's soldiers stayed behind. The king had brought Queen Ricomana, who welcomed their guests and especially Pleasure-of-my-life, since she had been Princess Carmesina's servant. Then they made their way to the palace, followed by a great crowd of commoners.

On their arrival, Philip took Tirant and the King of Fez by the hands, while the queen did likewise with Pleasure-of-my-life. Thus they entered a richly carpeted hall hung with silk and gold tapestries, where they beheld a great table heaped with gold and silver, for King Philip was rather greedy and had amassed a huge treasure. When everyone had entered, he urged Tirant to be seated, but the captain refused until the two monarchs had preceded him. Tirant sat facing King Philip, Pleasure-of-my-life ate between him and his queen, and, entertained by trumpeters and other musicians, they all dined with great gusto.

After the meal, Tirant and King Philip excused themselves, leaving the two queens, the King of Fez, and a multitude of knights and ladies in the hall, where they began to dance and make merry while their captains discussed the war.

Once the Breton had described his tribulations in Barbary, Our Lord's subsequent favors, and the emperor's predicament, King Philip declared: "Lord brother, I have gathered all the horses, armor, and infantry I need. Only the cavalry remains, and I can summon them within two hours."

Tirant replied: "Sire, please send criers through the city calling everyone to the ships at sundown, for I wish to depart this very evening."

The king quickly dispatched a chamberlain to summon his men. Then the two lords returned to the great hall, where they took their ease for a while with the queen.

Having drawn Pleasure-of-my-life aside, Queen Ricomana inquired about her mistress, to which the damsel replied that she could never recite all Carmesina's perfections or praise her enough. After touching on the princess's love affair with great gentility and discretion, she began to flatter Ricomana like a master of the art. Pleasure-of-my-life swore that only Tirant's beloved could equal the queen's beauty and wisdom, and our damsel said many other things to please Her Majesty.

The festivities continued until it was time for supper, which everyone ate with abundant pleasure. When the meal ended, Tirant asked King Philip to prepare to sail before nightfall, and they all said goodbye to those who were staying behind. The king appointed the Duke of Messina, who was Ricomana's cousin, viceroy in his absence, and having done everything necessary, the two knights boarded their ships. They weighed anchor at the first watch, and God sent them such favorable winds that they quickly reached Vlonë, where our knight's captains awaited them.

As soon as Tirant sighted their vessels, he sent the brig to tell them to hoist sail and follow him.

Here the book leaves Tirant and returns to King Escariano.

· CDIX ·

*H*OW KING ESCARIANO BAPTIZED EVERYONE IN HIS KINGDOM

King Escariano and his wife made their way to Ethiopa, where his vassals welcomed them with great honor, offered the queen valuable gifts, and rejoiced to hear about all the lands their lord had conquered.

A few days after his arrival, King Escariano summoned his knights to a parliament in the city of Trogodita, and when they all had gathered he made the following appeal: "Barons, I wish to inform you of my noble deeds, as I am sure you will delight in our new-found prosperity.[53] As you know, I was captured by a captain named Tirant lo Blanc, but that valiant knight generously freed me, became my brother-in-arms, and gave me the Princess of Tlemcen, whom I cherish more than the entire world. He also made me King of Tunis, for which I am further in his debt, and now he has asked me to help reconquer the Greek Empire. Therefore, I beg you: accompany me to Constantinople, as I promise to pay you well and see to all your needs."

They affirmed their fealty and vowed to die defending his honor in Constantinople or anywhere else. Having acknowledged their good will, King Escariano asked them to gather everything they needed and said he would reward them when they reassembled in Trogodita. Then he sent criers through his kingdom announcing that any foreigner or native who wished to serve in his army should come to that same city, where he would be generously paid.

Meanwhile, the virtuous queen pondered how she might spread Christianity with the help of many clergymen and two bishops she had brought from Constantine. As soon as they reached Trogodita, she asked them to start preaching, and a multitude of Ethiopians were baptized out of either duty or faith. Then the queen built churches and monasteries, to which the king allotted generous annuities. The bishops consecrated them and many natives chose to become monks, while the friars from Barbary were named abbots and the aforesaid bishops received wealthy dioceses. She urged all those who felt the call to go through the kingdom, preaching and baptizing anyone who wished to convert.

At that time the Ethiopians, who knew nothing of marriage, held their women in common and no man knew his father, which made them the most ignoble nation on earth.[54] Queen Emeraldine therefore ordered her subjects to marry, whereby all their subsequent children were legitimate.

In the south of King Escariano's lands there was a huge volcano that belched fire continually into the ocean, and his kingdom also had vast uninhabited deserts that stretched as far as Arabia.[55]

When his army was in order, the monarch offered to pay them, though many refused, and upon counting his cavalry, he found that he had two hundred and twenty thousand strong and able horsemen. King Escariano made great profits from his royal mines, and except for the Great Khan he was the mightiest lord on earth.

Having organized his affairs and appointed viceroys, King Escariano reviewed his troops and set a date for their departure. Then he collected horses and elephants to carry food, tents, and artillery, as well as great herds of cattle and other livestock for his men to eat. The queen assembled her finest robes and jewelry, which she entrusted to a multitude of ladies and damsels, some of whom were black and some white, for the whites were Tunisians and the blacks Ethiopians. She took such an large wardrobe because she had promised to attend Tirant's wedding, at which Lord Agramunt and Pleasure-of-my-life also planned to marry.

Once everything was in order, King Escariano and his army set out, and after fifty days he reached Shiraz on the border of Prester John's lands. King Escariano rested there and was splendidly entertained, for his subjects in that city had never seen him before.

Here the book leaves King Escariano and turns to Tirant's emissary Espercius.

· C D X ·

OF ESPERCIUS'S GOOD FORTUNE

After receiving King Philip's reply, Espercius took his leave of him and returned to Africa, while a few days later Tirant reached Palermo with his entire fleet, but their paths did not cross and Espercius continued on to Constantine, where they told him his lord had already left. Feeling most vexed, the knight took on fresh provisions, weighed anchor again, and upon reaching Palermo, found that the fleet had departed two weeks earlier. Espercius then set sail for Vlonë, where once again he learned that the Breton had left.

During Espercius's voyage to Constantinople, a storm arose and his ship was wrecked on the isle of Chios. Everyone perished except the knight and ten men, who then set out in search of something to eat.

As they walked, they met an aged shepherd pasturing a few sheep and asked him if there was a village nearby, to which he replied that there was only one small farmhouse, inhabited by four families who had been banished from Rhodes and lived in great poverty because the island was under a spell. Espercius begged him for food, saying they had eaten nothing for two days, and the kindly old man offered to share his meager lunch. He gathered his sheep and brought them to the farmhouse, where they divided what little there was. When they had finished eating, Espercius asked who had cursed such a fair place.

The shepherd said that since Espercius seemed a good man, he would recite the story: "My lord, Hippocrates, who once ruled both this isle and Crete,[56] had a beautiful daughter whom the goddess Diana changed into a dragon ten feet long. She is called the Lady of the Isles, and I have often seen her, for she haunts the crypt of an old castle you can see on that hill. She comes out twice or thrice a year and never harms anyone unless they trouble her, but the spell could be broken if some valiant knight kissed her lips. Once a knight from Rhodes bravely swore to do so and rode to the castle, but upon entering the crypt and spying the dragon's ugly head, the gentleman lost heart and fled in dismay. Seeing the dragon behind it, his horse went berserk and leapt off a cliff, whereby the hapless knight was killed for his cowardice.

"It happened that some time later a youth who knew nothing of all this came ashore, and as he was walking about the island in search of some amusement, he beheld the castle, whose crypt he resolved to enter. At the sight of the damsel combing her hair before a mirror surrounded by treasure, the youth decided that she was either mad or a prostitute expecting visitors. He stood there until she noticed his shadow on the wall and asked what he wanted, to which he replied: 'Fair lady, my sole desire is to be your servant.' She then asked if he was a knight, and after hearing that he was not, she said: 'Only one who has taken knightly vows can be my lord and master. Return to your ship, find someone to knight you, and await me tomorrow morning outside this castle. If you bravely kiss my lips, I shall do you no harm, for I am as you now see me, though a spell has changed my aspect. By kissing me, you shall win this treasure, my love, and the rule of these islands.'

"The young man left the crypt and hastened to his ship, where he was knighted. The next morning he went to kiss the damsel, but upon seeing her he fled in terror, while she pursued him, wailing sorrowfully as she ran. The knight quickly died, and such has been the fate of all others, but if one of them dared to kiss her he would be lord of this land."

When brave Espercius heard these words, he pensively asked: "Tell me, my good man: is this story true?"

The shepherd replied: "My lord, rest assured that I speak to you in all verity. Most of this happened in my lifetime, and I would not lie to you for anything."

Espercius decided to try his luck, as Our Lord could not have brought him there without a reason, and moreover, he was desperate since he could not leave the island. He said nothing to his companions lest they either join or seek to dissuade him, and, ready to kiss that dragon or die, he asked the old man how to reach the castle. That night they all slept in the shepherd's house.

Early the next morning, Espercius, who had not slept very well, rose and told his companions he was going to make water, but they paid no attention and went back to sleep. Once outside, he picked up a heavy staff, as he had no other arms, and stole away before anyone could notice his absence.

Soon the day dawned bright and clear, and having reached the dragon's lair, Espercius knelt and begged Our Lord for the courage to redeem that soul in torment.

Commending his soul to God, Espercius walked as far as he could into the crypt, and when he could see no more, he shouted so the dragon would hear him. She lumbered toward the knight with such a terrifying din that he fell to his knees and began to pray again. Then the dragon emerged, looking so ugly that Espercius shut his eyes, and at that moment he was truly more dead than alive.

As soon as the dragon saw him, it sweetly kissed his lips, whereupon Espercius fainted while the beast turned into a fair damsel. She placed his head in her lap, rubbing his temples and murmuring: "Brave knight, open your eyes and behold the glory that awaits you."

Espercius, however, did not recover for another hour, during which the gentle lady kept rubbing his temples and kissing him. At last he opened his eyes and, beholding the beautiful damsel, he pricked up his courage, rose to his feet, and said:

· CDXI ·

*E*SPERCIUS'S DECLARATION OF LOVE

"No mortal tongue could describe your gallant grace and perfection, which have captured my heart and enthralled my very soul. Love's flames leapt up within me when I first heard of your pulchritude, imbuing me with the courage to free you from your torments; but now that I have seen you I shall be enslaved forever, as your beauty will adorn my life and no man will be my equal, nor has anyone ever loved an unknown damsel as I have you. Trusting that my countenance will reveal what words cannot express, I await your commands and throw myself at your feet."

The damsel replied:

· CDXII ·

*T*HE DAMSEL'S REPLY

"Valiant knight, I can never thank you sufficiently, but I hope you will understand what mere words cannot express. I shall do my utmost to repay you, as you have risked your life for mine, and, conscious of your valor, I now offer you my love, thanking God for sending a knight of such peerless chivalry. Trust my devotion, which surpasses the limits of human nature, and rest assured that I shall do my best to make you happy."

Then she took his hand and led him to a splendid chamber, where she offered him both her body and her riches. Espercius thanked and kissed her more than a thousand times, and lest they waste another moment he carried her to the bed, upon which their love was quickly consummated.

·CDXIII·

*H*OW ESPERCIUS RETURNED TO HIS FRIENDS IN THE GENTLE LADY'S COMPANY

The next morning, Espercius led his lady to the shepherd's farmhouse, where his friends rejoiced to see their captain in such fair company, as they had feared that he might be dead or wounded. They bowed to the lady, whose every gesture breathed nobility, while she embraced them and did them great honor.

Once inside the shepherd's house, she thanked him and his wife, whom she promised to help in every way she could. Then she sent for clothes and money from her crypt, and adorned their abode most splendidly.

A while later some ships arrived, which Espercius and his lady hired to fetch settlers, with whom they populated the isle and built a noble city called Blessed Espertina. In addition, the monarchs constructed many other towns, villages, and castles, as well as generously endowed churches and monasteries in God's service. Espercius and his lady ruled that isle for many years, and their sons and daughters after them also reigned in peace and prosperity.

To avoid prolixity, the book now leaves Espercius and returns to Tirant.

TIRANT SUCCORS THE GREEK EMPIRE

·CDXIV·

*H*OW TIRANT SENT AN EMISSARY TO TELL THE EMPEROR HE WAS IN TROY

As soon as Tirant sighted Vlonë, he sent a galley to order the six cargo ships in its harbor to follow him. They quickly set sail, and after passing through the Dardanelles they all docked at Sigeum, which was once the noble and celebrated port of Troy.

Tirant took counsel with the two kings and his other barons, for he knew the sultan's fleet of more than three hundred vessels was anchored near Constantinople. After selecting an emissary named Sinegerus who spoke fluent Arabic, they told him to slip into the city at night and inform His Majesty that they were a hundred miles away. He committed his message to memory lest the Turks catch him and learn their plans.

This brave and eloquent knight was a Christian convert from the Tunisian royal family. Knowing that he had been a slave in Constantinople and therefore knew the city well, Tirant gave him his seal and a Saracen lackey's clothes.

Thus disguised, Sinegerus set out in a brig that left him a league from the Turkish camp, which he carefully skirted on his way toward the city. Despite all his precautions, some Saracen scouts detained him, but he explained himself so shrewdly and in such good Arabic that they believed he was one of them. Upon reaching the city gates, he told the emperor's guards that he bore a message from Tirant, whereupon they brought him before their lord, who was finishing supper.

Sinegerus knelt, kissed the emperor's hand and foot, and gave him Tirant's seal, on which the lord recognized his captain's coat of arms. He then embraced his guest with great joy, while Sinegerus said: "Most excellent lord, rouse your spirits and trust Tirant, who with God's help will rout your foes tomorrow morning. Furthermore, he asks you to call your cavalry to arms and guard the city well, for once he has vanquished the Turkish fleet, they may assault Constantinople and seek to fortify themselves here. Without their fleet they will be doomed, as his army is mighty enough to destroy them all."

"Friend," replied the emperor, "we are comforted by your words, which I pray God will prove true. May brave Tirant quickly fulfill our noble wishes and his own."

His Majesty then told Hippolytus: "Tirant will attack the Turks tomorrow, wherefore it is imperative that you marshal our cavalry, constables, and infantry. Let each captain man his post lest our foes find us unprepared."

Hippolytus replied: "Sire, I am cheered by my master's coming, since he will save your empire, free his imprisoned comrades, and shield your subjects from apostasy."

Having taken his leave of the emperor, Hippolytus hastened to the central square, where he gathered his knights, constables, and infantry captains. Once they had assembled, he spoke these words: "Tirant, who is in Troy, will rout our foes tomorrow morning. Therefore collect your troops and man your posts, each in his allotted place, doing so as silently as possible lest the Turks be alarmed."

Praising God for His favors, they summoned their men and took up positions on the walls, where they spent a quiet but joyous night.

· CDXV ·

HOW SINEGERUS WENT TO PAY HOMAGE TO THE EMPRESS AND THE PRINCESS

Having delivered his message, Sinegerus asked if he might pay his respects to the empress and princess. The emperor quickly agreed, and so Tirant's emissary went to the empress's chamber, where after kissing the two ladies' hands, he knelt and spoke these words: "My lord and captain Tirant lo Blanc commends himself to Your Highnesses, whom he promises to soon salute in this palace."

Hearing that her beloved was nearby, Carmesina almost fainted for sheer joy, while excess of bliss made her speechless for some time. Once she had regained her senses, she and her mother welcomed the emissary, embracing and caressing him while they asked many questions. They were especially eager to know who was in Tirant's company.

The emissary replied that the King of Sicily had come with a mighty army, as had the King of Fez, his betrothed, and all the barons from Tunis and Tlemcen, as well as Spanish, French, and Italian knights who had been drawn to Tirant's glory. Likewise, Tirant's brave comrade-in-arms King Escariano was approaching by land: "And he commands a mighty host of infantry and cavalry. His queen, who is with him, longs to behold your angelic beauty, for she herself ranks among the world's fairest ladies and is possessed of every virtue."

Then he said Pleasure-of-my-life had come that the royal family might attend her wedding. He recounted Tirant's African campaign, not neglecting to mention that he had given everything away, and indeed, he praised our knight so much that all the paper and ink on earth would not suffice to record it.

Having heard all Tirant's noble deeds, the ladies marveled at the grace God had shown him and wept for joy to think he would soon restore their sovereignty, since they had given up hope and expected to be enslaved, dishonored, and defiled any day. The princess was especially delighted at the Queen of Ethiopia's coming, for she had heard of her beauty and was eager to be her friend. So great was their pleasure in Sinegerus's words that they stayed up talking late into the night.

When they parted at last, the empress stayed in her chamber while Sinegerus accompanied Carmesina to her door. As they walked arm in arm, she asked why he had kissed her hand thrice, to which he replied that Tirant had ordered him to do so and to apologize on his behalf, nor would he dare to face her unless she pardoned his suspicions.

The princess replied: "Knight, inform my lord that where there is no fault there is no need for forgiveness, but should he wish to atone for his affronts, let him hasten to my side. My fondest hope is that he will give me the happiness I have so longed for. Tell him not to fret, as I shall quickly grant all his wishes."

Having bidden her goodnight, Sinegerus retired to the splendid lodgings prepared for him.

That evening Hippolytus had the city well guarded. None of the watchmen slept, both for fear of the Turks and because they eagerly awaited Tirant's attack in the morning.

Here the book leaves the emperor in his well-guarded city and turns to the Easygoing Widow, alias the Bedeviled.

·CDXVI·

*H*OW THE EASYGOING WIDOW SLEW HERSELF FOR FEAR OF TIRANT

Tirant's approach dismayed the Easygoing Widow, who said her heart ailed her and retired to her chamber, where she wept and beat her breast, considering herself as good as dead, for she knew that Pleasure-of-my-life had unmasked her treachery. She trembled to think of facing Carmesina once her wickedness was revealed, and on the other hand, her love for Tirant augmented her despair.[1]

She spent the whole night imagining things and battling within herself, uncertain of what to do or whom to ask for advice, but finally she acted in the manner of most women, whose fickleness makes them err when their need is greatest. She decided to poison herself so subtly that no one would detect her deed, since otherwise they might burn her body or feed it to the dogs.

She poured some orpiment she used to make depilatories into a cup of water, and after drinking it, she opened her door, undressed, and got into bed. When she was lying down, she started screaming so loudly that her maids, who slept nearby, heard the cries and rushed to her aid, but they found the widow already in her death throes.

Roused by the ensuing uproar, Carmesina and her mother hurried to the widow's chamber, while the emperor also awoke thinking the Turks had stormed his city or that his daughter was in danger. So great was his distress that he fainted and his servants had to call the doctors, whereupon the empress and princess left the widow and hastened to his side. Beholding him more dead than alive, Carmesina wept bitterly, but the physicians soon revived her father, who then asked what had caused such a commotion and whether the Turks had attacked. After learning that the Easygoing Widow had suffered a heart attack and was close to death, he dispatched his physicians to treat her, but just as they arrived, her soul entered Pluto's tenebrous kingdom.

Carmesina mourned the widow's passing and ordered her body placed in a fine coffin. On the morrow, the royal family, their court, and all the aldermen and distinguished citizens accompanied her to the Hagia Sophia, where she was solemnly laid to rest.

Here the book leaves the Easygoing Widow and recounts Tirant's speech to his knights:

· CDXVII ·

TIRANT'S SPEECH TO HIS TROOPS

"Battles are easier though no less honorable when knights are certain of their holy cause, wherefore we should delay no longer but have at them, valiant warriors! Rouse your slumbering ardor and defeat those cursed infidels, whom we shall pursue as they flee, exalting our faith and confounding their heresy! If we slay these damned souls and win eternal glory for our own, our fame will live forever as we sail victory's prosperous seas; and you, worthy kings, to whom I especially appeal: choose honor over life and let your bravery be an example, for if we fight courageously the day will be ours!"

· CDXVIII ·

HOW TIRANT CAPTURED THE TURKISH FLEET

Once Sinegerus had left, Tirant reviewed his battalions, deciding which vessels should give battle first and which should follow them. Then he told some captains to sound their trumpets, bugles, and clarions at the moment of attack, while other crews let out bloodcurdling war cries and fired bombards at the Turks.

After setting out very quietly at sunrise, they sailed all day and night, and Our Lord favored the Christians by making the day so foggy that neither friends nor foes could see them. They attacked the infidels two hours before dawn with such a din of horns, war cries, and artillery that the very earth seemed about to collapse. Tirant's men lit ten fires on each of their ships, and when the sleeping Turks heard the noise and saw the dreadful flames, they hastily surrendered without a struggle. The slaughter was astonishing to behold, as the Christians beheaded all their prisoners.

Those who dived overboard and swam to safety brought these sad tidings to their masters, who, fearing for their lives, mounted their steeds and stationed their squadrons along the shore.

Seeing the Turkish fleet in his power, Tirant fell to his knees and cried: "Oh mighty and clement Lord, I thank You for Your favors and for letting me capture three hundred ships without a single casualty!"

Their victory had been so swift that the sky was just growing light.

Those within Constantinople were overjoyed and amazed, for all the world's navies seemed to have gathered there, but they still feared an attack by the Turkish infantry.

Awakened by this tumult, the emperor rose from his bed and rode through the city with his few remaining knights, urging the townspeople to make ready to defend themselves if necessary and cheering them with the thought that their sorrows would soon end.

The Turks, however, were too dismayed to contemplate an attack, and knowing they were trapped, they posted all their troops along the shore.

When Tirant had manned the captured vessels, they sailed away toward the Aegean, for he still hoped to take his foes by surprise, while the Turks thought he was content with his remarkable victory.

Tirant sailed west all day until he was out of sight, but as soon as night fell, he ordered his ships to put about.

You should know that Constantinople, a splendid city surrounded by mighty walls, is built upon a triangular peninsula whose sides face the Aegean, the Black Sea, and the kingdom of Thrace. Tirant disembarked four leagues from the Turkish camp, bringing his men, horses, provisions, and artillery ashore so quietly that no one heard him.

When everyone was mounted and the pack mules had been loaded, they rode along a broad river till they reached a big stone bridge. Tirant had his men camp there, with the river between them and their adversaries in case the Turks attempted an assault during the night. Since his own tent was on the bridge, no one could cross without his knowledge, and his many bombards were so positioned that if the Turks came they would be well served. Then he sent scouts to the enemy camp with orders to warn him of any suspicious movements.

As soon as they were encamped, Tirant sent a messenger to Constantinople with this letter to the emperor:

· CDXIX ·

T IRANT'S LETTER TO THE EMPEROR

Most Serene Lord: God has granted us three hundred well-stocked Turkish ships that with your leave I intend to unload, that I may release the vessels I hired from further service, for our captured fleet will suffice to blockade the enemy, nor can they escape by land, as we have encamped near the stone bridge. If they wish to depart, they will be forced to surrender, but Your Highness should have his city well guarded lest the Saracens seek to storm it when their supplies give out. Finally, please tell me where to discharge the provisions, since, having brought enough food for ten years and trusting that God will soon grant our wishes, I await Your Majesty's speedy reply.

· CDXX ·

*H*OW THE WORTHY KNIGHT SINEGERUS RETURNED TO TIRANT'S CAMP

Once Tirant had finished, he gave the letter to his chosen messenger: a Greek named Carillo who knew the country well and who that night made his way along the back roads to Constantinople. The Turks neither saw nor heard him, and when he reached one of the city gates, the guards took him into custody and brought him before the emperor. His Majesty read the letter with great satisfaction, praising God for His abundant blessings, and then summoned his wife and daughter, who rejoiced in Tirant's victory.

The emperor also sent for Hippolytus, who said: "Sire, you will recall how often I urged you to trust Tirant, since I knew he would not abandon you as long as he lived. Therefore be of good cheer, as he will soon give you victory."

The emperor replied: "By God, captain, we are astonished at Tirant's deeds, and I swear by my crown to reward him in such fashion that he and his friends will be more than content. Now please take an inventory of all the food in my palace and city, that we may respond to our captain's questions."

Hippolytus made a thorough search with the aid of men experienced in such matters, and, after finding enough food for three months he returned to the emperor and said: "Your Majesty should know that we have provisions for three or possibly four months, and you may be certain that Tirant will send us more if we need it."

Then the emperor dictated a long letter, telling Tirant everything he had decided, and once he had finished, he summoned Sinegerus, to whom he said: "Please take this to Tirant and recount everything you have seen."

Having kissed the emperor's hand and foot, Sinegerus went to pay his respects to the empress and Carmesina, who asked him to remind Tirant that she would pine away and die if she did not see him. The knight replied that he would do her bidding, whereupon the gentle maiden embraced him and, disguised as Saracens, the two messengers left at midnight. They followed the same route Carillo had come by till they spied the bridge where Tirant had camped, and upon entering his tent at daybreak, they found him already up and about.

Our knight was delighted to see them and asked Sinegerus how the emperor and his princess fared, to which Sinegerus replied by describing what he had seen and repeating Carmesina's messages. When Tirant heard her words, tears of pity streamed down his cheeks, and for a long while he was silent as he thought of the princess's love and prayed for her well-being. Once his face had regained its normal color, Sinegerus gave him the emperor's letter, which was of the following tenor:

· C D X X I ·

*T*HE EMPEROR'S LETTER TO TIRANT

My son, we are greatly cheered by your coming, as all Greeks are beholden to you for delivering us. Your noble servant Hippolytus has taken good care of the city, nor does a more valiant knight except yourself dwell upon this earth. His deeds alone have saved us, he has slain innumerable Saracens, and furthermore he reports that we have many soldiers and enough food for three months. Though our greatest fear was starvation, our minds are now at rest, and we pray you not to risk your life, for the Turks are in your power and you can decide when and where you wish to fight them.

A third of the food should be taken to my castle in Sinope, where it will be safe and you can send for it as you need it; another third should be discharged in Pera, along with five hundred soldiers; and the rest should be stored in Constantinople, since once this is done, you may freely release as many hired ships as you like. I think it would be wise for the rest to anchor near us, as the Turks will then have to fear an attack from three quarters and their forces will be divided, with some troops on the shore, others around the city, and still others near your camp.

I have nothing to add except that if you need money, send one, two, or as many galleys as you like and I shall quickly provide it.

· C D X X I I ·

*H*OW THE SARACENS TOOK COUNSEL AND RESOLVED TO SEND TWO EMISSARIES TO TIRANT

Upon learning that Tirant's men were encamped near the bridge, the Turks were filled with dismay, as their provisions would only last two months, but nonetheless they bravely held council to discuss their plight. The following kings attended: the King of Aleppo, the King of Syria, the King of Cracow, the King of Assyria, the King of Hyrcania, the King of Daresten, the Grand Karaman's son, the Prince of Scythia, and innumerable other lords whom the book omits to avoid prolixity.

Many favored an assault on the city, which they thought contained enough food to support them till help came. Others wished to attack Tirant's camp, for he was too brave not to risk his life and they had many valiant warriors who might easily kill him. Even if they did not triumph, they said it was better to die like knights than to be slaughtered like sheep, and if Fortune gave them victory, they could either depart or continue the siege till the Greeks capitulated.

Still others thought it better to sue for peace or a truce, and so in the end they decided to send emissaries, since if Tirant refused to see them they could still try the other methods: to storm the city or, failing that, to die sword in hand like ardent warriors.

Having made up their minds, they chose the Princes of Karaman and Scythia, two eloquent knights experienced in warfare. They were to estimate the size of Tirant's army and determine how it was arrayed, and the kings instructed them in everything else they had to say and do.

The emissaries donned splendid brocade jubbahs and set out with two hundred unarmed cavalry, but first they sent a messenger to ask Tirant for safe-conduct, which he granted.

· CDXXIII ·

*H*OW TIRANT HAD THE FOOD DISCHARGED AND RELEASED THE HIRED SHIPS FROM FURTHER SERVICE

Having read the emperor's letter, Tirant summoned the Marquis of Liçana, who was his admiral, and told him to settle accounts with the captains of the hired ships. Once he had paid them generously, he was to divide the food, sending one third to the castle at Sinope and another to the castle at Pera. Then he could arm the remaining ships and send them to Constantinople: "And after they have unloaded, tell them to bombard the Turkish camp."

As soon as he had his orders, the admiral returned to the fleet and paid its captains, to whom he gave a thousand extra ducats apiece as well as whatever they had looted. Then he told them where to discharge their cargoes and said they could depart when they had finished.

Some ships set out for Sinope, which is fifty miles southwest of Constantinople sailing toward the Aegean, while others made for Pera, where they were welcomed with great joy.

When the valiant captain of Pera learned that Tirant had sent provisions, he gave his saviors a triumphant welcome and offered them splendid lodgings. The townspeople unloaded the food with great rejoicing, for their need had been great and our knight alone had saved them.

After discharging their cargoes, the ships set sail for home.

· CDXXIV ·

*H*OW TIRANT SENT THE QUEEN OF FEZ TO CONSTANTINOPLE WITH THE REMAINING SHIPS

After releasing the hired vessels, Tirant's admiral armed the remaining ones, which included four hundred and thirty-five ships, galleys, galliots, and smaller craft. The marquis kept two well-armed galleys anchored near the mouth of the river in case Tirant needed them.

When everyone was ready to sail, the admiral went to Tirant's camp and told him all his orders had been duly carried out. Then Tirant summoned the Queen of Fez and said: "Sister, I beg you to accompany these ships to Constantinople and comfort the lady who holds my heart in thrall. I fear that in my absence she may pine away and die, yet you know that if I visit her, the whole camp will be in danger, whereas you will find both happiness and comfort in the city. Employ your angelic wisdom to plead my case as you did before, and say I shall rejoin her as soon as I can. It is my fondest wish, for an hour without her seems a year, and after God there is no one I so long to see, obey, and serve."

The gracious queen forbade Tirant to continue and sweetly replied: "Lord brother, your wish is my command, nor could I repay the many honors you have showered upon me. Do not think me so ungrateful as to forget my obligations or your deserts, and if I sought to serve you before, I should now do so a thousand times more. Only you, who are the flower of chivalry, deserve to possess my lady's body, wherefore, my lord, I am at your command, and though I had a hundred lives I would risk them all for you."

Then they embraced and Tirant kissed her cheek, saying: "My lady, I can never repay your kindness, and I trust that you will bring my sufferings to an end. God willing, I shall reward you twice as well in the future."

Having told her to gather what she needed for the journey, Tirant returned to his tent and summoned the admiral, to whom he said: "Marquis, prepare to sail for Constantinople as soon as the queen is ready."

The admiral left Tirant and boarded one of his ships, on which the queen and her damsels departed the next morning. Tirant, the King of Sicily, and five hundred soldiers escorted her to the dock and then returned to their camp while the admiral weighed anchor.

· CDXXV ·

*H*OW THE TURKISH EMISSARIES ARRIVED AT TIRANT'S CAMP

When the sultan's emissaries reached the stone bridge, they were welcomed by five hundred warriors on richly caparisoned Sicilian chargers. These knights escorted their guests to the captain's tent, which was hung with the finest Parisian scarlet brocade the world had ever seen.

The Kings of Fez and Sicily and Tirant's other barons honored their foes as befitted their lofty station, but Tirant refused to negotiate immediately and sent them to splendid tents, where they were abundantly served with meat, fowl, and wines.

The Saracens were awed by the mighty chargers, the knights wearing Italian-style plumed helmets, and the four thousand horsemen on armored mounts who patrolled the camp. Beholding our knight's disciplined cavalry and concluding that all pagandom could not defeat them, the emissaries feared their journey had been in vain and that Tirant would slay them without mercy, as his army was so well positioned that no infidel could escape alive. Furthermore, they saw that since they could only fight Tirant on his terms, he might easily force them to die of starvation.

The emissaries spent all day and night pondering these gloomy prospects, and the next morning Tirant summoned his companions to Mass. When the service had ended, he sent for his guests, whom he asked to sit down and explain what they desired.

They urged the Grand Karaman's son to speak first, as he was the greatest lord among them, whereupon he rose, bowed to Tirant, and made the following proposals:

· CDXXVI ·

*T*HE EMISSARY'S PROPOSALS

"Mighty captain, you surely realize how many men will soon perish and that your own camp will be strewn with the corpses of dead warriors. Alas, you will see this river swell with blood, while the moans of the dying rise to Heaven and rouse the immutable planets' pity. Far from daunting us, such thoughts only ennoble our knightly spirits, but to avoid needless inhumanity we have come on the Grand Turk's and the sultan's behalf. They offer you a three-month truce or a hundred and one year peace treaty, under which they promise to succor your friends and oppose your enemies. Furthermore, they will quit the Greek Empire and all its castles, towns, and lands, freeing their prisoners and paying any reasonable tribute not prejudicial to their royal sovereignty. If, on the other hand, you prefer to prepare for war, you will quickly see cruel and bloody battles."

· CDXXVII ·

*H*OW TIRANT HELD COUNCIL TO DETERMINE HIS REPLY

Tirant was very pleased by the Turkish proposals, as he saw that his labors would soon be crowned with success, but being a prudent captain, he told the emissaries to await his reply.

On the morrow, Tirant summoned his kings, dukes, and noble lords to Mass. When the service had ended and each man was seated according to his rank, Tirant called for order and began to speak thus: "Illustrious lords and brothers, you know the Turkish emissaries have sued for peace or a truce, but before accepting their proposals, we should consider our glory as victors. Moreover, we should be mindful that by killing or capturing an entire army, we shall dismay all infidels, avenge the afflicted Greeks, and make our peace more secure. Therefore, I think we can best serve the emperor by demanding unconditional surrender and letting them do their worst if they are not satisfied, since we need only wait for them to die of starvation. We could also attack, but I believe that would be foolish, as they are desperate and many of us would surely come to harm. By merely blocking their escape, we can win the spoils of war, yet all the same, lords and brothers, I think we should first consult the emperor. Now let each man speak his mind, for you will all share the honor."

· CDXXVIII ·

THE KING OF SICILY'S OPINION

When Tirant had finished, Philip asked the King of Fez to speak. He refused, whereupon the Sicilian monarch asked his other comrades' views, but they all deferred to the noble lord and insisted that he precede them. Finally he removed his hat and uttered these words: "Mirror of divine wisdom, new star guiding us to peace and justice, peer of Solomon! Virtuous captain, you do not need our advice, yet to please you I declare that I also think the emperor should be consulted. Let him discuss these matters with his council and do as he sees fit, since his honor is more at stake than yours or mine. Nonetheless I am certain that he will accept your proposals, which are so useful and honorable that no worthy knight would contradict them, for you nobly strive to protect your men, discomfit your enemies, and reward your followers. I shall now let these other lords compensate for my omissions."

· CDXXIX ·

HOW THE KING OF FEZ SPOKE FOR HIMSELF AND THE OTHER BARONS

Having applauded Philip's speech, the assembled barons asked the King of Fez to speak on their behalf, and when everyone was silent, he rose and uttered these words: "Experience teaches men how to circumvent dangers, as no one need regret deeds done with deliberation, wherefore, brave captain, I need add nothing to your words except to agree that we should consult His Majesty the emperor. I urge you to send a messenger as soon as possible, that we may quickly respond to these pagan emissaries."

Tirant said it would be done, and each man returned to his tent.

· CDXXX ·

H OW TIRANT'S FLEET ARRIVED IN CONSTANTINOPLE

Tirant's fleet had such propitious weather that it reached Constantinople the same day, arriving two hours before Phoebus completed his rounds. His ships, which appeared clothed in victory's triumphant robes, saluted the noble city with clarions, trumpets, bombards, and joyous cries.

Both gentlefolk and commoners lined the walls to behold their saviors, while the imperial flag fluttered beside Tirant's and all the church bells rang.

As the aged emperor was on his way to the sea, one of his knights announced that the Queen of Fez was aboard. He quickly sent word to Carmesina, who rode with Hippolytus till they overtook him and who then asked Tirant's companion to escort the queen ashore.

The knight rejoiced at the sight of his splendidly dressed friend, for there had always been great love between them, and the queen asked after Carmesina, to which he replied that she awaited them.

Two well-dressed courtiers rowed her and Hippolytus ashore in a boat lined with brocade, and soon they were surrounded by noble knights and gentlewomen.

Seeing her maiden arrive in such royal style, the princess dismounted in her honor, while Pleasure-of-my-life fell at her feet and tried to kiss them, but Carmesina raised her up, kissed her lips, and led her to greet the emperor, who welcomed his favorite damsel with great honor. Then they left the port and made their way to the imperial palace, where the empress greeted one and all with sovereign joy. She was particularly happy to see Pleasure-of-my-life, who knelt and kissed her hands and feet as a loyal vassal.

The old emperor then told Hippolytus to unload the ships, and, after replying that work had already begun, he returned to the port, where his men spent the night going back and forth in every boat they could find. By daybreak, the grain, wine, oil, salt pork, honey, and everything else was safely stored in warehouses.

The next morning, His Majesty invited the admiral's retinue to lunch, at which they appeared in brocade and gold robes with heavy gold chains around their necks. The victors, who despite the city's recent shortages were served a feast of abundant fowl and exquisite wines, spent that day making merry with the gentle ladies, while their celebration was ennobled by many games and dances.

When night fell, the admiral asked his lord's leave to depart so they could start bombarding the Turkish camp in the morning. The emperor replied: "Admiral, there is nothing I would like better," whereupon the marquis took his leave of the royal ladies and led his men back to their ships.

They set out during the first watch, and as soon as they spied the Turkish camp, they fired their hundreds of bombards in unison. The Saracens were thrown into confusion and hurriedly donned their armor, for they thought the Christians were about to land.

· CDXXXI ·

THE PRINCESS'S CONVERSATION WITH THE QUEEN OF FEZ

On the night of the fleet's arrival, Carmesina invited Pleasure-of-my-life to share her bed, where the two damsels might talk to their hearts' content. Once they were alone, the princess told her friend: "Most cherished sister, your absence has tormented me beyond endurance, and especially when I thought you might have drowned in my service. Tirant was to blame, for he left without bidding me farewell, and the thought of his cruelty made me wish to die in sorrow. Tears flowed from my eyes, mingling with my laments as I sighed over the empire's impending doom and my own dishonor and enslavement. The worst was to think I had offended my beloved, wherefore I resolved to enter a convent and spend my days in contemplation, praying the Virgin to send the Angel of Consolation to save my old father from captivity, and now that merciful lady has sent me her Son's grace.

"I am cheered by your prosperity and much indebted to Tirant, but please tell me how I offended him and why he parted so hastily from one who was always obedient and spoke nothing but words of love. He must have been jesting, as so good a knight could not show ingratitude, yet my memory of your past services also calms my troubled soul. Please assure me of his devotion, for my love has grown in your absence and I shall die if I do not see him soon."

Having uttered these dolorous words, Carmesina burst into tears. The good queen comforted her, and when the princess had regained her composure, our damsel began to speak in this fashion:

· CDXXXII ·

*T*HE QUEEN'S REPLY TO CARMESINA

"I have no wish to utter words that may offend Your Highness, when merely to think them sorely troubles my soul. Tomorrow, if you wish, we may speak of these matters, though I fear your heart will ache to imagine such wickedness. You may be certain of one thing: you did nothing wrong. Knowing the truth, Tirant now repents, and you should pardon his suspicions, for he was deceived by an evil woman whom both of you trusted, but let us avoid subjects that can only cause you pain, as with his arrival your sorrow will turn to joy. You would be amazed if you knew how much he adores you, and therefore, my lady, you have good reason to requite his love. Your knight's immortal deeds in Barbary were done solely to share your bed, nor should your spirit fail you now when all your troubles are over. Trust me, my lady, to reunite you with Tirant, whose only wish is to serve and honor Your Highness. I saw with my own eyes how love brought him back, though he might have wed the fair Queen of Tlemcen and ruled all Barbary. This queen is beholden to him for many kind services, and, having heard of your splendor, she is eager to be your friend.

"My lady, does this brave knight not deserve your worthy person? What king ever conquered so many lands and kept nothing for himself? Tirant gave everything to his companions, yet the more he gives the more he has, as his generosity wins men's love and loyalty. Therefore lay aside gloomy thoughts and if you love yourself forget your sorrow, which can only harm your soul and afflict your noble body. Your beauty is renowned, but you must now be fairer than ever, since many people of every station will soon come to behold you, and your wedding will be ennobled by a multitude of kings, dukes, and lords, all of whom must think you peerless in lineage, grace, and virtue, for, having once been your servant, I would sooner die than hear the contrary."

· CDXXXIII ·

*T*HE PRINCESS'S REPLY

"It grieves me, wise queen, to hear your entreaties, for while things one has no hope of regaining are easily forgotten, my grief comes from craving what someday I shall possess. Here you see anger and sorrow, sadness and longing, since when two souls unite in desiring what is close at hand yet denied them, they burn more fiercely than if their object were distant. Sister, though in the past I sometimes scorned your wise counsel, from this moment on I shall heed your commands."

The queen replied: "My lady, should you do so, I shall give you more joy than you expect."

They spent most of the night talking, as the princess was delighted to have Pleasure-of-my-life's company again, but finally the queen said: "My lady, sleep now lest your beauty suffer."

And so they did.

· CDXXXIV ·

*H*OW TIRANT WENT TO CONSTANTINOPLE AND SPOKE WITH THE EMPEROR

Seeing his lords in agreement, Tirant decided that he had reached his goal: he had an excuse to visit his mistress, and since the Turkish proposals involved his honor above all others', he decided to call upon her father himself, thereby both assuring the empire's peace and reposing tranquilly in his lady's arms.

That night, after entrusting his camp to the Kings of Sicily and Fez, he sailed to Constantinople, which was twenty miles distant.

Having gone ashore in disguise with one trusted servant, Tirant went to the city gates and announced that he was an emissary. The guards quickly admitted him and he made his way to the palace, but as the emperor was abed, our knight went to the Queen of Fez's chamber, where the damsel, who had been praying, embraced him and cried: "Tirant, what joy to see you! Now I have greater reason to thank God, who despite my unworthiness has granted my pleas. As I spoke the last words, I know not what angel made me turn, whereupon I beheld you, the most virtuous of mortals. Lord worthy of all glory, you shall now be paid for your travails with sweet solace, and if you like, I shall give you what you have long desired, but should you scorn my advice, I shall forsake you and return to Fez."

Tirant quickly replied: "Lady sister, if I ever disobeyed you, I now apologize and swear by my chivalry to follow all your instructions, which might have helped me in the past had I been wise enough to heed them."

"Well then," said the queen, "let us see what you can do. Enter the lists and prove your mettle, for no worthy knight would lose this joust.

Now wait here, while I go and ask the princess to spend the night with me."

The queen entered Carmesina's chamber as she was about to retire, and upon beholding her friend, Tirant's beloved asked: "Why are you in such a hurry, sister?"

The queen joyously whispered: "My lady, come sleep with me tonight. I have many things to tell you, as a galley from Tirant's camp has arrived and a man has come ashore with tidings of your knight."

The princess happily agreed, since the two damsels slept together whenever they wished to share some intimacy.

The queen then took Carmesina's hand and they returned to her chamber, which she found well perfumed according to her instructions. After helping the princess disrobe, her damsels departed, leaving their mistress to her enamored champion.

Once they had left, the queen dismissed her own maidens, saying she was going to finish her prayers and go to sleep. Then she entered the alcove where Tirant was hidden and whispered: "Glorious captain, take off everything but your shirt, and hurry to the side of one who loves you more than life. Dig in your spurs and show her no mercy, for if you spurn my advice you will never enjoy her favors."

Having heard the queen's words, Tirant knelt and replied:

· CDXXXV ·

TIRANT'S LOVING THANKS TO THE QUEEN

"Lady sister, with strong chains you bind me, for though I were your slave I could not repay you. You offer me glory, delight, and Heaven in a mortal body, nor would all my past and future spoils suffice to show my gratitude. I can only thank you with love as true as yours, and I hope I shall live to help you as you have helped me."

"Lord Tirant," replied the queen, "say no more, as time wasted can never be recovered. Quickly undress."

Brave Tirant removed his shoes and threw all his clothes but his shirt on the floor. Then the queen led him to Carmesina, saying: "My lady, here is that blessed knight whom Your Highness so desires. Give him the pleasant company he expects, thinking only of the present, since no one on earth can foresee the future."

The princess cried: "False sister, I never thought you would betray me, but I trust that Tirant's virtue will compensate for your wickedness."

Do not think Tirant was idle during this argument, for his hands were speedily going about their business. The queen left them alone and lay down on a couch while the princess turned to our knight, who was trying to conclude the battle, and spoke these words:

· CDXXXVI ·

*H*OW TIRANT WON THE BATTLE AND FORCED HIS WAY INTO THE CASTLE²

"Tirant, do not change our glorious reunion into bitter woe but calm yourself, my lord, and abjure bellicose violence, for a delicate damsel cannot resist a knight. Do not treat me thus, as love's battles should be won through clever flattery and sweet deception, nor should you employ treachery except against infidels. Do not cruelly defeat one already vanquished by love! Will you brutally prove your mettle against a helpless damsel? Give me part of your manhood that I may resist you! Oh my lord, how can you delight in forcing me? Oh, how can you hurt the one you love? By your virtue and nobility, please stop before you hurt me! Love's weapons should not cut; love's lance should not wound! Alas, cruel false knight, be careful or I shall scream! Lord Tirant, show your compassion and pity a helpless damsel! You cannot be Tirant! Woe is me! Is this what I longed for? Oh, my life's hope, you have slain your princess!"

Do not think the princess's pleas persuaded Tirant to leave the job unfinished, but although he won the battle, his beloved also fainted. He leapt out of bed, thinking that he had killed her, and summoned the queen to help revive his lady.

Pleasure-of-my-life quickly rose and found a bottle of rice water, which she sprinkled on the princess's face while rubbing her temples. When Carmesina had finally recovered, she heaved a great sigh and said:

· CDXXXVII ·

*H*OW THE PRINCESS GENTLY REBUKED TIRANT

"Tokens of love should not be taken by cruelty, and now, lord captain, I begin to doubt your virtue. Can such a fleeting pleasure justify abusing

your beloved? You might have waited till our wedding day before entering my chastity's harbor, but you have not behaved like a knight or
revered me as a princess. I fear that righteous wrath and the loss of my
scarlet maidenhead will so weaken my offended delicacy that I shall soon
enter Pluto's kingdom, whereby you will change our celebration into a sad
funeral."

Refusing to let the afflicted princess continue, the queen turned to her
and said: "Alas, lady fool, you are a great one for acting pitiful, but no
knight's arms ever hurt a damsel! May God let me die as sweetly as you
pretend to have been killed, and may I catch your disease if you are not
cured by morning!"

The princess, who was still mourning her lost virginity, made no reply,
whereupon Tirant climbed back into bed and the queen left them alone.
They spent the rest of the night in those pleasant games lovers are wont to
play.

· CDXXXVIII ·

*H*OW THE LOVERS MADE PEACE AND TIRANT RECOUNTED HIS ADVENTURES

During the night, Tirant told his lady of the travails he had endured for
love of her and then happily recounted his triumphant victories. After
reciting everything in order, he swore that nothing meant as much as
having won her.

Once the princess had regained her composure, she also described her
life in his absence. Spurning all pleasures, she had spent her days in
constant prayer that alone had sustained her till his joyous return. Many
other delicate words accompanied by enamored sighs passed between
them, and as they talked they often felt the effects of libidinous desire.

As soon as the queen, who was in charge of the business, beheld the
sun's first rays, she thought of how love's bliss often make suitors feel
invincible. She rose, approached the couple, and said that since God had
given them a pleasant night, she hoped their day would be equally sweet.
They kindly thanked her but went on gaily playing and showing their joy,
whereupon the damsel told Tirant: "Lord of the Greek Empire, if you
wish to preserve your honor, rise now and leave this chamber as quickly as
you can."

Tirant, who would have liked that night to last a year, kissed the
princess many times and begged her to forgive him.

The princess replied: "Lord Tirant, my heart inclines to clemency but only if you return, for I cannot live without you now that I truly know what love is. Having captured me by force of arms, you must never forsake me, as you took my life, liberty, and person, yet you now seek to restore them. I accept in hope of your coming victory, which pleases me only because it will increase your might."

· CDXXXIX ·

*T*IRANT'S REPLY

When the noble lady had finished, Tirant replied: "My hope and joy, how can I thank you for pardoning my sweet offense? Having seized my reward without your leave, I am now all the more your prisoner and wish only to lie forever in your arms! You need not request what love forces me to offer, and I shall quickly return, for my sole desire is to obey you."

Once they had parted with a passionate kiss, the queen took Tirant's hand and led him to a hidden door in the garden. He tried to kiss her hands as they were walking, but she refused and asked: "Lord Tirant, how do you like what you waited so long to win?"

Tirant replied: "Lady sister, my tongue could never express my gratitude, though if God lets me finish what I have begun, I shall certainly reward you."

The queen curtsied and said: "Lord Tirant, you have already honored me far beyond my deserts, nor could I ever repay all your generous favors. I pray God will bless you as your nobility deserves."

After parting from his friend with many bows and courteous words, Tirant went to Hippolytus's lodgings while the queen returned to Carmesina, with whom she got into bed where our knight had been, and both damsels slept until late that morning.

· CDXL ·

*H*OW TIRANT WENT TO SPEAK WITH THE EMPEROR

Feeling delighted at his lord's return, Hippolytus threw himself at Tirant's feet and tried to kiss them, but our valiant knight refused and instead embraced his vassal with great joy, for they had not seen each other since that fateful storm. When they had talked for a while, Hippolytus went to inform the emperor that his captain wished to speak with him in secret.

His Majesty replied that he was most eager to greet Tirant, who he supposed had come on matters of great moment.

Hippolytus returned to his lodgings and repeated the emperor's words. After disguising themselves, the two friends slipped into the palace, where they found the emperor dressing in his rooms.

As soon as Tirant beheld His Majesty, he threw himself at his feet and tried to kiss them, but the aged lord refused, raised him up, and kissed his lips. Then the emperor led him into another chamber and bade him sit down beside him. Tears rolled down His Highness's cheeks as joy mingled with bitter memories, and only after calming his troubled spirit could he utter these solemn words:

· CDXLI ·

THE EMPEROR'S WORDS TO TIRANT

"Magnanimous captain and best-beloved son, we rejoice in your coming and thank you for your services. I trust that you will quickly deliver us from the Turkish peril, and knowing that you must have come on some urgent matter, I shall speak no further until I learn what it is."

When the emperor had finished, Tirant replied:

· CDXLII ·

TIRANT'S REPLY TO THE EMPEROR

"Excellent lord, I wish to inform you of certain Turkish proposals that I cannot accept without first receiving orders. I therefore urge you to summon your council, as the emissaries have offered an indefinite truce or peace for one hundred and one years, during which time they will be your allies, aiding your friends and opposing your enemies. Furthermore, they will quit your empire, restore everything they have conquered, and free every Christian captive in their lands, but if you reject these proposals, I shall prepare for battle, since they will appear before my camp as soon as they can."

The emperor replied: "Virtuous son and captain, we trust your good will and prudence, but to please you I shall gladly summon my council."

Meanwhile, Tirant went to pay his respects to the empress and Carmesina, whom he found together in the princess's chamber, where she was pretending to be ill and her mother was attending her. The empress embraced Tirant and made great joy of him, while her daughter was cooler lest anyone realize what had passed between them.

They spoke of many things and the princess repeatedly asked for news of King Escariano, to which Tirant replied: "My lady, I received a letter from him three days ago, asking me not to attack until he arrives two weeks hence."

The princess said: "Lord captain, my fondest wish is to behold his queen, whom men call the fairest lady on earth."

Tirant replied: "Your Highness, such is the case, and only your beauty and virtue excel those of the queen, who is just as eager to meet you and to gaze upon your perfections."

As they were chatting and taking their ease, the mournful Stephanie entered dressed in a tertiary's dark grey habit, for on the day of Diaphebus's capture she had entered a convent, where she planned to remain until the end of her life.

She threw herself at Tirant's feet, weeping and moaning as she cried:

· CDXLIII ·

*T*HE DUCHESS OF MACEDONIA'S LAMENT AT TIRANT'S FEET

"Oh honest ladies and chaste widows, console the grieving duchess! Cover my face, abundant in bitter tears, with wrinkled sheets and black mantles! Hold up my heavy body weighed down by slavery's chains! Aid me, oh ladies, with pitiful words and sad exclamations, as I beg our conquering captain for mercy! Show your compassion, Tirant, taking pity not on me but on that knight who was once my sole earthly joy, for when your cousin was taken prisoner, he left me and Macedonia desolate, and you should blush with shame and rage to imagine him in shackles. Take revenge on his captors, and Stephanie will be forever in your debt."

Refusing to let the duchess kneel before him, Tirant raised her up, kissed her, and uttered these words of comfort:

· CDXLIV ·

HOW TIRANT COMFORTED THE DUCHESS OF MACEDONIA

"Constant hardships and grief have taught me to aid the sorrowful, and especially when their troubles are shared by many, wherefore, my lady, I shall respond to your just request. Weep no more, as you will soon see I have not forgotten you, and I swear that within a month the duke will hold you in his arms."

Hearing Tirant's kind and humble words, the duchess fell at his feet and tried to kiss them, but he raised her up, took her hands, and sat down beside her.

While Tirant was comforting Stephanie, the emperor told his councilors of the Turkish proposals.

Once they heard the good news, they fell to arguing and disputing, for some favored slaying the Turks, who then would never dare to return, but others felt that was imprudent, as trapped men often fight desperately and the infidels would have to surrender when their provisions gave out. Still others said the wisest course would be to make peace while holding the sultan, Grand Turk, and other kings till the conquered lands and prisoners had been restored, since a massacre might drive their foes to elect other monarchs and continue the war.

Having discussed their differences, the councilors took a vote and then sent for the emperor, to whom they addressed the following words: "Holy Majesty, we have resolved that if you wish to avoid bloodshed and enjoy a peaceful old age, you should accept the Turkish offers, holding the Grand Turk and the sultan until they fulfill their promises and letting the other Saracens depart on foot and unarmed."

The emperor was pleased by their advice, and so the council ended.

Then His Majesty went to the princess's chamber, where he found brave Tirant. The emperor took his hand, bade him sit down beside him, and uttered these words:

·CDXLV·

HOW THE EMPEROR TOLD TIRANT WHAT HIS COUNCIL HAD DETERMINED

"My son, to lighten part of your burden, I am willing to make peace, and those in my council also favor such a course, but first I wish to hear your opinion."

Tirant replied: "Your Majesty should know that I also took counsel with my captains, whose views accorded with those of your advisors. It seems that Providence has made us all of one mind, wherefore I await Your Highness's commands."

When Tirant had finished, the emperor said: "Since God's divine clemency offers us such good fortune, I beg you to quickly reply to the emissaries."

Tirant said he would do so and took his leave of the imperial ladies, who urged him to free the Greek Empire as quickly as he could.

Tirant replied: "Ladies, may God permit me to do so."

The Queen of Fez accompanied our knight to the door and made him promise to return that evening.

Tirant retired to Hippolytus's lodgings and remained there till the sun had set. Then he disguised himself, slipped through the garden, and entered the palace, where he found the queen and Carmesina eagerly awaiting him. The ladies welcomed their captain with sovereign joy, and the three of them entered Pleasure-of-my-life's bedchamber.

The lovers played and took their ease with amorous pleasantries until bedtime, whereupon Carmesina undressed, the queen dismissed her damsels, and Tirant climbed in beside his lady, who welcomed him far more affectionately than the night before. After positioning them in the lists and arranging the joust, the queen went to sleep feeling certain the battle would never end.

Being a brave warrior, Tirant slept not a wink that night, for those who are dauntless in warfare should also be so in bed. As the dawn began to break, he told Carmesina: "My lady, I must leave you, since I swore to be in my camp by sunrise."

The princess replied: "My lord, this parting grieves me, as the sorrows I felt before have now multiplied a thousandfold. Promise not to tarry lest you cause my death, nor would I let you depart were our need not so dire."

When Tirant heard these words, he rose, began to dress, and, after bidding his lady farewell with passionate kisses and abundant tears, he left through the garden and hastened to Hippolytus's lodgings.

As soon as Hippolytus saw his master, he rose and accompanied him to the city walls, where Tirant climbed in a boat and they rowed him to the galley, whose crew set sail as quietly as they could and quickly reached their camp.

They arrived less than an hour after sunrise and were welcomed by the Kings of Sicily and Fez, who spent the rest of that day making merry with their captain. Tirant told them the emperor's will, and they were content with his decision.

·CDXLVI·

TIRANT'S REPLY TO THE TURKISH EMISSARIES

The next morning, Tirant summoned his great lords to Mass, and once the service had ended, he sent a messenger to fetch the emissaries.

They appeared splendidly attired in the Saracen style and solemnly escorted by knights from Tirant's camp. Before setting out, the emissaries had their horses saddled that they might leave as soon as they obtained a reply.

Upon entering Tirant's tent, the emissaries bowed deeply and sat down before our knight, who began to speak in this manner: "Valiant warriors must carefully ponder their actions, for only chivalry and courage can win glorious fame. A sage's wisdom will increase if he makes prudence his counselor, and thus, brave barons, I wished to consult our worthy emperor. We know your lives are in our hands, and we are aware of your cruelty, but that you may know our lord's magnanimity, he is willing to spare you, though only if the sultan, the Grand Turk, and all your other monarchs will consent to be his hostages till we recover the empire. Likewise, you must send him your Christian prisoners and slaves while your soldiers return home on foot and unarmed. Furthermore, once you fulfill his conditions he is willing to make peace for one hundred and one years and be your ally against other infidels. If you are not satisfied with these terms, prepare for your deaths, as I swear that mercy will be shown to no man."

The emissaries thanked Tirant for his kind reply and asked for three days to consult with their comrades. When our knight had granted their request, they returned to their camp, rejoicing in the knowledge that their lives would be spared.

Upon their arrival, they described Tirant's might and magnificence, as he commanded the finest knights on earth. They told their masters about his noble feasts and repeated his words, while the Turks, who were dismayed by everything they had heard about their foes, felt grateful to have escaped Tirant's wrath so easily.

On the morrow, the Saracen lords held council and decided to surrender. The emissaries then returned to Tirant's camp, where they were welcomed with great honor, as both victors and vanquished were weary of battle.

The emissaries informed Tirant that their masters would obey his commands, to which he replied: "When they have surrendered, I shall give the others safe-conduct, and on my faith as a knight, I promise no harm will befall them."

The emissaries humbly agreed, and upon reaching their camp, they found twenty-two lords gathered and ready to set out. To avoid prolixity I shall omit their names, but I can tell you they were too hungry to dawdle along the way. They bowed before Tirant, who, after welcoming them with great honor, served them a meal truly fit for such mighty lords, since the food was as splendid and abundant as it would have been in a great city. After the feast, Tirant brought them aboard two galleys and set sail for Constantinople.

As soon as the emperor learned of their arrival, he knelt and uttered this prayer:

· CDXLVII ·

*T*HE EMPEROR'S PRAYER

"Immense and inscrutable Lord, Creator, Omnipotent King of Kings, for whose supreme soul no deed is impossible: I thank You for the grace You show me despite my sins, for not only have You delivered us but You have restored our imperial scepter! Though knowledge of my failings sometimes made me doubt the outcome, I never lost faith in Your infinite mercy, and thus shall Your worshippers confound all depraved heretics, taking refuge in You till they reach Your blessed shore."

Having finished his prayer, the emperor sent a messenger to inform his wife and daughter of Tirant's arrival. The princess was so delighted that she almost fainted from sheer joy, but when she had recovered, the noble lady dressed carefully, knowing that many sovereigns would shortly behold her.

Then the emperor told Hippolytus to have the palace courtyard adorned with silk and shaded by great awnings of colored cloth. He also ordered three platforms erected: a high one covered with cloth of gold, a lower one covered with silk, and another nearby bearing his innumerable gold and silver vessels.

·CDXLVIII·

*H*OW TIRANT ARRIVED IN TRIUMPH AND WAS WELCOMED WITH GREAT HONOR

The commoners' joy at Tirant's approach was indescribable, and they thanked God for delivering them from past and future ills. Men and women thronged the docks to watch their saviors arrive, while many voices shouted: "Long live the noble captain who preserved us from slavery!"

Hippolytus then boarded Tirant's galley, where he bowed and told him: "My lord, the emperor invites you to come ashore."

Tirant said he would gladly do so, and once his galleys had docked, they threw down the ladders and their prisoners disembarked. The city officials were waiting to welcome our knight, who bowed to them in return and followed them to the palace.

Upon entering the courtyard, they saw the emperor on his throne atop the highest platform with the empress on his left and Carmesina on his right, sitting slightly forward in token of her coming succession. Her yellow damask gown, ennobled by sparkling rubies, diamonds, sapphires, and emeralds, had a thick band around the bottom, embroidered with oriental pearls and enameled flowers. She was bareheaded except for her golden tresses, which were gathered in a diamond clasp and fell loosely onto her shoulders. A flashing ruby hung between her breasts, and she had donned a black velvet shawl decorated with handsome pearls.

Tirant then mounted the platform, approached His Majesty, and knelt to kiss his hand, but the lord gently raised him up and kissed him on the lips. The sultan kissed His Highness's hand and foot, as did the other captured lords, and after welcoming them with a smile, the emperor sent them to another platform.

Tables were quickly brought forth, and the guests were seated in order of rank, while Hippolytus acted as imperial steward. Five ate at the emperor's table: himself, the empress, Tirant, Carmesina, and the Queen of Fez, each of whom had a separate platter and a servant in attendance. Tirant sat opposite his lady, and all the prisoners were served with reverence, for though infidels, they were nonetheless mighty lords of high degree. Astonished by the exquisite dishes and fine wines, they declared that Christians ate with better grace than Saracens.

When they had finished, Tirant obtained his lord's leave to oversee the Turks' departure, whereupon our knight's company boarded their galleys and weighed anchor.

At the sight of them in the distance, the admiral ordered all his trumpets, bugles, and clarions blown, and his sailors cheered as he boarded Tirant's galley and asked: "My lord, what are your wishes?"

Tirant replied: "Send your ships to collect the enemy soldiers and take them away."

The admiral then returned to his galley and ordered his fleet to approach shore, where one of the sultan's knights told the infidels to go aboard. Too hungry to delay, the soldiers left their horses, armor, clothes, and tents behind as they hastened to board the ships, which carried them to the other side of the Dardanelles and then returned for more. You can imagine how many there were, since over four hundred vessels had to make ten trips.

After the Saracens had departed, Tirant's men scrambled for their share of the spoils, and in truth the Turkish camp was the richest the world had ever seen, for they had sacked the entire empire and had the booty there with them. It did them little good, but those who pillaged their camp were rich for life.

When everything had been taken, Tirant sent his men back to their camp. Then he, the two kings, and many other barons went to pay their respects to the emperor, while the fleet set out to meet them in Constantinople.

· CDXLIX ·

HOW THE EMPEROR HAD THE HOSTAGES PLACED UNDER GUARD

Once the feast had ended, Hippolytus told the hostages to follow him, and after bowing to the royal table, they descended from their platform. Having led the Grand Turk and sultan to a fair chamber with silk hangings and a fine bed, he said: "Sires, the emperor asks you to accept his hospitality and hopes you will be forbearing if he does not honor you as you deserve."

The sultan replied: "Brave knight, we shall be forever in his debt, as he has treated us more like brothers than prisoners, and our sole desire is to serve him loyally."

Hippolytus told four pages never to leave the chamber and to fetch whatever they requested.

The remaining prisoners were divided among the other towers, in which they occupied splendid rooms with silk hangings and canopied beds. There were servants to do their bidding as well as vigilant soldiers, and thus they were both well guarded and well attended.

Knowing that Tirant, the two kings, and many other lords were on their way, the emperor ordered the courtyard left as it was and told his steward to gather many kinds of fowl, while Hippolytus prepared good lodgings for their guests.

· CDL ·

HOW THE KINGS OF SICILY AND FEZ PAID THEIR RESPECTS TO THE EMPEROR

A few days later, upon learning that Tirant's company was a league away, the emperor sent his court to meet them while he himself rode to the city gates. The empress, Carmesina, and the Queen of Fez also donned their finest robes for the guests, who within a few minutes had reached the walls of Constantinople.

When His Majesty spied them, he spurred his mount and rode to salute the victors, whereupon everyone dismounted and King Philip stepped forward. He fell to his knees to kiss the emperor's hand, but the lord raised him up and kissed him thrice on the lips. Then Tirant and the King of Fez did likewise and the other knights followed suit, while the aged emperor did them all great honor.

Having thus shown their joy, they remounted and entered the city behind Tirant, who was followed by the emperor with the kings on his right and left. They rode in this order until they reached the palace, where the ladies greeted their deliverers most graciously. Then King Philip took the empress's arm, as did the King of Fez with Carmesina and Tirant with the Queen of Fez, and in this fashion they mounted the emperor's platform, upon which they chatted and made merry for some time.

Tirant's companions were dazzled by the beautiful ladies, and especially the princess, who wore a crimson dress adorned with gold brocade. A thick band encircled the bottom, studded with big pearls, rubies, sapphires, emeralds, and enameled jasmine flowers, while over her dress she had donned a black satin mantle from France, whose edging, cape, and sleeves were decorated with gold and enamel. She wore a belt of gold sprinkled with diamonds, rubies, balases, sapphires, and emeralds. A carbuncle hung between her breasts, held in place by a gold chain, and her blond tresses were set off by a gold and enamel coronet.

After they had conversed awhile, the emperor invited them to table, at which King Philip sat beside the empress and the King of Fez ate between Pleasure-of-my-life and Carmesina.

The emperor begged Tirant to join them, but he insisted on acting as steward, and the rest of his knights ate on another platform where they were nobly entertained by singers and musicians.

As soon as they had finished eating, the dances began, and the King of Fez asked the empress to be his partner, to which she replied that although she had not danced in many years, she would do her utmost to please His Majesty. They danced splendidly to several tunes, as in her youth she had been most graceful, and all the other knights and ladies then followed suit.

The courtyard was full of commoners, either watching the festivities or joining them, for their joy at Tirant's bloodless victory was a wonder to behold, and triumphal celebrations ennobled the entire city for a week. In the morning everyone went to church, and after lunch the galas began.

When night fell, the dancing stopped and, once supper had been served by torchlight, the lords bade everyone goodnight and retired to their lodgings, which were magnificently adorned, as such noble knights deserved.

King Philip ate and slept with Tirant lest his affair come to light, but every day the Breton pressed his suit, begging Carmesina to wed him.

The princess replied:

· CDLI ·

THE PRINCESS'S REPLY TO TIRANT

"Oh most virtuous of mortals, you need not beg for what I desire, or do you think I would ungratefully withhold your guerdon? Let your spirit not be vexed if we must yet wait awhile, but rather rejoice in the glory you and your friends have lately won, for you need only be crowned emperor now that my father has promised to abdicate."

Refusing to let her continue, Tirant gently replied: "Exalted lady, you have so perturbed my thought and tongue that I can scarcely respond, but may God forbid me to be crowned in your father's lifetime, as a lord of such excellence should not be deposed, nor do I wish to be more than his son and his daughter's slave."

Weeping with gratitude at Tirant's words, Carmesina threw her arms around him and said: "My lord and greatest treasure, no mortal tongue could describe your virtue, and I pray God to let you rule this empire and myself."

Thus did the lovers part with many enamored words.

· CDLII ·

HOW TIRANT ASKED THE EMPEROR'S LEAVE TO RECONQUER THE LOST TERRITORIES, AND OF HIS BETROTHAL TO CARMESINA

Tirant spent a night of amorous imaginings as he waited for Phoebus's rays to illumine the East, and the next morning he went before His Majesty, to whom he said: "Provident lord, you will recall the sultan's and Grand Turk's promise to restore your empire. With your leave, I shall free and enlarge it either peacefully or by force, and should Fortune favor us, you will regain the lands ruled by Justinian."

The emperor replied: "Ardent captain, though we can never repay your services, we present all our lands to you and your companions. Furthermore, if you will have her, we offer our daughter Carmesina, as I am too old to defend or rule my realms, and moreover I am certain that you will honor me as a father."

Tirant threw himself at the emperor's feet, humbly kissed them, and replied: "Sire, may God forbid me to accept the empire in your lifetime, nor would I prefer ten kingdoms to virtuous Carmesina, who is the only reward I desire for my labors."

Seeing Tirant's gentility, His Majesty led him to the princess's chamber, where she was sitting on a dais attended by her ladies and King Philip.

Everyone bowed before the emperor, who seated himself with Carmesina on his right, Tirant on his left, and King Philip before them. Then he turned to his daughter and said: "My child, you know how well Tirant has served us and championed our empire, wherefore we now wish to offer him our greatest treasure. Take him as your lord and husband, for such is our command."

The princess modestly replied: "Benign and clement lord, I am honored that you consider me sufficient guerdon, for in truth I am unworthy to remove Tirant's shoe, but if he will have me, I shall gladly obey your orders."

The emperor summoned his archbishop while the couple stood speechless for sheer joy, and when the cleric arrived, His Majesty told him to betroth the lovers.

Once they were engaged, there was a great and joyous feast attended by the emperor and empress, King Philip of Sicily, Lord Agramunt of Fez and Bougie, Queen Pleasure-of-my-life, Tirant's admiral the Marquis of Liçana, the Viscount of Branches, Tirant's servant Hippolytus, Almedixer, Lord Espercius of Espertina, Lord Melquisedec of Montagata, many other knights and ladies, and a vast crowd of commoners. As was proper on such an occasion, delicious cakes and marzipan in imperial abundance were served from enameled gold and silver platters, while the carpets and tapestries, the nuptial chamber, the daises and curtains were of a pomp and luxury never seen before. There were musicians in the towers and at the windows of the great halls, playing trumpets, bugles, clarions, tambourins, flageolets, musettes, and kettledrums with such clamor and magnificence that even the saddest hearts rejoiced. In the chambers and alcoves one heard cymbals, flutes, viols, and voices sweetly singing in angelic harmony, while in the great halls, lutes, harps, and other instruments lent grace and measure to the dancing courtiers.

Such triumph and splendor had never been seen before by Greeks or foreigners, who all cheered Tirant's betrothal, which would assure their peace and prosperity. The celebrations lasted a week, both in the palace and the city.

The emperor dispatched criers to announce with trumpets and kettledrums that Tirant would be his heir, whereupon everyone swore fealty to their future emperor, who from that day on was called Caesar by one and all. The criers' announcement was of the following tenor:

· CDLIII ·

*T*HE EMPEROR'S ANNOUNCEMENT

Hear ye, hear ye! The emperor reminds all Greeks of the memorable deeds performed by his valiant captain and noble knight, Tirant lo Blanc of Saltrock, through whom the empire has not only been succored, delivered, and freed from oppression, danger, and slavery, but also given honor, riches, abundance, peace, joy, and glory. All this Tirant did for God and our imperial sovereignty, with unprecedented travails both corporal and spiritual; and since courageous deeds should be duly guerdoned, His Imperial Majesty sought to abdicate in Tirant's favor, but the brave captain refused, accepting only the succession, wherefore our most illustrious and Christian princess has been betrothed to this knight, whom His Highness commands all and sundry to hold, consider, and deem a worthy Caesar, our future emperor, and our present prince and captain general. May his reign be glorious, and may all Christians praise God's favors, nor should any man claim that he was not duly notified.

All the townsfolk responded with one voice: "Long live the emperor's angelic virtue! Long live the new Caesar, our honor and glory!"

· CDLIV ·

HOW TIRANT AND HIS ARMY SET OUT TO MEET KING ESCARIANO

After proclaiming Tirant Caesar, the emperor led his guests to the palace, while our knight's woes redoubled at the thought of leaving his lady. That his task might end more quickly, he resolved to set out immediately, but he dreaded separation from his beloved and feared that Fortune might snatch her from him.

Then word came that King Escariano's host was in the land of the Pechenegs, which borders on the empire, and knowing that if his friend reached Constantinople, the festivities would never end, Tirant decided to intercept him and take him on his campaign.

Having reached this decision, the brave Caesar gathered his captains, who then bade the emperor farewell and returned to their lodgings. That night, Tirant had the Grand Turk and sultan write letters of credence, which, translated into our language, were of the following tenor:

· CDLV ·

THE SULTAN'S LETTER OF CREDENCE

I, Baralinda, sovereign prince of Mohammed's faith, scorning worldly riches but glorying in my might, inform all my kaids, governors, cadis, captains, and vassals that, to free us and our comrades, they must honor and obey Tirant lo Blanc, Caesar of the Greek Empire, and quickly execute everything ordered by my messenger, the Prince of Karaman. Written and signed in the palace prison of Constantinople in the month of Ramadan, the seventh year of my reign.

The Grand Turk, who also called himself the Subjugator of Turkey and the Avenger of Trojan Blood, wrote a similar letter ordering all the occupied lands restored to Tirant, and he entrusted this letter to the Prince of Scythia.

Having taken his leave of the imperial family, Tirant returned to camp with his companions and the two Saracen knights. Upon their arrival, his trumpeters called the soldiers to arms, and the next morning they set out to meet King Escariano, while sending a courier to ask him to remain wherever he was.

· CDLVI ·

*T*IRANT'S LETTER TO KING ESCARIANO

To my beloved brother-in-arms, the King of Tlemcen, Tunis, and Ethiopia: I, Tirant lo Blanc of Saltrock, Captain and Caesar of the Greek Empire, greet my noble comrade King Escariano, in whose coming we rejoice, and that we may welcome you fitly, we beg you to stay wherever you are, for we have already vanquished the Turkish host. I know you will be pleased to hear of my betrothal, as I am well aware of the love and good will you bear me.

The letter delighted King Escariano, who marveled at Tirant's prowess and decided to encamp near the noble city of Strenes, which lies on the banks of a broad river about five days from Constantinople. The courier then returned to his captain, whom he informed of the black's whereabouts.

Tirant proceeded to the fair city of Sinope, where his two Saracen emissaries gave the Turkish captain their letters of credence. After reverently kissing and reading the missives, he swore to obey all his masters' commands.

Having received the captain's surrender, Tirant and his men occupied the city, whose Greek inhabitants rejoiced and whose Christian renegades returned to their faith. Our knight drove out the Saracens and appointed a good Christian captain, while messengers brought the keys to ten fortified towns, from which Tirant's lieutenants quickly evicted the remaining Turks.

Then the Christians set out for the pleasant city of Adrianople, where they repeated everything they had done in Sinope. The neighboring towns and castles capitulated and offered costly gifts, as did those they passed through between Adrianople and Strenes.

When Tirant was only half a league from Strenes, King Escariano learned of his approach and rode forth to meet him.

Once the two friends had embraced, Tirant asked King Escariano to join forces with him, to which the black gladly consented and warmly kissed the kings. Then they all remounted and rode toward the camp, where Tirant was welcomed by the Queen of Ethiopia.

Our knight sent his emissaries to warn the inhabitants of Strenes that if they chose to fight, he would spare no one, young or old.

Upon reaching the gates, they asked for the captain and gave him their letters, which he accepted with reverence and swore to obey, as he had received his title from the sultan.

The Prince of Karaman said: "Captain, on your sovereign's behalf I order you to pay homage to the Grand Imperial Caesar, and furthermore, I warn you that should you refuse, he will spare no one."

The captain replied: "Brave and noble emissaries, tell your Caesar I shall be more obedient than if he were the emperor himself."

The captain's men quickly opened the gates, which the Christian lords entered to the accompaniment of kettledrums, trumpets, clarions, and tambourins. They were given splendid lodgings, and our knight received many fine gifts.

Tirant told his soldiers to camp outside the city, for though large, it could not accommodate even a third of their troops, all of whom were given everything they needed.

Tirant then asked the king and queen to rest for a week, since their journey had lasted more than a hundred days. In his eagerness to fight the Turks, King Escariano had come by forced marches, and his men and horses were close to exhaustion.

Many sweet words passed between Tirant and his friends as they took their ease in Strenes. Our knight recounted his glorious exploits and praised the generous emperor, who had appointed him Imperial Caesar and successor to the crown. He also described the treaties the Grand Turk and the sultan had signed, while consenting to remain as hostages till the empire had been restored: "And therefore, lord and brother, I beg you to join me in this campaign, knowing that between God's help and our mighty armies we shall best all our foes. I also ask you to send your queen to Constantinople till we complete our conquests, as I know my princess's fondest wish is to behold her."

King Escariano replied:

· CDLVII ·

*H*OW KING ESCARIANO AGREED TO SEND HIS WIFE TO CONSTANTINOPLE

"Lord of the Greek Empire and brother, my tongue could never express our joy at your good fortune, nor should you beseech one whom you may command as your humble vassal, as I would follow you to Hell and owe more to you than to my father."

After thanking King Escariano for his gallant words, Tirant gathered five hundred soldiers and many lords to escort the queen to Constantinople. Our knight, King Escariano, and the other monarchs accompanied her for a league, whereupon they parted company and she continued on her way.

· CDLVIII ·

*H*OW TIRANT AND HIS ARMY SET OUT FROM STRENES

When the queen had departed, Tirant told his friend: "Lord brother, let us set out, as your men are rested and I long for my beloved, though I fear that cruel Fortune will deny me such joy."

King Escariano replied: "May God reward you as you deserve and grant all your wishes; I am ready to march whenever you like."

The two armies then broke camp and made for Stagira, a Thracian walled city with well-proportioned towers.

As soon as they arrived, Tirant sent his emissaries to the Turkish captain, who saw them approaching and rode out to meet them.

After reading the letters, he promised to open the gates immediately and then went to Tirant's camp, where he knelt before him and said:

· CDLIX ·

*H*OW THE CAPTAIN OF STAGIRA GAVE TIRANT THE KEYS TO THE CITY

"Your glorious fame, noble captain, draws all knights to your banner, and the great God whom you champion is the source of your peerless valor. I obeyed the Grand Turk, who had made me his captain, but deeming myself freed from all such vassalage, I offer you the service of one who, desiring no other lord but God, implores you to baptize him and gives you these keys."

Tirant replied: "Wise men always obtain what they desire, emerging from defeat stronger than they were before. Mindful of your wisdom, I shall gladly accept your fealty, confirming your captaincy in the emperor's name and mine. If Fortune favors me, I shall make you a great lord."

The Turkish captain, who was still kneeling, kissed Tirant's hand and said: "My lord, I bless your favors, which I surely do not deserve. May God let me help you convert all Saracens and make you emperor."

After ordering their men to pitch camp nearby, Tirant, King Escariano, and the other barons entered Stagira, where they were joyously welcomed by the Greek townspeople. Tirant received many gifts and his companions were well lodged, while the soldiers in his camp were feasted with abundant food.

The next morning, since Tirant's new captain had asked to be baptized, our knight ordered a bishop in his company to reconsecrate the church and to have its baptismal fonts readied for use. The bishop quickly obeyed, and when the church had been reconsecrated, they erected a handsome altar with an image of Our Lady.

Then Tirant, his companions, and the captain made their way to the church, followed by most of the Turks in the city. A splendid Mass began, as Tirant and King Escariano had brought their cantors, whose sweet voices filled the infidels with awe at Christian liturgy.

After the service, a priest baptized the new captain, whose godfather was King Escariano and who therefore was christened Sir John Escariano, while his wife was christened Angela and Tirant was her godfather. When the five sons had embraced Christianity, Tirant knighted, horsed, and armed them. Two thousand other Saracens also turned to God that morning, for the inhabitants of Stagira revered their captain's wisdom.

Tirant also reconverted the renegade Greeks, making them swear fealty to him and the emperor. All infidels who clung to their faith were expelled from the city, which is Aristotle's birthplace and whose inhabitants worship him as a saint.[3]

During Tirant's stay, his emissaries rode through the countryside, ordering the nearby towns to dispatch representatives with their keys, while our knight appointed new Christian captains to rule Thrace.

Then they left Stagira and rode to the Macedonian city of Olympia,[4] which lies not far from Mount Olympus, one of the world's loftiest mountains. They were welcomed with special joy since the Macedonians knew Tirant was their duke's cousin, and to atone for their renegade

Greek captain, they offered our knight lavish gifts from their prosperous land. Within a few days, the entire duchy had been recovered.

After leaving Macedonia, Tirant set out for Trebizond and forced its immediate surrender, as his army of over four hundred thousand struck fear into infidel hearts. His troops, who were from all nations, could storm any citadel, and within a month the whole province of Trebizond was in his hands.

While they were in Trebizond, one hundred and eighty-three prisoners arrived under Diaphebus's command, for the others—and they were many—had died in battle or in prison. The survivors had been brought from Alexandria by one of the sultan's knights who, following Tirant's instructions, had ordered the kaids to place their captives on a ship, which then sailed to Trebizond, where a joyous welcome awaited them.

Tirant asked for the Duke of Macedonia, and Diaphebus was brought before him, but Stephanie's husband was so altered that our knight could scarcely recognize him: pale and emaciated, with a beard down to his waist and hair to his shoulders. All the prisoners were attired in yellow burnooses and blue turbans.

Upon beholding Tirant, Diaphebus fell at his feet and tried to kiss them, but the Caesar raised him up and kissed him on the lips. Tears ran down our knight's cheeks as he sighed deeply and spoke these words:

· CDLX ·

*T*IRANT'S WORDS OF LOVE AND COMFORT TO THE DUKE OF MACEDONIA

"My eyes cannot help weeping at what they behold, nor can my heart keep from mourning your woeful aspect. Since you suffered for my sake, I humbly apologize, yet faith in God's mercy has now brought us joy, for not only have we triumphed but we have also freed you. This is what most delights me, though I am pleased by the others' freedom, and therefore be of good cheer, as your duchess sends this letter."

Weeping bitterly, the duke replied: "Lord Tirant, I rejoice in your sight as the ancient prophets in Purgatory did at Our Savior's coming. You, who are our salvation, our life, and our redemption, threw open those dungeon gates and sundered the chains that bound us. Our past hardships are as nought beside our present consolation, and to fight beneath your banner is our greatest satisfaction."

Then the duke read his wife's letter, which was of the following tenor:

· CDLXI ·

THE DUCHESS OF MACEDONIA'S LETTER TO HER HUSBAND

Extreme joy and sorrow have so besieged my weary heart that only a miracle has kept your Stephanie alive. When we meet, you will behold the suffering in my pale visage, while my brain has grown so addled that I scarcely know what I say, wherefore I kneel at your feet, kissing the chains that bind us both, begging you to pity one who loves you more than life, nor do I recite my woes as proof of devotion, since I would endure many more to shield you from harm. To think of the glory you deserve makes me feel that I should only lament your misfortunes, for what eyes can keep from weeping over so fine a duke enslaved by infidels, and what heart is so hard that it would not break at the thought of your torments? My lord, do not think I never imagine you in prison, where I see your long, white beard covering the chest on which I laid my head. I envisage your sunken eyes and skeletal body, though I know your every gesture will breathe nobility, and as I ponder your agonies, I claw my face and tear my hair, lamenting those afflictions that lacerate both our souls. Your yellow burnoose stained with tears, and that blue turban on a head that deserves a crown, have robbed me of all my joy and solace. I wear grey sackcloth over the hair shirt against my skin to show my anguish as I pray, sigh, and pine for your return. To match your chains I wear a tight girdle, while to match your shackles I go barefoot, and as long as you are imprisoned, I shall continue to renounce the world, remaining locked in this convent until you rescue your duchess. Hurry, my lord! You are the key to my dungeon, the scepter of my rule, the crown of my glory, my desolation's only cure! Bring the bright dawn that will end my dark night!

The duke, who had wept for joy at the sight of Tirant and his redemption, now sobbed with bitter grief over his beloved duchess's letter.

· CDLXII ·

HOW ALL THE OTHER PRISONERS PAID THEIR RESPECTS TO TIRANT

The Marquis of Saint George then knelt before our knight, who smiled, raised him up, and kissed him on the lips, whereupon his brother the

Duke of Pera, the Prior of Saint John, and the other lords followed suit while Tirant welcomed them with love and abundant joy.

Likewise, the Duke of Macedonia paid his respects to the three kings, who honored him both for his bravery and because he was Tirant's cousin.

Tirant quickly clothed the prisoners, gave them splendid mounts, and offered all the pleasures he could devise to restore their spirits.

He also informed Stephanie that her husband would soon be with her, for in her grief she had refused to take part in the festivities at her lady's betrothal.

The knights feasted and took their ease in Trebizond till they were strong enough to leave.

· CDLXIII ·

HOW THE QUEEN OF ETHIOPIA ARRIVED IN CONSTANTINOPLE AND THE HONORS SHE RECEIVED

As soon as the emperor learned of Queen Emeraldine's approach, he asked Carmesina to welcome their guest. The princess then dressed as splendidly as she could, while three hundred noblewomen and knights made ready to accompany her.

Before departing, the princess told her servants to erect a scarlet brocade pavilion one league beyond the city, and when they arrived, she and her ladies entered the huge tent, whose size you can imagine, for the Queen of Ethiopia's retinue could also fit inside it.

The knights rode on till they met the queen, whom they saluted and led to the princess's pavilion, which was cunningly adorned with embroidered birds and animals.

Learning that noble Carmesina was inside, the queen entered the pavilion and fell to her knees. Tirant's beloved then raised her up, kissed her three times in sign of love, and asked the worthy lady to sit down beside her.

Though the wise princess had learned many languages from foreigners who had passed through Constantinople, she was especially well versed in Latin, whose grammar and poetry she had studied. After promising to attend Tirant's wedding, the queen had also learned Latin, and so they exchanged many courtesies as gallant ladies are wont to do.[5]

The princess was dazzled by the queen's resplendent beauty, which she considered far greater than her own or anyone else's, while the queen, for her part, was awed by the princess and declared that nowhere on earth could such comeliness be found.

After they had spoken for a while, the two goddesses remounted without taking their delighted eyes off each other, and the other ladies rode behind them as they made their way to the city.

The princess took her friend's hand as they approached the city gates, where the emperor and empress awaited them on horseback. The queen tried to kiss Their Majesties' hands, but the emperor refused and embraced her, as did the empress, who also kissed her three times on the lips.

The emperor and empress led the way, followed by the princess and the Queen of Ethiopia, the Queen of Fez, the Duchess of Macedonia, the other ladies, and a multitude of commoners. On their arrival, the queen was shown to a splendid chamber with gold and silk hangings, where they left her to rest and recover from her journey. She was abundantly served with everything she needed, and fine lodgings were prepared for those in her retinue.

The next day, His Highness invited her to eat in the great hall. Beholding his guest in her finest clothes and escorted by all her ladies, the emperor asked her to sit between the empress and the Queen of Fez, while the queen's noblemen ate at another table and her ladies sat with the imperial maidens. Bands of musicians played an astonishing array of instruments on platforms nearby as the lords dined in great triumph, attended by knights in gold and brocade robes.

After lunch, the assembled lords and ladies began to dance with the Queen of Ethiopia, who had donned a green brocade dress trimmed with rubies, diamonds, and emeralds, all worked into handsome and subtle designs. Her black damask mantle was adorned with gold and enamel, while a gold chain set with diamonds and rubies sparkled upon her neck and her hair shone like spun gold beneath its jeweled tiara, nor was the stone on her forehead less dazzlingly radiant.

Astounded by her beauty, the courtiers marveled at Tirant's virtue, for he had spurned the fair queen and kept faith with his beloved.

Upon hearing these rumors, the princess resolved to teach them the truth, since when the two ladies stood together Carmesina clearly outshone the queen.

While His Majesty's guests were dancing, a messenger entered the hall and approached Stephanie, before whom he knelt and took out a letter, saying: "My lady, reward me as the bearer of joyous tidings, for your husband and his companions have been freed and are in Trebizond."

The duchess fainted for sheer joy, whereupon a great uproar ensued as everyone stopped dancing and hastened to fetch rice water. They splashed some in the duchess's face and she recovered her senses, but an hour passed before she could speak or read the letter, which proved to contain words of the following tenor:

· CDLXIV ·

*T*IRANT'S LETTER TO STEPHANIE

Mindful of your sadness, I have striven to ease your woes, for I wished to reap the first fruits of your delight. Beloved duchess, banish care from your heart, as your duke and my favorite cousin is now free, happy, and in good health. He will soon return to your side, cheered by seven great joys: joy in captivity's end, joy in newfound freedom, joy in health, joy in honor, joy in your sight, joy in riches and triumph, and joy in the happy life ahead. I have no message for His Majesty, with whom I spoke not long ago.

When Stephanie had read the letter, she gave a thousand ducats to Tirant's messenger, who thanked her profusely and went away feeling very content. Then she knelt before the emperor and handed the missive to him, whereupon he ordered all the church bells rung.

The townsfolk hoped they would now live in peace and prosperity, but Providence did not suffer their merriment to long endure.

Once Tirant had feasted Diaphebus and his companions, he gave them leave to go to Constantinople, where the emperor and empress welcomed them with great honor, but let us now leave His Majesty's festivities and turn to our knight's exploits.

· CDLXV ·

*H*OW TIRANT LEFT TREBIZOND AND RECOVERED MANY OTHER PROVINCES

As soon as Diaphebus had left, Tirant and King Escariano called their men to arms and rode to Vidin, which was six days away. All the infidels in their path surrendered without resistance.

After accepting their submission and leaving garrisons in the towns, the Christians went on to free the provinces of Hungary, Bosnia, Serbia, and Epirus. Each of them contains a multitude of cities, towns, and villages, whose inhabitants welcomed their liberation from the Turks' evil rule.

Having subdued the cities of Arcadia, Tegea, and Turina, they set out for Persia and conquered it by force of arms, since it had not been ruled by the sultan or Grand Turk. They also occupied the rich market city of Tabriz, as well as Bukhara and Samarkand on the Ganges.[6]

Tirant recovered so many lands and provinces that it would be a great task to recite them, for by his diligence and chivalry he recovered all of Greece and Asia Minor, Persia, Thessalonica (where Gallipoli is), the Peloponnesus, and Arta and Vlonë in Albania. Likewise, he sent his fleet under the Marquis of Liçana to recapture all the islands that had been lost to the Turks, including Corfu, Lesbos, Naxos, Melos, Scarpanto, Lemnos, and many others the book omits to avoid prolixity.[7]

· CDLXVI ·

HOW THE ADMIRAL RETURNED IN TRIUMPH TO CONSTANTINOPLE, WHERE THE EMPEROR REWARDED HIM WITH THE DUKE OF PERA'S DAUGHTER

Once the admiral had recaptured all the islands—some peacefully and others by force—his fleet returned to Constantinople in great triumph. As his men entered the harbor, they cheered and fired bombards, while townspeople lined the city walls to welcome their champions. Then the admiral and his knights saluted the emperor, who greeted them warmly as they kissed his hand and foot.

His Majesty made the marquis governor of the islands he had reconquered, declaring him and his successors imperial admirals in perpetuity. Moreover, he granted him an annuity of one hundred thousand ducats and fair Eliseu, the empress's maid in waiting and the widowed Duke of Pera's only daughter. Her father had wooed the princess but had lost her to Tirant.

The admiral thanked the emperor, saying he prized the wife even more than the annuity, and to celebrate their betrothal, the festivities began again, as the Dukes of Macedonia and Pera, the Marquis of Saint George, the Prior of Saint John of Jerusalem and the other freed prisoners had recently arrived.

For love of the two queens, Carmesina ennobled the celebrations with her presence, and to reward the knights His Majesty arranged marriages for them with imperial damsels, giving them estates where they might dwell in honor and prosperity. He postponed their marriages until Tirant's wedding day, but Fortune decreed otherwise, for God created us to attain bliss not in this world but in the next. Men often pay little heed to such matters, since brave knights perform immortal deeds every day, as did Tirant lo Blanc in Barbary and the Greek Empire, though alas, he did not live to see the fruits of his labor.

· CDLXVII ·

HOW TIRANT CAUGHT THE DISEASE THAT KILLED HIM

My weary hand must now write of man's ignorance of his fate, for Tirant never received the guerdon he expected. He should serve as an example to those who sell their souls for power or pleasure, as such vain, pompous fools waste their wretched lives.

Tirant's company set out for his wedding feast in Constantinople, where the emperor made a breach in the walls so our knight's triumphal chariot could enter. The army halted in Adrianople, which is a day's ride from the capital, because His Majesty had asked them to wait there until he sent word.[8]

One morning Tirant was taking his ease with King Philip and King Escariano, and as they strolled along a river that flowed near the city walls he suddenly felt a sharp pain in his side. His two friends carried him back into the town, where they put him to bed and summoned their doctors, who tried many remedies but to no avail.

Fearing his hour was at hand, our knight called for a priest and they brought his confessor, who was a Franciscan friar and a master of theology.[9] Tirant then diligently confessed his sins, as he could feel the pain growing.

While he was confessing, the King of Fez dispatched a messenger to fetch the emperor's physicians, though he feared that their captain might die before they came.

After Tirant had confessed, he asked to take Communion, weeping and praying to the Host in the following manner:

· C D L X V I I I ·

*T*IRANT'S PRAYER TO THE *CORPUS DOMINI*

"Oh Savior of Mankind, Infinite Lord, staff of life, priceless treasure, incomparable joy, sinners' advocate and unfailing defense, oh God's true flesh and blood, meek immaculate lamb sacrificed to redeem us, shining mirror wherein divine mercy is reflected, King of Kings whom all creatures obey, immense, humble, sweet and merciful God! How can I repay the love You have shown me? Not only did You descend to save me from perdition, but You were tortured and killed, offering Your body to cleanse my wicked soul. Now I humbly request true repentance and forgiveness, for though You have preserved me from many perils, I see my hour has come and obediently accept death as due penance for my sins. Lord, preserve my faith, as I wish to live and die a Christian, and show Your clemency that, lamenting my sins and blessing Your holy name, I may go before You and beg for absolution."

Having spoken these words, Tirant wept and took Communion, while all those present said he had spoken more like a saint than a knight. After setting his soul in order, he dictated his last will and testament:

· C D L X I X ·

*T*IRANT'S WILL

Since death is the lot of all, a wise man will ensure that when he leaves this vale of tears and returns to Our Creator, he may account for his use of the wealth entrusted to him. Therefore I, Tirant lo Blanc of Breton Saltrock lineage, knight of the Order of the Garter and Imperial Caesar, finding myself mortally ill but in full possession of my faculties, now dictate my last will and testament before the Kings of Ethiopia, Sicily, and Fez.

My executors shall be Carmesina, Princess of the Greek Empire, and my noble cousin Diaphebus, Duke of Macedonia, to whom I commend my soul.

I beg them to distribute a hundred thousand ducats of my wealth at their own discretion, and furthermore I ask them to send my body to the Church of Our Lady in Brittany, where my worthy ancestors lie in their tombs.

Moreover, I bequeath a hundred thousand ducats to each relative who attends my funeral and fifty thousand more to every one of my servants. The heir to my wealth and privileges shall be my nephew and servant Hippolytus, who shall inherit all my rights and dispose of them as he sees fit.

Having finished his will, Tirant dictated a note to the princess.

· CDLXX ·

*T*IRANT'S FAREWELL NOTE TO THE PRINCESS

Seeing that death draws nigh and will not long stay its hand, I can only bid you a sorrowful farewell.

Alas, it seems that Fortune will steal my reward, though could I die in your arms, death would not appear so cruel. I beg you to remain alive and pray for my sinful soul, which now must sadly return to its Maker.

Were I to behold or address you, I am certain that you would save me, but as I cannot, I have decided to pen this tearful missive. My affliction is great, for death creeps ever closer and my pain is such that I can scarcely lift my hand. I commend all my companions and servants to Your Highness.

—Your Tirant, who kisses your hands and feet and commends his soul to you

AFTER TIRANT'S DEATH

·CDLXXI·

*H*OW THE EMPEROR SENT DIAPHEBUS AND HIPPOLYTUS WITH THE DOCTORS, AND HOW TIRANT DIED ON HIS WAY TO CONSTANTINOPLE

Tirant then asked the kings to take him to Constantinople, for his greatest woe was to die without Carmesina, whose sight he still thought might restore him to health.

They granted his request, since all the doctors' efforts had been for nought, and hoping love might succeed where medicines had failed, they placed Tirant on a stretcher, which four men lifted onto their shoulders. The kings escorted him, leaving their army in Adrianople.

Plunged into despair by the King of Fez's letter, the emperor summoned his physicians, the Duke of Macedonia, and Hippolytus, whom he asked to mount their horses and ride to Adrianople. They left without a word lest the noble princess take ill as well.

After riding for half a day, they encountered Tirant, whose bearers set down the stretcher while Diaphebus asked: "Cousin, how fares Your Lordship?"

Our knight replied: "Friend, I rejoice to behold you and I beg you and Hippolytus to bid me farewell."

The two Bretons wept as they kissed their captain, who commended both his soul and his beloved to them, but the duke replied: "My lord, how can so valiant a warrior be thus dismayed? Trust in God's mercy, for He will surely cure you."

As he was speaking, Tirant suddenly cried: "Jesus, Son of David, forgive me! I believe, I confess, I repent, I beg for mercy! Virgin Mary, guardian angel Michael, do not forsake me! Jesus, I place my soul in Your hands!"

With these words he expired, leaving his handsome body in the duke's arms.

Everyone wept and cried aloud, as Tirant had been loved by all.

Finally, after many tears, King Escariano drew the Kings of Sicily and Fez, the Duke of Macedonia, and Hippolytus aside. They resolved to embalm Tirant's corpse in Constantinople and send it to Brittany, but they asked King Escariano not to enter since the emperor did not know him, nor was it a fit time for the two monarchs to meet.

Late that night they reached the city and parted from King Escariano, who returned to Adrianople, grieving all the while. The others brought our knight's body to a house where doctors could embalm it.

Once that had been accomplished, Tirant's friends dressed him in a brocade doublet and a sable-lined brocade robe of state. Then they bore him to the Hagia Sophia, where they placed him and his sword upon a bier.

When the emperor learned of Tirant's demise, he rent his imperial robes and stepped down from his throne, uttering the following lamentation:

· C D L X X I I ·

*T*HE EMPEROR'S LAMENT

"Today I have lost my scepter and my triumphant crown lies in the dust, as Fortune has snatched away my right arm and the pillar upon which my empire rested. Oh unjust Death who robs us of such a knight while allowing innumerable infidels to prosper: in slaying Tirant you have undone me as well, but although I shall die, may his glorious fame endure forever! Oh celestial hierarchies, place him among the elect, and you, Prince of Darkness, laugh if you can! Our enemies will soon rejoice, for invincible Tirant has now been vanquished, and only I, the forsaken emperor, must weep at his funeral. May clouds hide the sun lest even the moon reflect its light; may gales shake the earth, high mountains fall, and rivers halt; may clear water mix with sand and be imbibed by my subjects, as they grieve like turtledoves bereft of their mates; and may the sea abandon its fish and mermaids, that they too may mourn our woes! Lament, oh sweet sirens, the death of our phoenix; howl, savage beasts, and may birds cease to sing! Would that I might die and bear my affliction to Pluto's realm, there to make Ovid forge verses worthy of our champion, but as I must live, I shall put away my golden robes, strip my palaces of their rich purple, and cover myself with sackcloth, while my subjects dress in black and bells toll in chaos, thus mourning a loss of which my tongue cannot bear to speak."[1]

The emperor spent most of the night lamenting, and with the dawn he went to ensure that Tirant's funeral was worthy of such a lord.

The princess, who marveled to hear everyone weeping and feared for her father's life, leapt out of bed clad only in her nightdress. Upon reaching the window, she saw Diaphebus and many others, who did nothing but tear their hair and beat their heads against the wall.

"By the One God I beg you," cried the princess, "to disclose the cause of your grief."

The widow Montsanto replied: "My lady, someone must inform you that Tirant has passed away and returned to his Maker. He lies in the cathedral, where your father is weeping inconsolably."

At first Carmesina was speechless, but then she began to sob and cried: "Fetch my wedding gown, as I have not yet donned it."

It was quickly brought forth, whereupon the widow Montsanto asked: "My lady, how can you dress for a wedding when such an admirable knight has just perished in your father's service? Everyone else is wearing black, yet you, who should grieve the most, are attired in this unheard-of fashion!"

"Do not fret, lady widow," replied the princess, "for I shall reveal my sorrow when the moment comes."

Once she had dressed, the anguished princess and her ladies went to the cathedral.

When she reached the bier and saw Tirant, her heart almost broke, but she forced herself to climb the steps and throw herself upon his corpse, sobbing and lamenting thus:

· CDLXXIII ·

*T*HE PRINCESS'S LAMENT

"Oh monstrous, two-faced Fortune always tormenting the wretched Greeks, now you have truly displayed your power! You envy the courageous and despise the defenseless, for though we surely wept enough for my brother and our imperiled lands, you now undo my joy, my father's comfort, and the hope of our nation, destroying not only Tirant but our empire and dynasty. Oh inexorable Fates who part me from this glorious knight: at least allow me to kiss him until my aching heart is comforted!"

The lady embraced him with such force that she broke her nose and blood trickled down her face, filling all the onlookers with sorrow and compassion. Then she said: "Since Fortune has thus ordained, I shall never smile again but shall seek Tirant in Heaven, serving him in death as I could not in life. Save your tears, ladies and damsels, for you will soon mourn two corpses. Alas, woe is me, where is my Tirant, yet he is here before my eyes, dead and covered with my blood! Oh Tirant, take my kisses, sighs, and sobs, but leave me that shirt I gave you in sign of love and which, placed in our tomb, shall be cleansed by my bitter tears."

Having spoken these words, she fainted upon his corpse, from which they quickly raised her while the doctors brought cordials and smelling salts.² When she had recovered, the half dead lady again threw herself on Tirant and kissed his cold mouth. Unable to utter even words of sorrow, she tore her hair, clothes, and skin, as her warm tears mingled with Tirant's cold ones. With trembling hands, she opened his eyes and touched them with her own, so that Tirant seemed to mourn Carmesina's bereavement. Having spent all her tears, she began to weep blood, lamenting with words that would have softened steel, flint, or diamonds.

· CDLXXIV ·

H OW THE PRINCESS CONTINUED TO LAMENT OVER TIRANT'S BODY

"Words cannot describe the torments of grief, for though my whole body were covered with mouths, it could not express my woe. Often, in my imagination, I foresaw this dreadful moment, nor should you, my soul, expect to be long parted from Tirant. After my burial, I shall follow him to Heaven or Hell, where just as we were joined in life, so shall we be in death."

Then she cried: "Who will reunite my soul with Tirant? Alas, I was surely born beneath an evil star, as on that ill-omened day the sun was in eclipse, the waters were turbid, the heat was stifling, and my mother nearly perished. Would that I had died myself and thus avoided such pain, wherefore I beg the King of Heaven to foil any who seek to stop me."

Dismayed by his daughter's laments, the aged emperor cried: "This damsel's grief will only cease when she joins Tirant! Therefore, my lords, remove her to the palace either willingly or by force."

It was quickly done, while her father followed, saying: "May the wretched be comforted by our tears and lamentations, since we can truly say the pillar of chivalry is dead, and you, daughter and successor: control your grief or you will kill me. Do not show your sorrow lest you be punished as a false accuser, though you have nothing to regret and are innocent of all blame. Therefore, dry your eyes and show a cheerful countenance to your subjects."

The princess replied: "Alas, my lord, you engendered a wretched daughter! Do you believe you can console me for Tirant's sad demise? I cannot restrain my tears, which well up like boiling water!"

Unable to bear the sight of his afflicted daughter, the emperor left the room, whereupon Carmesina sat down and said: "Come, my faithful maidens, and help me to disrobe. You will have time enough for weeping, but first take off my veil and other garments."

Assuming as modest a pose as she could, the princess then declared: "I, who thought to rule an empire, now ask you to mourn Tirant. Oh worthy knight, we beat our breasts and tear our hair in sorrow, mourning one who was our shield and our ardent sword in warfare, nor should you think, Tirant, that you will fade from my memory, since as long as I live I shall lament your passing. Therefore, dear damsels, help me end my life in sorrow."

The city rang with their cries, while the damsels cursed cruel Fortune. The doctors said she could not live long, as blood was trickling from her mouth.

When the empress learned of Carmesina's condition, she hurried to the maiden's chambers, where at first she stood speechless before her daughter's grief, but then she roused herself and said: "My child, please pity yourself and me. Is this the joy I expected of you? Is this the wedding that would have cheered your parents and subjects? Is this the season for imperial marriages? Is this how you adorn your marriage bed? Are these the songs one hopes to hear at noble celebrations? Tell me, my daughter: where are your parents' nuptial blessings? Alas, woe is me, I possess nothing but grief and bitterness, and wherever I turn I behold distress and sorrow! I see the emperor upon the floor, surrounded by damsels with disheveled hair and bloody faces. What day was ever so doleful? All the monks are weeping and none can sing. Tell me: what holiday is everyone celebrating? Woe unto the mother who bore such a daughter! I ask you, my child, to be of better cheer and to comfort your anguished parents, who raised you with such love."

She was overcome by grief and could speak no more.

· CDLXXV ·

*T*HE PRINCESS'S REPLY TO HER MOTHER

"Were my death not imminent," the princess replied, "I would take my own life, for how can I rejoice after losing such a peerless knight? In his tender youth he subdued widely scattered lands, and his fame will endure for centuries and millenia. He never shrank from battle but avenged the wrongs we Greeks had suffered, bravely pursuing our foes and driving them from the empire, while likewise he freed a multitude of knights from infidel dungeons, nor did any mortal dare to resist him as he expelled our enemies and imprisoned their chieftains, but why should I speak when I do not fear death, which can only reunite us and end my sufferings? Oh grief, let this wretched damsel die as she lived, and fetch my worthy father that he may witness and recall my end."

When her father had come, she begged him and her mother to lie on either side of her, and once they had done so, the princess spoke these words:

· C D L X X V I ·

*H*OW THE PRINCESS SET HER SOUL IN ORDER AND PUBLICLY CONFESSED HER SINS

"Have no fear, my heart, of praising brave Tirant, whose sole flaw was that he lacked a drop of royal blood. I shall lay aside earthly vanities and do what I must, as my soul longs to leave my body and fly to his side, wherefore I beg you to summon my confessor [who was a Franciscan abbot of great learning and saintly life]."

When he had come, the princess said: "Father, I wish to confess before everyone, and since I had no shame in erring, I shall have none in repentance. Before God, the Holy Virgin, all the saints in Heaven, and you, my spiritual father, I, an unworthy sinner, affirm the tenets of our Catholic Church, in whose faith I shall live and die, abjuring anything contrary to it. I confess my sin in taking money from my father's treasury that Tirant might appear more generous than other lords and I beg my father to forgive me, deeming it part of my inheritance, just as I sincerely ask God for due penance and atonement. Furthermore, father, I sinned greatly in allowing Tirant to deflower me before our wedding, for which I ask Christ's forgiveness and due penance from you. Moreover, I confess that I neither loved nor served God as I should but squandered most of my time on vanities useless to my soul, and I also confess that I have disobeyed my parents. I beg Christ to forgive all other sins of word, thought, or deed that I cannot recall. Father, absolve me, for my contrition is sincere."

After asking her for a general declaration of faith, the confessor absolved her of all blame and penance, as a papal bull entitled the Emperors of Constantinople and their descendants to absolution on their deathbeds.

Once she had been absolved, the princess devoutly took Communion, while everyone marveled at her steadfast faith and many prayers, which would have moved even the steeliest heart to tears.

Having set her soul in order, she summoned the imperial secretary and told her father: "Sire, with your leave I shall now dispose of my goods [for she possessed the wealthy county of Benaixí and many valuable clothes and jewels]."

The emperor replied: "My daughter, do as you like, since if you die I shall lose my life and everything I cherish in this world."

The princess thanked him and turned to face the secretary, who then recorded her last will and testament:

· CDLXXVII ·

*T*HE PRINCESS'S WILL

Since all earthly things are transient and no mortal can escape his fate, the wise ensure that when their pilgrimage ends, they can account for themselves before their Maker. Therefore, I, Princess Carmesina of the Greek Empire, being mortally ill but in full possession of my faculties, make my last will and testament in my parents' presence and Jesus Christ's name.

My executors shall be Diaphebus of Macedonia and his wife, Stephanie, to whom I commend my soul. I ask them to bury me with Tirant, that, though parted in life, we may be joined in death until the end of eternity.

Furthermore, my county, clothes, and jewels shall be sold to pay my damsels' dowries according to each one's rank and condition. I empower my executors to make any other payments they deem beneficial to my soul, while all my remaining wealth and prerogatives shall accrue to the empress, whom I appoint my sole and perpetual heiress.

When the princess had disposed of her soul and earthly goods, she bade her parents farewell, kissing their hands and begging their forgiveness.

"Alas," she cried, "I fear my death will slay the emperor, who pulls me one way just as Tirant pulls me another!"

Her afflicted father saw she was at death's door and, beside himself with agony, he tried to rise and leave the room, but instead he fainted and fell to the floor. They carried him to his chamber and put him to bed, where he gave up the ghost before his daughter.

The cries and laments over his death were so loud that the empress heard them and hurried to his side, but she arrived too late. Think how wretched she must have felt, as her husband, daughter, and son-in-law were being snatched away, nor had such grief and anguish ever been seen in one day.

Upon learning of the emperor's death, Carmesina told his knights: "Help me sit up and heed my words, for being my father's appointed successor, I now order you by your oaths of fealty to fetch his body and Tirant's."

They were obliged to obey her, and as soon as they had returned, Carmesina ordered them to place the emperor on her right hand and Tirant on her left. She lay between them, kissing her father many times and Tirant still more often as she cried: "Woe is me, my love has changed to cruel distress! Oh Death: take up arms and slay me as I desire! Grief has driven me half mad and I would kill myself if fear did not restrain me, since on one side I see the emperor and on the other this peerless knight! Let death come when it will, but You, oh Lord, for whom all is possible: do as You did with Lazarus and thereby show Your might, awakening this man that I too may recover. Should You refuse and condemn me, the world will never forget that I died for love. Oh Jesus Christ, I feel my soul take flight and my legs and feet grow numb! Embrace me, oh sisters, and share my afflictions!"

The Queens of Ethiopia and Fez, Stephanie, the empress, and the others tearfully kissed Carmesina's lips as they bade her a sad farewell.

Then the princess begged their forgiveness and said: "I go to seek joy and comfort with the man I was to wed and who, had he lived, would have married a hundred of you with handsome dowries, but as Fortune has ordained otherwise, of what shall I complain: of love, of misfortune, or of my little hope? The water in my baptismal font was cursed, and my entire life has been unlucky, wherefore, unjust Fortune, do not stay your hand but let me behold Heaven's glory, where Tirant's resplendent soul awaits me."

Then she asked for the cross and devoutly prayed:

· CDLXXVIII ·

*T*HE PRINCESS'S PRAYER ON HER DEATHBED

"Oh Lord Jesus who perished on the true cross to redeem mankind from sin: I beg a drop of Your agony to atone for my failings. Lend me the grief and compassion to lament Your sufferings for my sake, while I thank and praise You for letting me die a Christian. I confess that I have erred, but I wish to mend my ways, firmly believing that no one can be saved except through Christ's passion. Lord, I place Christ's death between me and my sins and between You and Your judgment, throwing myself upon Your mercy and invoking Your holy clemency. I depart from this world in the name of the Father who created me in His image, the Son who died to free me, and the Holy Ghost who gives me grace. Oh angels and archangels, thrones and dominions, principalities and powers, holy patriarchs and prophets, apostles, martyrs, confessors, virgins, widows, celebates, and all the saints in Heaven: let me dwell in peace within God's glorious city.

"Oh Lord of Mercy who forgives the repentant sinner: pity Your fallen servant and hear her humble pleas! Cleanse what has been corrupted by vice and Satan's treachery, granting me redemption, Almighty Father whose mercy I implore. Deliver me, just as You delivered Noah from the flood and Elias and Enoch from Hell's eternal torments! Preserve my soul as you preserved Isaac from Abraham's knife, Lot from the destruction of Sodom and Gomorrah, and Moses from the pharoah! Shield me as you shielded Daniel in the lion's den; Shadrach, Meshach, and Abednego in the fiery furnace; Judith from Holofernes; Abraham from the Chaldeans; Job from his torments; David from Saul and the giant Goliath; Saint Peter and Saint Paul from prison; and Saint Thecla from her torturers! Welcome Your own creature, as it was You who fashioned me, and save me from the Prince of Darkness, dressing my soul in celestial garb! Let it drink from the fountain of life, be crowned among the holy martyrs, and behold Your splendor amid the cherubim and seraphim. Oh God of love and goodness, place my soul among Your saints!"

As she uttered these words, a host of radiant angels descended and bore her away with Tirant, who had been awaiting his beloved.

· CDLXXIX ·

*T*HE LAMENTATIONS OVER THE PRINCESS'S DEATH

Thus was the Greek imperial dynasty extinguished when after countless hardships the emperor thought to win repose, wherefore no man should trust worldly prosperity, as pride too often goes before a fall.

The laments over Carmesina's death echoed through the city, redoubling the people's grief at their monarch's demise, and the poor empress fell in a swoon from which her doctors could not rouse her. Afraid that she too was dead, Hippolytus beat his breast, but he stayed by his mistress, rubbing her temples and sprinkling rice water on her face till an hour later she recovered and they carried her to her bed.

Hippolytus kissed and comforted his lady, whom he reminded of his undiminished love, while the empress, for her part, cherished him more than herself or Carmesina.

Do not think Hippolytus was overly distressed, since as soon as Tirant died he realized that he would be emperor, and still more after His Majesty and Carmesina passed away. He was certain that the enamored empress would lay aside her shame and take him as her husband and son, for old ladies usually wish to marry their sons to repair and atone for the sins of their youth.

After they had talked awhile and Hippolytus's kisses had assuaged her grief, the empress said: "Son and lord, please arrange the funeral rites for my husband, daughter, and son-in-law, that afterward you and I may fulfill our desires."

Having heard these amorous words, Hippolytus kissed her lips and swore to obey her. Then he went to the princess's chamber, where the three corpses lay, and had Tirant's body carried to its bier in the cathedral. He also summoned surgeons to embalm Carmesina and the emperor, who was to recline upon a much higher and more splendid bier in the Hagia Sophia. It was hung with cloth of gold, as such a noble monarch deserved, while the angelic princess lay on Tirant's right.

Hippolytus dispatched criers to direct the mourners to a certain house, where sackcloth would be distributed to the court and foreigners, who within a day were all dressed in black. The knight also invited every nearby priest, monk, and nun, twelve hundred of whom came to the funeral in Constantinople.

Having decided to hold the last rites two weeks after the emperor's death, Hippolytus summoned His Majesty's barons from the field or their estates and sent a messenger to invite King Escariano, on his and the empress's behalf, to honor Tirant and Carmesina at their solemn obsequies. King Escariano replied that he would gladly do so, though he had hoped to enter Constantinople in a more joyous fashion, and after telling his captains to await him in Adrianople, he and a few servants set out for the capital.

· CDLXXX ·

HOW TIRANT'S COMPANIONS HELD COUNCIL TO CHOOSE A NEW EMPEROR

Hippolytus then called the Kings of Sicily and Fez, the Duke of Macedonia, the Marquis of Liçana, the Viscount of Branches, and Tirant's other friends and relatives to council. When they had gathered, he said: "My lords, you are not unaware of the harm done by Tirant's death, for he would have become emperor and given us titles and rich estates. Now that we have lost him, we must determine what to do about the empress who, though old, will be wooed by many foreign monarchs. When she dies her husband may very well abuse us, wherefore I think we should choose one of our company to reward his fellows, and I ask for your opinions on this weighty matter."

Once King Philip had risen and praised Hippolytus's words, the King of Fez, who was Tirant's oldest relative, said: "Lords and brothers, let us first read Tirant's and the princess's wills."

Having approved his suggestion, they summoned Tirant's and the emperor's secretaries, who read the wills and then were dismissed by the knights, to whom Diaphebus said: "My lords, our choice is clear, since Tirant transferred all his prerogatives to Hippolytus, and moreover, I see that Carmesina made the empress her successor. Knowing that Hippolytus and Her Majesty are old friends, we can do but one thing: marry them and make our comrade emperor, whereby we shall both do justice and confirm our new titles."

The Marquis of Liçana said: "My lords, I think the duke's advice is good, as we already have wives and such was Tirant's desire."

The others agreed, and so they unanimously elected Hippolytus, who swore to reward them in such fashion that they would be well satisfied, and whose wedding they resolved to celebrate soon after the funeral.

· CDLXXXI ·

*H*OW KING ESCARIANO REACHED CONSTANTINOPLE AND PAID HIS RESPECTS TO THE EMPRESS

That evening King Escariano arrived at the palace, where Queen Emeraldine and Hippolytus showed him to his lodgings. The Kings of Fez and Sicily, Diaphebus, and many other barons visited their friend, who after talking with them awhile went to pay homage to the empress.

Upon beholding Her Majesty, King Escariano bowed deeply, while she took his hand and bade him sit down beside her. Then King Escariano said: "Your glorious fame, lady empress, constrains me to honor you, both for your great merits and for love of Tirant. At his request I left my lands, and my queen accompanied me to attend his wedding, but now that he and his princess have passed away, I hope to serve you in their stead."

When King Escariano had finished, the empress softly replied: "I am comforted by your generous words, which I shall always remember. Our Lord, you, and Tirant have restored our empire, but it was dearly bought with the three noblest souls on earth, wherefore I cannot rejoice, having lost what I most cherish, and I shall be forced to spend the rest of my life in mourning."

The empress was so overwhelmed that she burst into tears, and to keep her company King Escariano also began to cry. After they had wept awhile, he spoke of more pleasant matters that they discussed late into the night, and by the time they went to bed she felt much better.

Hippolytus spent that night with the empress, telling her what he and his companions had decided: "They want me to marry you, and though I am unworthy to be your servant, I hope you will accept me as your humble slave. Trust your Hippolytus, whose sole desire is to obey you."

The empress replied: "My son, you know how much I long to be your wife, and though I am old, you will never find another so devoted. I swear to make you rich and honored, for your gentility is my only joy."

Hippolytus tried to kiss her hands and feet, but the empress refused and instead embraced him tightly, whereupon they spent a pleasant night together, heedless of those who lay in state.

Before Phoebus's rays illuminated the earth, Hippolytus rose in excellent spirits and went to welcome the Greek barons, who found the city lit by countless candles and torches. Many noblemen enhanced the emperor's funeral, while all the commoners lamented their noble lords' passing and the priests and monks chanted so dolefully that the cruelest heart would have been moved to tears. Carmesina's last rites were held on the morrow, and Tirant's the day after, with comparable pomp and glorious ceremony.

Everyone mourned so much in those three days that a year passed before they wished to weep again, and once the funerals had ended, they placed the emperor in a beautiful jasper tomb inlaid with gold and azurite and inscribed with his arms. He had ordered it long before, in anticipation of his demise. Tirant and Carmesina were placed in a large wooden coffin, that their bodies might be taken to Brittany.

When all this had been done, King Philip, Lord Agramunt, and Diaphebus went to see King Escariano. They told him about their council and Hippolytus's election, to which King Escariano replied: "I am delighted at your wise decision, as he is a worthy knight who deserves to rule the empire."

The black and his comrades then set out to visit the empress, and all together they were the noblest emissaries who ever called upon man or woman. After welcoming them with abundant honor and taking King Escariano and King Philip by the hands, she sat down between them on the imperial dais, while Tirant's brother-in-arms began to speak thus:

· CDLXXXII ·

*H*OW TIRANT'S COMPANIONS ASKED THE EMPRESS TO WED HIPPOLYTUS

"Our knowledge of your kindness, noble lady, emboldens us to ask a favor, for to alleviate your distress and soothe your afflicted spirit, I and my companions thought you might wish to reign in company. The affairs of state would not then weigh so heavily upon you, and since we treasure your honor and virtuous majesty, we offer you a knight so brave that your soul will be comforted and your person venerated. Therefore, I beg you to take no offense at my words but to remember that your empire's prosperity is due to Tirant lo Blanc, who willed his prerogatives to our comrade Hippolytus. As you lack the strength to keep your barons in check or defend them from the infidels who encircle your realms, we ask and advise you to marry this knight, who loves and reveres Your Majesty above all others. He is experienced and valiant enough to rule this empire, and we trust that you will reply with wisdom and gentility."

Upon hearing King Escariano's words, the delighted empress replied:

· CDLXXXIII ·

*T*HE EMPRESS'S REPLY

"I can scarcely reply, magnanimous lords, to an offer as difficult to accept as to reject, and my heart is buffeted by tempestuous winds, for if your request is just, I shall be forced to consent, but if you look well, you will see I have ample cause for refusal. Being too old to bear children, I do not wish to remarry, wherefore I beg you to excuse me lest I set a bad example."

The King of Fez boldly replied: "Most excellent lady, I hope you and these lords will forgive me, but I cannot bear to hear you speak against your heart, honor, and fame. Though Providence has made you mistress of the Greek Empire, you can neither rule nor defend it, and thus I again beseech you to heed our counsel. We offer a champion who will protect your lands, whose inhabitants will rejoice when they learn that he was Tirant's companion."

With mingled shame and sweetness, the empress replied: "Beloved lords, I trust that you would never betray my honor, and henceforth I shall freely place myself in your hands."

They bowed, thanked her, and hastened to Hippolytus's chamber, where they joyously told him what his mistress had said.

The knight knelt and thanked them, feeling himself the luckiest of mortals, whereupon they escorted him to his lady's rooms and summoned a bishop, who betrothed the couple before all the imperial ladies. Everyone was much solaced, since they were weary of mourning and had feared it might last for many months or years.

As news spread through the city, the commoners also rejoiced and thanked God, for they loved Hippolytus and remembered how well he had defended them during the siege.

On the morrow, Hippolytus and the empress donned their finest robes, while the ladies prepared to celebrate with their mistress. The palace was adorned with more gold and silk hangings than had ever been seen before.

To ennoble the wedding feast, Hippolytus ordered Lord Agramunt, the Marquis of Liçana, the Viscount of Branches (who was engaged to one of the widow Montsanto's daughters), and many other betrothed knights and barons to be married with him. There were twenty-five couples in all, but to avoid prolixity the book does not list them.

When everyone had dressed, Hippolytus led the way, followed by the empress, who was escorted by King Escariano and King Philip, and the other brides accompanied by many dukes, counts, and marquises. Their procession slowly made its way to the cathedral, where Hippolytus was crowned emperor after swearing to defend the Holy Mother Church. Once the imperial vassals had sworn fealty to him, he and the empress were wed, as were all the other couples in order of rank.

After hearing Mass, they returned to the palace in the same order, accompanied by a multitude of trumpets, clarions, bugles, tambourins, flageolets, and other instruments. The abundance of their wedding feast would tax one's powers of description, as would the graceful dances that followed it, but an idea can be formed from the station of those present. The celebrations lasted two weeks, and every day there were dances, jousts, tournaments, and other festivities to help people forget their past woes.

Once the celebrations had ended, King Escariano and his queen set out with a splendid escort, as the emperor, the kings, and many knights accompanied them for a league.

King Escariano then marshaled his troops and returned to Ethiopia, where he was joyously welcomed by his vassals and subjects.

· CDLXXXIV ·

*H*OW THE NEW EMPEROR SUMMONED TIRANT'S SOLDIERS, PAID THEM GENEROUSLY, AND BADE THEM FAREWELL

When Hippolytus had returned to Constantinople, he summoned Tirant's soldiers, whom he rewarded most generously, bestowing gifts upon many, and likewise he paid Tirant's servants in accord with their master's will.

Once this had been done, King Philip said: "Sire, I have no further business here, and with your leave I shall depart."

The emperor replied: "Lord and brother, I thank you for your good will and services. We shall be forever in your debt, nor should you hesitate to request our aid."

After giving him many gifts and jewels for his queen, Hippolytus paid Philip's knights so well that they declared him the most generous lord on earth. The Marquis of Liçana then went to ready thirty ships for the king's departure, and within two days they were all armed and provisioned.

King Philip gathered his knights but left many of his horses behind, and, bidding one and all farewell, he set sail for Sicily.

· CDLXXXV ·

*H*OW THE EMPEROR SENT TIRANT'S AND THE PRINCESS'S BODIES TO BRITTANY

Once King Philip had left, the emperor asked the King of Fez and the Viscount of Branches to take Tirant's and Carmesina's remains to Brittany. They said they would gladly obey for love of their dead captain, and Hippolytus had the admiral prepare forty galleys to escort them.

The emperor then ordered the wooden coffin covered with delicately enameled gold plates, while Tirant and the princess were attired in robes of gold brocade that would never rot.

The coffin was taken aboard one of the galleys, along with Tirant's banners and tunics, which would be placed above his tomb. Hippolytus also gave the King of Fez two hundred thousand ducats for our knight's last rites in Brittany.

As soon as everything was in order, the King of Fez, his queen, and the

Viscount of Branches bade everyone farewell and set sail for Tirant's homeland.

They docked at the city of Nantes, where, after the Duke and Duchess of Brittany had welcomed them, the lovers' coffin was brought to the cathedral by a procession of priests, monks, and nuns, who placed it in a tomb supported by four lions. It was made of white alabaster, with an inscription carved in gold Greek letters:

> *This knight who in arms was a phoenix*
> *and the lady whose beauty was peerless*
> *lie together in this little tomb.*
> *The world resounds with their immortal fame:*
> *Tirant lo Blanc and noble Carmesina.*

The lions and tomb, which were cunningly inlaid with gold, azurite, and colored enamel, were flanked by four angels: two on the right holding Tirant's arms and two on the left bearing the princess's escutcheon. The tomb stood in a vaulted chapel whose porphyry arches rested upon jasper columns and whose keystone, of solid gold inlaid with precious gems, showed an angel holding Tirant's sword stained by the blood of many battles. The chapel floor was marble, the walls were adorned with scarlet brocade, and only the lovers' tomb was uncovered. Outside, one could behold the shields of those Tirant had bested in single combat, while above his triumphal arch, panels depicted some of his wondrous victories. His armor and trappings hung nearby, along with his garter embroidered with many pearls, sapphires, and balases. Flags and banners of many vanquished cities and provinces also hung from the cathedral vault, beside Tirant's and the virtuous princess's devices: gold tongues of fire on a scarlet field, and scarlet flames upon gold. In the gold flames were the letters C.C.C. and in the scarlet ones T.T.T., signifying that Tirant's love was purified by Carmesina's flames, just as the princess ardently mingled with Tirant's devotion.

These lines were sculpted in gold above their tomb:

> *May love, which joined them together in life,*
> *and tragically parted them from this wretched world,*
> *reunite them again in their noble sepulcher.*[3]

· CDLXXXVI ·

*H*OW TIRANT'S BODY WAS HONORED IN BRITTANY

Mere words could not describe Tirant's funeral rites, at which the duke, the duchess, and his relatives mourned him, for they knew of his immortal deeds and the high rank he had won. His parents had passed away during his absence.

The King of Fez spent the two hundred thousand ducats well and rejoiced to see his family, but after six months in Brittany, he decided to depart.

He, his queen, and the Viscount of Branches then bade the Bretons farewell and set sail for Morocco.

Our Lord gave them such good weather that they soon reached Tangier, where the monarchs and their retinue disembarked while the Viscount of Branches went on to visit Hippolytus, who welcomed him with great joy upon his return to Constantinople.

The viscount told him they had carried out all his orders, and the emperor, who had purchased the princess's county of Benaixí for three hundred thousand ducats, bestowed it upon him in reward for his services. Then he gave those who had married the princess's and the empress's damsels fine estates where they might dwell in honor. They were all most grateful, and Hippolytus gradually arranged marriages for his remaining knights.

· CDLXXXVII ·

*H*OW, AFTER FREEING THE SULTAN AND GRAND TURK, THE EMPEROR BECAME THEIR ALLY

Fortune so favored Hippolytus and he was such a brave knight that he conquered many provinces, amassed a great fortune, and was both loved and feared by his subjects and neighbors.

Within a few days of his coronation he freed the sultan, the Grand Turk, and his other Saracen hostages, with whom he made peace for one hundred and one years, showing them such honor that many became his allies. Then the emperor gave them two galleys and let them sail for home.

Hippolytus lived to a ripe old age but the empress died within three years of their marriage, and shortly after her death, he married an English princess who was fair, chaste, humble, and devout. The good lady bore him two daughters and three sons, who grew up to be brave and worthy knights. The eldest, named Hippolytus after his father, performed many valiant deeds that the book does not recount but leaves to the histories written about him. Before dying, his father endowed all his relatives and servants with rich estates.

The emperor and empress, who both passed away in their old age, were laid to rest in a splendid tomb he had ordered, and you may be certain that after their virtuous reign, they both went straight to Heaven.

Deo Gratias

Thus ends the story of that valiant and spirited knight Tirant lo Blanc, Prince and Caesar of Constantinople. This book was translated from English into Portuguese, and thence into Valencian vernacular, by the brave and magnificent knight Sir Joanot Martorell. Owing to his untimely death, he was unable to complete his task, the last quarter of which was finished, at the request of that noble lady Dona Isabel de Lloris, by the magnificent knight Sir Martí Joan de Galba. Should any faults be found herein, he hopes they will be attributed to his ignorance and prays Our Lord Jesus Christ, in His infinite goodness, to reward him for his labors with the glory of Paradise. Likewise, if anything uncatholic should be discovered in this book, he rues the day he wrote it and submits to the Church's correction.

PUBLISHED IN THE CITY OF VALENCIA,
NOVEMBER 20, 1490 A.D.

· Notes ·

Translator's Foreword

1. Miguél de Cervantes Saavedra, *Don Quijote de la Mancha,* pt. 1, ch. 6. All translations into English are mine.

2. "Carta de batalla por *Tirant lo Blanc,*" *Revista de Occidente* 70 (1969):2, 3.

3. For a fuller account of modern Catalan history, see David H. Rosenthal, "New Day for Catalonia," *Inquiry* 1:12 (May 1, 1978):13–17 and the introduction to the same author's *Modern Catalan Poetry: An Anthology* (St. Paul: New Rivers Press, 1979).

4. The novel has been translated into Italian (1538), French (1737?), and twice into Castilian (1511 and 1969). Only the Castilian translations are currently in print.

5. The most coherent theory of exactly which author wrote what is Joan Coromines's "Sobre l'estil i manera de Martí Joan de Galba i els de Joanot Martorell" in *Lleures i converses d'un filòleg* (Barcelona: El Pi de Tres Branques, 1971), 363–378.

6. Joanot Martorell and Martí Joan de Galba, *Tirant lo Blanc,* introd. Martí de Riquer (Esplugues de Llobregat: Ariel, 1979), 7. The originals of all citations from *Tirant* and from Martorell's correspondence can be found in this edition (page numbers are indicated parenthetically). Unless otherwise noted, I follow Riquer's account of Martorell's life and *Tirant*'s sources.

7. See Justina Ruiz de Conde, *El amor y el matrimonio secreto en los libros de caballerías* (Madrid: Aguilar, 1948). Chapter 3 (101–170) is entirely devoted to *Tirant.*

8. Document first reprinted by Jordi Rubió Balaguer in the "Literatura Catalana" section of *Historia general de las literaturas hispánicas* (Barcelona: Vergara, 1953), 3:860 and cited by Riquer in *Història de la literatura catalana* (Esplugues de Llobregat: Ariel, 1964), 2:648.

9. The work can now be read in Pere Bohigas's *Tractats de cavalleria* (Barcelona: Barcino, 1947), 43–77 and in the above-mentioned edition of *Tirant,* 1235–1251.

10. Included in *Obres essencials* (Barcelona: Selecta, 1957), 1:515–545.

11. *Le rommant de Guy de Warwik et de Herolt d'Ardenne,* ed. D. J. Conlon (Chapel Hill: University of North Carolina, 1971) and *Guy de Warewic,* ed. Alfred Ewart (Paris: E. Champion, 1933).

12. Much of my information on Martorell's England and English sources is taken from William J. Entwistle's "Observacions sobre la dedicatòria i primera part del *Tirant lo Blanch,*" trans. Jordi Rubió Balaguer, *Revista de Catalunya* 7 (1927):381–398 and "*Tirant lo Blanch* and the Social Order at the End of the 15th Century," *Estudis Romànics* 2 (1949–1950):149–164.

13. Bohigas, *Tractats* 43.

14. Entwistle, "Observacions" 394.

15. The poem, entitled "Romanç de la armada del Soldà contra Rodes, fet per Francesc Ferrer," is reprinted with notes and commentary by Lluís Nicolau d'Olwer in "Un témoignage catalan du siège de Rhodes en 1444," *Estudis Universitaris Catalans* 12 (1927):376–387.

16. The connection between Tirant and Thoisy was first proposed in one of the major contributions to scholarship on *Tirant*: Constantin Marinesco's "Du nouveau sur *Tirant lo Blanch,*" *Estudis Romànics* 4 (1953–1954):137–203.

17. Cited in Marinesco, "Du nouveau" 160.

18. Hunyadi was first indicated as a model by Marinesco, "Du nouveau" 164–177.

19. Ronald Cohen, *The Kanuri of Bornu* (New York: Holt, Rinehart and Winston, 1967), 16.

20. This information first appears in Marinesco, "Du nouveau" 189–193.

21. *Orígenes de la novela* (Madrid: Consejo Superior de Investigaciones Científicas, 1954), 400.

Dedication

1. This dedication, which at one time provoked heated debates among scholars as to what light it might shed on *Tirant,* was shown by Martí de Riquer to have been largely plagiarized from the dedication to Don Enrique de Villena's *Los doce trabajos de Hércules* (Burgos, 1499), a work that Villena translated from his own original Catalan version. The only known copy of this version, which was dedicated to the Valencian knight Pero Pardo, remains in the possession of a bibliophile who refuses to permit its publication (see Riquer, *Nuevas contribuciones a las fuentes de* Tirant lo Blanch [Barcelona: Biblioteca Central, 1949], 8–10).

2. "Valencian vernacular" here refers to what modern linguists would call the Valencian dialect of Catalan.

Prologue

1. Possibly: "Quam multas nobis imagines, non solum ad intuendum, verum etiam ad imitandum, fortissimorum virorum expressas scriptores et graeci et latini reliquerunt?" (Pro Archia 6).

2. "When a strong man armed keepeth his palace, his goods are in peace" (Luke 11:21). Unless otherwise noted, all scriptural references are to the King James Version of the Bible or (in the case of the Apocrypha) to *The Oxford Annotated Bible with the Apocrypha* (New York: Oxford University Press, 1965).

William of Warwick

1. In the original *Guy of Warwick,* the invaders of England are Danes. In Martorell's first draft (*William of Warwick*) they become Moors under the Kings of Tangier and Gibraltar. They remain Moors in *Tirant* but are led by the King of Canary. It should be noted that in the early Middle Ages (except on the Iberian Peninsula, naturally), there was considerable confusion in Western Europe between pagans in general and Saracens.

2. Or possibly Killingworth, according to William J. Entwistle's hypothesis in "Observacions" 389–390. The castle is called "Alimburg" in *Tirant.*

3. The historical Richard de Beauchamp, Earl of Warwick, accepted the surrender of Rouen in 1419 and in 1430 presided over the court that sentenced Joan of Arc to death (see Joseph A. Vaeth, *Tirant lo Blanch* [New York: Columbia University Press, 1918], 133–139).

4. According to Entwistle (395), this is probably "Çalla bem Çalla," a Moorish defender of Ceuta often mentioned in Gomes Eanes de Zurara's Portuguese chronicles.

5. The author here is probably thinking of the wedding of Henry VI of England and Margaret of Anjou, celebrated in Tours in May 1444, and the celebrations at the queen's coronation, followed by a three-day tournament, in Westminster in May 1445 (see Riquer, *Tirante el Blanco* [Madrid: Espasa-Calpe, 1974], 1:96 and Entwistle 394).

Tirant and the Hermit

1. This "Tiranian March" is an invention of Martorell's.

2. As has been mentioned in the Foreword (ix), this chapter and the following ones are based upon Ramon Llull's *Libre de l'orde de cavalleria* and not Honoré Bouvet's *Arbre des batailles.*

3. This story would seem to provide indirect evidence that Martorell never revised *Tirant,* since we see here an alternate version of the deliverance of Constantinople that is never mentioned in the later "Tirant Succors the Greek Empire" episodes.

4. Ps. 109, which begins: "Hold not thy peace, O God of my praise . . ."

5. An Albanian chieftain who held off the Ottomans until his death in 1468.

The Festivities in England

1. This mention of prostitutes and pimps, as well as the quarrel between the guilds in the preceding chapter, offer the first signs of broad humor and sexuality in *Tirant.* The manner in which these qualities creep into the book as it progresses suggests that Martorell's style and literary personality evolved as he went along, without any final attempt to unify his novel's tone.

2. This meant that the knights who chose "real arms" (or "arms of war") would also be required to have jousting points on their lances. These points were often preferred in tournaments because they were more likely to fell opponents than to kill or seriously wound them.

3. Elaborate artifices of this type, as well as food for one and all, were not uncommon in late medieval celebrations. Some examples Martorell might have had in mind were the festivities at Lille (1454), the coronation of Martin I of Aragon in Saragossa (1399), or Henry VI's triumphant entry into London in 1432.

4. This comment refers to a late Greek legend (recounted in Statius's *Achilleid*) in which Thetis, learning from an oracle that her son Achilles would die in the Trojan War, made him dress as a woman and live among King Lycomedes's maidens.

Tirant's Exploits in England

1. Tirant fears that private duels might be forbidden outside the official jousts overseen by the King of England.

2. There is abundant evidence of duels such as this one in the Middle Ages, with

minimal protection and weapons devised to ensure a speedy outcome (for assorted examples, see Riquer, *Cavalleria fra realtà e letteratura nel Quattrocento* [Bari: Adriatica Editrice, 1970], 251–258).

3. Such battles between knights and animals were common in chivalric literature (e.g., the lion in Chrétien de Troyes's *Yvain* or the "beste glatissant" in the prose version of *Tristan*) and should not be taken as an example of Martorell's humor (see Sylvia Roubaud, "Chevalier contre chien: l'étrange duel du Tirant lo Blanc," *Mélanges de la Casa de Velásquez* 6 [1970]:131–160).

4. See note 2, "The Festivities in England."

5. Kyrieleison of Muntalbà's humorous name (which later attracted Cervantes's notice) was probably intended to satirize Don Gonçalbo de Híjar, Lord of Montalbán, to whom Martorell sent various abusive cartels of defiance between April 1446 and April 1450.

6. This was a common procedure in fifteenth-century cartels of defiance. The authenticity of the document was proven by the signature, a seal with the knight's arms, and the capital letters ABC, along which the sheet containing the letter in duplicate was torn in half, thus "proving" that the copy sent was identical to that retained by the challenger.

The Order of the Garter

1. Polydore Vergili, in his *Anglicae historiae* (Basil, 1534), does not name this woman, but English tradition identifies her as Katherine Montacute, Countess of Salisbury, or "the Fair Maid of Kent." Martorell's reason for naming her "Honeysuckle" ("Madresilva" in the original) is unknown.

2. As is well known, the standard traditional form is "Honi soit . . ."

3. Tirant's inclusion in the Order of the Garter has a historical parallel in the election of the Spanish knight-errant Francis de Suriene, called "l'Arragonoiz," in 1447 (see Albert Van de Put, *Hispano-Moresque Ware of the Fifteenth Century* [London: The Art Worker's Quarterly, 1911], 88).

Tirant in Sicily and Rhodes

1. A reference to the Valencian pope Calixtus III's efforts to have his nephew Rodrigo Borgia inherit the kingdom of Naples after Alphonse the Magnanimous's death in 1458. See Marinesco, "Du nouveau" 179–181.

2. This legend can be found in various French texts, e.g., Olivier de la Marche's fifteenth-century *Mémoires* (introd. xiv): "Auquel Clovis monstra Dieu par moult de fois qu'il le voulait appeller en son service, comme de luy envoyer les trois fleurs de lys."

3. The word for "inn" here is "alfóndec," defined in Antoni Alcover's and Francesc de B. Moll's *Diccionari català-valencià-balear,* 2nd ed. (Palma de Majorca: n.p., 1975–1977) as a building in many commercial towns where outside merchants could find inns, storerooms, and stalls for their transactions. A clause from a 1403 treaty is then cited: "xvii, Item, que los catalans e cicilians e los sotmesos dels dits Reys de Sicilia e de Arago hagen en Tunis e en les altres terres del dit Rey de Tunis alfondech per lur habitació, ab botigues, forns, e totes jurisdiccions e sgleya; e que alcuna persona stranya no hi puxa star o habitar sino ab volentat de aquells catalans o sicilians."

4. For the sources of the philosopher's story, see Foreword, xi herein and Riquer, *Nuevas contribuciones*, 21–27.

5. Matt. 7:19.

Expedition with the King of France

1. "Dry Mass," celebrated on ships, was unconsecrated lest the vessel's rocking spill the wine.

Tirant in the Greek Empire

1. This same emperor, also called "Frederic" in ch. 146, is later called "Henry" in ch. 186, perhaps in reference to the Latin Emperor Henry I (1205–1218). The sultan referred to a few lines below is the Mameluke Sultan of Egypt (later also called the "Sultan of Babylon," this being one of the titles habitually used by Mameluke rulers).

2. This is a pun (repeated in the following chapter) on "d'amar" ("from loving") and "de mar" ("from the sea"), pronounced similarly in the eastern dialect of Catalan spoken around Barcelona, though not, interestingly enough, in the western dialect spoken around Valencia.

3. An allusion to Aristotle's definition of friendship as a kind of attraction between like spirits in *Nicomachean Ethics* 8.1.1155a.

4. An untranslatable pun, in the original "Una val mil e mill no valen una." "Mil" is "a thousand" and "mill" is "millet."

5. This description of the princess is very close to that of Helen of Troy in Jacme Conesa's Catalan translation (1374) of Guido delle Colonne's *Historia destructionis Troiae* (in Catalan *Les històries troyanes de Guiu de Columpnes*, ed. Ramon Miquel y Planas [Barcelona: Biblioteca Catalana, 1916], 101).

6. After her brother's death and her sister's marriage, the princess is now the heiress apparent to the imperial throne, whereas "infanta" refers to any daughter of a monarch except the firstborn.

7. This story about the isle of Tenedos is taken from Ramon Muntaner, who in his fourteenth-century Catalan *Crònica* (ch. 214) states that on the island: "havia una ídola, e venien-hi un mes de l'any tots los honrats hòmens de Romania, e honrades dones, a romeria."

8. This legend comes from the apocryphal Pseudo Matthaei 23 (my translation): "And it came to pass that when the most blessed Mary went into the temple with the little child, all the idols prostrated themselves upon the floor."

9. In the word *cadenat* ("padlock"), the first letter is Carmesina's initial and the last is Tirant's.

10. This legend about Constantine the Great appears in various places, among them Brunetto Latini's *Li livres dou tresor* 1.87.

11. This is the knight Fonseca (Fontseca in Catalan), whom Cervantes mentions in his praise of *Tirant,* but who appears only once in the novel, leading one to suppose that Cervantes opened it at random in search of another name and happened upon this one.

12. Many of the Italian knights listed here were Alphonse the Magnanimous's allies in the struggle to impose his son Ferrante as King of Naples, whereas those mentioned as

serving the Muslims favored the house of Anjou against the Aragonese pretender. See Marinesco, "Nuevas notas sobre *Tirant lo Blanch*," *Boletín de la Real Academia de Buenas Letras de Barcelona* 28 (1959–1960):363.

13. It was a medieval custom to eat from the plate of a person one wished to honor. See Rubió Balaguer, *Vida española en la época gótica* (Barcelona: Alberto Martín, 1943), 241.

14. The reference here is to a medieval torture.

15. In MS. 7811 (fol. 262v.) at the Spanish Biblioteca Nacional in Madrid, which contains Joanot Martorell's cartels of defiance and a number of other texts related to our novel, there is a letter from the Mameluke sultan to King John of Cyprus which is, as Samuel Gili Gaya noted (in "Noves recerques sobre *Tirant lo Blanch*," *Estudis Romànics* 1 [1947–1948]:138, 139), the model for this letter. It begins: "Jacomach, per la permisió de Déu omnipotent gran soldà de Babilònia, senyor de dos temples, ço és a saber, del Sant Temple de Salamó de la ciutat de Jerusalem e del Sant Temple de Mecha, senyor e deffenedor de tot lo poble morisch qui és e habita sots lo cel celestial, mentenedor e deffenedor de la sancta fe e de la sancta doctrina del nostre sanct propheta Mahomet, la qual fe aquells que la tenen en llur fi dóna consolació e glòria sens fi . . ."

16. "To turn a white face to someone" is an Arabic expression, meaning "to behave honestly, benignly," which also appears in the copied letter.

17. This "citation" reappears in ch. 357 of *Tirant*, though in the latter case a knight's wife is added to his riches, honor, and life.

18. Lake Trasimene (or Trasimeno) in central Italy, the setting for one of Hannibal's greatest victories, appears here transformed into a river in Asia Minor.

19. See note 12, "Tirant in the Greek Empire."

20. Hippolytus, here presented as a Greek, will later be declared French (ch. 234), then of Tirant's Saltrock lineage (ch. 238), and finally Tirant, in his testament, will call him his nephew (ch. 469).

21. The terms "Turks" and "Saracens" (often "Moors" in the original, "Moor" being a generic term for Muslims in Iberian languages), are used interchangeably throughout the novel.

22. See note 4, "Tirant and the Hermit."

23. The rest of this chapter is copied, with minor variations and corruptions, from a Catalan translation of a Latin epistle Petrarch sent Niccolò Acciauoli, which appears in *Familiarum rerum* 12.2. The translation may be found in the same MS. 7811 (fols. 75r.–82r.) in the Spanish Biblioteca Nacional that includes the sultan's letter cited in ch. 135 of *Tirant*, the first draft of *William of Warwick*, and Martorell's cartels of defiance.

24. Cicero places these words in the mouth of Manius Curius (*De senectute* 16.56).

25. Sallust *De bello Iugurthino* 10.4.

26. Seneca *Ad Lucilium* 3.3.

27. Cicero *De amicitia* 21.76.

28. The words of Domitianus, according to Suetonius in *Domitianus* 9.

29. This anecdote can be found in the chapter entitled "Quomodo medicus Alexandri potionem sibi dedit ex qua statim convaluit Alexander" in *Historia Alexandri Magni regis Macedonia de preliis* (Argentine [Strasbourg], 1494), fol. B5.

30. Suetonius *Augustus* 51.

31. Seneca *Thyestes* 612.

32. *Ab urbe condita* 28.27.7.

33. Virgil *Aeneid* 6.853.

34. Virgil *Eclogae* 10.69.

35. *Somnium Scipionis* 9.29.

36. Another contradiction involving Hippolytus, whom Tirant knighted in ch. 140.

37. Possibly a locality mentioned in medieval letters as being on the Bosporus (see Marinesco "Du nouveau" 186).

38. This curious "albarà" ("vow") imitates a document common among fifteenth-century Valencian knights preparing to fight a secret duel, who would specify the conditions of the encounter, its few witnesses, and the dishonor those denying the bout's validity would incur. Marriage vows of this sort, however, may have also been relatively common, since the poet Joan Berenguer de Masdovelles (mid-fifteenth century) refers in one of his poems to an "albarán" written by his lady the day he won her (see Riquer, *Cavalleria* 310).

39. Promulgated in 18 B.C.

40. This paragraph was standard in chivalric vows.

41. The princess, therefore, was fourteen too, since in ch. 119 we are told that the two damsels were the same age.

42. John 20:29.

43. "Grand Karaman" ("Gran Carmany" in the original) was one of the titles given to the Emirs of Karaman (or Karamania) in Anatolia. One of them, Ibrahim Beg (1421–1455), formed an alliance with the Pope, Venice, and Aragon against the Ottomans. Jaume Vilargut, Martorell's friend, had been imprisoned by the Grand Karaman and therefore could inform our author about him (see Foreword, xi).

44. Originally, a couple in 11 of Ovid's *Heroides*. Macareus, however, was the brother and Canace the sister.

45. This speech, up to "hold my tongue," copies a cartel of defiance sent by Joanot de la Serra to Bernat de Vilarig (both Valencian knights) contained in MS. 7811 at the Biblioteca Nacional in Madrid (fol. 350 r.). Since the letter is dated December 30, 1452, and Riquer has demonstrated that it was copied by Martorell and not vice versa (*Tirante* 3: 334), these episodes in *Tirant* must date from 1453 at the earliest.

46. First reference to "the book," perhaps indicating Galba's intervention (see Riquer's introd. to *Tirant lo Blanc* [Barcelona: Selecta, 1947], 144–149).

47. Ps. 90:4.

48. This female army is reminiscent of the "ladies' tournaments," literary pieces in which the ladies of some country, region, or court were celebrated in military terms (e.g., the Occitan troubadour lyrics "Carros" by Raimbaut de Vaqueiras and "Treva" by Guilhem de Tor). The origin lies in courtly mimes (in this regard, Riquer cites Andrea Pulega, *Ludi e spettacoli nel Medioevo: i tornei di dame* [Milan, 1970]).

49. This is the first time Pyramus's and Richard's deaths are mentioned.

50. A name possibly suggested by the Albanian nobleman Simon Atisfieri or Altafoglia, who was a relative of Scanderbeg's.

51. On the last day of the celebrations at Charles the Bold's and Margaret of York's wedding in 1474, we read that: "sur la fin du disner se levèrent roys d'armes et heraulx . . . et vindrent crier devant la personne de monseigneur le duc: 'Largesse!' comme il est de coustume" (La Marche 2.4).

52. See the fabliau "Des trois meschines": "Quar, si le sanc ert el talon, / Sel feroit ele amont venir, / Et le vis vermeil devenir;" (eds. Anatole de Montaiglon and Gaston Raynaud, *Recueil général et complet des fabliaux* [Paris: Librairie des Bibliophiles, 1878], 3:77).

53. This naval strategem is also described by Francesc Eiximenis: "E de fet de mar havem vist sovint que trenta galees ne prenien cent per esta manera, car les trenta venien en descuyt e havien ab si qualsque cent laüts detràs, portants falles enceses soptosament, axí que apparia un infinit stol; e per esta via les trenta galees, firent vigorosament, tolien lo cor e·l poder als contraris, e·ls vencien" (*Dotzè del Chrestià* or *Regiment de prínceps e de comunitats* [Valencia, 1484] ch. 230).

54. This list of great men fooled by women refers to a number of popular medieval legends. For Virgil and the pannier, see Domenico Pietro Antonio Comparetti's *Virgilio nel Medio Evo* (Florence: La Nuova Italia, 1896), 1:111. Another legend asserts that Aristotle fell in love with a damsel who later saddled and rode him (see Joachim Storost's "Femme chavalchant Aristotle" in *Zeitschrift für französische Sprache und Literatur* 66 (1956):186–201. In regard to Hippocrates, the famous doctor, it was believed that his own wife had killed him (see Ferdinand Lot, *Etudes sur le Lancelot en prose* [Paris: E. Champion, 1918], 208).

55. Prov. 30:18–20. The lines that follow are by Guillem de Cervera (also known as Cerverí de Girona, fl. 1250–1280), whose Rhymed Proverbs 423 and 424 constitute a gloss on the Biblical passage. See also Lluís Nicolau d'Olwer, "Sobre les fonts catalanes del *Tirant lo Blanch*," *Revista de Bibliografia Catalana* 5 (1905):23.

56. Riquer attributes this idea to Saint Isidor and cites a passage from the *Etimologies* ("Mulier preferetur viro, scilicet: Materia, quia Adam factus de limo terrae, Eva de costa Adae; loco: quia Adam factus extra Paradisium, Eva in Paradiso") that I have been unable to locate. The argument is then reproduced in Cerverí de Girona's poem "Maldit bendit."

57. This speech reappears, with slight variations, in ch. 328. The debate between Courage and Wisdom is itself one version of the medieval and Renaissance debate between the Pen and the Sword. The ideas expressed here parallel and are sometimes phrased identically with those of two other works: *Doctrina moral*, by the Majorcan Nicolau de Pax (fl. 1373–1419; see also Nicolau 24–27) and ch. 71 of Gutiérrez Diez de Games's (ca. 1379–1450) *El Victorial*. In Riquer's opinion (*Tirante* 3:55), the three works share a common source but did not influence each other.

58. See note 1, "Tirant in the Greek Empire."

59. Here Martorell plagiarizes (from "How well I remember" to "the morning's light") part of a pseudo-Ovidian epistle from Troilus to Cressida in the fifteenth-century *Bursario*, a work attributed to Juan Rodríguez de la Cámara or del Padrón.

60. In a song ("Amors m'envida e·m somo") by the thirteenth-century troubadour Daude de Prades, we find: "Franca piucella de sazo / mi platz, qand m'es de bel parer, / E·is vai de josta mi sezer, / Qan·sui vengutz en sa maiso; / e si·l vuoill baisar la maissella / o·il estreing un pauc la mamella, / no·is mou ni·s vira ni s'esglaia, / anz poigna cum vas mi m'atraia, / tro que·l baisars en sia pres / e·l doutz tocars de luoc deves."

61. We find many fifteenth-century helmets with as much or more ornamentation. For example, an inventory of the Valencian knight Jaume Guillem Escrivà's goods mentions a jousting helmet adorned with a black leg and its legging (see Riquer, *L'arnès del cavaller* [Esplugues de Llobregat: Ariel, 1968], 120). Other bizarre adornments in the miniatures in René d'Anjou's *Livre des tournois* (1460–1465; published in 1946 as *Traité de la forme et devis d'un tournoi* [Paris: Editions de la Verve]) include trees, bears, deer, dogs with bones in their mouths, bearded men, etc. This detail in *Tirant*, then, is typical of its era.

62. Brittany, Diaphebus's homeland.

63. A play on words, "seques amors" (or "dry loves") in the original being the English sycamore tree.

64. This viscount is inspired by a historic personage: the Portuguese knight Alvaro Vaz de Almada, who served King Henry V of England, became Count of Abranxes in Portugal, and was invited to join the Order of the Garter (see Rui de Pina's [1440–1521] *Cronica d'el-rei D Affonso V*, ch. 31). His son, João de Almada, Count of Abranxes (often spelled "Branches" by himself and others), accompanied the constable Don Pedro of Portugal to Barcelona when he was proclaimed King of Aragon in opposition to Joan II. João de Almada was also given a horse by Don Ferdinand of Portugal, to whom Martorell dedicates *Tirant,* while living in Barcelona with his first cousin Don Pedro, "King of the Catalans" (see Riquer, "La batalla a ultranza entre João de Almada y Menaut de Beaumont," in *Homenaje a Jaime Vicens Vives* [Barcelona: Universidad de Barcelona, 1965], 1:579–590).

65. In the original "francs-arquers," a militia founded in France in 1448 and consisting of the kingdom's best archers, who were selected by their parishes and paid by the king (see Philippe Contamine, *Guerre, état et société à la fin du Moyen Age* [Paris: Presses Universitaires de France, 1972], 337–366).

66. Here the "King Arthur episode" begins. It is identified as a masque rather than a supernatural element both by the fact that it begins as the meal ends and by the words in ch. 202, referring to the emperor, empress, and princess: "They were dazzled by what they had seen, for everything *seemed* done by magic" [italics mine]. Such elaborate "numbers" were not uncommon at fifteenth-century banquets. Much of the material in this episode was inspired by or copied from Guillem Torroella's *La faula* (before 1375; see also Pere Bohigas, "La matière de Bretagne en Catalogne," *Bulletin Bibliographique de la Société Internationale Arthurienne* 13 [1961]:90–92).

67. Taken from Cerverí de Girona's "moral poem": "Lo vers de cels que fan perdre el mon: Princep enic e bisbe negligen . . . e seynor ses vertat . . . paubre'ergoyllos. Jove antic e desobedient . . . veyls luxurios . . . poble ses ley, fat."

68. A knight's armor, in the middle of the fifteenth century, weighed between fifty-five and sixty-six pounds (see Riquer, *L'arnès* 97).

69. Arturo Farinelli, in *Italia e Spagna* (Turin: Fratelli Bocca, 1929, 1:77) mentions several Spanish medieval texts, including *Tirant,* that echo Petrarch's Sonnet 136 ("Fiamma dal ciel sulle tue treccie piova").

70. "Nulla (res) carius constat, quam quae pretibus empta est," Seneca *De beneficiis* 2.1.4. Thus does Dante quote the phrase in the *Convivio* (1.8), though modern editions render it as "Nulla aulla."

71. See note 52, "Tirant in the Greek Empire."

72. Possibly Rom. 5:58: "But God commendeth his love toward us, in that, while we were yet sinners, Christ died for us."

73. No connection has thus far been found between this story and the Arthurian legends involving Uther Pendragon.

74. Riquer suggests (*Tirante* 3:175) that this story may bear some vague relation to the characters and plot of the fifteenth-century *Pierres de Provença,* the motifs in Philippe de Remis's (d. 1296) *Roman de la Manekine,* and the latter's many imitations and derivations.

75. Prov. 10:4: "He becometh poor that dealeth with a slack hand; but the hand of the diligent maketh rich."

76. Eiximenis gives the following advice on selecting warriors: "E ja a XIII anys faràs que començ l'om d'armes a exercitar si mateix . . . e si d'officis specials los has a elegir, no elegesques pescadors ne caçadors ne hòmens molls, mas ferrers, fusters, carnicers e pedrers, e caçadors de porcs salvatges, e hom de vergonya qui tema e·s confona fugir (*Dotzè del Chrestià,* ch. 217).

77. Weeks, not years, have passed since Tirant first saw Carmesina.

78. This story is taken directly from 2, 4 of Boccaccio's *Decameron:* "Landolfo Ruffolo, impoverito, divien corsale e da' genovesi preso, rompe in mare, o sopra una cassetta, di gioie carissime piena, scampa, e in Gurfo ricevuto da una femmina, ricco si torna a casa sua" (see Farinelli 1:364, 365).

79. This scene constitutes a legitimate marriage (see Ruiz y Conde 162–168). In the Middle Ages, church law permitted marriage by mutual consent ("per verba de prae-senti").

80. This strange tradition can be found in Sir John Mandeville's *Travels* (ch. 4): "Et sachiés que Saint Jehan fist là faire sa fosse en sa vie, et puis se coucha par dedenz tous vis. Et pour ce dient aucuns que il ne mourut point, mais que il se repose jusques au jour du jugement." It is believed that our author read these lines, because they are followed in *Travels* by the story of Hippocrates's daughter turned into a dragon (ch. 410 in *Tirant*). If the dragon episode was written by Galba, as most scholars think, then this episode also was probably written by Martorell's successor.

81. This episode had a number of literary consequences. It was the basis for Ludovico Ariosto's story of Ginevra and Dalinda and Polinesso and Ariodante in *Orlando furioso*, canto 5 (see Pio Rajna, *Le Fonte dell 'Orlando furioso* [Florence: Sansoni, 1900], 149). The idea is taken up by Bandello (*Le novelle* 1.22), in which Peter the Great of Aragon plays a role, and thence, through a French translation of Bandello by Francois de Belleforest (*Histoires tragiques*), to Shakespeare, who uses it in *Much Ado About Nothing* (see Riquer, *Tirant* [Selecta], 181–185).

82. See note 44, "Tirant in the Greek Empire."

Tirant in North Africa

1. This episode about Pleasure-of-my-life's shipwreck and rescue by the Moor is more or less inspired by 5, 2 of the *Decameron:* "Gostanza ama Murtuccio Gomìto, la quale, udendo che morto era, per disperata sola si mette in una barca, la quale dal vento fu trasportata a Susa; ritruòval vivo in Tunisi, palesaglisi, ed egli grande essendo col re per consigli dati, sposatala, ricco con lei in Lìpari se ne torna" (see Farinelli 1:366, 367). The imitation continues in ch. 350 of *Tirant*.

2. "Cabdillo sobre los cabdillos" in the original, a translation of the Turkish honorary title "beylerbey."

3. The kingdom of Tlemcen (west of Tunis) was annexed by Morocco (here called the kingdom of Fez) in 1389.

4. An imitation of the opening words of the *Decameron:* "Umana cosa è aver compas-sione agli afflitti."

5. This passage is based on the well-known anecdote about Scipio's arrival in Africa, recounted by Frontinus (*Strategemata* 1.12.1). Eiximenis also relates it: "Gal·lus Fabi, emperador dels tartres, sí feya son poder de esquivar fetilleries e de girar en bé tots senyals qui vinguessen, car si en l'entrada de la terra que volia conquerir caygués en terra, deya que era senyal que la terra lo volia per senyor" (ch. 246).

6. As we shall see later, this King Escariano shares many of Prester John of the Indies' hypothetical traits.

7. Perhaps Prov. 13:7: "There is that maketh himself rich, yet hath nothing: there is that maketh himself poor, yet hath great riches."

8. The "Hispania Ulterior" of the Romans.

9. The rest of this speech is taken from book 5 of Bernat Metge's *Lo somni*. Metge, for his part, followed Petrarch's Latin epistle to Anna, Emperor Charles IV's wife (*Familiarum rerum* 21.8), Boccaccio's *De claribus mulieribus,* and Valerius Maximus' *Factorum dictorumque memorabilium* (see Nicolau 27–35).

10. This anecdote appears in Metge and his sources, but makes no mention of the name Mirilla or Saint John Lateran.

11. An imitation of the anecdote about Zopyrus in the siege of Babylon, recounted by Heroditus (3:153–160). Here it may be taken from one of the numerous works that repeat it, e.g., Frontinus's *Strategemata* 3.3.4.

12. During parts of the thirteenth and fourteenth centuries, there was an independent kingdom of Bougie.

13. Probably Lake Tana in Ethiopia, mentioned by Mandeville in ch. 18.

14. This phrase is taken from one of Joan Roís de Corella's letters in the epistolary debate with the Prince of Viana (see *Obres completes,* Roís de Corella, ed. Jordi Carbonell, [Valencia: Albatros, 1973], 1:90 and Moll, "Rudiments de versificació en el *Tirant lo Blanch,*" *Bolletí del Diccionari de la Llengua Catalana* 16 [1934]:181).

15. The beginning of this chapter is an almost exact reproduction of Carmesina's speech in ch. 181 (see note 57, "Tirant in the Greek Empire," in which sources are indicated).

16. Here Boccaccio, as author of *Il Filostrato,* whose protagonists are Troilus and Cressida, is added.

17. Wisd. 8:10–14: "Because of her I shall have glory among the multitudes and honor in the presence of the elders, though I am young. . . . Because of her I shall have immortality, and leave an everlasting remembrance to those who come after me. I shall govern people, and nations will be subject to me."

18. Valencia, according to Ptolemaic astronomy, is in the fourth clime, which is the sun's sphere (Moon, Mercury, Venus, Sun). In addition, Arab texts declare that the sun's reflection in the Albufera (a lagoon near the city) increases the brightness of Valencian skies.

19. The king interprets Saint Christopher, with the Christ child on his shoulder, after his own lights.

20. This technique is also described by Eiximenis: "Si los assetjants caven dejús lo mur, a açò los assetjats deuen haver l'ull obert. . . . Aprés, si d'açò han sospita, posen al peu del mur, endins, bacins buyts, e attenen si faran poch ne molt de so, car si·u fan, senyal és que la terra dejús se mou per aquells qui fan les caves dejús lo mur" (ch. 309).

21. This strategem is also described by Frontinus: "Hispani contra Hamilcarem boes vehiculis adjuntos in prima fronte constituerunt, vehiculaque taedae, sebi, et sulphuris plena, signo pugnae dato, incenderunt; actis deinde in hostem bubus consternatam aciem perruperunt" (*Strategemata* 2.4.17).

22. This "miracle," fairly common in medieval literature but somewhat at odds with Martorell's viewpoint, is often cited as one indication that the African episodes of *Tirant* were written by Galba.

23. This strategem can be found in Frontinus: "Atheas, rex Sytharum, quum adversus ampliorem Triballorum exercitum configeret, jussit a feminis et pueris omnique inbellit turba, greges asinorum ac boum ad postreman hostium aciem admoveri, et erectas hastas praeferre. Famam deine diffudit, tamquam auxilia sibi ab ulterioribus Scythis adventarent; qua adserveratione averit hostem" (*Strategemata* 3.4.20).

24. The imitation of Boccaccio continues here (see note 1, "Tirant in North Africa").

25. In the original "algemia," meaning "foreign" in Arabic, a word used by Spanish Muslims to refer to the Romance vernaculars spoken by Christians.

26. These words have never been found in Saint James's writings, nor have all the other passages cited by Pleasure-of-my-life and Tirant in these chapters been identified.

27. Another quotation from Boccaccio (see note 4, "Tirant in North Africa").

28. This citation, which vaguely recalls 10.121–128 in the first book of Lucan's *Bellum civile,* is attributed to the otherwise unknown "poet Geber," who is also mentioned in Eiximenis's discussion of the most propitious astrological signs for knights: "per què posà Geber en los seus júys astròlechs, que tots los marcials aptes són a batallar" (ch. 224).

29. Another slip on (probably) Galba's part, since Pleasure-of-my-life has no way of knowing the princess's whereabouts.

30. A repetition of the citation in ch. 137 (see note 17, "Tirant in the Greek Empire").

31. Another indication of Galba's authorship of this part of *Tirant,* since Martorell was clearly a great admirer of the English.

32. Eccl. 1:2: "Vanity of vanities, saith the Preacher, vanity of vanities; all is vanity."

33. In Vulgate (Job 7:1): "Militia est vita hominis super terram."

34. 1 Cor. 11:26.

35. Ecclus. 6:14: "A faithful friend is a sturdy shelter: he that has found one has found a treasure."

36. Possibly Rom. 8:38, 39: "For I am persuaded, that neither death, nor life . . . shall be able to separate us from the love of God, which is in Christ Jesus Our Lord."

37. Eccl. 3:1.

38. Matt. 7:17, 18.

39. Bornu, now in northeastern Nigeria, is accurately located here on the frontier between Barbary and Black Africa.

40. This character, hitherto called the Marquis of Luçana in the original, is henceforth referred to as the Marquis of Liçana, probably because our author was thinking of the Valencian Maça de Liçana family, involved in various duels and feuds.

41. Constantine, in fact, is an inland city in Algeria.

42. The frequent mention of various languages from now on is usually taken as a sign of Galba's authorship, whereas in Martorell's part of the book, Sicilians, Englishmen, Turks, Greeks, etc. generally understand each other without difficulty (see Riquer, *Tirante* 4:260).

43. Imitation of the second sonnet of Dante's *Vita nuova:* "O voi che per la via d'amore passate, / attendete e guardate / s'elli e dolore alcun, quanto'l mio grave."

44. Another indication of Galba's authorship, since Martorell always treats the Genoese with profound antipathy.

45. This friar appears to be the same one previously identified as Valencian (chs. 330 and 372). The mention of his linguistic accomplishments may suggest the hand of Galba.

46. Ps. 99:32.

47. Ecclus. 23:27.

48. In fact, Luke 12:49.

49. 1 Cor. 2:5.

50. Prov. 15:27.

51. Marinesco ("Du nouveau" 189–193), advances the hypothesis that this King Escariano is a fictionalized version of Prester John of the Indies, King of Ethiopia, with whom Alphonse the Magnanimous exchanged emissaries (see Foreword, xiv herein). In regard to the Tigris, Latini says: "Mais par deriere vers midi sont les desers de Etyope sur la mer ocheaine, et le fleuve de Tygre, ki engendre Nile, ki divise la terre d'Affrike et celui d'Etyope, ou li etyopiien havitent." (1.124.3)

52. In fact, Vlonë is an Albanian port on the Adriatic.

53. Heroditus (4.183) situates the "Troglodites" ("cave-dwellers") in Ethiopia. Following his lead, Latini (1.124.4) states: "La sont les gens de Namazoine et de Trogodite et les gens des Amans, ki font les maisons de sel."

54. Likewise, Latini states (1.124.5): "Et sachiés que les gens d'Etyope et de Garremans no sevent que mariages soit, ains ont entre'aus femes communes a tous; et por ce avient ke nus n'i conoist peres, s meres non, por quoi il sont apelé les main nobles gens du monde."

55. Latini continues: "Et sachiés que en Etyope sus la mer vers midi est un grant tertre ki giete grant plenté de feu ardant tozjors sans estanchier. Outre ces gens sont il li tres grant desiert, ou nules gens ne reperent, jusque en Arrabe." (1.124.5)

56. From here through "the rule of these islands," our author translates part of ch. 4 of Mandeville's *Travels.* We know the book had already been translated into Catalan because of an item in an inventory of Antoni Coll's goods (Barcelona, 1484): "Ítem un altre libre de forma de full comú, scrit en paper en vulgar, apellat Johan de Mandavila. Comense en los capítols: 'Ací comense lo libre de Joan de Manda'; e acaba en la primera pàgina: 'lo soldà'. Stà com cubert de cuyro vermell" (Marimón Madurell and Jordi Rubió Balaguer, *Documentos* [Barcelona: Gremio de Editores, de Libreros, y de Maestros Impresores, 1955], 44). Riquer suggests (*Tirante* 5:36) that the legend about Hippocrates's bewitched daughter may be of Byzantine origin and due either to confusion with the doctor's nephew Dracon or to traditions connected with the cult of Asclepius, the mythological doctor. The *Travels,* originally written in French (1361), was translated into English and all the major Romance languages.

Tirant Succors the Greek Empire

1. Another contradiction involving Hippolytus, who was present when Pleasure-of-my-life explained the widow's ruse. Since the knight remained in Constantinople, one would imagine he had also told the princess, yet she appears unaware of the trick.

2. The military metaphors, as well as the lively style, of these chapters have led several scholars to attribute them to Martorell (see Riquer, *Tirante* 5:105).

3. Mandeville has this to say about Stagira, a city in Chalcidice: "En ce pays fu Aristocles nez en une cité que on appelle Strageres, assez près de la cité de Trachie; et a Stageres gist il, et ya un autel sur sa tumbe, et fait on grant feste de li tous les ans, aussi comme il fust saint" (ch. 3). Four lines before this quotation, Mandeville enumerates the islands that appear in ch. 465 of *Tirant.*

4. In fact, the city of Olympia lies in the Peloponnesus. Mandeville is also the source of this error: "Vers la fin de Machidoine il a une montaigne qui es appellée Olimpius, qui depart Macedoine et Trachie" (ch. 3).

5. Another realistic reference to linguistic matters.

6. Again, our author makes use of Mandeville's *Travels,* in which Tabriz ("Taurisse," ch. 16), Bukhara ("Boutera," ch. 28), and Samarkand ("Sarnagan," ch. 28) are mentioned.

7. In Mandeville (ch. 3), "Colcos, Lesbrie, Nurtaflaxon, Melo, Capace, Lempne." In these and other reconquered territories, I follow Riquer's and Marinesco's interpretations of their identities (see note 3, "Tirant Succors the Greek Empire").

8. Roger de Flor died in Adrianople, though by assassination, not from disease.

9. János Hunyadi, another possible model for Tirant, died August 11, 1456, attended by the Franciscan friar Giovanni di Capistrano (see Marinesco, "Du nouveau" 174).

After Tirant's Death

1. This lamentation, from the beginning of the chapter, is written in versified prose in the original. Hendecasyllables abound in it, many of them reminiscent of Joan Roís de Corella (see Moll, "Rudiments" 179–182).

2. This paragraph resembles a passage that can be found in Roís de Corella's "La història de Lèander i Hero" (*Obres completes,* 1:180; see also Riquer, who, in *Nuevas contribuciones* 18–20, argues that Galba plagiarized Corella and not vice versa).

3. Another borrowing from Roís de Corella's "La història de Lèander i Hero" (182).

Alonso, Dámaso. "*Tirant lo Blanc,* novela moderna." *Revista Valenciana de Filología* 1 (1951):179–215; rpt., in abridged form, in *Primavera temprana de la literatura europea.* Madrid: Guadarrama, 1961, 201–253.

Amador de los Rios, José. *Historia crítica de la vida española.* Madrid: José Rodríguez et al, 1865, 7:385–391.

Boehne, Patricia. *Dream and Fantasy in Fourteenth- and Fifteenth-Century Catalan Prose.* Barcelona: Hispam, 1975.

Bohigas, Pere, ed. *Tractats de cavalleria.* Barcelona: Barcino, 1947.

———. "La matière de Bretagne en Catalogne." *Bulletin Bibliographique de la Société Internationale Arthurienne* 13 (1961):92–94.

Capmany, Maria Aurèlia. *La dona a Catalunya.* Barcelona: Edicions 62, 1966, 54–57.

Coromines, Joan. "Sobre l'estil i manera de Martí Joan de Galba i els de Joanot Martorell." In *Lleures i converses d'un filòleg.* Barcelona: El Pi de Tres Branques, 1971, 363–378.

Eiximenis, Francesc. *Dotzè del Chrestià.* Valencia: Lambert Palmart, 1484.

Entwistle, William J. "Observacions sobre la dedicatòria i primera part del *Tirant lo Blanch.*" Trans. Jordi Rubió Balaguer. *Revista de Catalunya* 7 (1927):381–398.

———. "*Tirant lo Blanch* and the Social Order at the End of the Fifteenth Century." *Estudis Romànics* 2 (1949–1950):149–164.

Farinelli, Arturo. "Nota sulla fortuna del Boccaccio nella Ispagna nell'Età Media." In *Italia e Spagna.* Turin: Fratelli Bocca, 1929, 1:362–369.

Ferrer, Francesc. "Romanç de la armada del Soldà contra Rodes." Ed. Lluís Nicolau d'Olwer. In "Un témoignage catalan du siège de Rhodes en 1444." *Estudis Universitaris Catalans* 12 (1927):376–387.

Froissart, Jean de. *Les chroniques de sire Jean de Froissart.* Ed. Jean Alexandre Buchon. 3 vols. Paris: A. Desrez, 1838–1840.

Gili Gaya, Samuel. "Noves recerques sobre *Tirant lo Blanc.*" *Estudis Romànics* 1 (1947–1948):135–147.

Givanel Mas, Joan. "Estudio crítico de la novela caballeresca *Tirant lo Blanch.*" *Archivo de Investigaciones Históricas,* 1 (1911):213–248, 319–348 and 2 (1911):392–445, 477–513; rpt. Madrid: V. Suárez, 1912.

Guy de Warewic. Ed. Alfred Ewart. Paris: E. Champion, 1933. See also *Le rommant de Guy de Warwik et de Herolt d'Ardenne.* Ed. D. J. Conlon. Chapel Hill: Univ. of North Carolina, 1971.

La Marche, Olivier de. *Mémoires.* Eds. Jules d'Arbaumont and Henri Beaune. 4 vols. Paris: Société de l'Histoire de France, 1883–1888.

Latini, Brunetto. *Li livres dou tresor.* Ed. Francis J. Carmody. Berkeley: Univ. of California Press, 1947.

Lot, Ferdinand. *L'art militaire et les armées au Moyen Age.* 2 vols. Paris: Payot, 1946.

Mandeville, Sir John. *Mandeville's Travels.* Ed. Malcolm Letts. 2 vols. London: Hakluyt Society, 1953.

Marinesco, Constantin. "Du nouveau sur *Tirant lo Blanch.*" *Estudis Romànics* 4 (1953–1954):137–203.

———. "Nuevas notas sobre *Tirant lo Blanch.*" *Boletín de la Real Academia de la Historia* 28 (1956):287–305.

McNerney, Kathleen. *Tirant lo Blanc Revisited: A Critical Study.* Detroit: Medieval and Renaissance Monograph Series, 1983.

Menéndez y Pelayo, Marcelino. *Orígenes de la novela*. Madrid: Bailly-Ballière e Hijos, 1905, 1:251–258; rpt. Madrid: Consejo Superior de Investigaciones Científicas, 1954, 393–401.

Moll, Francesc de B. "Els refranys del *Tirant lo Blanch*." *Bolletí del Diccionari de la Llengua Catalana* 15 (1933):169–172.

———. "Rudiments de versificació en el *Tirant lo Blanch*." *Bolletí del Diccionari de la Llengua Catalana* 16 (1934):179–182.

Muntaner, Ramon. "Crònica." In *Les quatre grans cròniques*. Ed. Ferran Soldevila. Barcelona: Selecta, 1971, 667–942.

Nicolau d'Olwer, Lluís. "Sobre les fonts catalanes del *Tirant lo Blanch*." *Revista de Bibliografía Catalana* 5 (1905):5–37.

———. "*Tirant lo Blanc:* examen de algunas cuestiones." *Nueva Revista de Filología Hispánica* 15 (1961):131–154.

Pierce, Frank. "The Role of Sex in *Tirant lo Blanch*." *Estudis Romànics* 10 (1962):291–300.

Riquer, Martí de. *Nuevas contribuciones a las fuentes de* Tirant lo Blanch. Barcelona: Biblioteca Central, 1949.

———, ed. *Lletres de batalla, cartells de deseiximents i capítols de passos d'armes*. 3 vols. Barcelona: Barcino, 1963–1968.

———. *Història de la literatura catalana*. Esplugues de Llobregat: Ariel, 1965, 2:632–721.

———. *L'arnès del cavaller: armes i armadures catalanes medievals*. Esplugues de Llobregat: Ariel, 1968.

———. *Cavalleria fra realtà e letteratura nel Quattrocento*. Bari: Adriatica Editrice, 1970.

Rubió Balaguer, Jordi. *Vida española en la época gótica*. Barcelona: Alberto Martín, 1943.

———. "Literatura catalana." In *Historia general de las literaturas hispánicas*. Barcelona: Vergara, 1953, 3:859–862.

Ruiz de Conde, Justina. *El amor y el matrimonio secreto en los libros de caballerías*. Madrid: Aguilar, 1948, 101–170.

Vaeth, James A. Tirant lo Blanch: *A Study of its Authorship Principal Sources and Historical Setting*. New York: Columbia University Press, 1918.

Vargas Llosa, Mario. "Carta de batalla por *Tirant lo Blanc*." *Revista de Occidente* 70 (1969):1–21; rpt. as introd. to *Tirante el Blanco*. 2 vols. Madrid: Alianza Editorial, 1969.